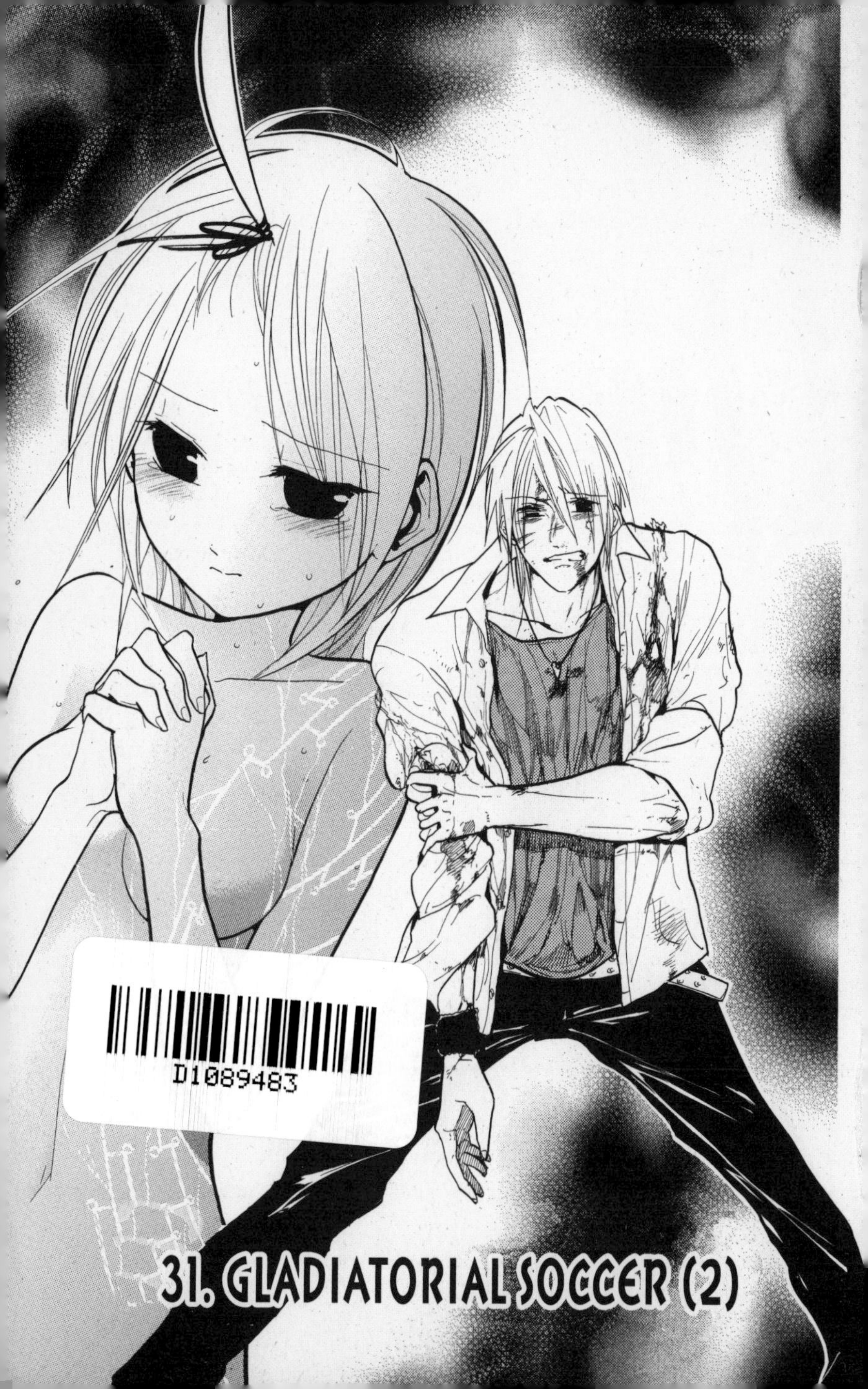
31. GLADIATORIAL SOCCER (2)

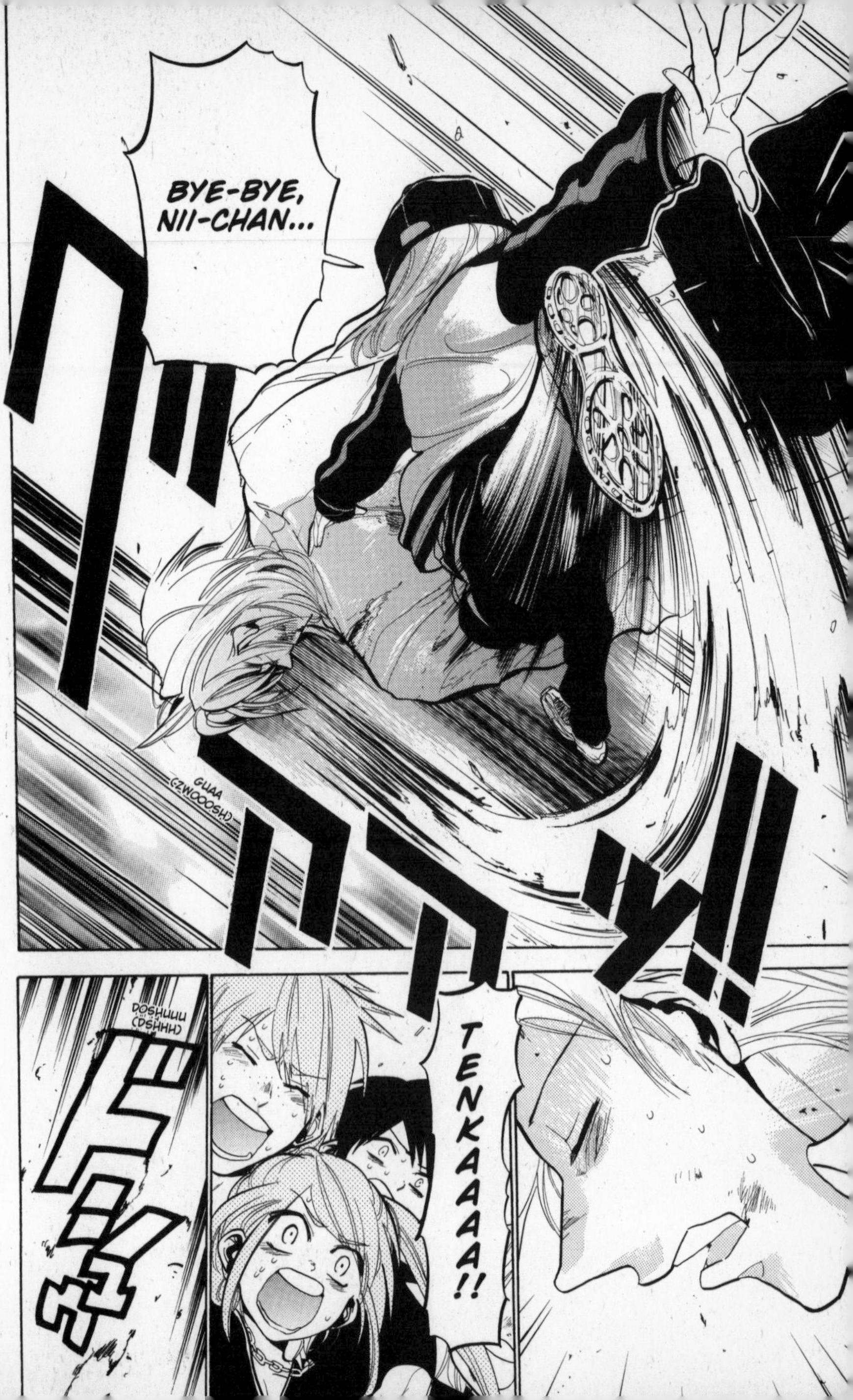
BYE-BYE, NII-CHAN...
GUAA (ZWOOOSH)
TENKAAAAAA!!
DOSHUUU (DSHHH)

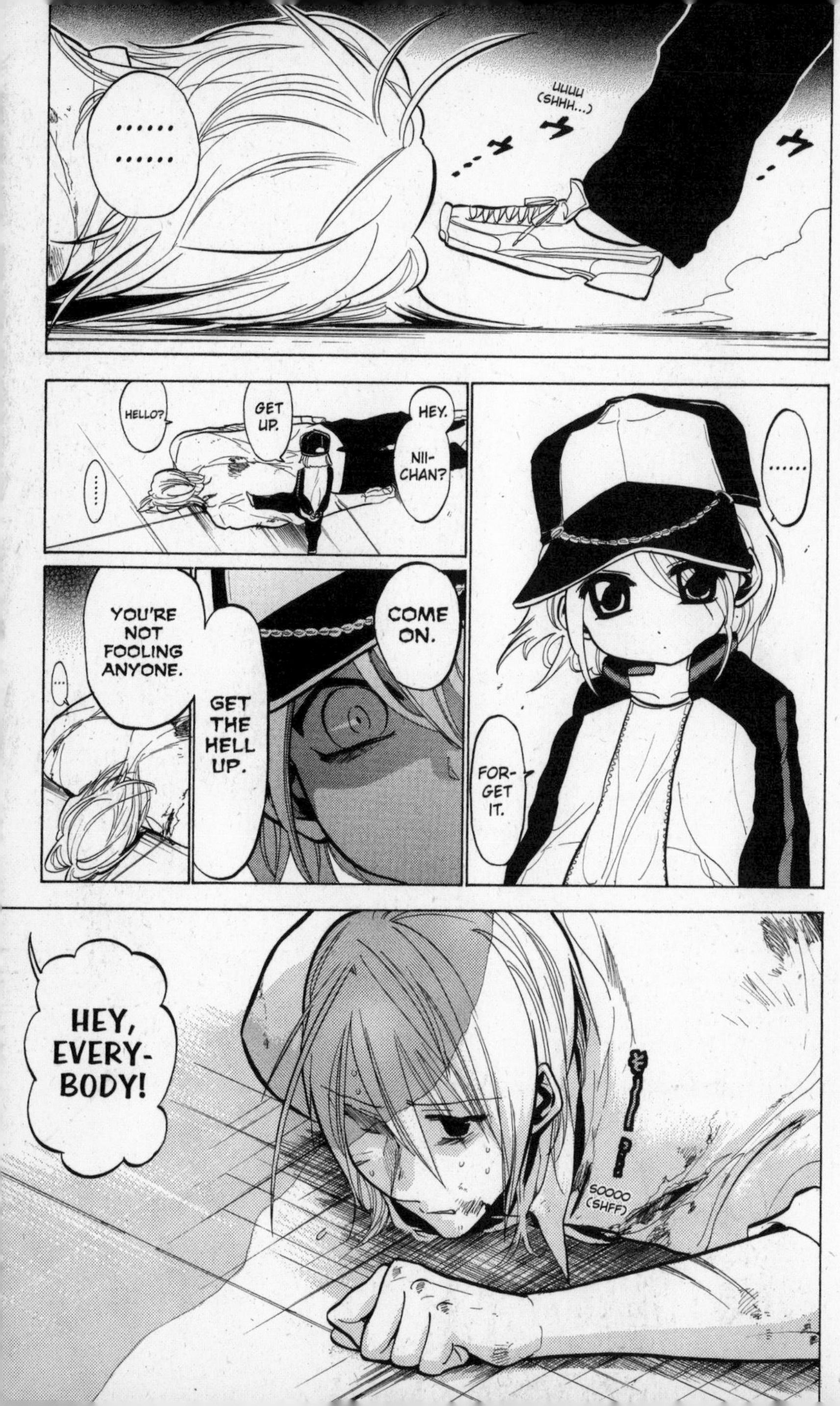
uuuu (SHHH...)
......
......
......
FOR-GET IT.
HEY.
NII-CHAN?
GET UP.
HELLO?
......
COME ON.
YOU'RE NOT FOOLING ANYONE.
GET THE HELL UP.
...
SOOOO (SHFF)
HEY, EVERY-BODY!

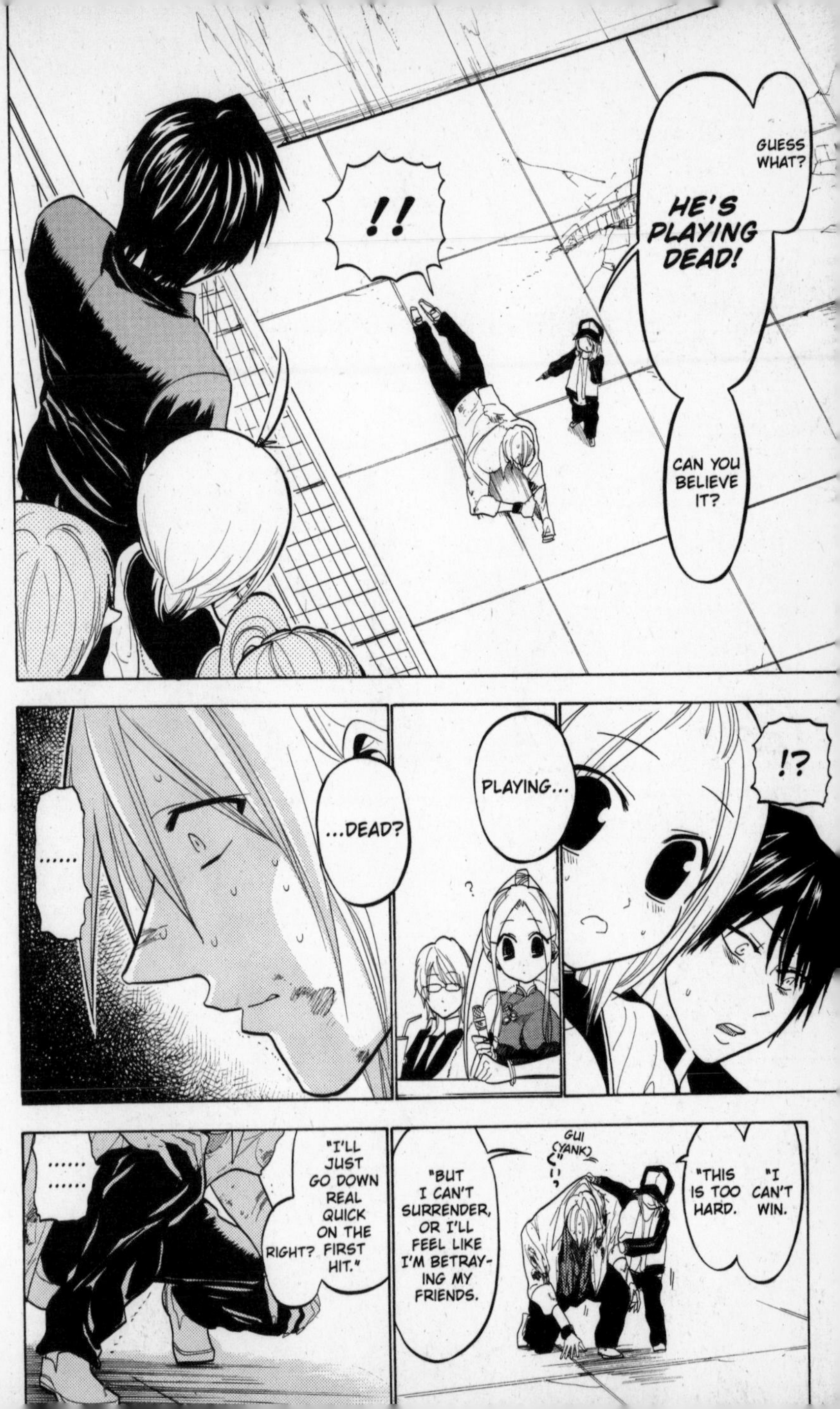
GUESS WHAT? HE'S PLAYING DEAD! CAN YOU BELIEVE IT?
!!
!?
PLAYING...
...DEAD?
......
"I CAN'T WIN.
"THIS IS TOO HARD.
GUI (YANK)
"BUT I CAN'T SURRENDER, OR I'LL FEEL LIKE I'M BETRAYING MY FRIENDS.
"I'LL JUST GO DOWN REAL QUICK ON THE FIRST HIT."
RIGHT?
....

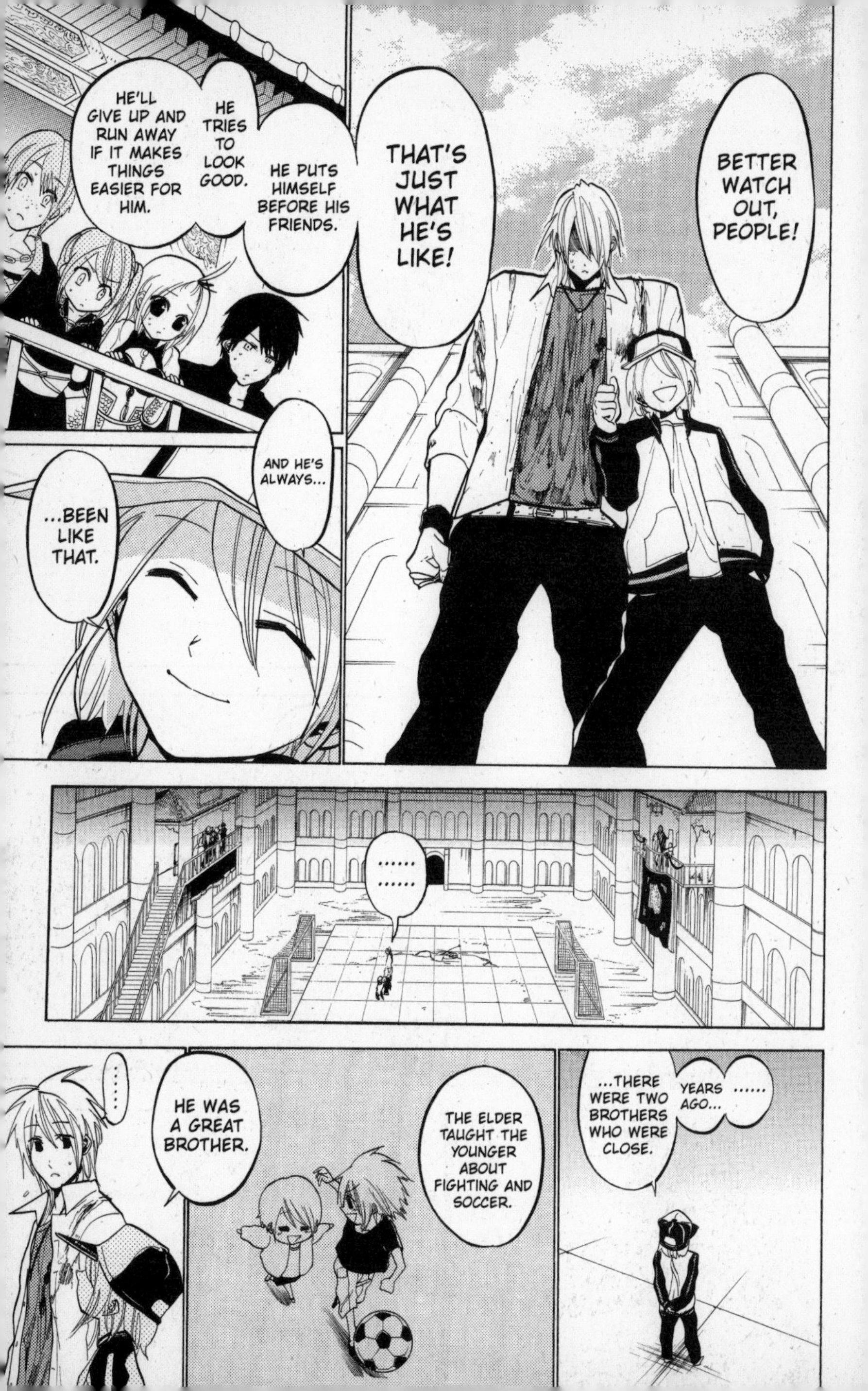
BETTER WATCH OUT, PEOPLE!
THAT'S JUST WHAT HE'S LIKE!
HE PUTS HIMSELF BEFORE HIS FRIENDS.
HE TRIES TO LOOK GOOD.
HE'LL GIVE UP AND RUN AWAY IF IT MAKES THINGS EASIER FOR HIM.
AND HE'S ALWAYS...
...BEEN LIKE THAT.
......
......
......
YEARS AGO...
...THERE WERE TWO BROTHERS WHO WERE CLOSE.
THE ELDER TAUGHT THE YOUNGER ABOUT FIGHTING AND SOCCER.
HE WAS A GREAT BROTHER.
......

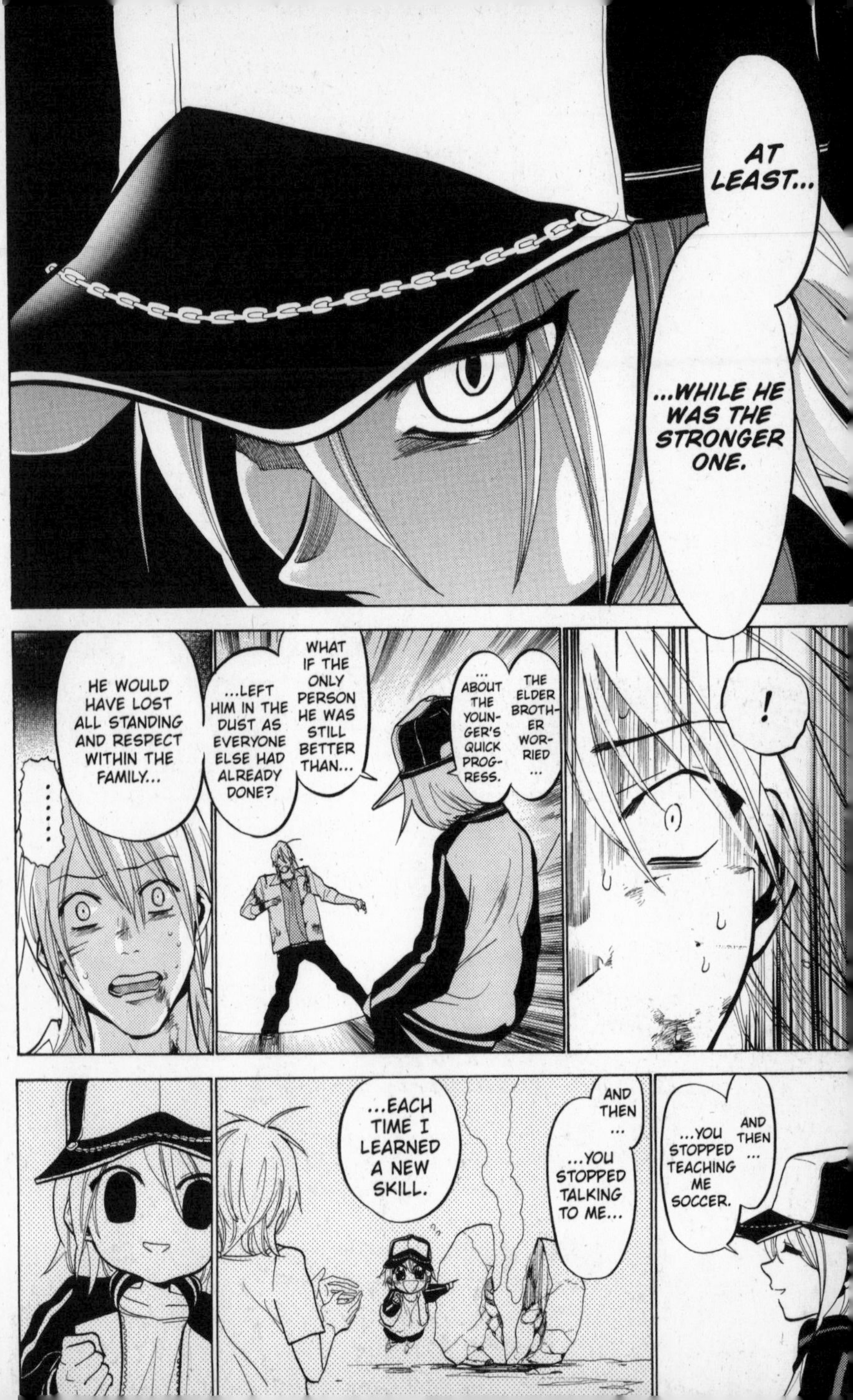
AT LEAST...
...WHILE HE WAS THE STRONGER ONE.
!
THE ELDER BROTHER WORRIED...
...ABOUT THE YOUNGER'S QUICK PROGRESS.
WHAT IF THE ONLY PERSON HE WAS STILL BETTER THAN...
...LEFT HIM IN THE DUST AS EVERYONE ELSE HAD ALREADY DONE?
HE WOULD HAVE LOST ALL STANDING AND RESPECT WITHIN THE FAMILY...
......
AND THEN...
...YOU STOPPED TEACHING ME SOCCER.
AND THEN...
...YOU STOPPED TALKING TO ME...
...EACH TIME I LEARNED A NEW SKILL.

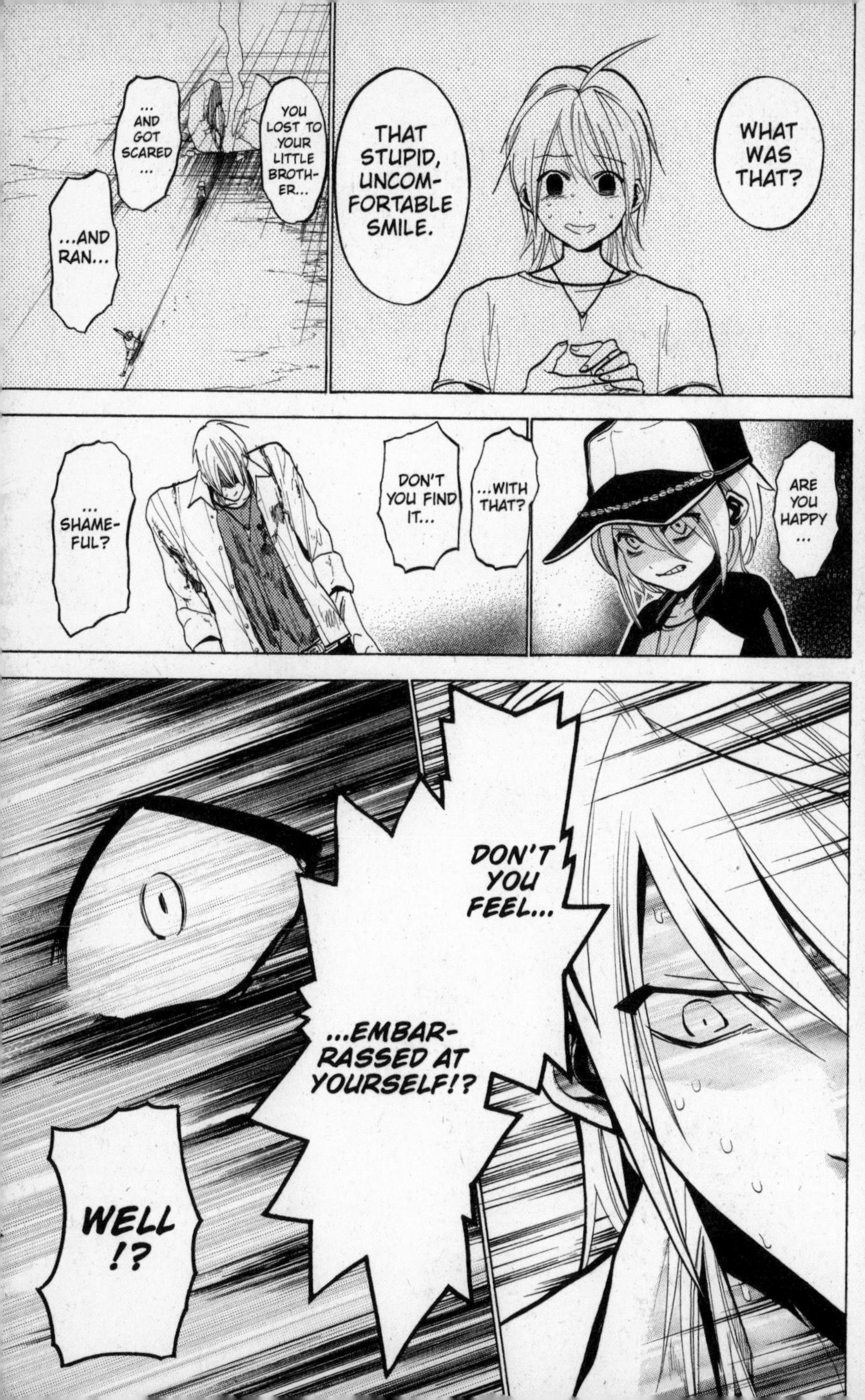
WHAT WAS THAT?
THAT STUPID, UNCOMFORTABLE SMILE.
YOU LOST TO YOUR LITTLE BROTHER...
... AND GOT SCARED ...
...AND RAN...
ARE YOU HAPPY ...
...WITH THAT?
DON'T YOU FIND IT...
... SHAMEFUL?
DON'T YOU FEEL...
...EMBARRASSED AT YOURSELF!?
WELL !?

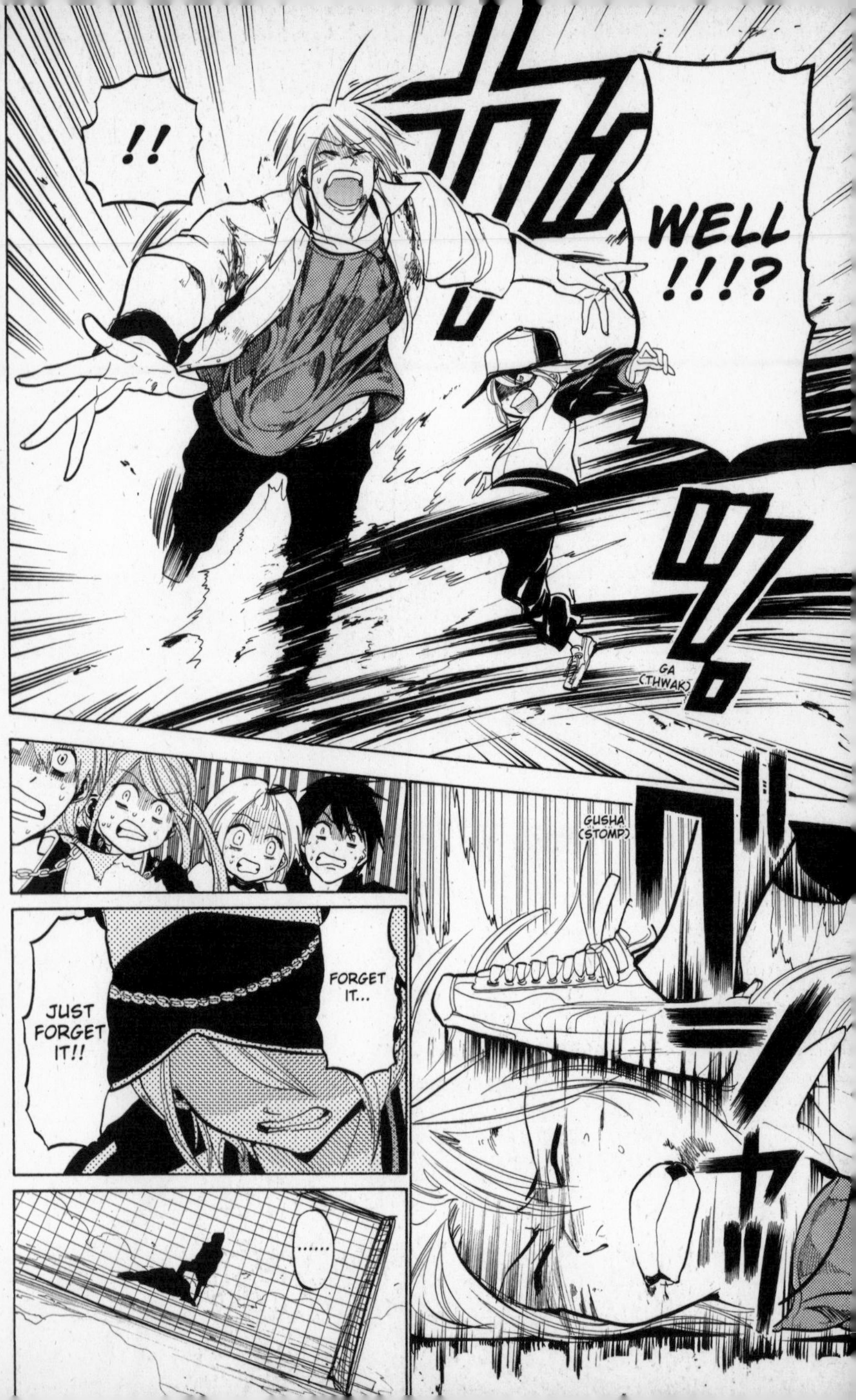
WELL!!!?
!!
GA (THWAK)
GUSHA (STOMP)
FORGET IT...
JUST FORGET IT!!
......

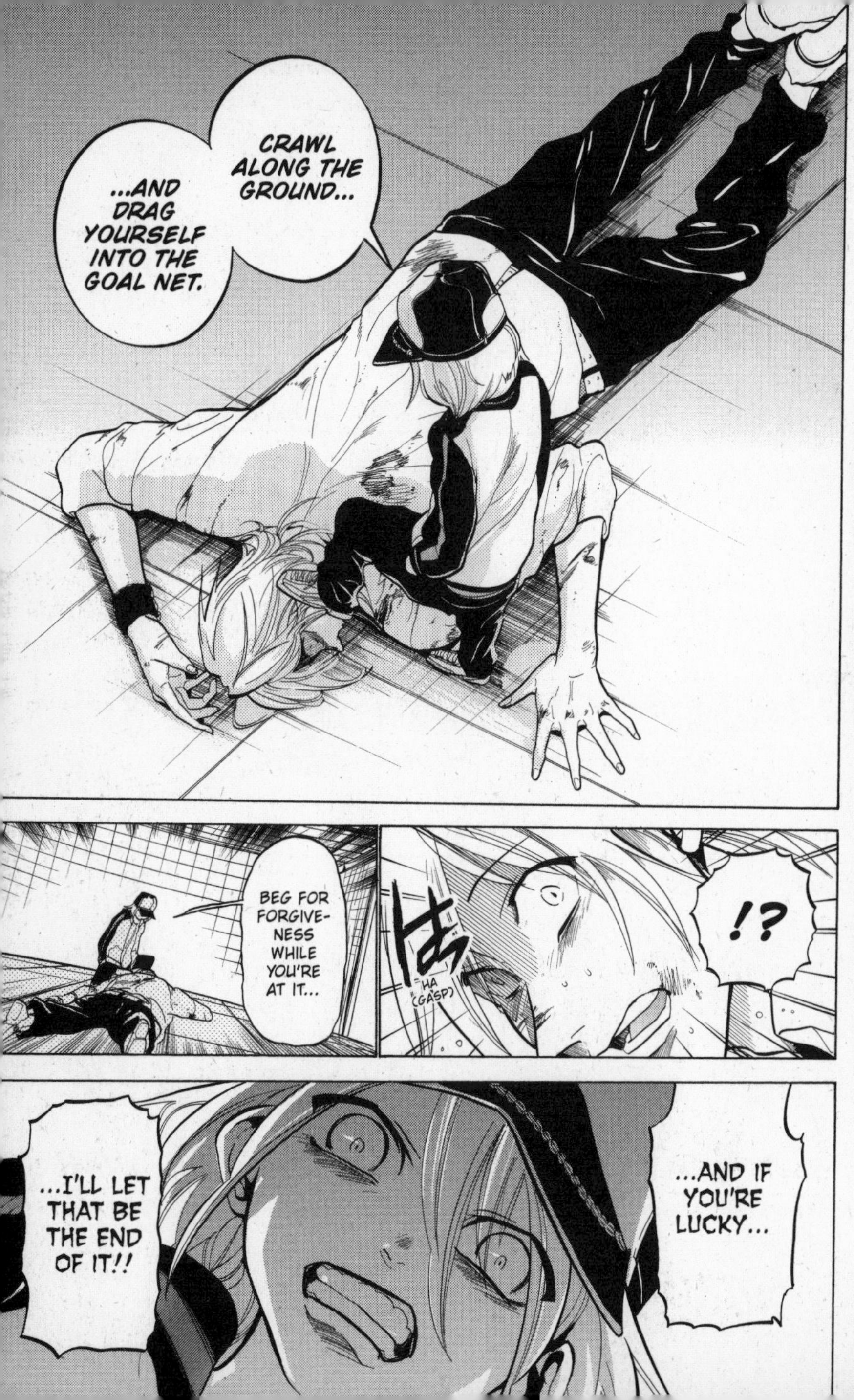
CRAWL ALONG THE GROUND...
...AND DRAG YOURSELF INTO THE GOAL NET.
!?
はっ
HA (GASP)
BEG FOR FORGIVE-NESS WHILE YOU'RE AT IT...
...AND IF YOU'RE LUCKY...
...I'LL LET THAT BE THE END OF IT!!

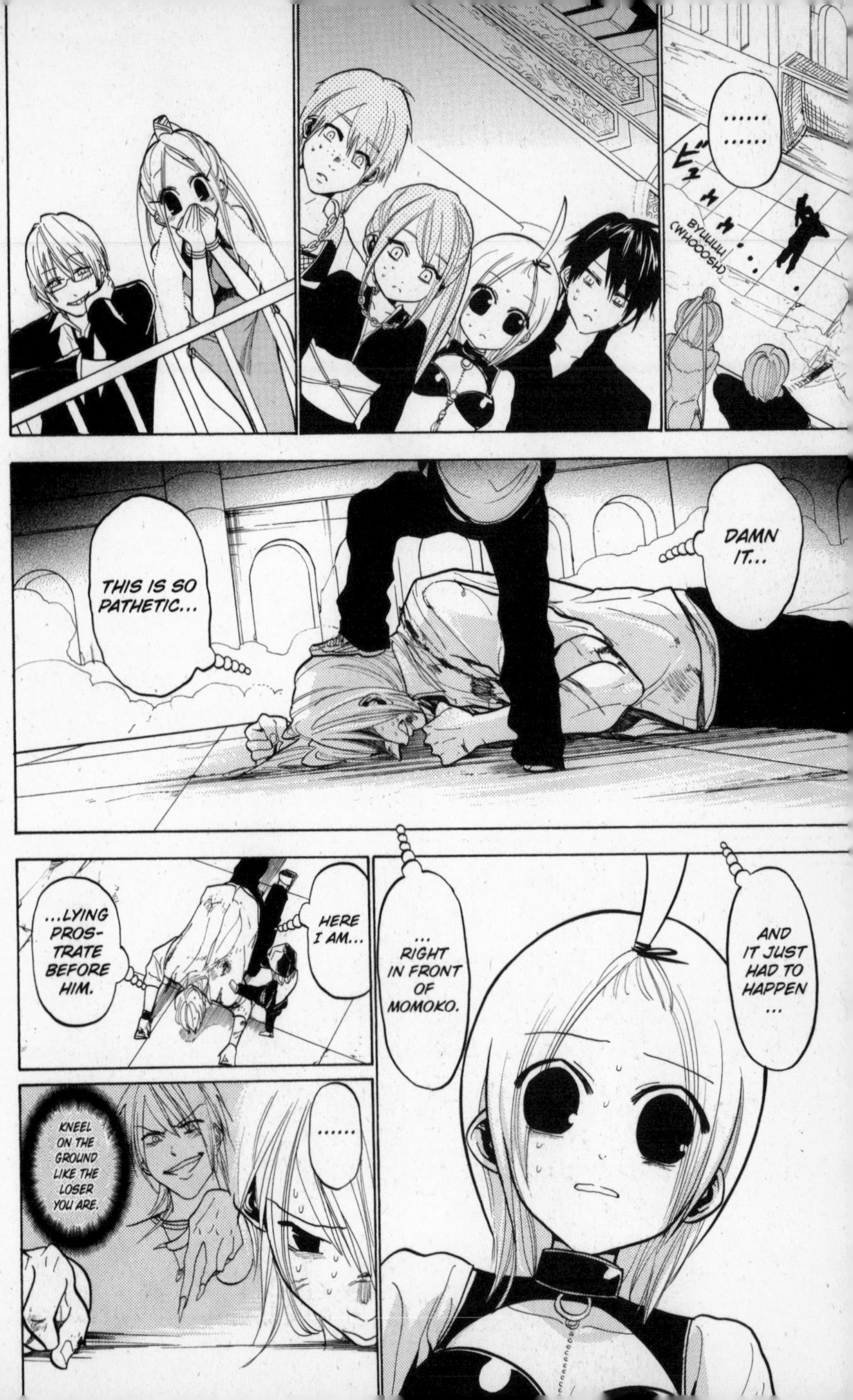
......
......
BYUUUU
(WHOOOSH)
DAMN IT...
THIS IS SO PATHETIC...
AND IT JUST HAD TO HAPPEN...
...RIGHT IN FRONT OF MOMOKO.
HERE I AM...
...LYING PROS-TRATE BEFORE HIM.
......
KNEEL ON THE GROUND LIKE THE LOSER YOU ARE.

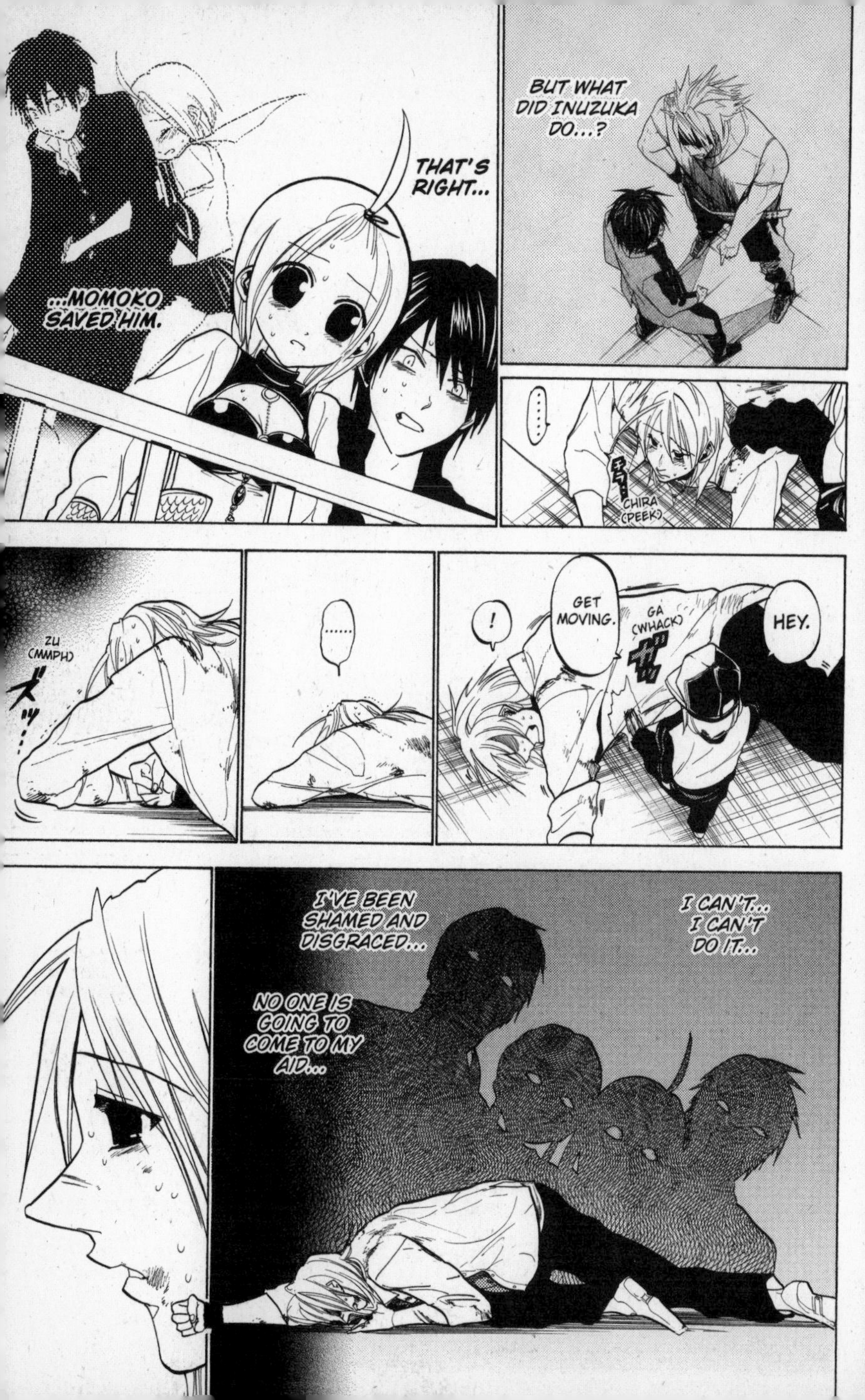
BUT WHAT DID INUZUKA DO...?
......
CHIRA (PEEK)
THAT'S RIGHT...
...MOMOKO SAVED HIM.
HEY.
GA (WHACK)
GET MOVING.
!
......
ZU (MMPH)
I CAN'T... I CAN'T DO IT...
I'VE BEEN SHAMED AND DISGRACED...
NO ONE IS GOING TO COME TO MY AID...

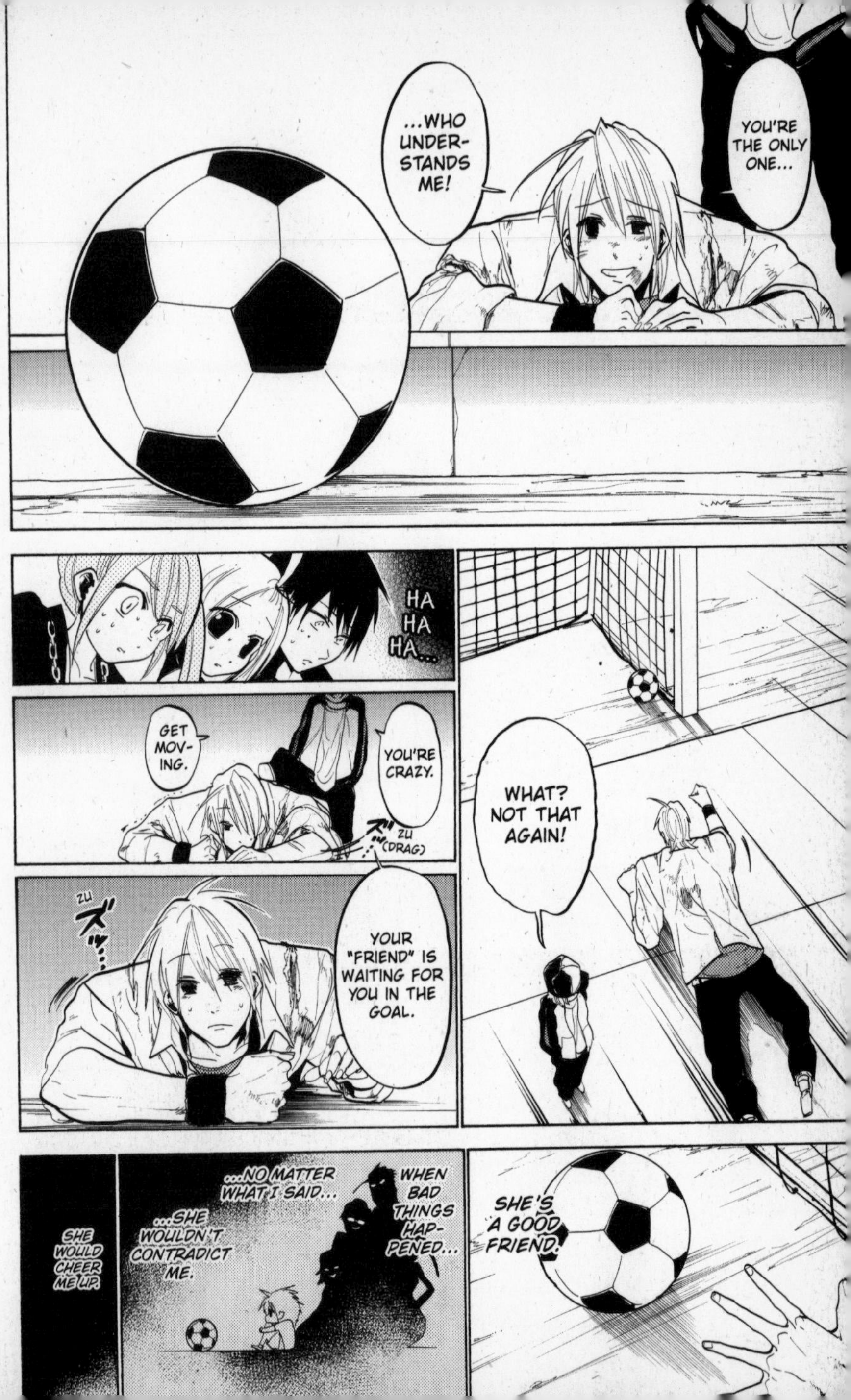
YOU'RE THE ONLY ONE...
...WHO UNDER-STANDS ME!
HA HA HA...
WHAT? NOT THAT AGAIN!
YOU'RE CRAZY.
GET MOV-ING.
ZU (DRAG)
YOUR "FRIEND" IS WAITING FOR YOU IN THE GOAL.
ZU
SHE'S A GOOD FRIEND.
WHEN BAD THINGS HAP-PENED...
...NO MATTER WHAT I SAID...
...SHE WOULDN'T CONTRADICT ME.
SHE WOULD CHEER ME UP.

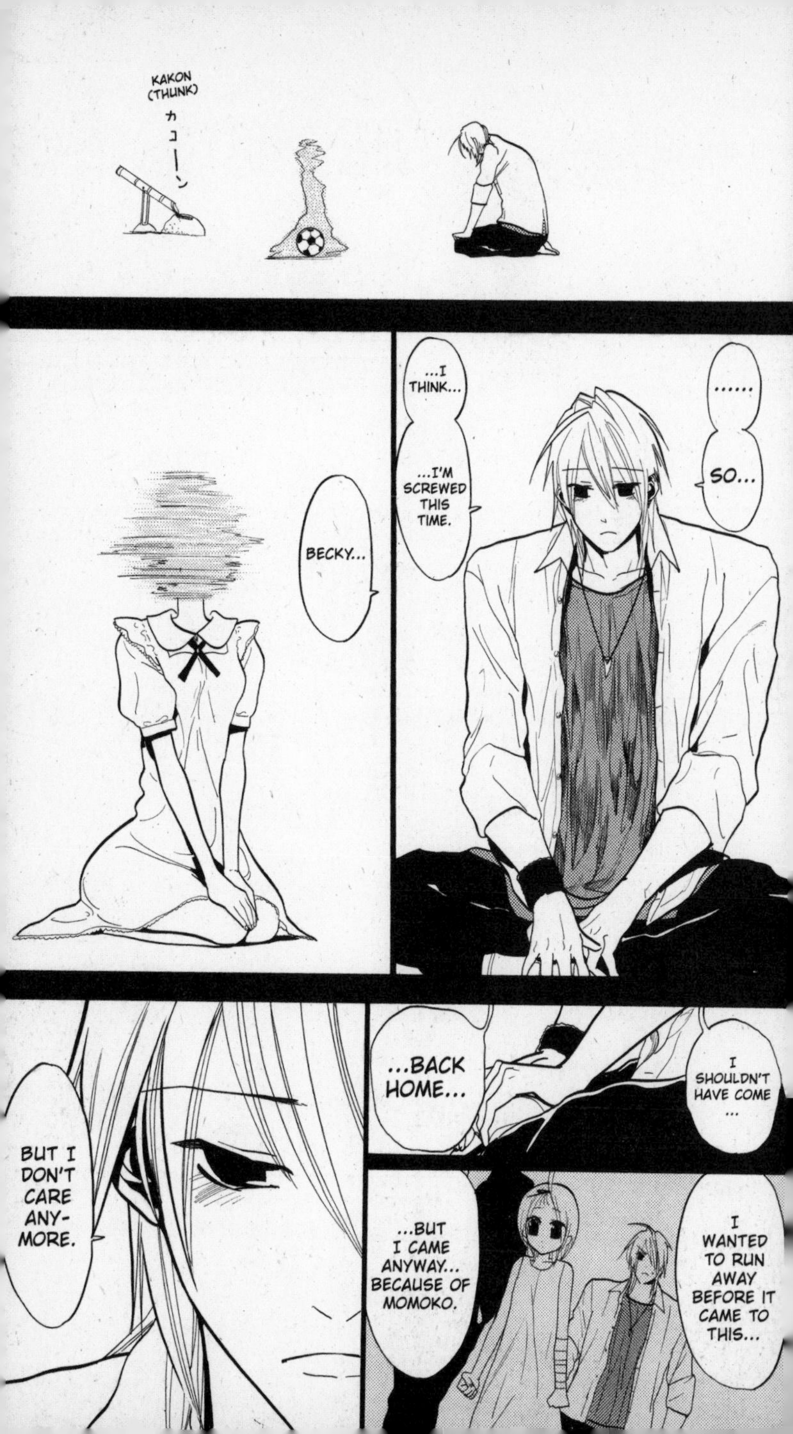
KAKON (THUNK)
カコーン
......
SO...
...I THINK...
...I'M SCREWED THIS TIME.
BECKY...
I SHOULDN'T HAVE COME ...
...BACK HOME...
I WANTED TO RUN AWAY BEFORE IT CAME TO THIS...
...BUT I CAME ANYWAY... BECAUSE OF MOMOKO.
BUT I DON'T CARE ANY-MORE.

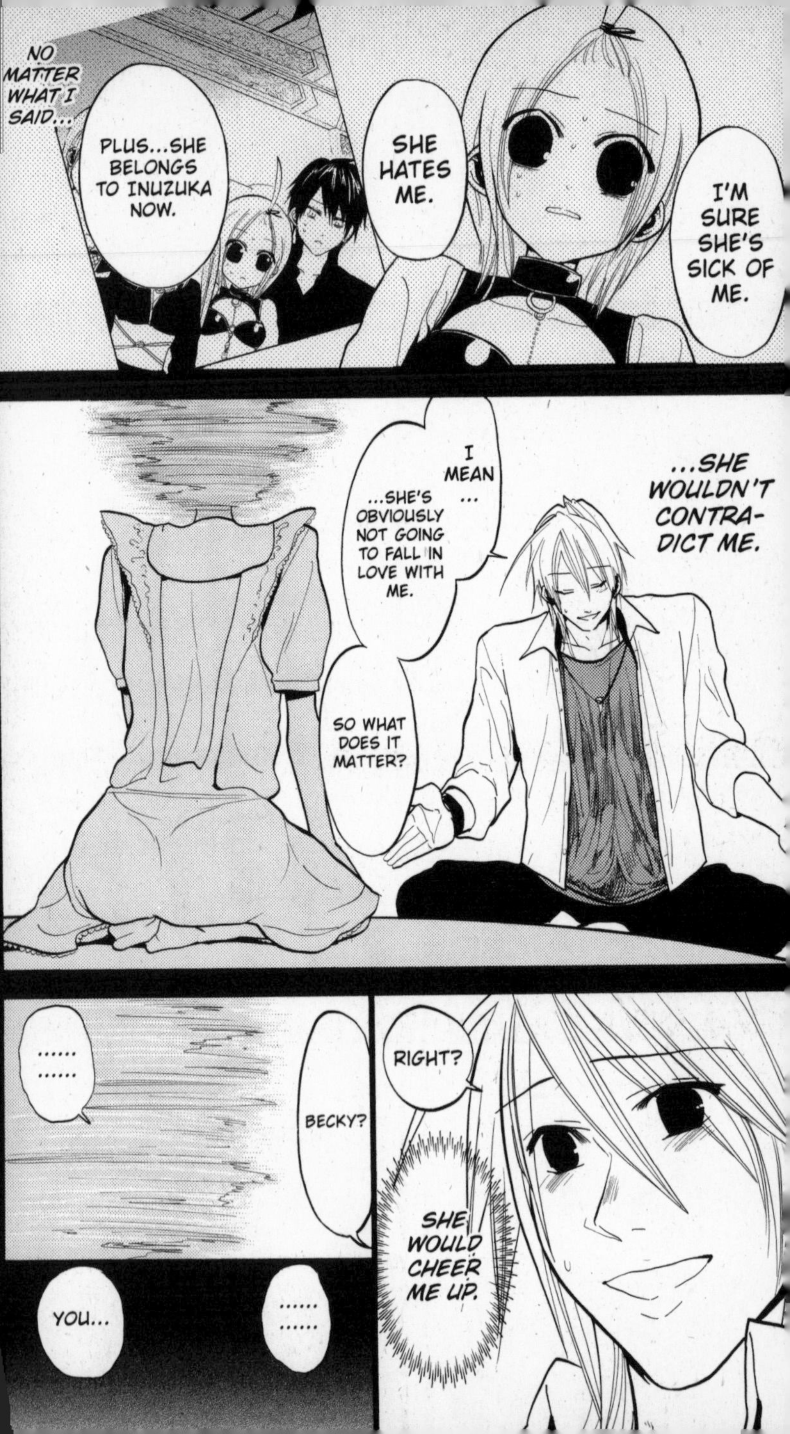

I'M SURE SHE'S SICK OF ME.
SHE HATES ME.
PLUS...SHE BELONGS TO INUZUKA NOW.
NO MATTER WHAT I SAID...
...SHE WOULDN'T CONTRA-DICT ME.
I MEAN...
...SHE'S OBVIOUSLY NOT GOING TO FALL IN LOVE WITH ME.
SO WHAT DOES IT MATTER?
RIGHT?
BECKY?
SHE WOULD CHEER ME UP.
....
....
YOU...

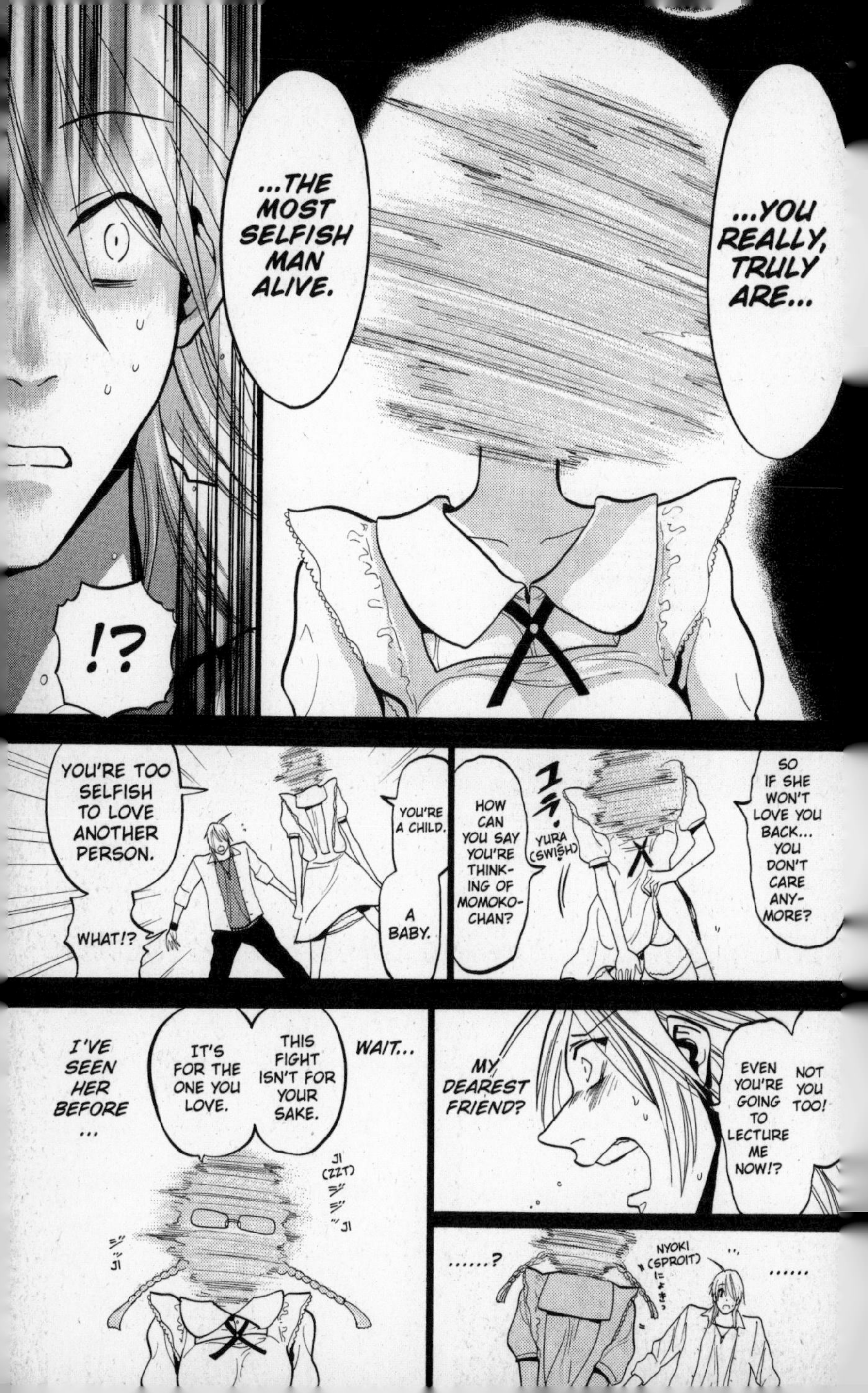
...YOU REALLY, TRULY ARE...
...THE MOST SELFISH MAN ALIVE.
!?
SO IF SHE WON'T LOVE YOU BACK... YOU DON'T CARE ANYMORE?
YURA (SWISH)
HOW CAN YOU SAY YOU'RE THINKING OF MOMOKO-CHAN?
YOU'RE A CHILD.
A BABY.
YOU'RE TOO SELFISH TO LOVE ANOTHER PERSON.
WHAT!?
NOT YOU TOO!
EVEN YOU'RE GOING TO LECTURE ME NOW!?
MY DEAREST FRIEND?
......
NYOKI (SPROIT)
......?
WAIT...
THIS FIGHT ISN'T FOR YOUR SAKE.
IT'S FOR THE ONE YOU LOVE.
I'VE SEEN HER BEFORE...
JI (ZZT)
JI
JI

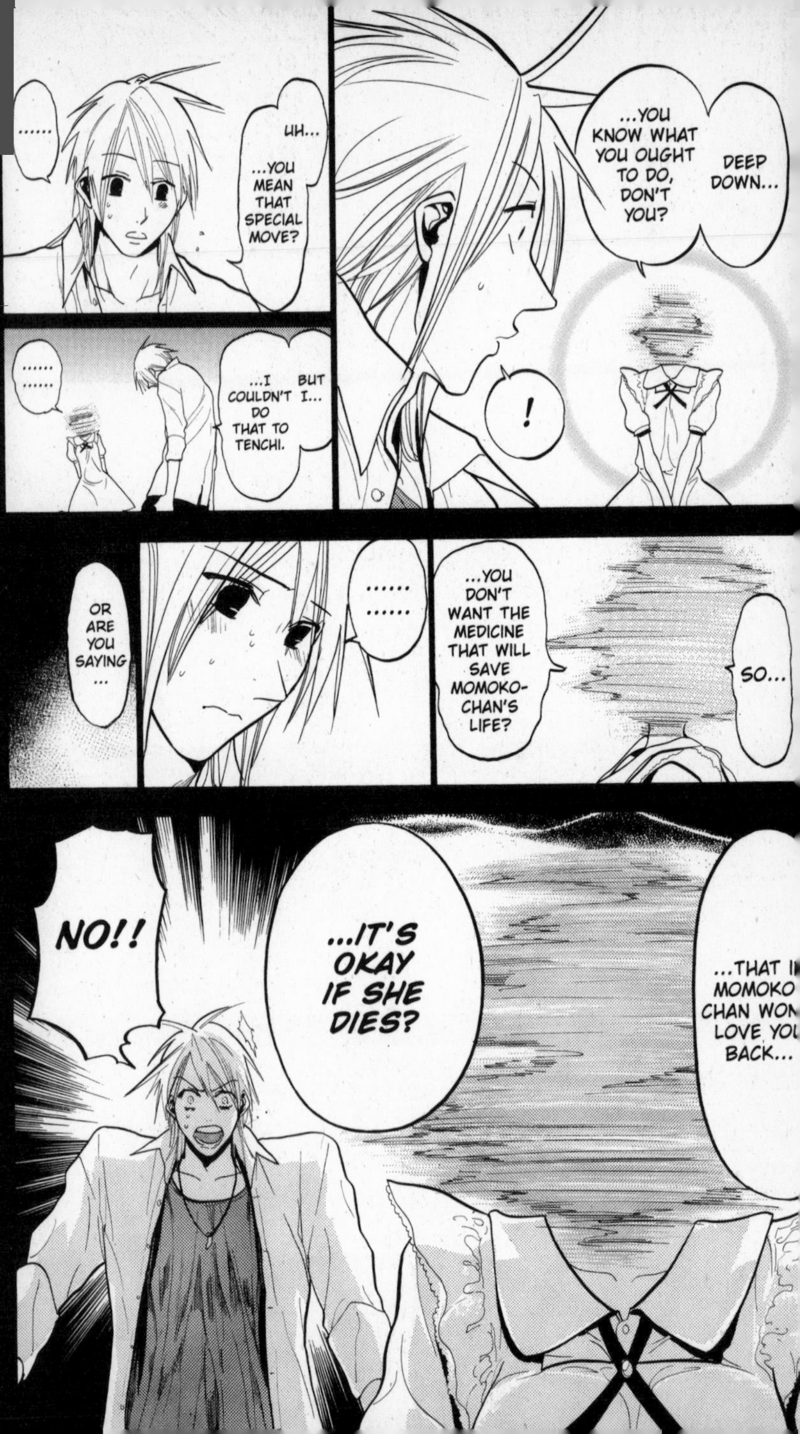
DEEP DOWN...
...YOU KNOW WHAT YOU OUGHT TO DO, DON'T YOU?
!
UH... ...YOU MEAN THAT SPECIAL MOVE?
......
BUT I... ...I COULDN'T DO THAT TO TENCHI.
....
SO...
...YOU DON'T WANT THE MEDICINE THAT WILL SAVE MOMOKO-CHAN'S LIFE?
....
OR ARE YOU SAYING ...
...THAT I MOMOKO CHAN WON LOVE YO BACK...
...IT'S OKAY IF SHE DIES?
NO!!

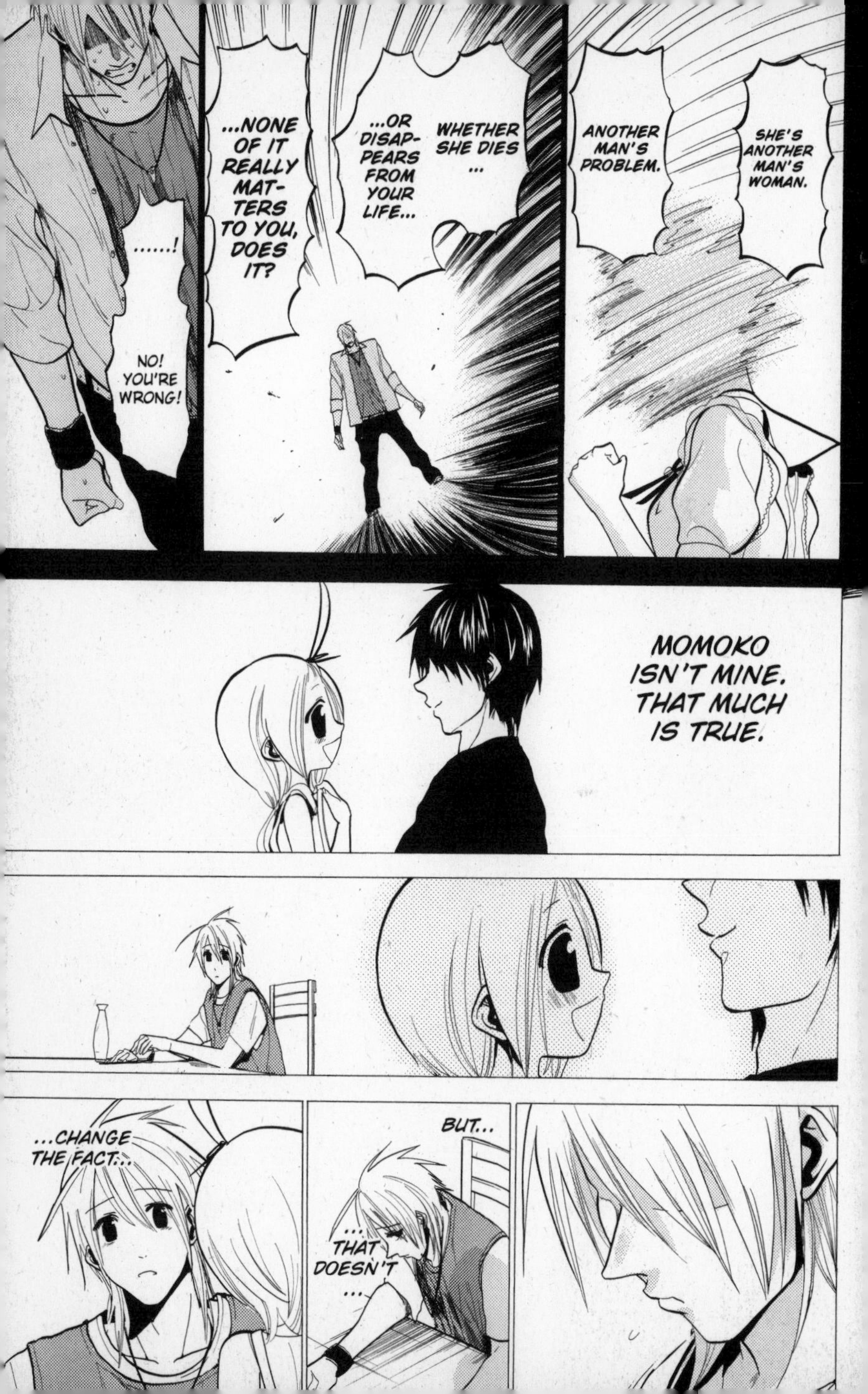
SHE'S ANOTHER MAN'S WOMAN.
ANOTHER MAN'S PROBLEM.
WHETHER SHE DIES ...
...OR DISAPPEARS FROM YOUR LIFE...
...NONE OF IT REALLY MATTERS TO YOU, DOES IT?
......!
NO! YOU'RE WRONG!
MOMOKO ISN'T MINE. THAT MUCH IS TRUE.
BUT...
...THAT DOESN'T ...
...CHANGE THE FACT...

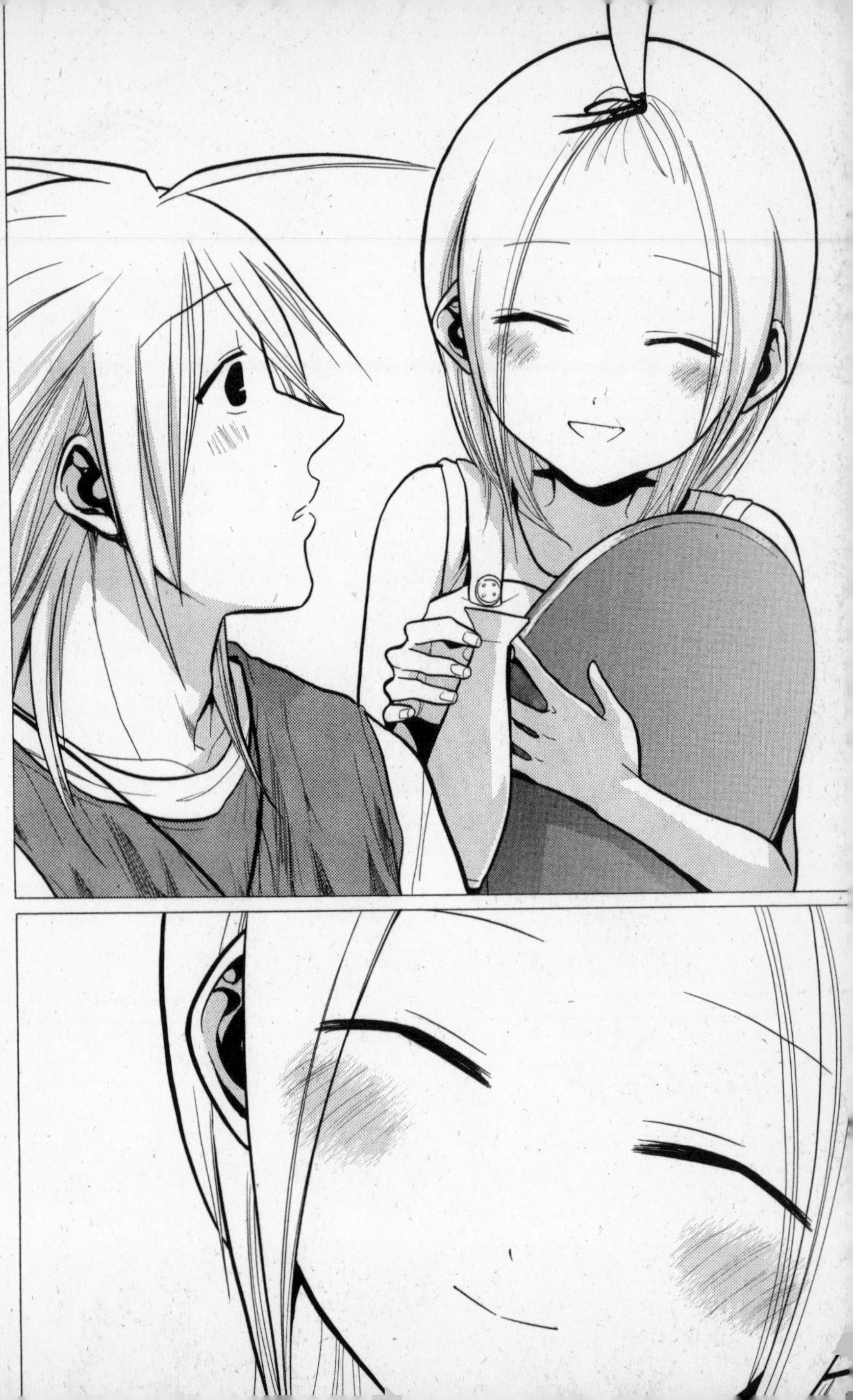

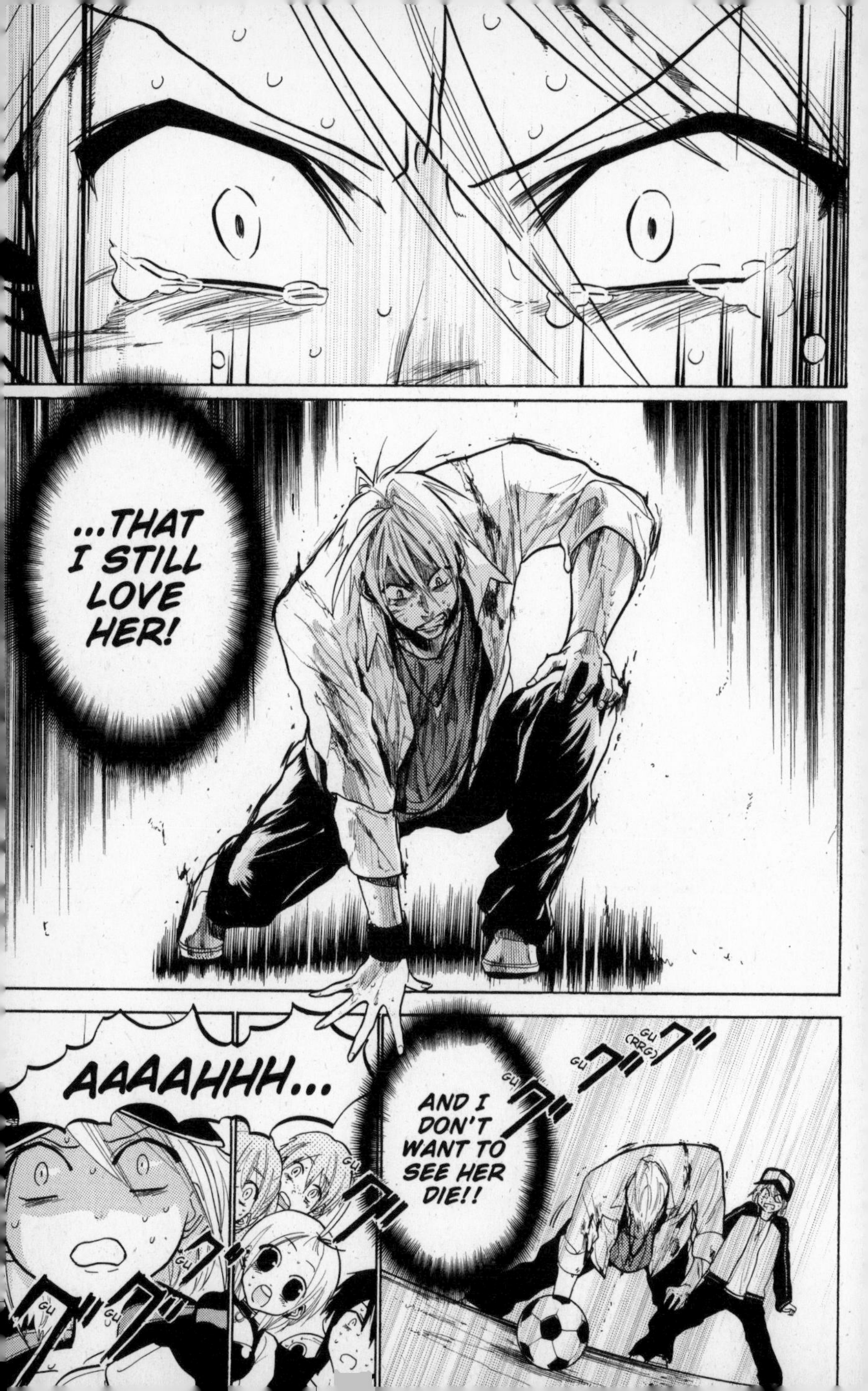
...THAT I STILL LOVE HER!
GU (RRG)
GU
GU
AND I DON'T WANT TO SEE HER DIE!!
AAAAHHH...
GU
GU
GU
GU

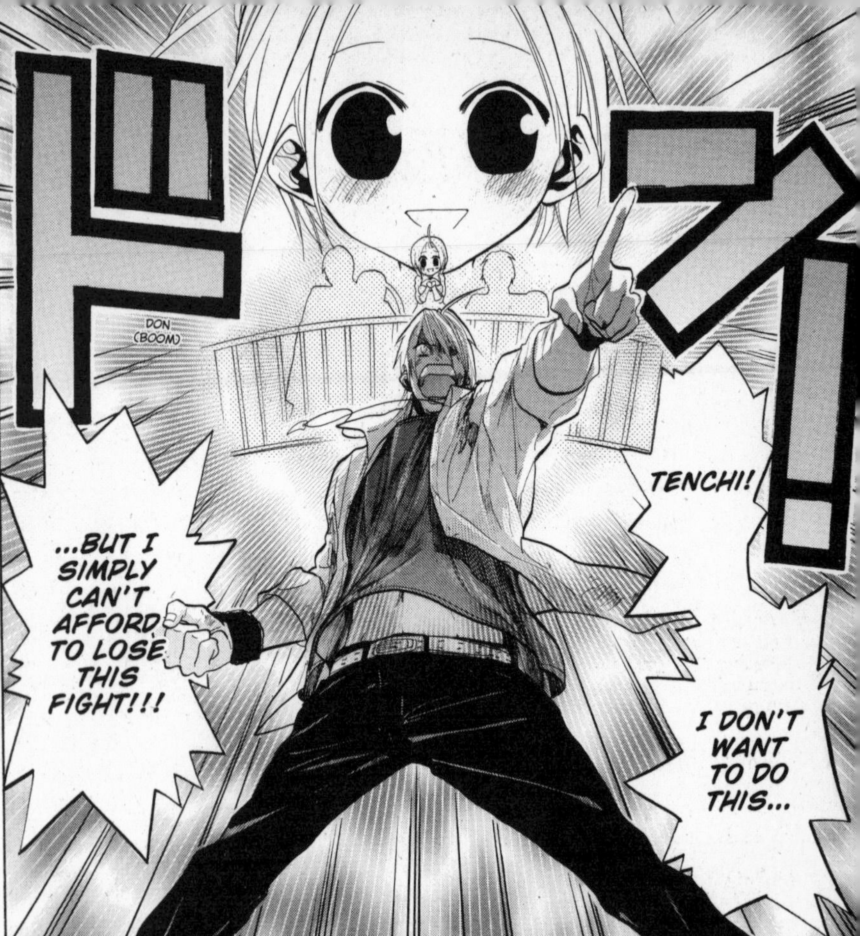
DON
(BOOM)
TENCHI!
I DON'T WANT TO DO THIS...
...BUT I SIMPLY CAN'T AFFORD TO LOSE THIS FIGHT!!!
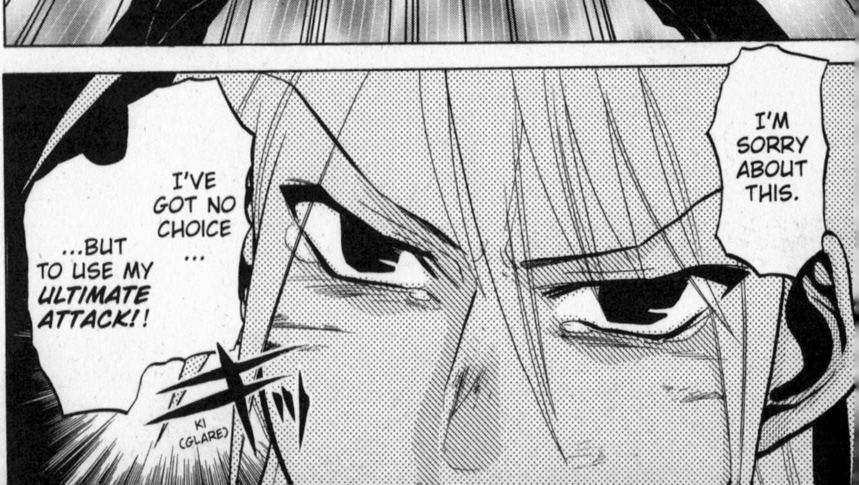
I'M SORRY ABOUT THIS.
I'VE GOT NO CHOICE ...
...BUT TO USE MY ULTIMATE ATTACK!!
KI
(GLARE)

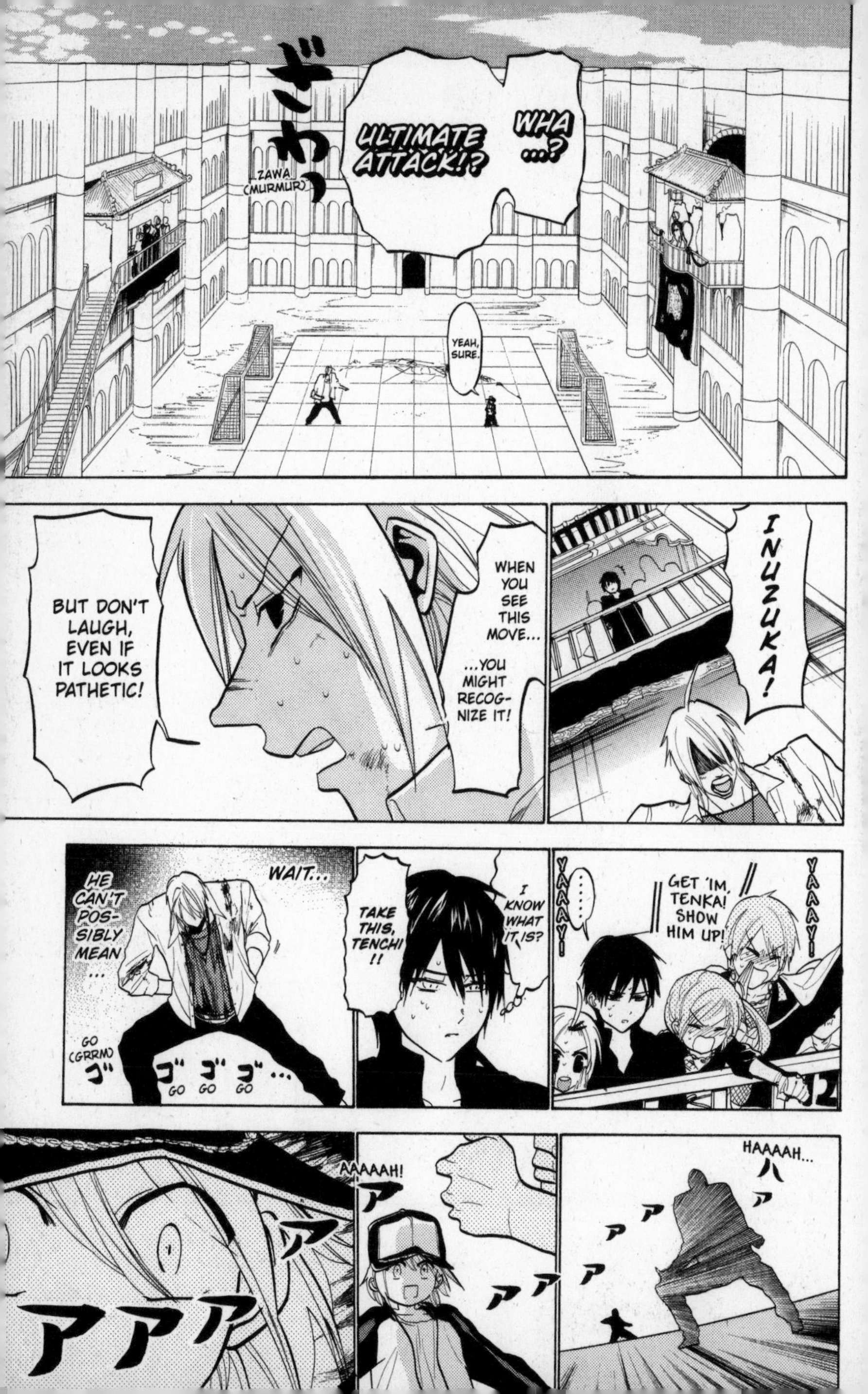
WHA ...?
ULTIMATE ATTACK!?
ざわっ
ZAWA (MURMUR)
YEAH, SURE.
INUZUKA!
WHEN YOU SEE THIS MOVE...
...YOU MIGHT RECOGNIZE IT!
BUT DON'T LAUGH, EVEN IF IT LOOKS PATHETIC!
YAAAAY!
GET 'IM, TENKA! SHOW HIM UP!
......
YAAAAY!
I KNOW WHAT IT IS?
TAKE THIS, TENCHI!!
WAIT...
HE CAN'T POS-SIBLY MEAN...
GO (GRRM)
ゴ
ゴゴゴ...
GO GO GO
HAAAAH...
ハアアアアアア
AAAAAH!
ア
アアアア

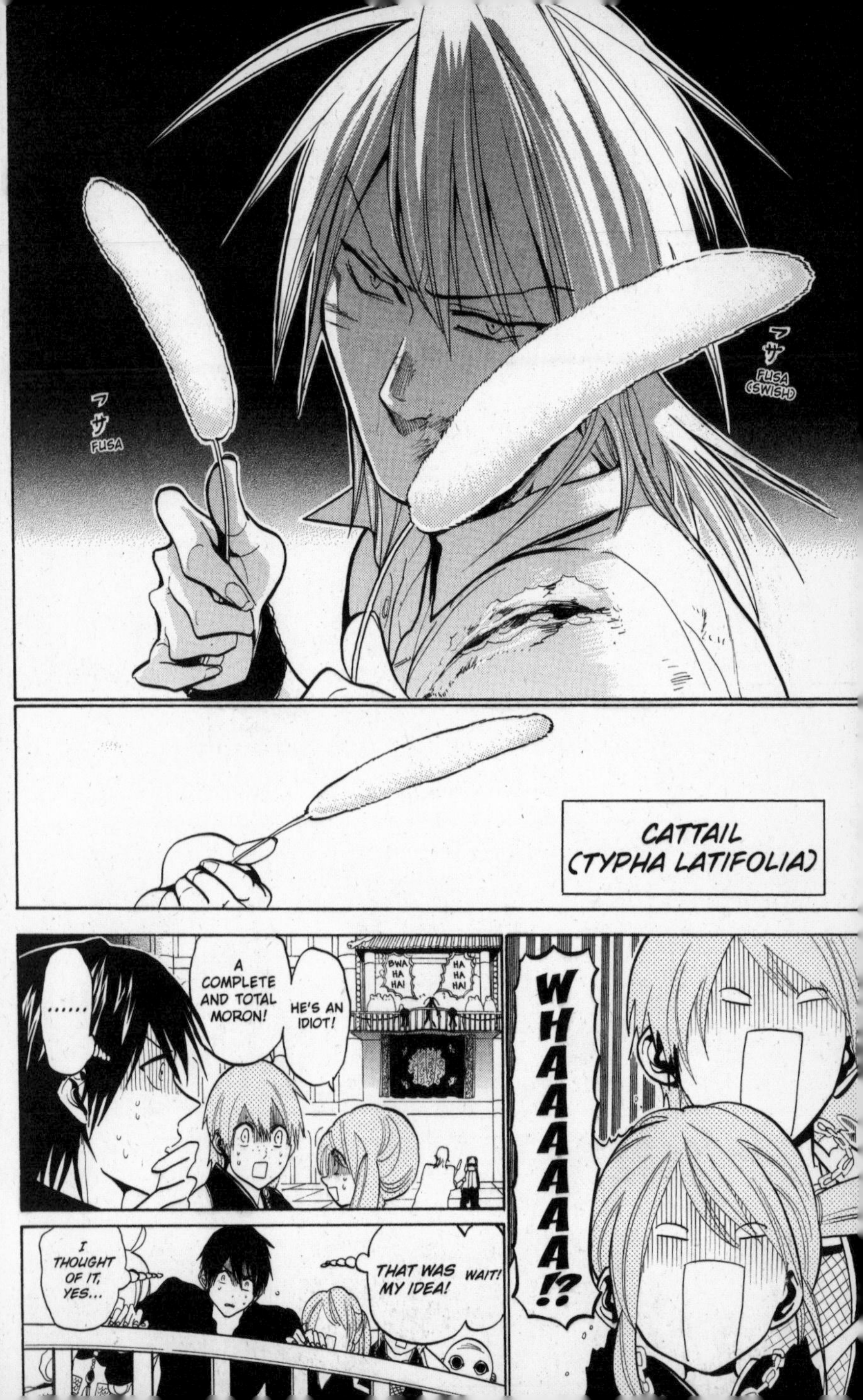
フサ
FUSA (SWISH)
フサ
FUSA
CATTAIL (TYPHA LATIFOLIA)
WHAAAAAAAAA!?
HA HA HA!
BWA HA HA!
HE'S AN IDIOT!
A COMPLETE AND TOTAL MORON!
......
WAIT!
THAT WAS MY IDEA!
I THOUGHT OF IT, YES...

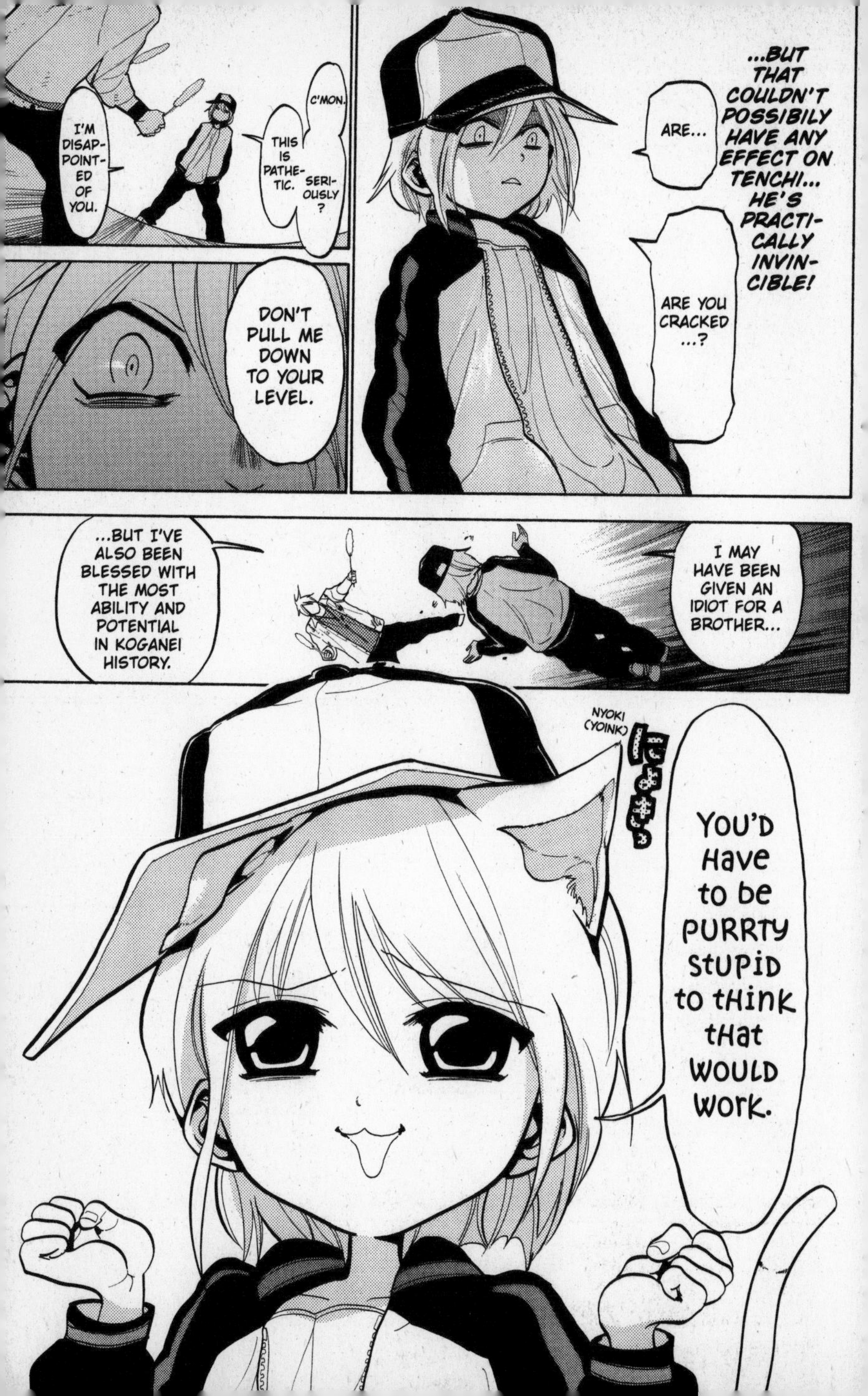
...BUT THAT COULDN'T POSSIBILY HAVE ANY EFFECT ON TENCHI... HE'S PRACTICALLY INVINCIBLE!
ARE...
ARE YOU CRACKED ...?
C'MON.
THIS IS PATHETIC.
SERIOUSLY?
I'M DISAPPOINTED OF YOU.
DON'T PULL ME DOWN TO YOUR LEVEL.
I MAY HAVE BEEN GIVEN AN IDIOT FOR A BROTHER...
...BUT I'VE ALSO BEEN BLESSED WITH THE MOST ABILITY AND POTENTIAL IN KOGANEI HISTORY.
NYOKI (YOINK)
YOU'D HAVE TO BE PURRTY STUPID TO THINK THAT WOULD WORK.

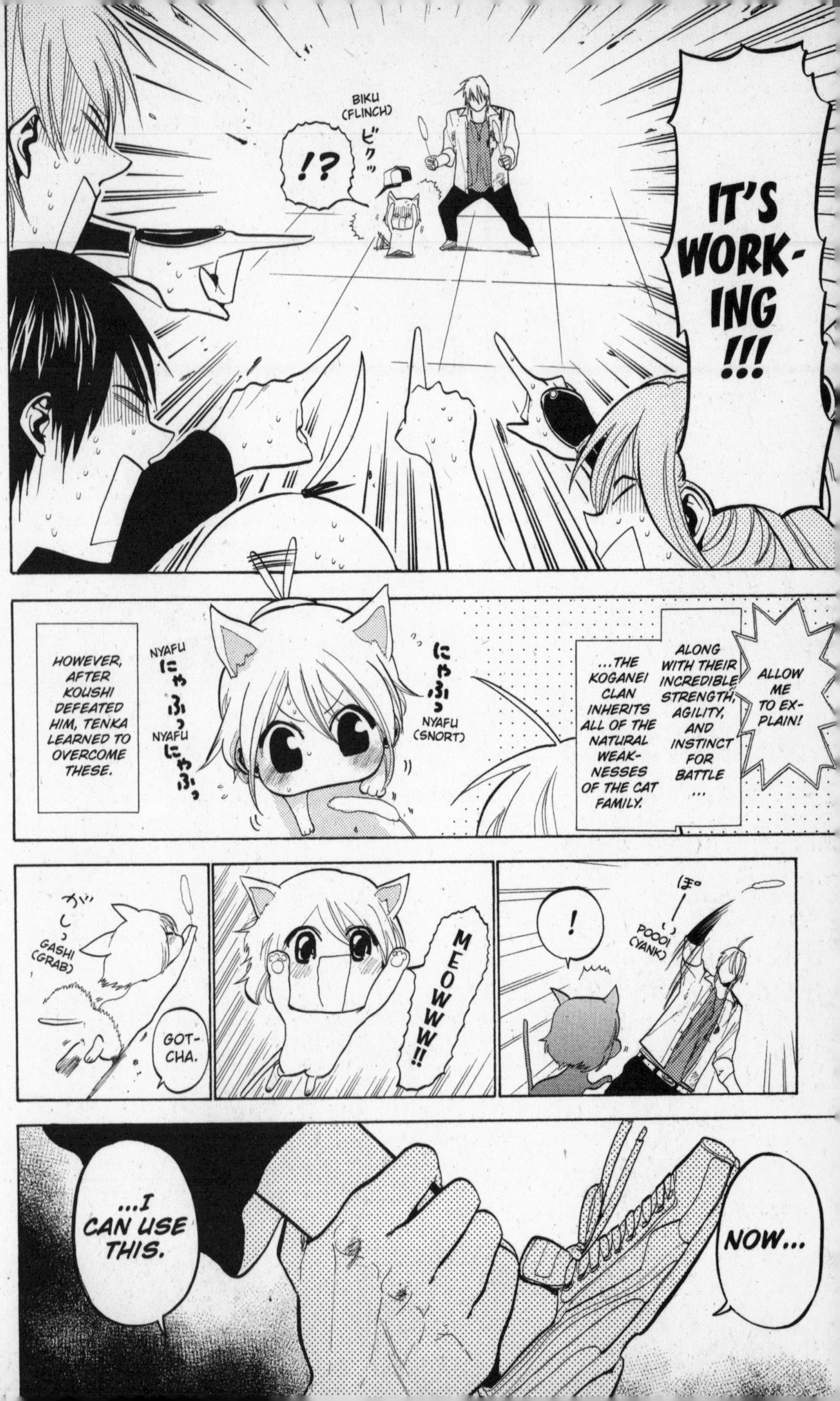
IT'S WORKING!!!
BIKU (FLINCH)
ビクッ
!?
ALLOW ME TO EXPLAIN!
ALONG WITH THEIR INCREDIBLE STRENGTH, AGILITY, AND INSTINCT FOR BATTLE ...
...THE KOGANEI CLAN INHERITS ALL OF THE NATURAL WEAKNESSES OF THE CAT FAMILY.
にゃふっ
NYAFU (SNORT)
NYAFU にゃふっ
NYAFU にゃふっ
HOWEVER, AFTER KOUSHI DEFEATED HIM, TENKA LEARNED TO OVERCOME THESE.
ぽー(い)
POOOI (YANK)
!
MEOWWW!!
がしっ
GASHI (GRAB)
GOT-CHA.
NOW...
...I CAN USE THIS.

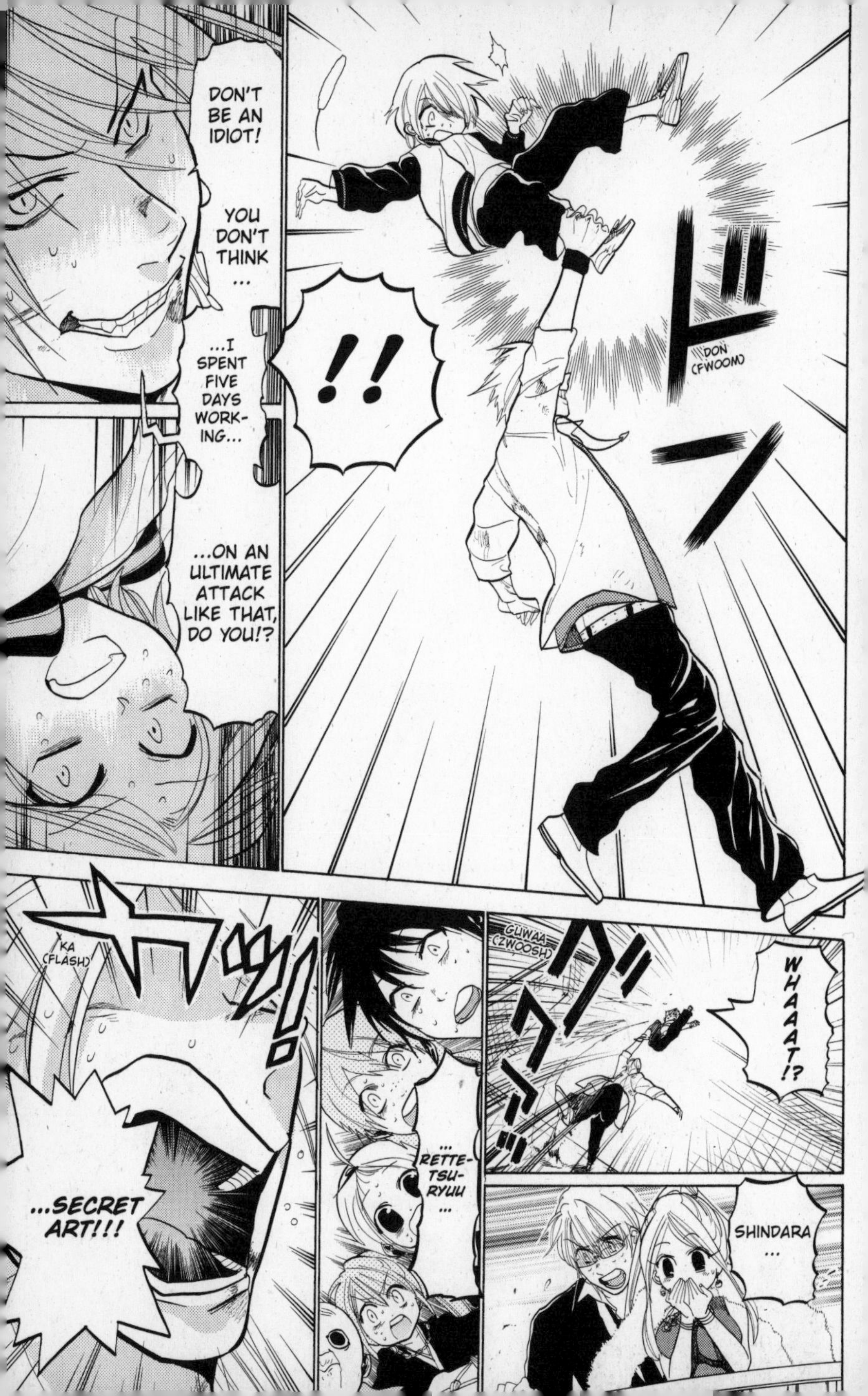
!!
DON (FWOOM)
DON'T BE AN IDIOT!
YOU DON'T THINK ...
...I SPENT FIVE DAYS WORK-ING...
...ON AN ULTIMATE ATTACK LIKE THAT, DO YOU!?
GUWAA (ZWOOSH)
WHAAAT!?
SHINDARA ...
... RETTE-TSU-RYUU ...
KA (FLASH)
...SECRET ART!!!

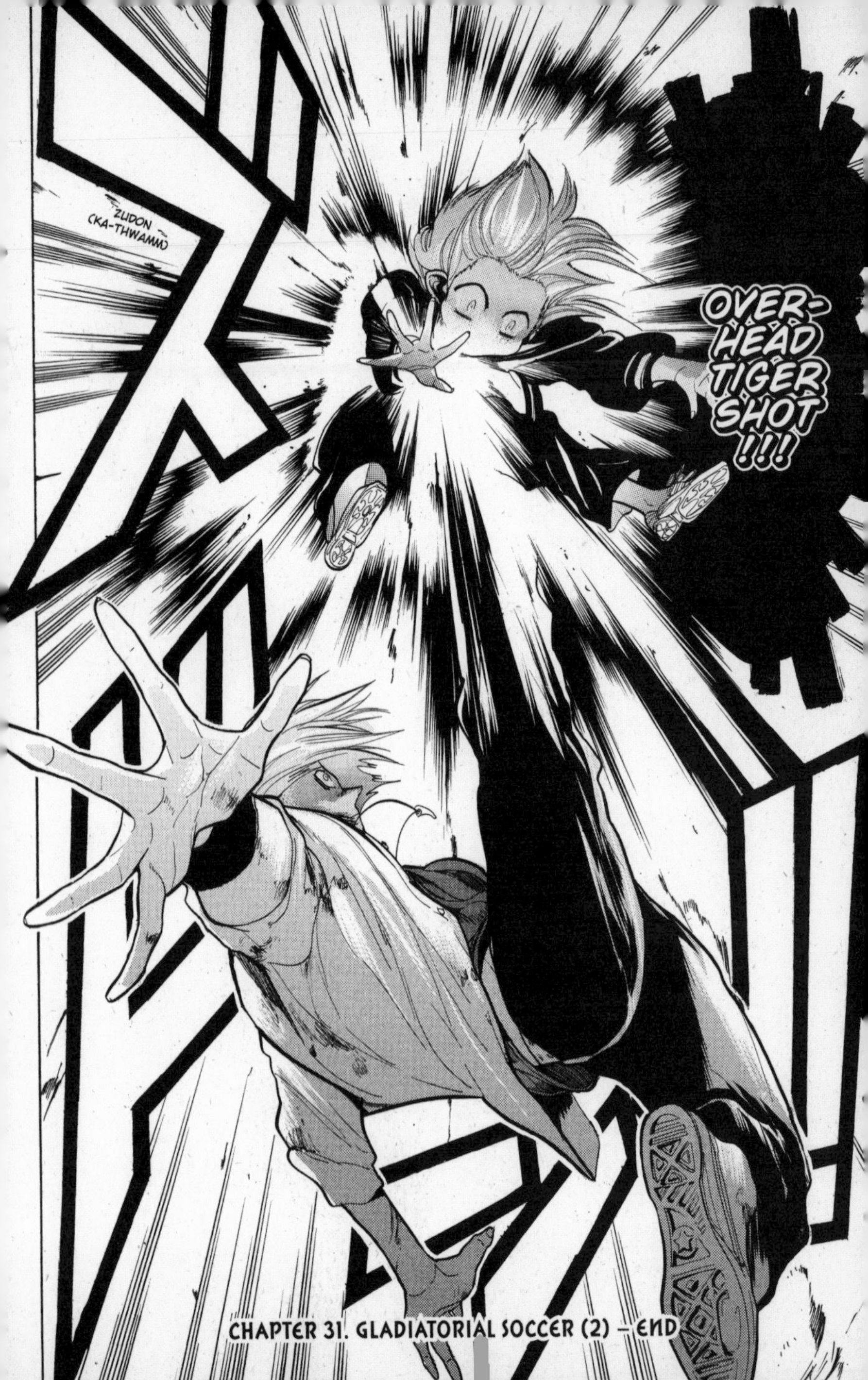
OVER-HEAD TIGER SHOT!!!
ZUDON (KA-THWAMM)

CHAPTER 31. GLADIATORIAL SOCCER (2) – END

32. GLADIATORIAL SOCCER (3)

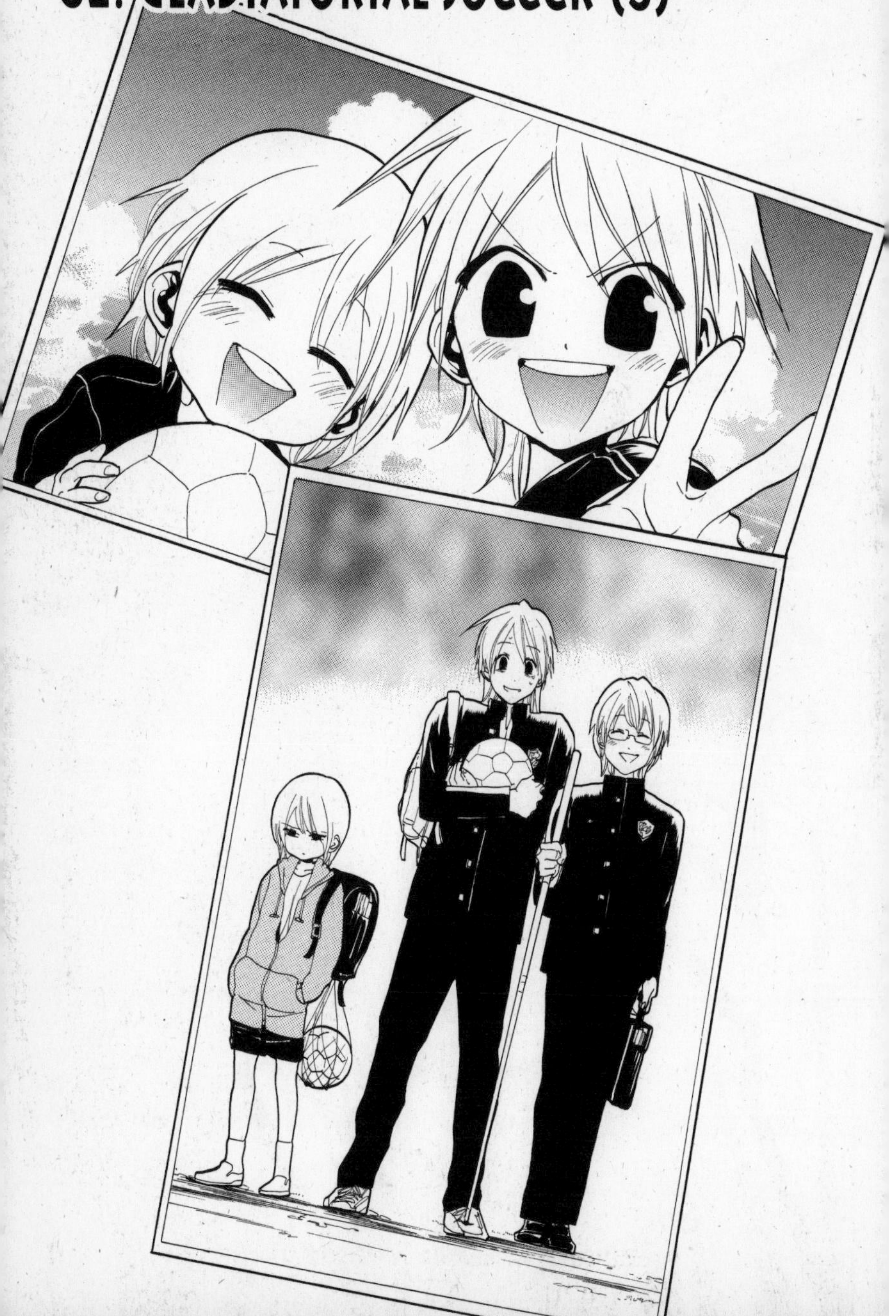

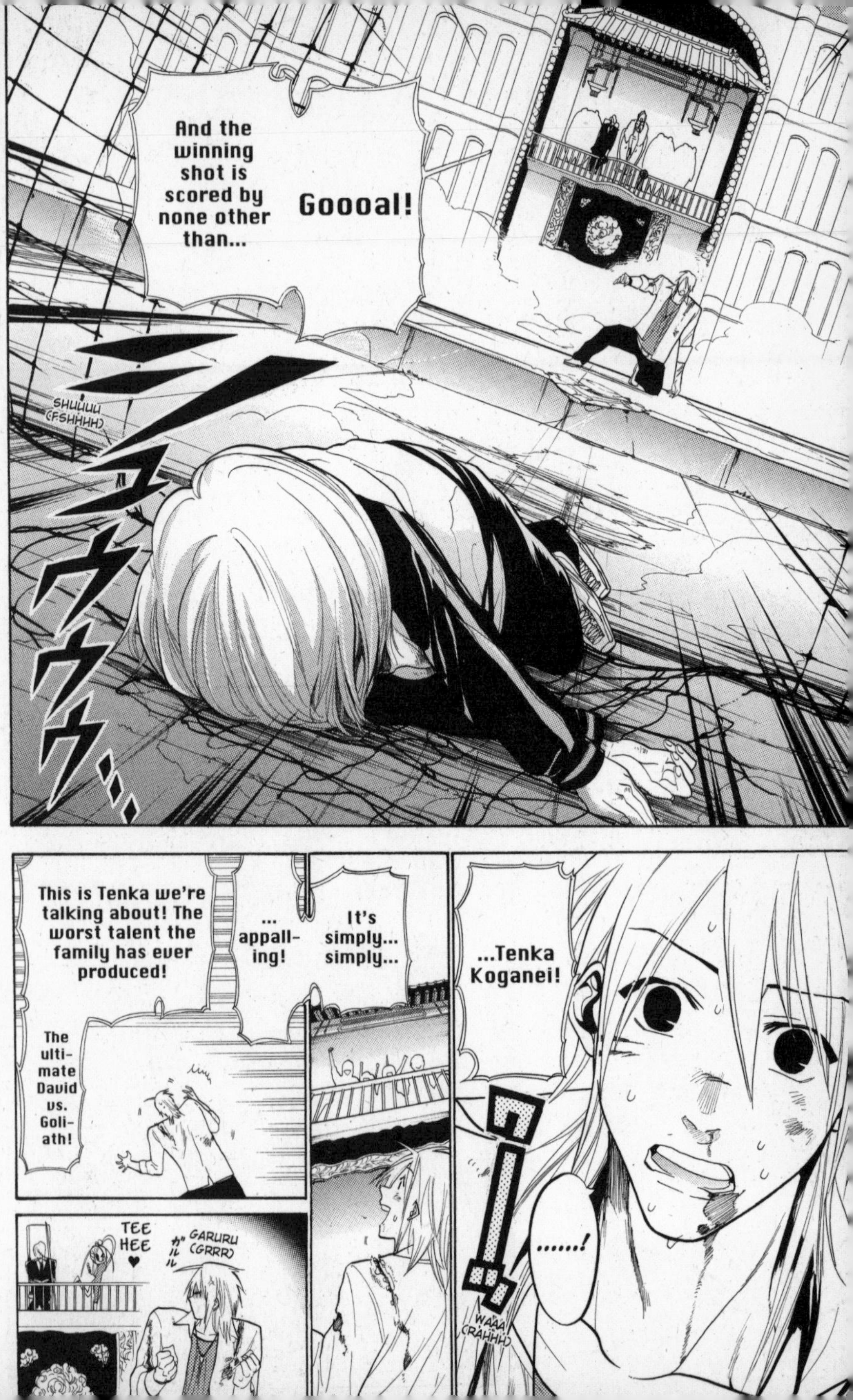
Goooal!
And the winning shot is scored by none other than...
SHUUUU (FSHHHH)
...Tenka Koganei!
WAAA (RAHHH)
......!
It's simply... simply...
... appall-ing!
This is Tenka we're talking about! The worst talent the family has ever produced!
The ultimate David vs. Goliath!
TEE HEE ♥
GARURU (GRRR)

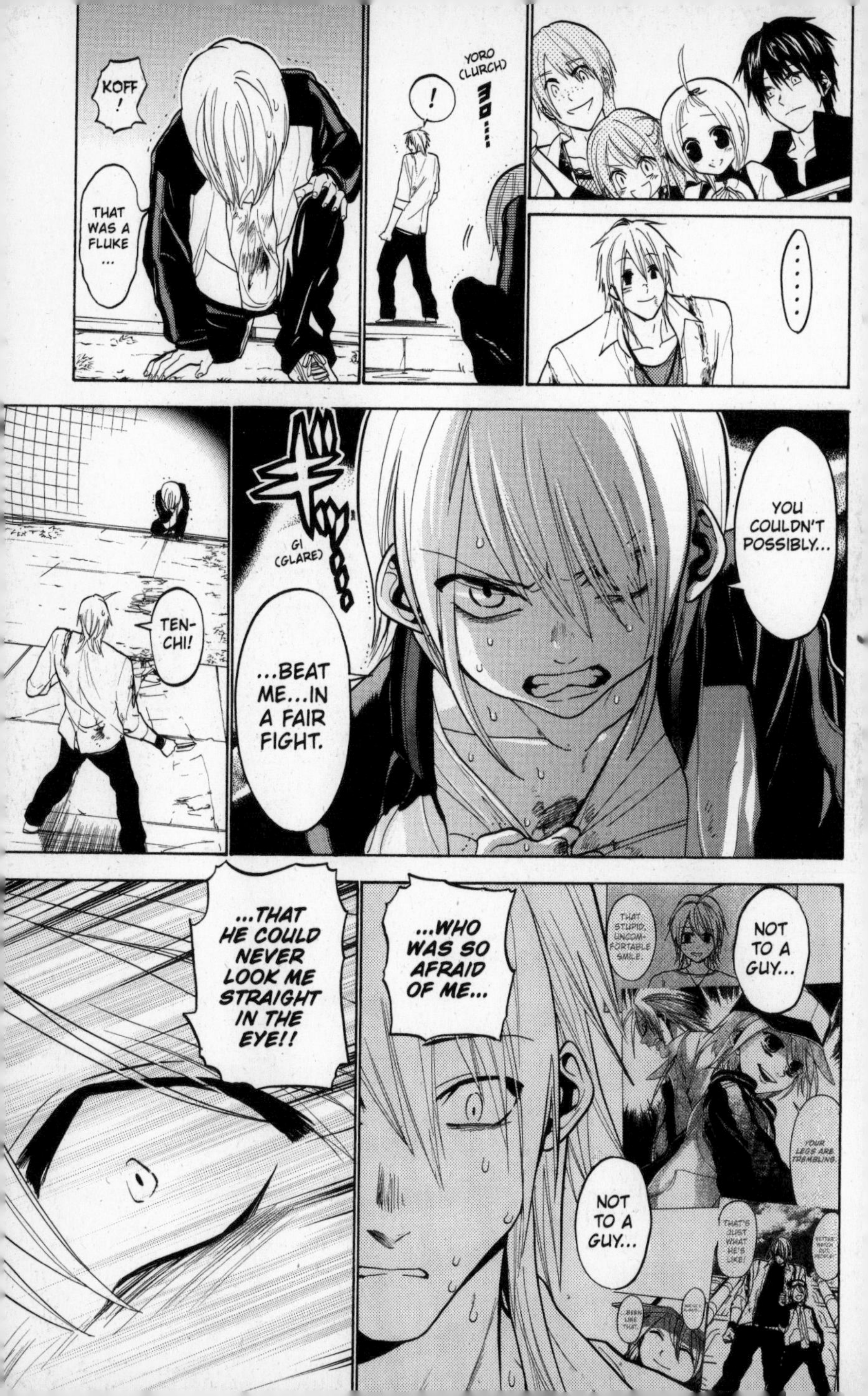
......
YORO (LURCH)
ヨロ…
!
KOFF!
THAT WAS A FLUKE...
YOU COULDN'T POSSIBLY...
GI (GLARE)
...BEAT ME...IN A FAIR FIGHT.
TEN-CHI!
NOT TO A GUY...
THAT STUPID, UNCOMFORTABLE SMILE.
YOUR LEGS ARE TREMBLING.
THAT'S JUST WHAT HE'S LIKE!
...BEEN LIKE THAT.
NOT TO A GUY...
...WHO WAS SO AFRAID OF ME...
...THAT HE COULD NEVER LOOK ME STRAIGHT IN THE EYE!!

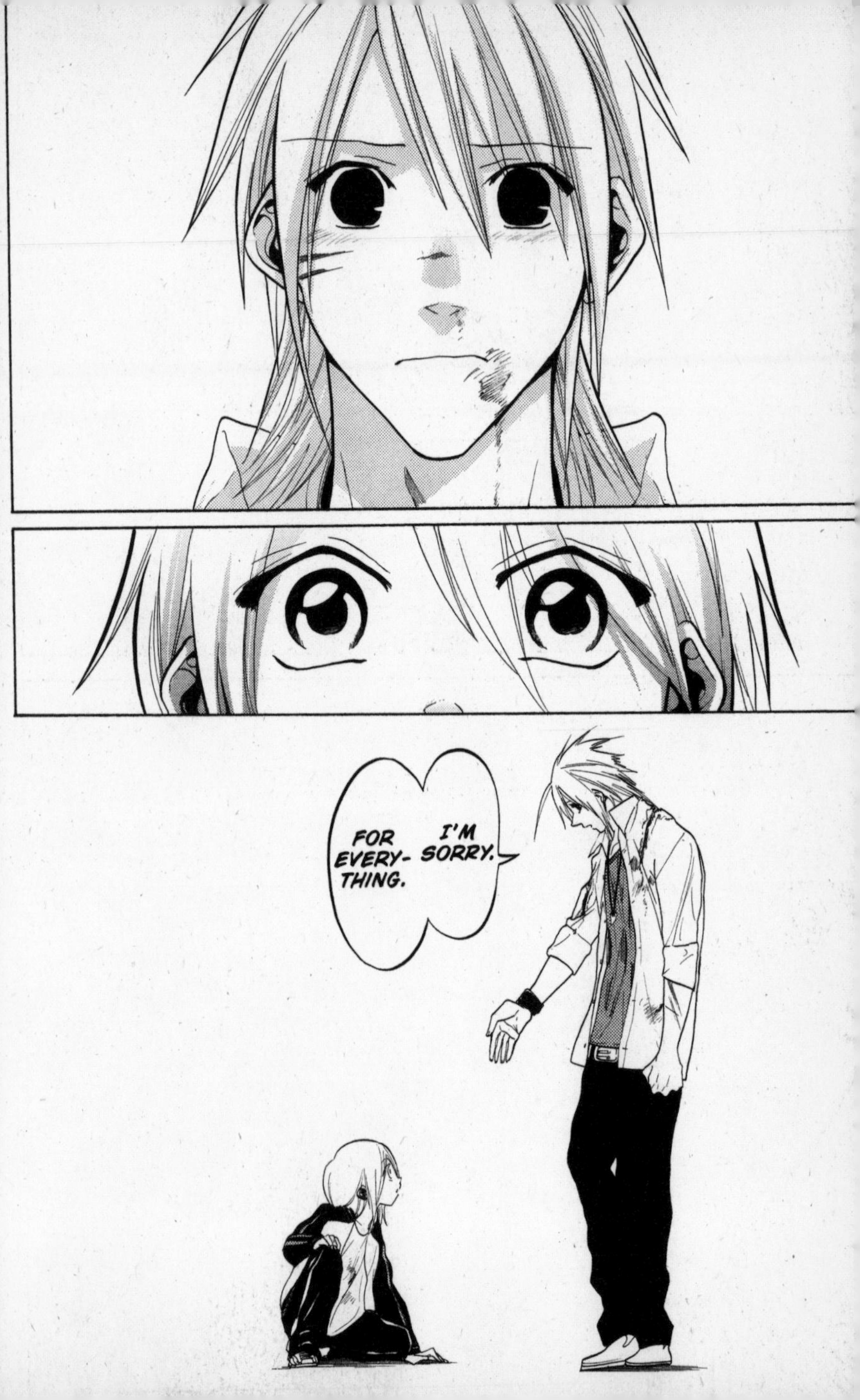
I'M SORRY. FOR EVERYTHING.

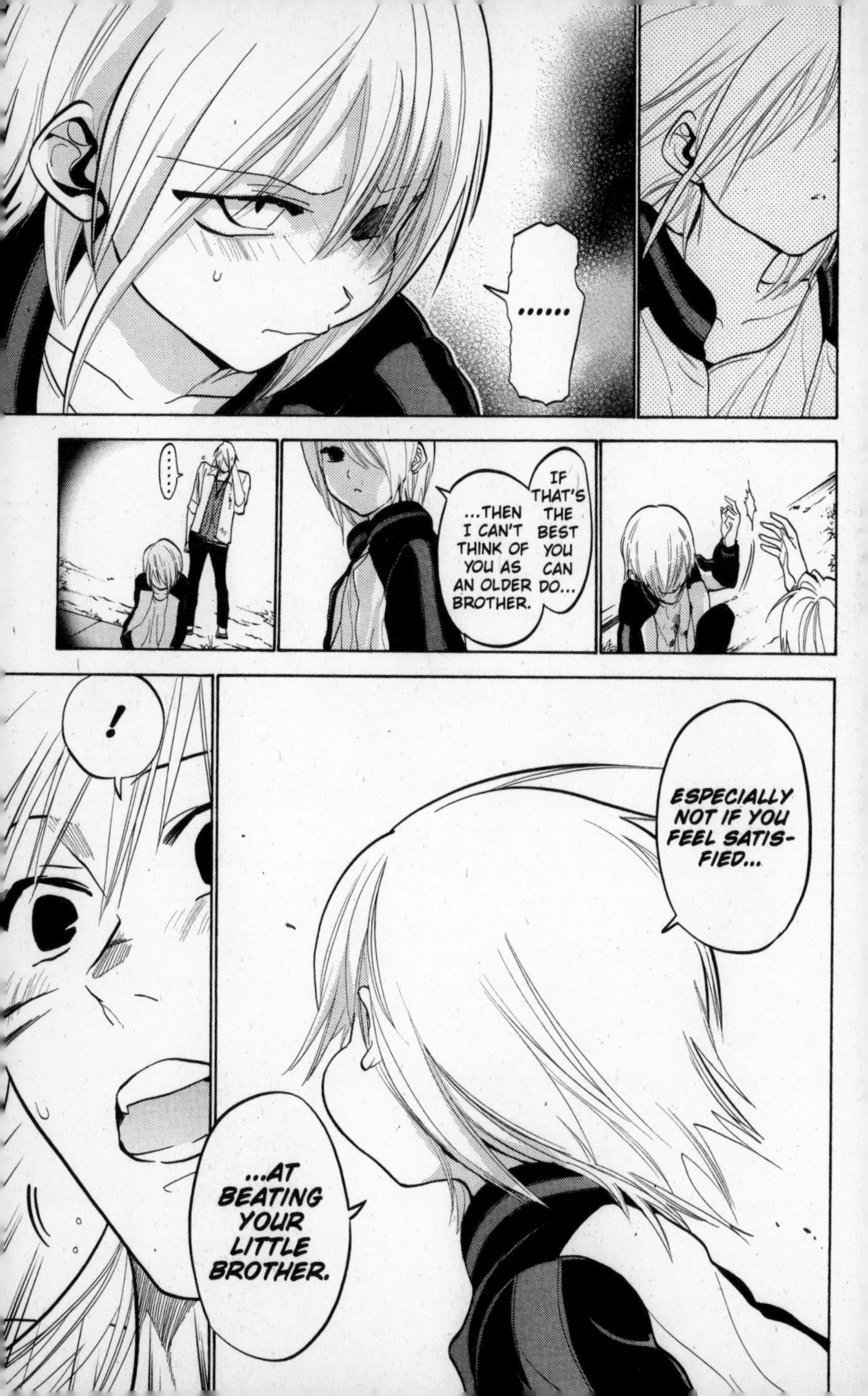
......
IF THAT'S THE BEST YOU CAN DO...
...THEN I CAN'T THINK OF YOU AS AN OLDER BROTHER.
.....
ESPECIALLY NOT IF YOU FEEL SATIS-FIED...
...AT BEATING YOUR LITTLE BROTHER.
!

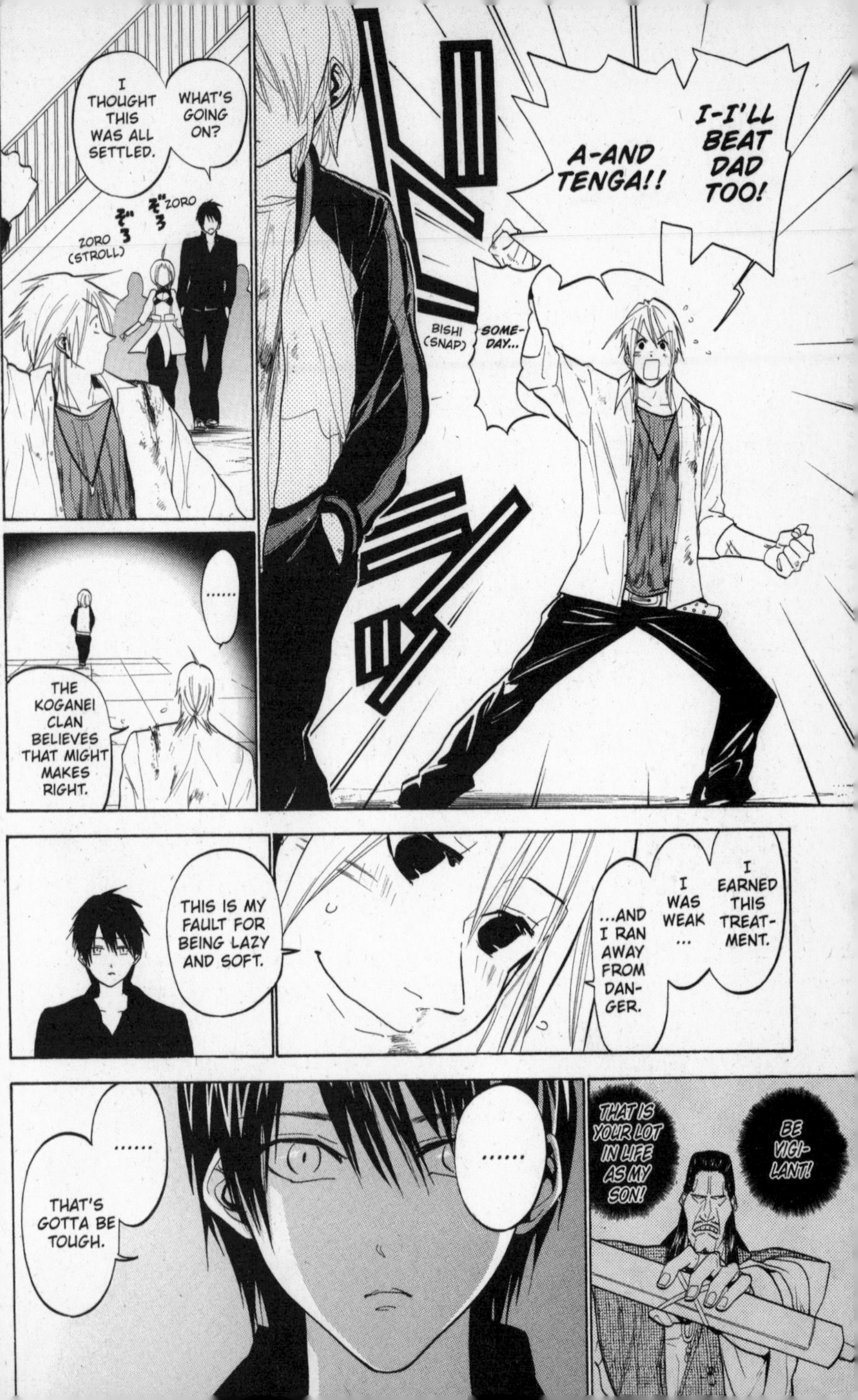
I-I'LL BEAT DAD TOO!
A-AND TENGA!!
SOME-DAY...
BISHI (SNAP)
WHAT'S GOING ON?
I THOUGHT THIS WAS ALL SETTLED.
ぞろ ZORO
ぞろ ZORO (STROLL)
......
THE KOGANEI CLAN BELIEVES THAT MIGHT MAKES RIGHT.
I EARNED THIS TREATMENT.
I WAS WEAK...
...AND I RAN AWAY FROM DANGER.
THIS IS MY FAULT FOR BEING LAZY AND SOFT.
BE VIGILANT!
THAT IS YOUR LOT IN LIFE AS MY SON!
......
......
THAT'S GOTTA BE TOUGH.

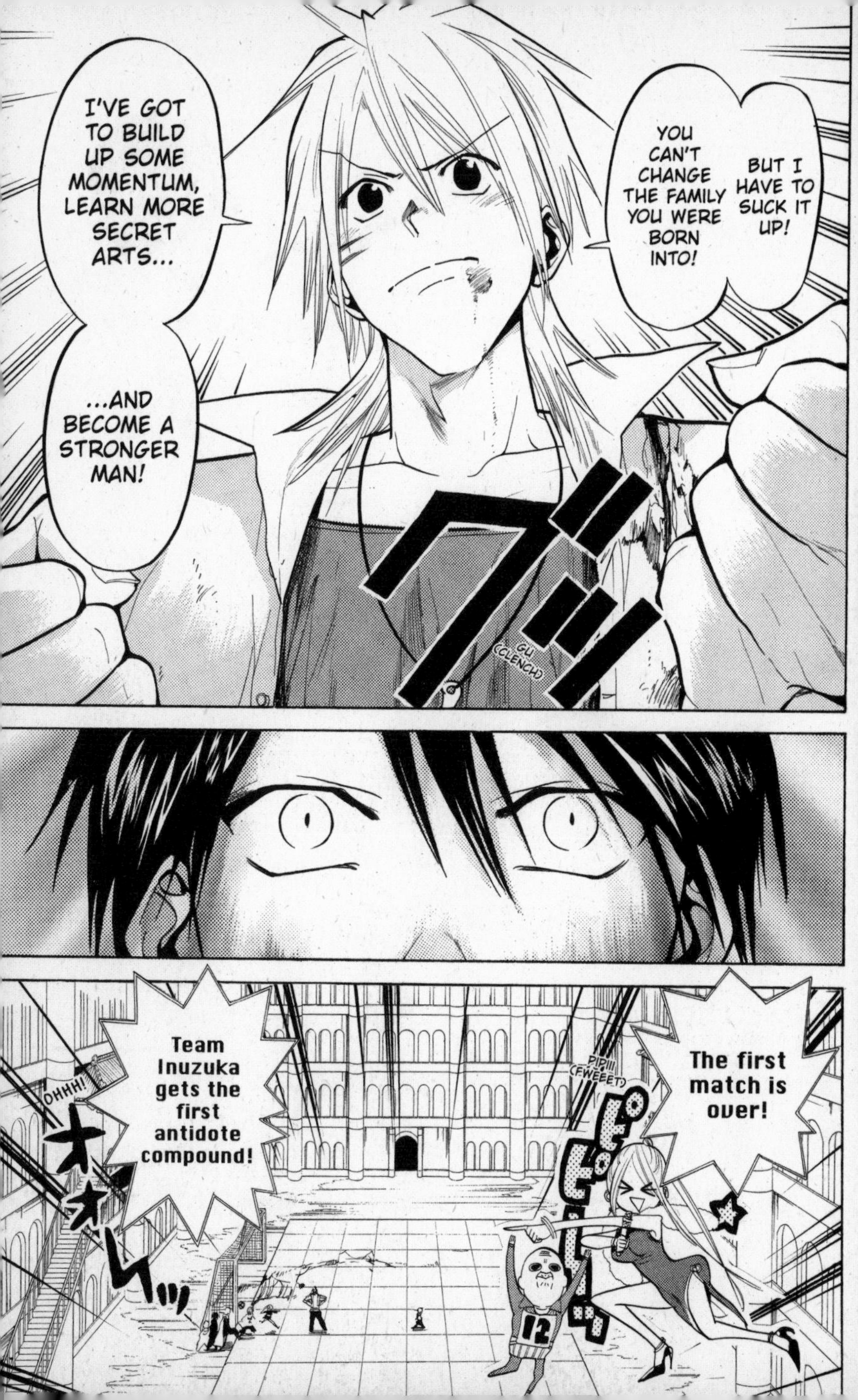
YOU CAN'T CHANGE THE FAMILY YOU WERE BORN INTO!
BUT I HAVE TO SUCK IT UP!
I'VE GOT TO BUILD UP SOME MOMENTUM, LEARN MORE SECRET ARTS...
...AND BECOME A STRONGER MAN!
GU (CLENCH)
The first match is over!
PIPIII (FWEEET)
Team Inuzuka gets the first antidote compound!
OHHH!

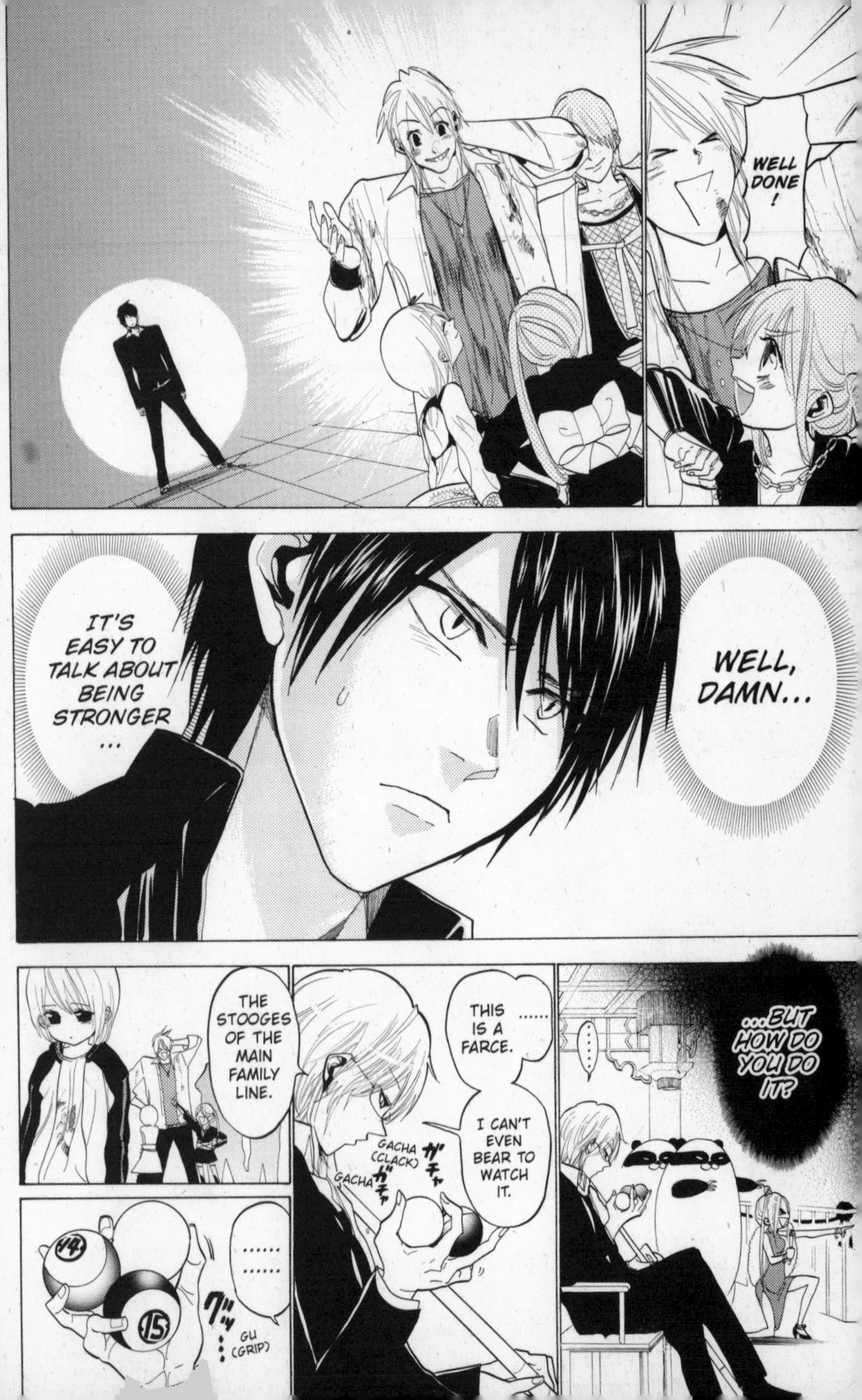
WELL DONE!
WELL, DAMN...
IT'S EASY TO TALK ABOUT BEING STRONGER...
...BUT HOW DO YOU DO IT?
......
THIS IS A FARCE.
......
I CAN'T EVEN BEAR TO WATCH IT.
GACHA (CLACK)
GACHA
THE STOOGES OF THE MAIN FAMILY LINE.
....
GU (GRIP)

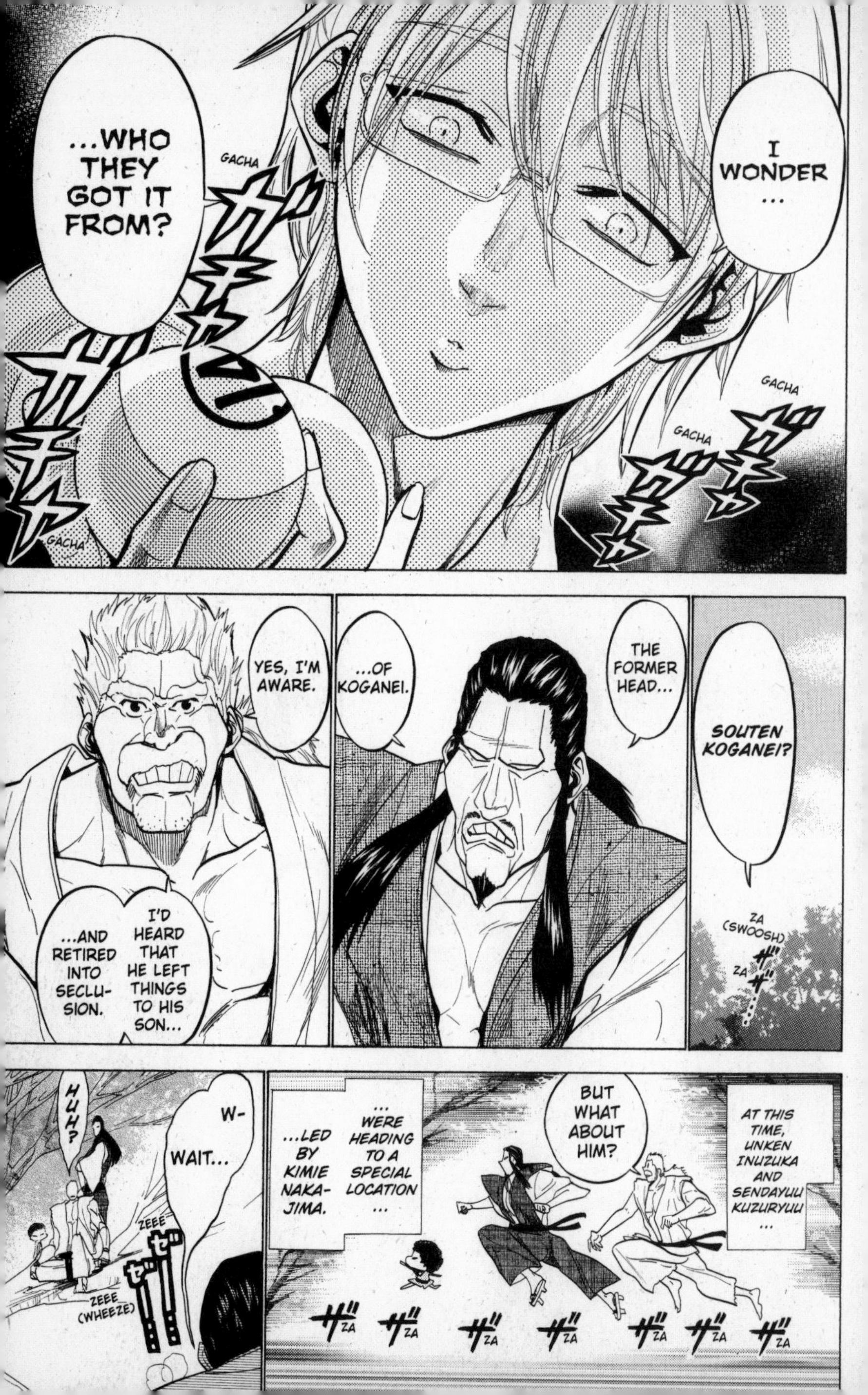
I WONDER ...
GACHA
GACHA
...WHO THEY GOT IT FROM?
GACHA
GACHA
SOUTEN KOGANEI?
ZA (SWOOSH)
ZA
THE FORMER HEAD...
...OF KOGANEI.
YES, I'M AWARE.
I'D HEARD THAT HE LEFT THINGS TO HIS SON...
...AND RETIRED INTO SECLU- SION.
AT THIS TIME, UNKEN INUZUKA AND SENDAYUU KUZURYUU ...
BUT WHAT ABOUT HIM?
... WERE HEADING TO A SPECIAL LOCATION ...
...LED BY KIMIE NAKA- JIMA.
ZA
ZA
ZA
ZA
ZA
ZA
ZA
W- WAIT...
HUH?
ZEEE
ZEEE (WHEEZE)

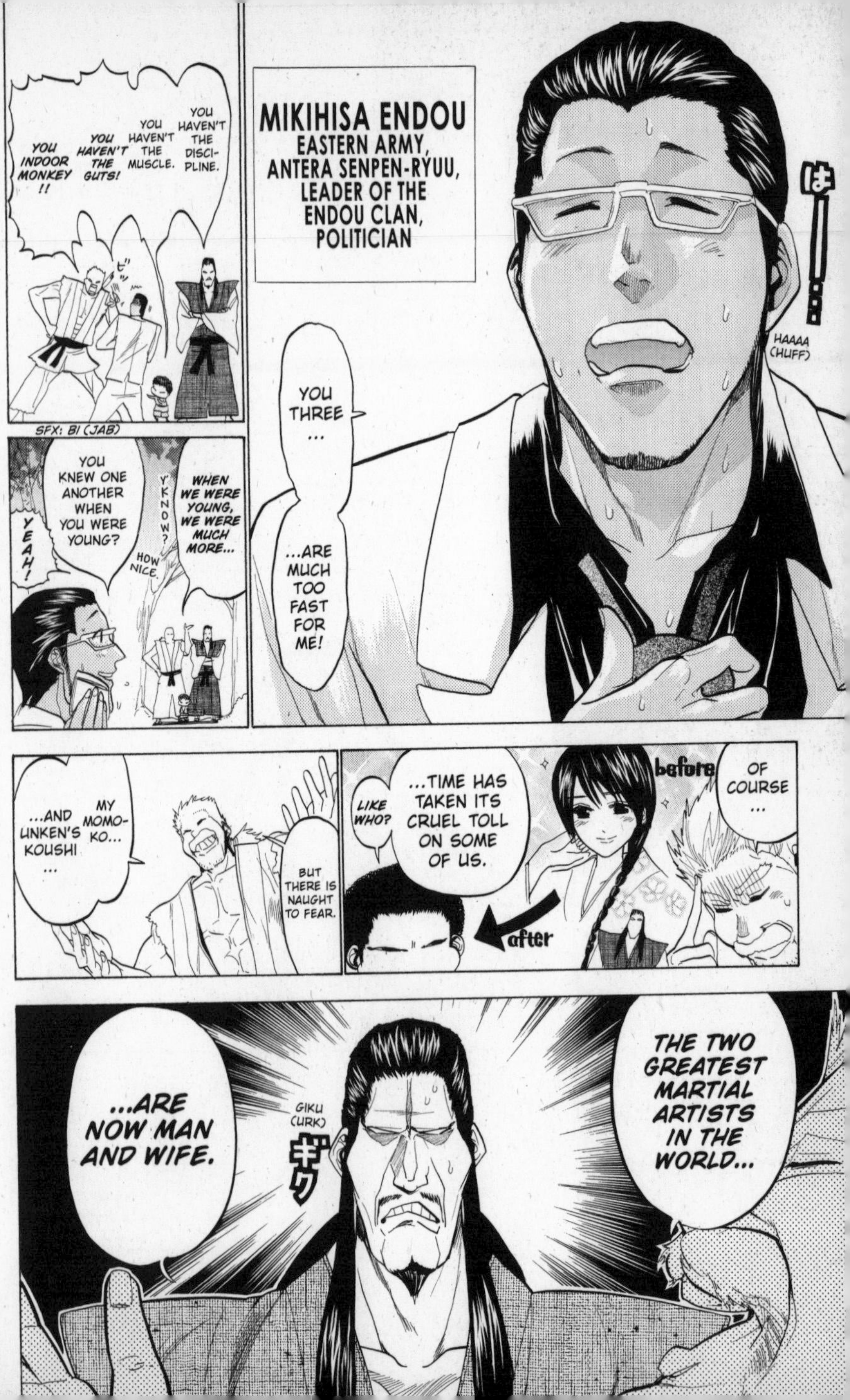
MIKIHISA ENDOU
EASTERN ARMY, ANTERA SENPEN-RYUU, LEADER OF THE ENDOU CLAN, POLITICIAN
HAAAA (HUFF)
YOU THREE ...
...ARE MUCH TOO FAST FOR ME!
YOU HAVEN'T THE DISCI-PLINE.
YOU HAVEN'T THE MUSCLE.
YOU HAVEN'T THE GUTS!
YOU INDOOR MONKEY !!
SFX: BI (JAB)
WHEN WE WERE YOUNG, WE WERE MUCH MORE...
Y'KNOW?
YOU KNEW ONE ANOTHER WHEN YOU WERE YOUNG?
HOW NICE.
YEAH!
OF COURSE ...
before
...TIME HAS TAKEN ITS CRUEL TOLL ON SOME OF US.
LIKE WHO?
after
BUT THERE IS NAUGHT TO FEAR.
MY MOMO-KO...
...AND UNKEN'S KOUSHI ...
THE TWO GREATEST MARTIAL ARTISTS IN THE WORLD...
GIKU (URK)
...ARE NOW MAN AND WIFE.

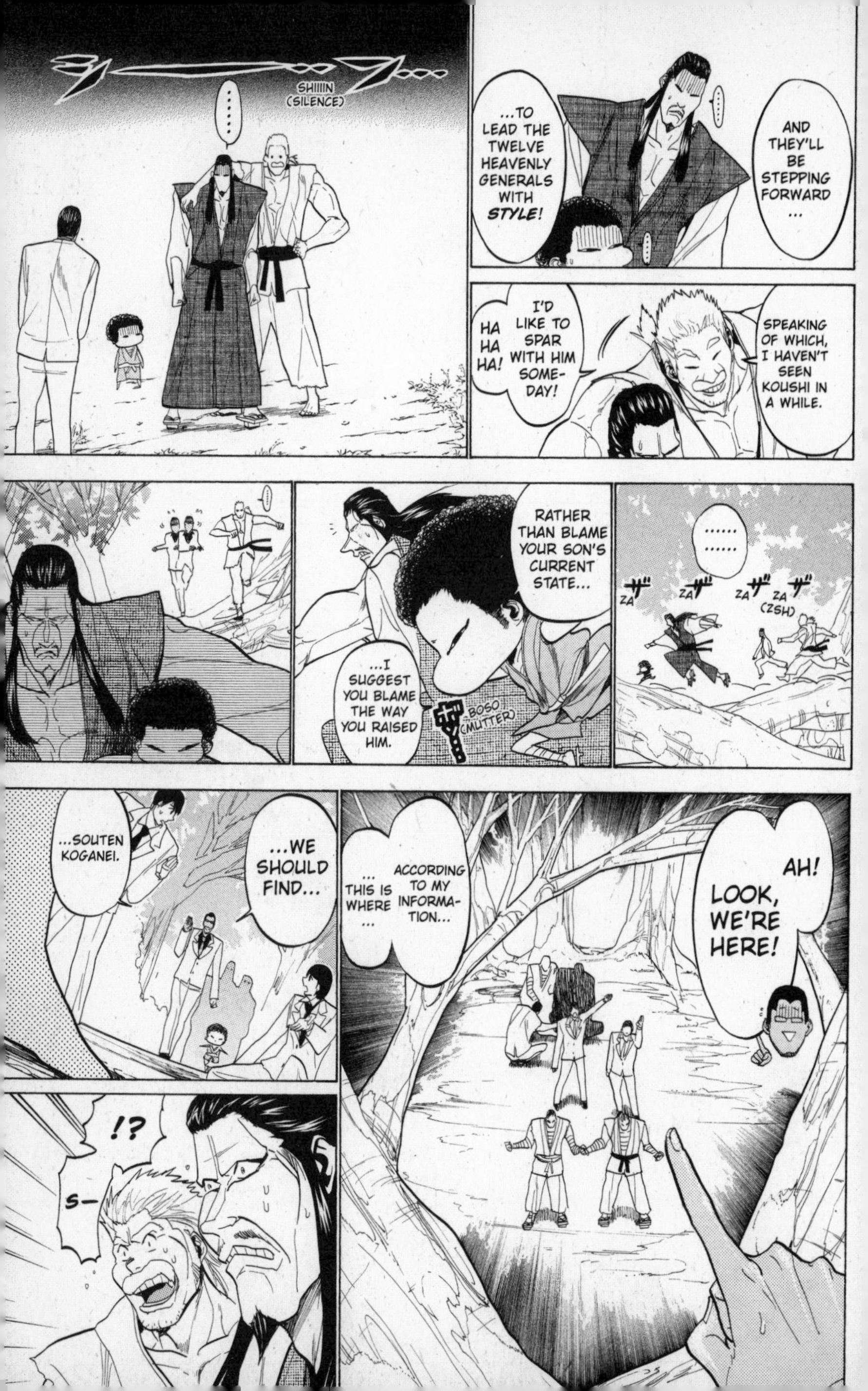
AND THEY'LL BE STEPPING FORWARD ...
...TO LEAD THE TWELVE HEAVENLY GENERALS WITH STYLE!
...
...
SPEAKING OF WHICH, I HAVEN'T SEEN KOUSHI IN A WHILE.
I'D LIKE TO SPAR WITH HIM SOMEDAY!
HA HA HA!
SHIIIN (SILENCE)
......
......
......
ZA ZA ZA ZA (ZSH)
RATHER THAN BLAME YOUR SON'S CURRENT STATE...
...I SUGGEST YOU BLAME THE WAY YOU RAISED HIM.
BOSO (MUTTER)
...
AH! LOOK, WE'RE HERE!
ACCORDING TO MY INFORMATION...
... THIS IS WHERE ...
...WE SHOULD FIND...
...SOUTEN KOGANEI.
!?
S—

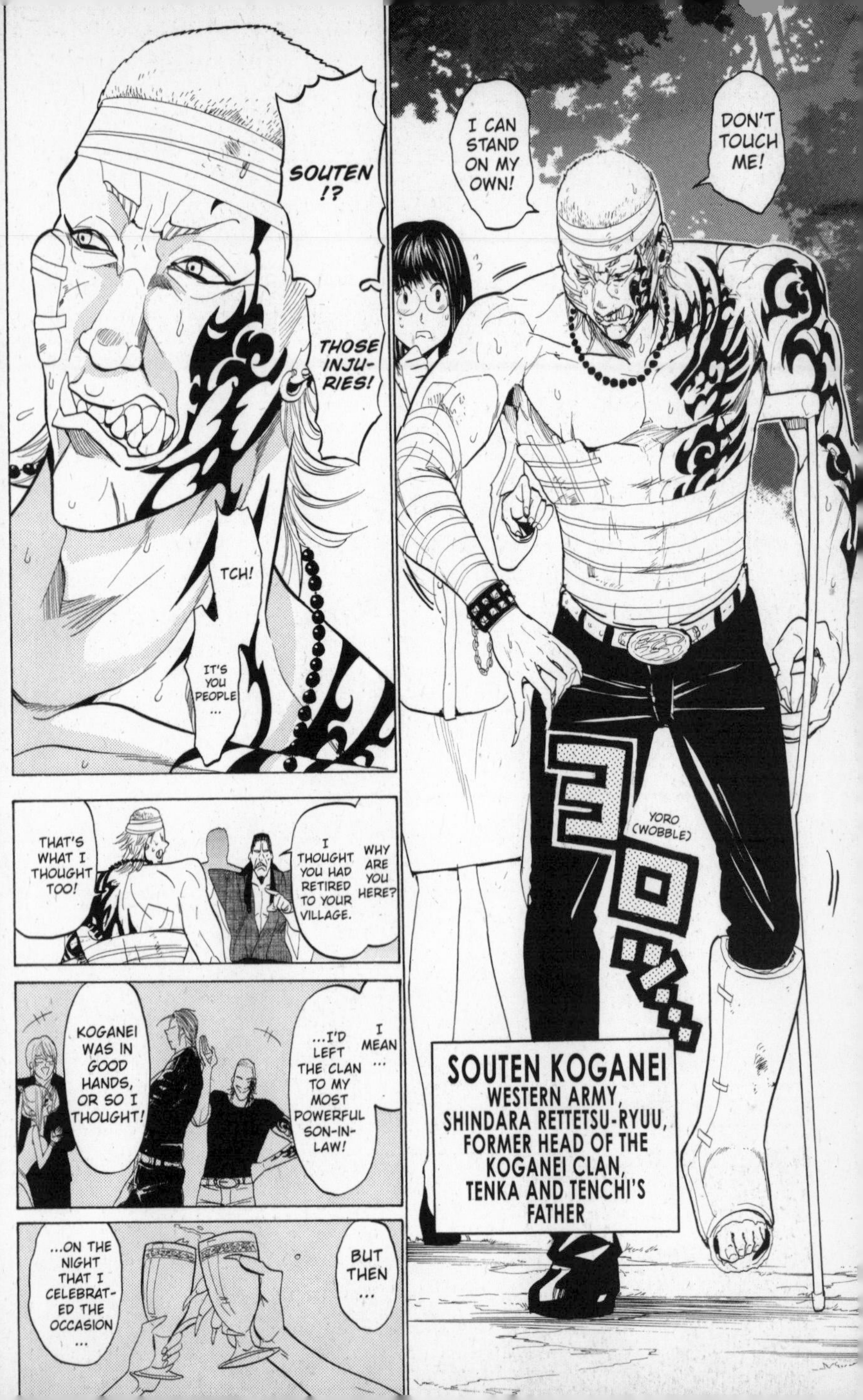
DON'T TOUCH ME!
I CAN STAND ON MY OWN!
YORO (WOBBLE)
SOUTEN KOGANEI
WESTERN ARMY, SHINDARA RETTETSU-RYUU, FORMER HEAD OF THE KOGANEI CLAN, TENKA AND TENCHI'S FATHER
SOUTEN !?
THOSE INJU-RIES!
TCH!
IT'S YOU PEOPLE ...
WHY ARE YOU HERE?
I THOUGHT YOU HAD RETIRED TO YOUR VILLAGE.
THAT'S WHAT I THOUGHT TOO!
I MEAN ...
...I'D LEFT THE CLAN TO MY MOST POWERFUL SON-IN-LAW!
KOGANEI WAS IN GOOD HANDS, OR SO I THOUGHT!
BUT THEN ...
...ON THE NIGHT THAT I CELEBRAT-ED THE OCCASION ...

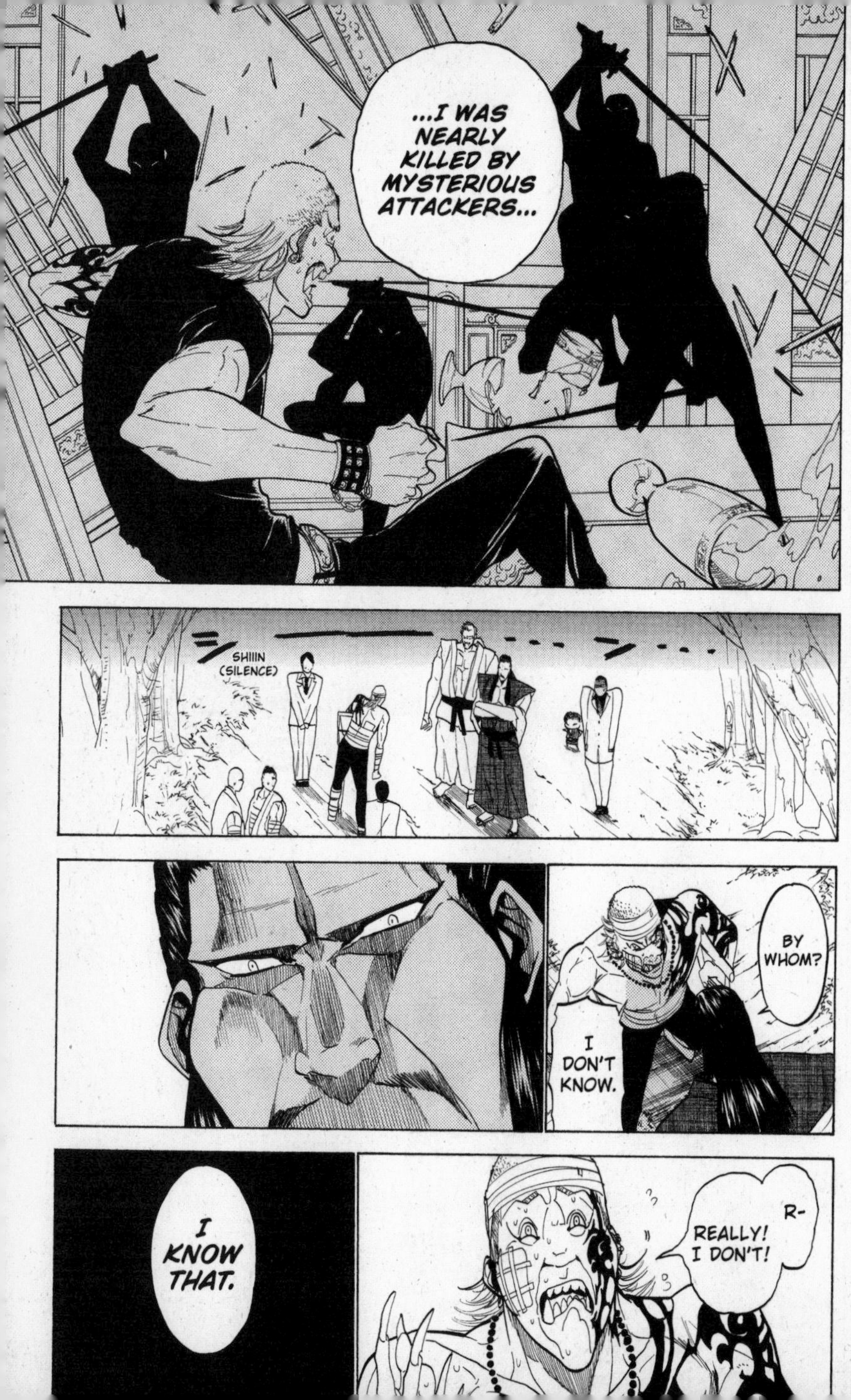
...I WAS NEARLY KILLED BY MYSTERIOUS ATTACKERS...
SHIIIN (SILENCE)
BY WHOM?
I DON'T KNOW.
R-
REALLY! I DON'T!
I KNOW THAT.

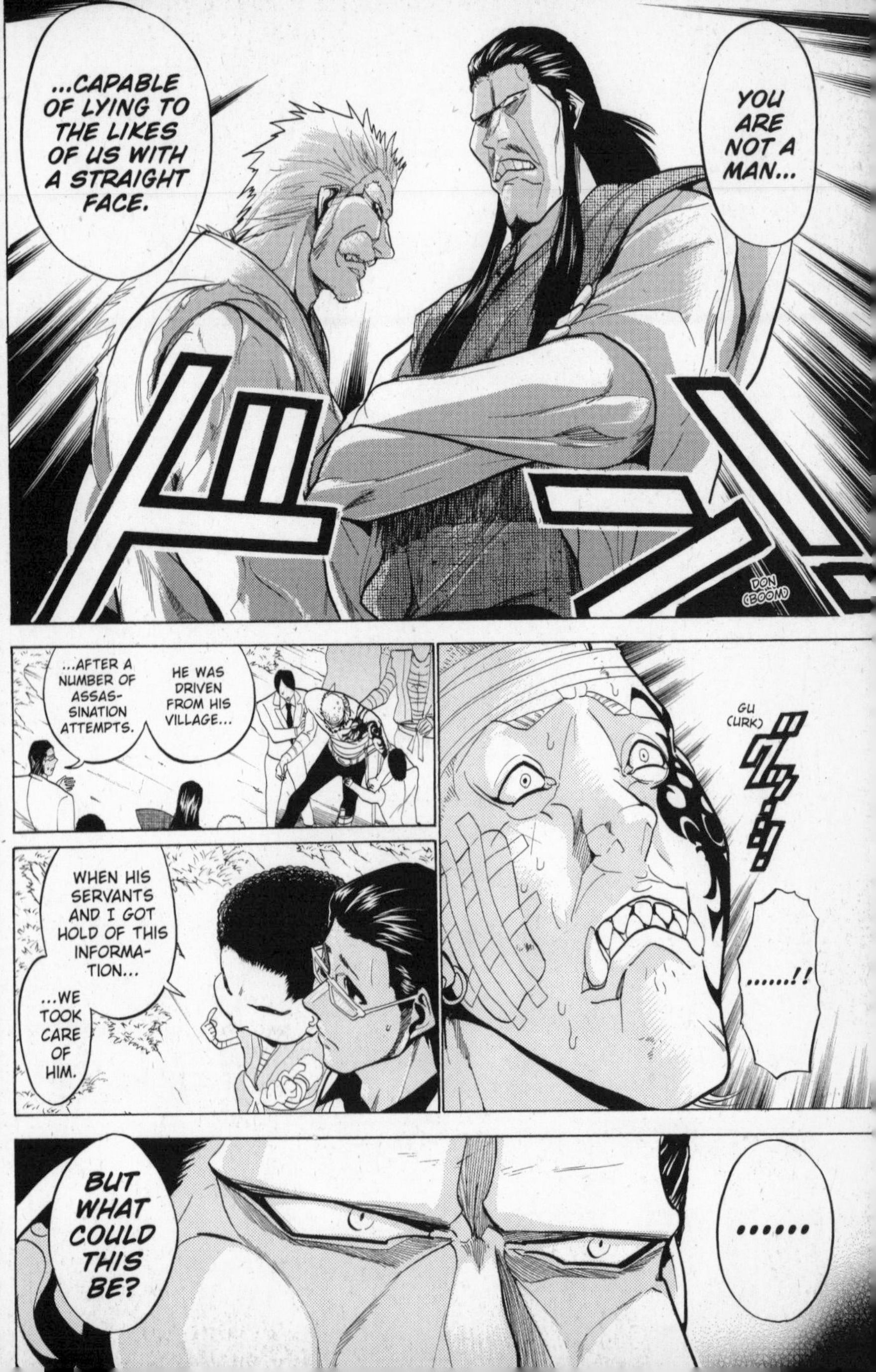
YOU ARE NOT A MAN...
...CAPABLE OF LYING TO THE LIKES OF US WITH A STRAIGHT FACE.
DON (BOOM)
GU (URK)
......!!
HE WAS DRIVEN FROM HIS VILLAGE...
...AFTER A NUMBER OF ASSAS-SINATION ATTEMPTS.
WHEN HIS SERVANTS AND I GOT HOLD OF THIS INFORMA-TION...
...WE TOOK CARE OF HIM.
......
BUT WHAT COULD THIS BE?

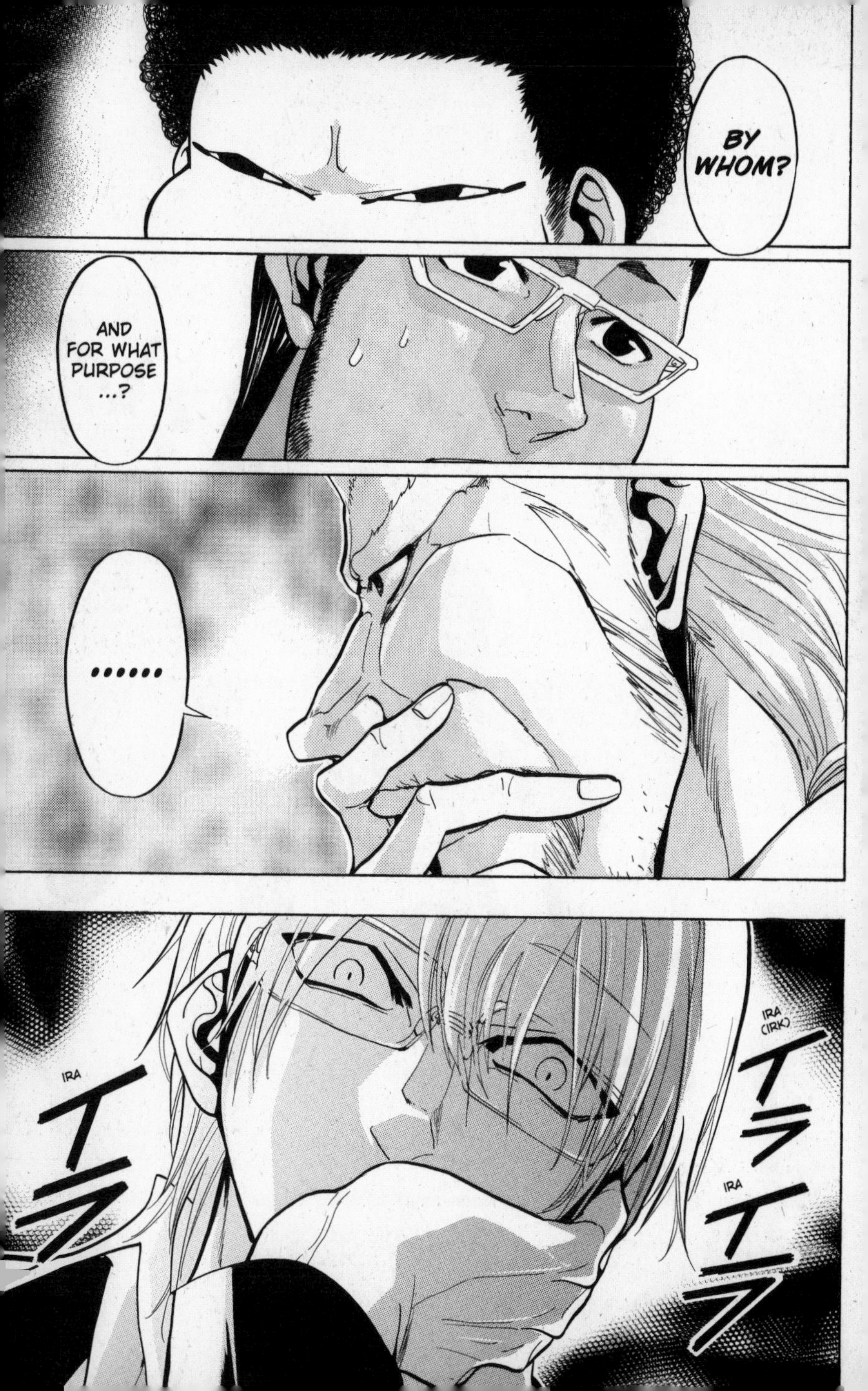
BY WHOM?
AND FOR WHAT PURPOSE ...?
......
IRA (IRK)
イラ
IRA
イラ
IRA
イラ

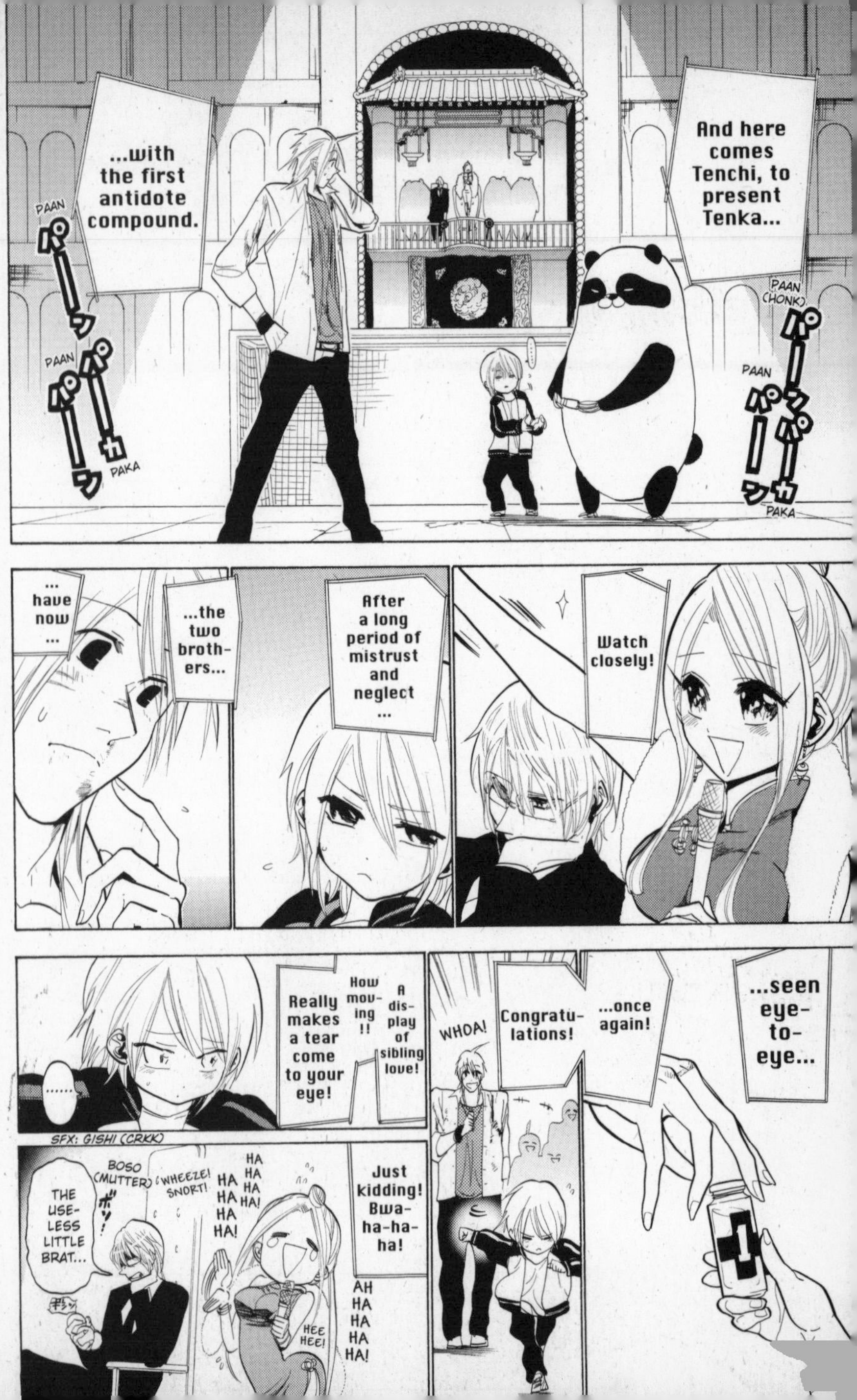
And here comes Tenchi, to present Tenka...
PAAN (HONK) PAAN PAKA
...
...with the first antidote compound.
PAAN PAAN PAKA
Watch closely!
After a long period of mistrust and neglect...
...the two brothers...
... have now ...
...seen eye-to-eye...
...once again!
Congratulations!
WHOA!
A display of sibling love!
How moving!!
Really makes a tear come to your eye!
......
SFX: GISHI (CRKK)
Just kidding! Bwa-ha-ha-ha!
HA HA HA HA!
HA HA HA HA!
AH HA HA HA HA!
HEE HEE!
WHEEZE! SNORT!
BOSO (MUTTER)
THE USELESS LITTLE BRAT...

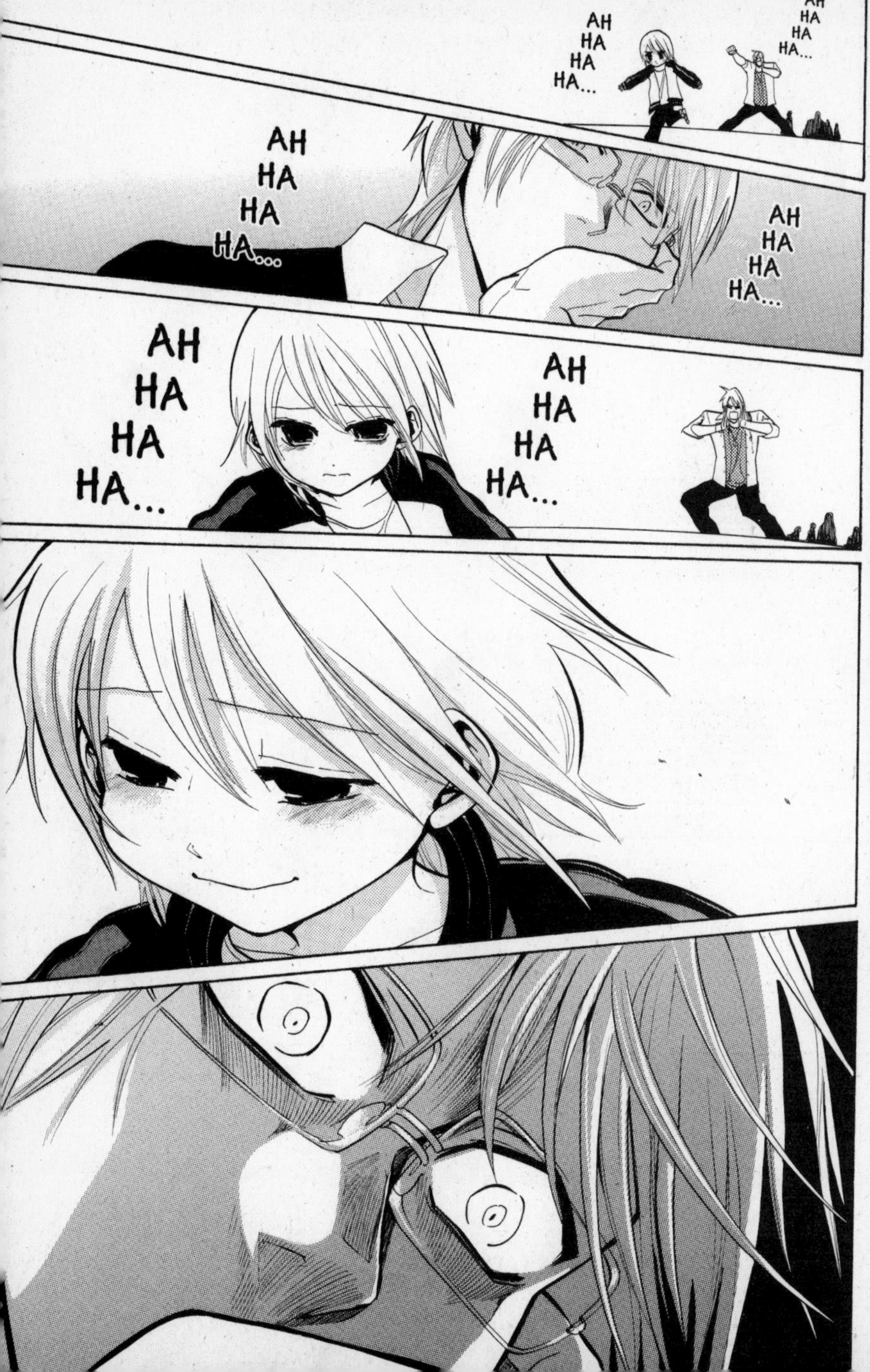
AH HA HA HA...
AH HA HA HA...
AH HA HA HA...
AH HA HA HA...
AH HA HA HA...
AH HA HA HA...

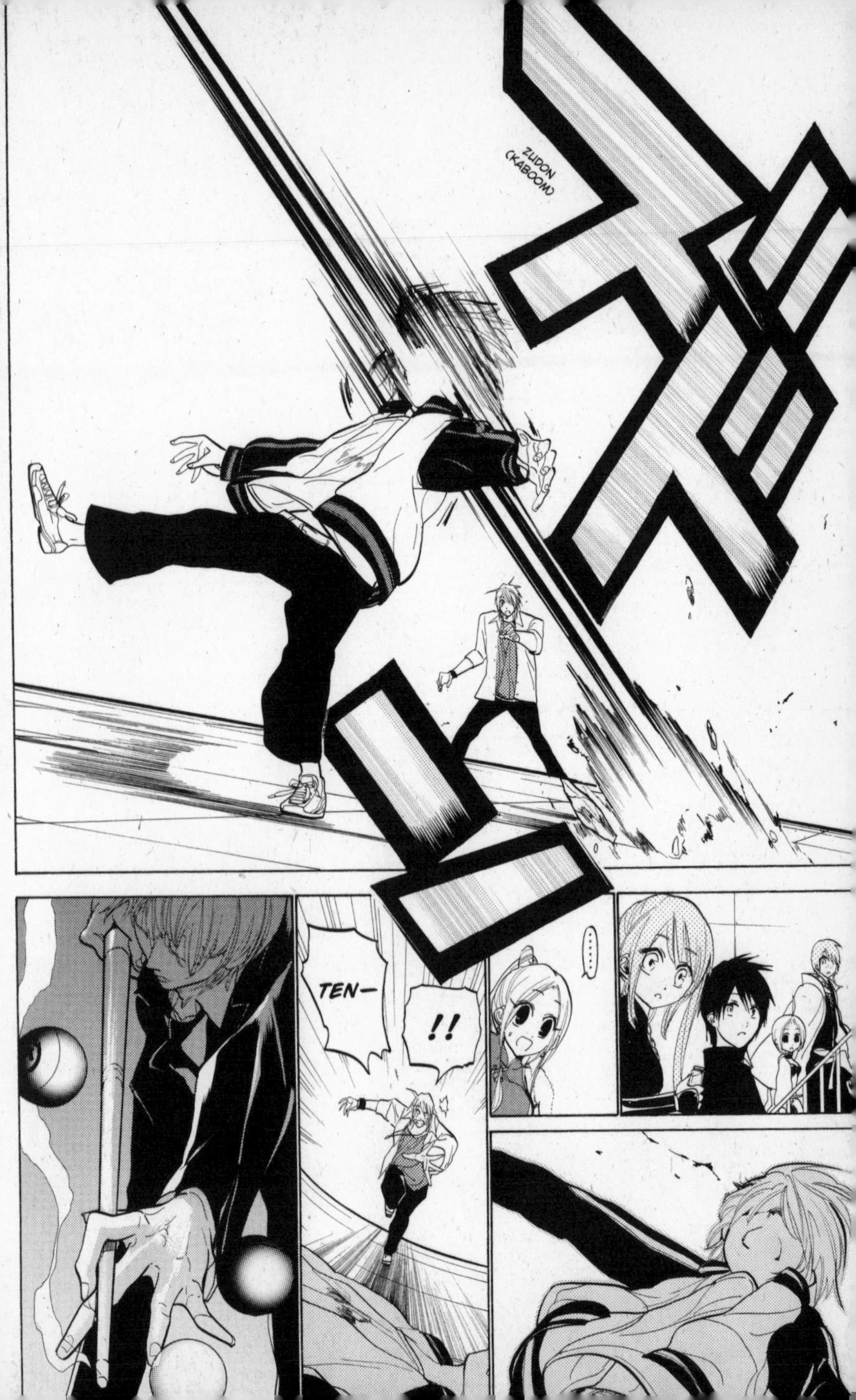
ZUDON (KABOOM)
......
TEN—
!!

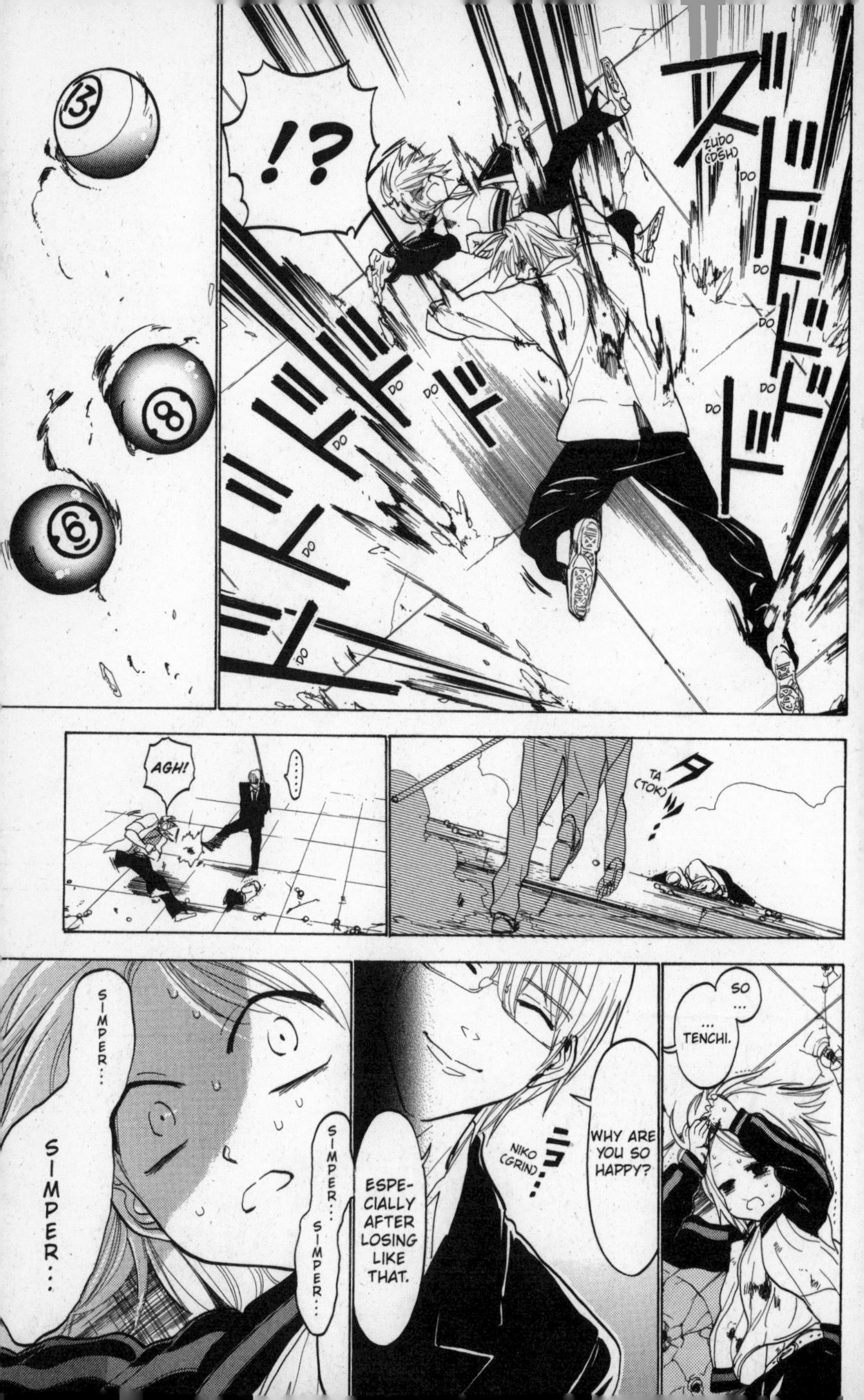
ZUDO (DOSH)
DO
DO
DO
DO
DO
!?
DO
DO
DO
DO
DO
TA (TOK)
AGH!
......
SO ...
... TENCHI.
WHY ARE YOU SO HAPPY?
NIKO (GRIN)
ESPE-CIALLY AFTER LOSING LIKE THAT.
SIMPER... SIMPER...
SIMPER... SIMPER...

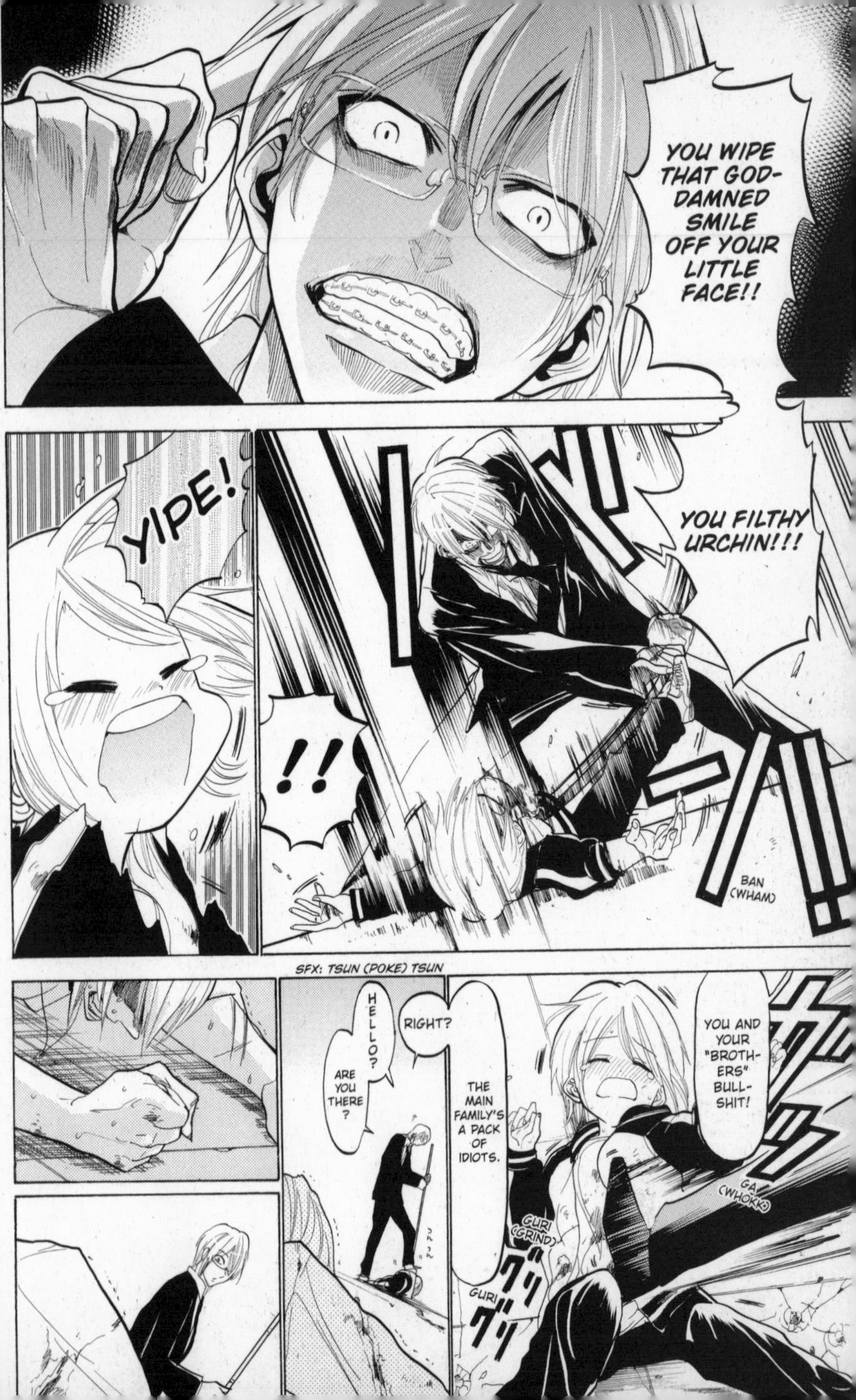
YOU WIPE THAT GOD-DAMNED SMILE OFF YOUR LITTLE FACE!!
YOU FILTHY URCHIN!!!
!!
BAN (WHAM)
YIPE!
SFX: TSUN (POKE) TSUN
YOU AND YOUR "BROTHERS" BULL-SHIT!
GA (WHOKK)
GURI (GRIND)
GURI
THE MAIN FAMILY'S A PACK OF IDIOTS.
RIGHT?
HELLO? ARE YOU THERE?

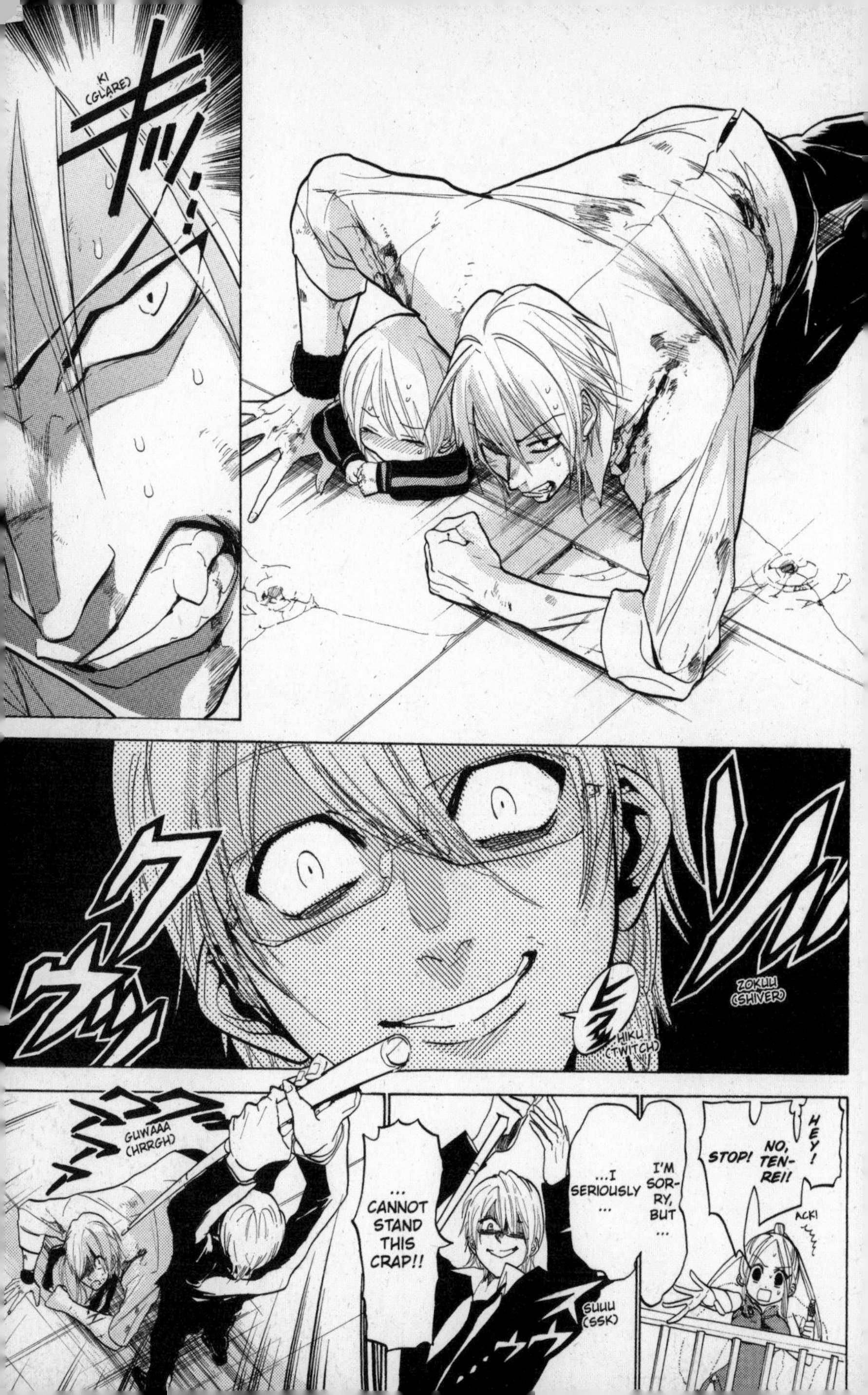
KI (GLARE)
ZOKUU (SHIVER)
HIKU (TWITCH)
HEY!
NO, TENREI!
STOP!
ACK!
I'M SORRY, BUT ...
...I SERIOUSLY ...
... CANNOT STAND THIS CRAP!!
SUUU (SSK)
GUWAAA (HRRGH)

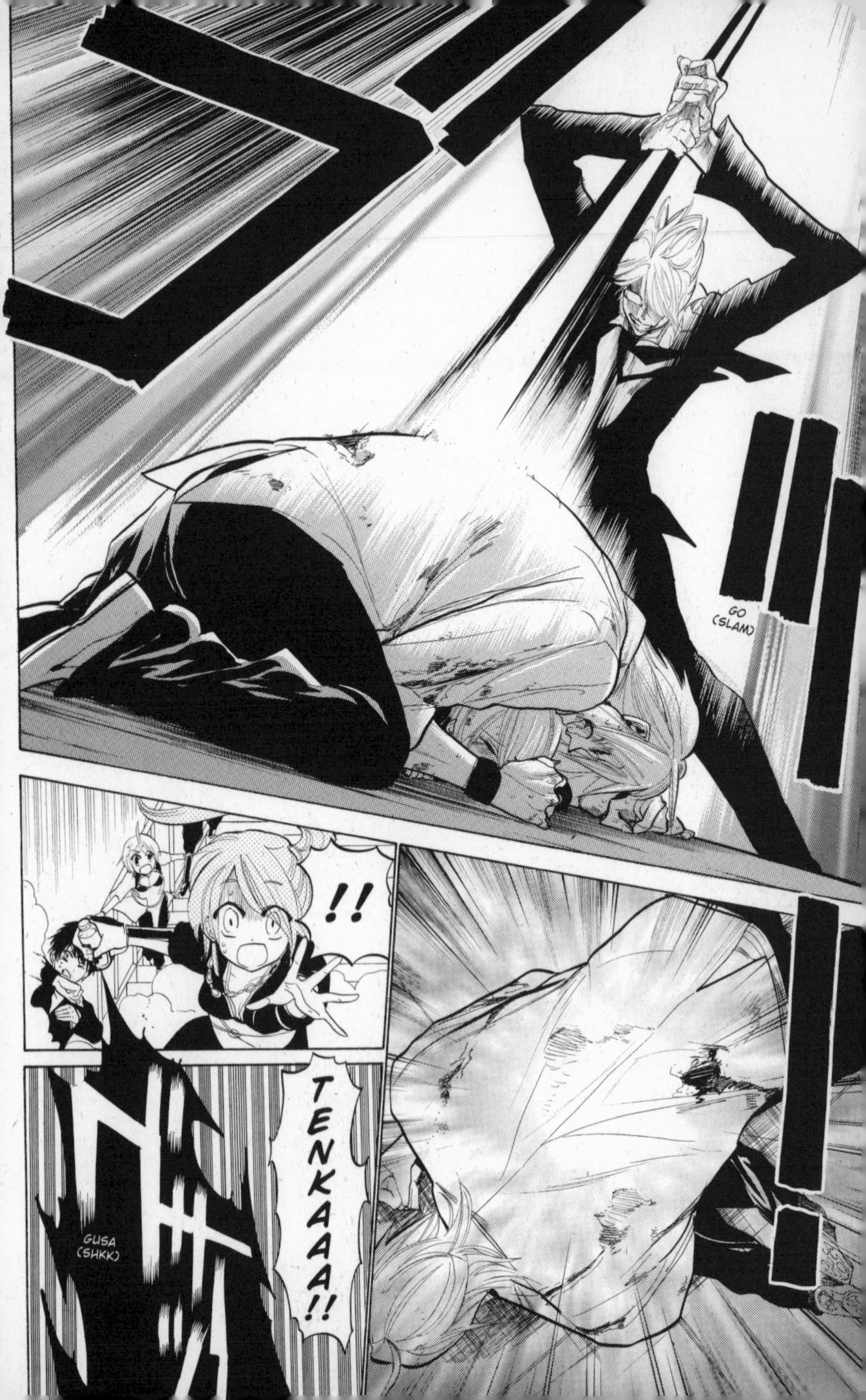
GO
(SLAM)
!!
TENKAAAA!!
GUSA
(SHKK)

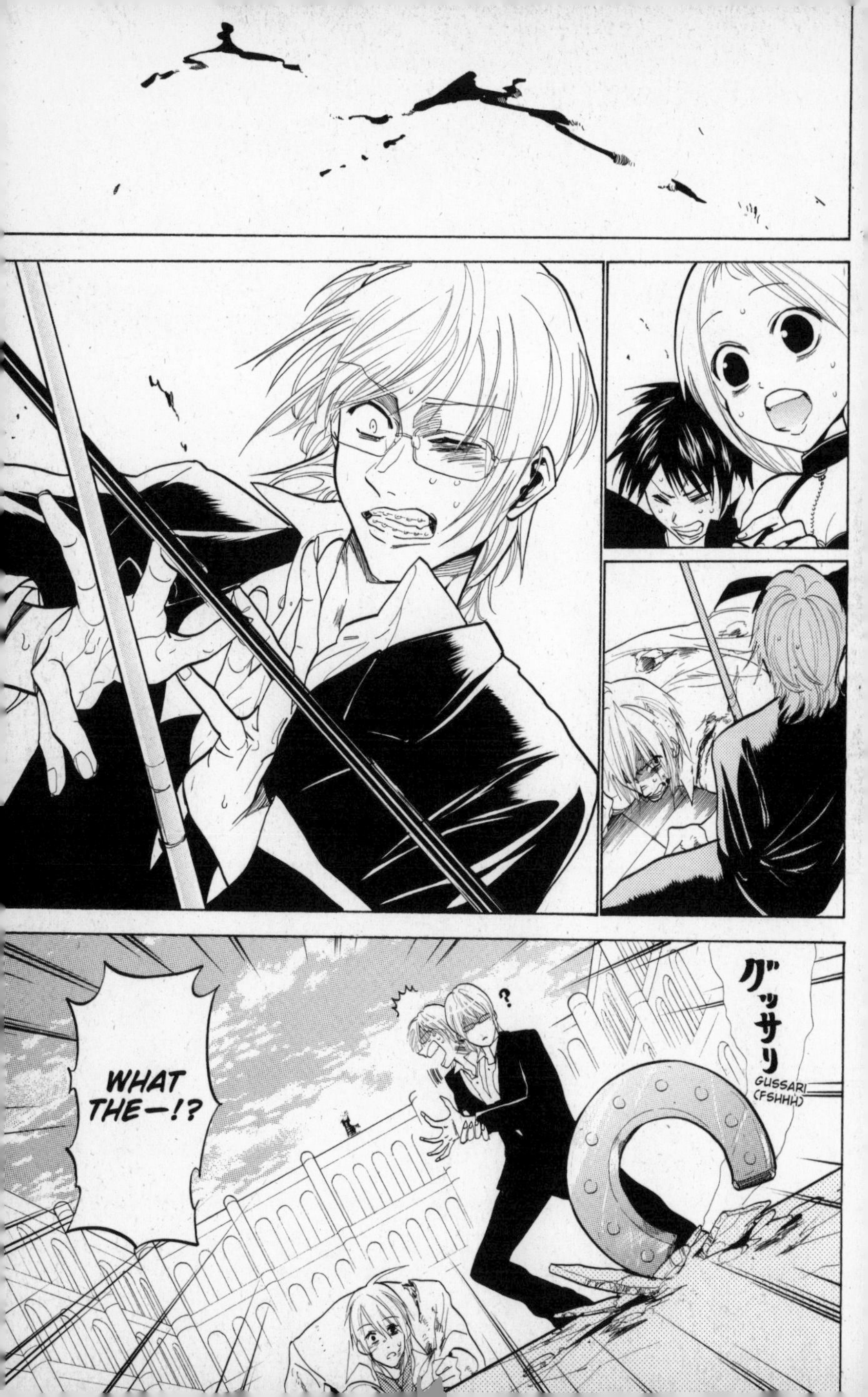
グッサリ
GUSSARI (FSHHH)
WHAT THE—!?

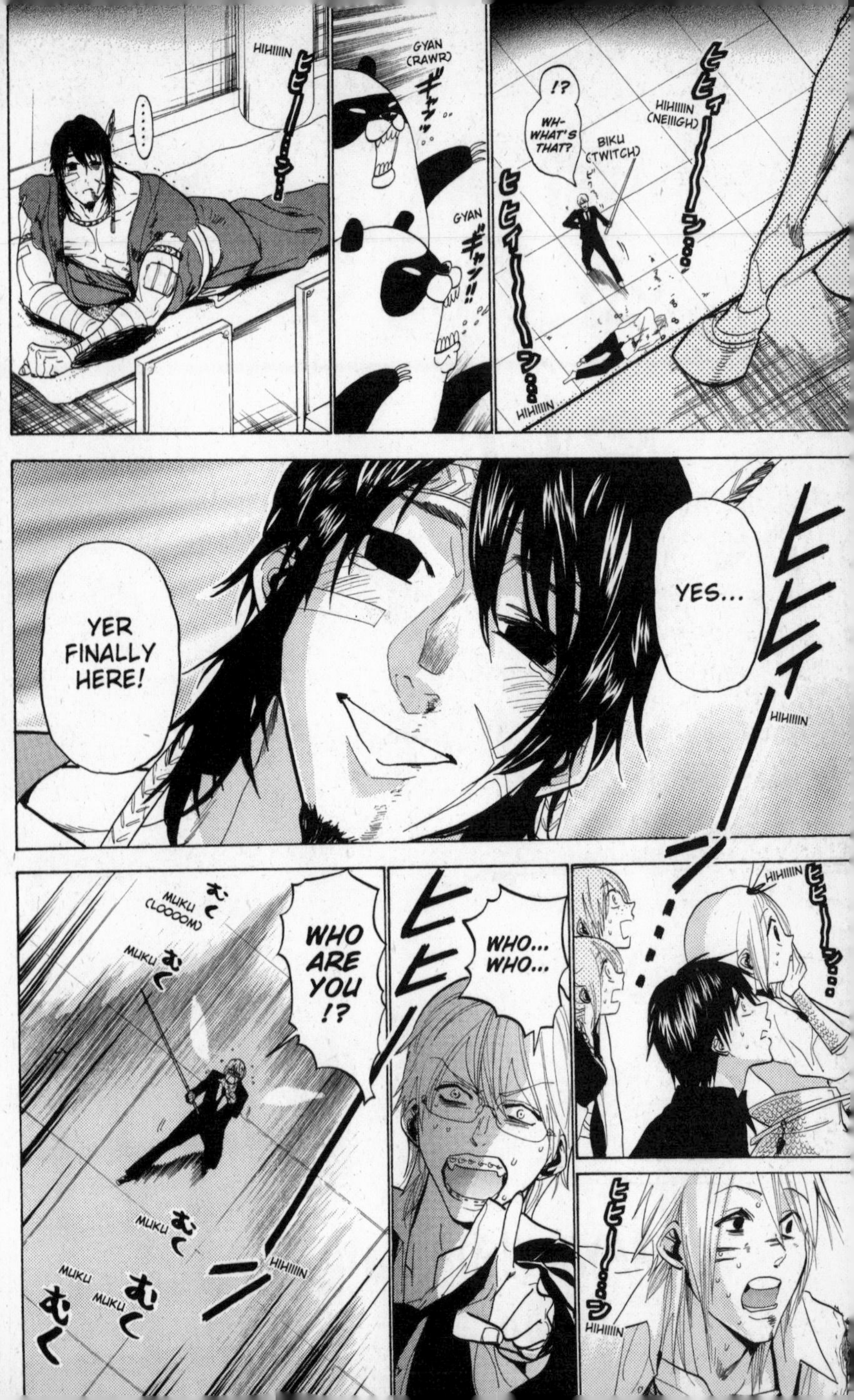
HIHIIIIN (NEIIIGH)
!?
WH-WHAT'S THAT?
BIKU (TWITCH)
HIHIIIIN
GYAN (RAWR)
GYAN
HIHIIIIN
……
YES...
HIHIIIIN
YER FINALLY HERE!
HIHIIIIN
HIHIIIIN
WHO... WHO...
WHO ARE YOU !?
HIHIIIIN
MUKU (LOOOOM)
MUKU
MUKU
MUKU
MUKU

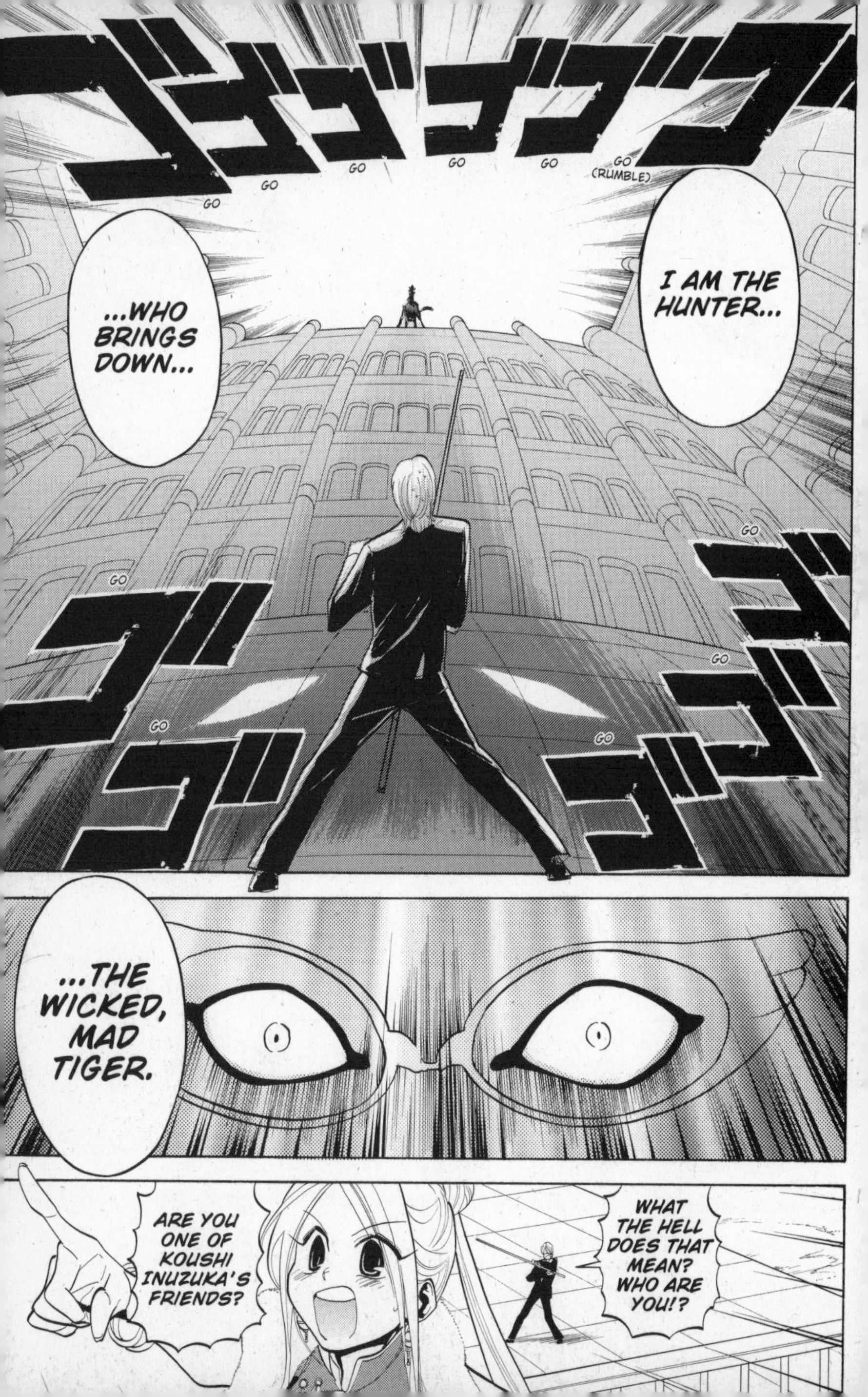
GO GO GO GO GO GO (RUMBLE)
I AM THE HUNTER...
...WHO BRINGS DOWN...
GO GO GO GO GO
...THE WICKED, MAD TIGER.
WHAT THE HELL DOES THAT MEAN? WHO ARE YOU!?
ARE YOU ONE OF KOUSHI INUZUKA'S FRIENDS?

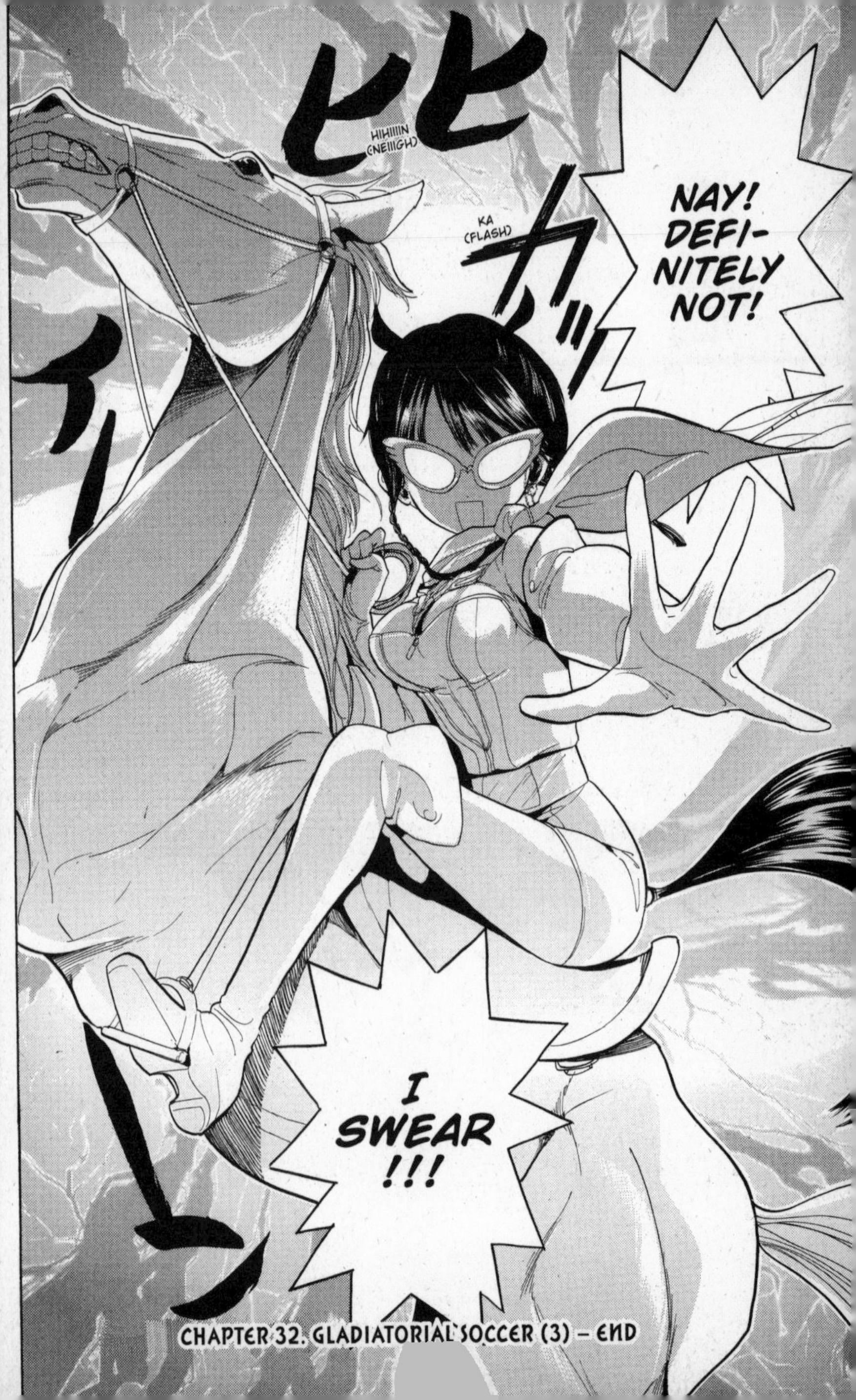
NAY! DEFI-NITELY NOT!
HIHIIIIN (NEIIIGH)
KA (FLASH)
I SWEAR !!!
CHAPTER 32. GLADIATORIAL SOCCER (3) – END

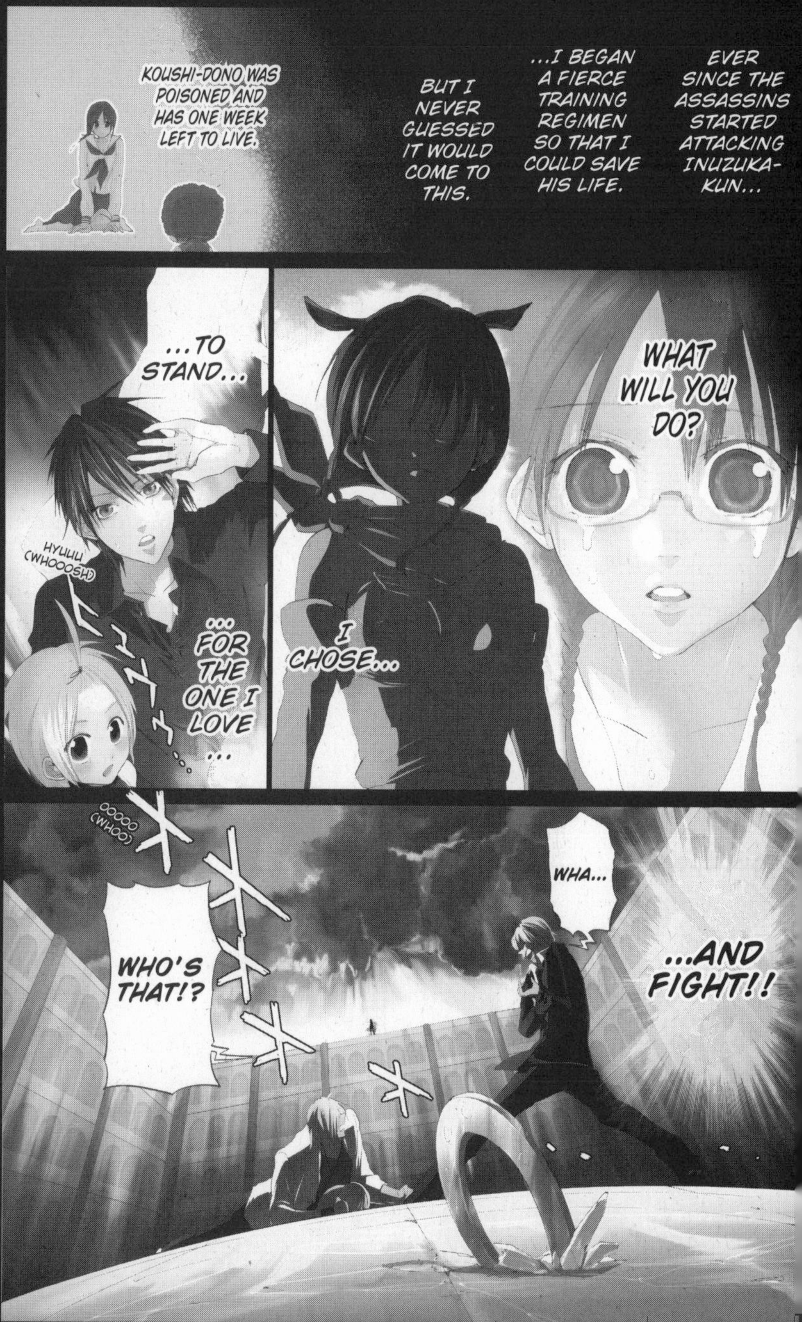
EVER SINCE THE ASSASSINS STARTED ATTACKING INUZUKA-KUN...
...I BEGAN A FIERCE TRAINING REGIMEN SO THAT I COULD SAVE HIS LIFE.
BUT I NEVER GUESSED IT WOULD COME TO THIS.
KOUSHI-DONO WAS POISONED AND HAS ONE WEEK LEFT TO LIVE.
WHAT WILL YOU DO?
I CHOSE...
...TO STAND...
...FOR THE ONE I LOVE...
HYUUU (WHOOOSH)
...AND FIGHT!!
WHA...
WHO'S THAT!?
OOOOO (WHOO)

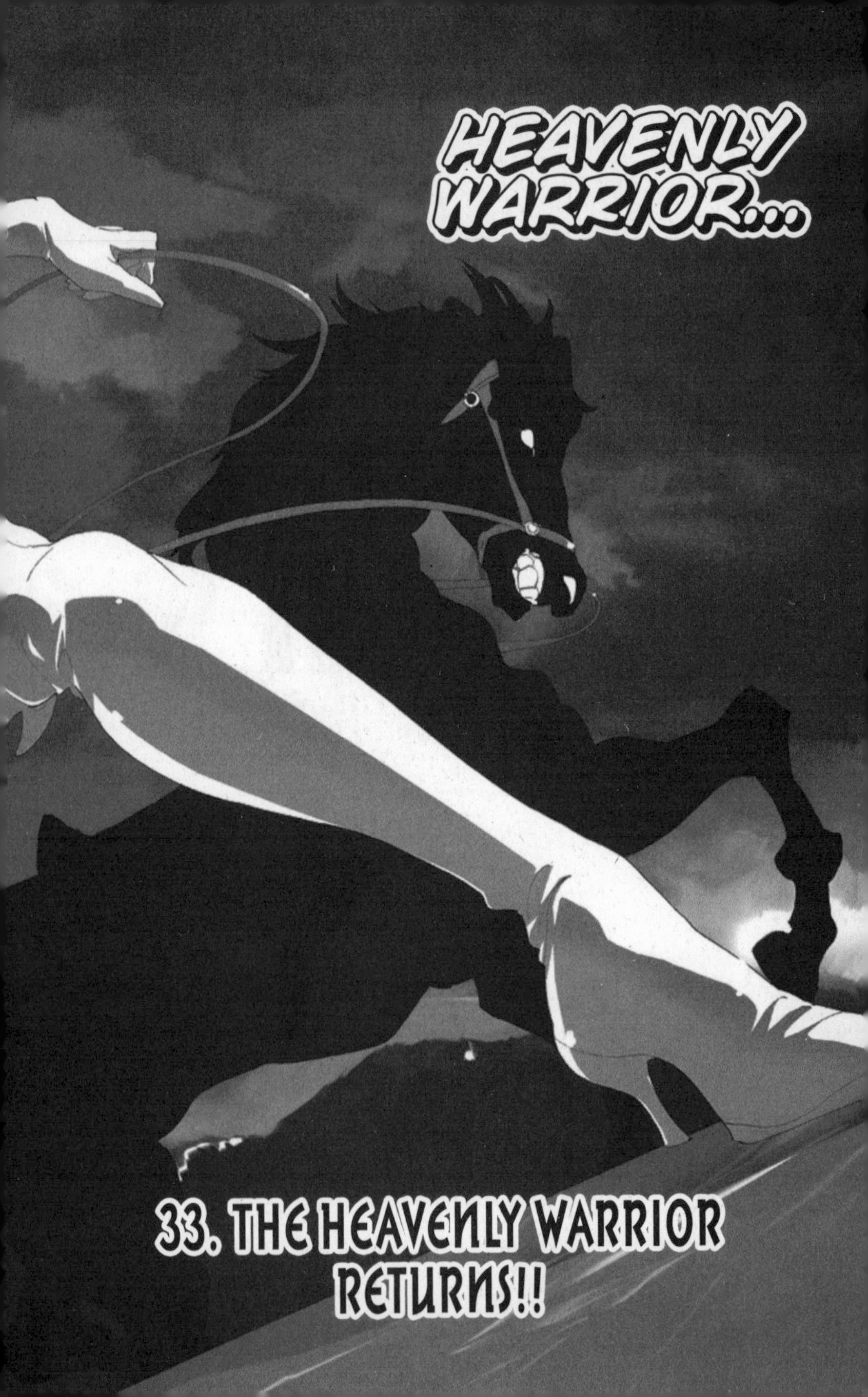
HEAVENLY WARRIOR...
33. THE HEAVENLY WARRIOR RETURNS!!

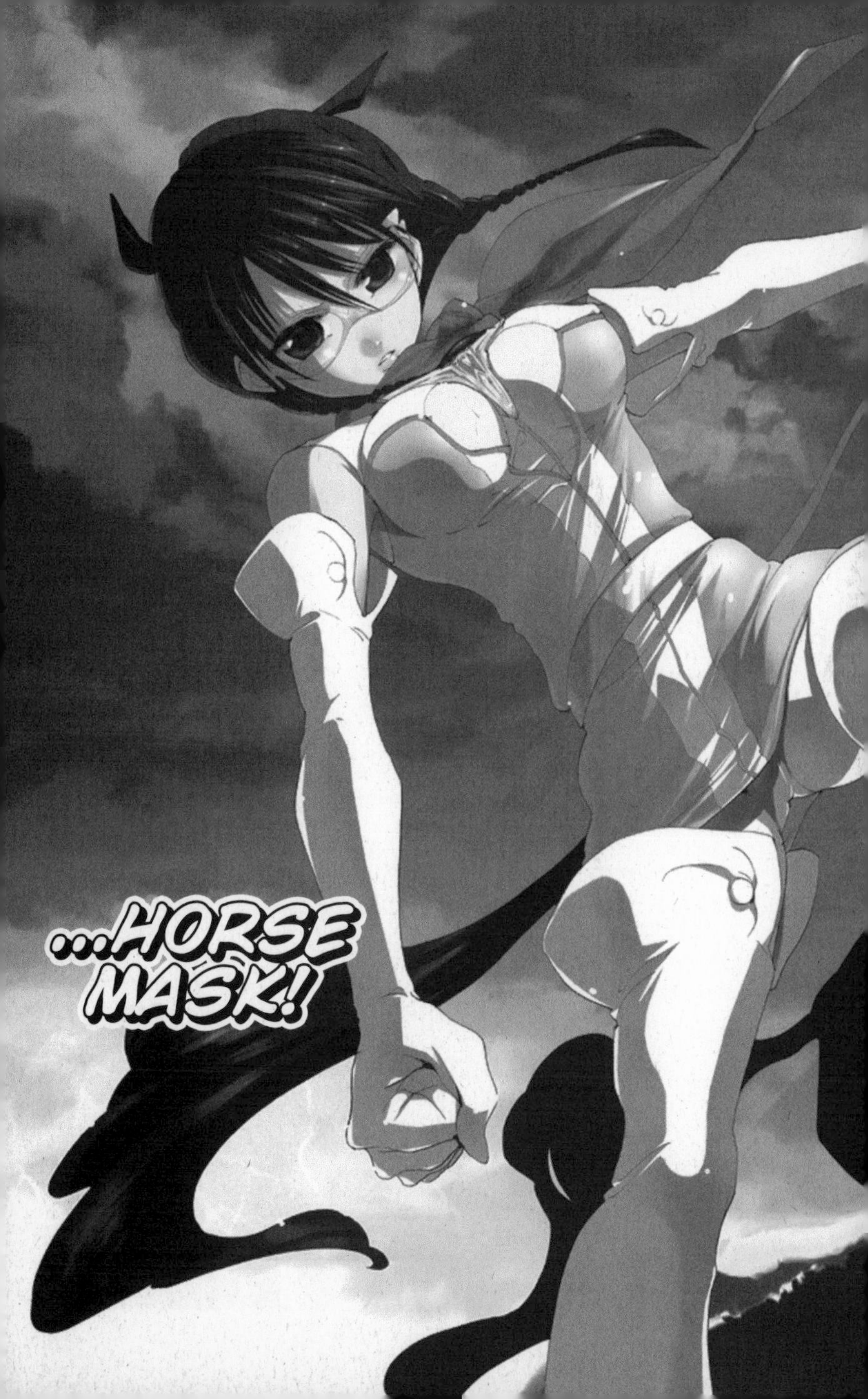
...HORSE MASK!

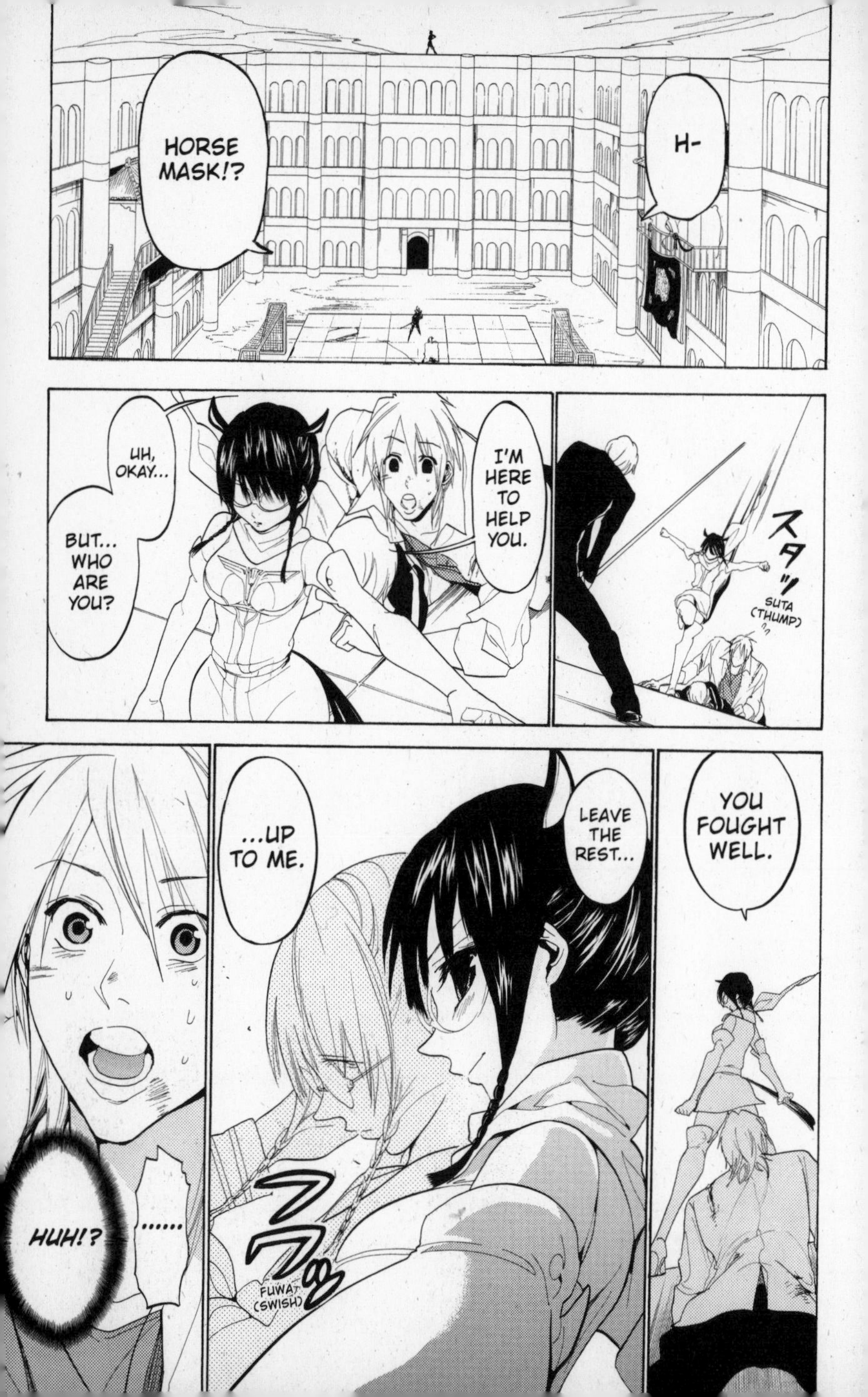
H-
HORSE MASK!?
スタッ
SUTA (THUMP)
I'M HERE TO HELP YOU.
UH, OKAY...
BUT... WHO ARE YOU?
YOU FOUGHT WELL.
LEAVE THE REST...
...UP TO ME.
FUWA (SWISH)
......
HUH!?

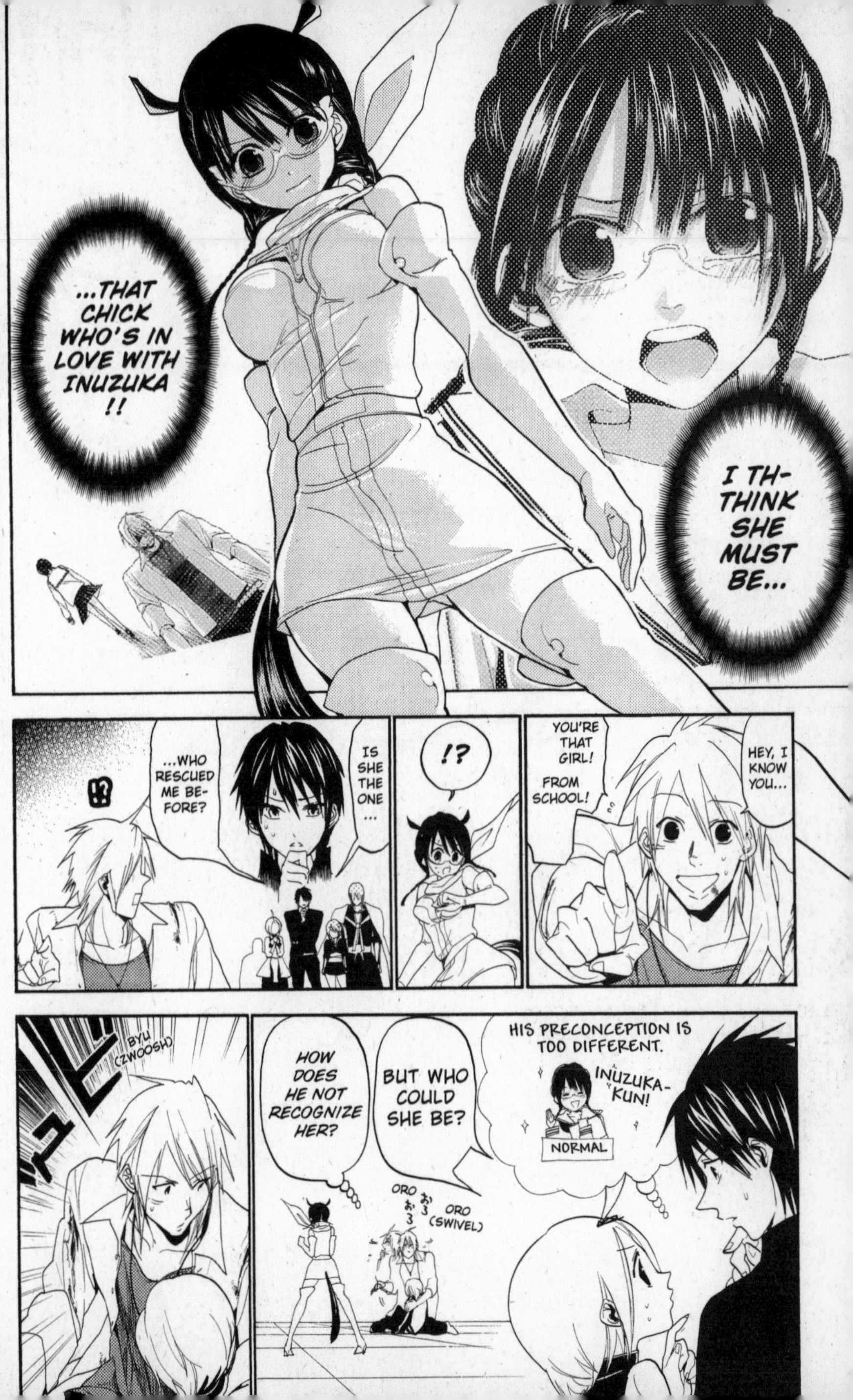
I TH-THINK SHE MUST BE...
...THAT CHICK WHO'S IN LOVE WITH INUZUKA!!
HEY, I KNOW YOU...
YOU'RE THAT GIRL! FROM SCHOOL!
!?
IS SHE THE ONE...
...WHO RESCUED ME BEFORE?
!?
HIS PRECONCEPTION IS TOO DIFFERENT.
INUZUKA-KUN!
NORMAL
BUT WHO COULD SHE BE?
HOW DOES HE NOT RECOGNIZE HER?
ORO おろ おろ ORO (SWIVEL)
BYU (ZWOOSH)

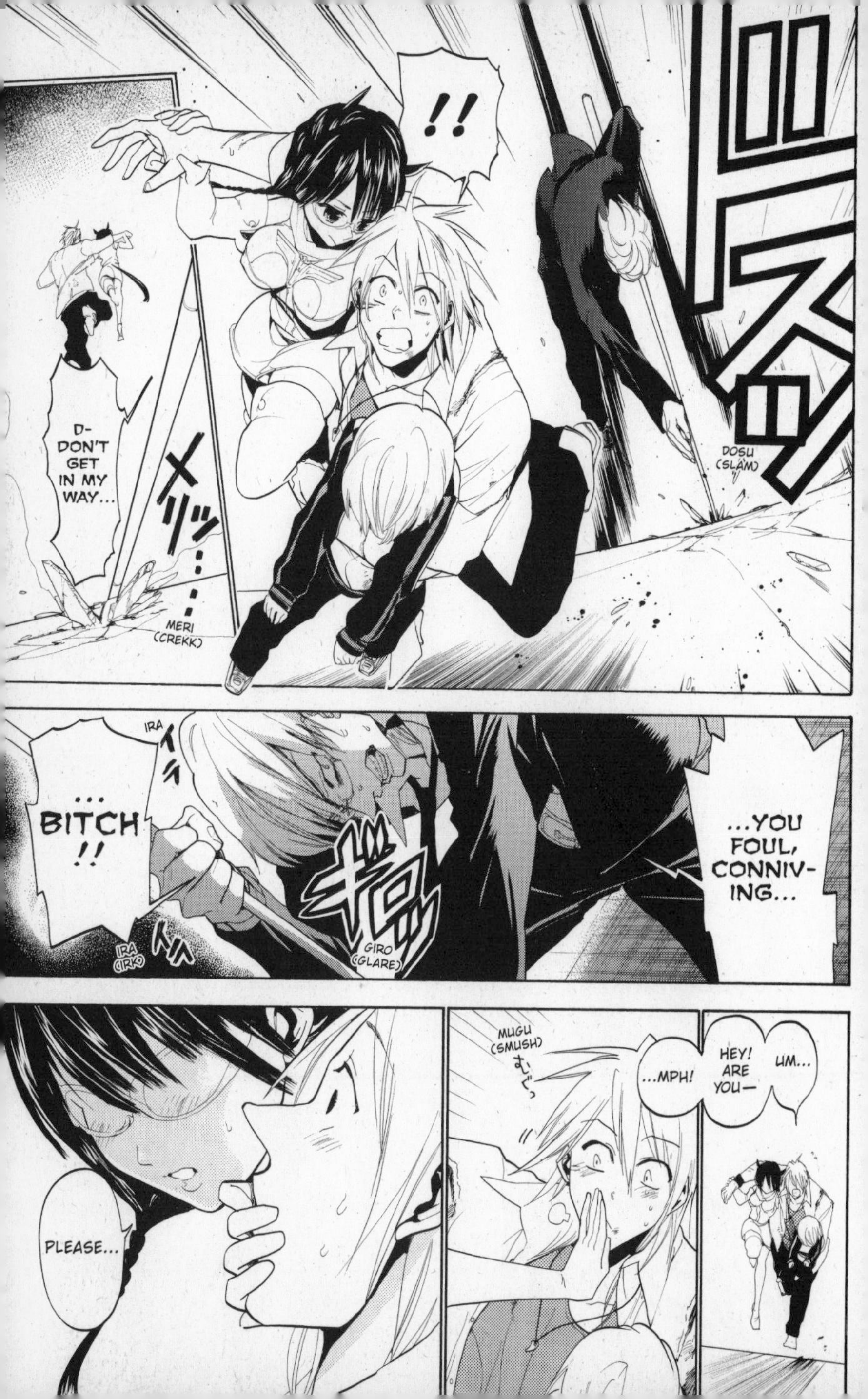
!!
DOSU (SLAM)
D-DON'T GET IN MY WAY...
MERI (CREKK)
...YOU FOUL, CONNIV-ING...
GIRO (GLARE)
IRA
...BITCH!!
IRA (IRK)
UM...
HEY! ARE YOU—
...MPH!
MUGU (SMUSH)
PLEASE...

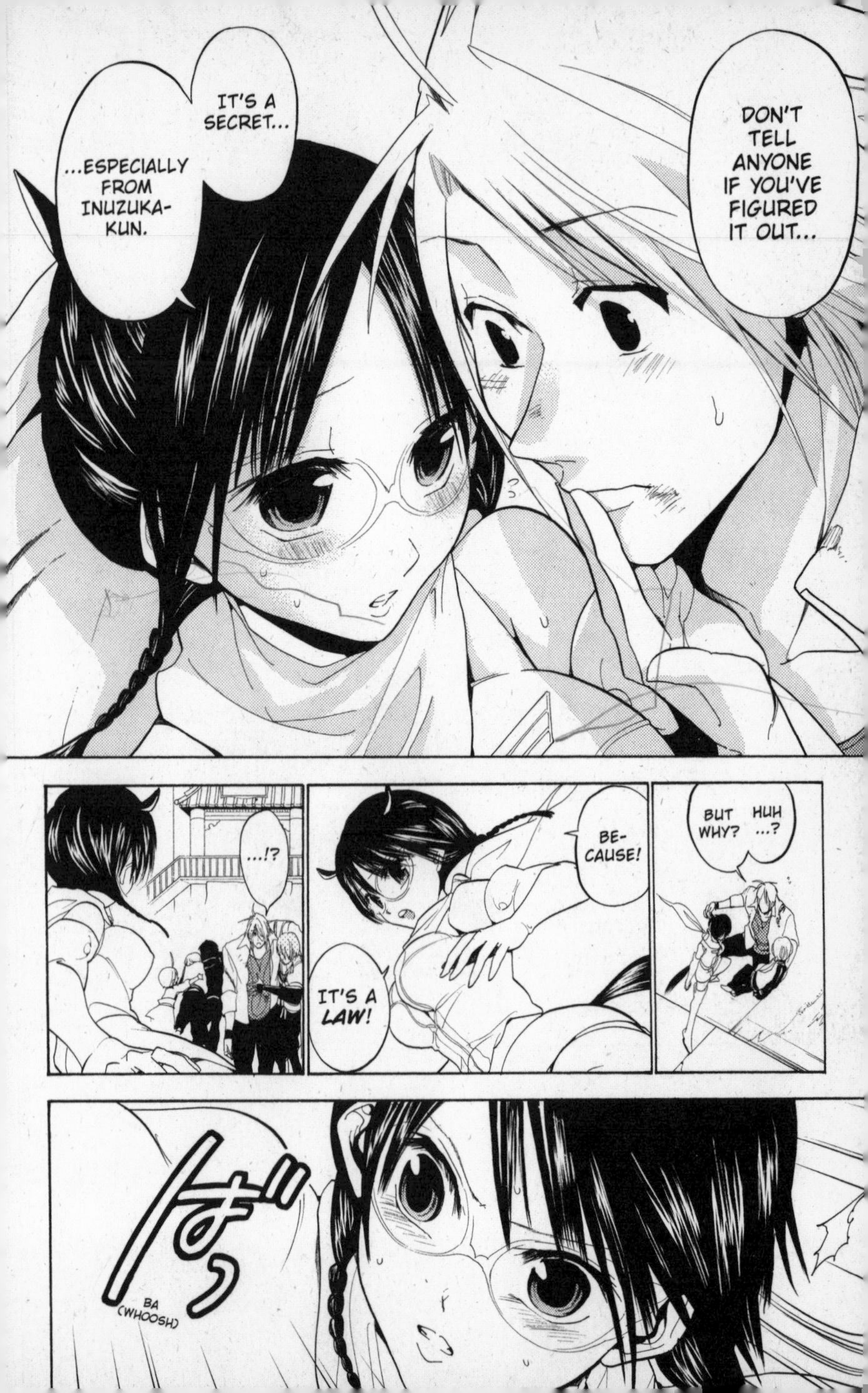
DON'T TELL ANYONE IF YOU'VE FIGURED IT OUT...
IT'S A SECRET...
...ESPECIALLY FROM INUZUKA-KUN.
HUH ...?
BUT WHY?
BE-CAUSE!
IT'S A *LAW*!
...!?
ばっ
BA (WHOOSH)

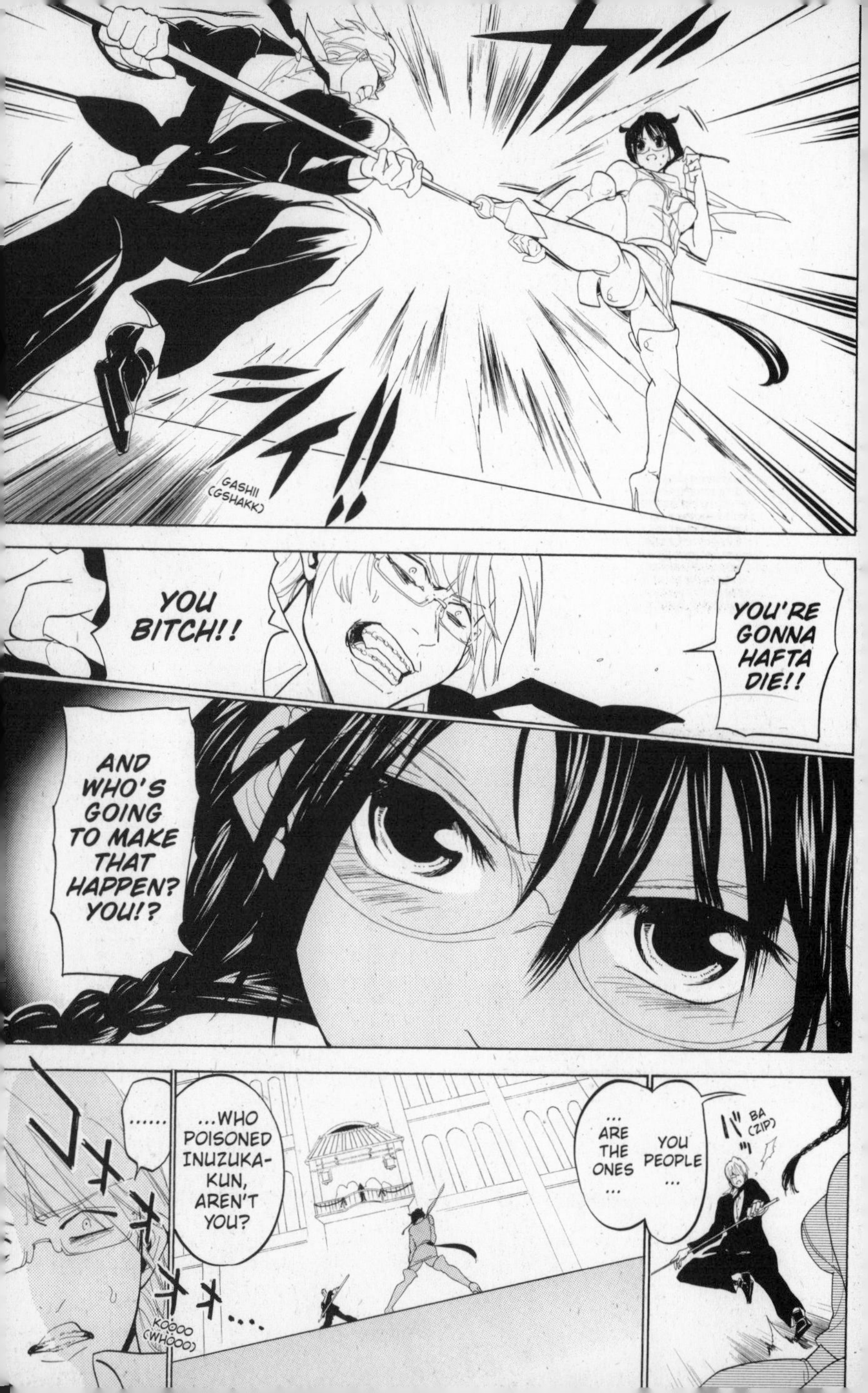
GASHII (GSHAKK)
YOU'RE GONNA HAFTA DIE!!
YOU BITCH!!
AND WHO'S GOING TO MAKE THAT HAPPEN? YOU!?
BA (ZIP)
YOU PEOPLE ...
... ARE THE ONES ...
...WHO POISONED INUZUKA-KUN, AREN'T YOU?
......
...
KOOOO (WHOOO)

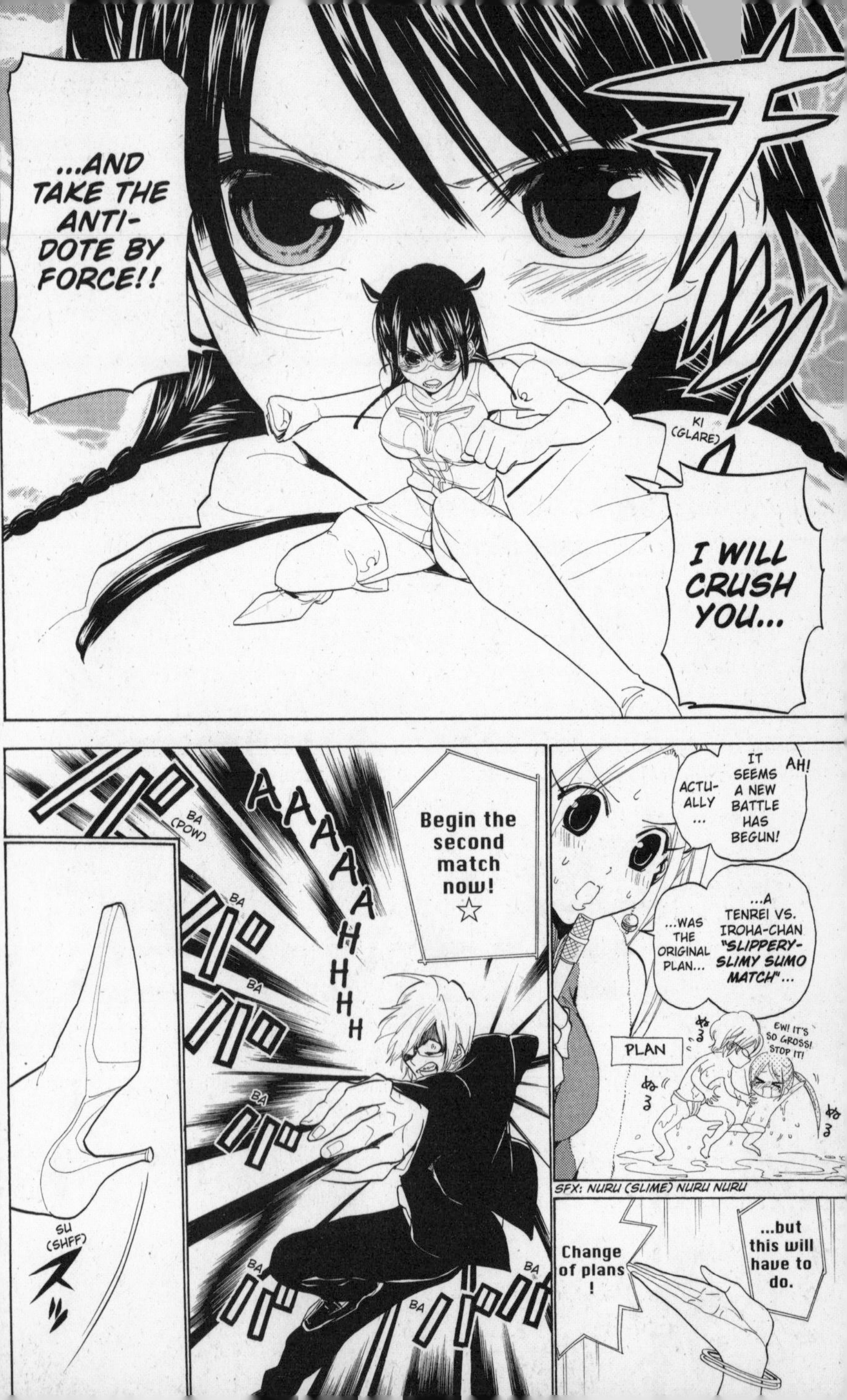
KI (GLARE)
I WILL CRUSH YOU...
...AND TAKE THE ANTI-DOTE BY FORCE!!
AH!
IT SEEMS A NEW BATTLE HAS BEGUN!
ACTU-ALLY...
...A TENREI VS. IROHA-CHAN "SLIPPERY-SLIMY SUMO MATCH"...
...WAS THE ORIGINAL PLAN...
PLAN
EW! IT'S SO GROSS! STOP IT!
SFX: NURU (SLIME) NURU NURU
...but this will have to do.
Change of plans!
Begin the second match now! ☆
AAAAAAHHHHH
BA (POW)
BA
BA
BA
BA
BA
BA
SU (SHFF)

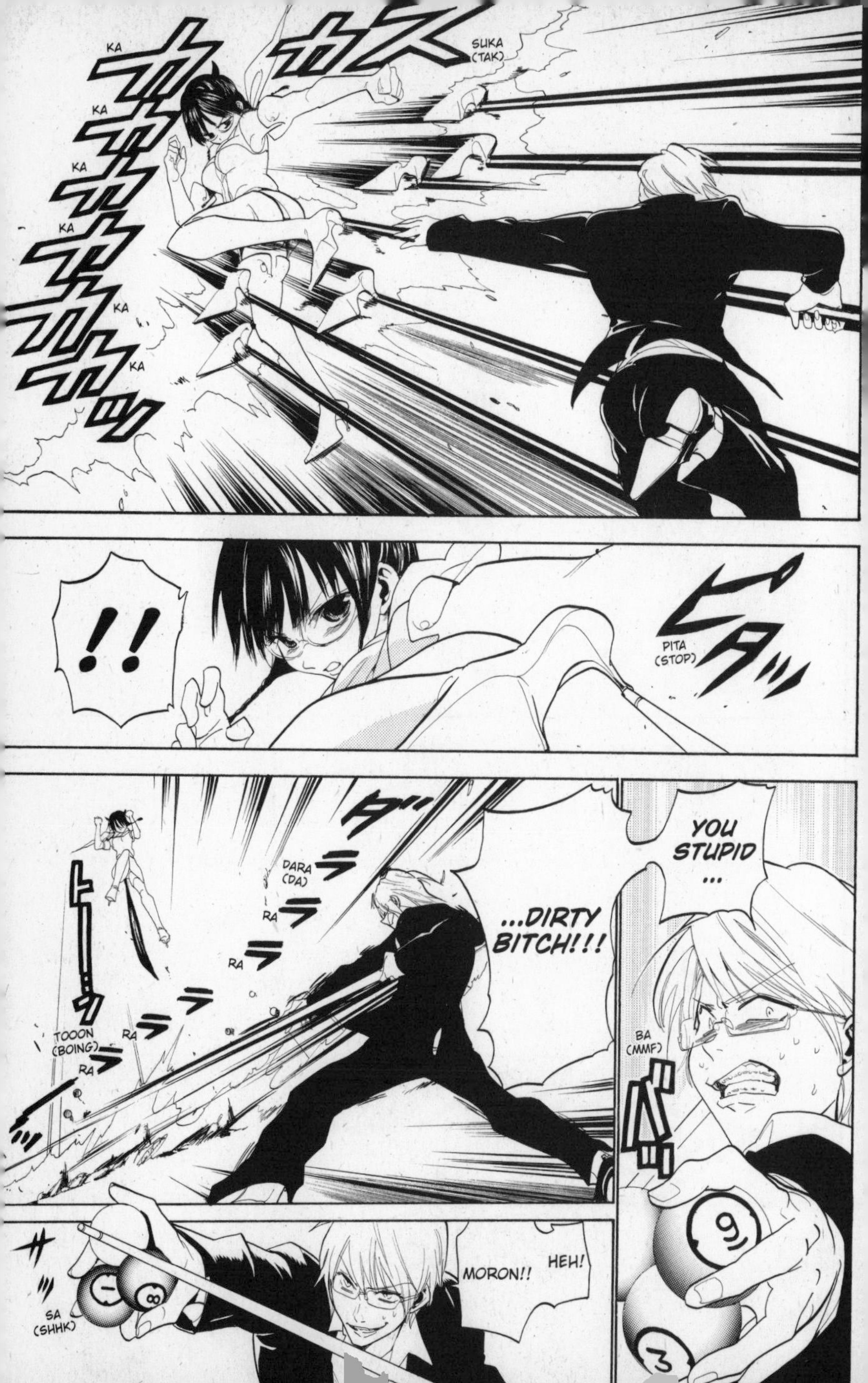
SUKA (TAK)
KA
KA
KA
KA
KA
KA
PITA (STOP)
!!
YOU STUPID ...
...DIRTY BITCH!!!
BA (MMF)
DARA (DA)
RA
RA
RA
RA
TOOON (BOING)
HEH!
MORON!!
SA (SHHK)

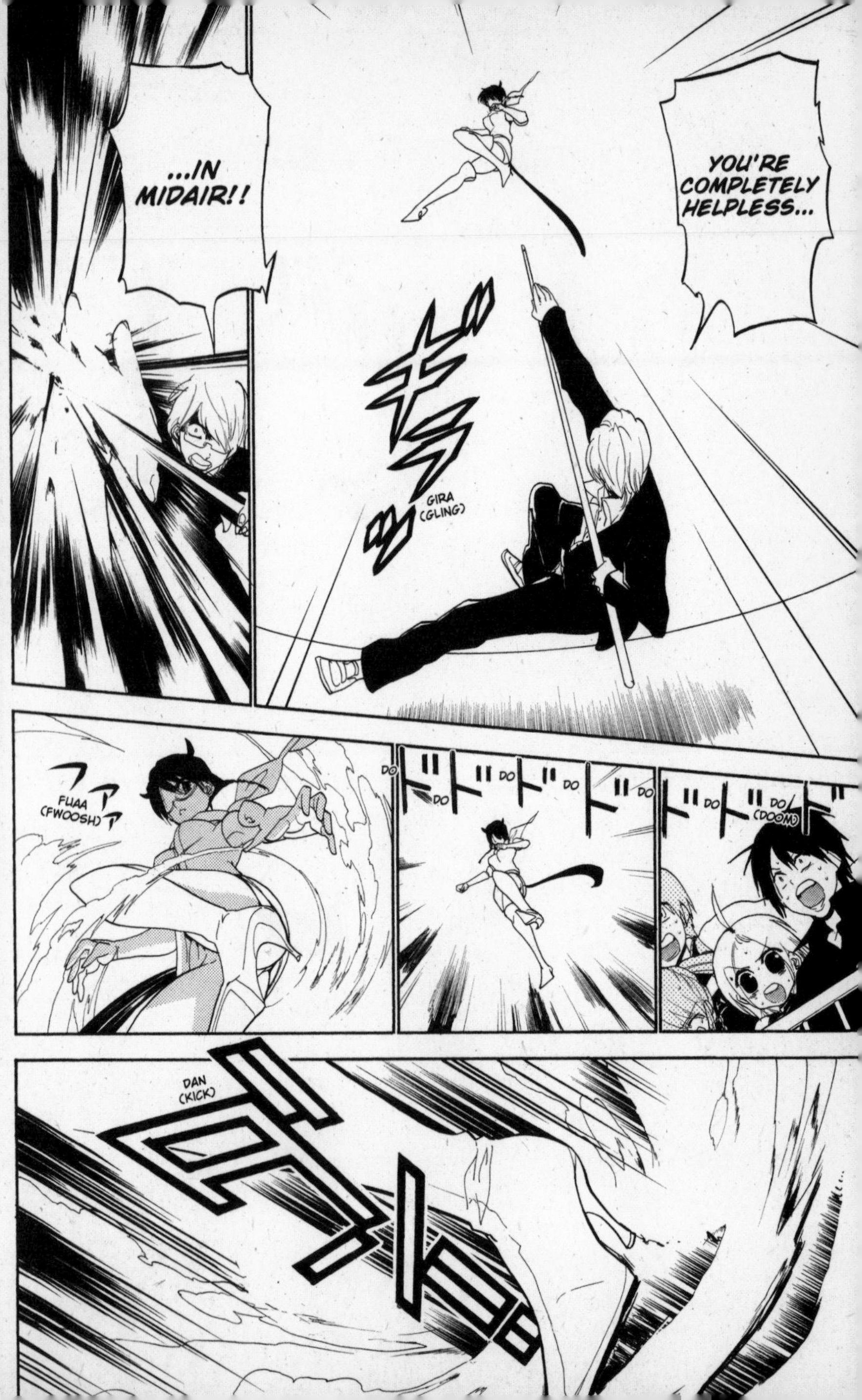
YOU'RE COMPLETELY HELPLESS...
GIRA (GLING)
...IN MIDAIR!!
DO DO DO (DOOM)
DO DO DO DO
FUAA (FWOOSH)
DAN (KICK)

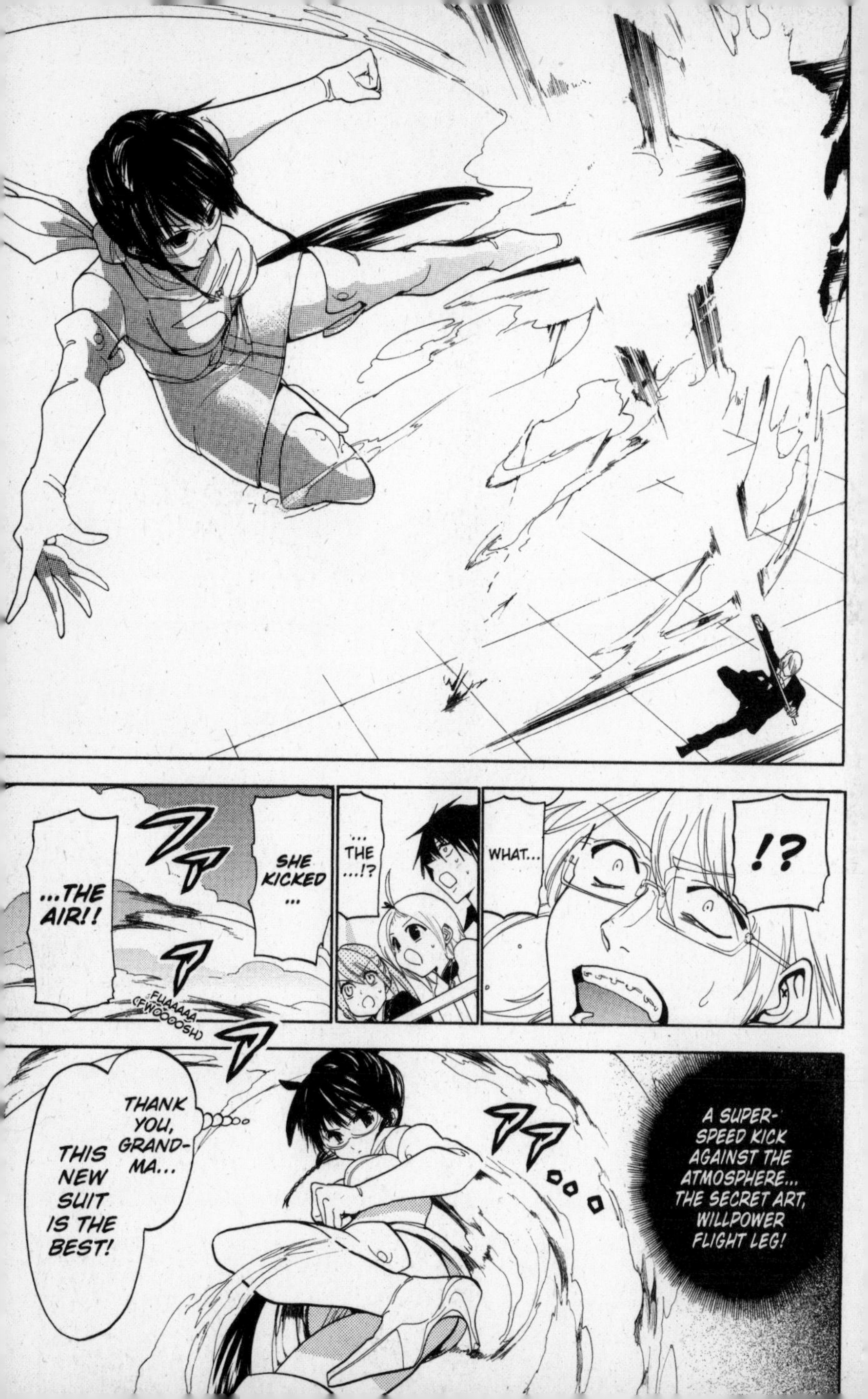
!?
WHAT...
...THE ...!?
SHE KICKED ...
...THE AIR!!
FUAAAAA (FWOOOOSH)
A SUPER-SPEED KICK AGAINST THE ATMOSPHERE... THE SECRET ART, WILLPOWER FLIGHT LEG!
THANK YOU, GRANDMA...
THIS NEW SUIT IS THE BEST!

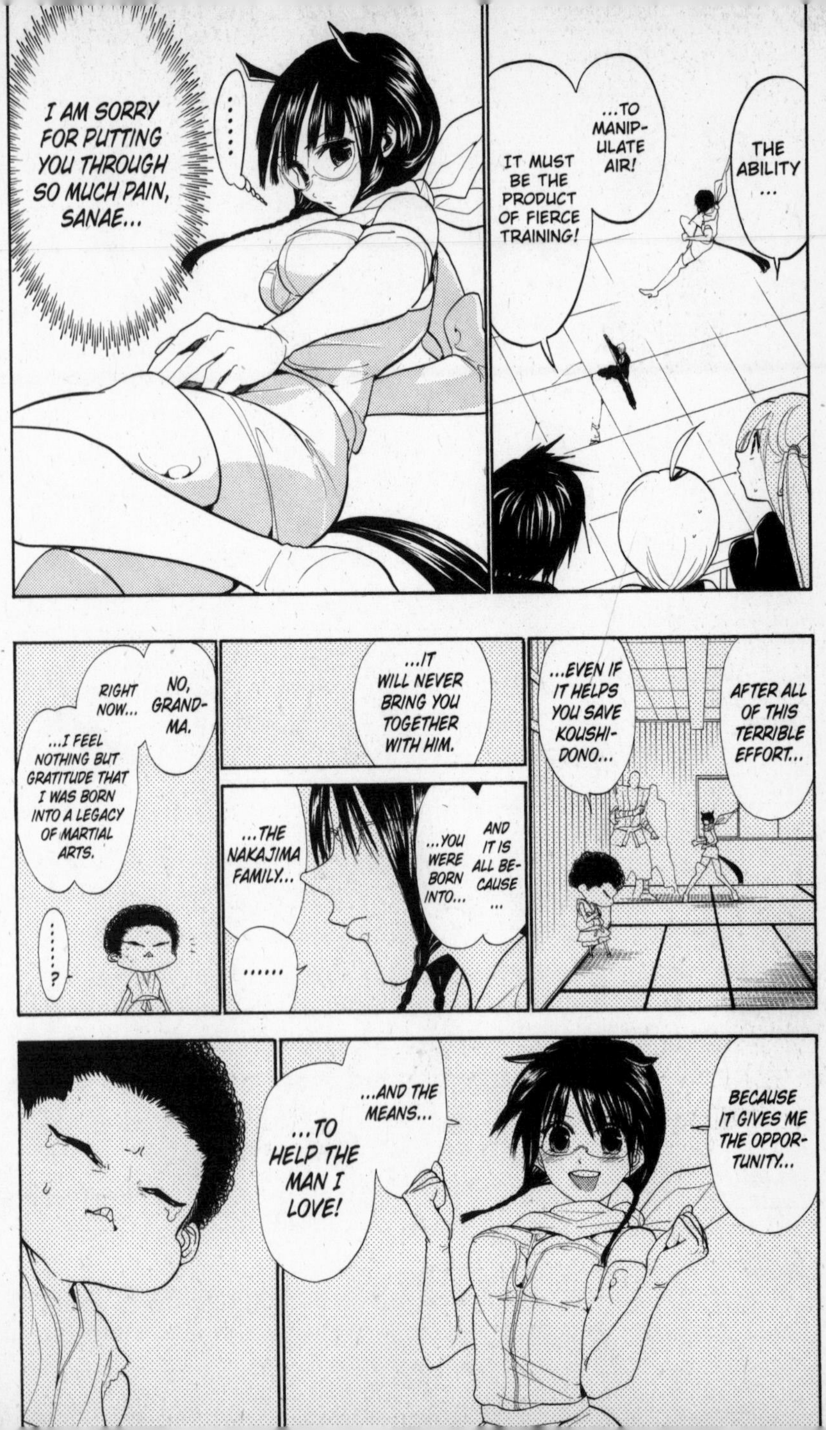
THE ABILITY ...
...TO MANIP-ULATE AIR!
IT MUST BE THE PRODUCT OF FIERCE TRAINING!
......
I AM SORRY FOR PUTTING YOU THROUGH SO MUCH PAIN, SANAE...
AFTER ALL OF THIS TERRIBLE EFFORT...
...EVEN IF IT HELPS YOU SAVE KOUSHI-DONO...
...IT WILL NEVER BRING YOU TOGETHER WITH HIM.
AND IT IS ALL BE-CAUSE ...
...YOU WERE BORN INTO...
...THE NAKAJIMA FAMILY...
......
NO, GRAND-MA.
RIGHT NOW...
...I FEEL NOTHING BUT GRATITUDE THAT I WAS BORN INTO A LEGACY OF MARTIAL ARTS.
......?
BECAUSE IT GIVES ME THE OPPOR-TUNITY...
...AND THE MEANS...
...TO HELP THE MAN I LOVE!

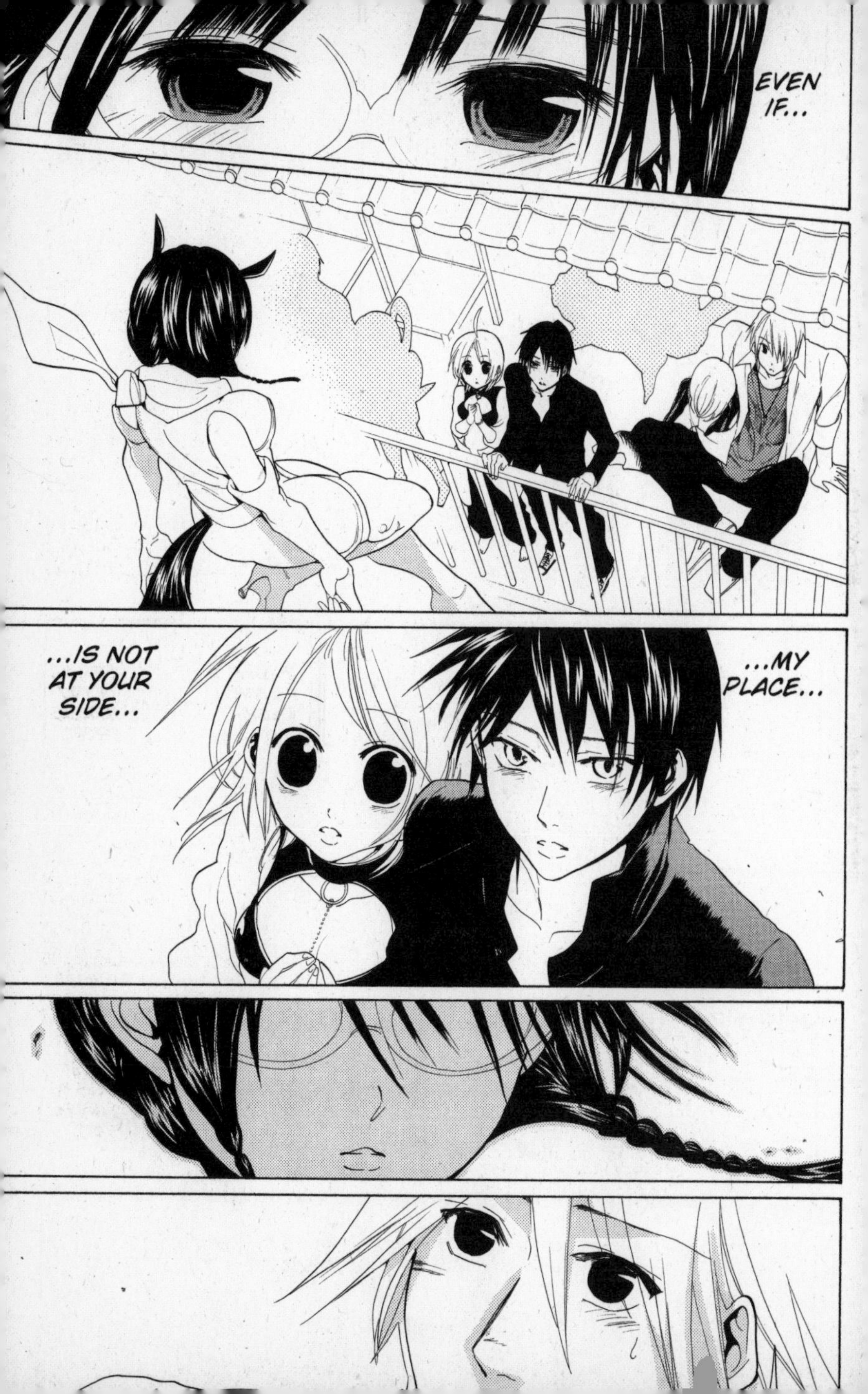
EVEN IF...
...MY PLACE...
...IS NOT AT YOUR SIDE...

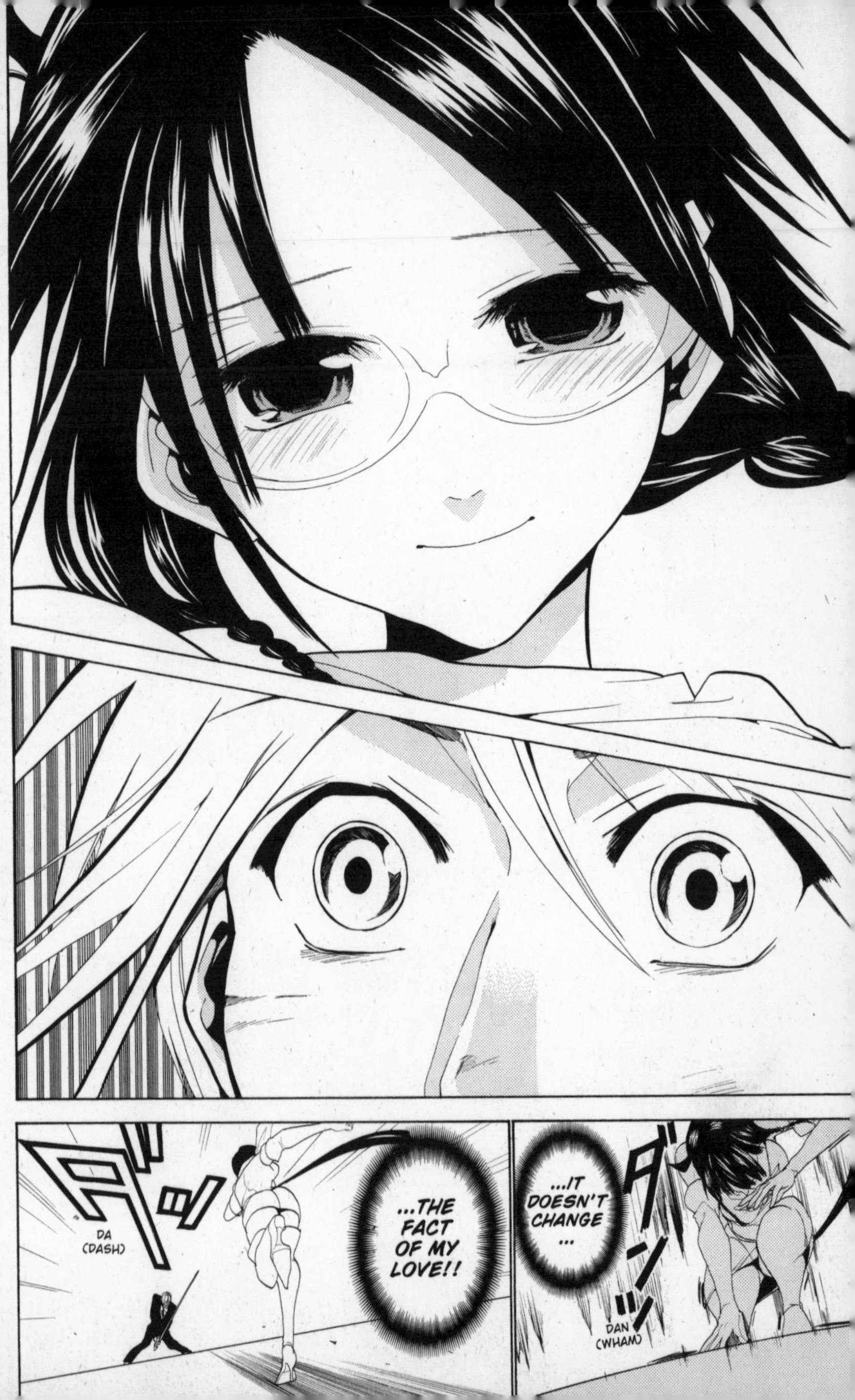

...IT DOESN'T CHANGE ...
DAN (WHAM)
...THE FACT OF MY LOVE!!
DA (DASH)

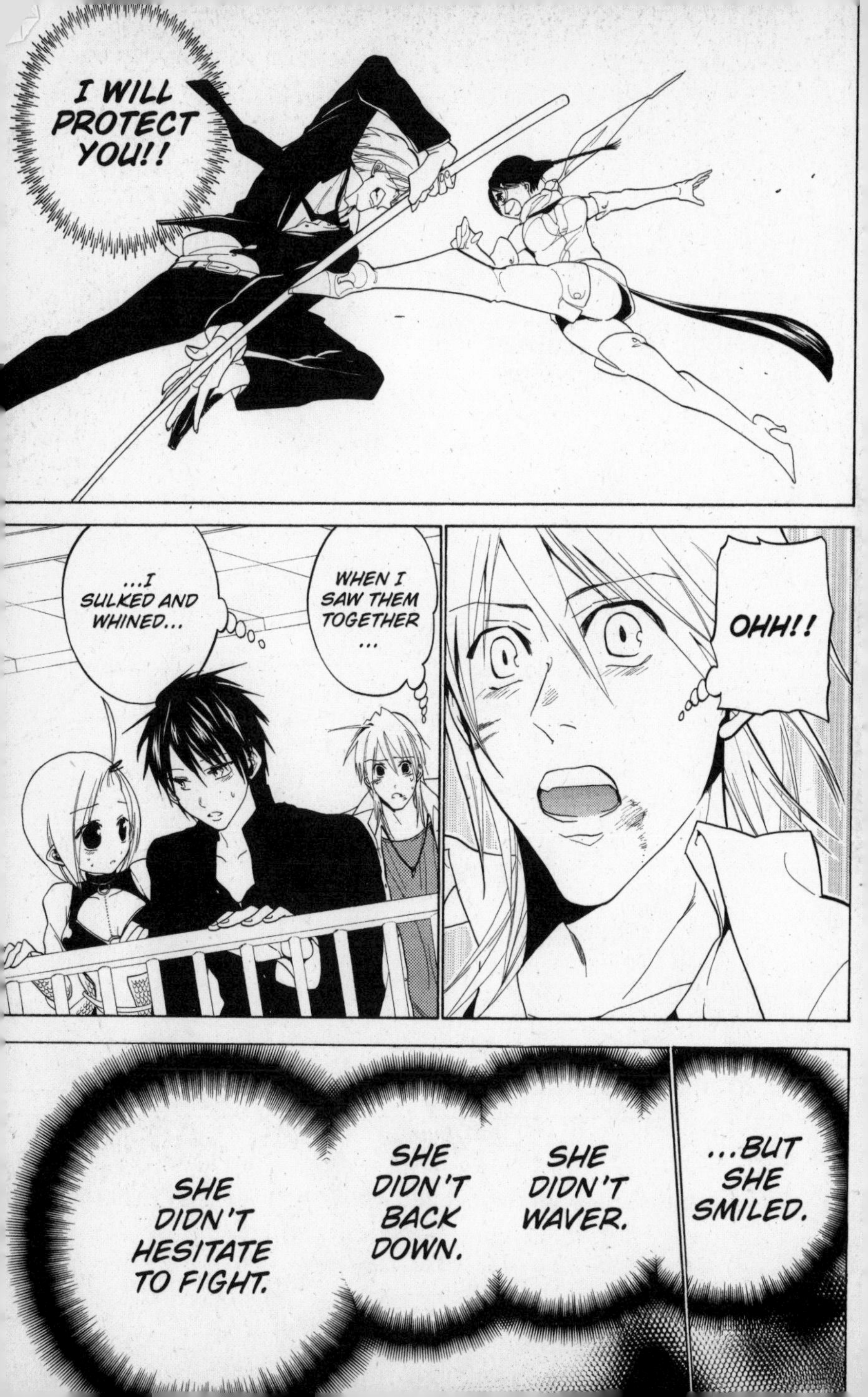
I WILL PROTECT YOU!!
OHH!!
WHEN I SAW THEM TOGETHER ...
...I SULKED AND WHINED...
...BUT SHE SMILED.
SHE DIDN'T WAVER.
SHE DIDN'T BACK DOWN.
SHE DIDN'T HESITATE TO FIGHT.

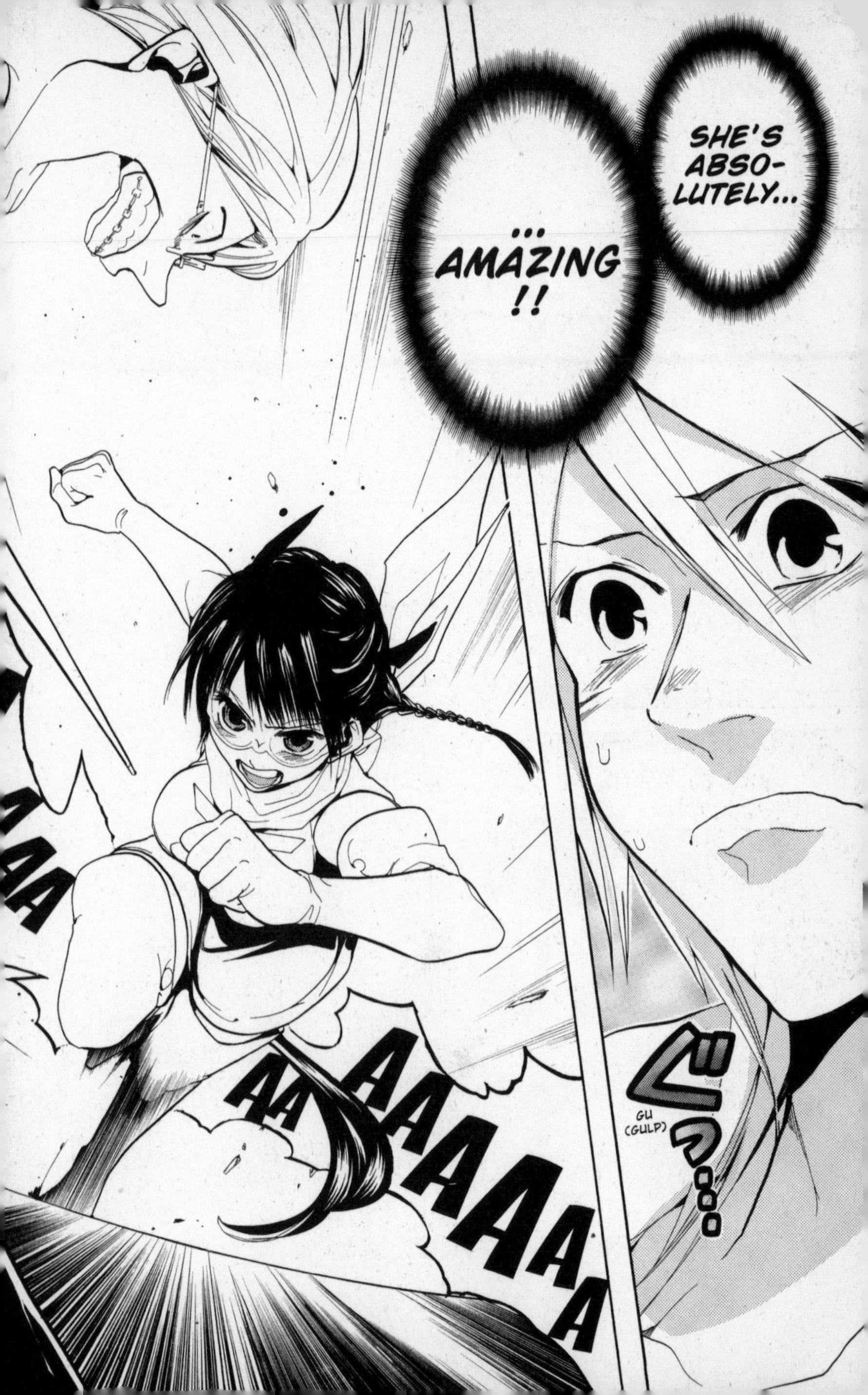
SHE'S ABSO-LUTELY...
...AMÄZING!!
AAAAAAAAAAAAAAA
グッ…
GU (GULP)

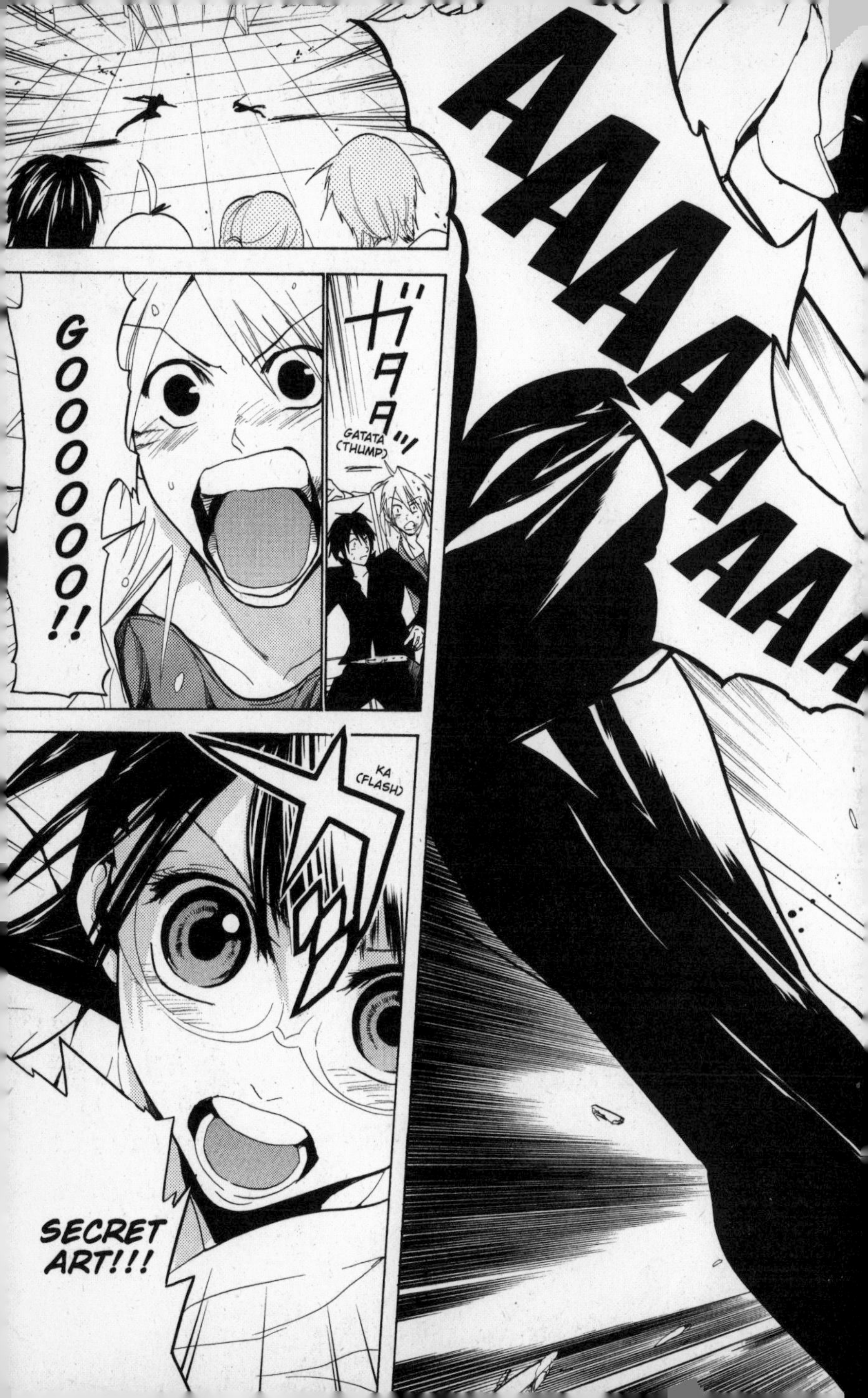
AAAAAAAAA
ガタタッ
GATATA (THUMP)
GOOOOOOOO!!
KA (FLASH)
SECRET ART!!!

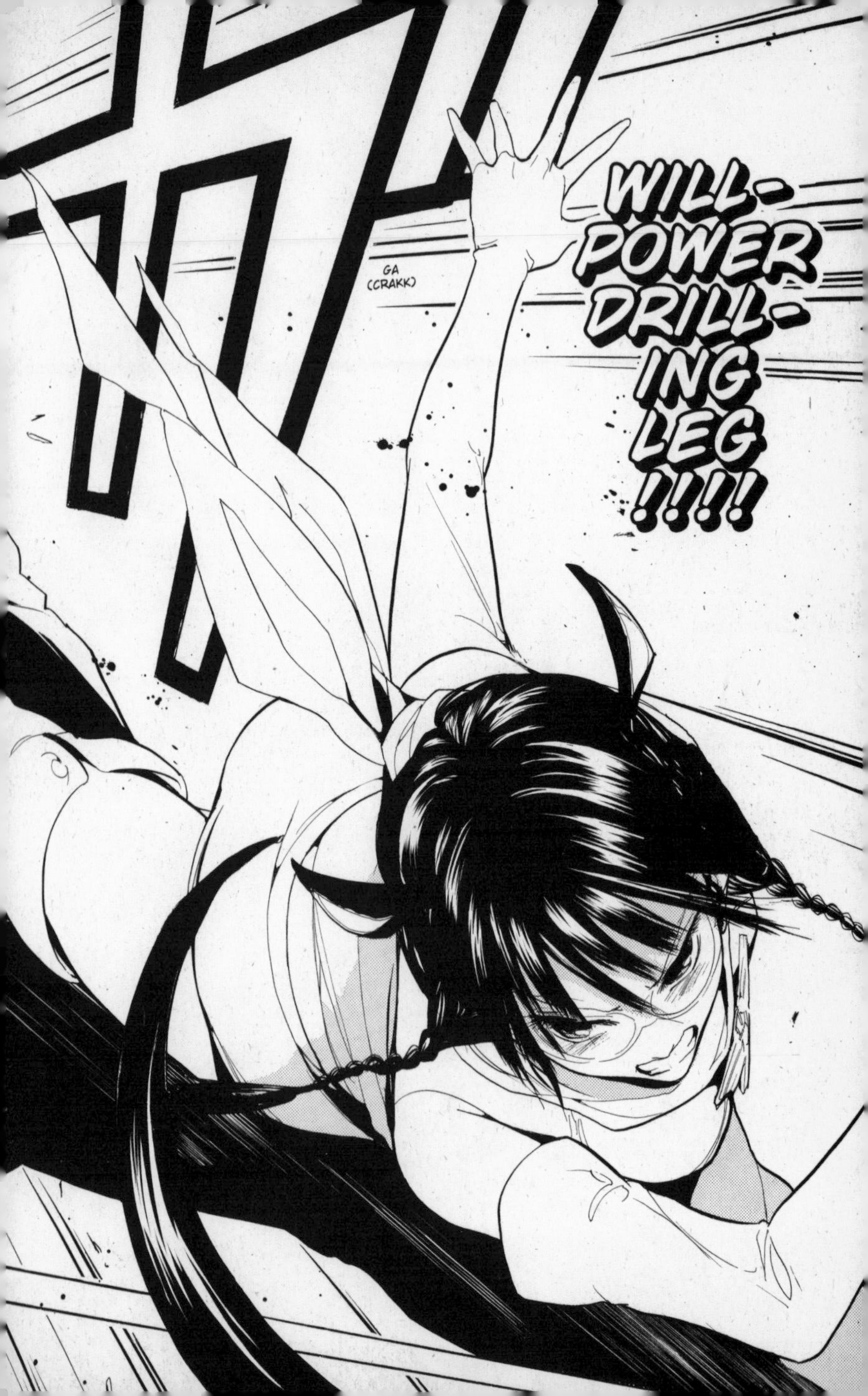
WILL-POWER DRILL-ING LEG !!!!
GA (CRAKK)

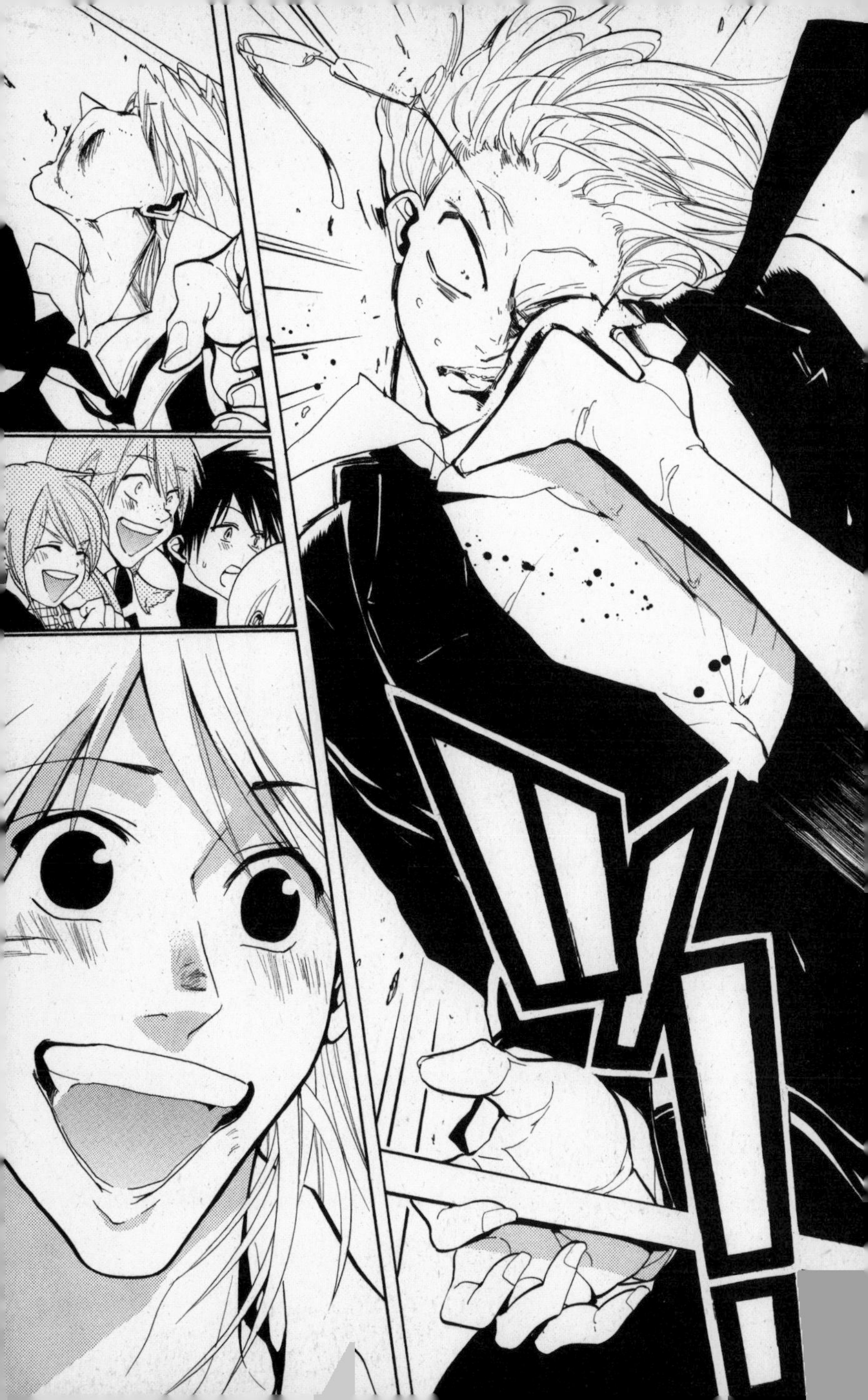

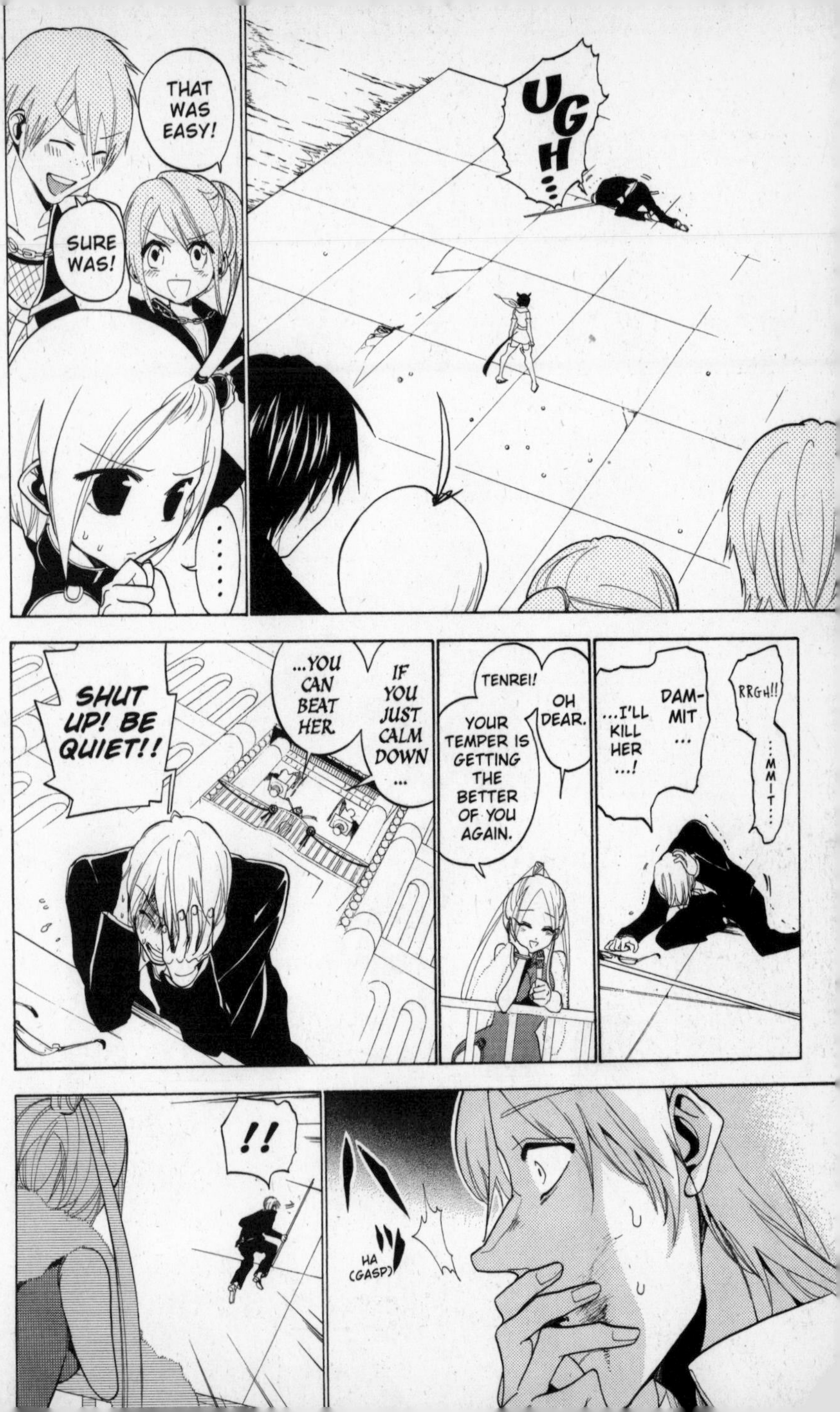
UGH...
THAT WAS EASY!
SURE WAS!
......
RRGH!!
...MMIT...
DAM-MIT...
...I'LL KILL HER...!
OH DEAR.
TENREI!
YOUR TEMPER IS GETTING THE BETTER OF YOU AGAIN.
IF YOU JUST CALM DOWN...
...YOU CAN BEAT HER.
SHUT UP! BE QUIET!!
HA (GASP)
!!

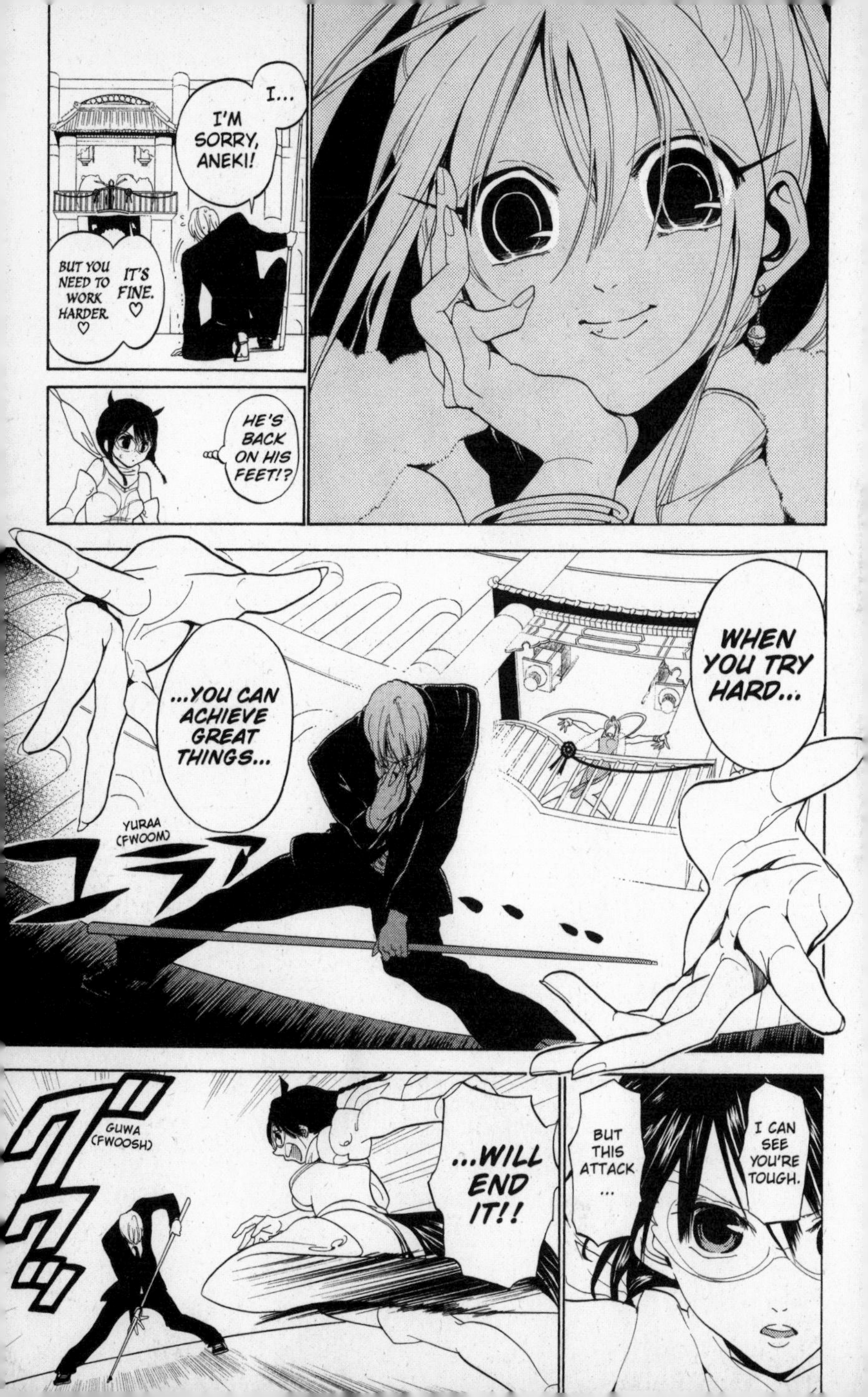
I...
I'M SORRY, ANEKI!
IT'S FINE. ♡
BUT YOU NEED TO WORK HARDER. ♡
HE'S BACK ON HIS FEET!?
WHEN YOU TRY HARD...
...YOU CAN ACHIEVE GREAT THINGS...
YURAA (FWOOM)
I CAN SEE YOU'RE TOUGH.
BUT THIS ATTACK ...
...WILL END IT!!
GUWA (FWOOSH)

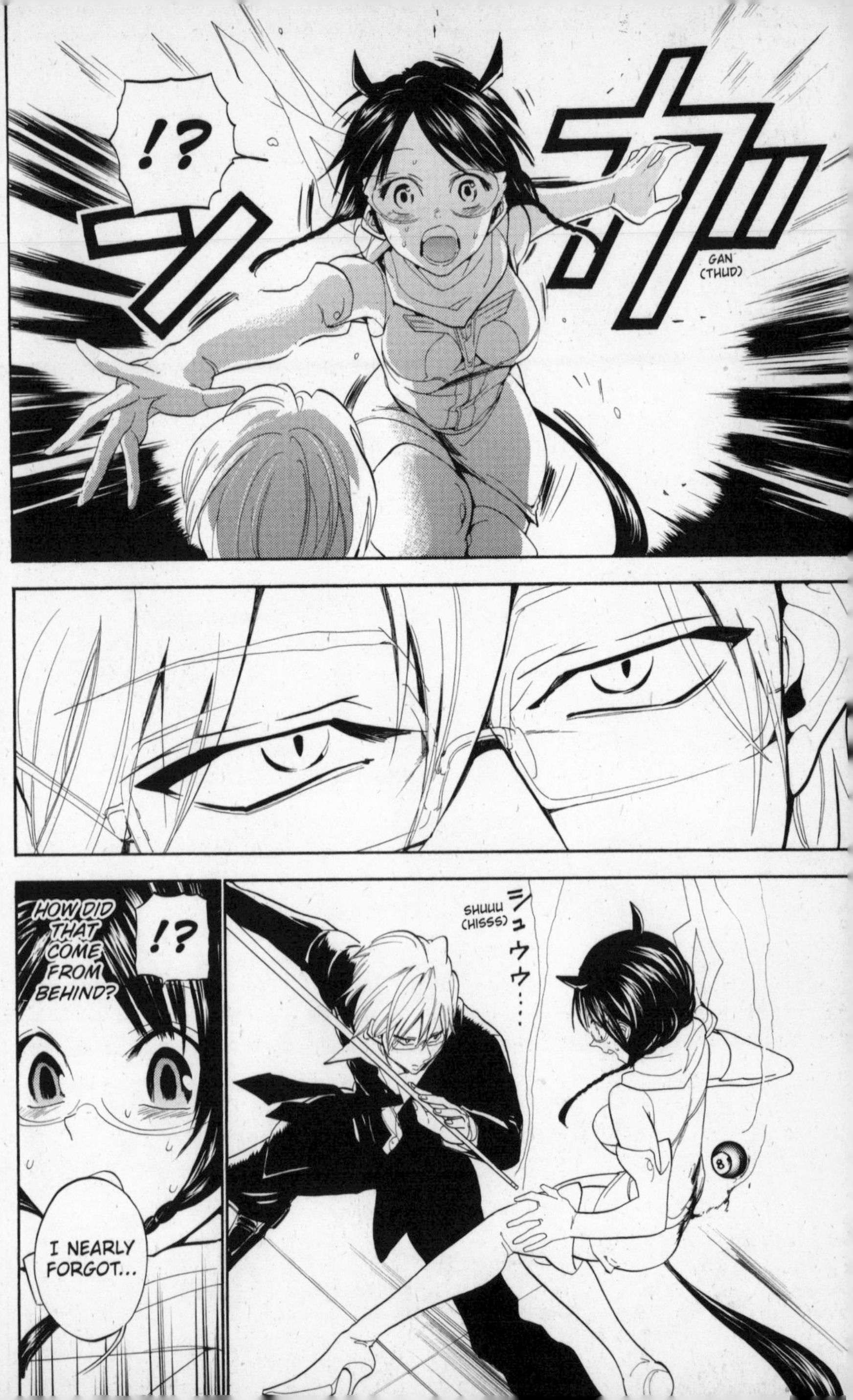

ガン
GAN (THUD)
!?
シュウウ…
SHUUU (HISSS)
HOW DID THAT COME FROM BEHIND?
!?
I NEARLY FORGOT...

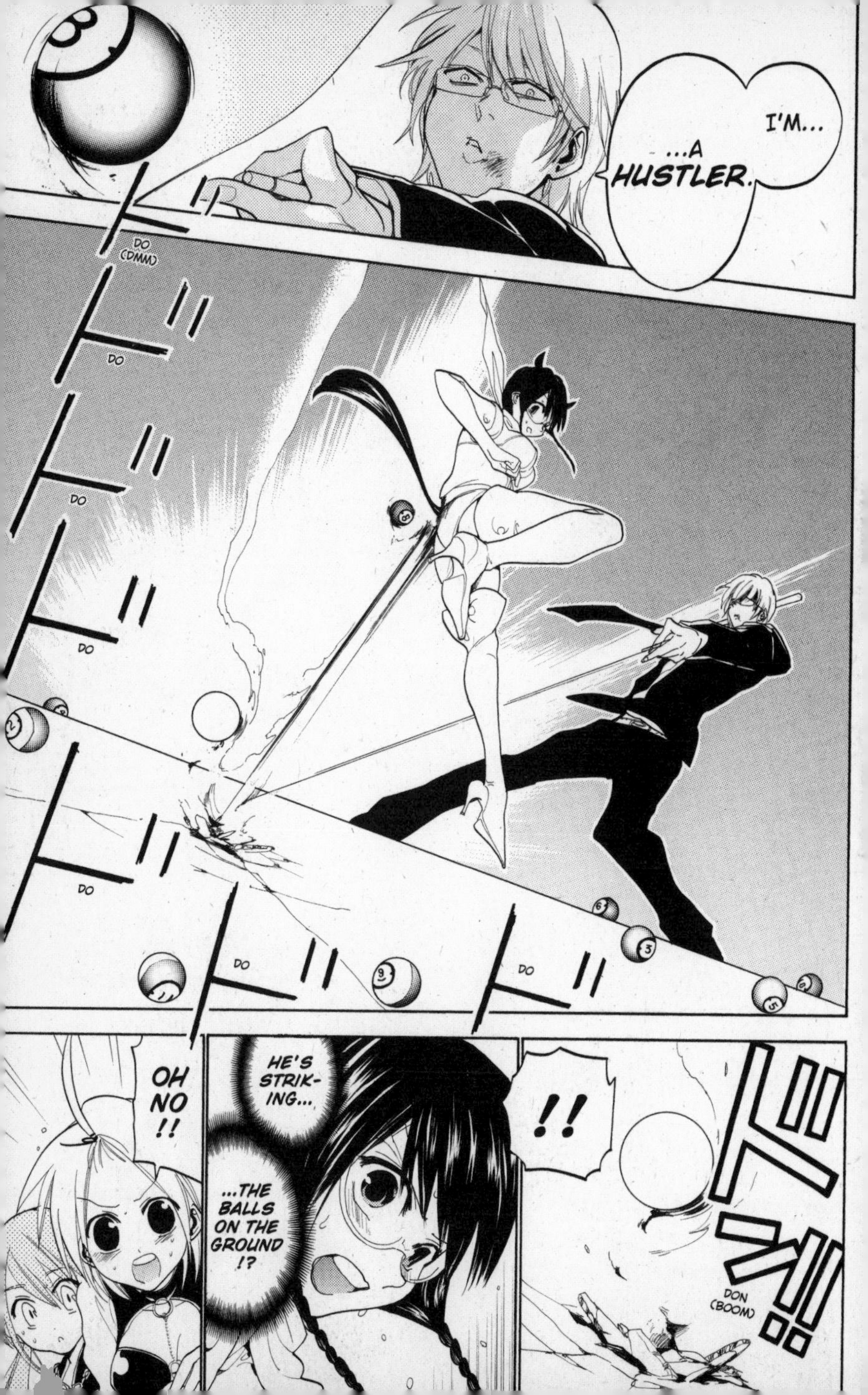
I'M...
...A HUSTLER.
DO (DMM)
DO
DO
DO
DO
DO
DO
DON (BOOM)
!!
HE'S STRIK-ING...
...THE BALLS ON THE GROUND!?
OH NO!!

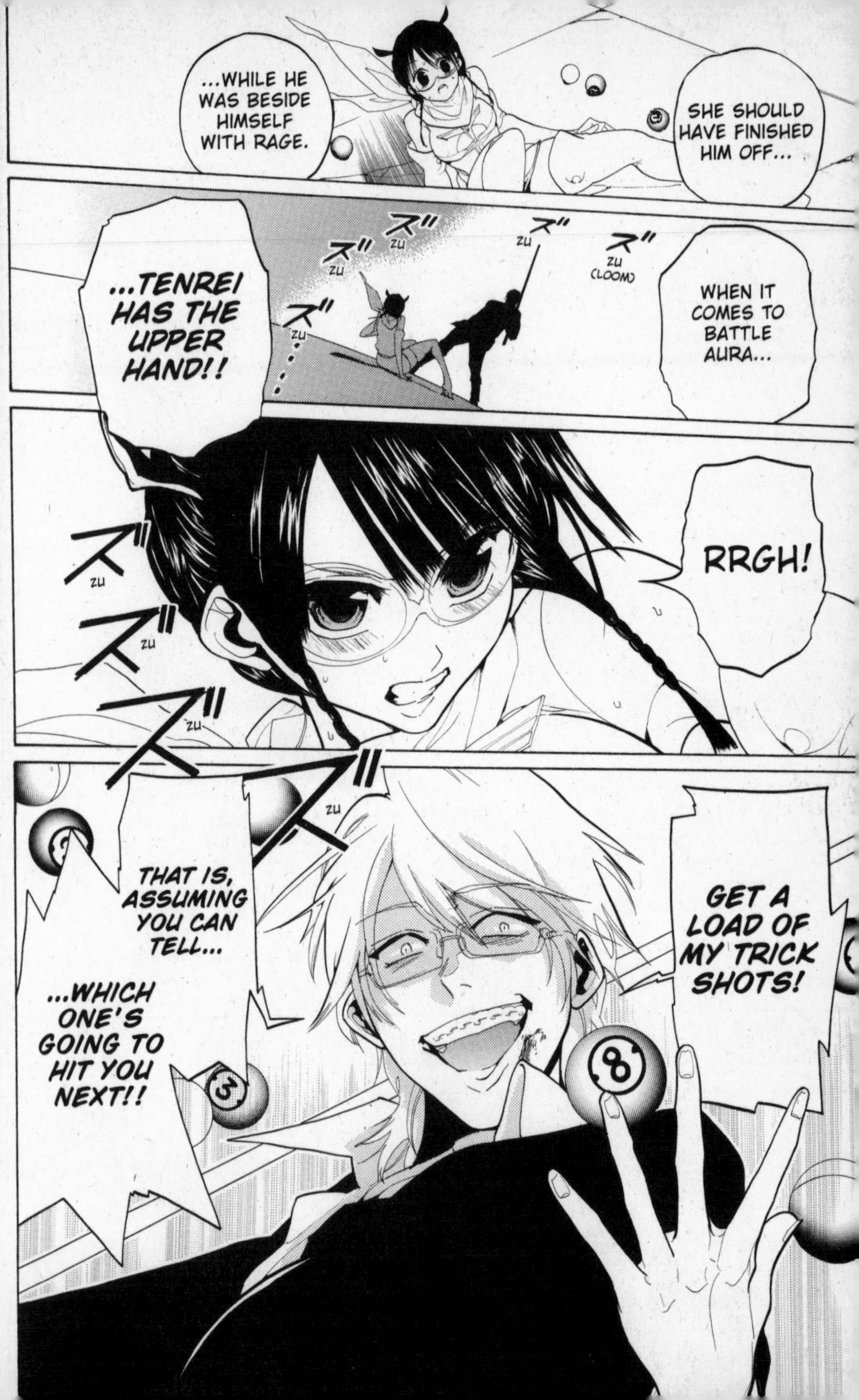
SHE SHOULD HAVE FINISHED HIM OFF...
...WHILE HE WAS BESIDE HIMSELF WITH RAGE.
WHEN IT COMES TO BATTLE AURA...
ZU (LOOM)
ZU
ZU
ZU
ZU
...TENREI HAS THE UPPER HAND!!
RRGH!
ZU
ZU
ZU
ZU
GET A LOAD OF MY TRICK SHOTS!
THAT IS, ASSUMING YOU CAN TELL...
...WHICH ONE'S GOING TO HIT YOU NEXT!!

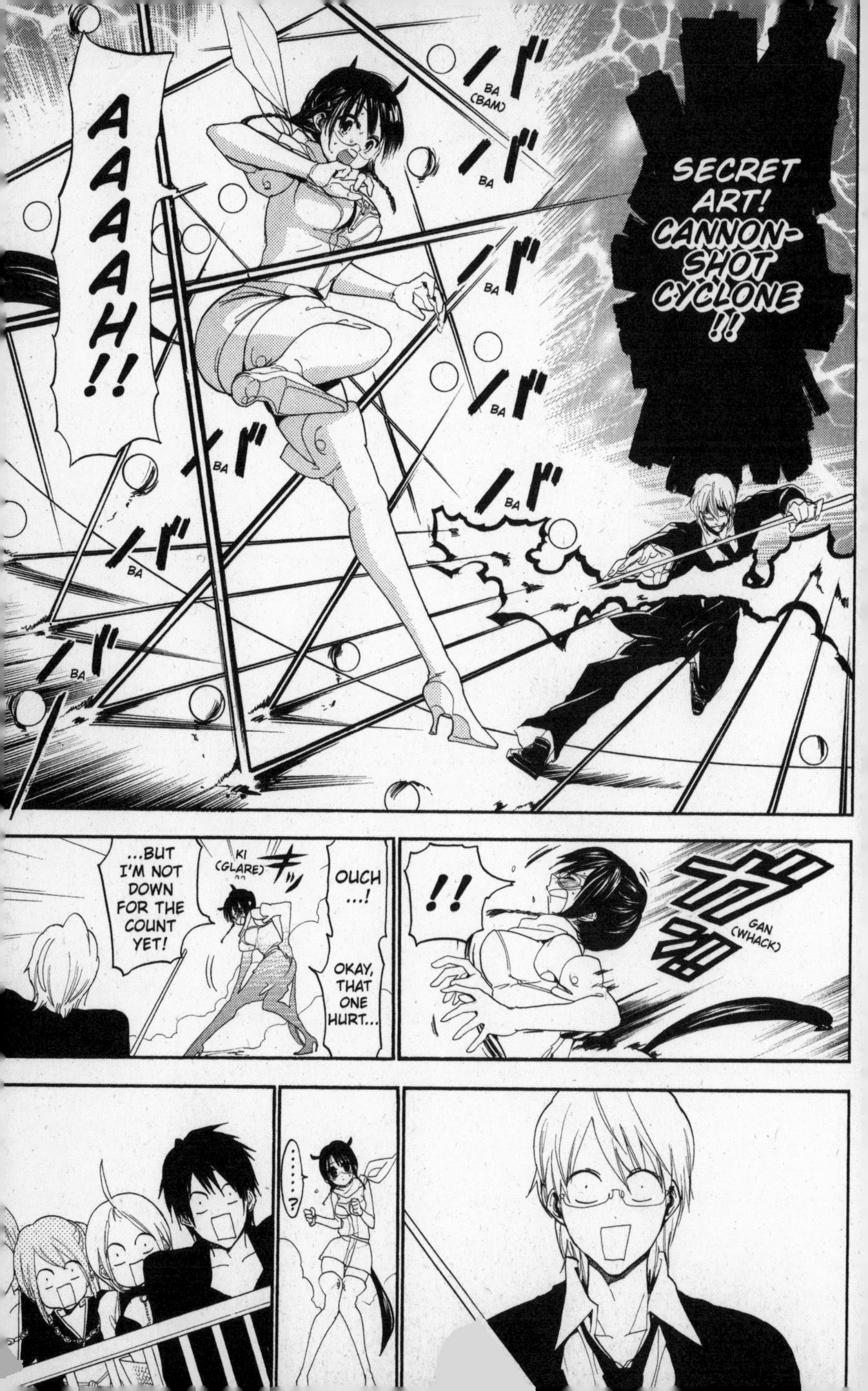
SECRET ART! CANNON-SHOT CYCLONE!!
BA (BAM)
BA
BA
BA
BA
BA
BA
BA
AAAAAH!!
!!
GAN (WHACK)
OUCH...!
OKAY, THAT ONE HURT...
KI (GLARE)
...BUT I'M NOT DOWN FOR THE COUNT YET!
......?

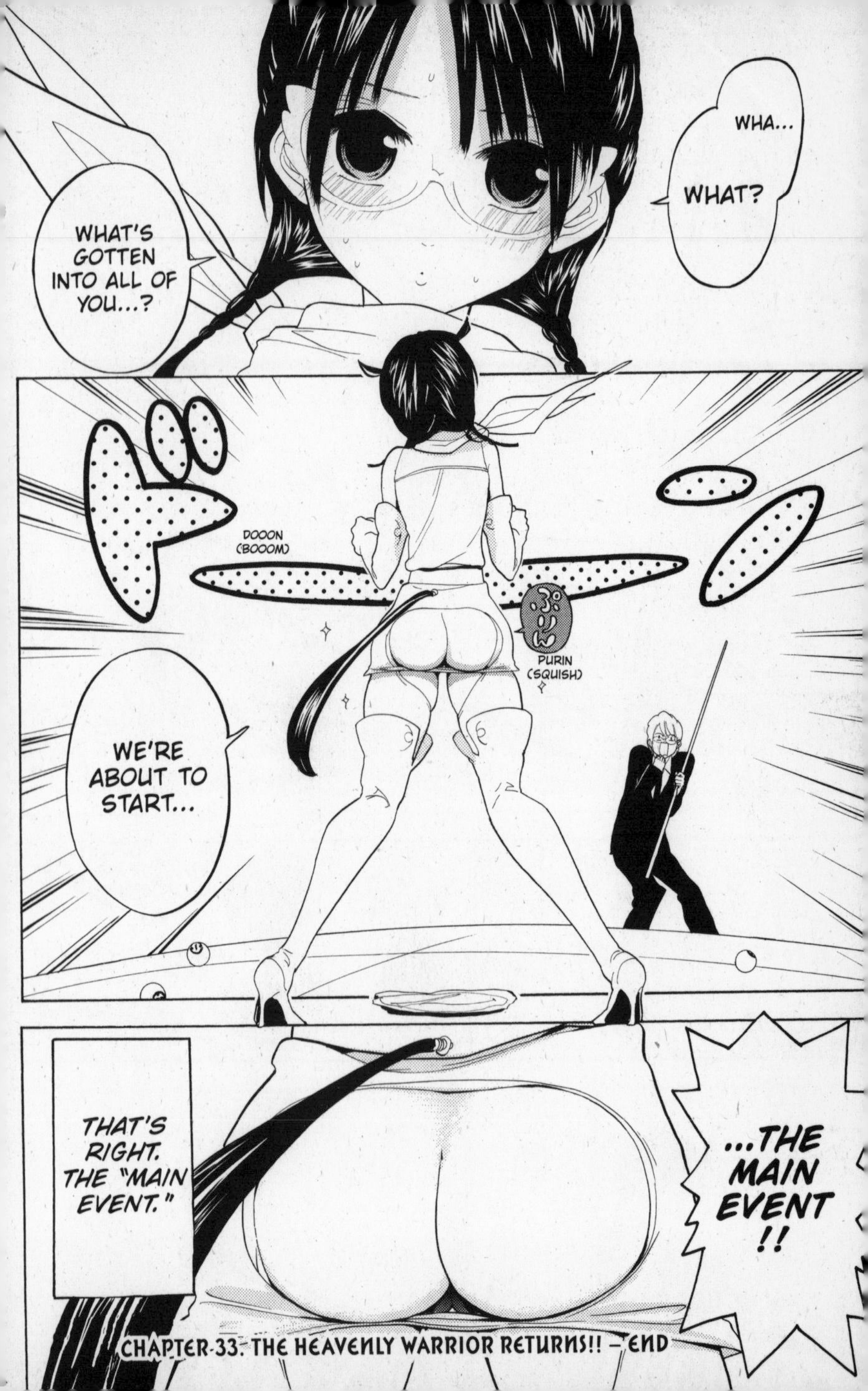
WHA...
WHAT?
WHAT'S GOTTEN INTO ALL OF YOU...?
DOOON (BOOOM)
ぷりん
PURIN (SQUISH)
WE'RE ABOUT TO START...
...THE MAIN EVENT!!
THAT'S RIGHT. THE "MAIN EVENT."
CHAPTER 33: THE HEAVENLY WARRIOR RETURNS!! — END

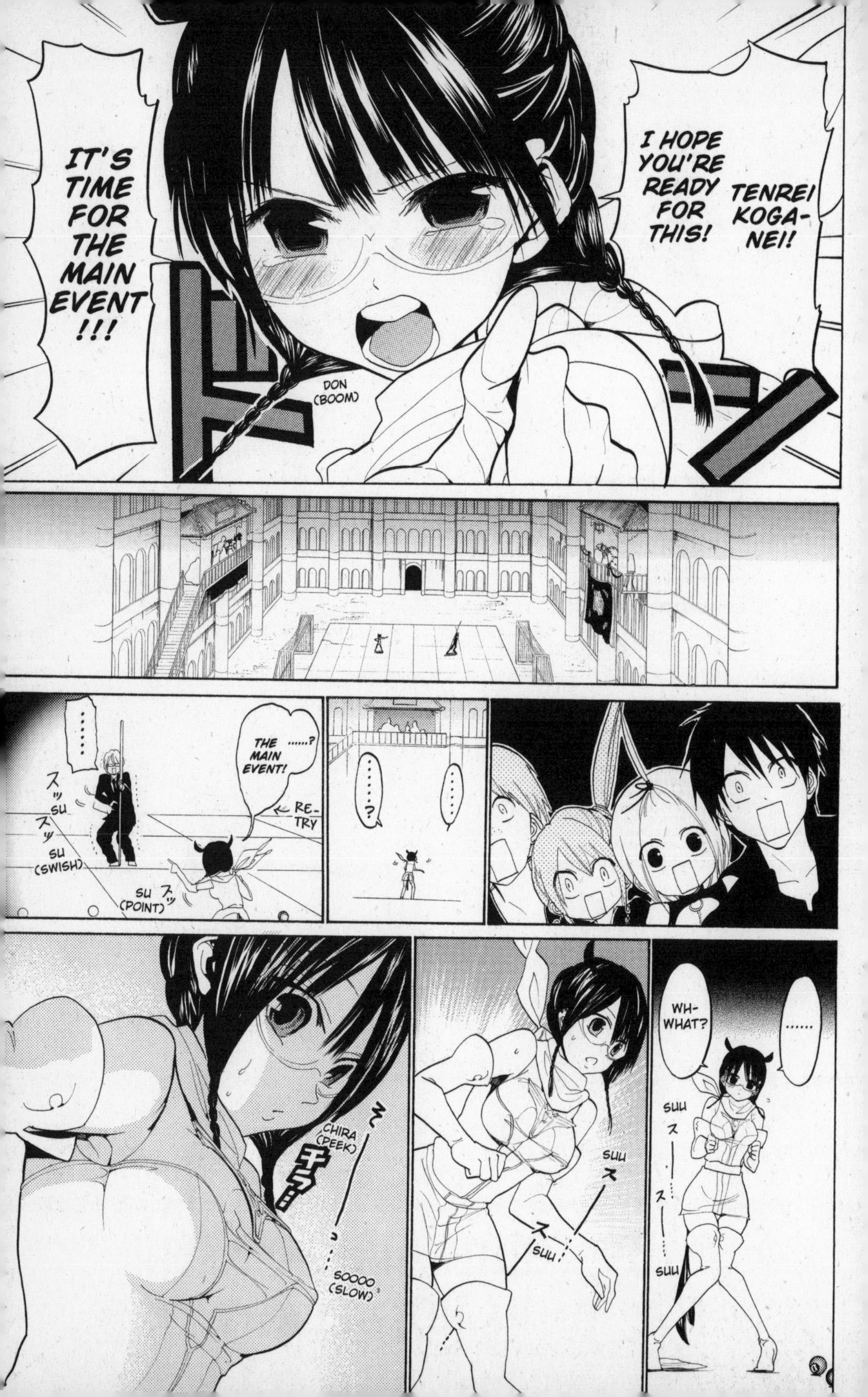
TENREI KOGA-NEI!
I HOPE YOU'RE READY FOR THIS!
IT'S TIME FOR THE MAIN EVENT!!!
DON (BOOM)
......
......?
THE MAIN EVENT! ......?
RE-TRY
......
SU
SU (SWISH)
SU (POINT)
WH-WHAT?
......
SUU
SUU
SUU
SUU
CHIRA (PEEK)
SOOOO (SLOW)

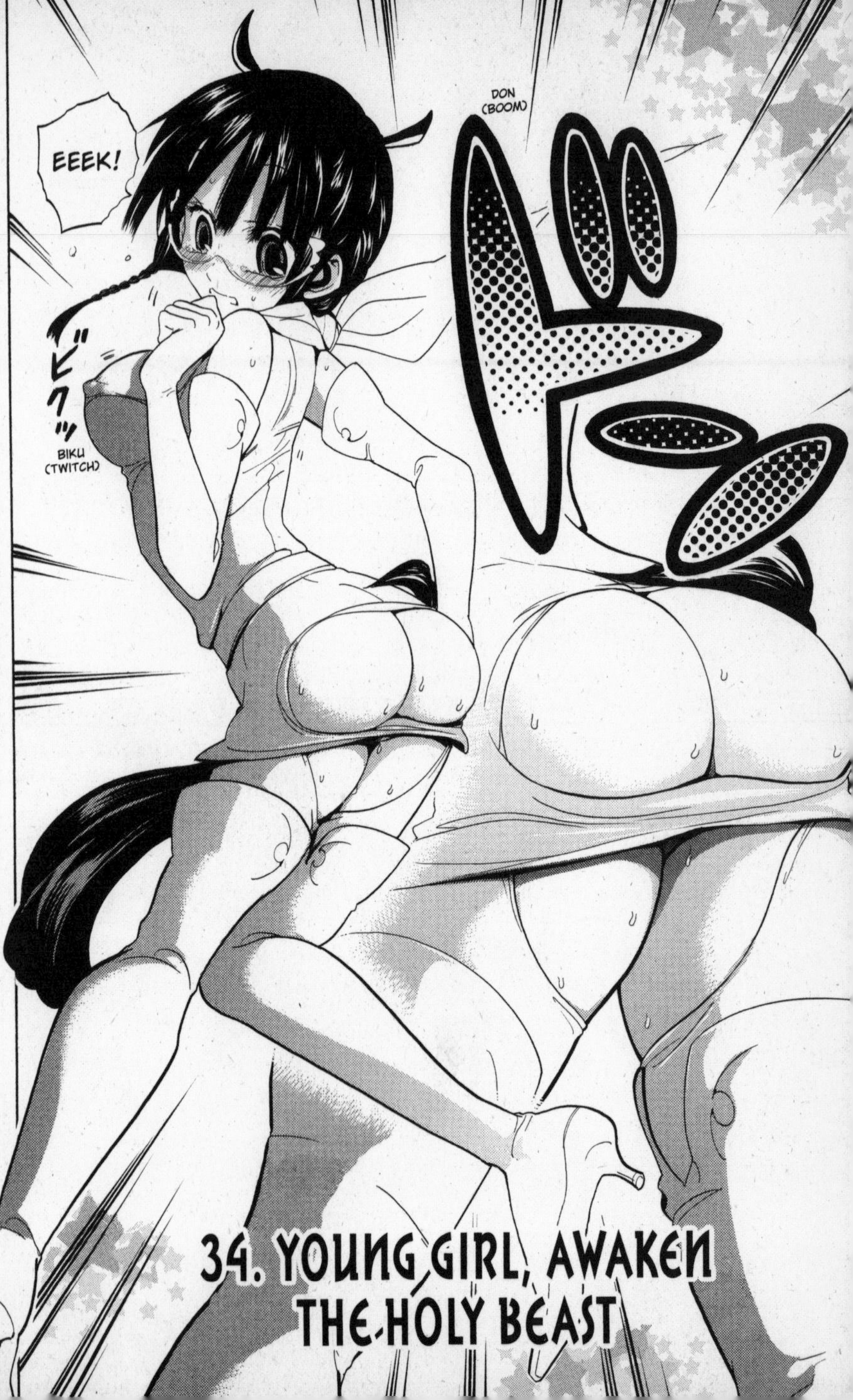
EEEK!
DON (BOOM)
ビクッ
BIKU (TWITCH)
34. YOUNG GIRL, AWAKEN THE HOLY BEAST

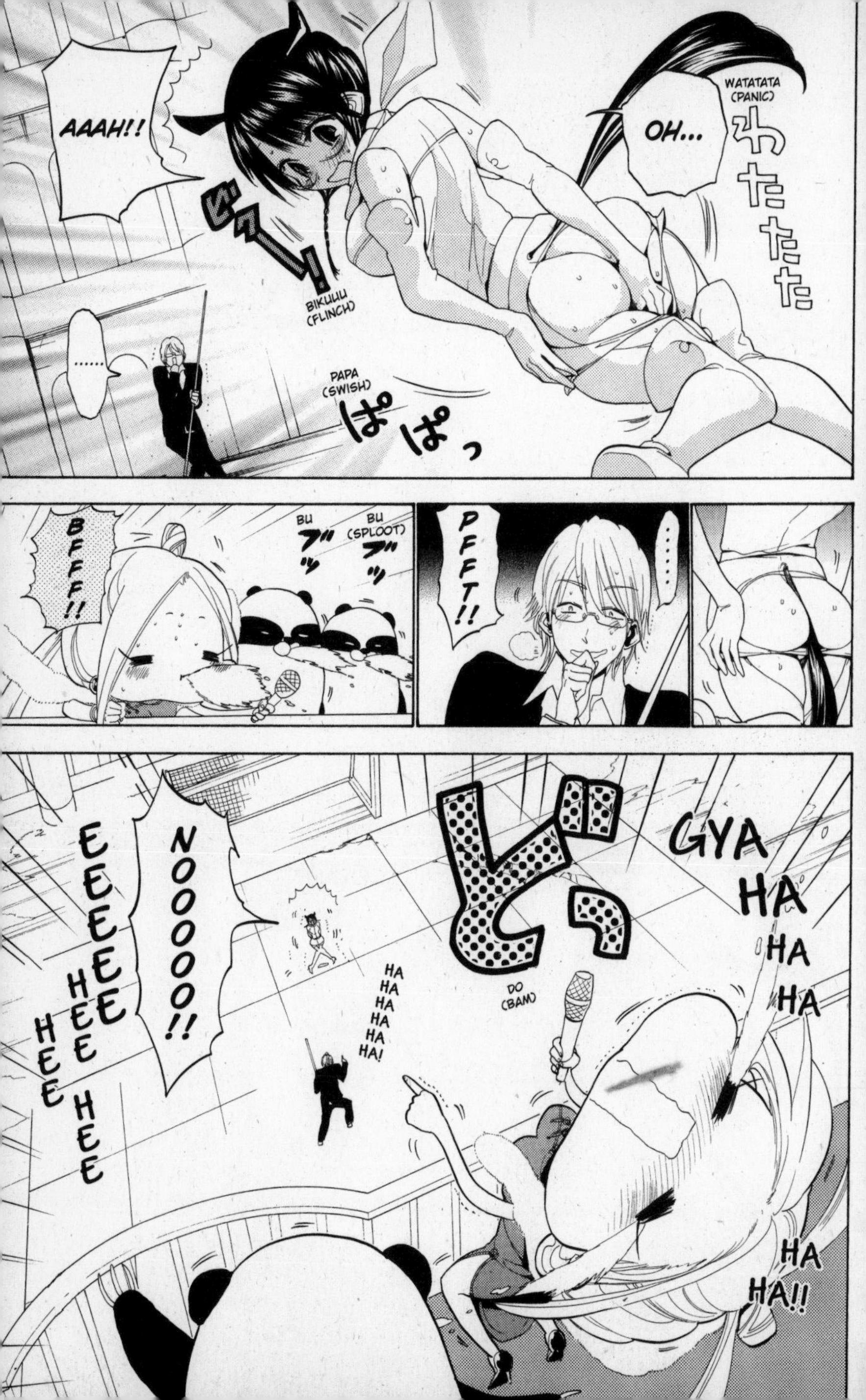
WATATATA (PANIC)
わたたたた
OH...
AAAH!!
BIKUUU (FLINCH)
PAPA (SWISH)
ぱぱっ
......
......
PFFT!!
BU BU (SPLOOT)
ブッ ブッ
BFFF!!
GYA HA HA HA
ど
DO (BAM)
HA HA!!
HA HA HA HA HA HA!
NOOOOOO!!
EEEEEEE
HEE HEE HEE HEE HEE HEE

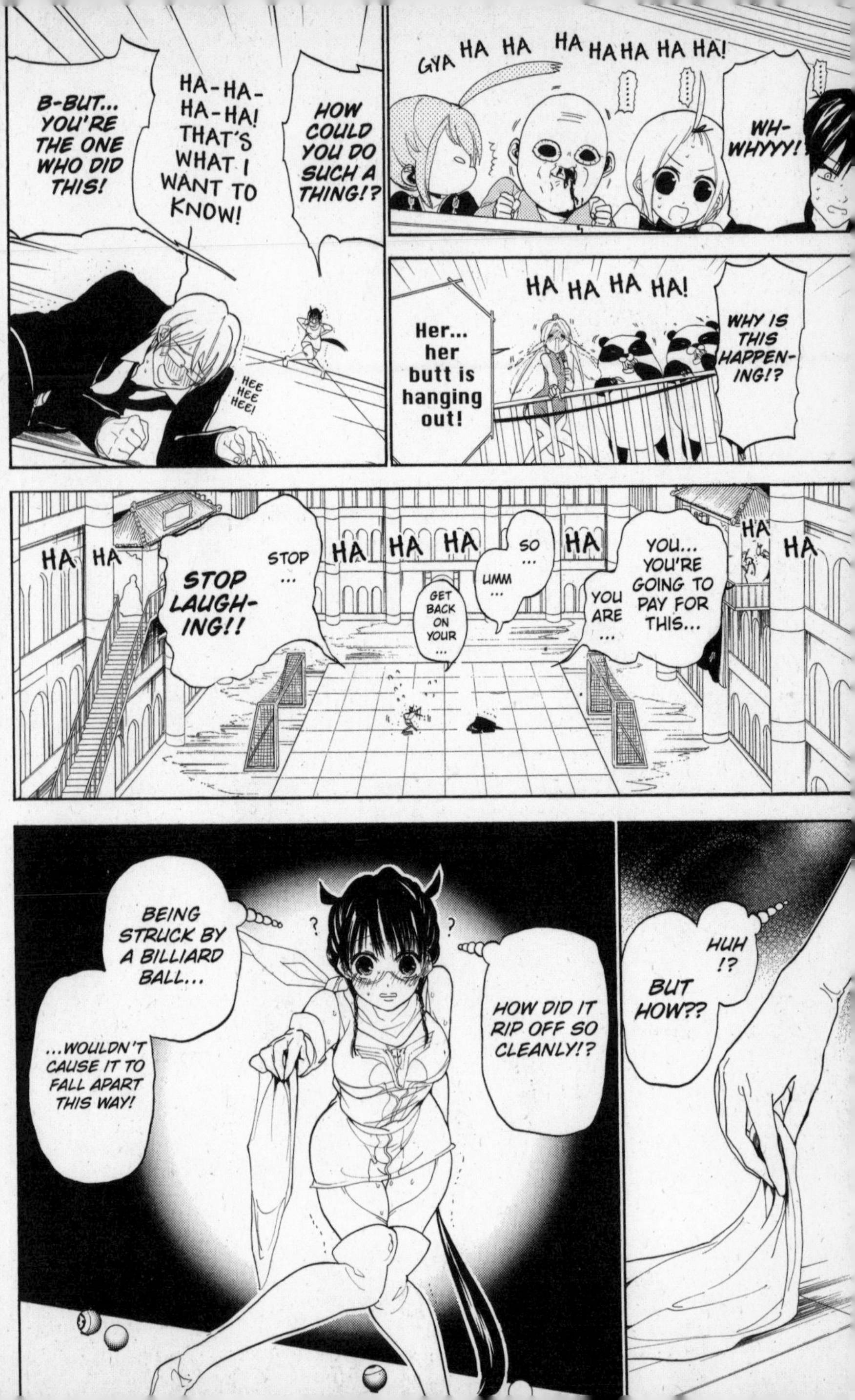

GYA HA HA HA HA HA HA HA!
WH-WHYYY!
HA HA HA HA!
WHY IS THIS HAPPEN-ING!?
Her... her butt is hanging out!
HOW COULD YOU DO SUCH A THING!?
HA-HA-HA-HA! THAT'S WHAT I WANT TO KNOW!
B-BUT... YOU'RE THE ONE WHO DID THIS!
HEE HEE HEE!
HA
HA
YOU... YOU'RE GOING TO PAY FOR THIS...
YOU ARE ...
HA
SO ... UMM ...
GET BACK ON YOUR ...
HA HA HA
STOP ...
STOP LAUGH-ING!!
HA HA
HUH!? BUT HOW??
HOW DID IT RIP OFF SO CLEANLY!?
BEING STRUCK BY A BILLIARD BALL...
...WOULDN'T CAUSE IT TO FALL APART THIS WAY!

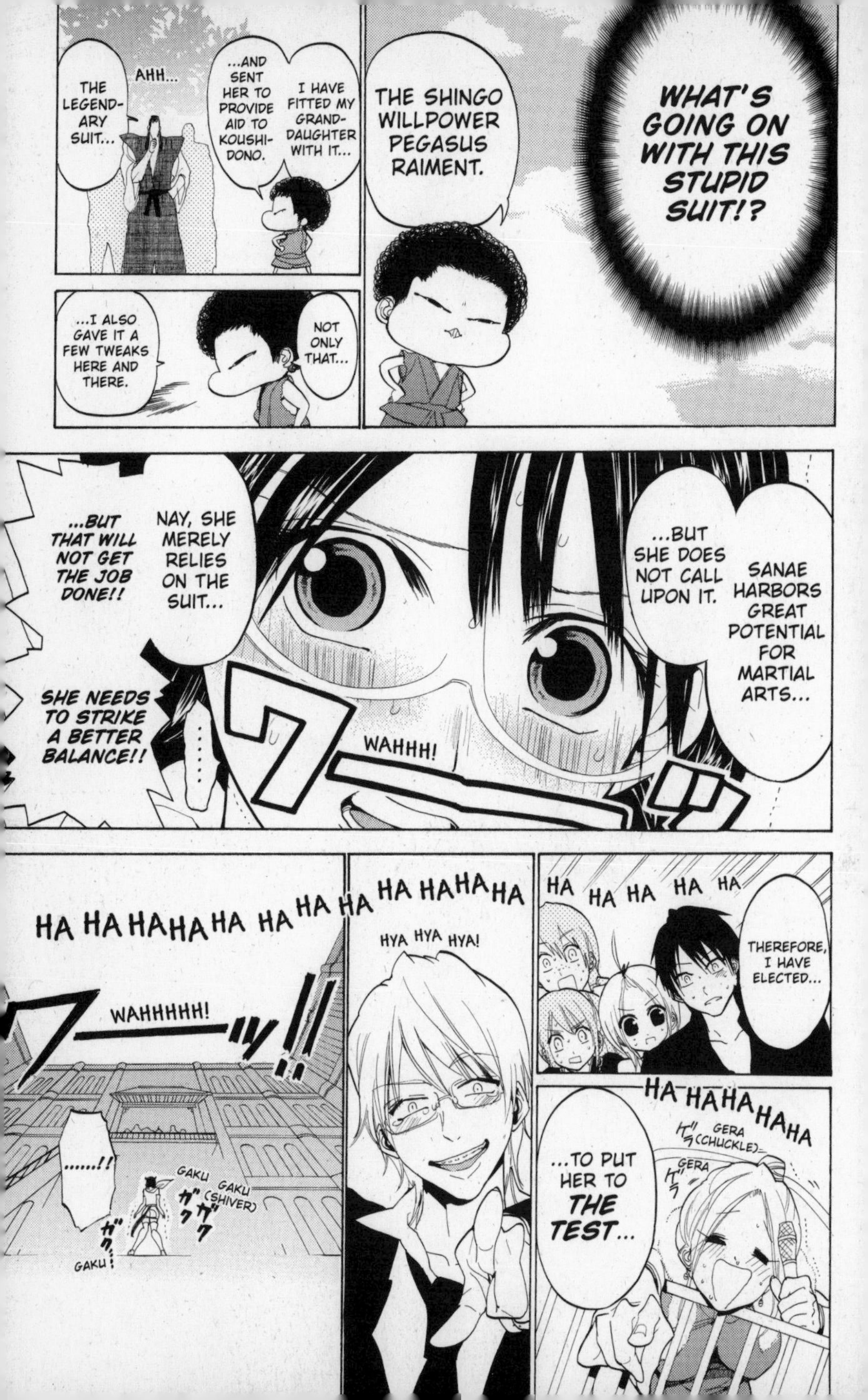
WHAT'S GOING ON WITH THIS STUPID SUIT!?
THE SHINGO WILLPOWER PEGASUS RAIMENT.
I HAVE FITTED MY GRAND-DAUGHTER WITH IT...
...AND SENT HER TO PROVIDE AID TO KOUSHI-DONO.
AHH...
THE LEGEND-ARY SUIT...
NOT ONLY THAT...
...I ALSO GAVE IT A FEW TWEAKS HERE AND THERE.
SANAE HARBORS GREAT POTENTIAL FOR MARTIAL ARTS...
...BUT SHE DOES NOT CALL UPON IT.
WAHHH!
NAY, SHE MERELY RELIES ON THE SUIT...
...BUT THAT WILL NOT GET THE JOB DONE!!
SHE NEEDS TO STRIKE A BETTER BALANCE!!
HA HA HA HA HA
THEREFORE, I HAVE ELECTED...
HA HA HA HA HA HA
GERA (CHUCKLE)
GERA
...TO PUT HER TO THE TEST...
HA HA HA HA HA HA HA HA HA HA HA HA HA
HYA HYA HYA!
WAHHHHH!
......!!
GAKU GAKU (SHIVER)
GAKU

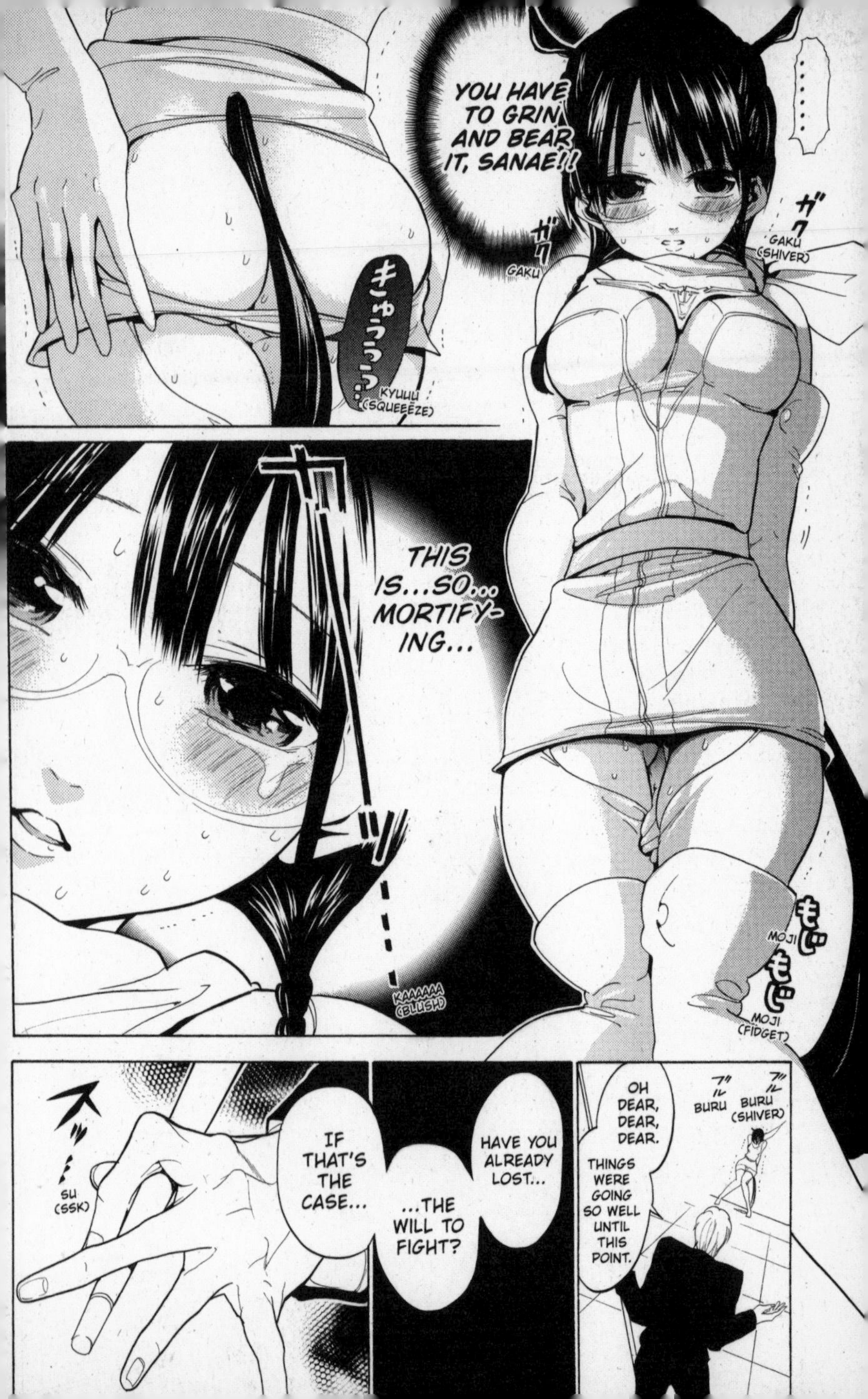
……
YOU HAVE TO GRIN AND BEAR IT, SANAE!!
ガク
GAKU (SHIVER)
ガク
GAKU
もじ
MOJI
もじ
MOJI (FIDGET)
きゅううう…
KYUUU (SQUEEEZE)
THIS IS…SO… MORTIFYING…
KAAAAA (BLUSH)
ブル
BURU (SHIVER)
ブル
BURU
OH DEAR, DEAR, DEAR.
THINGS WERE GOING SO WELL UNTIL THIS POINT.
HAVE YOU ALREADY LOST…
…THE WILL TO FIGHT?
IF THAT'S THE CASE…
スッ
SU (SSK)

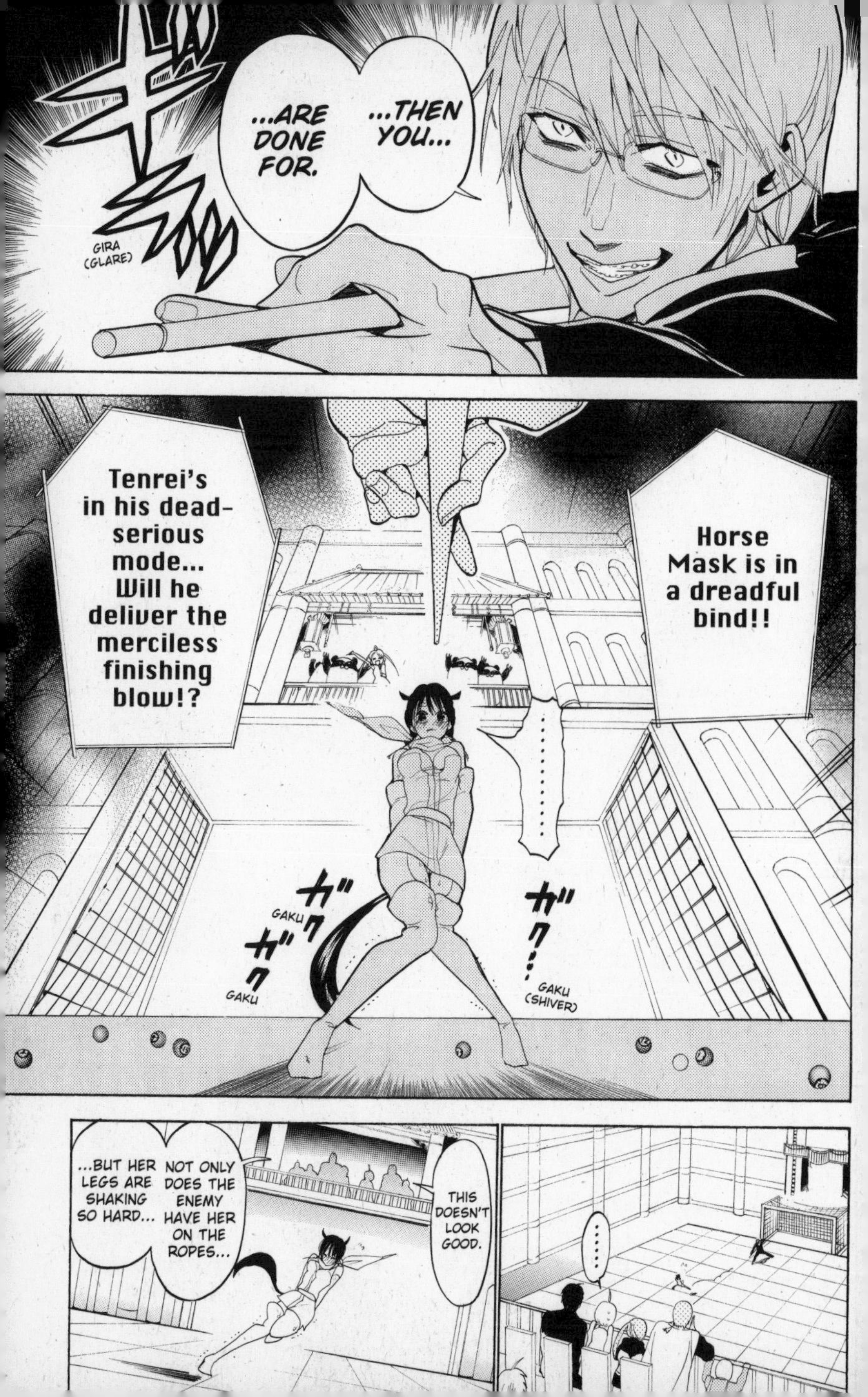
...THEN YOU...
...ARE DONE FOR.
GIRA (GLARE)
Horse Mask is in a dreadful bind!!
Tenrei's in his dead-serious mode... Will he deliver the merciless finishing blow!?
......
GAKU (SHIVER)
GAKU
GAKU
......
THIS DOESN'T LOOK GOOD.
NOT ONLY DOES THE ENEMY HAVE HER ON THE ROPES...
...BUT HER LEGS ARE SHAKING SO HARD...

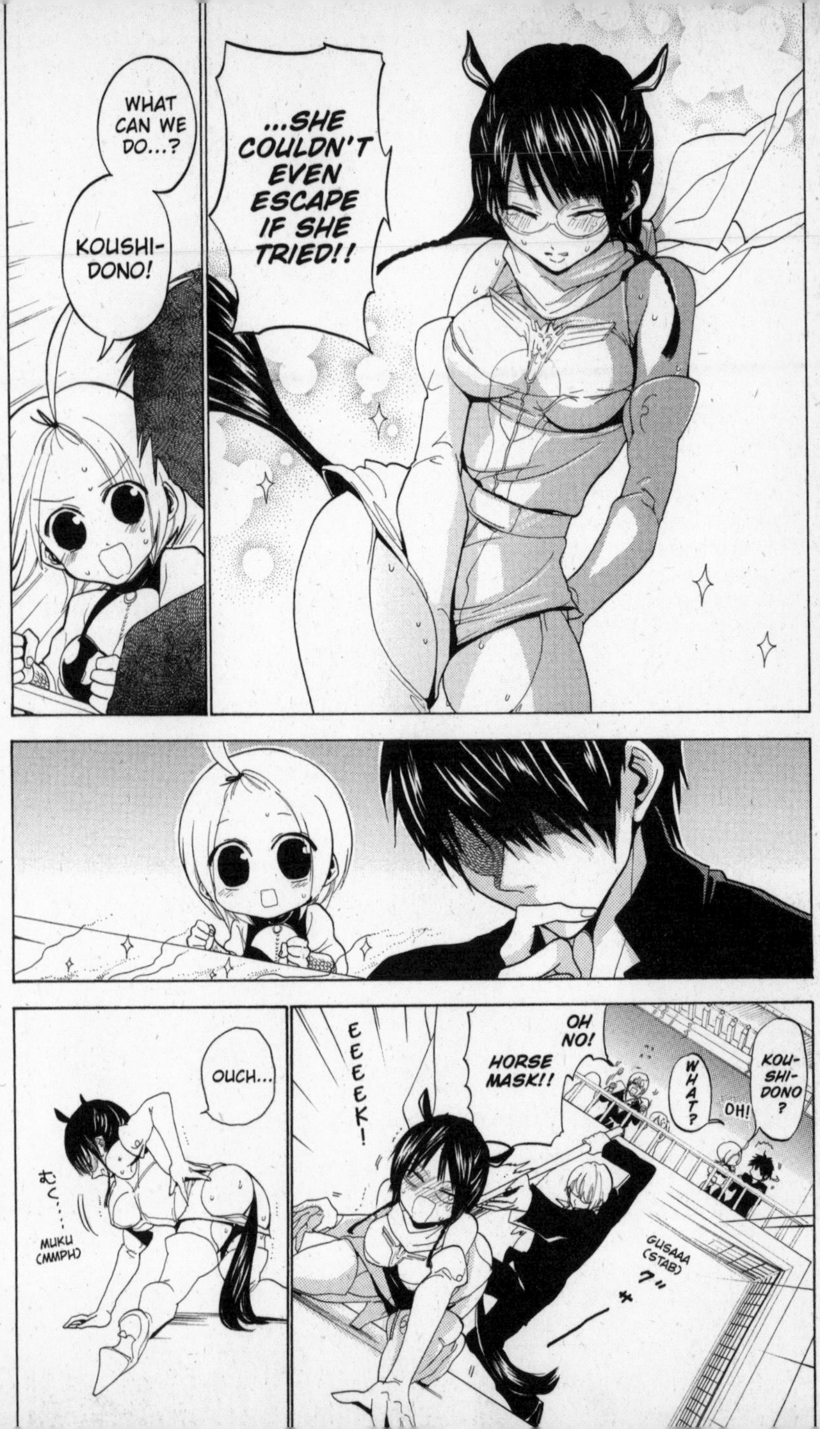
...SHE COULDN'T EVEN ESCAPE IF SHE TRIED!!
WHAT CAN WE DO...?
KOUSHI-DONO!
KOU-SHI-DONO?
OH!
WHAT?
OH NO!
HORSE MASK!!
EEEEEK!
GUSAAA (STAB)
OUCH...
むく…
MUKU (MMPH)

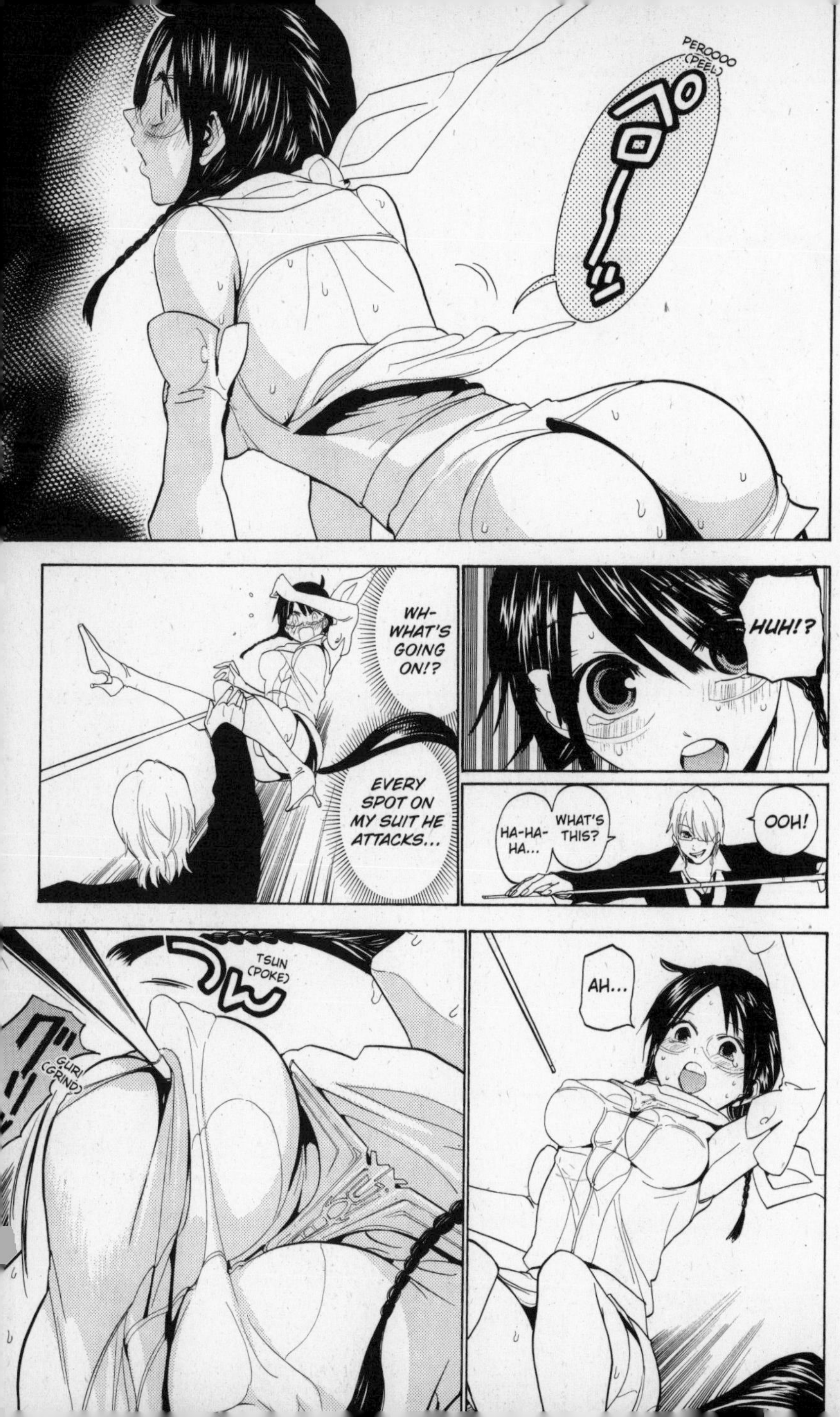
PEROOOO (PEEL)
HUH!?
OOH!
WHAT'S THIS?
HA-HA-HA...
WH-WHAT'S GOING ON!?
EVERY SPOT ON MY SUIT HE ATTACKS...
AH...
TSUN (POKE)
GURI (GRIND)

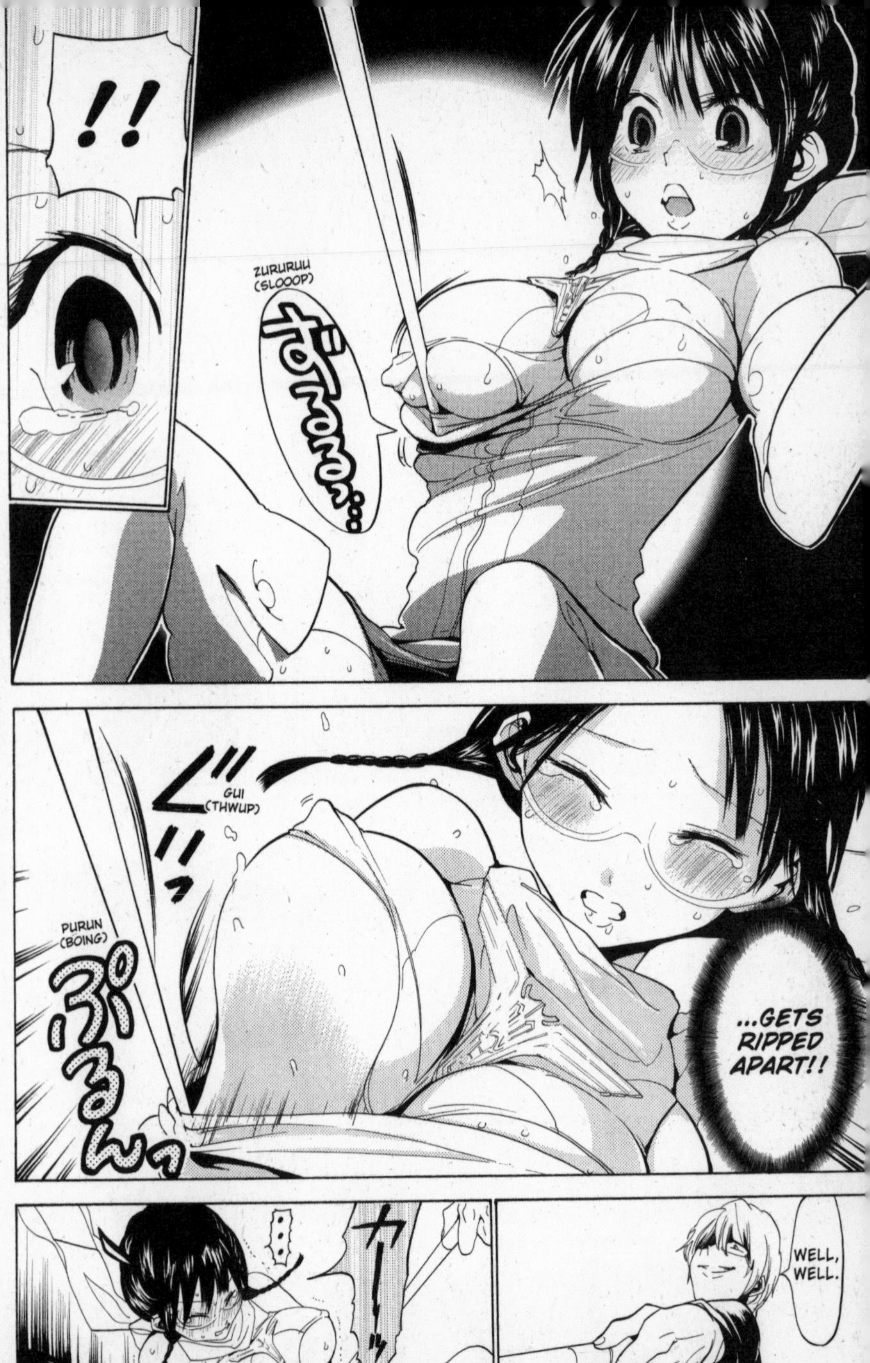
ZURURUU
(SLOOOP)
!!
...GETS RIPPED APART!!
GUI
(THWUP)
ぐいっ
PURUN
(BOING)
ぷるんっ
WELL, WELL.
...
KAAAA
(FLUSH)

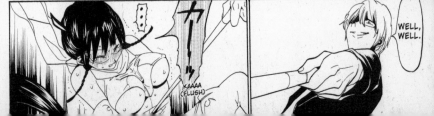

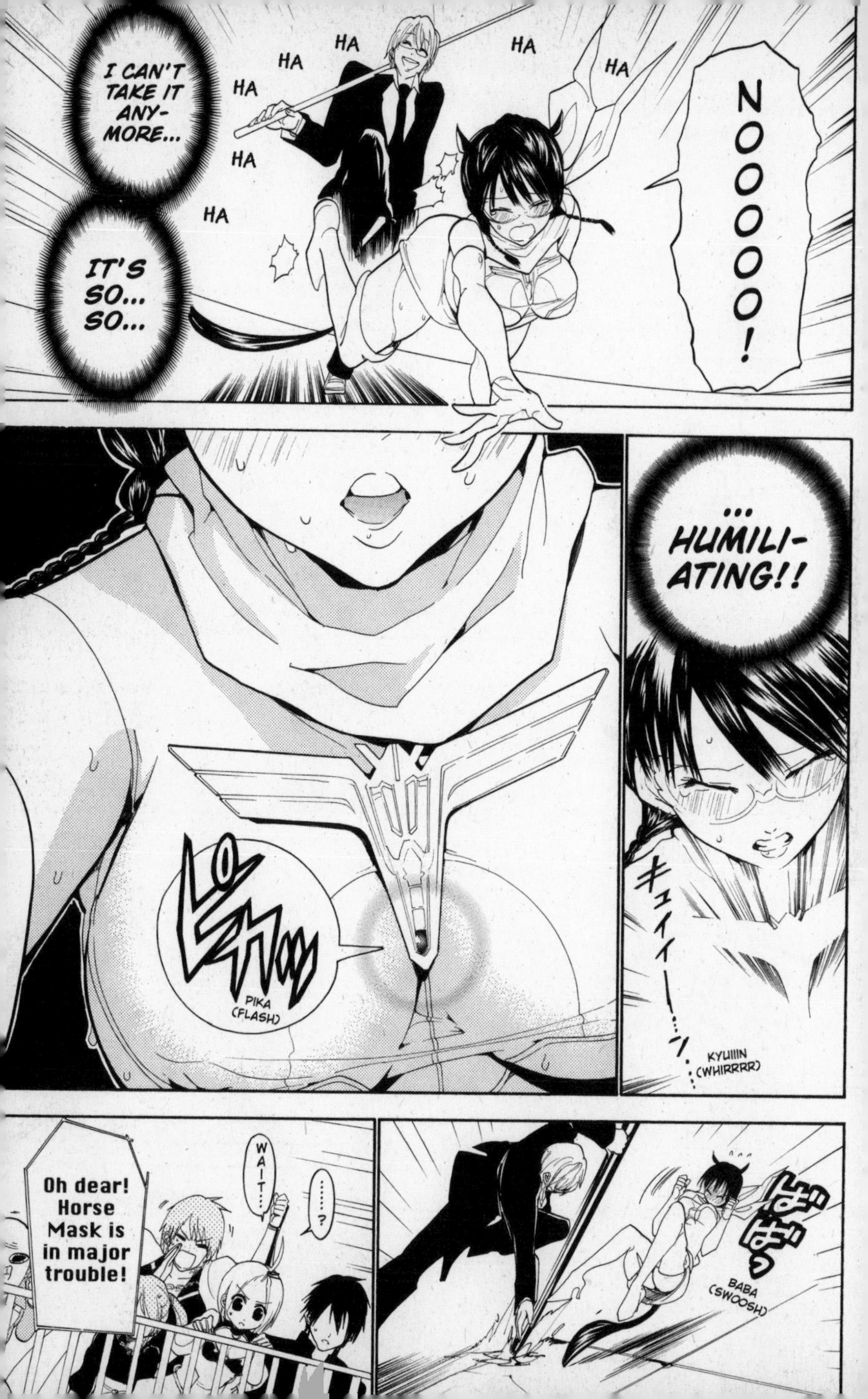
NOOOOOO!
HA
HA
HA
HA
HA
HA
HA
I CAN'T TAKE IT ANYMORE...
IT'S SO... SO...
... HUMILIATING!!
キュイイー…ン
KYUIIIN (WHIRRRR)
ピカッ
PIKA (FLASH)
ばばっ
BABA (SWOOSH)
WAIT...
......?
Oh dear! Horse Mask is in major trouble!

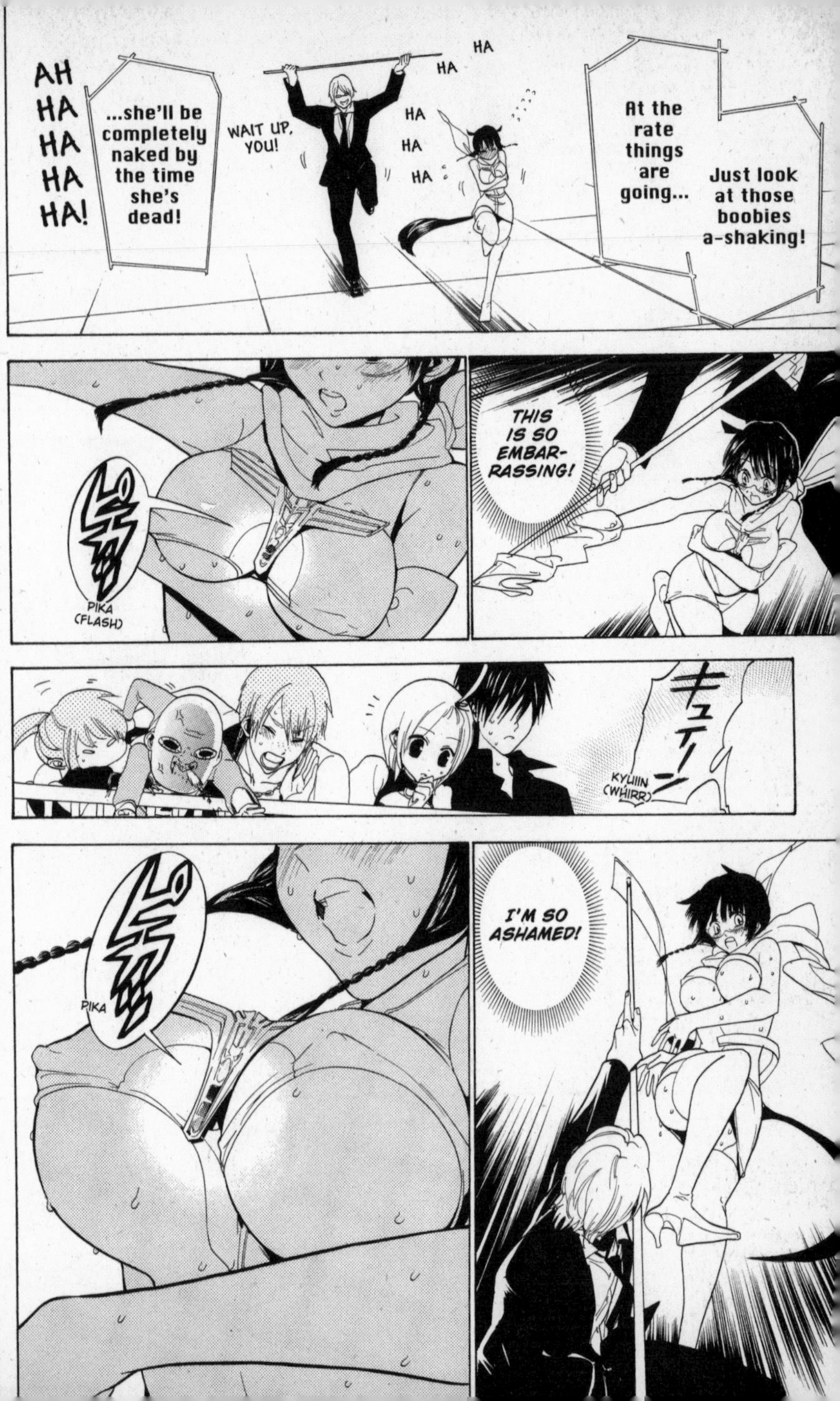

At the rate things are going...
Just look at those boobies a-shaking!
HA
HA
HA
HA
HA
WAIT UP, YOU!
...she'll be completely naked by the time she's dead!
AH HA HA HA HA!
THIS IS SO EMBARRASSING!
PIKA (FLASH)
KYUIIN (WHIRR)
I'M SO ASHAMED!
PIKA

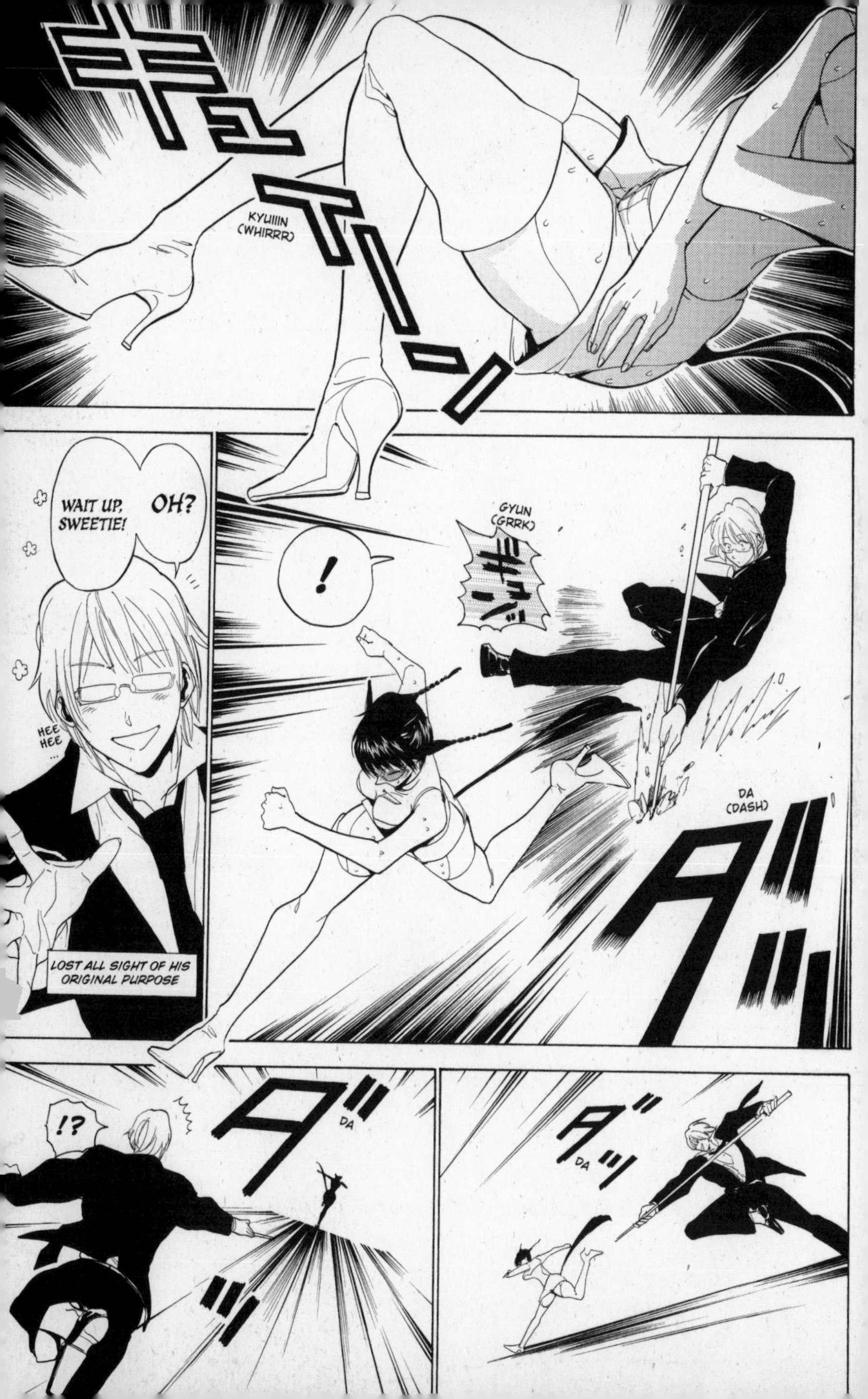
KYUIIIN
(WHIRRR)
GYUN
(GRRK)
!
DA
(DASH)
OH?
WAIT UP, SWEETIE!
HEE HEE ...
LOST ALL SIGHT OF HIS ORIGINAL PURPOSE
DA
!?
DA

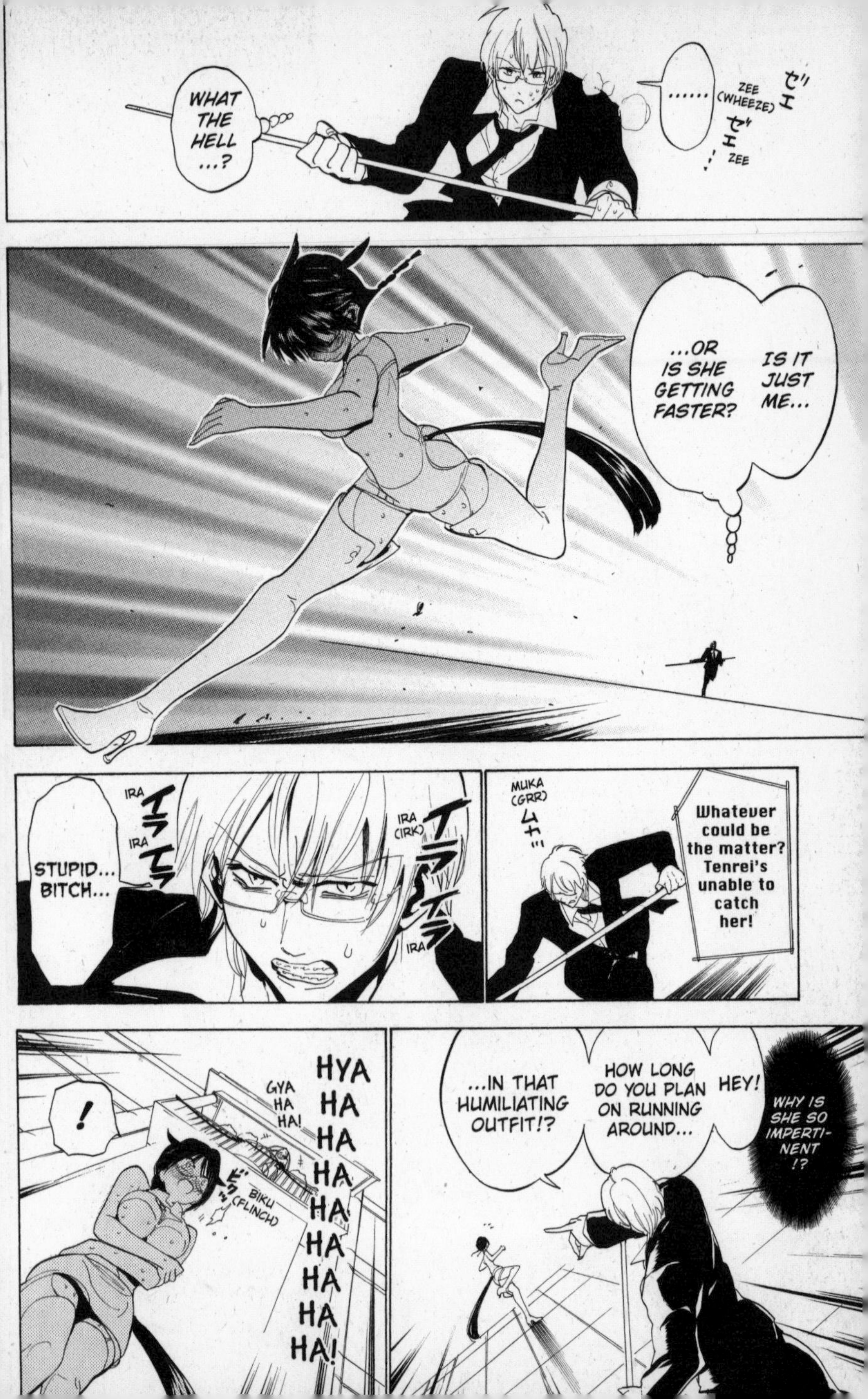
......
ZEE (WHEEZE)
ZEE
WHAT THE HELL ...?
IS IT JUST ME...
...OR IS SHE GETTING FASTER?
MUKA (GRR)
Whatever could be the matter? Tenrei's unable to catch her!
IRA (IRK)
IRA
IRA
IRA
STUPID... BITCH...
WHY IS SHE SO IMPERTI-NENT !?
HEY!
HOW LONG DO YOU PLAN ON RUNNING AROUND...
...IN THAT HUMILIATING OUTFIT!?
HYA HA HA HA HA HA HA HA HA HA!
GYA HA HA!
BIKU (FLINCH)
!

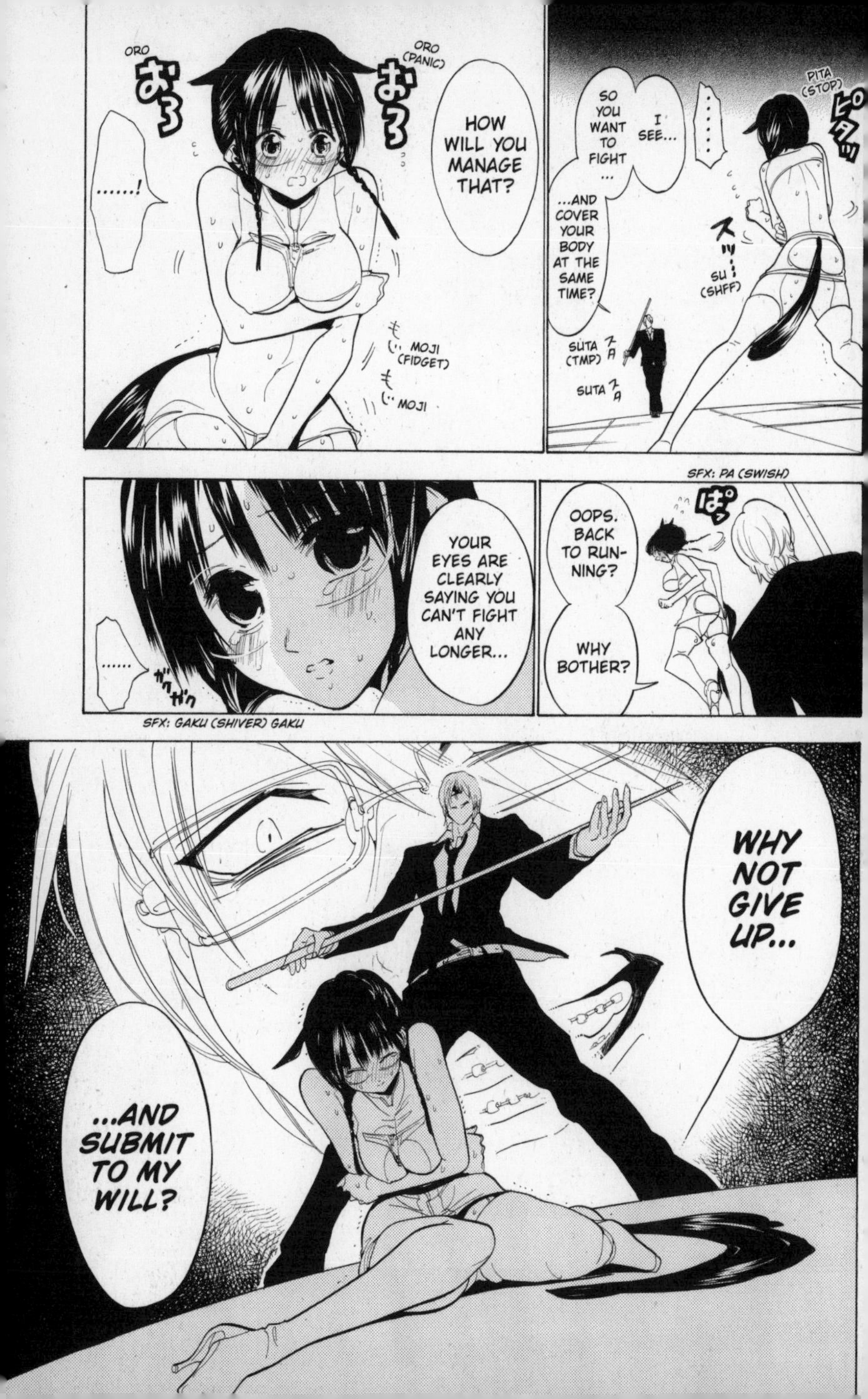
PITA (STOP) ピタッ
......
I SEE...
SO YOU WANT TO FIGHT...
...AND COVER YOUR BODY AT THE SAME TIME?
スッ SU (SHFF)
SUTA (TMP) スタ
SUTA スタ
ORO (PANIC) おろ
HOW WILL YOU MANAGE THAT?
ORO おろ
......!
もじ MOJI (FIDGET)
もじ MOJI
SFX: PA (SWISH) ぱっ
OOPS. BACK TO RUN-NING?
WHY BOTHER?
YOUR EYES ARE CLEARLY SAYING YOU CAN'T FIGHT ANY LONGER...
......
ガクガク
SFX: GAKU (SHIVER) GAKU
WHY NOT GIVE UP...
...AND SUBMIT TO MY WILL?

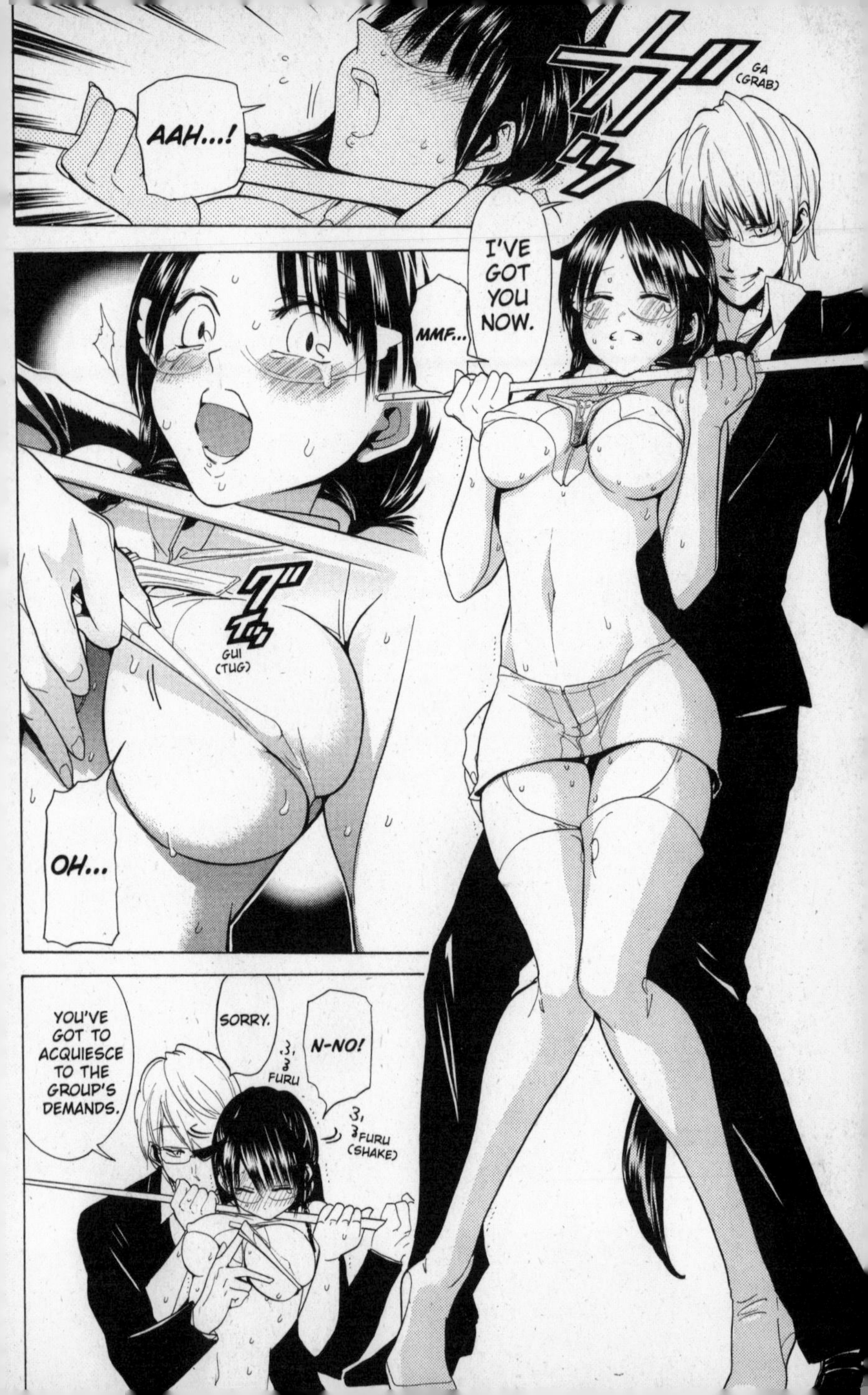
GA (GRAB)
AAH...!
I'VE GOT YOU NOW.
MMF...
GUI (TUG)
OH...
N-NO!
FURU FURU (SHAKE)
SORRY.
FURU
YOU'VE GOT TO ACQUIESCE TO THE GROUP'S DEMANDS.

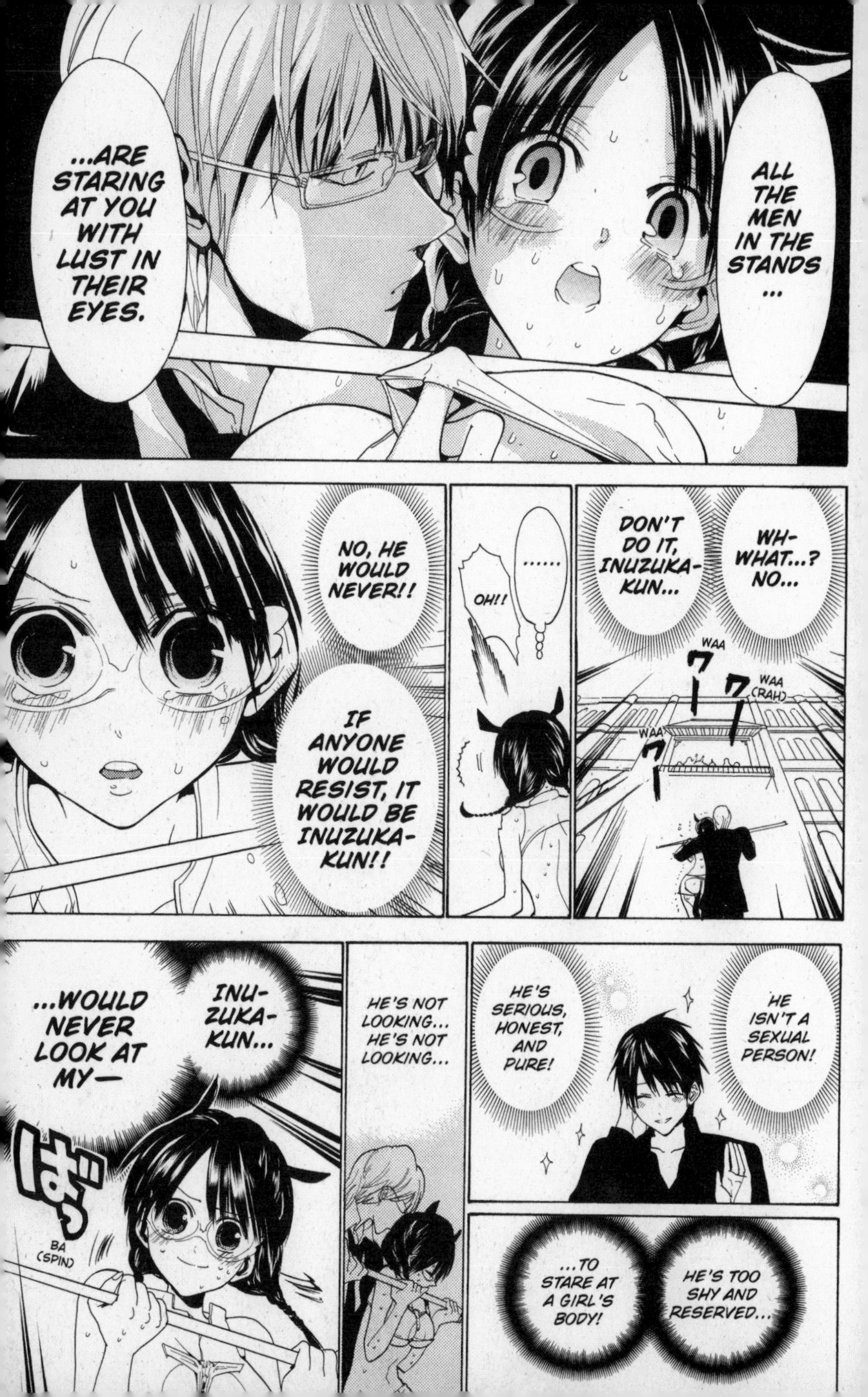
ALL THE MEN IN THE STANDS ...
...ARE STARING AT YOU WITH LUST IN THEIR EYES.
WH-WHAT...? NO...
DON'T DO IT, INUZUKA-KUN...
WAA
WAA (RAH)
WAA
OH!!
......
NO, HE WOULD NEVER!!
IF ANYONE WOULD RESIST, IT WOULD BE INUZUKA-KUN!!
HE ISN'T A SEXUAL PERSON!
HE'S SERIOUS, HONEST, AND PURE!
HE'S TOO SHY AND RESERVED...
...TO STARE AT A GIRL'S BODY!
HE'S NOT LOOKING... HE'S NOT LOOKING...
INUZUKA-KUN...
...WOULD NEVER LOOK AT MY—
BA (SPIN)

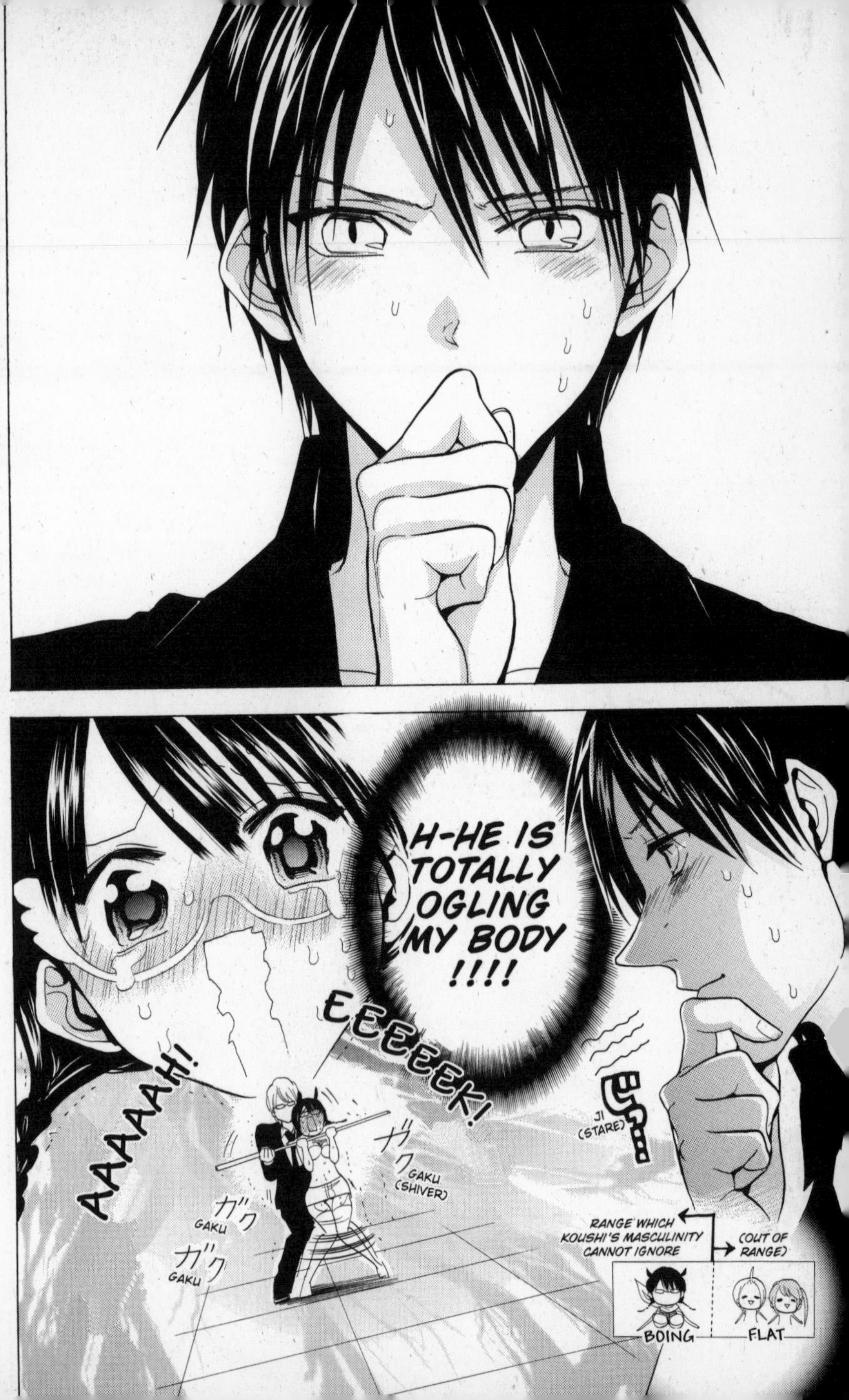
H-HE IS TOTALLY OGLING MY BODY !!!!
EEEEEEK!
AAAAAH!
JI (STARE)
RANGE WHICH KOUSHI'S MASCULINITY CANNOT IGNORE
(OUT OF RANGE)
BOING
FLAT
ガク
GAKU (SHIVER)
ガク
GAKU
ガク
GAKU

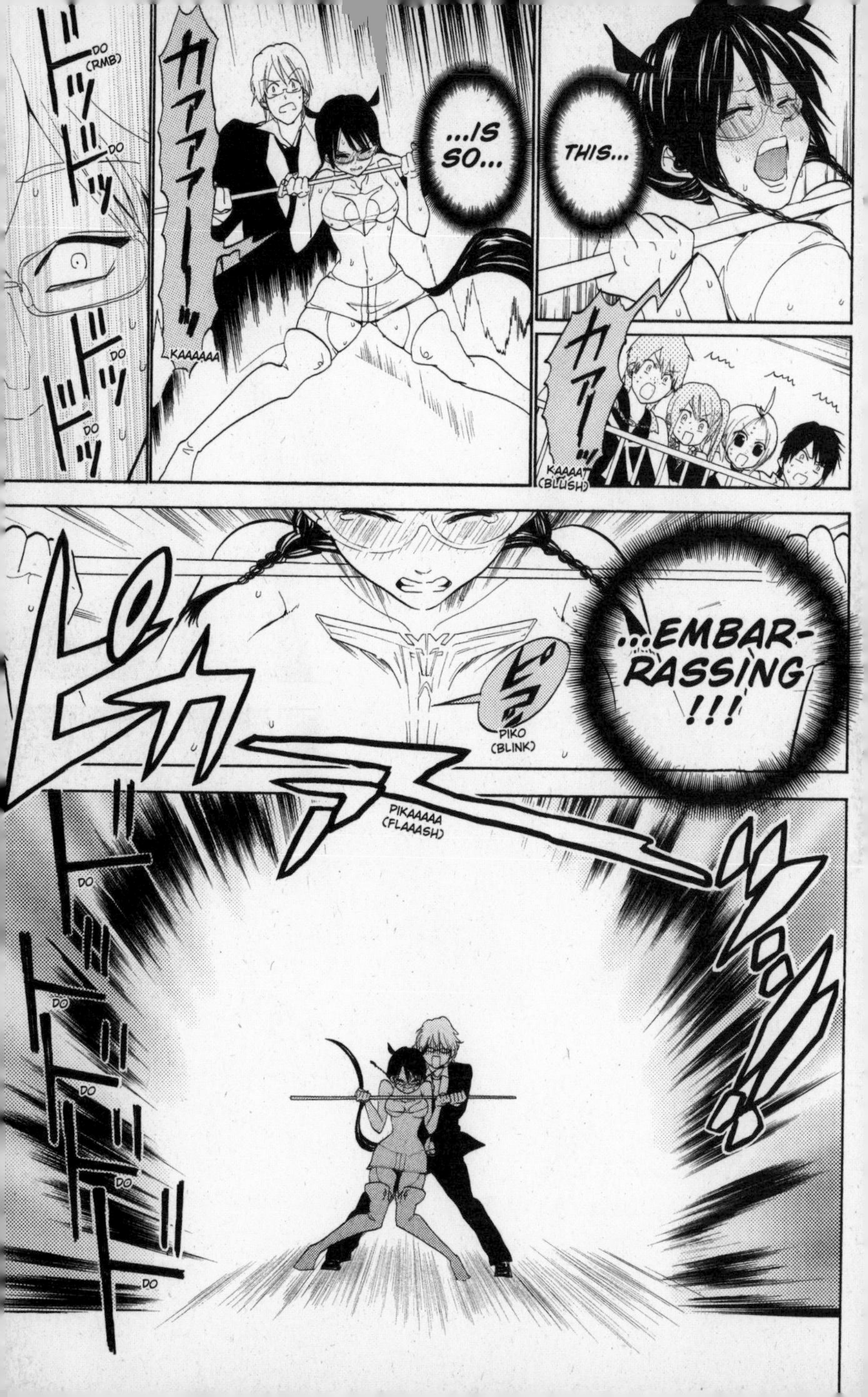
THIS...
KAAAAT (BLUSH)
...IS SO...
KAAAAAA
DO (RMB)
DO
DO
DO
...EMBAR-RASSING!!!
PIKO (BLINK)
PIKAAAAA (FLAAASH)
DO
DO
DO
DO
DO

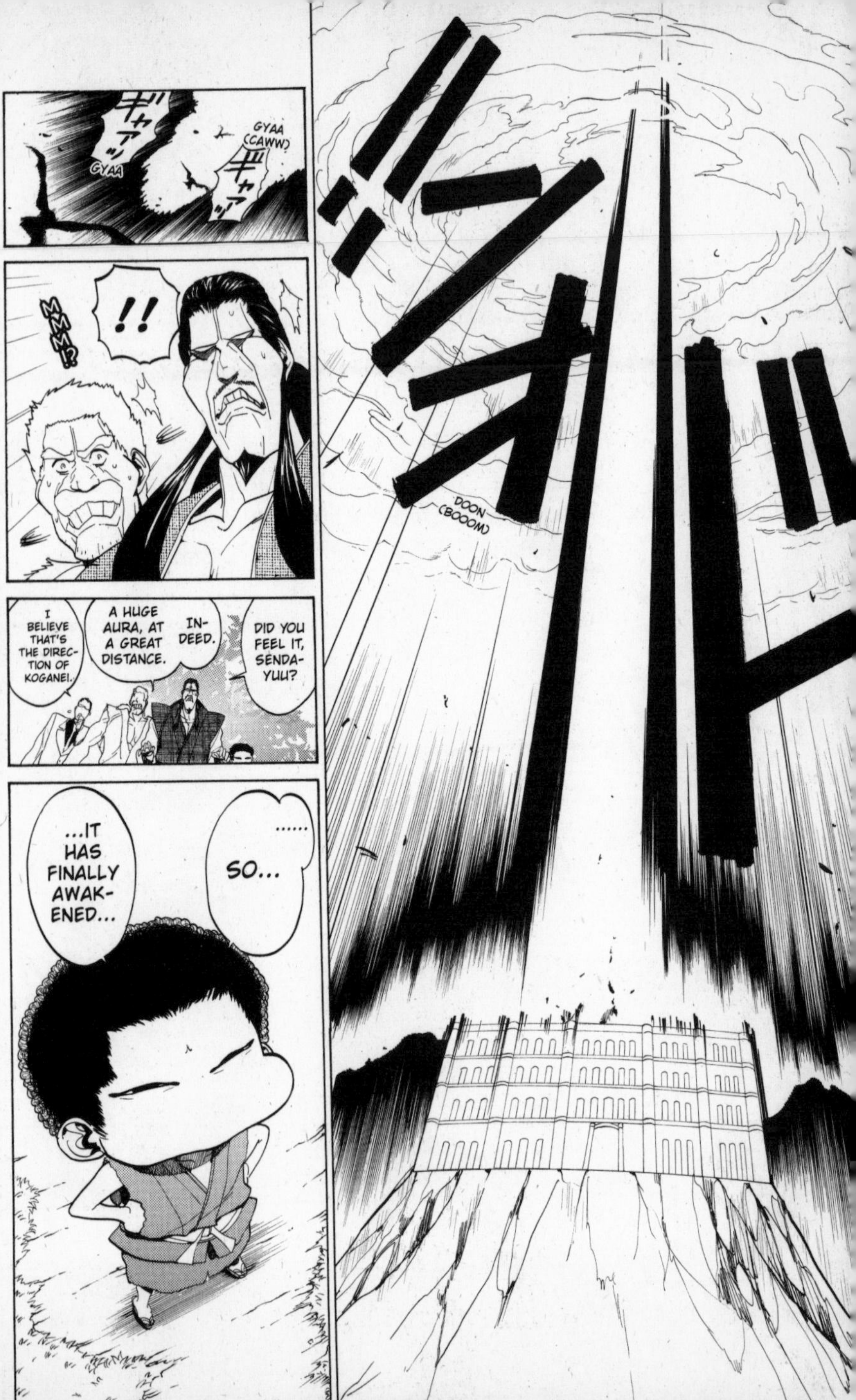
DOON (BOOOM)
GYAA (CAWW)
GYAA
!!
MMM!?
DID YOU FEEL IT, SENDA-YUU?
IN-DEED.
A HUGE AURA, AT A GREAT DISTANCE.
I BELIEVE THAT'S THE DIREC-TION OF KOGANEI.
......
SO...
...IT HAS FINALLY AWAK-ENED...

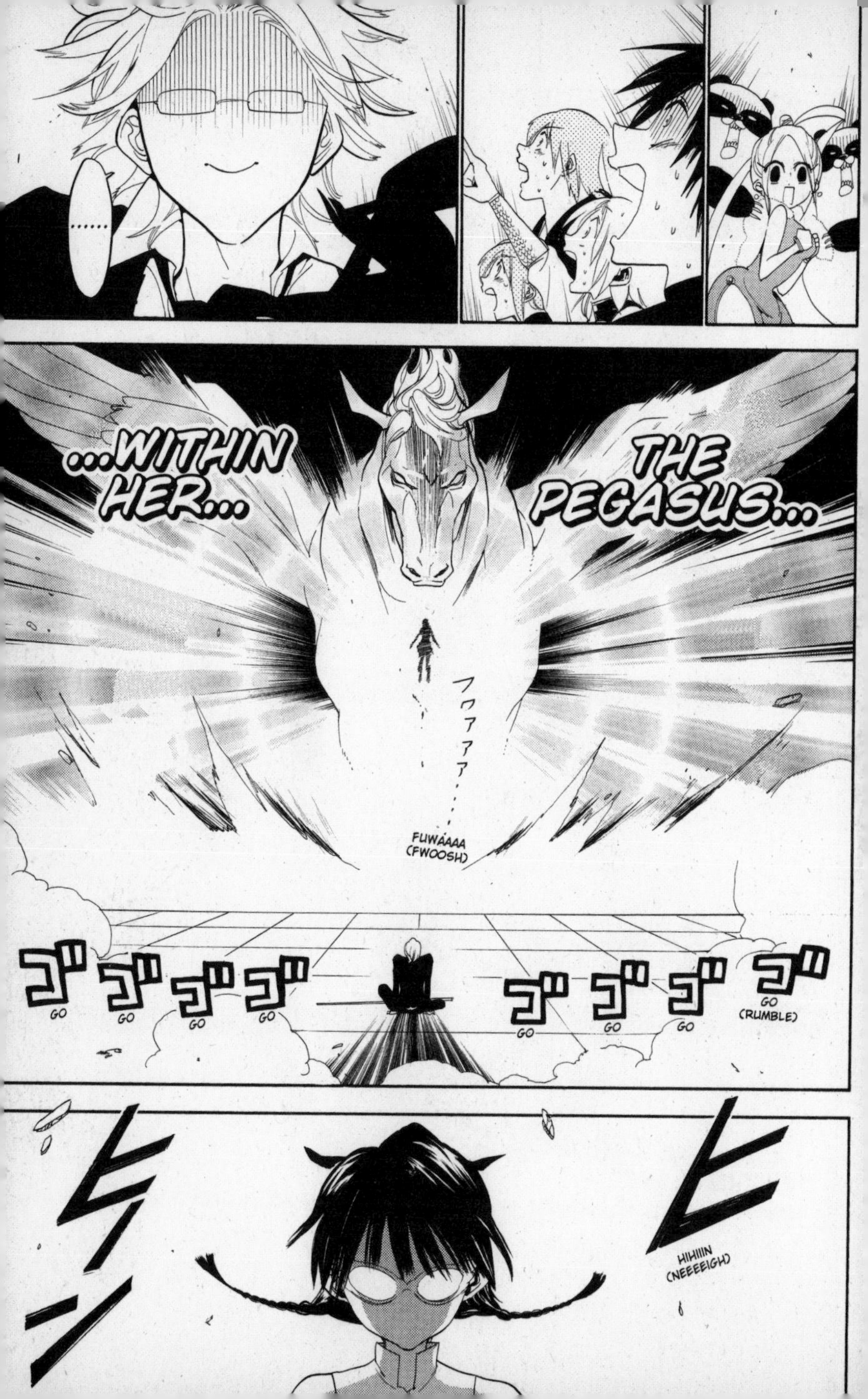
......
THE PEGASUS...
...WITHIN HER...
フワァァァ...
FUWAAAA (FWOOSH)
ゴ ゴ ゴ ゴ
GO GO GO GO
ゴ ゴ ゴ ゴ
GO GO GO GO (RUMBLE)
ヒ
HIHIIIN (NEEEEIGH)
ヒン

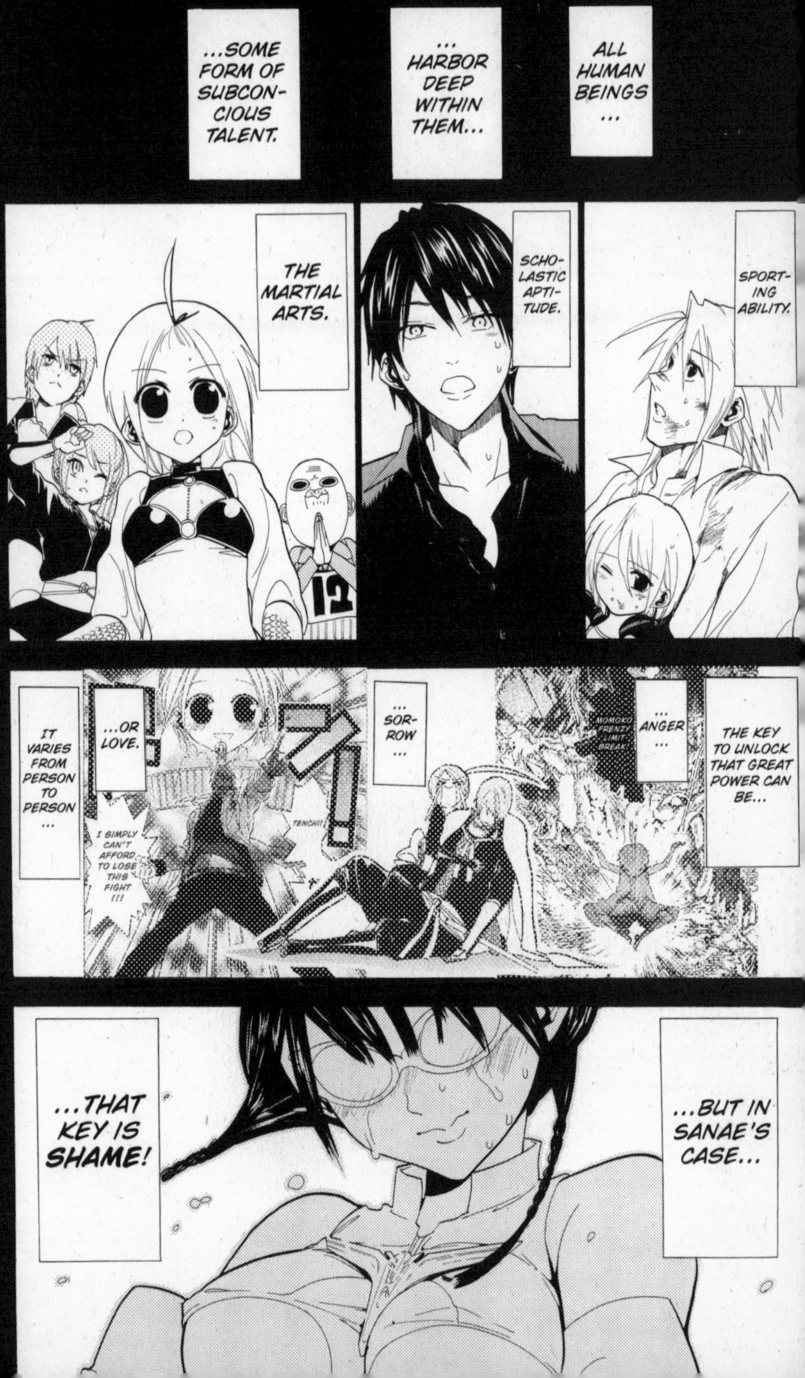
ALL HUMAN BEINGS...
...HARBOR DEEP WITHIN THEM...
...SOME FORM OF SUBCONCIOUS TALENT.
SPORTING ABILITY.
SCHOLASTIC APTITUDE.
THE MARTIAL ARTS.
THE KEY TO UNLOCK THAT GREAT POWER CAN BE...
...ANGER...
MOMOKO FRENZY LIMIT-BREAK!
...SORROW...
TENCHI!!
...OR LOVE.
I SIMPLY CAN'T AFFORD TO LOSE THIS FIGHT!!!
IT VARIES FROM PERSON TO PERSON...
...BUT IN SANAE'S CASE...
...THAT KEY IS SHAME!

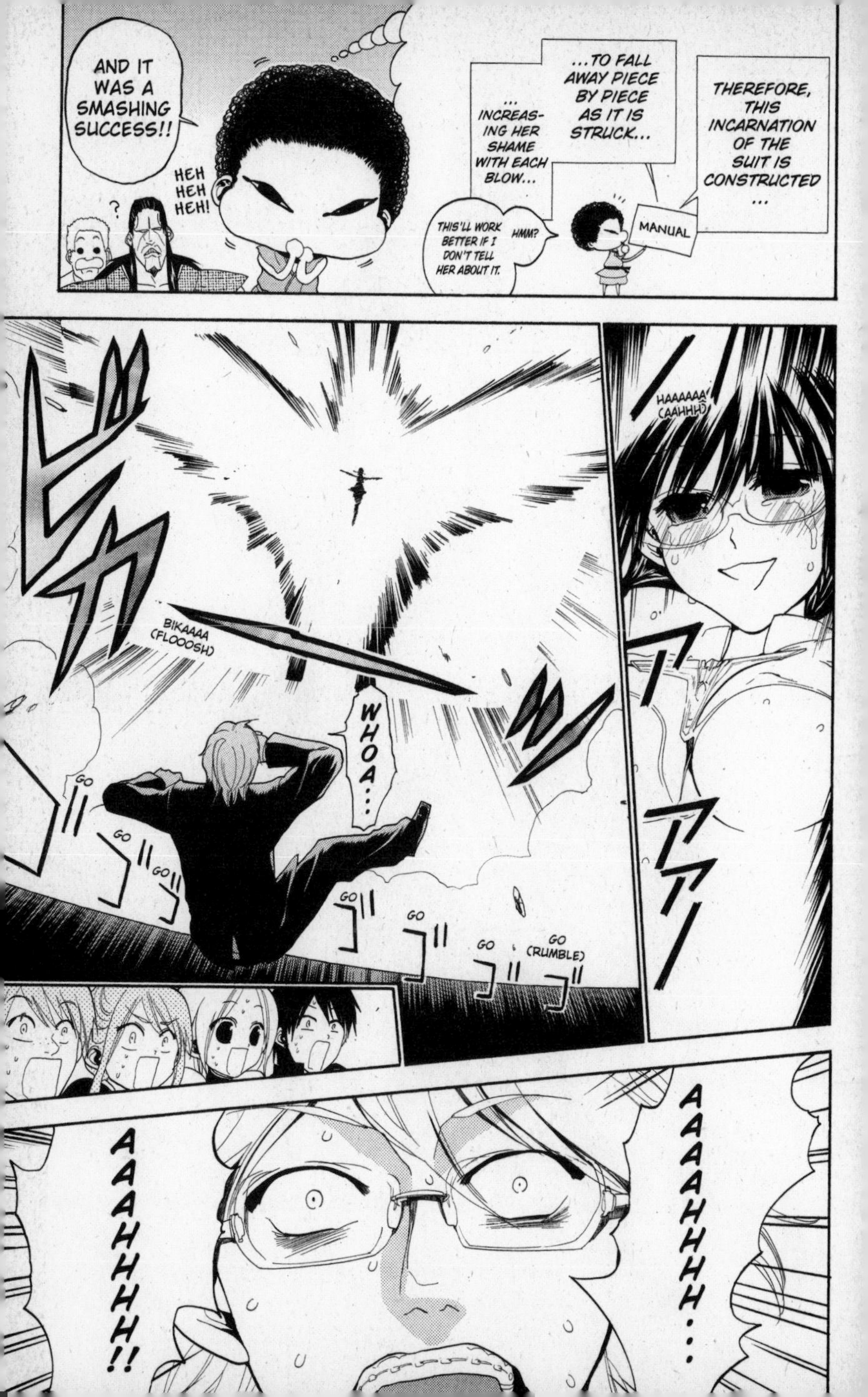
THEREFORE, THIS INCARNATION OF THE SUIT IS CONSTRUCTED...
...TO FALL AWAY PIECE BY PIECE AS IT IS STRUCK...
...INCREASING HER SHAME WITH EACH BLOW...
MANUAL
HMM?
THIS'LL WORK BETTER IF I DON'T TELL HER ABOUT IT.
HEH HEH HEH!
?
AND IT WAS A SMASHING SUCCESS!!
HAAAAAA (AAHHH)
BIKAAAA (FLOOOSH)
WHOA...
GO
GO
GO
GO
GO
GO
GO (RUMBLE)
AAAAHHHH...
AAAAHHHHH!!

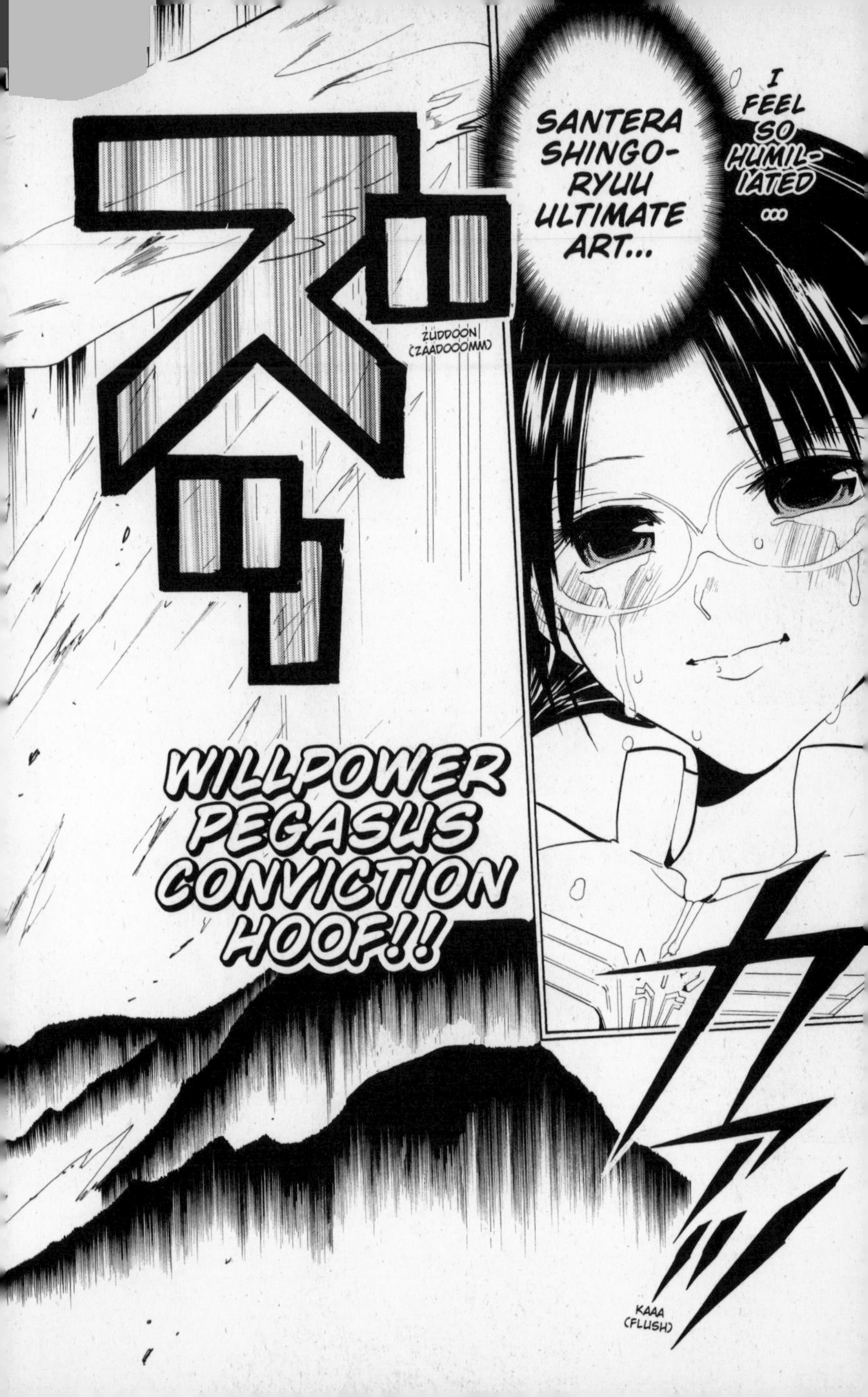
I FEEL SO HUMILIATED...
SANTERA SHINGO-RYUU ULTIMATE ART...
KAAA (FLUSH)
ZUDDOON (ZAADOOOMM)
WILLPOWER PEGASUS CONVICTION HOOF!!

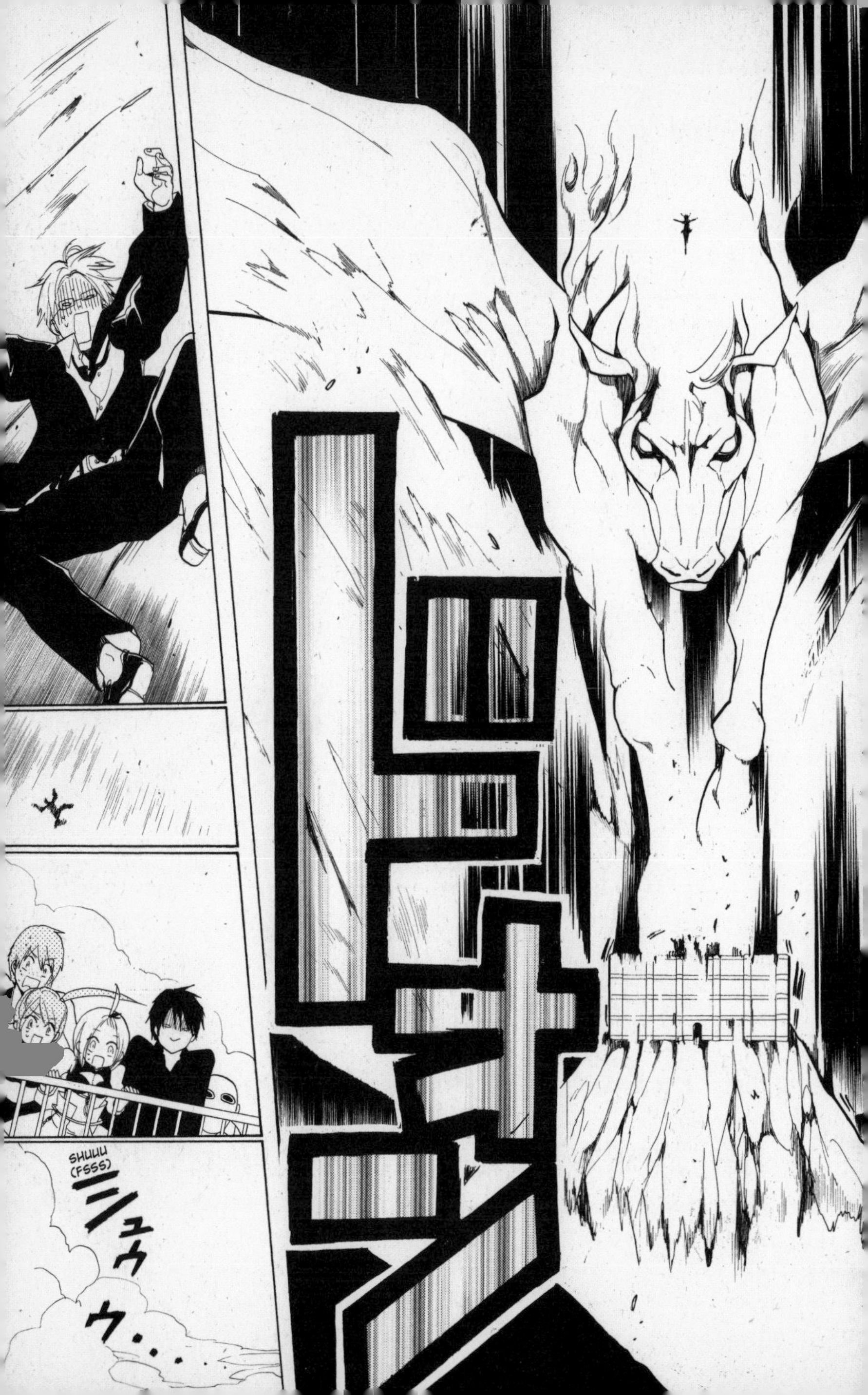
SHUUU
(FSSS)
シュウウ…

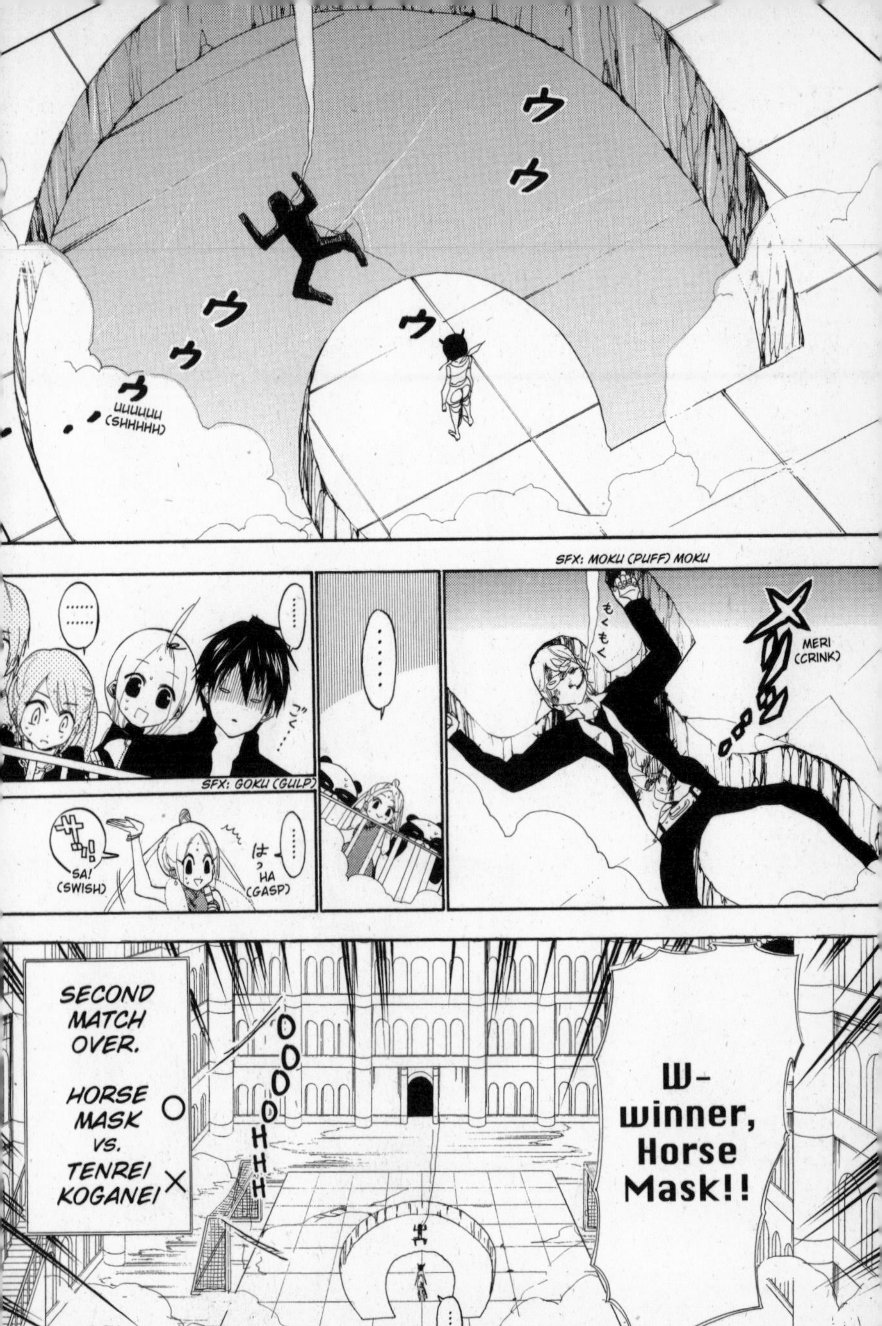
ウ
ウ
ウ
ウ
ウ
ウ
UUUUUUU (SHHHHHH)
もくもく
SFX: MOKU (PUFF) MOKU
MERI (CRINK)
......
ごく...
SFX: GOKU (GULP)
......
......
......
......
はっ
HA (GASP)
SA! (SWISH)
W-winner, Horse Mask!!
OOOOHHH
SECOND MATCH OVER.
HORSE MASK ○ VS. TENREI KOGANEI ×
......

CHAPTER 34: YOUNG GIRL, AWAKEN THE HOLY BEAST – END

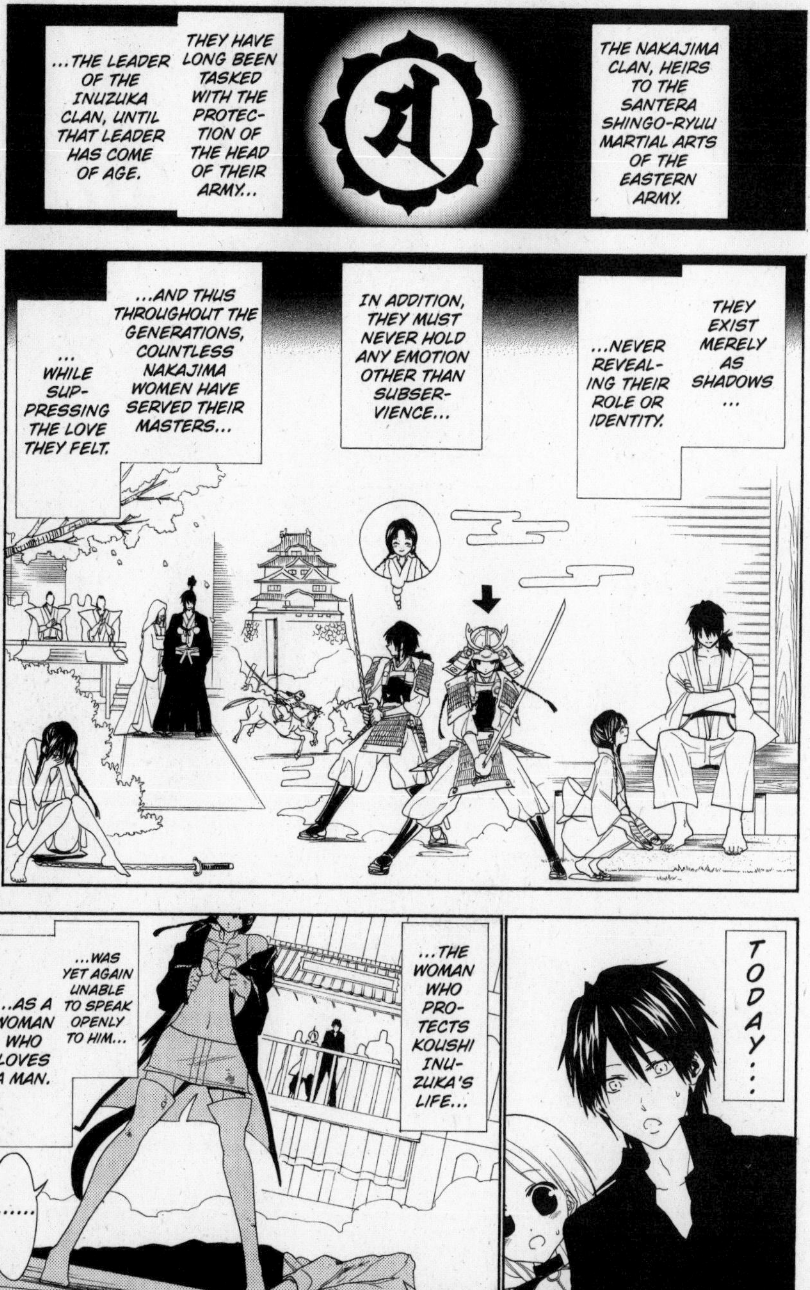
THE NAKAJIMA CLAN, HEIRS TO THE SANTERA SHINGO-RYUU MARTIAL ARTS OF THE EASTERN ARMY.
THEY HAVE LONG BEEN TASKED WITH THE PROTECTION OF THE HEAD OF THEIR ARMY...
...THE LEADER OF THE INUZUKA CLAN, UNTIL THAT LEADER HAS COME OF AGE.
THEY EXIST MERELY AS SHADOWS...
...NEVER REVEALING THEIR ROLE OR IDENTITY.
IN ADDITION, THEY MUST NEVER HOLD ANY EMOTION OTHER THAN SUBSERVIENCE...
...AND THUS THROUGHOUT THE GENERATIONS, COUNTLESS NAKAJIMA WOMEN HAVE SERVED THEIR MASTERS...
...WHILE SUPPRESSING THE LOVE THEY FELT.
TODAY...
...THE WOMAN WHO PROTECTS KOUSHI INUZUKA'S LIFE...
...WAS YET AGAIN UNABLE TO SPEAK OPENLY TO HIM...
...AS A WOMAN WHO LOVES A MAN.
......

35. TWO BLADES OF CONVICTION

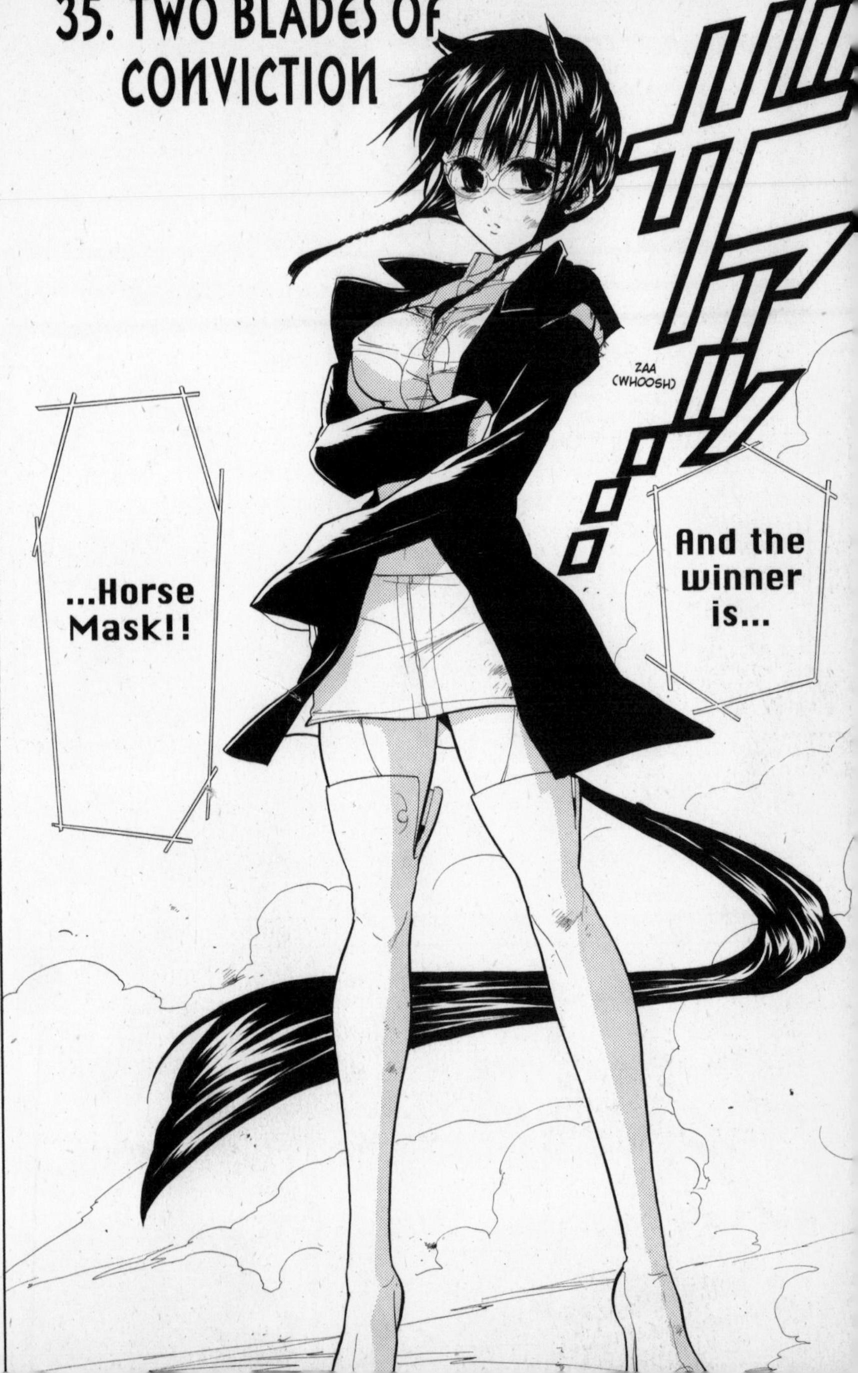
ZAA (WHOOSH)
And the winner is...
...Horse Mask!!

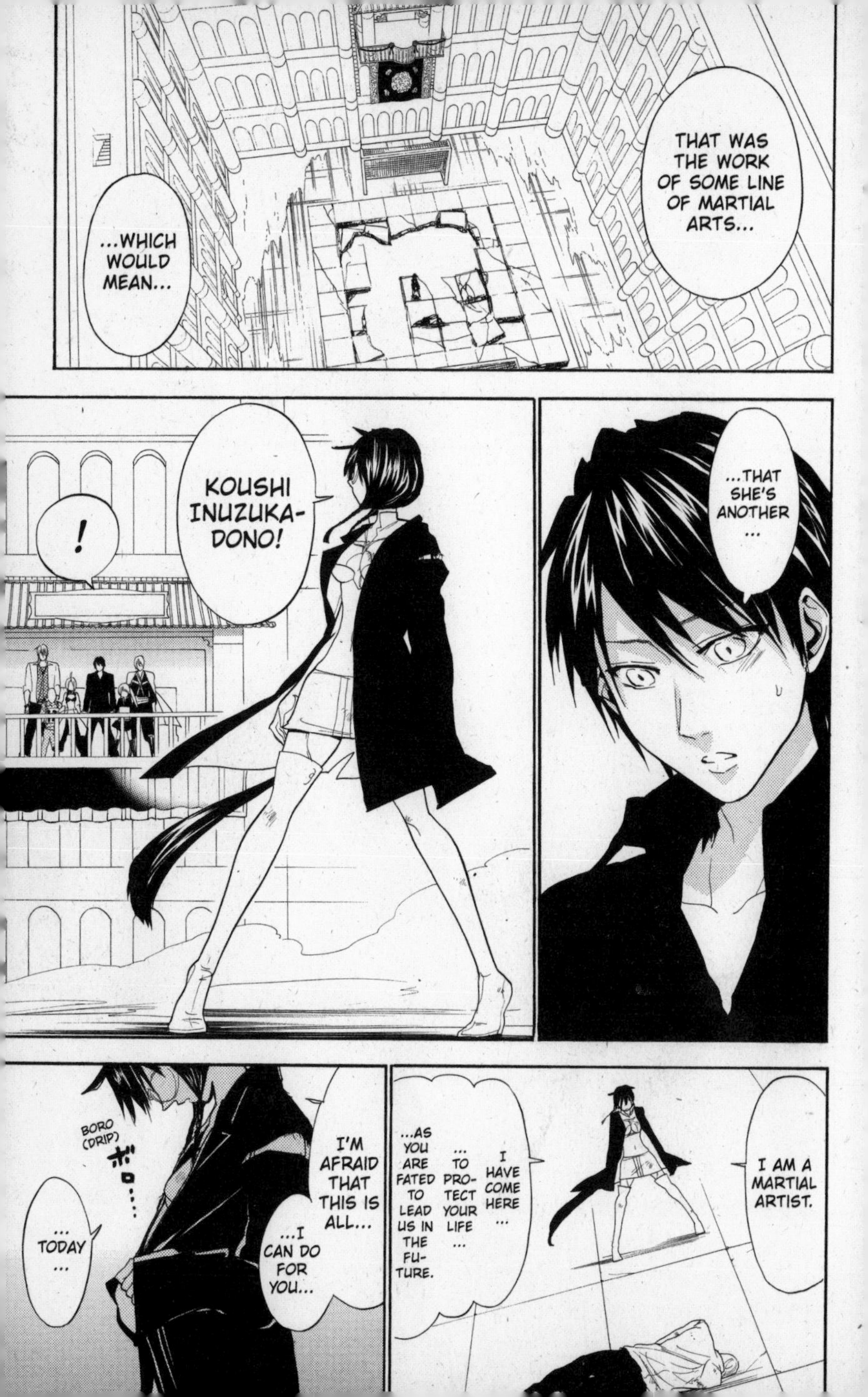
THAT WAS THE WORK OF SOME LINE OF MARTIAL ARTS...
...WHICH WOULD MEAN...
...THAT SHE'S ANOTHER ...
KOUSHI INUZUKA-DONO!
!
I AM A MARTIAL ARTIST.
I HAVE COME HERE ...
... TO PROTECT YOUR LIFE ...
...AS YOU ARE FATED TO LEAD US IN THE FUTURE.
I'M AFRAID THAT THIS IS ALL...
...I CAN DO FOR YOU...
BORO (DRIP)
... TODAY ...

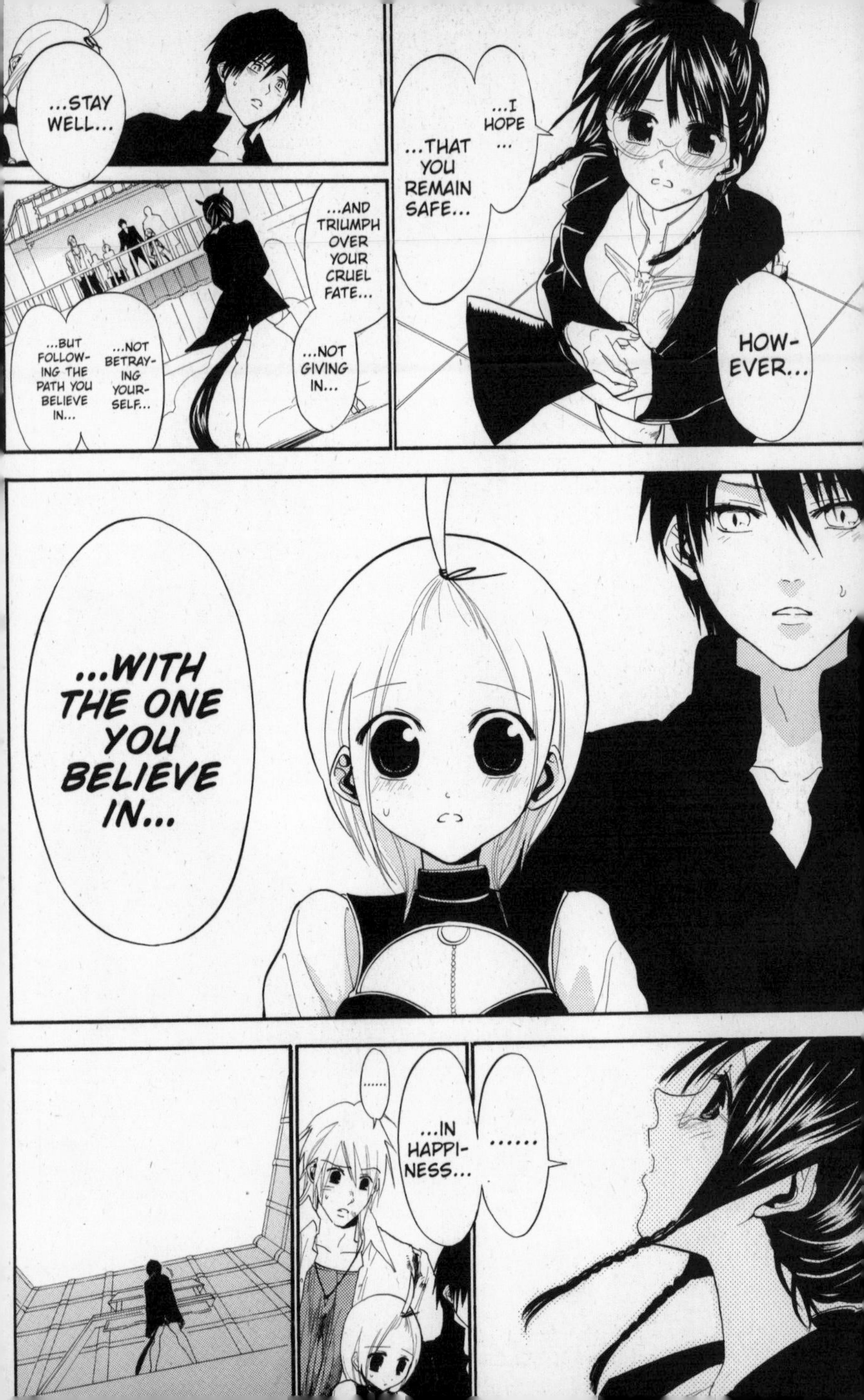

...I HOPE ...
...THAT YOU REMAIN SAFE...
HOW-EVER...
...STAY WELL...
...AND TRIUMPH OVER YOUR CRUEL FATE...
...NOT GIVING IN...
...NOT BETRAY-ING YOUR-SELF...
...BUT FOLLOW-ING THE PATH YOU BELIEVE IN...
...WITH THE ONE YOU BELIEVE IN...
......
...IN HAPPI-NESS...
......

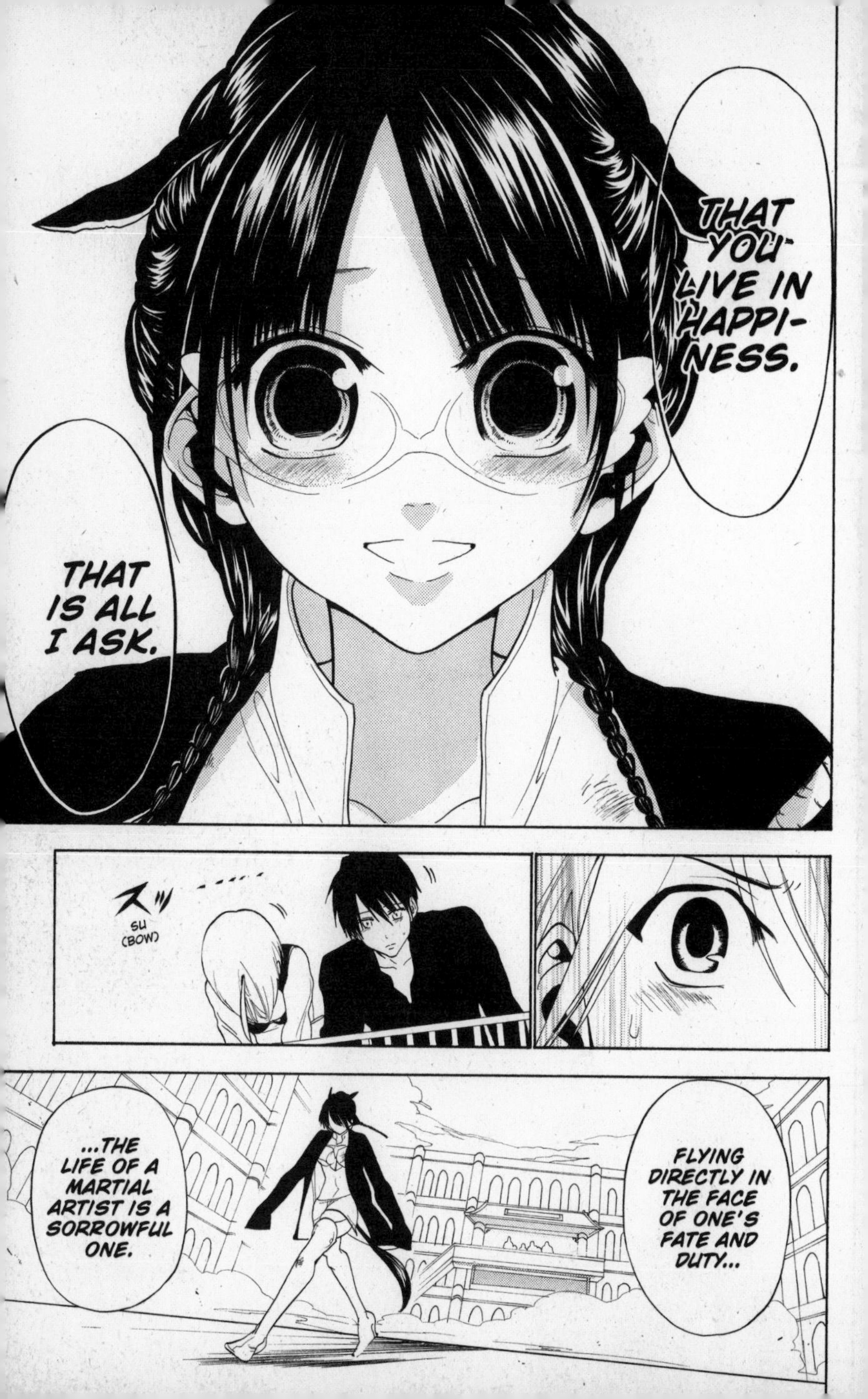
THAT YOU LIVE IN HAPPI-NESS.
THAT IS ALL I ASK.
スッ
SU (BOW)
FLYING DIRECTLY IN THE FACE OF ONE'S FATE AND DUTY...
...THE LIFE OF A MARTIAL ARTIST IS A SORROWFUL ONE.

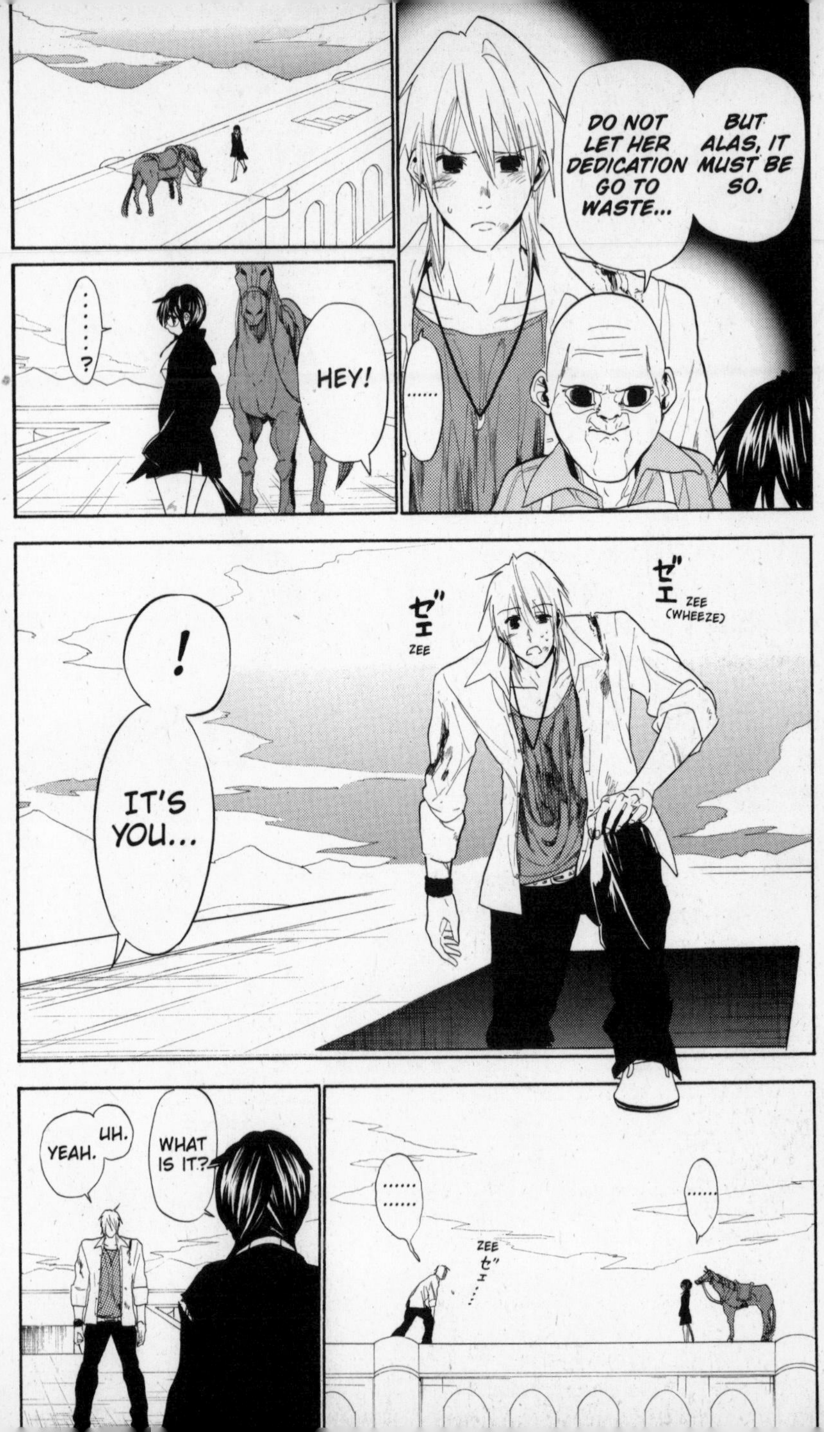
BUT ALAS, IT MUST BE SO.
DO NOT LET HER DEDICATION GO TO WASTE...
......
HEY!
......?
ゼェ
ZEE (WHEEZE)
ゼェ
ZEE
!
IT'S YOU...
......
ZEE
ゼェ...
......
......
WHAT IS IT?
UH. YEAH.

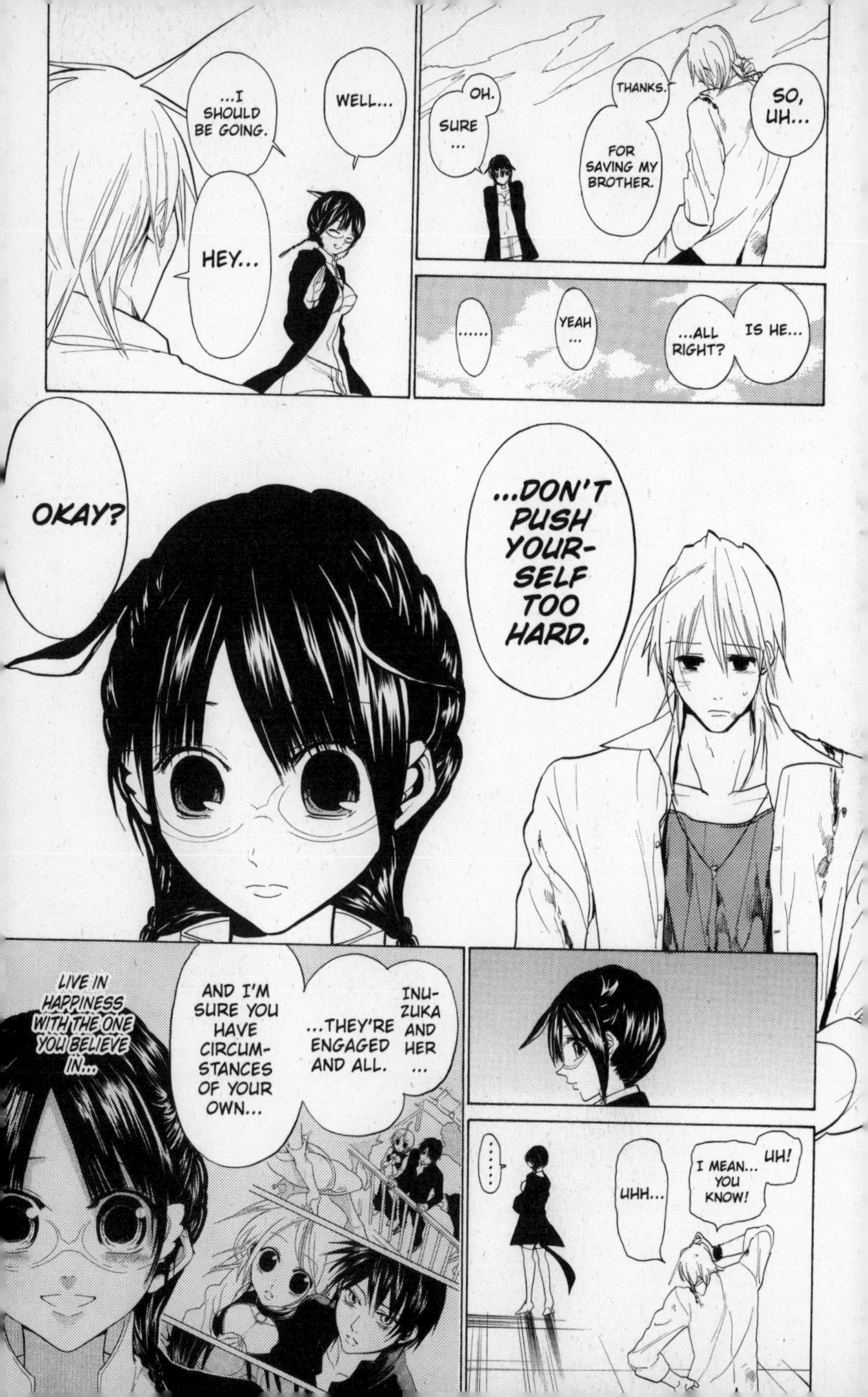
SO, UH...
THANKS.
FOR SAVING MY BROTHER.
OH. SURE...
IS HE...
...ALL RIGHT?
YEAH...
......
WELL...
...I SHOULD BE GOING.
HEY...
...DON'T PUSH YOUR-SELF TOO HARD.
OKAY?
UH! I MEAN... YOU KNOW!
UHH...
......
INU-ZUKA AND HER...
...THEY'RE ENGAGED AND ALL.
AND I'M SURE YOU HAVE CIRCUM-STANCES OF YOUR OWN...
LIVE IN HAPPINESS WITH THE ONE YOU BELIEVE IN...

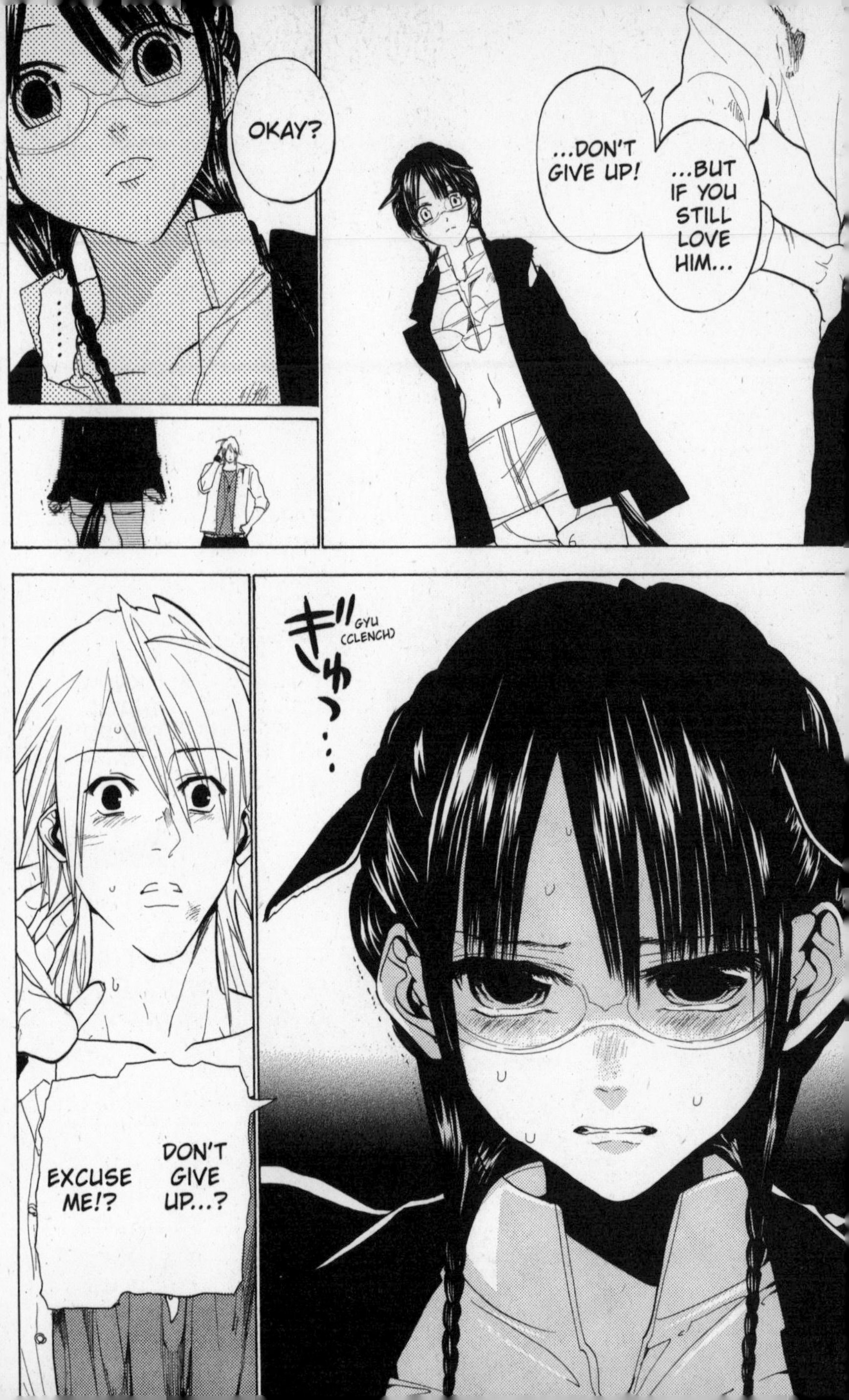
...BUT IF YOU STILL LOVE HIM...
...DON'T GIVE UP!
OKAY?
......
ぎゅっ…
GYU (CLENCH)
DON'T GIVE UP...?
EXCUSE ME!?

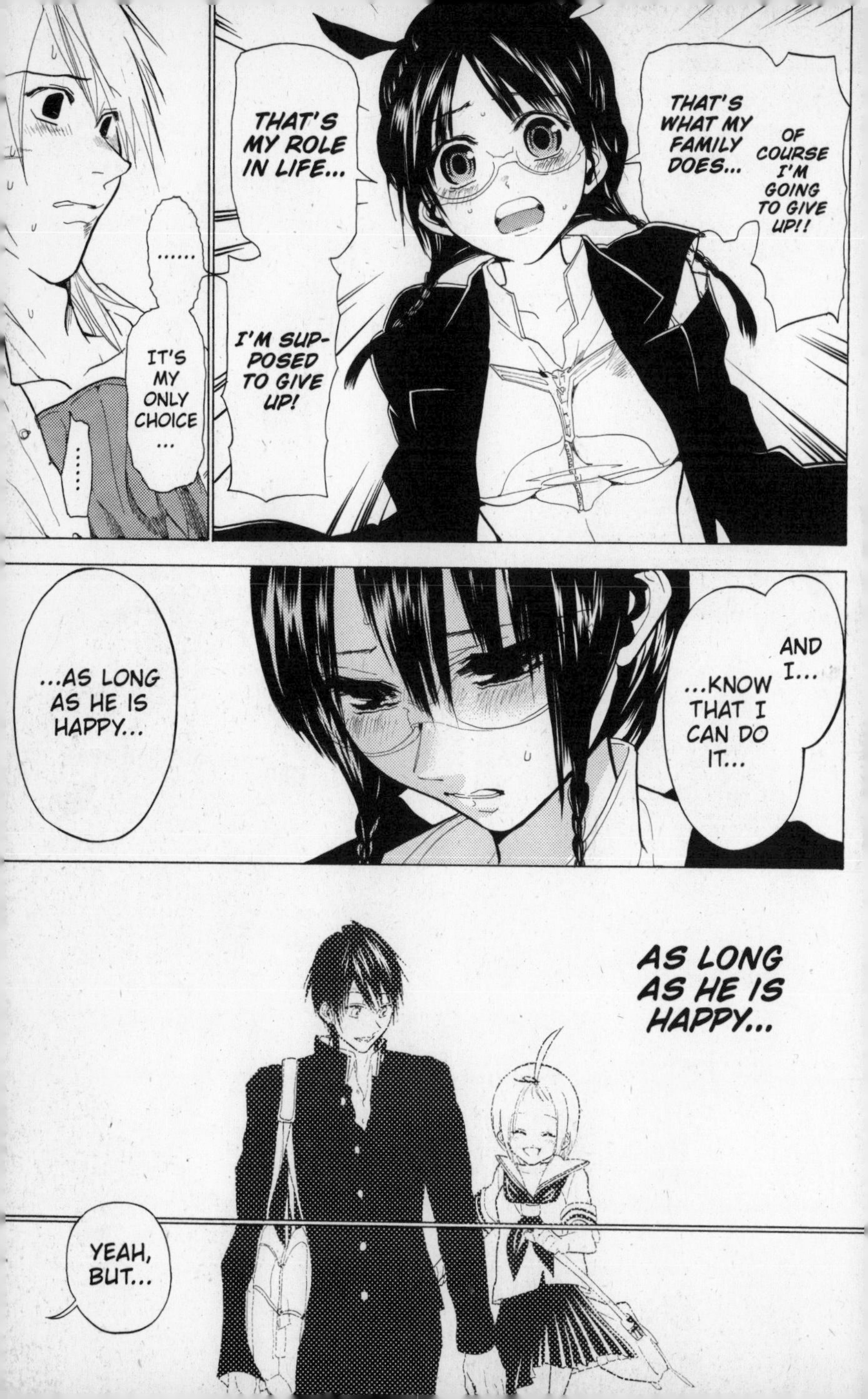
OF COURSE I'M GOING TO GIVE UP!!
THAT'S WHAT MY FAMILY DOES...
THAT'S MY ROLE IN LIFE...
I'M SUP-POSED TO GIVE UP!
......
IT'S MY ONLY CHOICE...
......
AND I...
...KNOW THAT I CAN DO IT...
...AS LONG AS HE IS HAPPY...
AS LONG AS HE IS HAPPY...
YEAH, BUT...

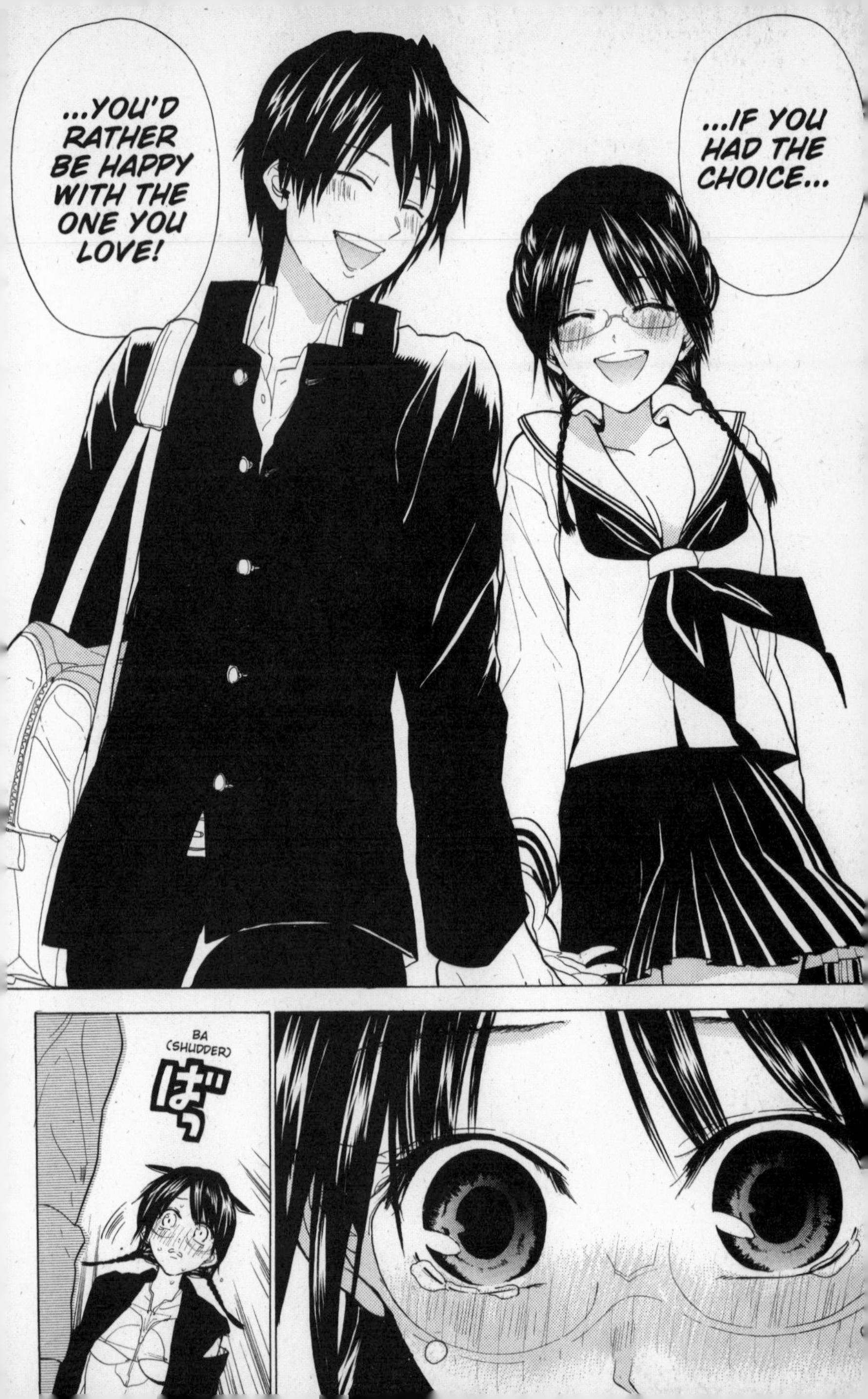
...IF YOU HAD THE CHOICE...
...YOU'D RATHER BE HAPPY WITH THE ONE YOU LOVE!
BA (SHUDDER)
ばっ

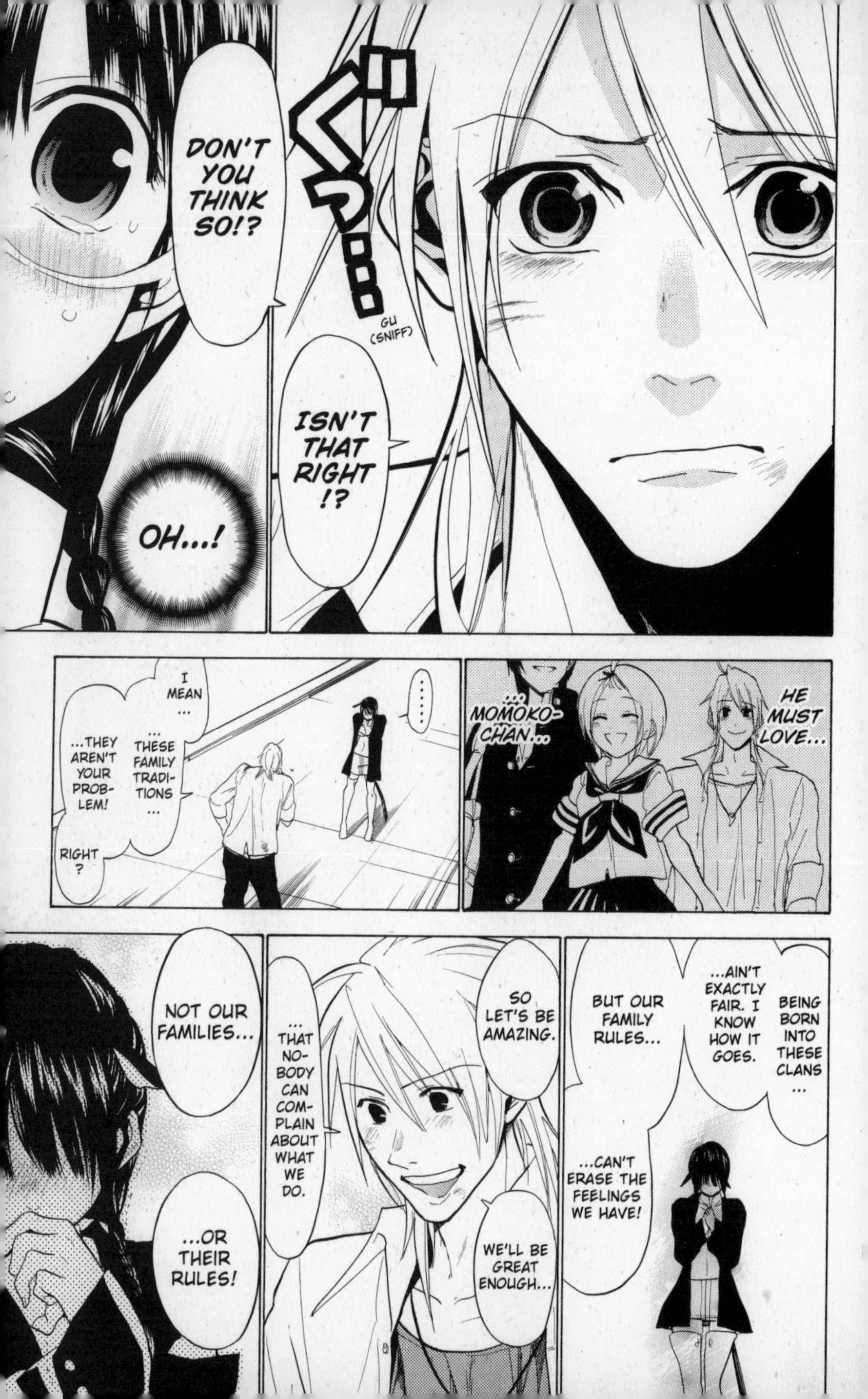
GU (SNIFF)
ISN'T THAT RIGHT !?
DON'T YOU THINK SO!?
OH...!
HE MUST LOVE...
...MOMOKO-CHAN...
......
I MEAN...
...THESE FAMILY TRADI-TIONS...
...THEY AREN'T YOUR PROB-LEM!
RIGHT?
BEING BORN INTO THESE CLANS...
...AIN'T EXACTLY FAIR. I KNOW HOW IT GOES.
BUT OUR FAMILY RULES...
...CAN'T ERASE THE FEELINGS WE HAVE!
SO LET'S BE AMAZING.
...THAT NO-BODY CAN COM-PLAIN ABOUT WHAT WE DO.
WE'LL BE GREAT ENOUGH...
NOT OUR FAMILIES...
...OR THEIR RULES!

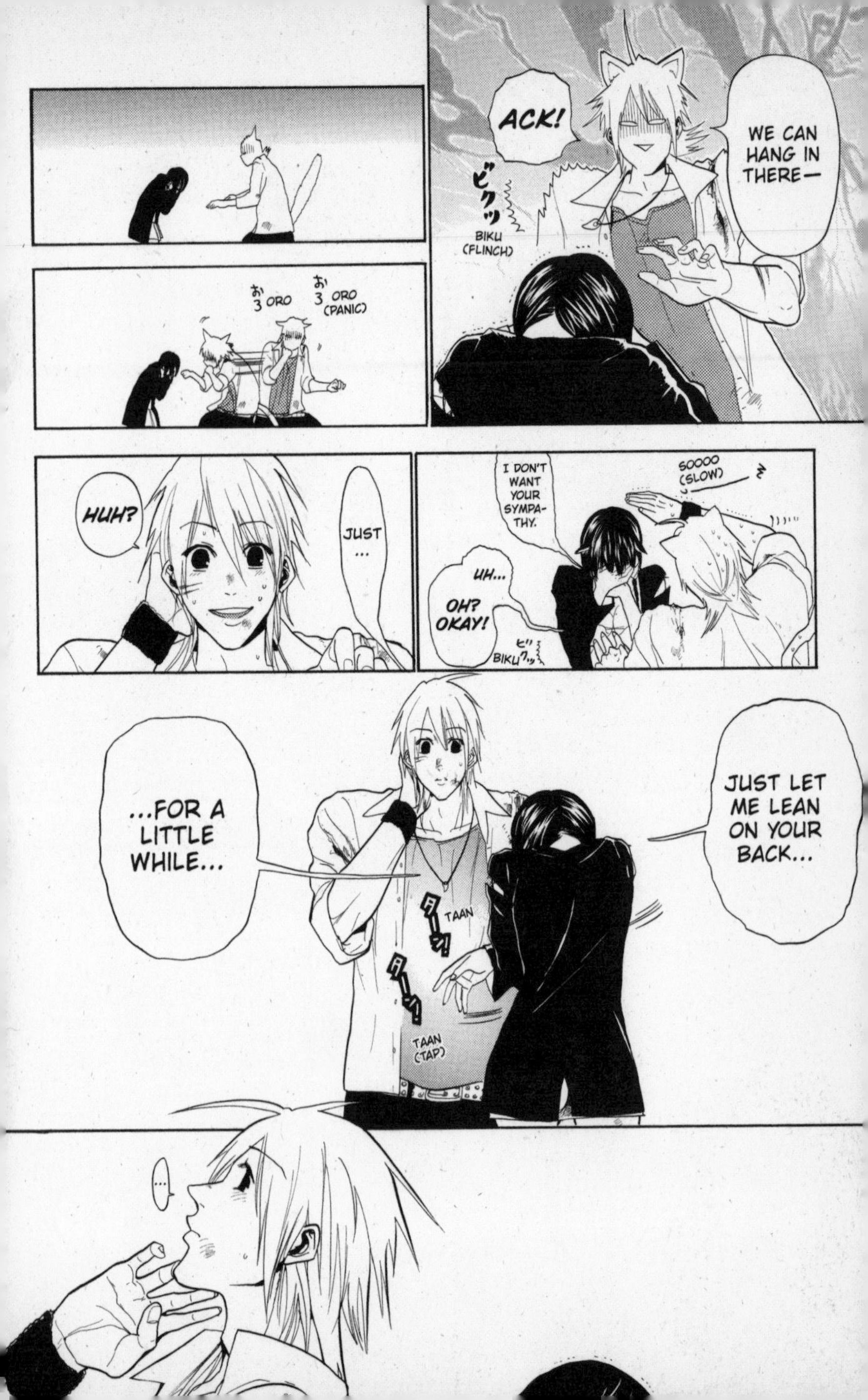
WE CAN HANG IN THERE—
ACK!
ビクッ
BIKU (FLINCH)
おろ ORO (PANIC)
おろ ORO
SOOOO (SLOW)
I DON'T WANT YOUR SYMPATHY.
UH... OH? OKAY!
ビクッ BIKU
JUST ...
HUH?
JUST LET ME LEAN ON YOUR BACK...
TAAN
TAAN (TAP)
...FOR A LITTLE WHILE...
...

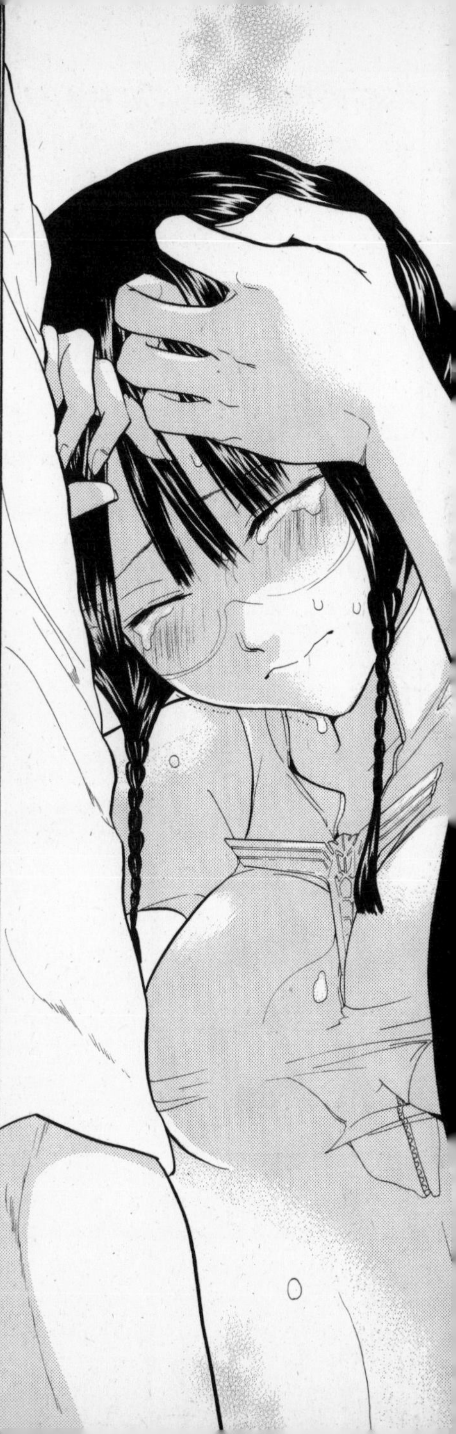

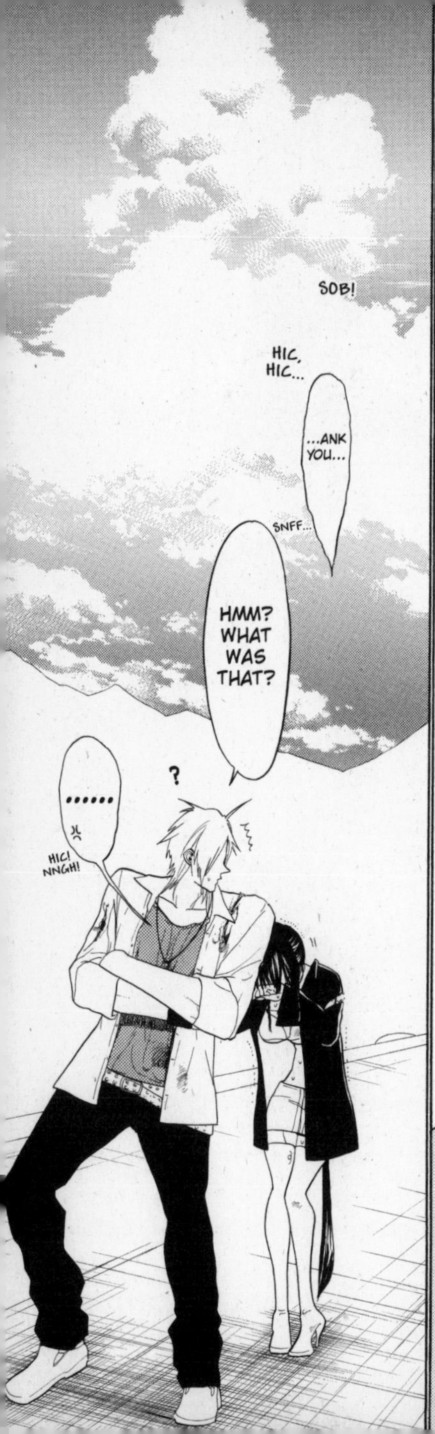
SOB!
HIC, HIC...
...ANK YOU...
SNFF...
HMM? WHAT WAS THAT?
?
......
HIC! NNGH!

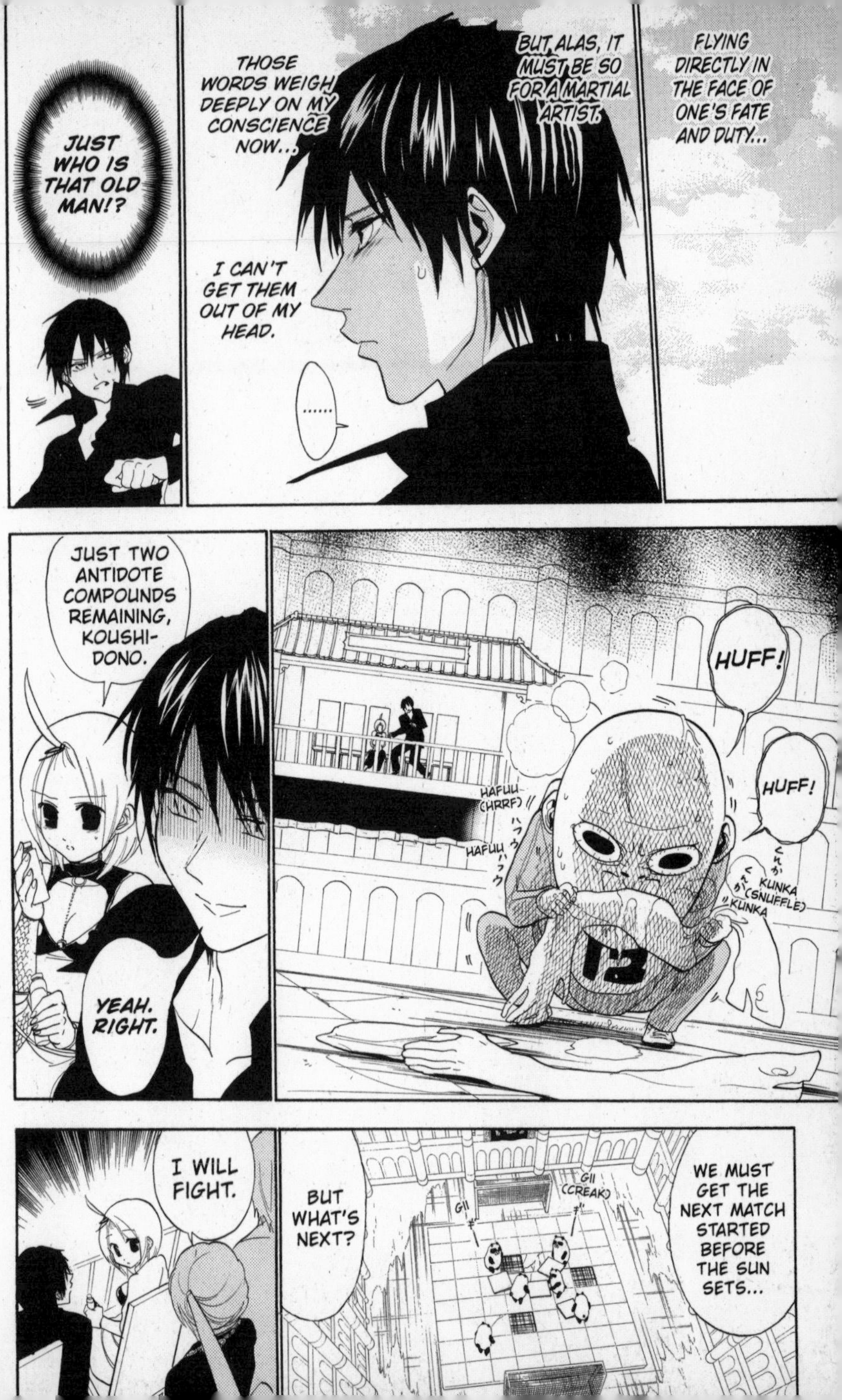
FLYING DIRECTLY IN THE FACE OF ONE'S FATE AND DUTY...
BUT ALAS, IT MUST BE SO FOR A MARTIAL ARTIST.
THOSE WORDS WEIGH DEEPLY ON MY CONSCIENCE NOW...
I CAN'T GET THEM OUT OF MY HEAD.
......
JUST WHO IS THAT OLD MAN!?
HUFF!
HUFF!
KUNKA (SNUFFLE) KUNKA
HAFUU (HRRF)
HAFUU
JUST TWO ANTIDOTE COMPOUNDS REMAINING, KOUSHI-DONO.
YEAH. RIGHT.
WE MUST GET THE NEXT MATCH STARTED BEFORE THE SUN SETS...
GII (CREAK)
GII
BUT WHAT'S NEXT?
I WILL FIGHT.

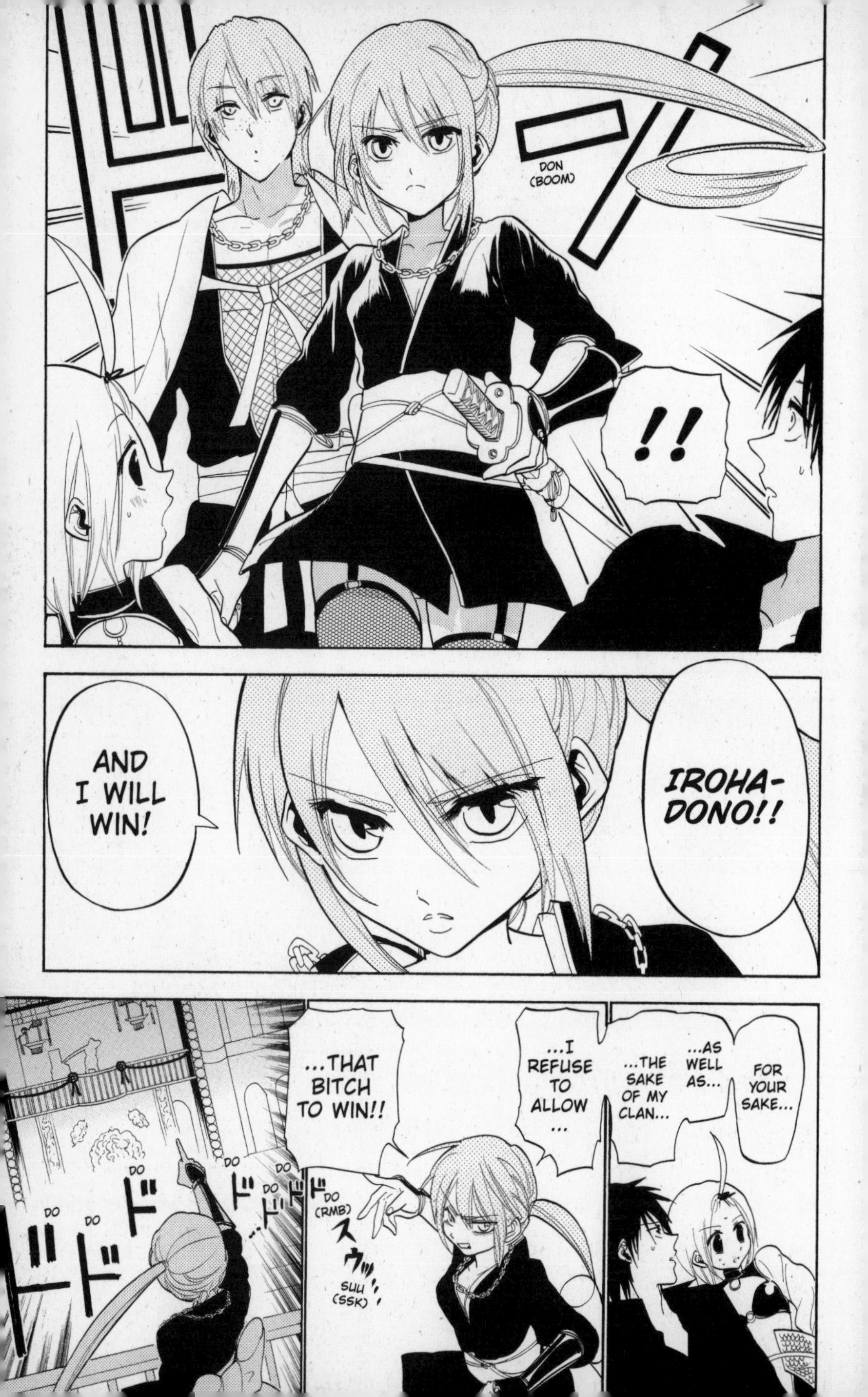
DON (BOOM)
!!
IROHA-DONO!!
AND I WILL WIN!
FOR YOUR SAKE...
...AS WELL AS...
...THE SAKE OF MY CLAN...
...I REFUSE TO ALLOW ...
...THAT BITCH TO WIN!!
SUU (SSK)
DO DO DO DO DO DO DO (RMB)

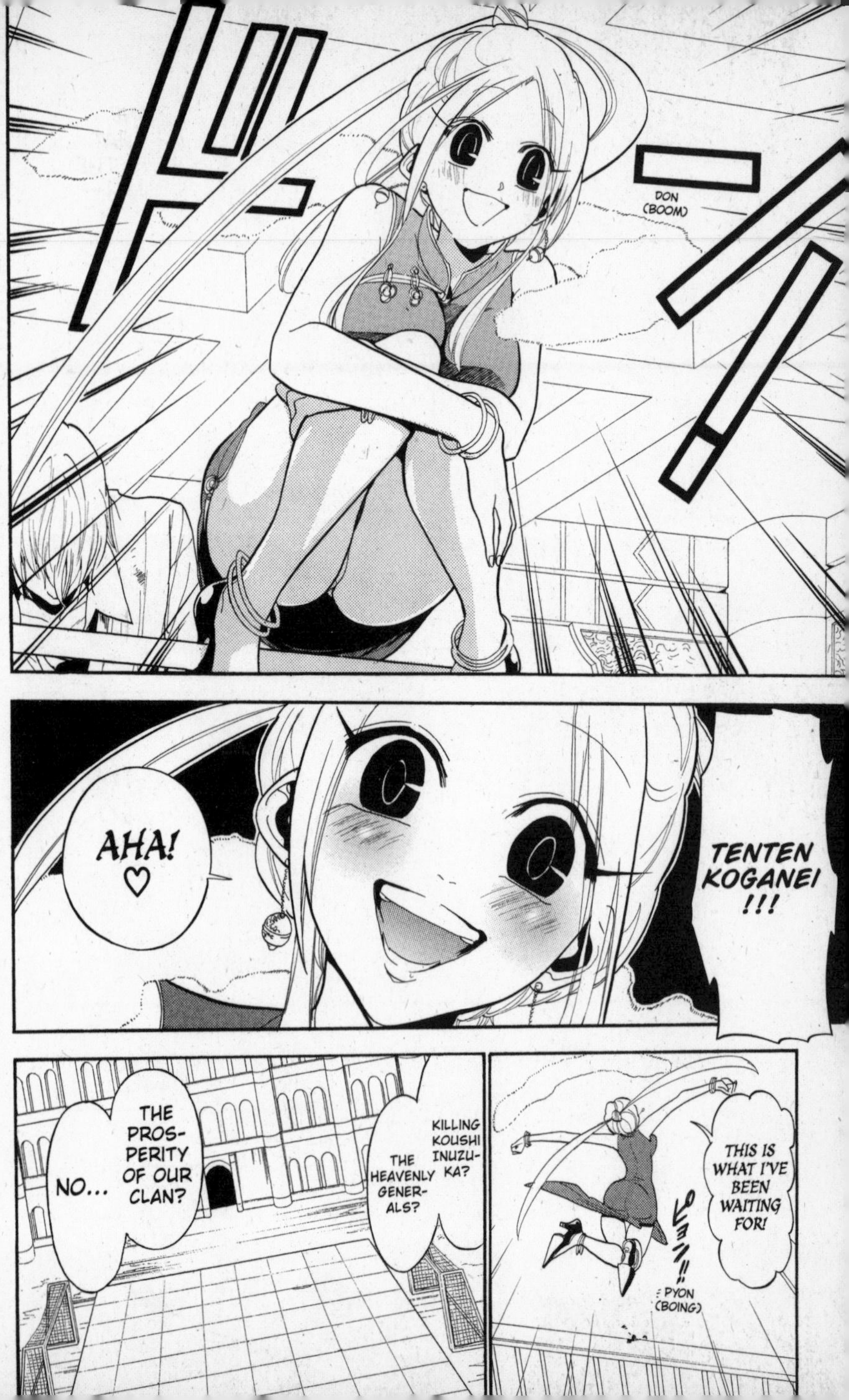
DON (BOOM)
TENTEN KOGANEI !!!
AHA! ♡
THIS IS WHAT I'VE BEEN WAITING FOR!
PYON (BOING)
KILLING KOUSHI INUZUKA?
THE HEAVENLY GENERALS?
THE PROSPERITY OF OUR CLAN?
NO...

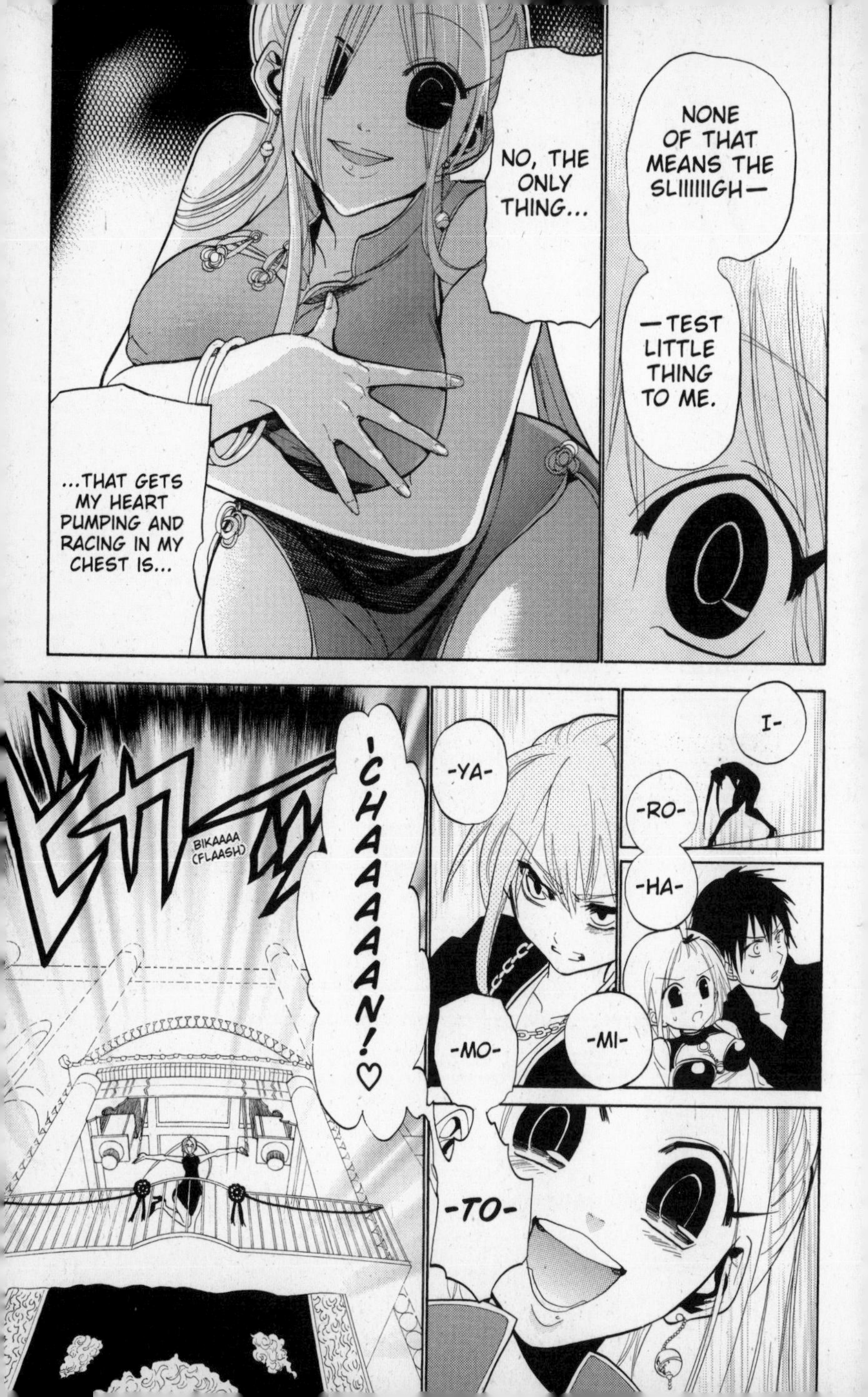
NONE OF THAT MEANS THE SLIIIIIIGH—
—TEST LITTLE THING TO ME.
NO, THE ONLY THING...
...THAT GETS MY HEART PUMPING AND RACING IN MY CHEST IS...
I-
-RO-
-HA-
-MI-
-YA-
-MO-
-TO-
-CHAAAAAAN!♡
BIKAAAA (FLAASH)

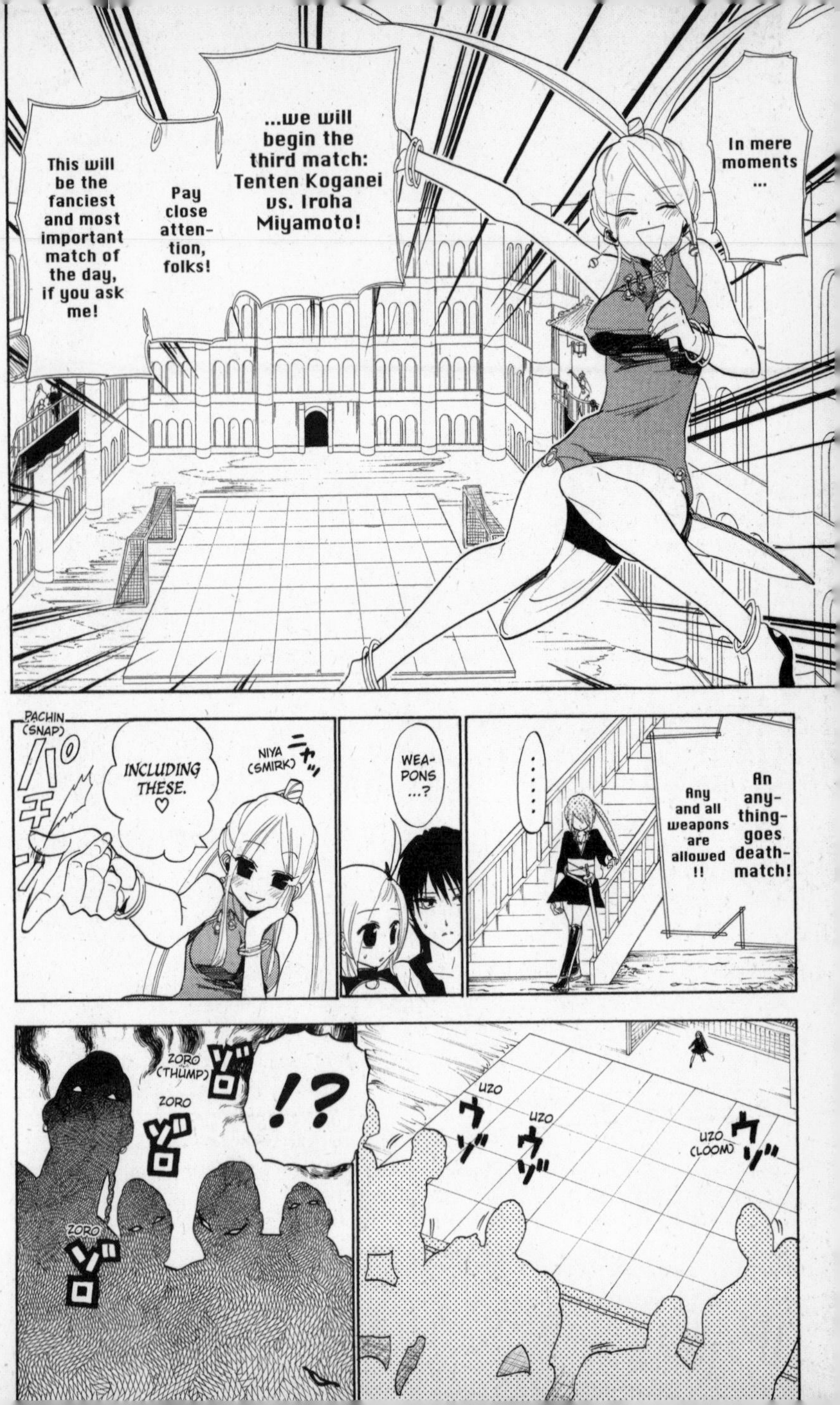
In mere moments ...
...we will begin the third match: Tenten Koganei vs. Iroha Miyamoto!
Pay close atten- tion, folks!
This will be the fanciest and most important match of the day, if you ask me!
An any- thing- goes death- match!
Any and all weapons are allowed !!
......
WEA- PONS ...?
NIYA (SMIRK)
INCLUDING THESE. ♡
PACHIN (SNAP)
UZO (LOOM)
UZO
UZO
!?
ZORO (THUMP)
ZORO
ZORO

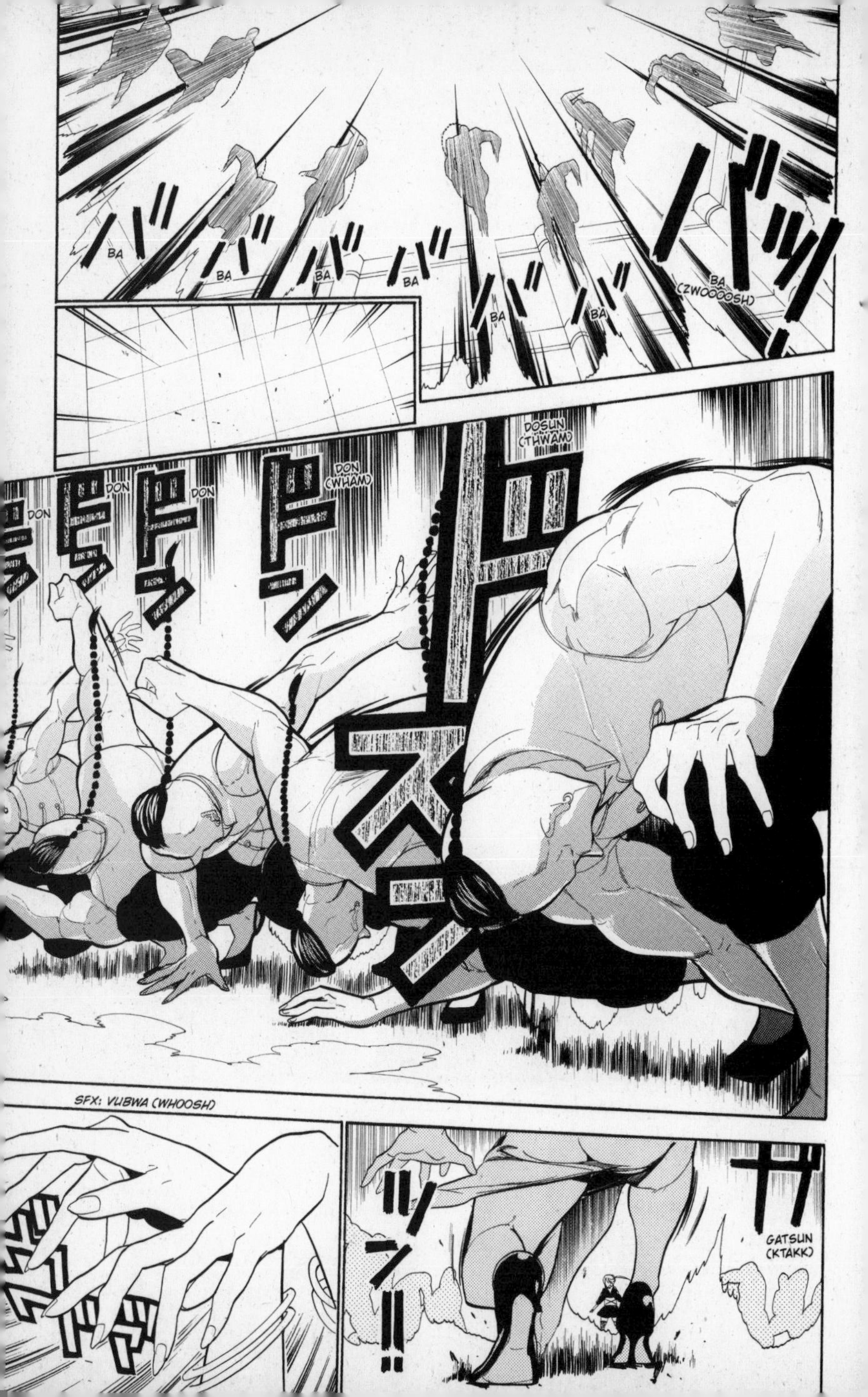
BA (ZWOOOSH)
BA
BA
BA
BA
BA
BA
DOSUN (THWAM)
DON (WHAM)
DON
DON
DON
GATSUN (KTAKK)
SFX: VUBWA (WHOOSH)

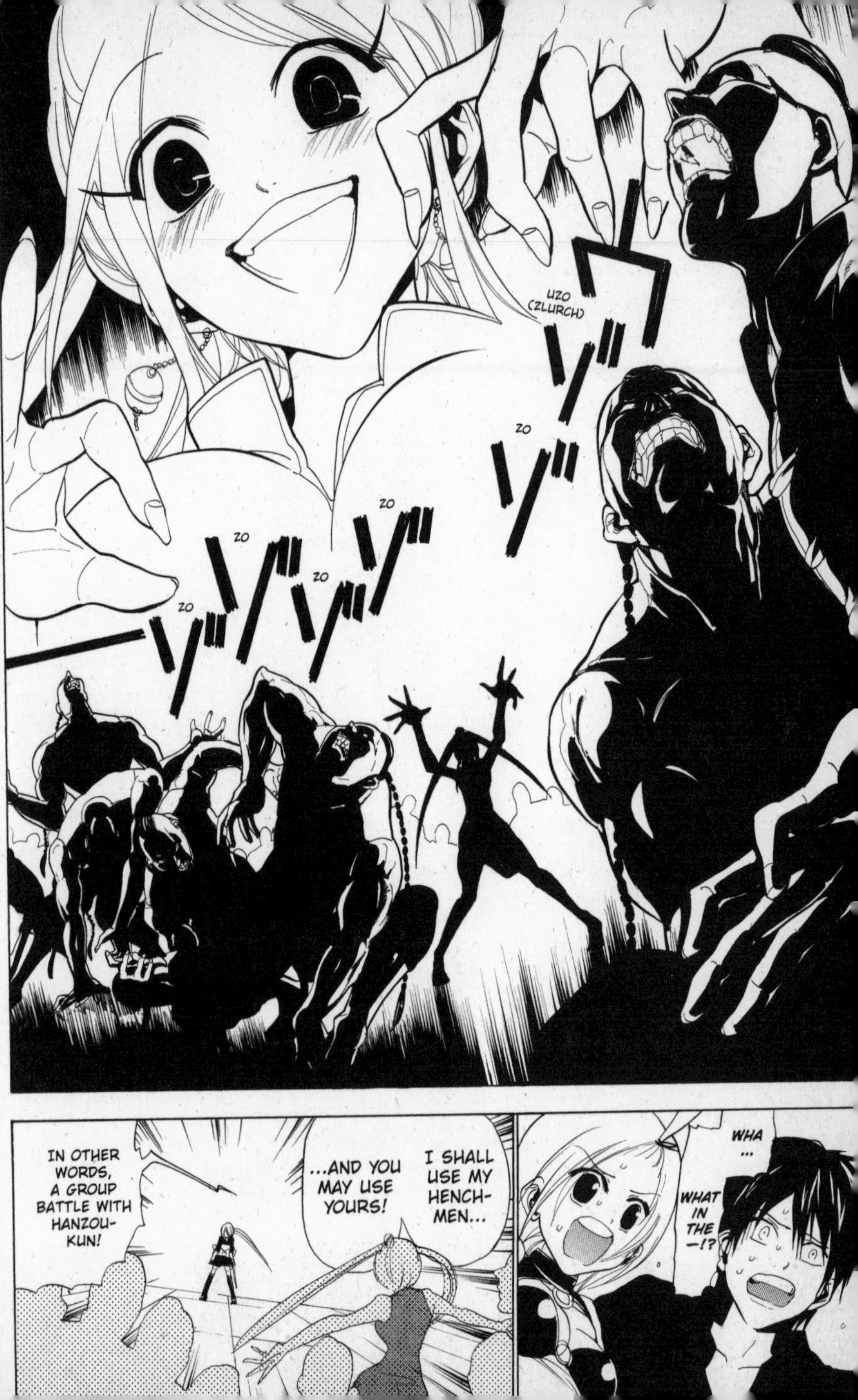
UZO
(ZLURCH)
ZO
ZO
ZO
ZO
ZO
WHA...
WHAT IN THE—!?
I SHALL USE MY HENCH-MEN...
...AND YOU MAY USE YOURS!
IN OTHER WORDS, A GROUP BATTLE WITH HANZOU-KUN!

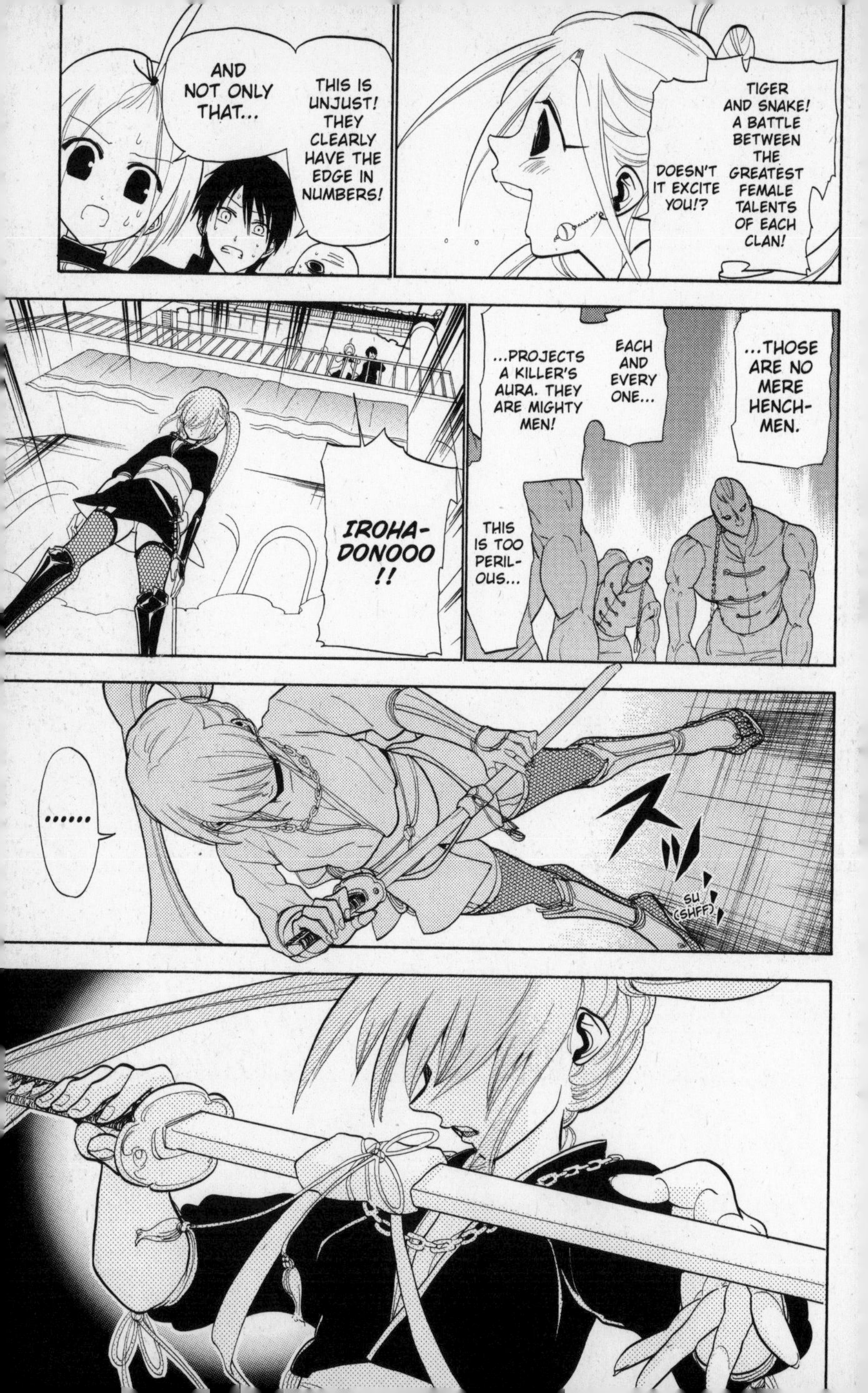
TIGER AND SNAKE! A BATTLE BETWEEN THE GREATEST FEMALE TALENTS OF EACH CLAN!
DOESN'T IT EXCITE YOU!?
THIS IS UNJUST! THEY CLEARLY HAVE THE EDGE IN NUMBERS!
AND NOT ONLY THAT...
...THOSE ARE NO MERE HENCH-MEN.
EACH AND EVERY ONE...
...PROJECTS A KILLER'S AURA. THEY ARE MIGHTY MEN!
THIS IS TOO PERIL-OUS...
IROHA-DONOOO!!
SU (SHFF)
......

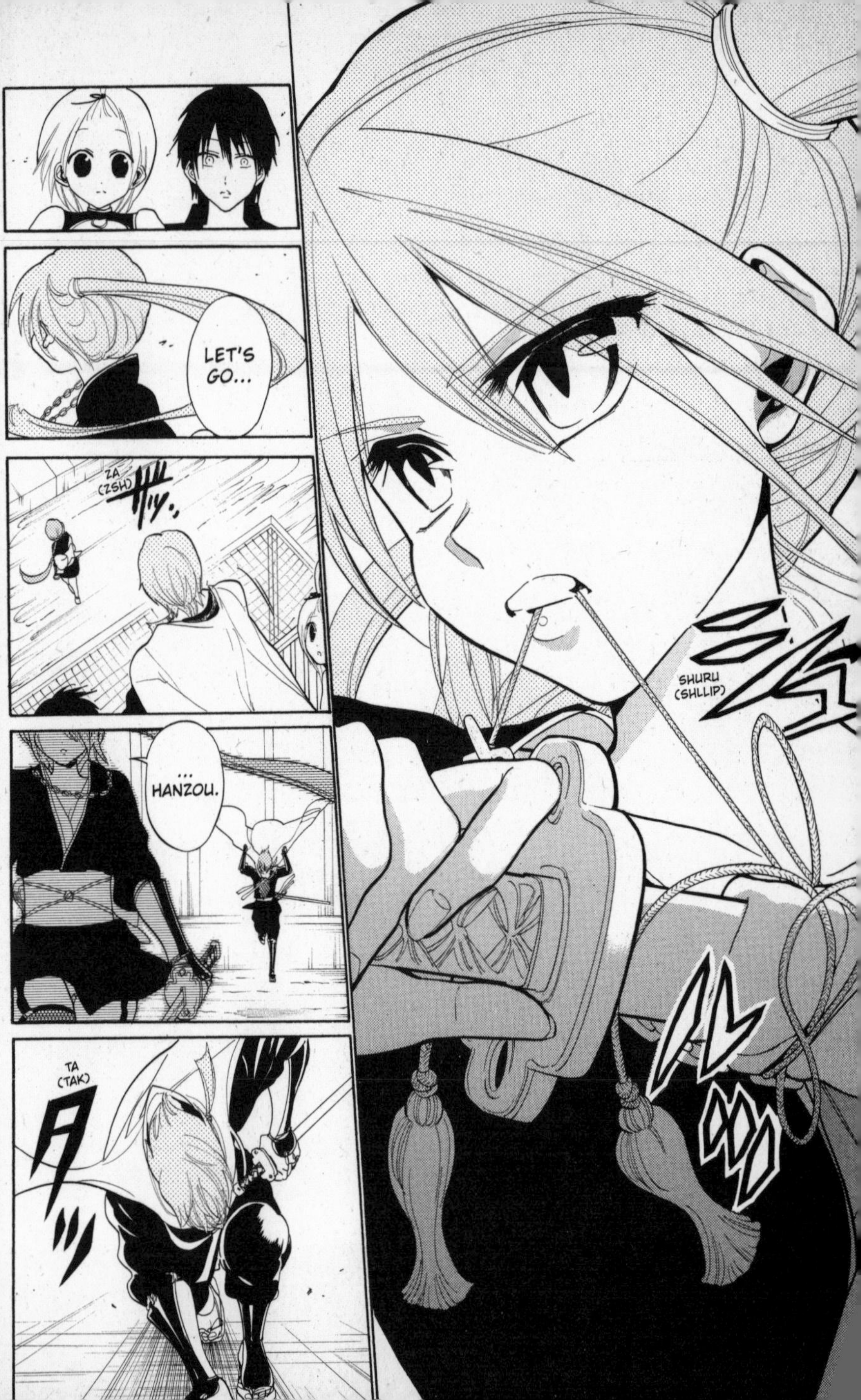
SHURU (SHLLIP)
LET'S GO...
ZA (ZSH)
... HANZOU.
TA (TAK)

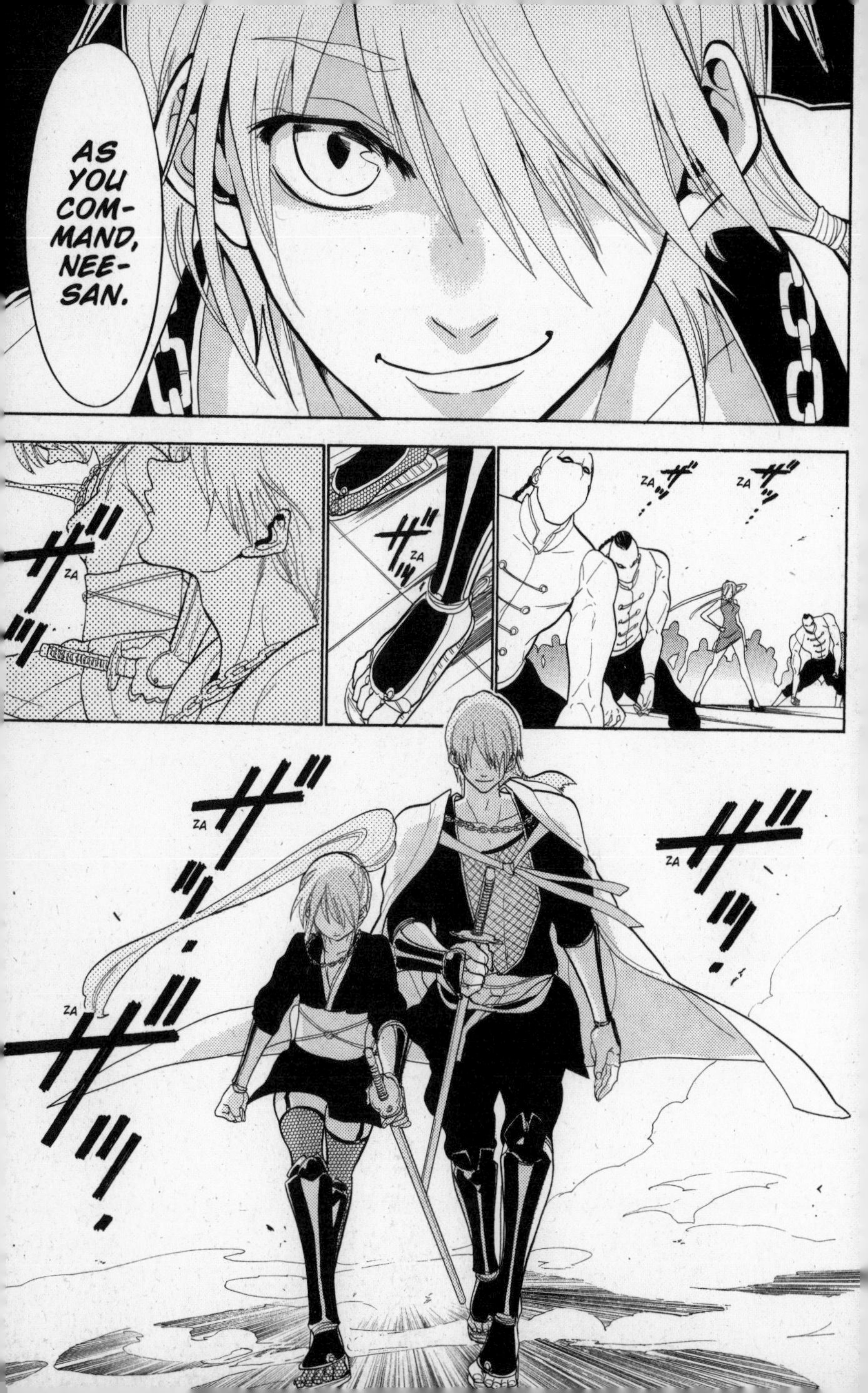
AS YOU COM-MAND, NEE-SAN.
ZA
ZA
ZA
ZA
ZA
ZA
ZA

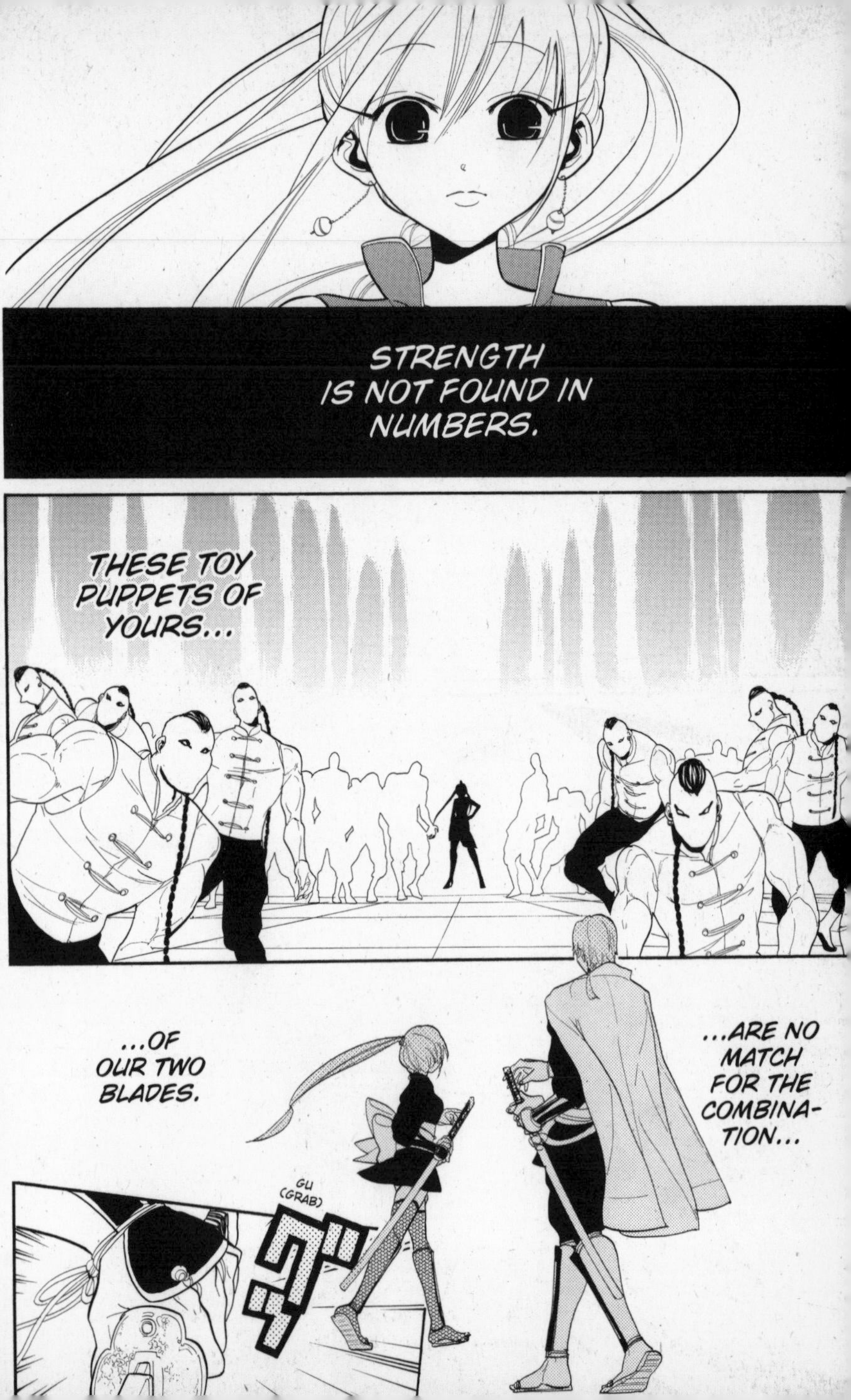

STRENGTH IS NOT FOUND IN NUMBERS.
THESE TOY PUPPETS OF YOURS...
...ARE NO MATCH FOR THE COMBINATION...
...OF OUR TWO BLADES.
GU (GRAB)

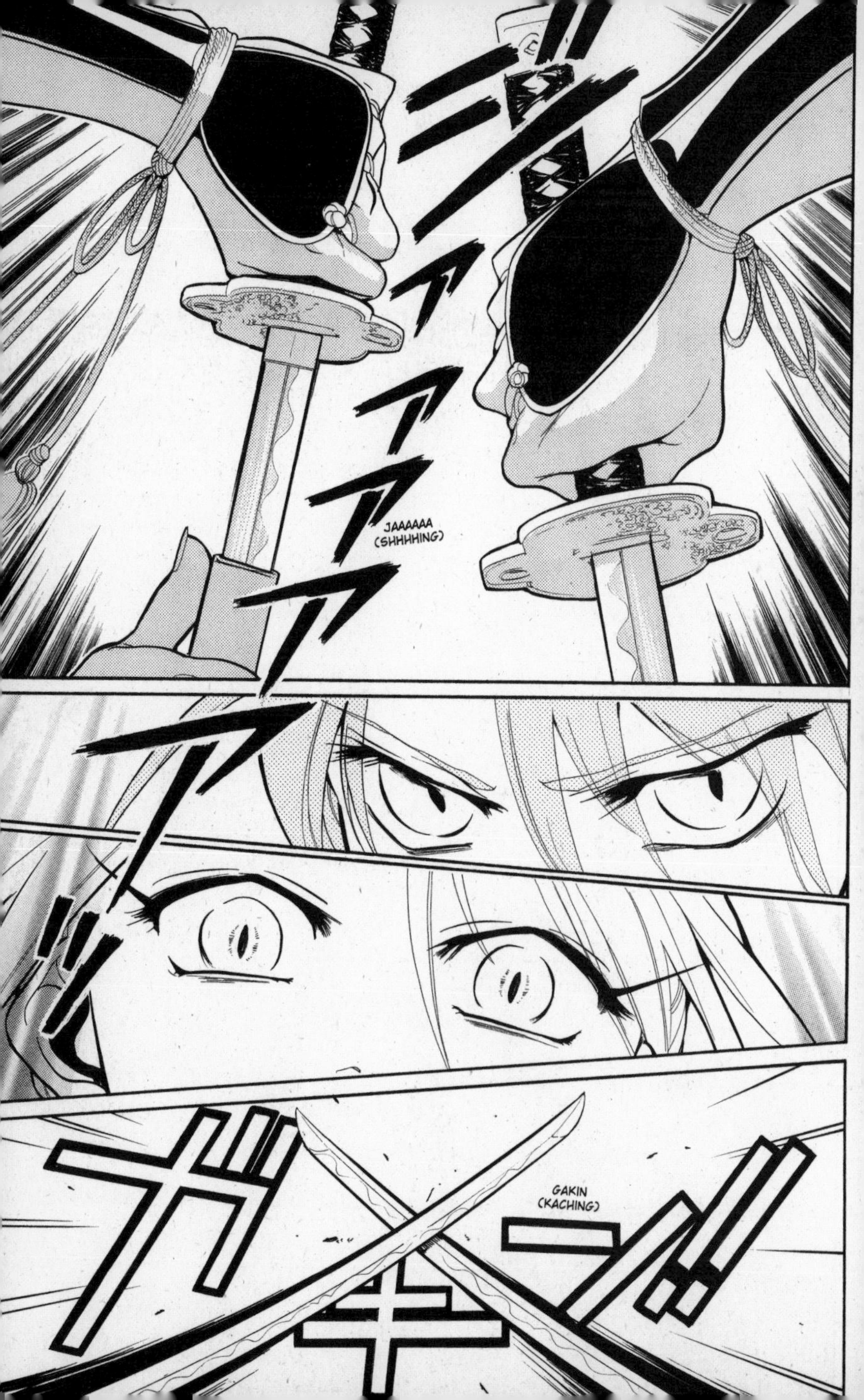
JAAAAAA
(SHHHHING)
GAKIN
(KACHING)

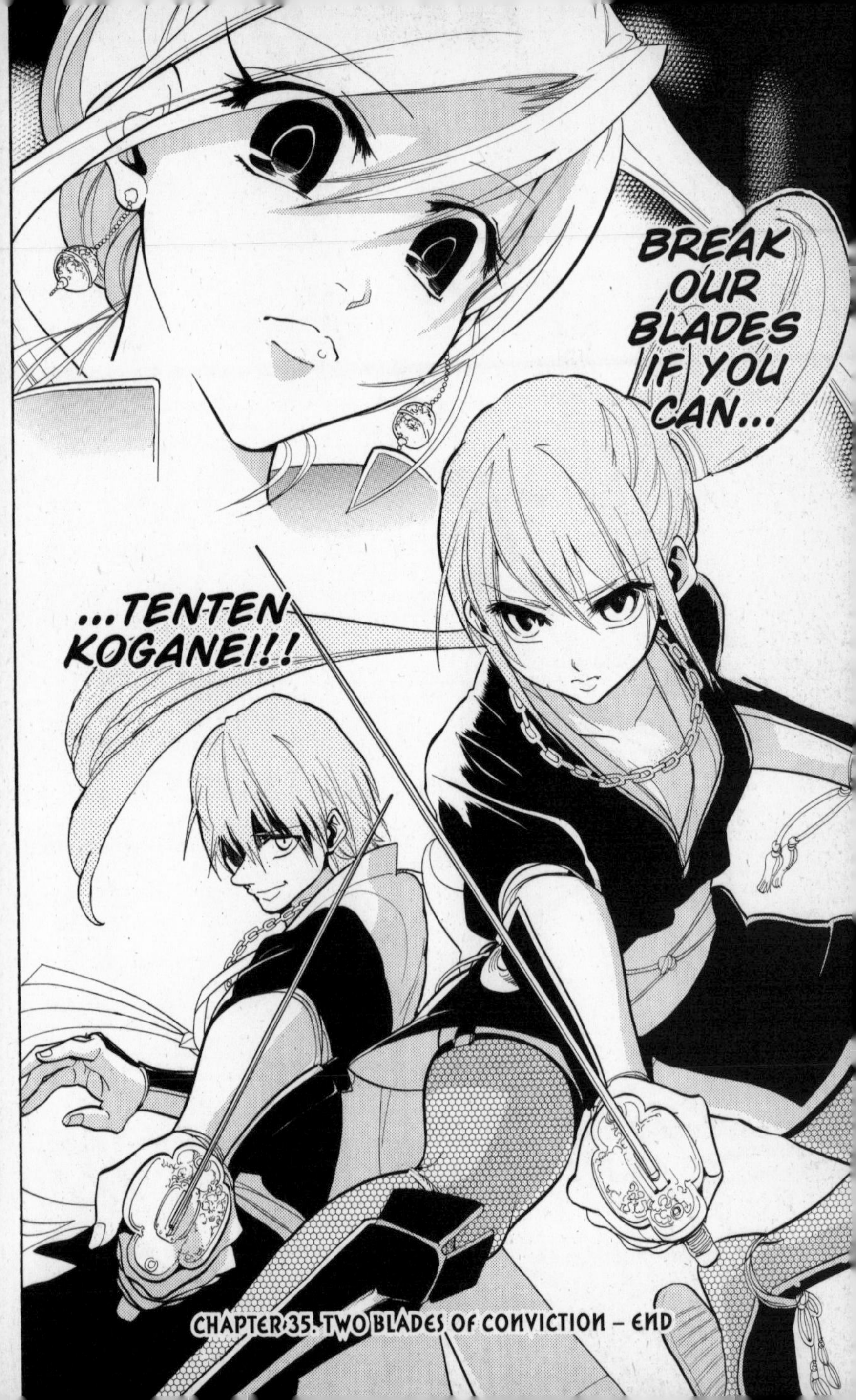
BREAK OUR BLADES IF YOU CAN...
...TENTEN KOGANEI!!
CHAPTER 35: TWO BLADES OF CONVICTION – END

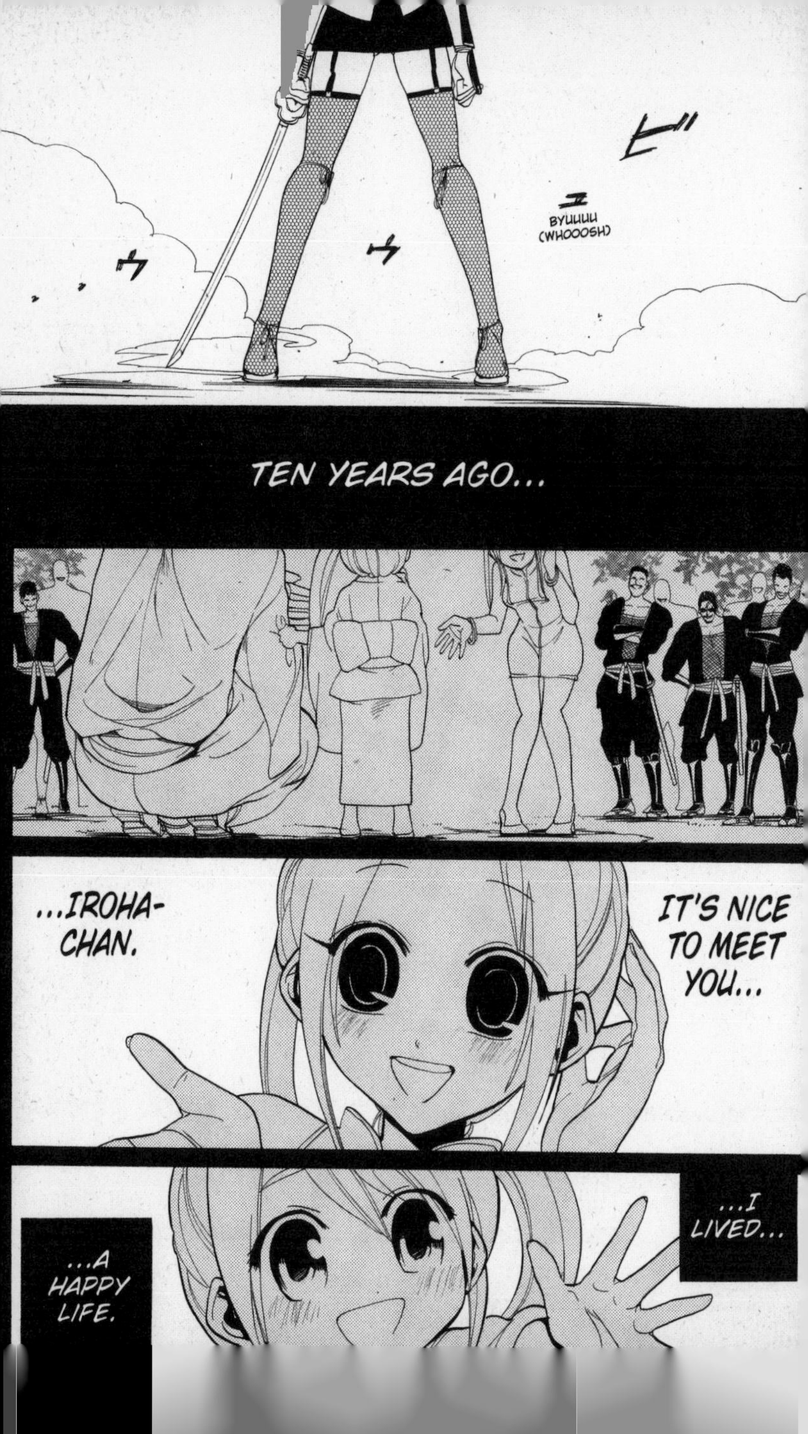
BYUUUU
(WHOOOSH)
TEN YEARS AGO...
IT'S NICE TO MEET YOU...
...IROHA-CHAN.
...I LIVED...
...A HAPPY LIFE.

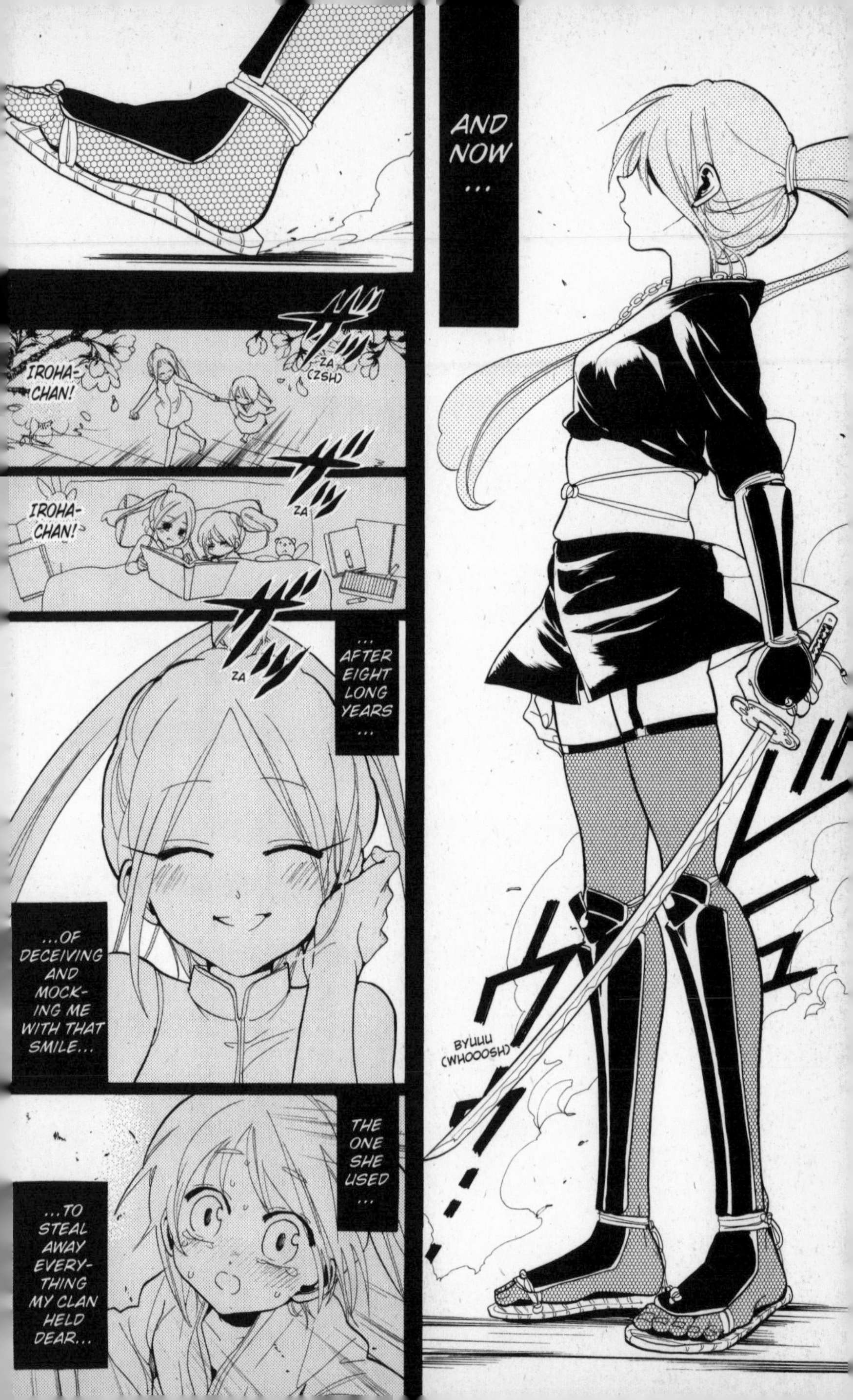
AND NOW ...
BYUUU (WHOOOSH)
ZA (ZSH)
IROHA-CHAN!
ZA
IROHA-CHAN!
ZA
... AFTER EIGHT LONG YEARS ...
...OF DECEIVING AND MOCKING ME WITH THAT SMILE...
THE ONE SHE USED ...
...TO STEAL AWAY EVERYTHING MY CLAN HELD DEAR...

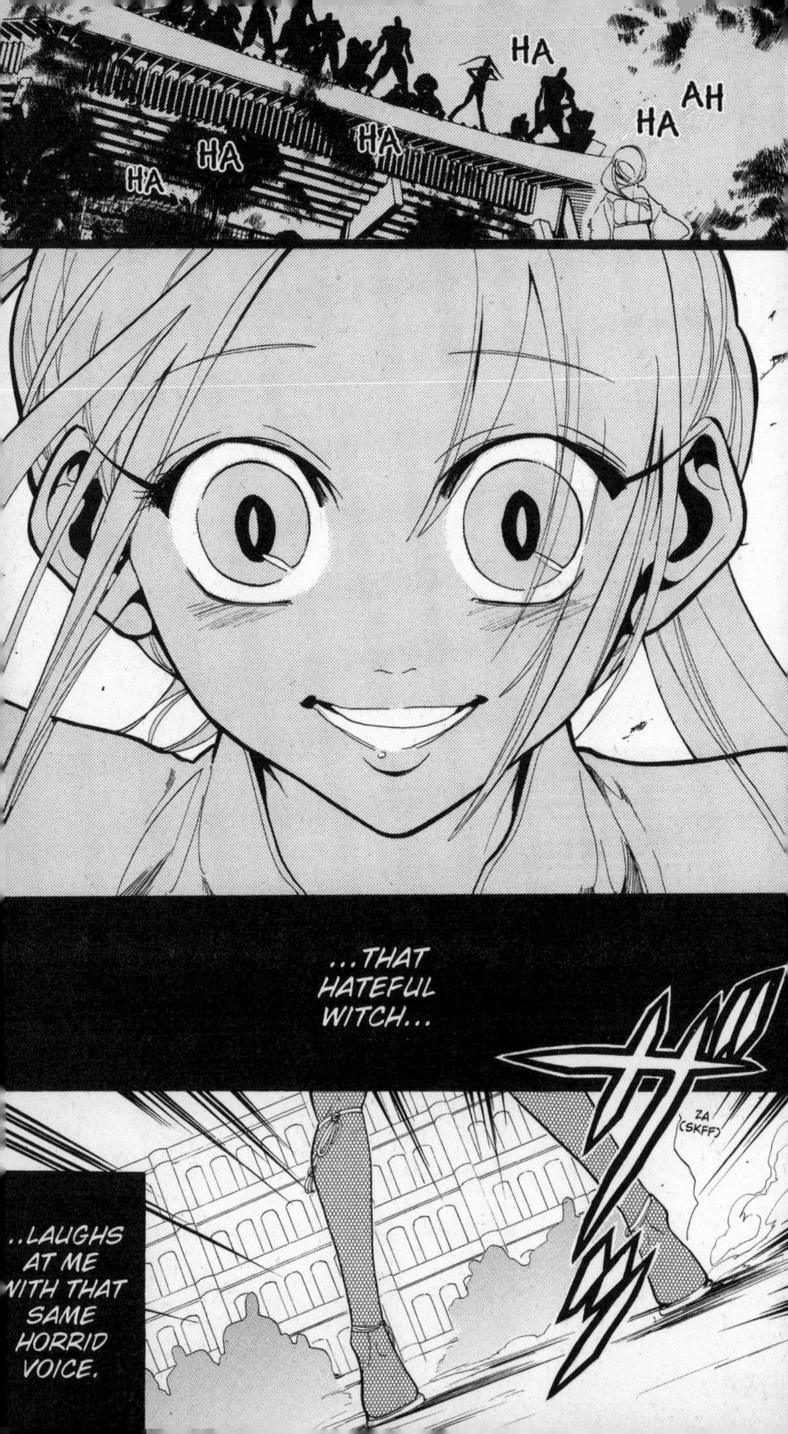
HA
AH
HA
HA
HA
HA
...THAT HATEFUL WITCH...
ZA (SKFF)
..LAUGHS AT ME WITH THAT SAME HORRID VOICE.

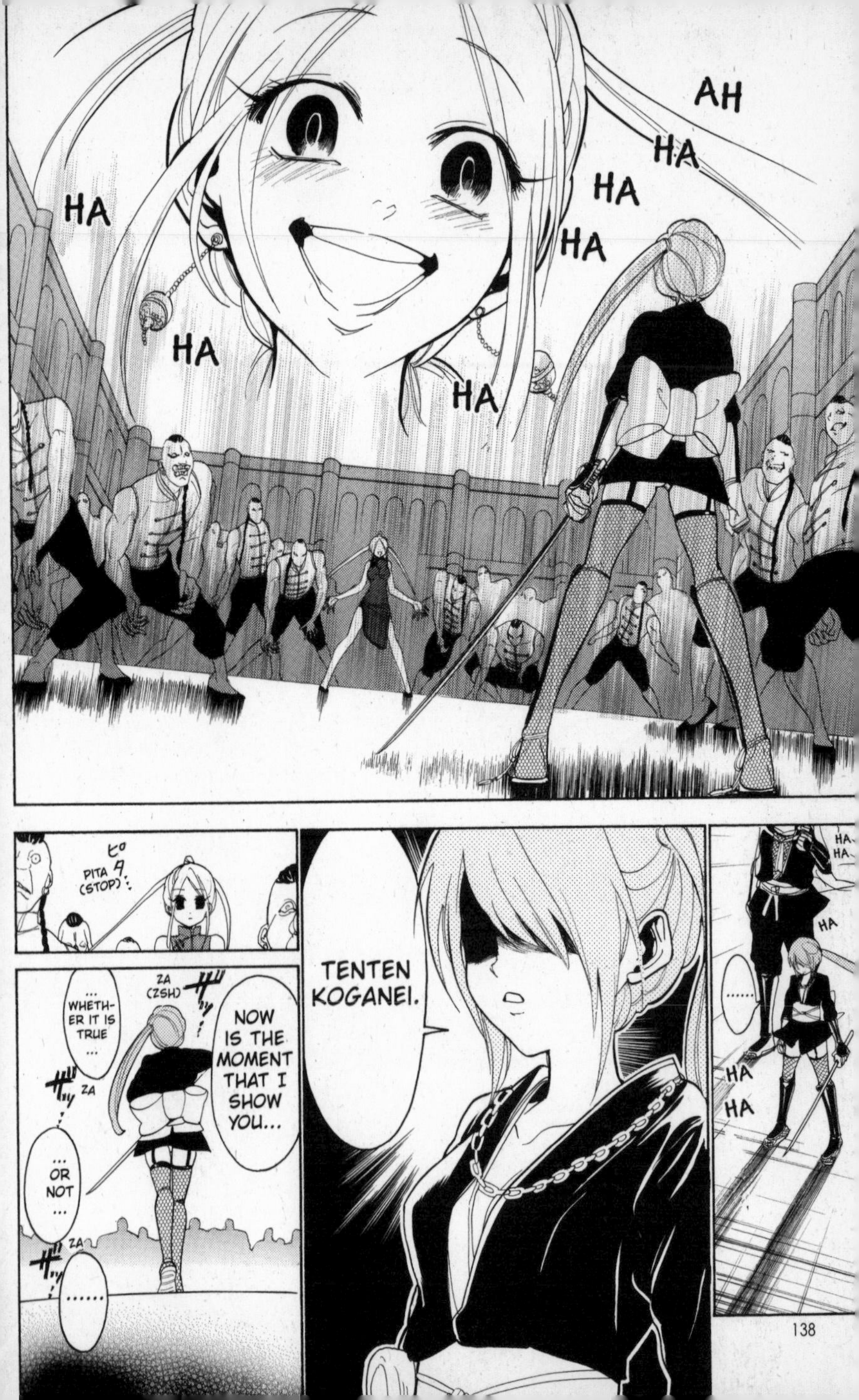
AH
HA
HA
HA
HA
HA
HA
HA-
HA-
HA
......
HA
HA
TENTEN KOGANEI.
ピタ
PITA (STOP)
ZA (ZSH)
NOW IS THE MOMENT THAT I SHOW YOU...
... WHETH-ER IT IS TRUE ...
ZA
... OR NOT ...
ZA
....

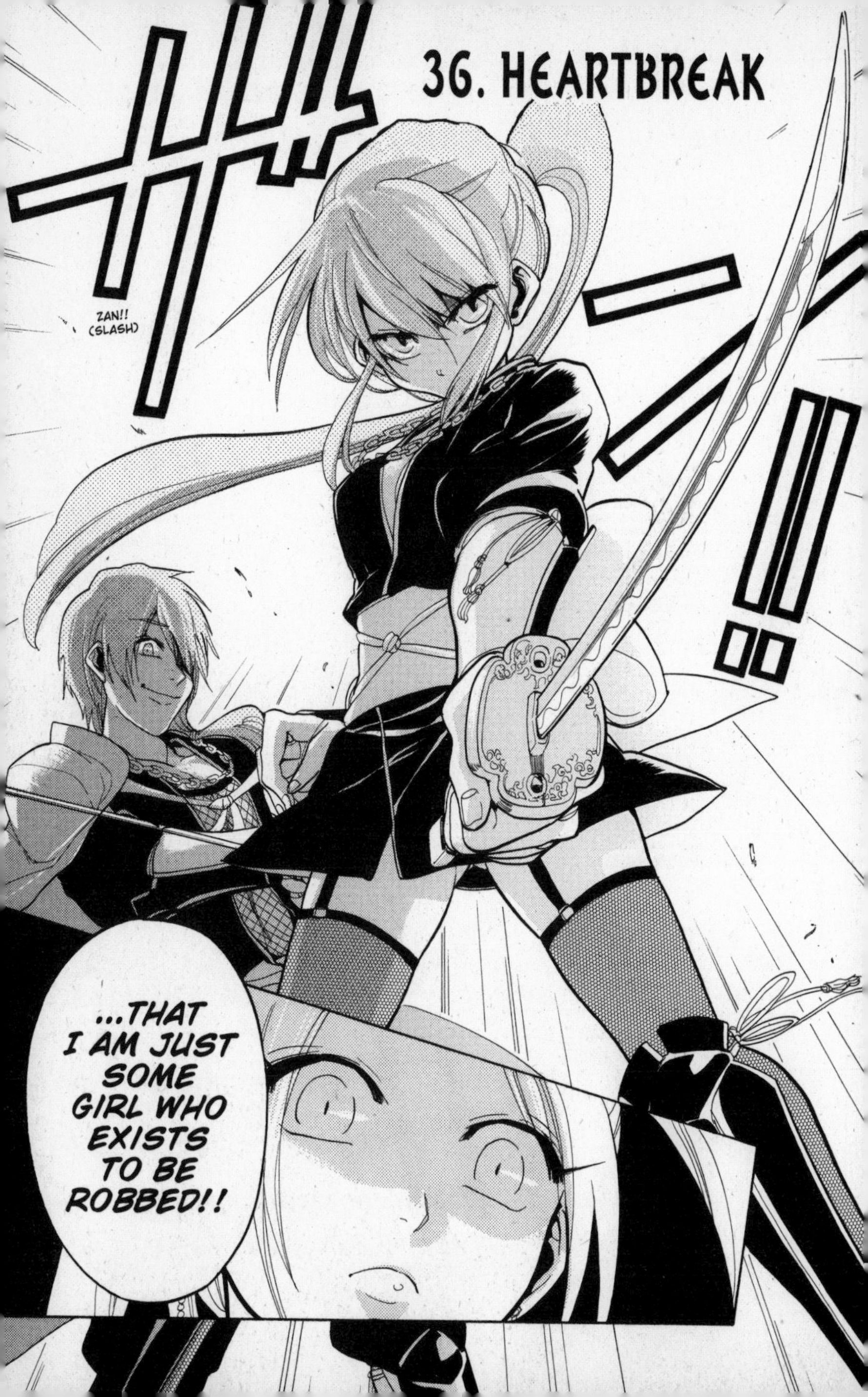
36. HEARTBREAK
ZAN!! (SLASH)
...THAT I AM JUST SOME GIRL WHO EXISTS TO BE ROBBED!!

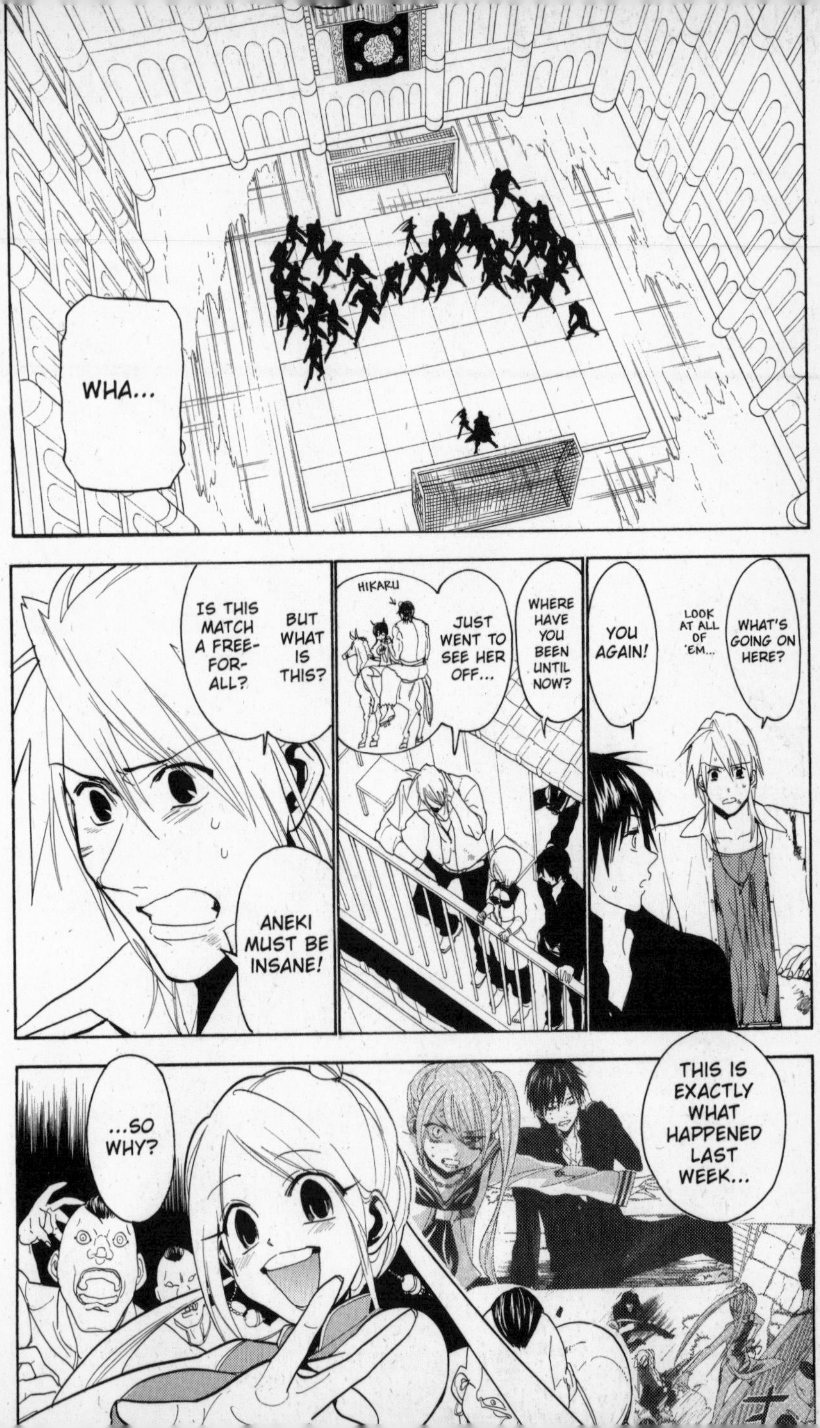
WHA...
WHAT'S GOING ON HERE?
LOOK AT ALL OF 'EM...
YOU AGAIN!
WHERE HAVE YOU BEEN UNTIL NOW?
JUST WENT TO SEE HER OFF...
HIKARU
BUT WHAT IS THIS?
IS THIS MATCH A FREE-FOR-ALL?
ANEKI MUST BE INSANE!
THIS IS EXACTLY WHAT HAPPENED LAST WEEK...
...SO WHY?

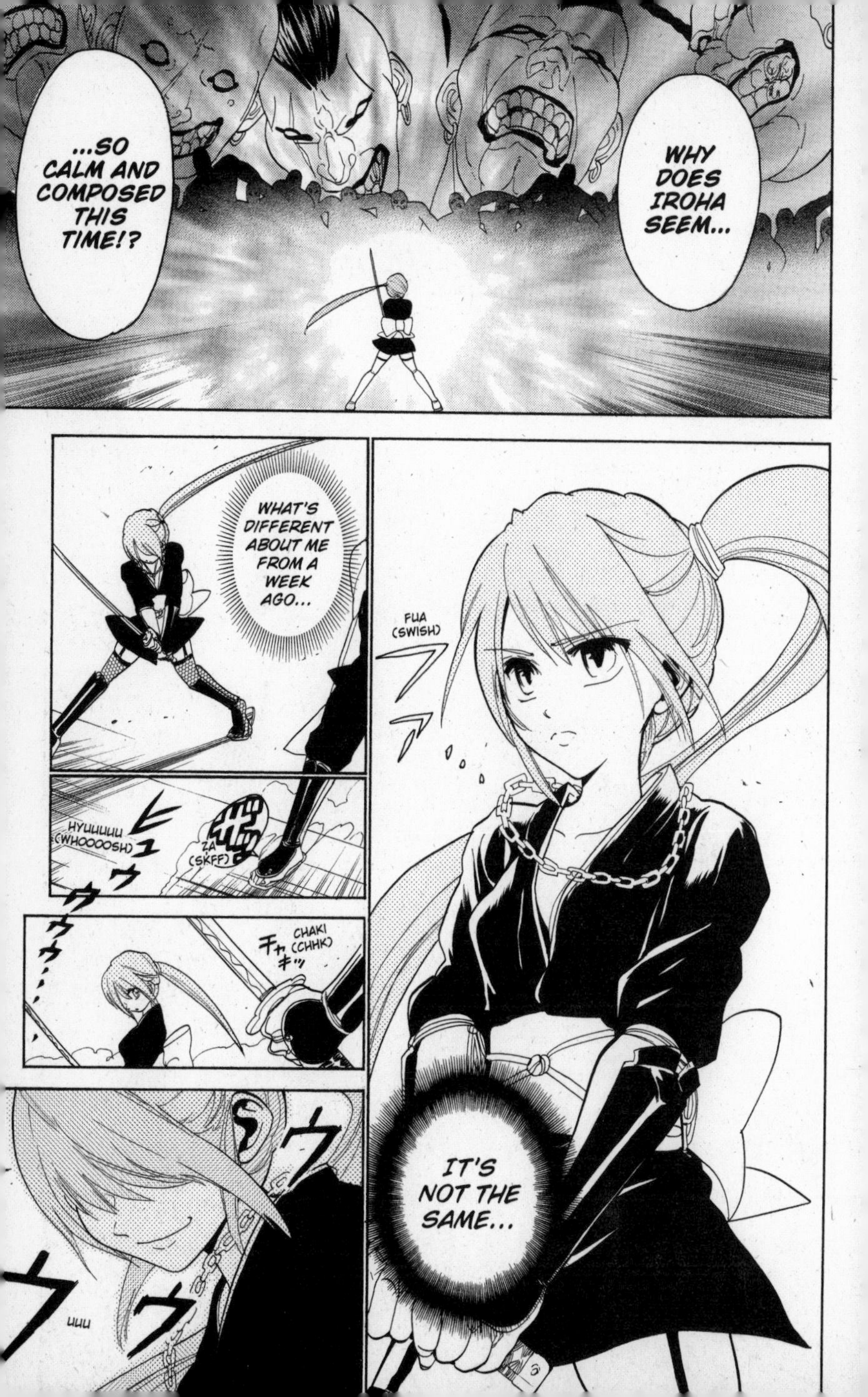

WHY DOES IROHA SEEM...
...SO CALM AND COMPOSED THIS TIME!?
FUA (SWISH)
IT'S NOT THE SAME...
WHAT'S DIFFERENT ABOUT ME FROM A WEEK AGO...
HYUUUUU (WHOOOOSH)
ZA (SKFF)
CHAKI (CHHK)
チャキッ
UUU

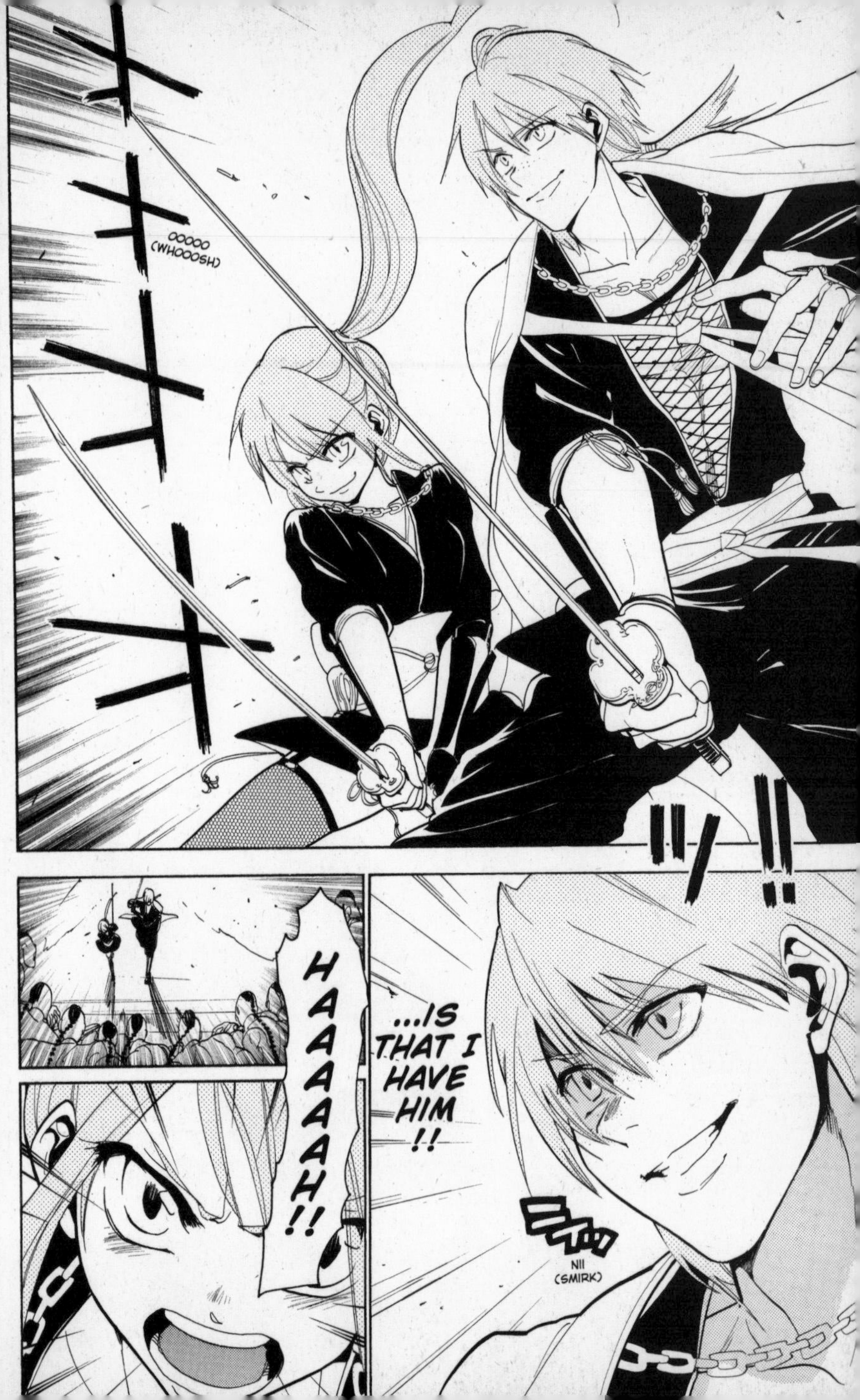
OOOOO (WHOOOSH)
...IS THAT I HAVE HIM!!
NII (SMIRK)
HAAAAAAAH!!

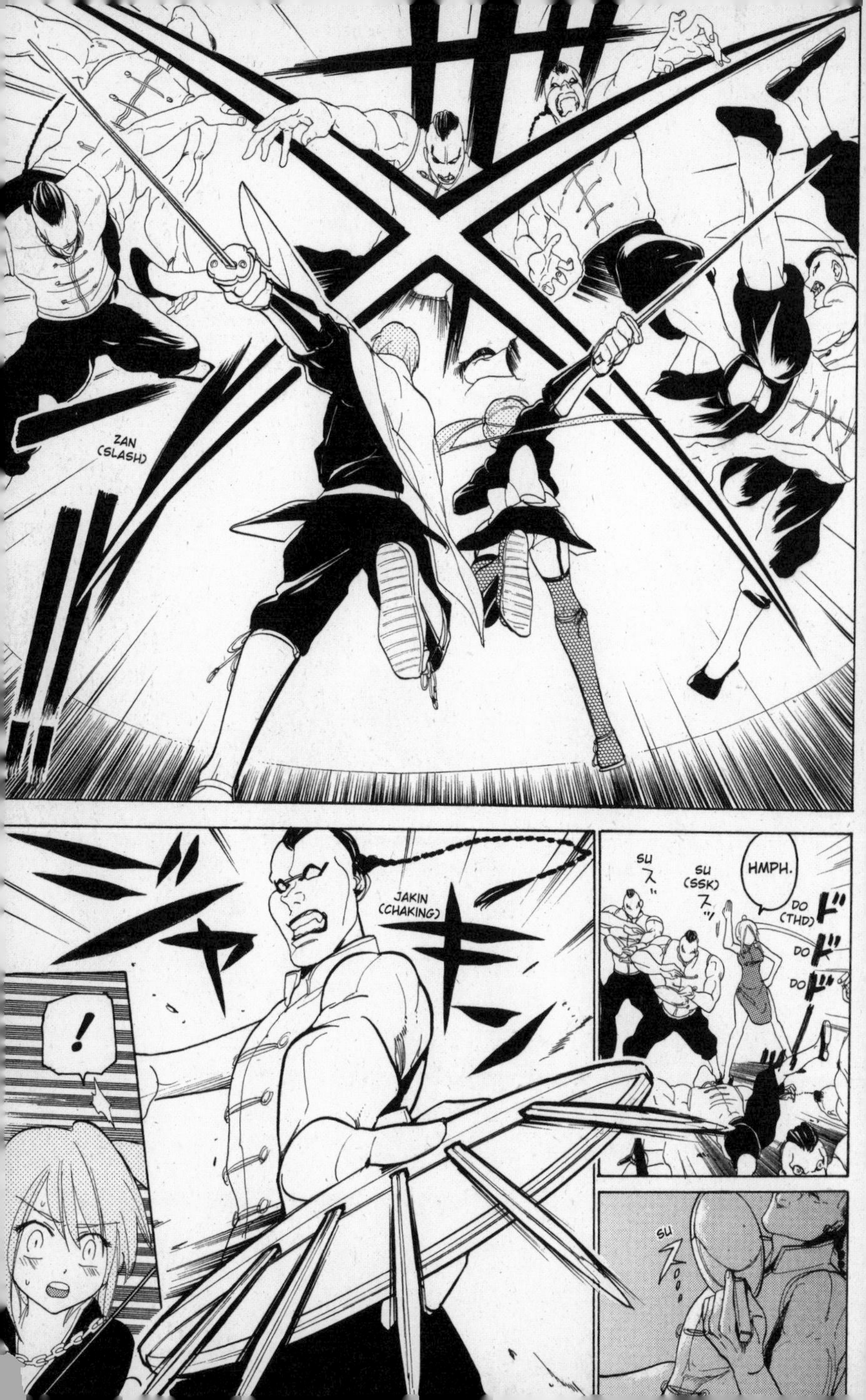
ZAN
(SLASH)
HMPH.
DO
(THD)
DO
DO
SU
(SSK)
SU
SU
JAKIN
(CHAKING)
!

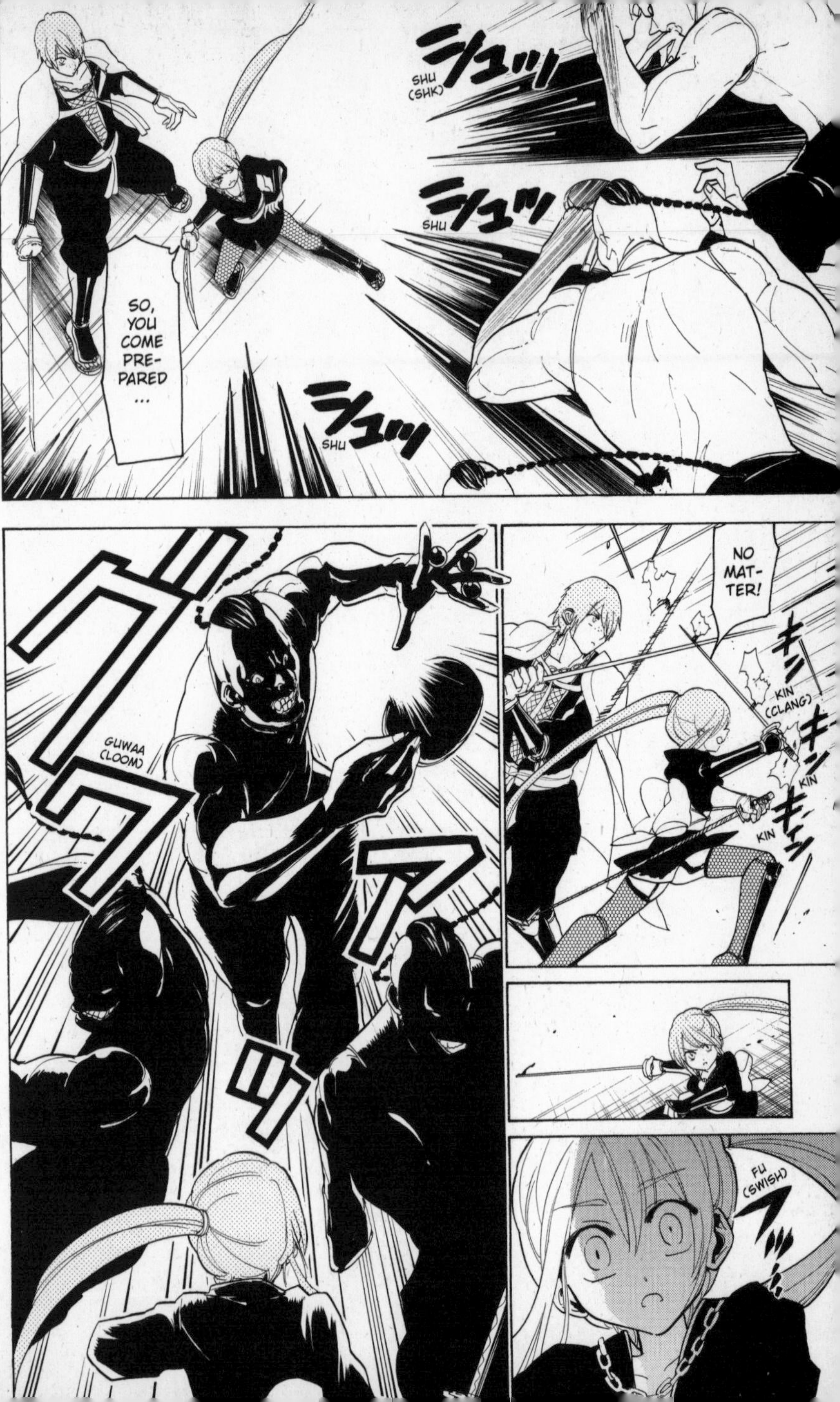
SHU (SHK)
SHU
SO, YOU COME PRE-PARED...
SHU
NO MAT-TER!
KIN (CLANG)
KIN
KIN
FU (SWISH)
GUWAA (LOOM)

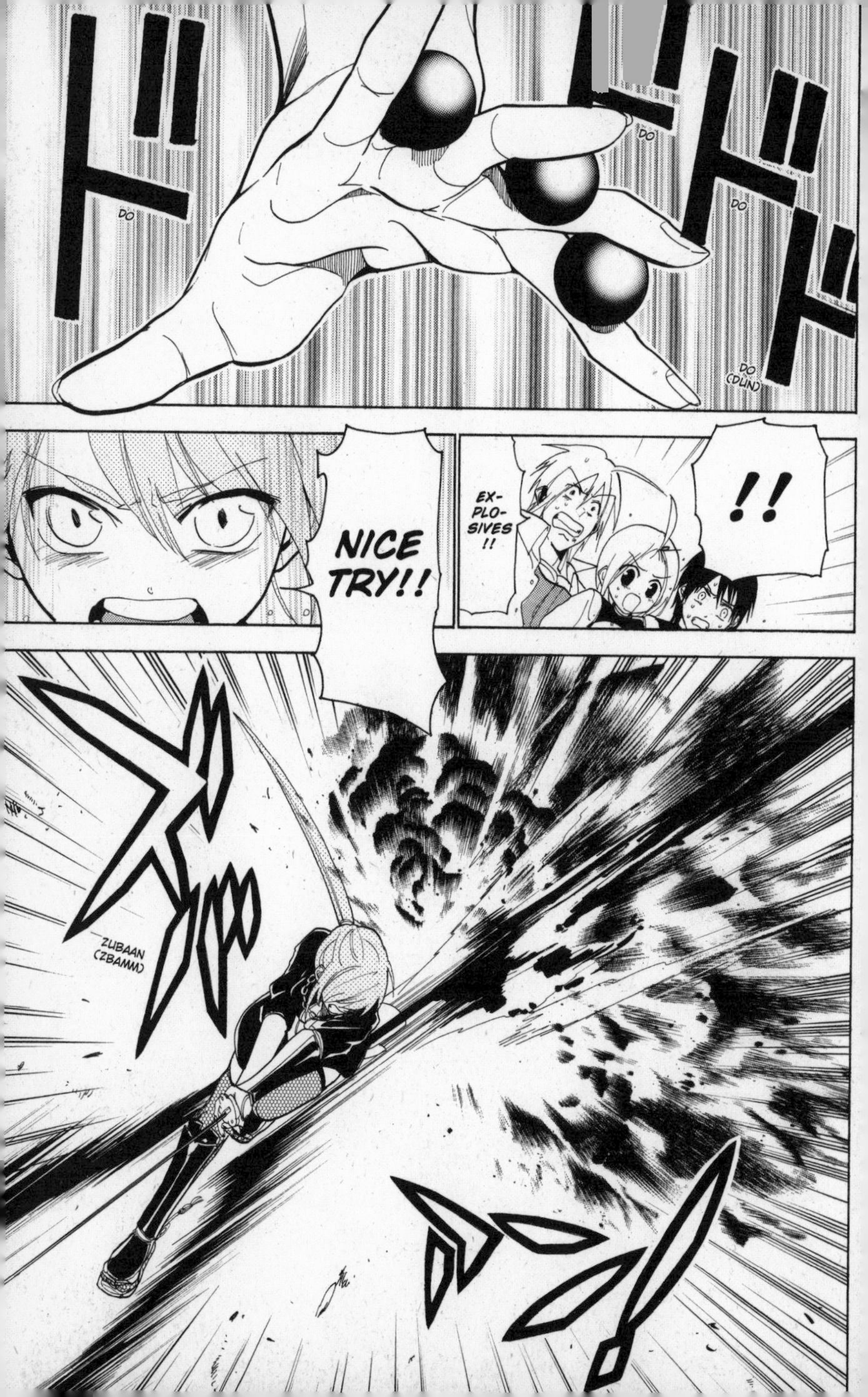
DO
DO
DO (DUN)
DO
!!
EX-PLO-SIVES!!
NICE TRY!!
ZUBAAN (ZBAMM)

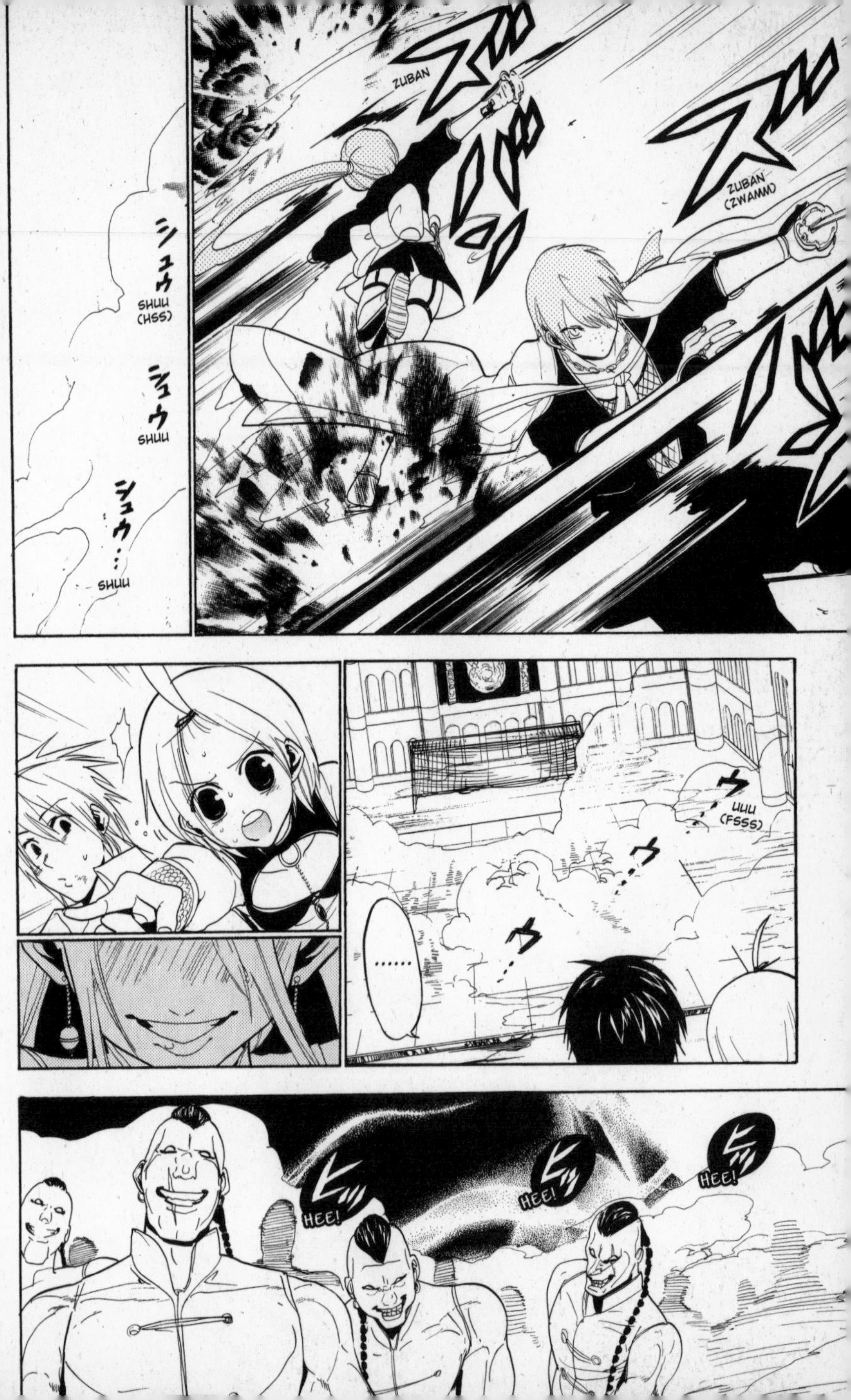

ZUBAN (ZWAMM)
ZUBAN
シュウ
SHUU (HSS)
シュウ
SHUU
シュウ…
SHUU
ウ
UUU (FSSS)
……
HEE!
HEE!
HEE!

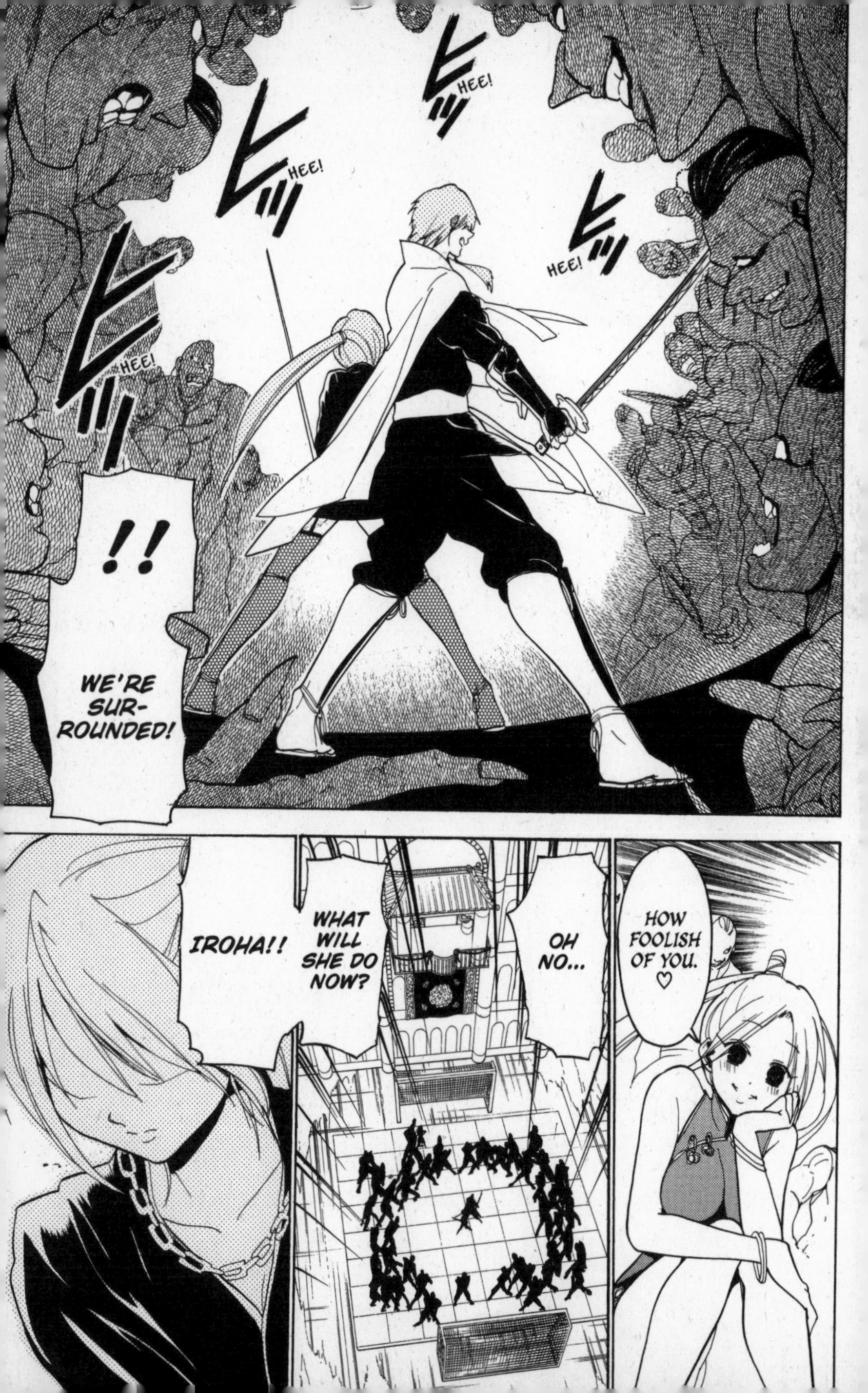
HEE!
HEE!
HEE!
HEE!
!!
WE'RE SUR-ROUNDED!
HOW FOOLISH OF YOU. ♡
OH NO...
WHAT WILL SHE DO NOW?
IROHA!!

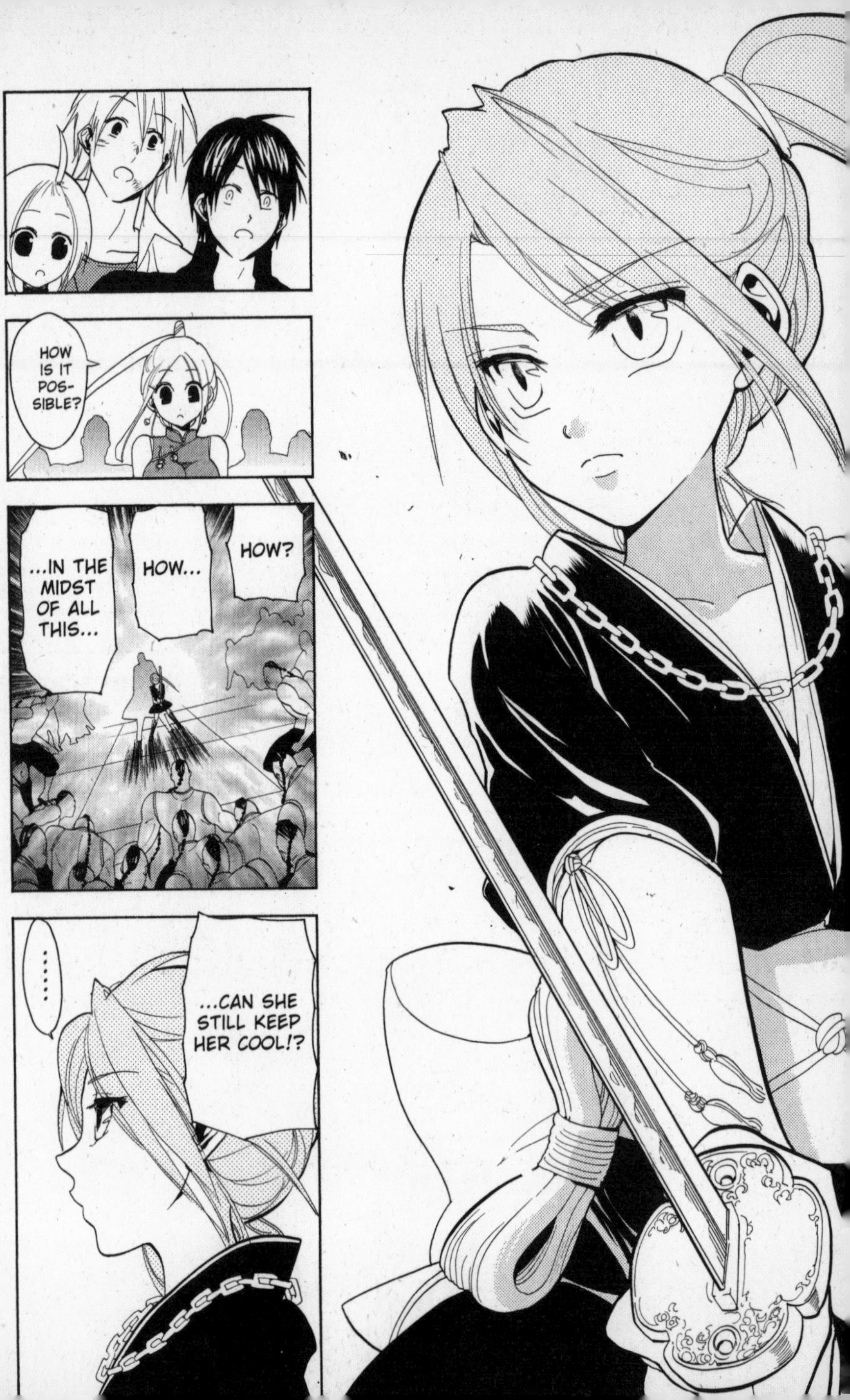
HOW IS IT POS-SIBLE?
HOW?
HOW...
...IN THE MIDST OF ALL THIS...
...CAN SHE STILL KEEP HER COOL!?
......

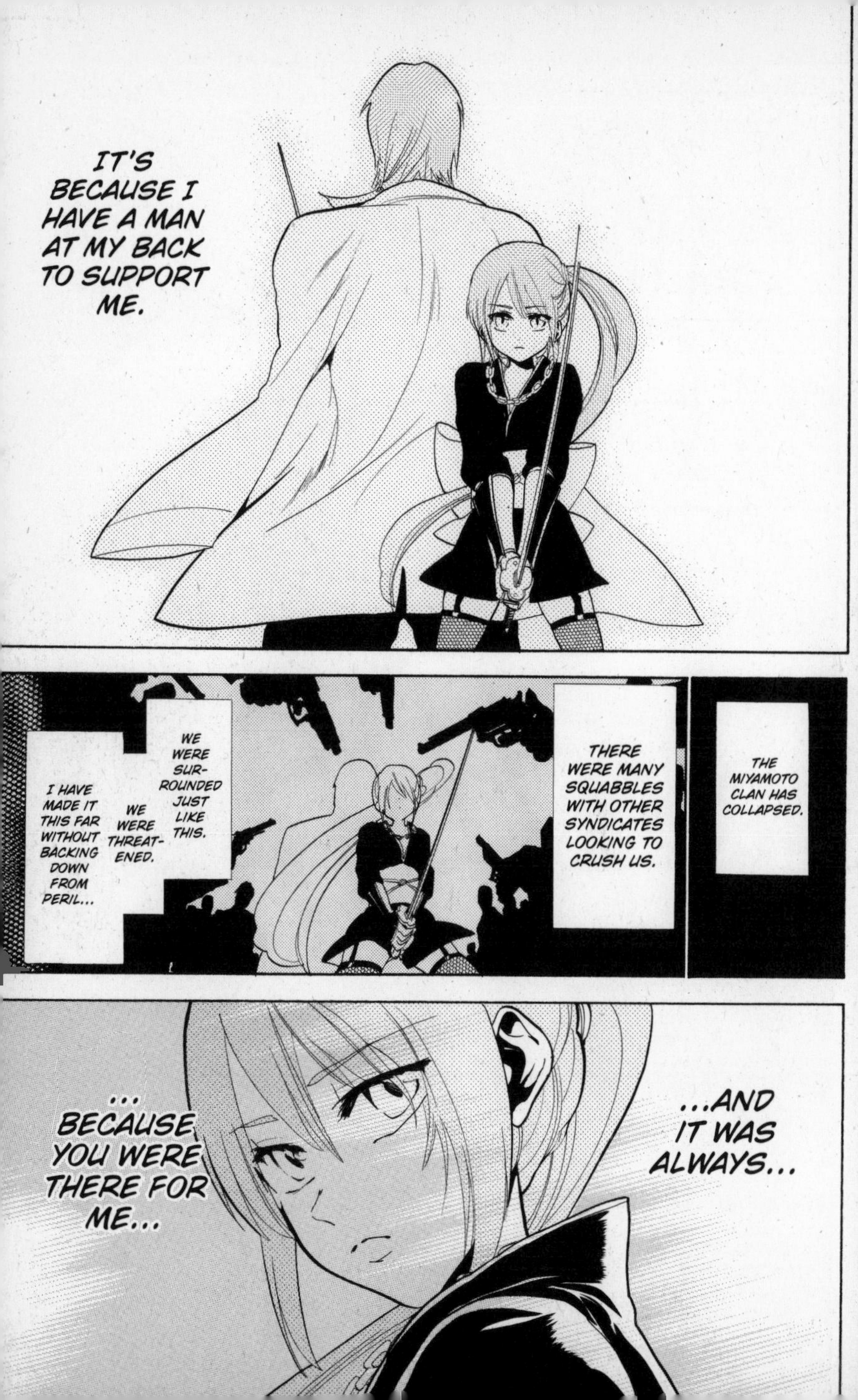
IT'S BECAUSE I HAVE A MAN AT MY BACK TO SUPPORT ME.
THE MIYAMOTO CLAN HAS COLLAPSED.
THERE WERE MANY SQUABBLES WITH OTHER SYNDICATES LOOKING TO CRUSH US.
WE WERE SUR-ROUNDED JUST LIKE THIS.
WE WERE THREAT-ENED.
I HAVE MADE IT THIS FAR WITHOUT BACKING DOWN FROM PERIL...
...AND IT WAS ALWAYS...
...BECAUSE YOU WERE THERE FOR ME...

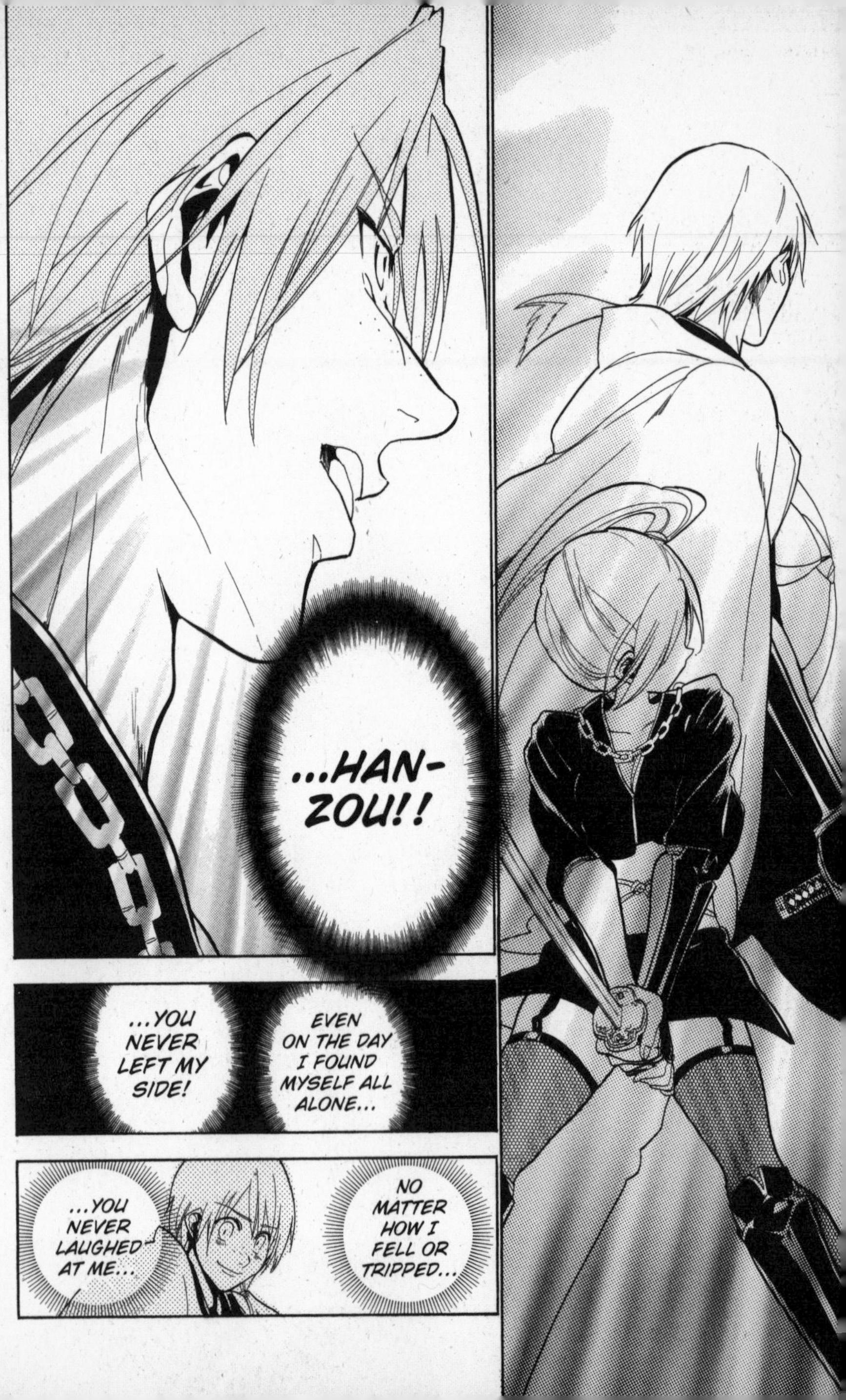
...HAN-ZOU!!
EVEN ON THE DAY I FOUND MYSELF ALL ALONE...
...YOU NEVER LEFT MY SIDE!
NO MATTER HOW I FELL OR TRIPPED...
...YOU NEVER LAUGHED AT ME...

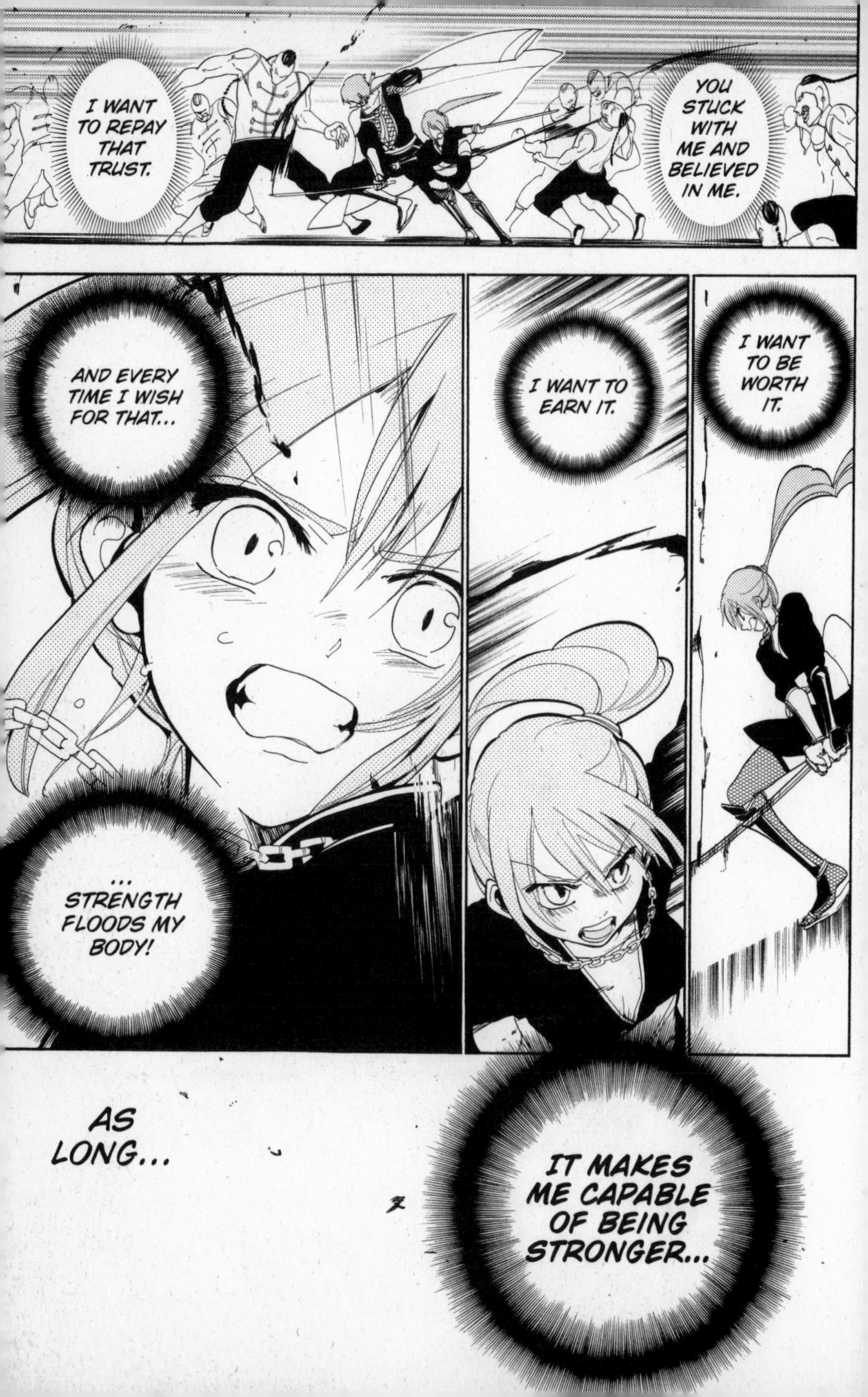
YOU STUCK WITH ME AND BELIEVED IN ME.
I WANT TO REPAY THAT TRUST.
I WANT TO BE WORTH IT.
I WANT TO EARN IT.
AND EVERY TIME I WISH FOR THAT...
... STRENGTH FLOODS MY BODY!
IT MAKES ME CAPABLE OF BEING STRONGER...
AS LONG...

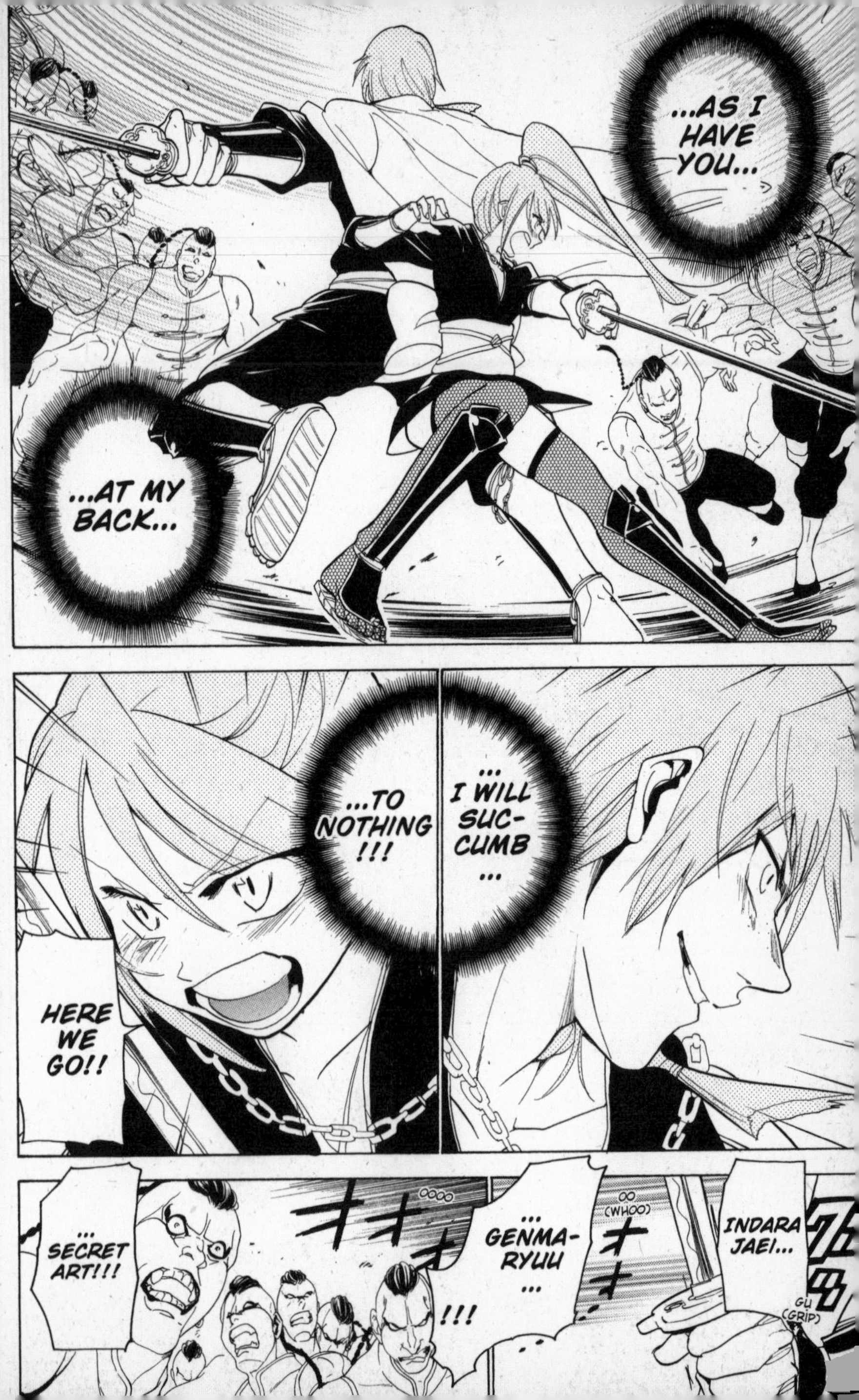
...AS I HAVE YOU...
...AT MY BACK...
... I WILL SUC-CUMB ...
...TO NOTHING!!!
HERE WE GO!!
INDARA JAEI...
GU (GRIP)
... GENMA-RYUU ...
OO (WHOO)
OOOO
!!!
... SECRET ART!!!

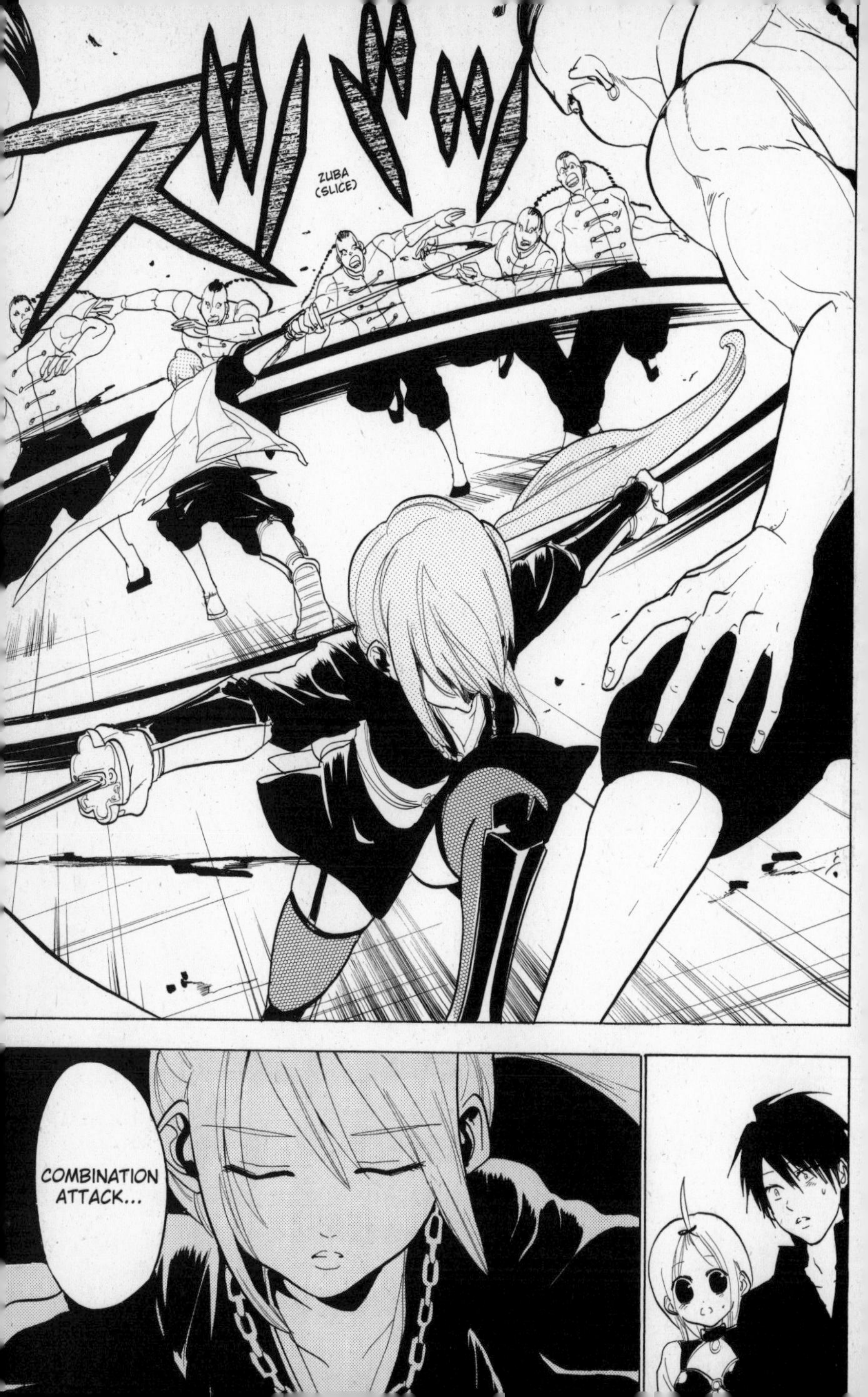
ZUBA (SLICE)
COMBINATION ATTACK...

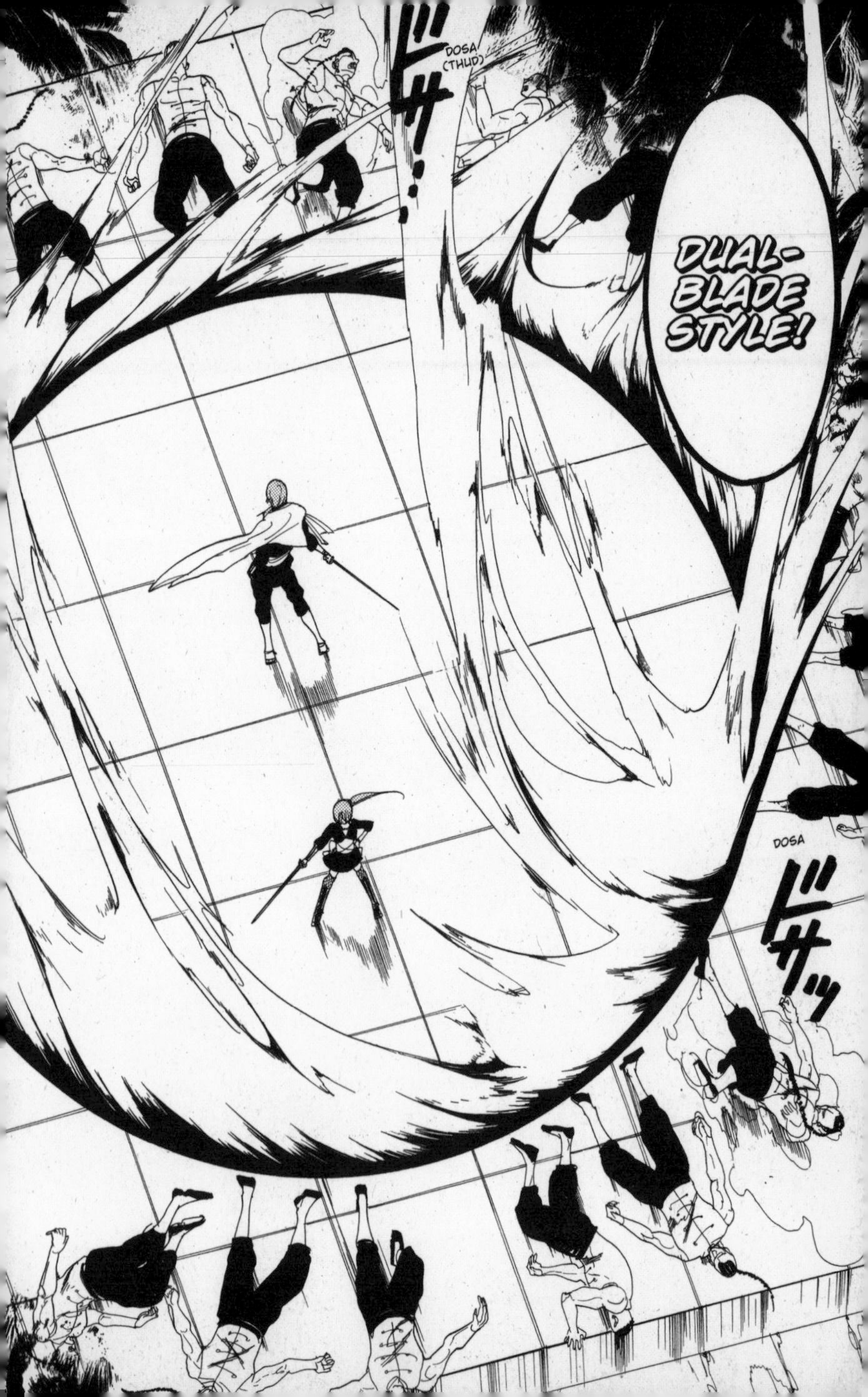

DUAL-BLADE STYLE!
ドサ!!
DOSA (THUD)
ドサッ
DOSA

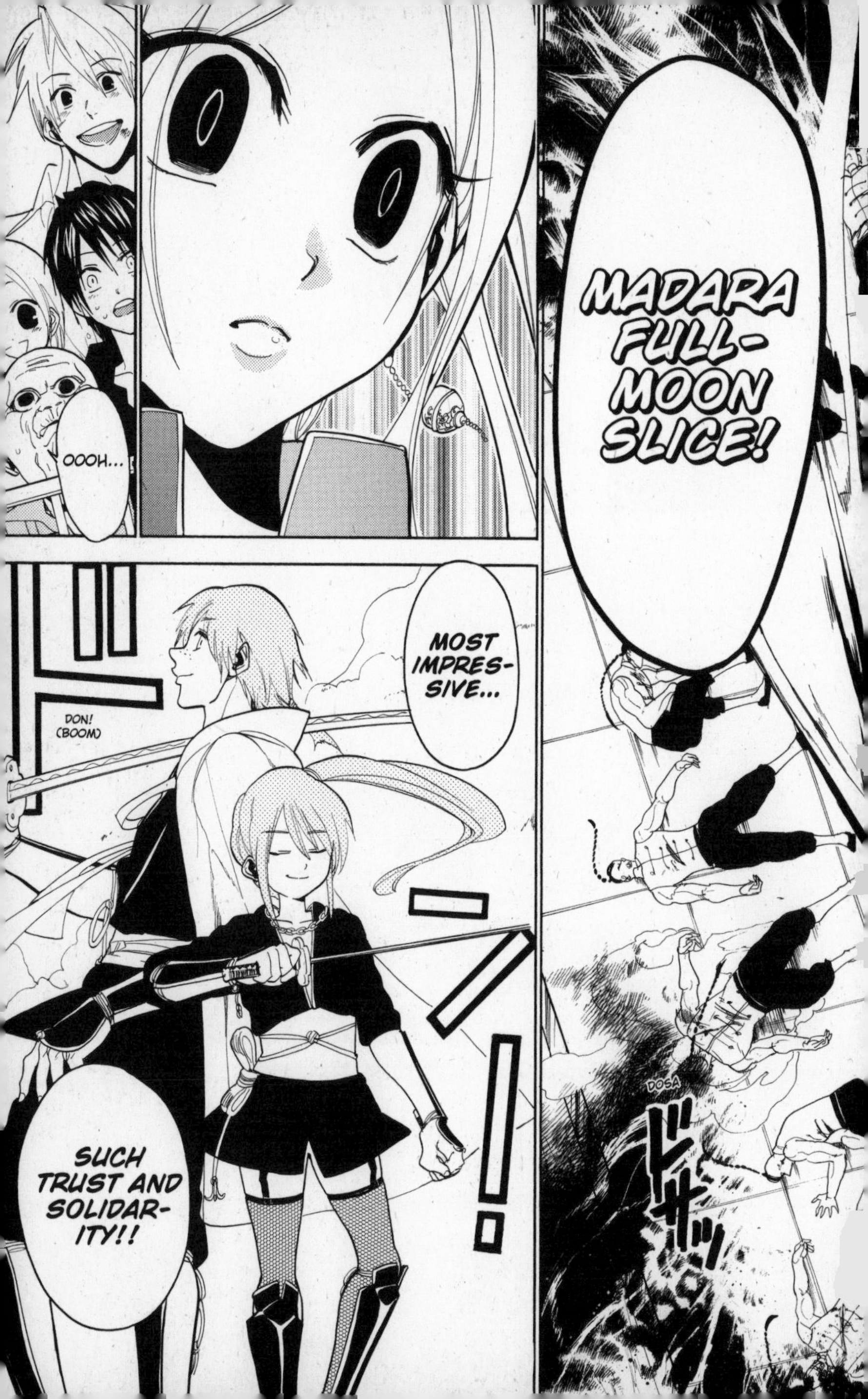
MADARA FULL-MOON SLICE!
DOSA
OOOH...
MOST IMPRES-SIVE...
DON! (BOOM)
SUCH TRUST AND SOLIDAR-ITY!!

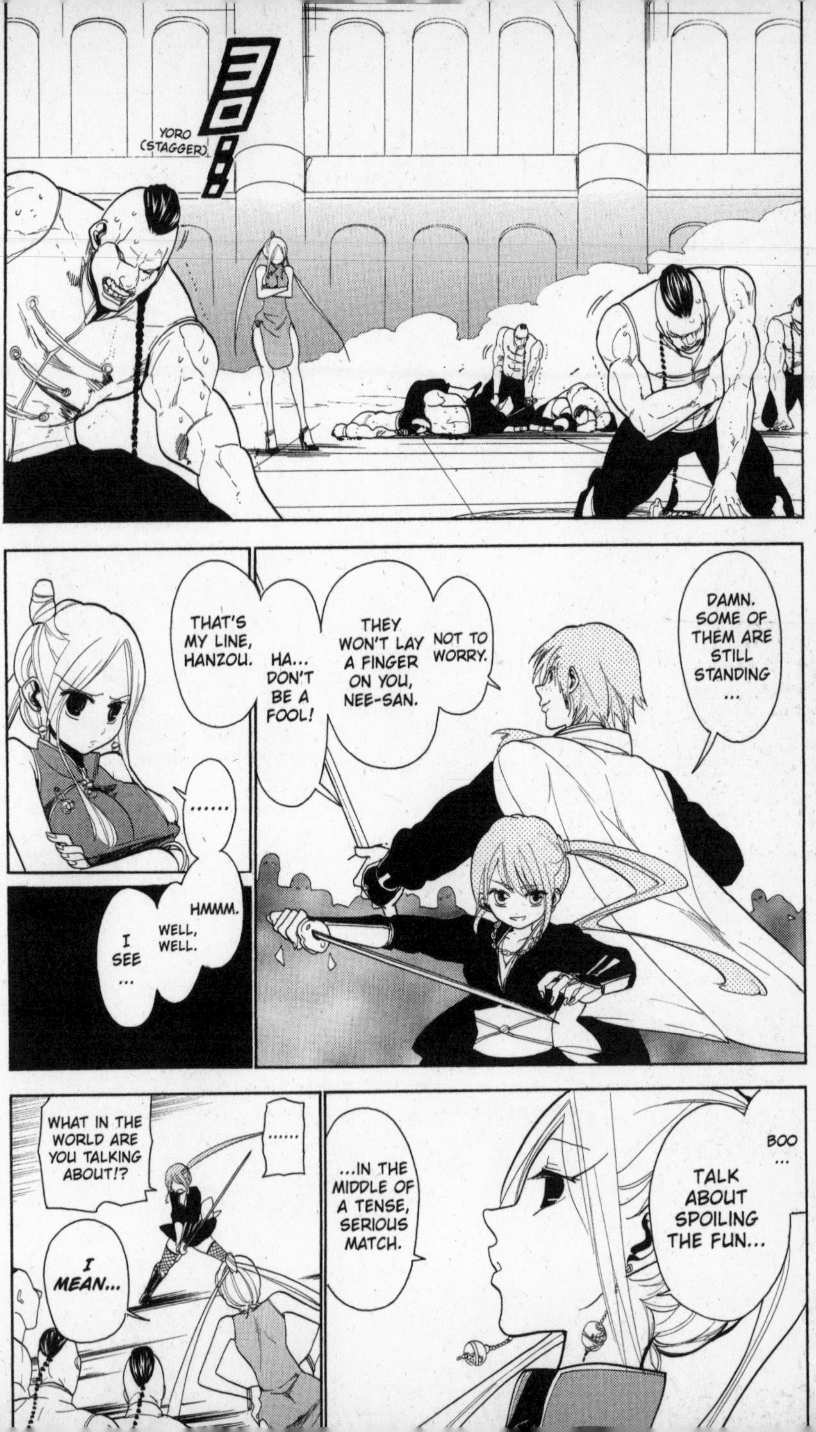
YORO (STAGGER)
DAMN. SOME OF THEM ARE STILL STANDING ...
NOT TO WORRY.
THEY WON'T LAY A FINGER ON YOU, NEE-SAN.
HA... DON'T BE A FOOL!
THAT'S MY LINE, HANZOU.
......
HMMM.
WELL, WELL.
I SEE ...
BOO ...
TALK ABOUT SPOILING THE FUN...
...IN THE MIDDLE OF A TENSE, SERIOUS MATCH.
......
WHAT IN THE WORLD ARE YOU TALKING ABOUT!?
I MEAN...

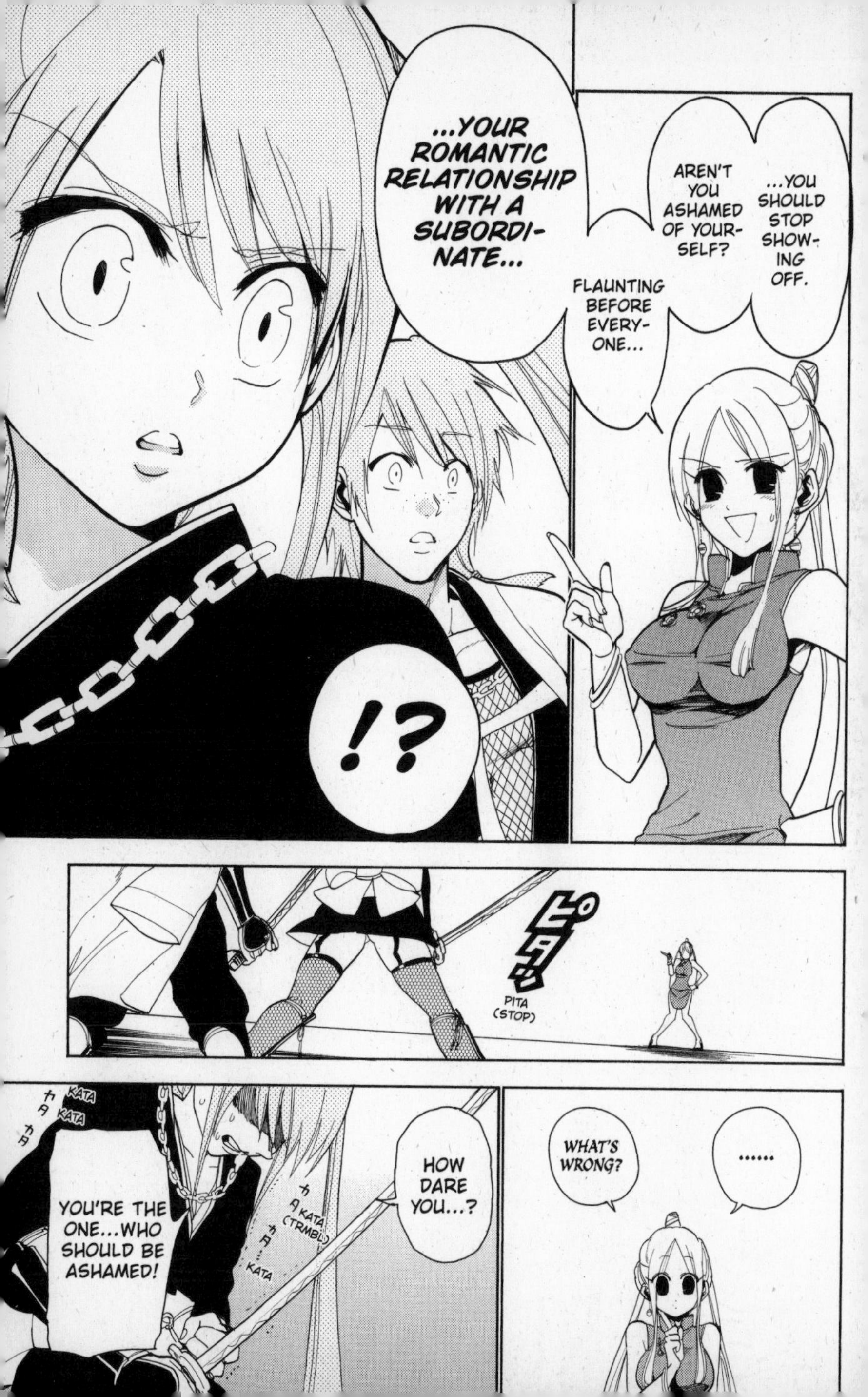
...YOU SHOULD STOP SHOWING-OFF.
AREN'T YOU ASHAMED OF YOUR-SELF?
FLAUNTING BEFORE EVERY-ONE...
...YOUR ROMANTIC RELATIONSHIP WITH A SUBORDI-NATE...
!?
ピタッ
PITA (STOP)
......
WHAT'S WRONG?
カタ KATA (TRMBL)
カタ... KATA
HOW DARE YOU...?
カタ KATA
カタ KATA
YOU'RE THE ONE...WHO SHOULD BE ASHAMED!

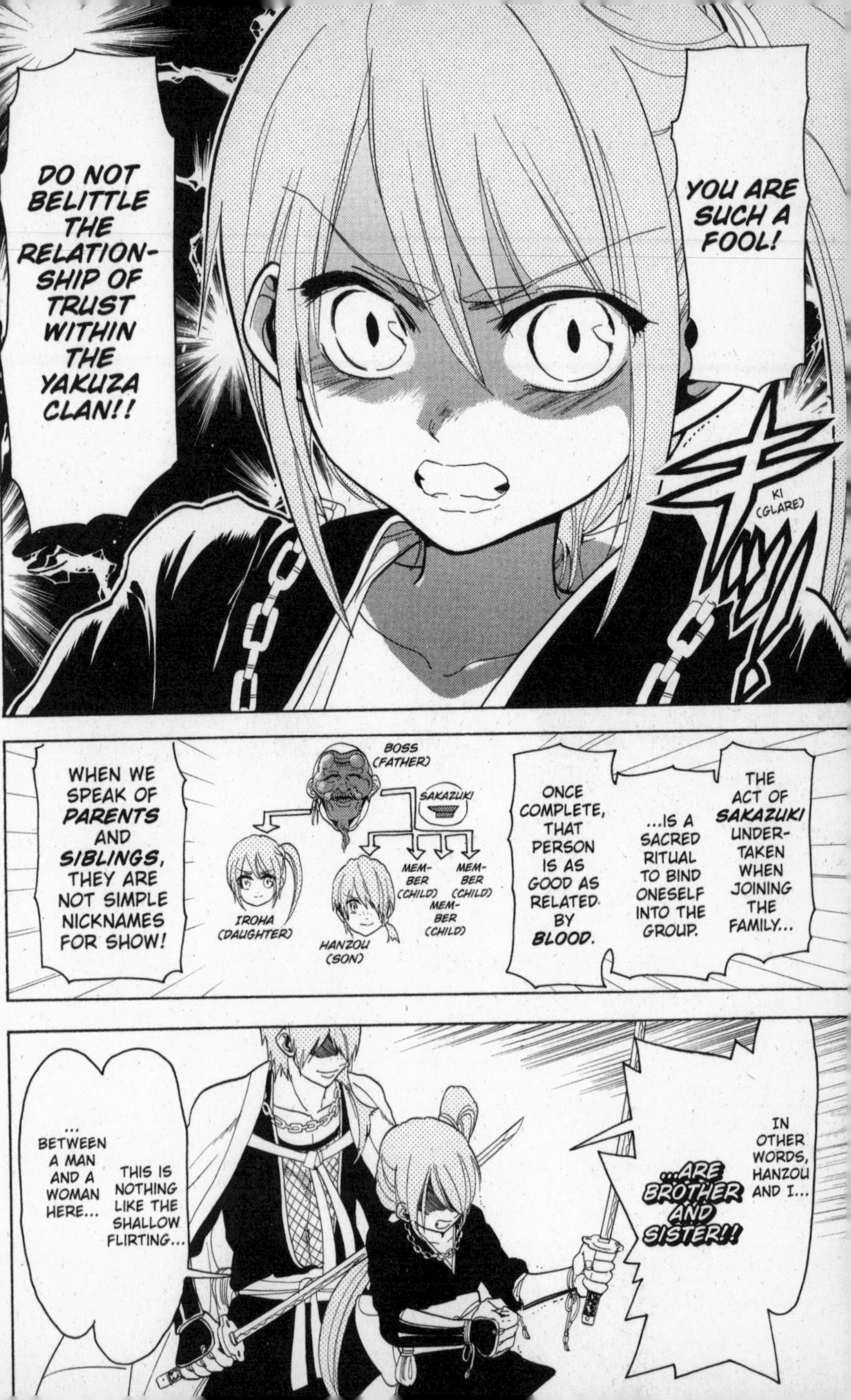
YOU ARE SUCH A FOOL!
DO NOT BELITTLE THE RELATIONSHIP OF TRUST WITHIN THE YAKUZA CLAN!!
KI (GLARE)
THE ACT OF SAKAZUKI UNDERTAKEN WHEN JOINING THE FAMILY...
...IS A SACRED RITUAL TO BIND ONESELF INTO THE GROUP.
ONCE COMPLETE, THAT PERSON IS AS GOOD AS RELATED BY BLOOD.
BOSS (FATHER)
SAKAZUKI
MEMBER (CHILD)
MEMBER (CHILD)
MEMBER (CHILD)
HANZOU (SON)
IROHA (DAUGHTER)
WHEN WE SPEAK OF PARENTS AND SIBLINGS, THEY ARE NOT SIMPLE NICKNAMES FOR SHOW!
IN OTHER WORDS, HANZOU AND I...
...ARE BROTHER AND SISTER!!
THIS IS NOTHING LIKE THE SHALLOW FLIRTING...
...BETWEEN A MAN AND A WOMAN HERE...

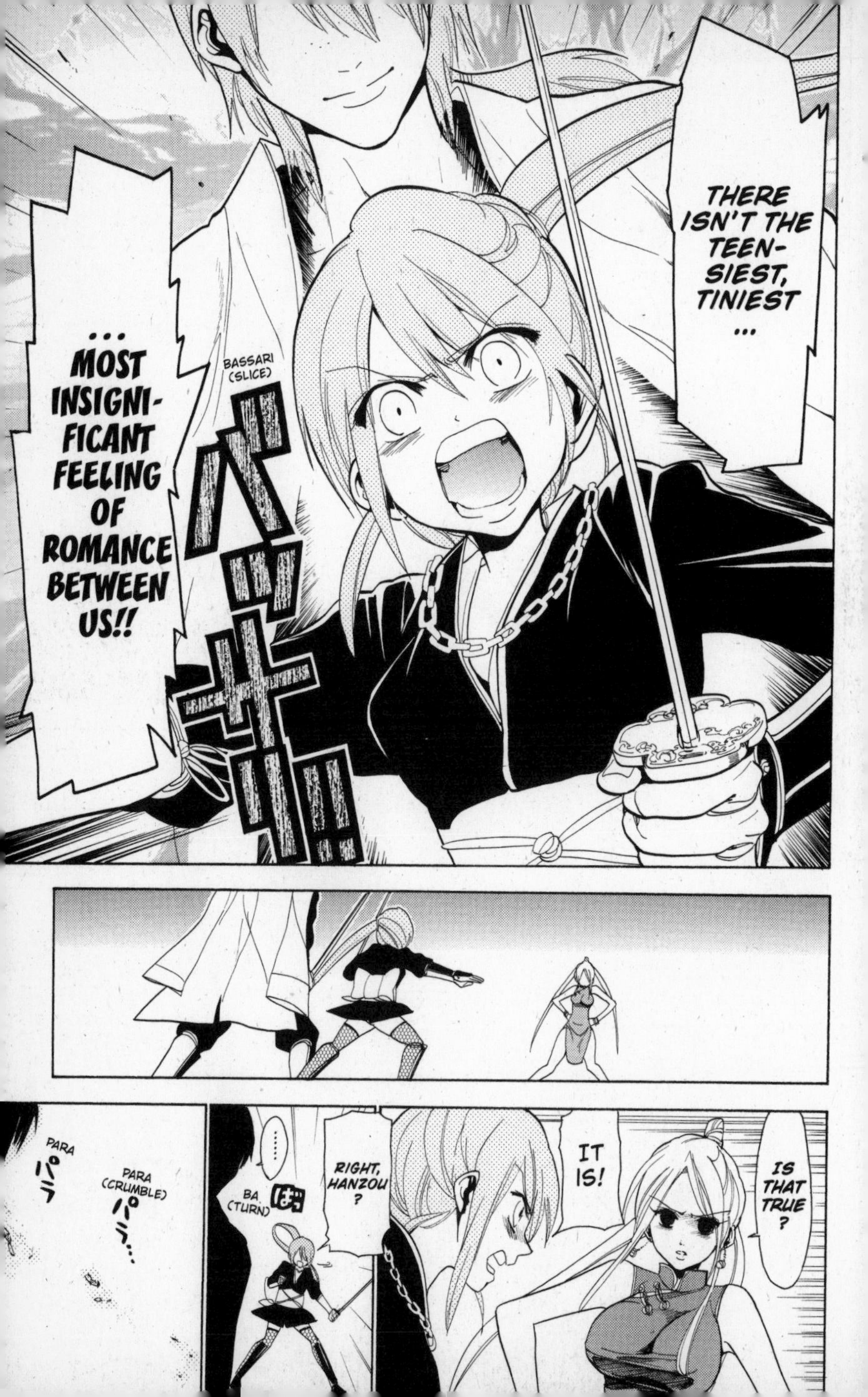
THERE ISN'T THE TEEN-SIEST, TINIEST ...
BASSARI (SLICE)
... MOST INSIGNI-FICANT FEELING OF ROMANCE BETWEEN US!!
IS THAT TRUE?
IT IS!
RIGHT, HANZOU?
......
BA (TURN)
ぱっ
PARA
パラ
PARA (CRUMBLE)
パラ…

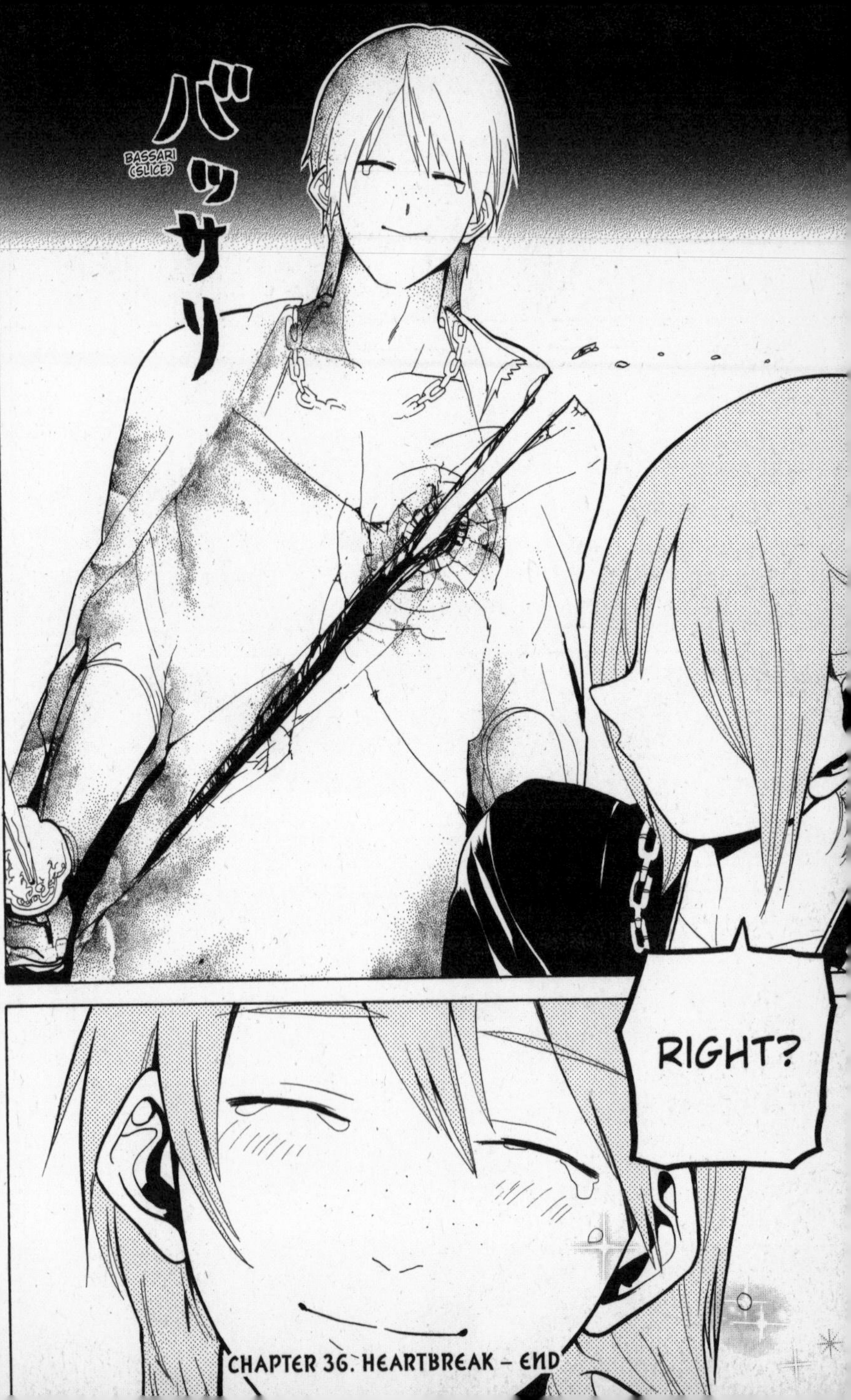
バッサリ
BASSARI (SLICE)
RIGHT?
CHAPTER 36. HEARTBREAK – END

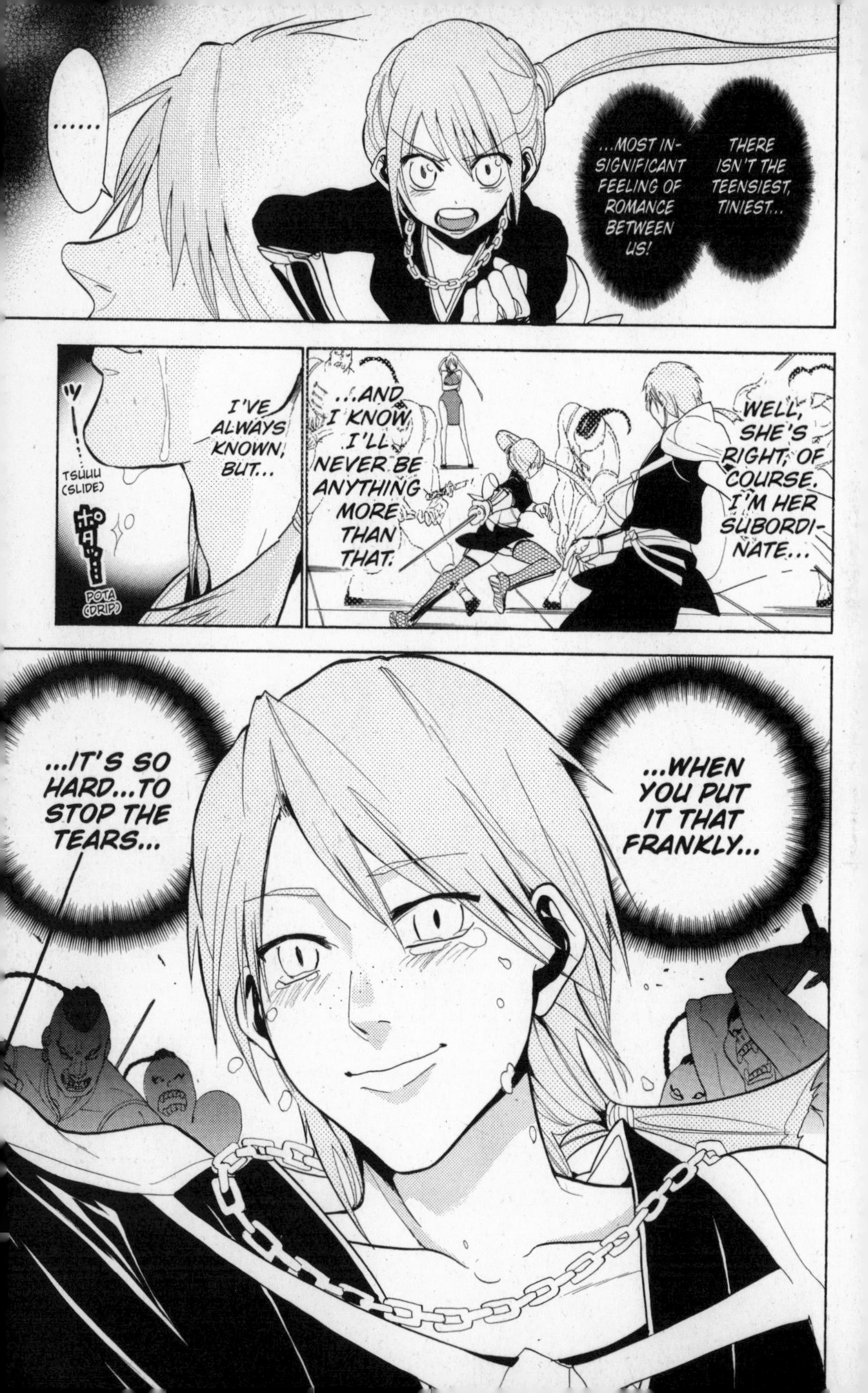
THERE ISN'T THE TEENSIEST, TINIEST...
...MOST IN-SIGNIFICANT FEELING OF ROMANCE BETWEEN US!
......
WELL, SHE'S RIGHT, OF COURSE. I'M HER SUBORDI-NATE...
...AND I KNOW I'LL NEVER BE ANYTHING MORE THAN THAT.
I'VE ALWAYS KNOWN, BUT...
TSUUU (SLIDE)
POTA (DRIP)
...WHEN YOU PUT IT THAT FRANKLY...
...IT'S SO HARD...TO STOP THE TEARS...

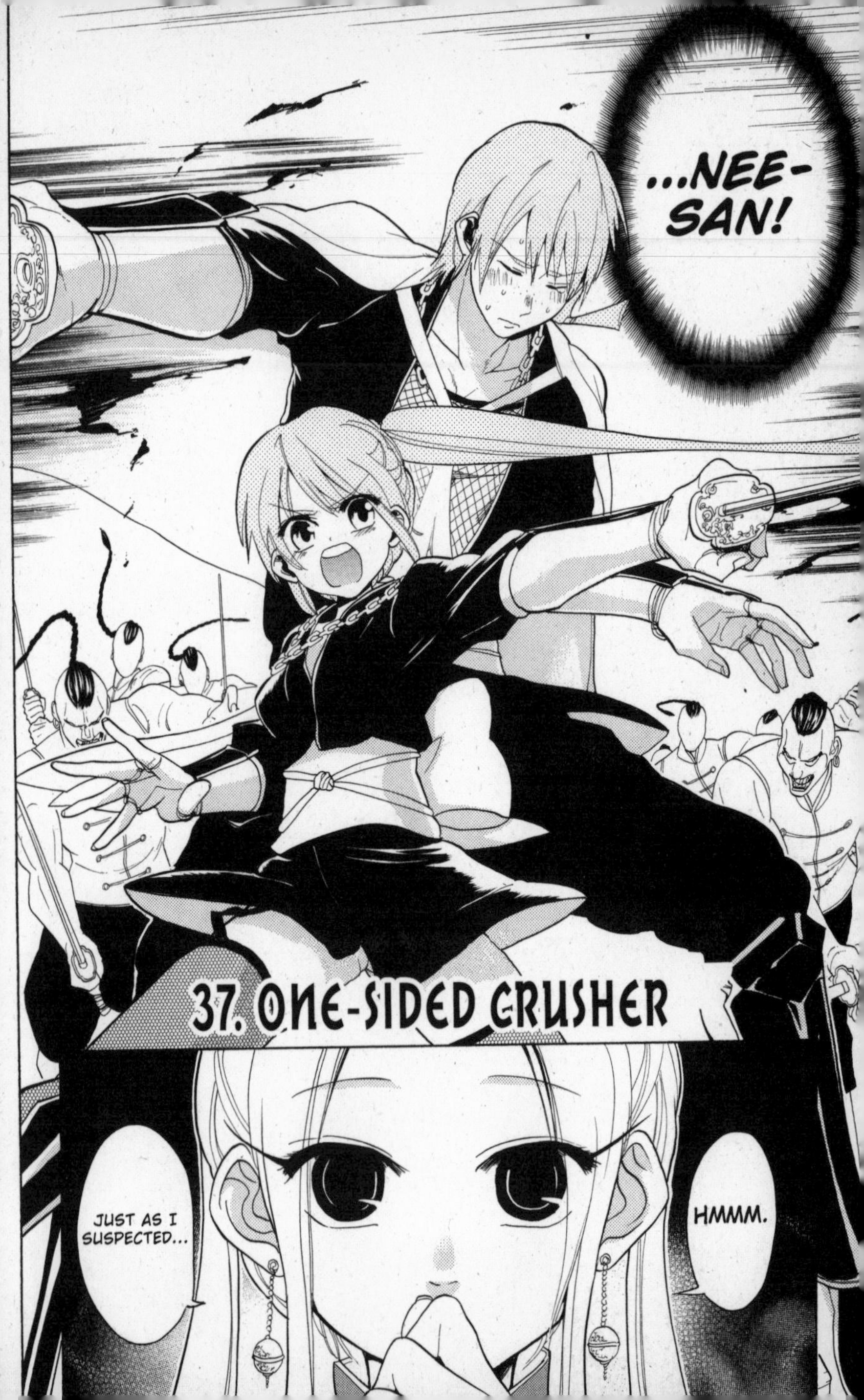
...NEE-SAN!
37. ONE-SIDED CRUSHER
HMMM.
JUST AS I SUSPECTED...

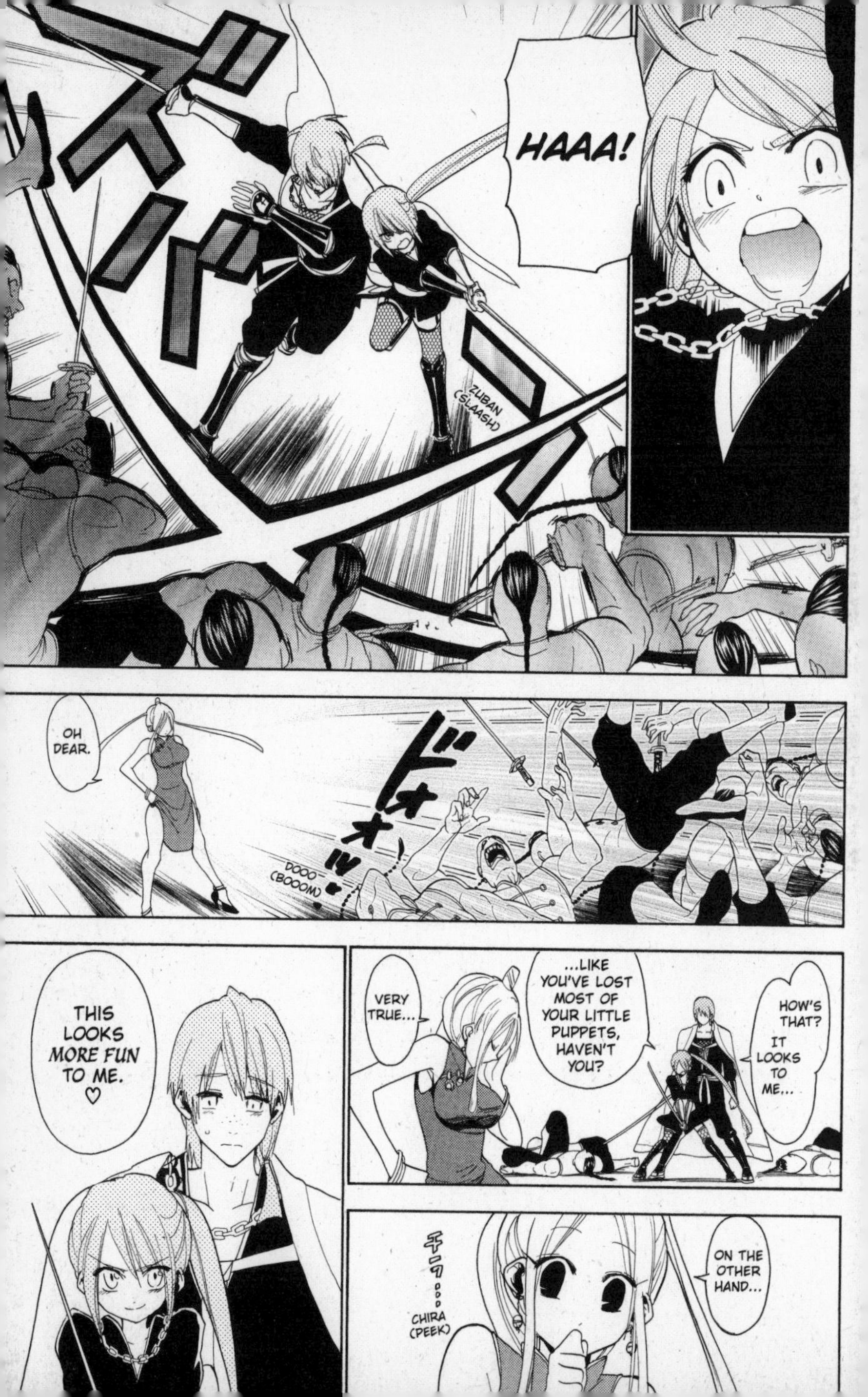
HAAA!
ZUBAN (SLAASH)
DOOO (BOOOM)
OH DEAR.
HOW'S THAT? IT LOOKS TO ME...
...LIKE YOU'VE LOST MOST OF YOUR LITTLE PUPPETS, HAVEN'T YOU?
VERY TRUE...
ON THE OTHER HAND...
CHIRA (PEEK)
THIS LOOKS MORE FUN TO ME. ♡

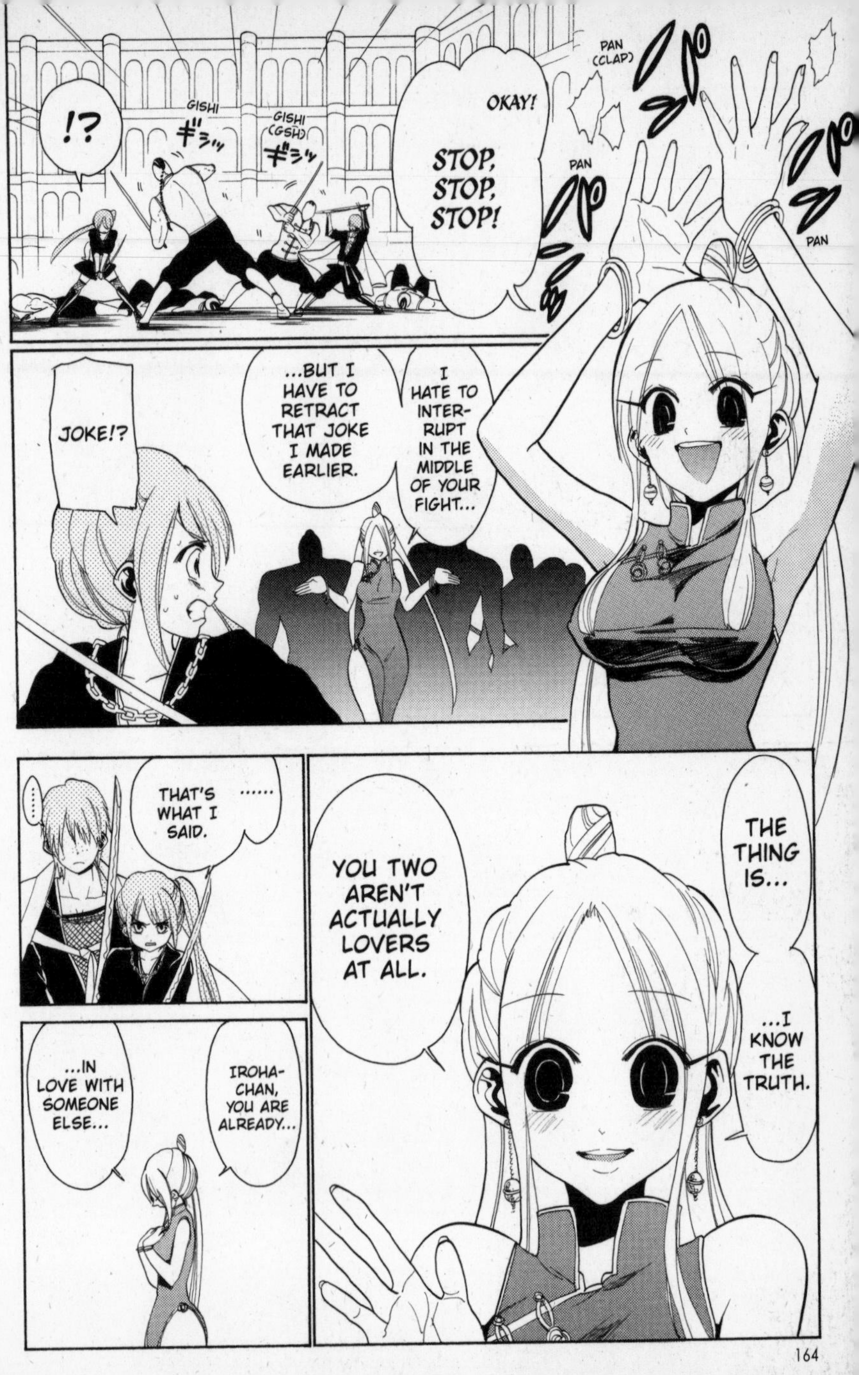
PAN (CLAP)
PAN
OKAY!
STOP, STOP, STOP!
PAN
GISHI (GSH)
GISHI
!?
I HATE TO INTER-RUPT IN THE MIDDLE OF YOUR FIGHT...
...BUT I HAVE TO RETRACT THAT JOKE I MADE EARLIER.
JOKE!?
THE THING IS...
...I KNOW THE TRUTH.
YOU TWO AREN'T ACTUALLY LOVERS AT ALL.
......
THAT'S WHAT I SAID.
...
IROHA-CHAN, YOU ARE ALREADY...
...IN LOVE WITH SOMEONE ELSE...

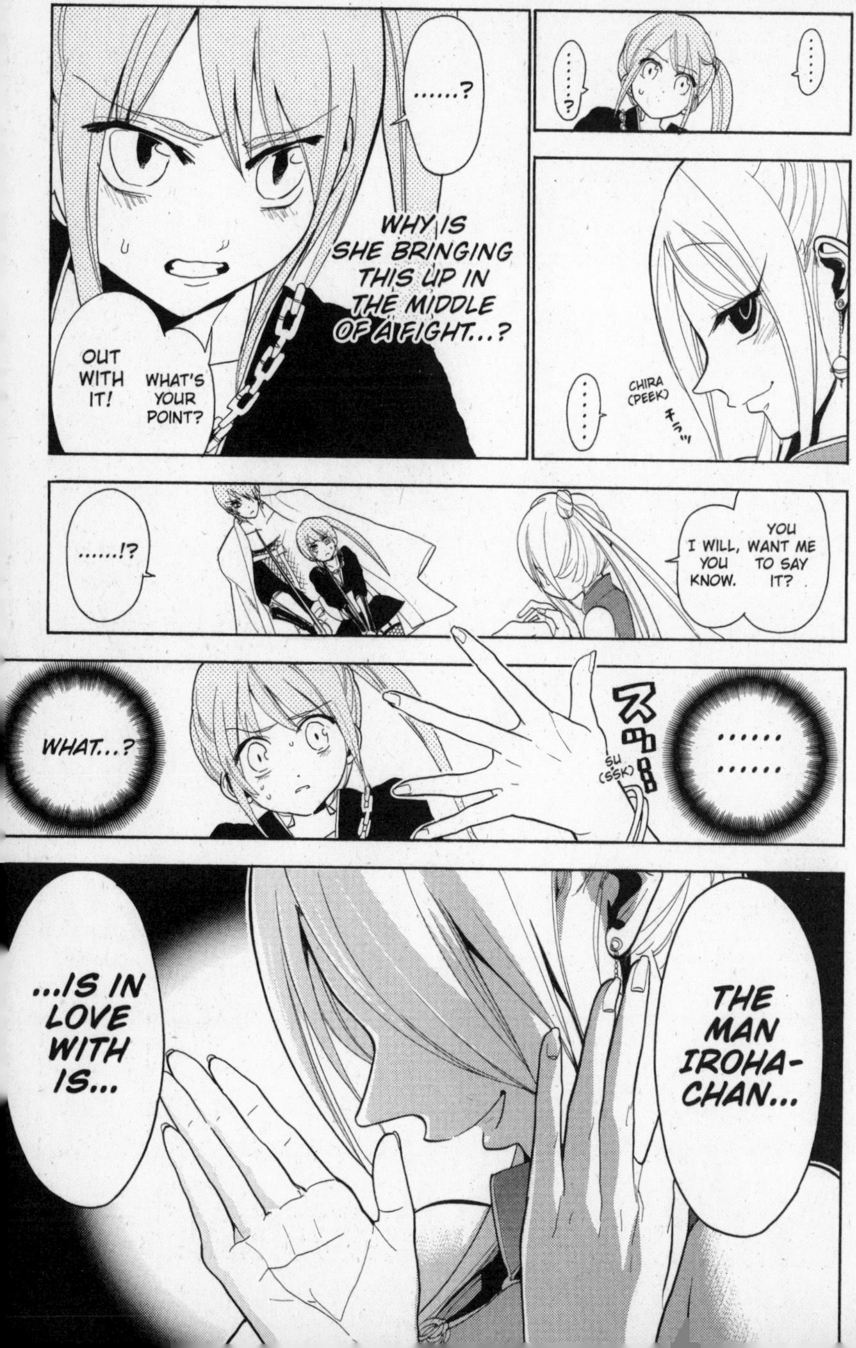
......
......?
......
CHIRA (PEEK)
......?
WHY IS SHE BRINGING THIS UP IN THE MIDDLE OF A FIGHT...?
WHAT'S YOUR POINT?
OUT WITH IT!
YOU WANT ME TO SAY IT?
I WILL, YOU KNOW.
......!?
....
SU (SSK)
WHAT...?
THE MAN IROHA-CHAN...
...IS IN LOVE WITH IS...

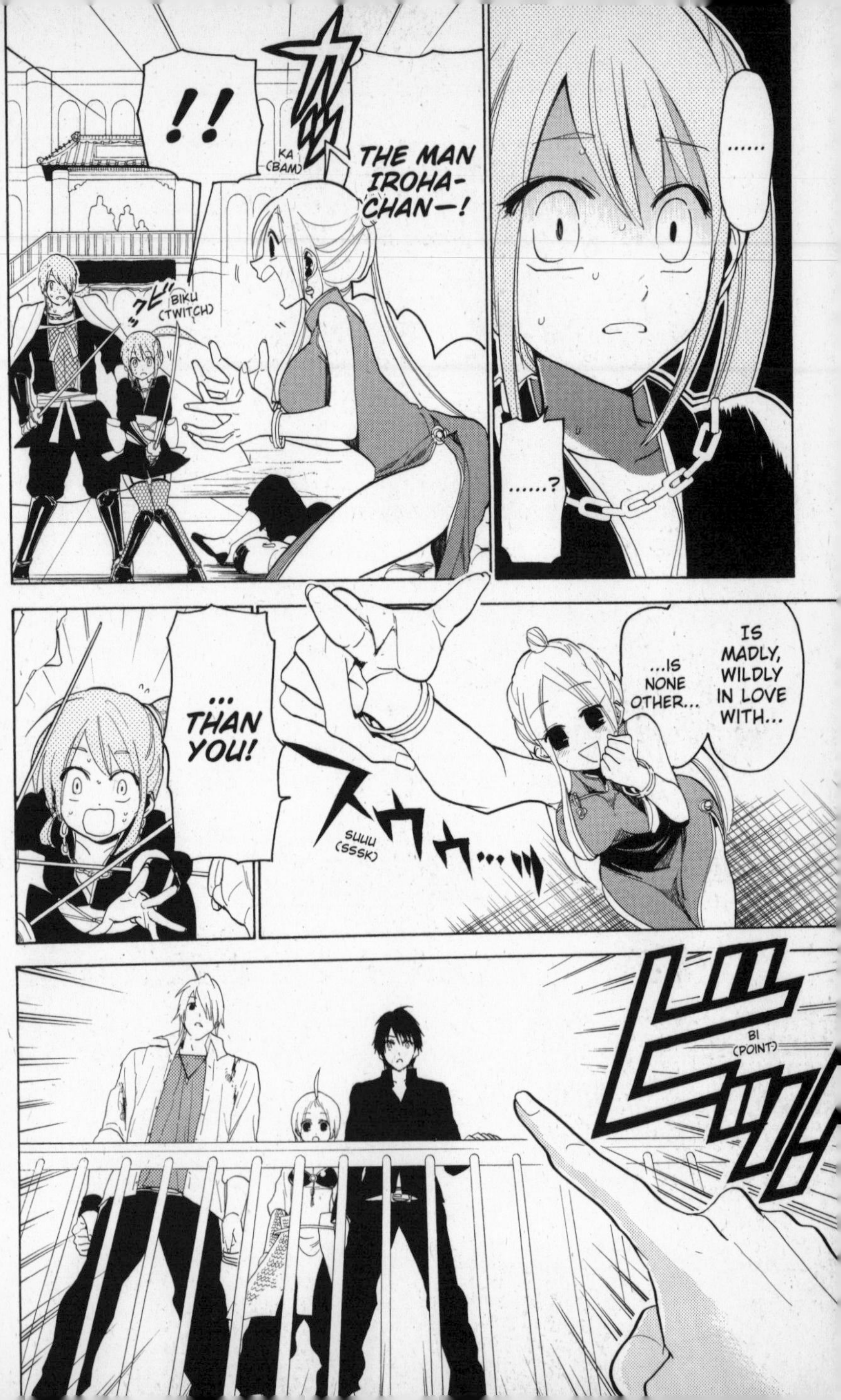
......
......?
KA (BAM)
THE MAN IROHA-CHAN—!
!!
BIKU (TWITCH)
IS MADLY, WILDLY IN LOVE WITH...
...IS NONE OTHER...
SUUU (SSSK)
... THAN YOU!
BI (POINT)

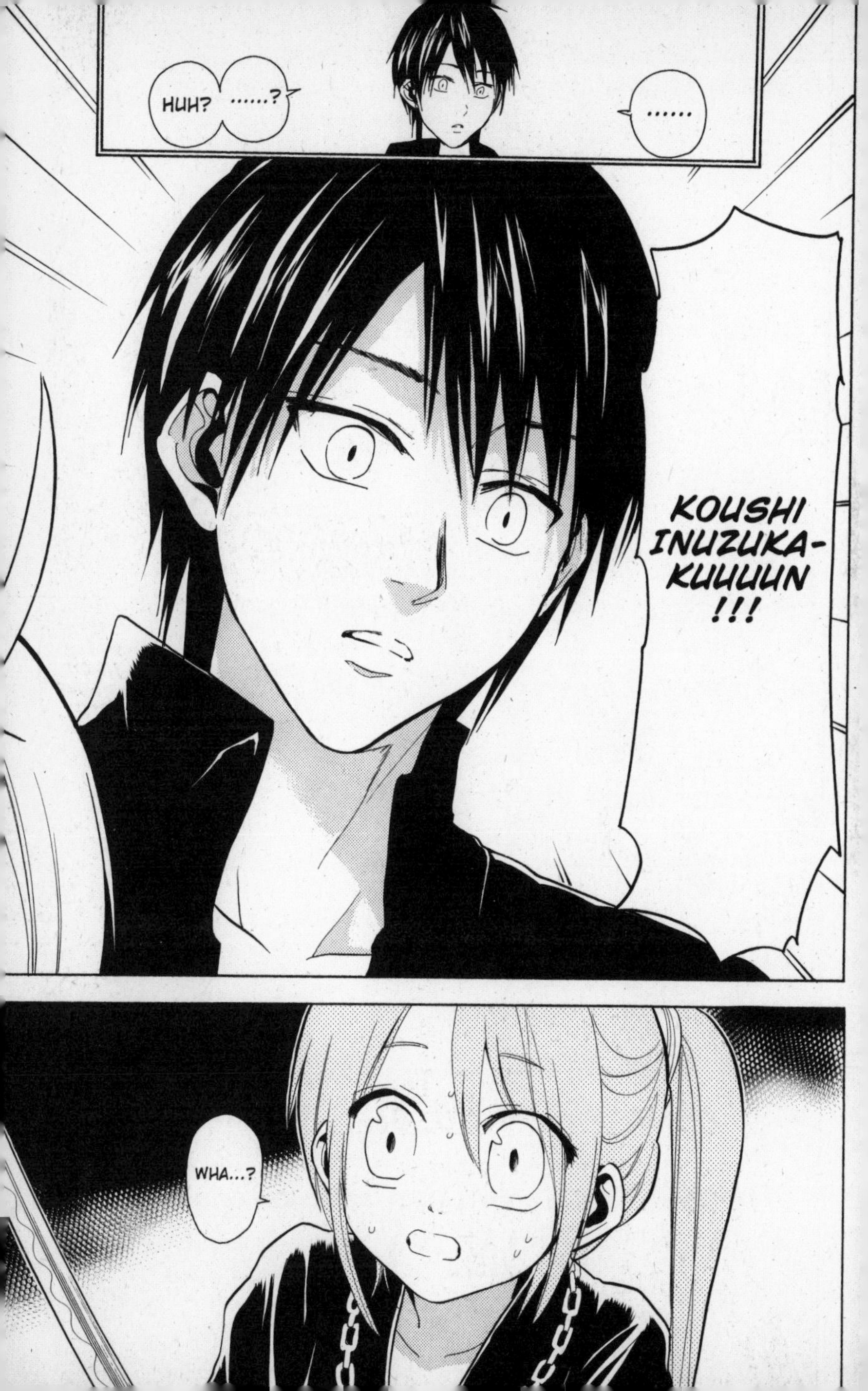

......
HUH?
......?
KOUSHI INUZUKA-KUUUUN !!!
WHA...?

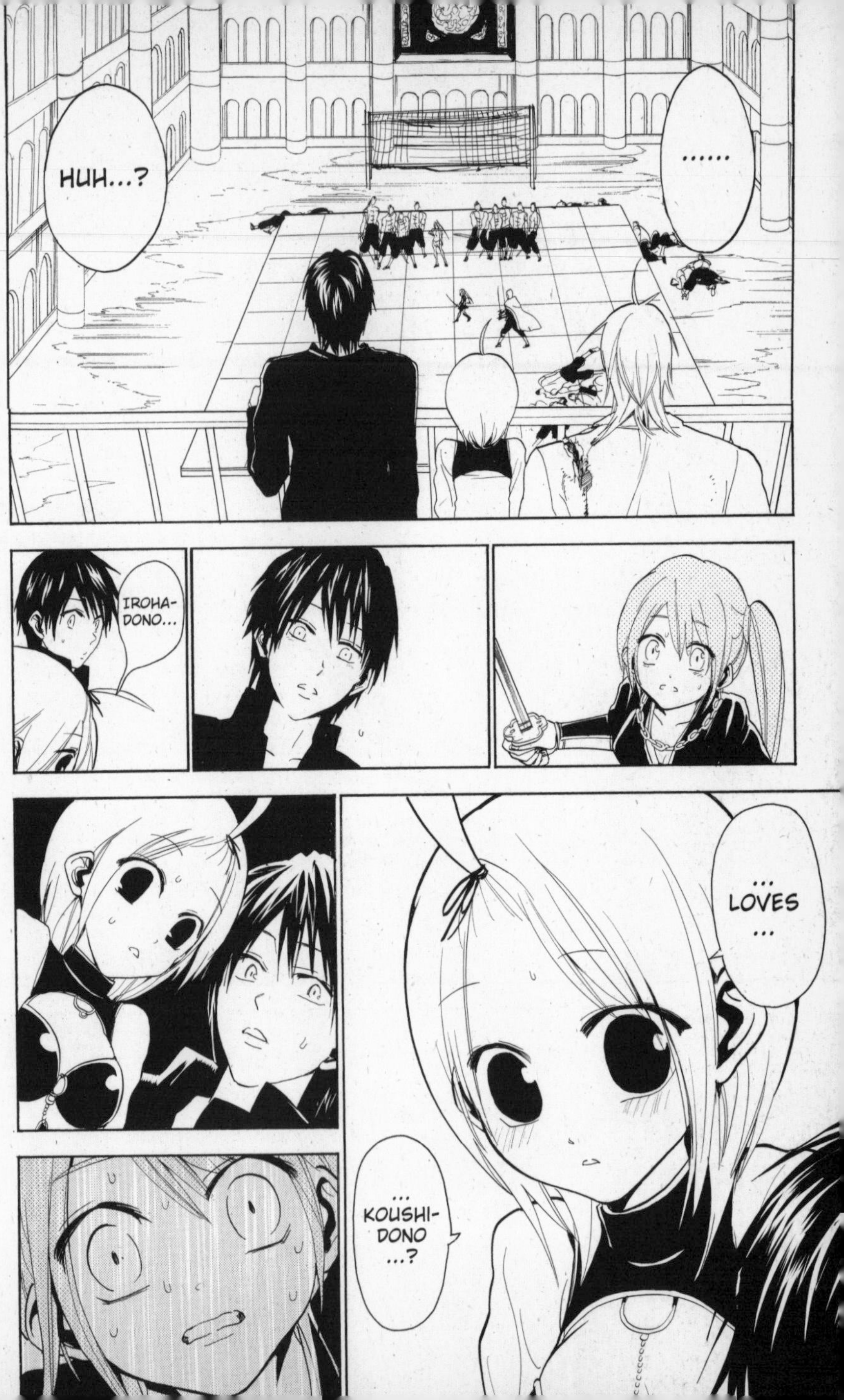
......
HUH...?
IROHA-DONO...
... LOVES ...
... KOUSHI-DONO ...?

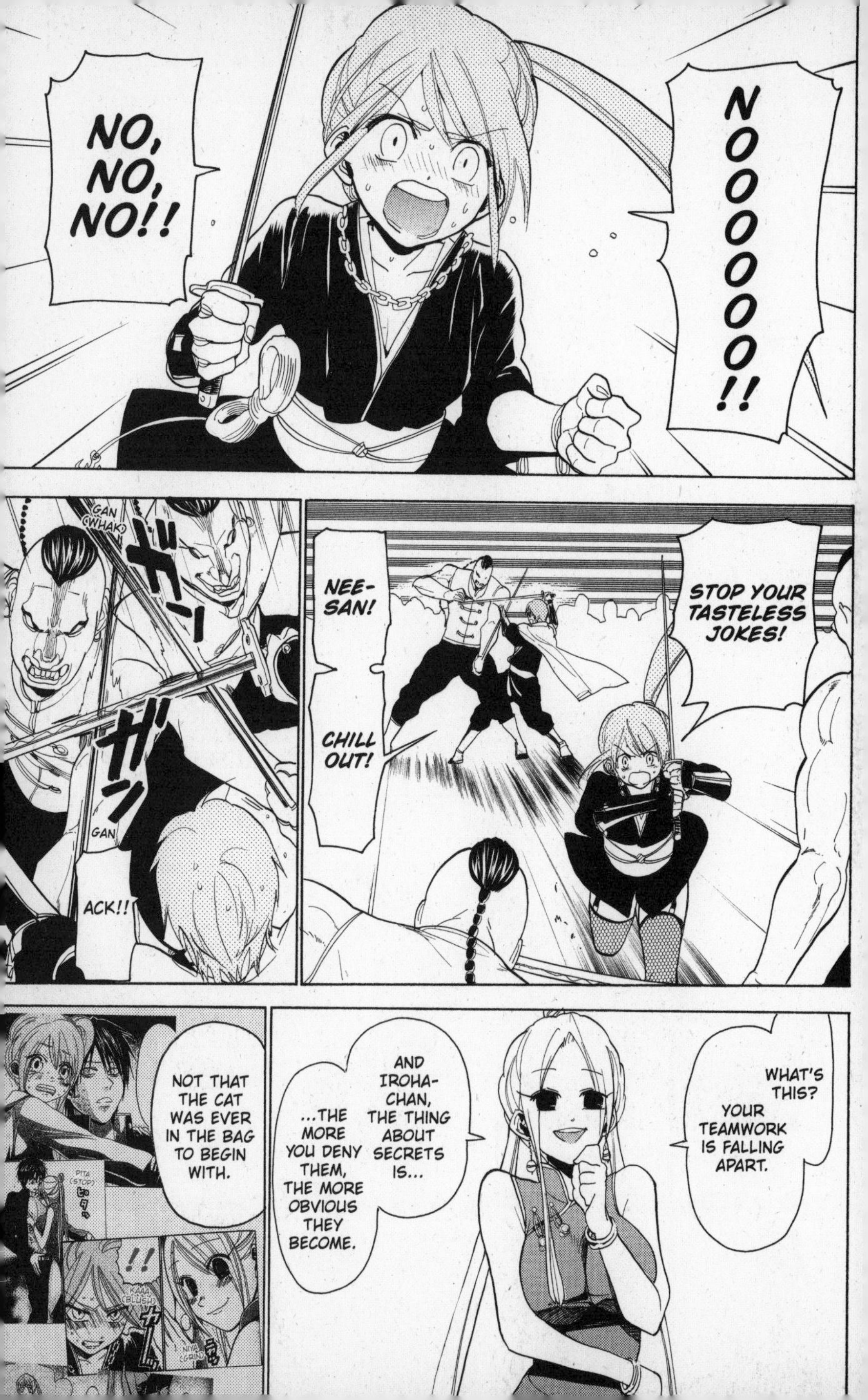
NOOOOOOO!!
NO, NO, NO!!
STOP YOUR TASTELESS JOKES!
NEE-SAN!
CHILL OUT!
GAN (WHAK)
ACK!!
GAN
WHAT'S THIS?
YOUR TEAMWORK IS FALLING APART.
AND IROHA-CHAN, THE THING ABOUT SECRETS IS...
...THE MORE YOU DENY THEM, THE MORE OBVIOUS THEY BECOME.
NOT THAT THE CAT WAS EVER IN THE BAG TO BEGIN WITH.
PITA (STOP)
!!
KAAA (BLUSH)
NIYA (GRIN)

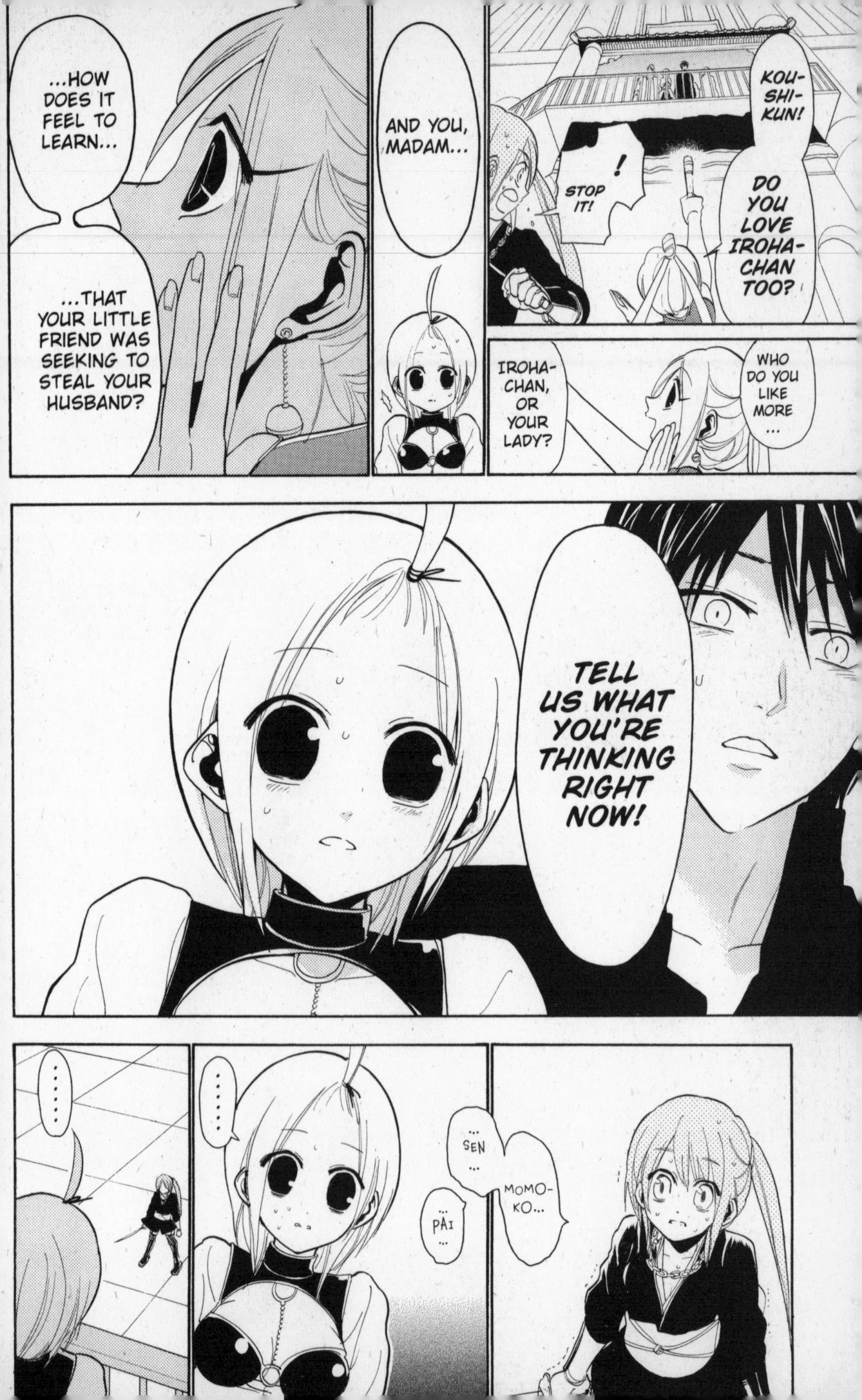
KOU-SHI-KUN!
DO YOU LOVE IROHA-CHAN TOO?
!
STOP IT!
WHO DO YOU LIKE MORE ...
IROHA-CHAN, OR YOUR LADY?
AND YOU, MADAM...
...HOW DOES IT FEEL TO LEARN...
...THAT YOUR LITTLE FRIEND WAS SEEKING TO STEAL YOUR HUSBAND?
TELL US WHAT YOU'RE THINKING RIGHT NOW!
...SEN...
MOMO-KO...
...PAI...
......
......

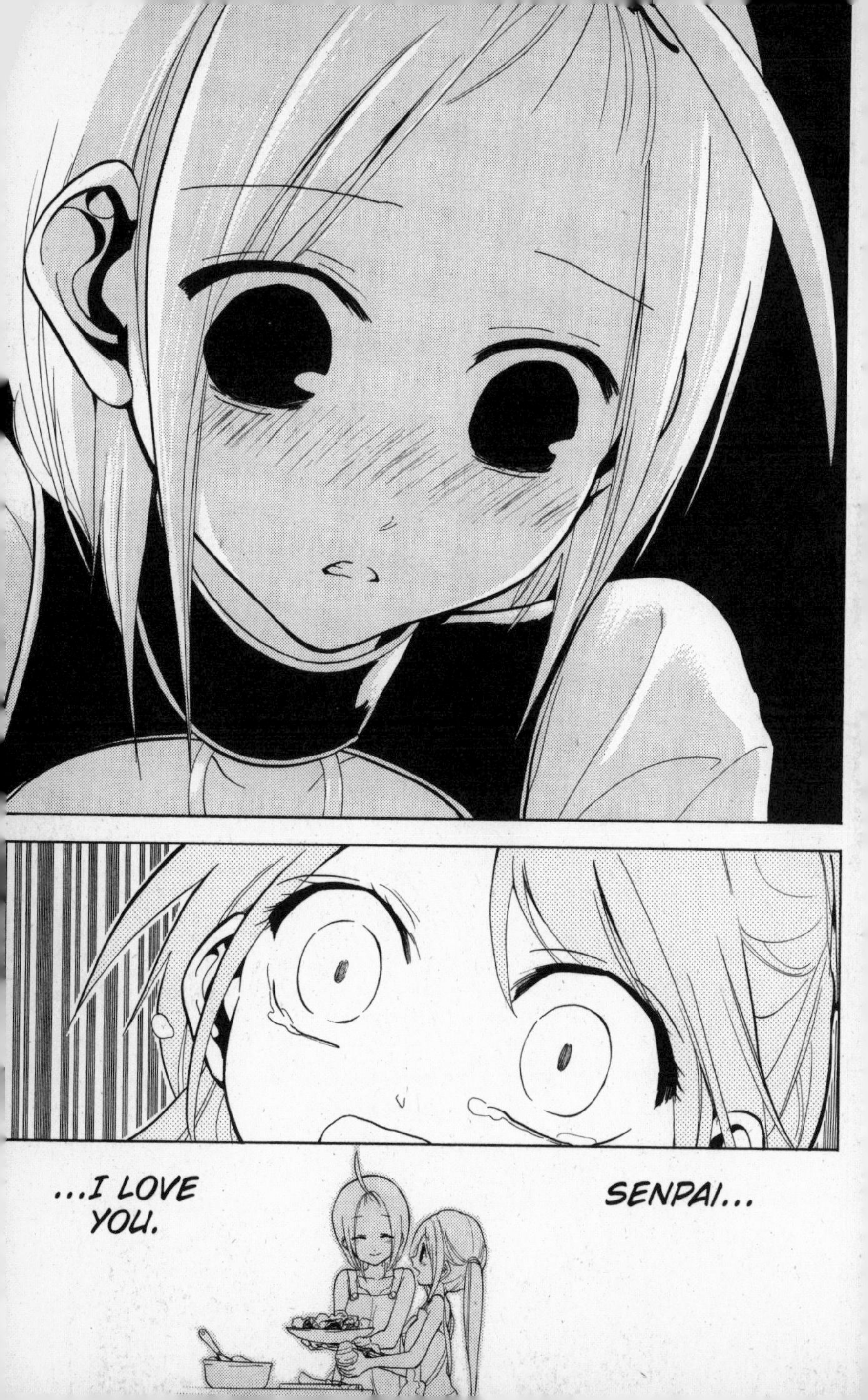
SENPAI...
...I LOVE YOU.

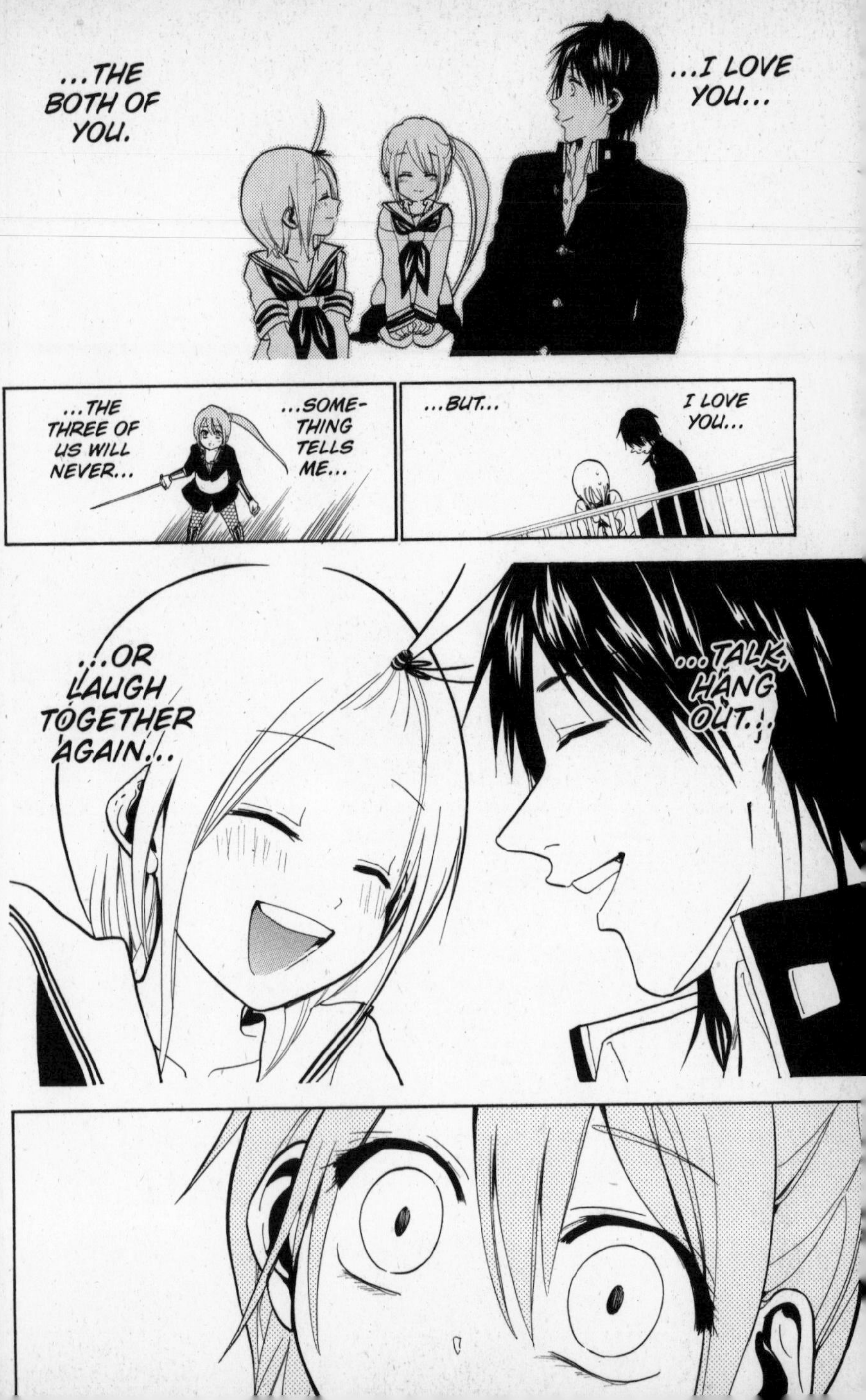
...I LOVE YOU...
...THE BOTH OF YOU.
I LOVE YOU...
...BUT...
...SOME-THING TELLS ME...
...THE THREE OF US WILL NEVER...
...TALK, HANG OUT...
...OR LAUGH TOGETHER AGAIN...

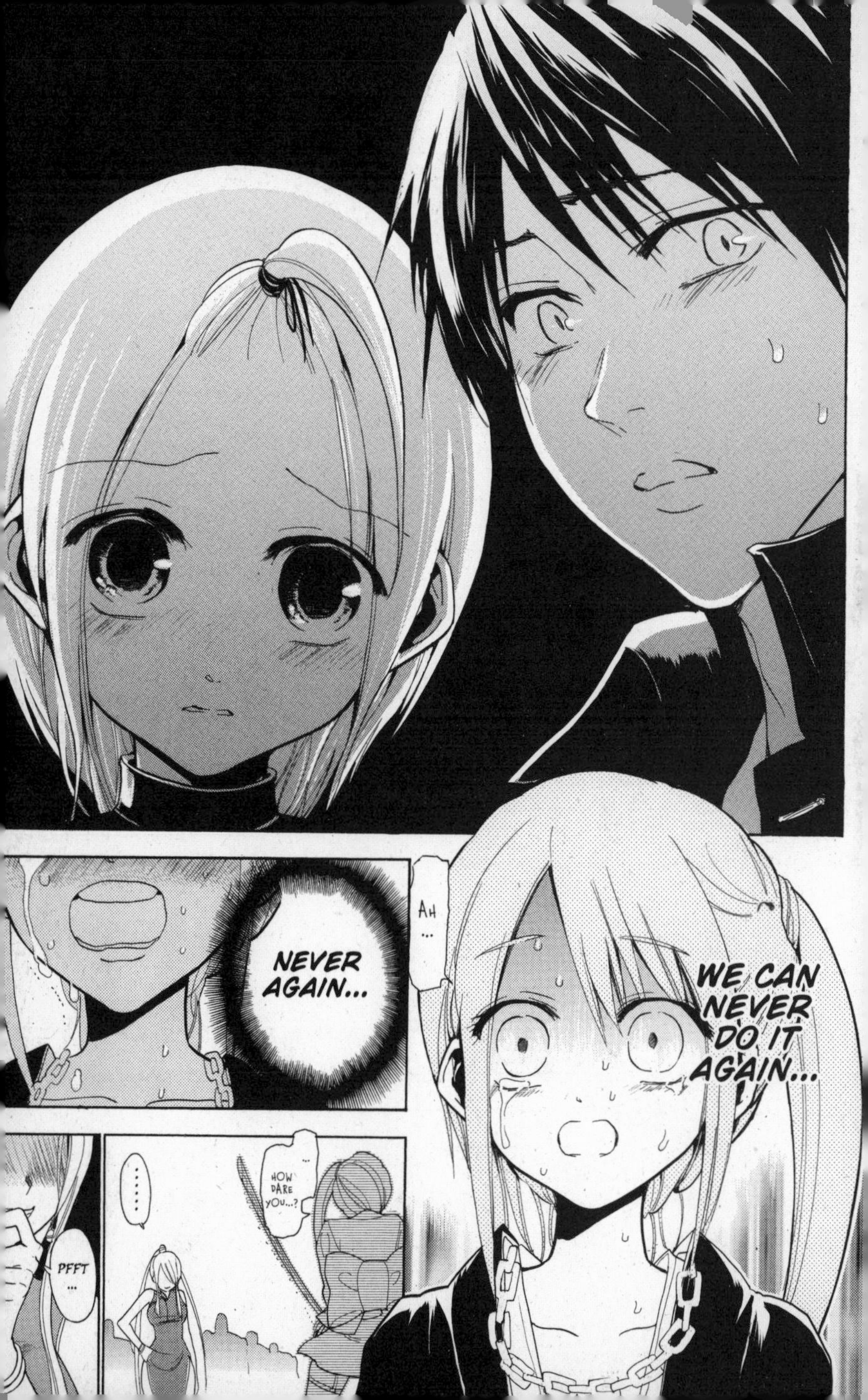
AH...
WE CAN NEVER DO IT AGAIN...
NEVER AGAIN...
... HOW DARE YOU...?
......
PFFT...

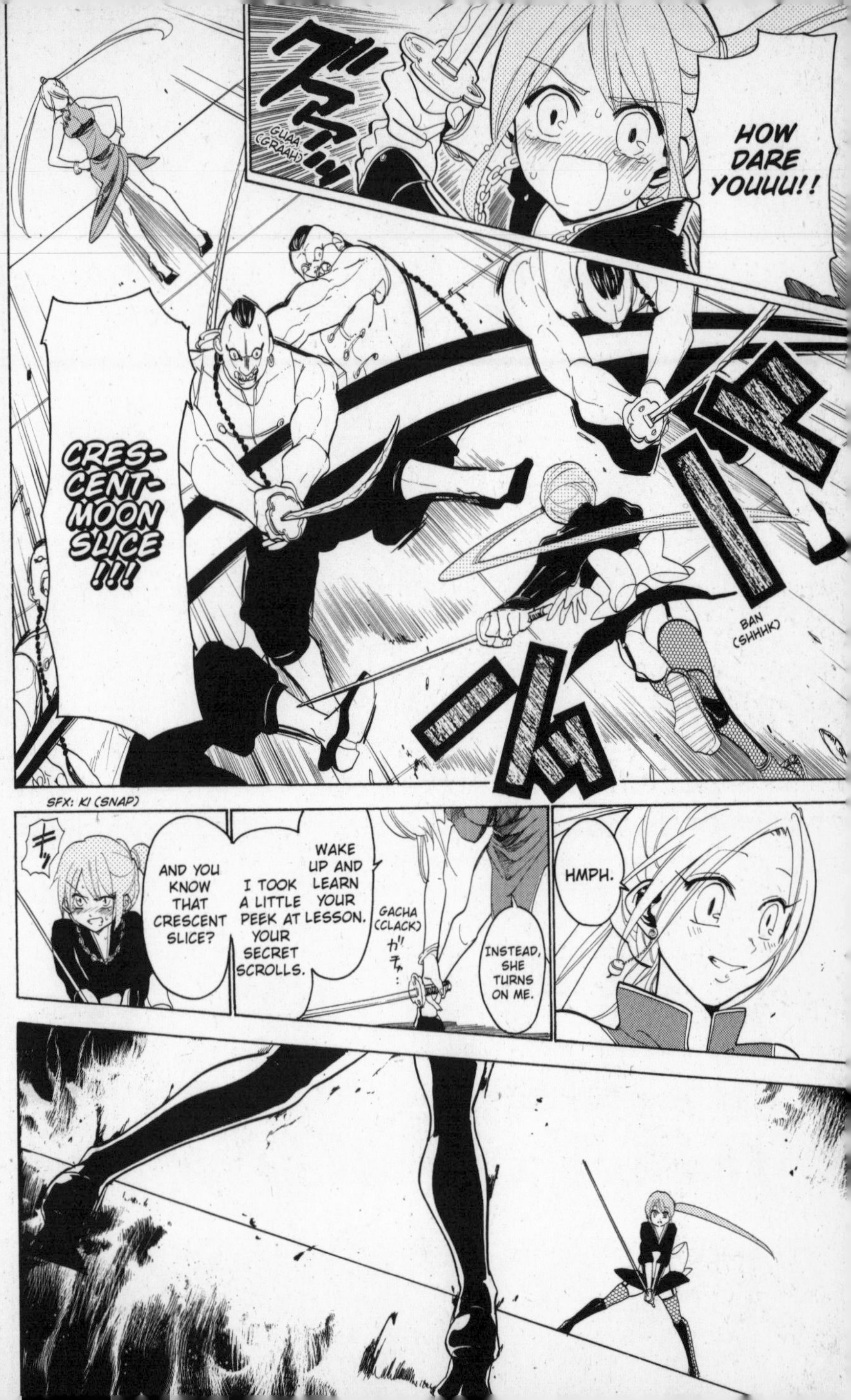
HOW DARE YOUUU!!
GUAA (GRAAH)
BAN (SHHHK)
CRES-CENT-MOON SLICE!!!
SFX: KI (SNAP)
HMPH.
INSTEAD, SHE TURNS ON ME.
GACHA (CLACK)
WAKE UP AND LEARN YOUR LESSON.
I TOOK A LITTLE PEEK AT YOUR SECRET SCROLLS.
AND YOU KNOW THAT CRESCENT SLICE?

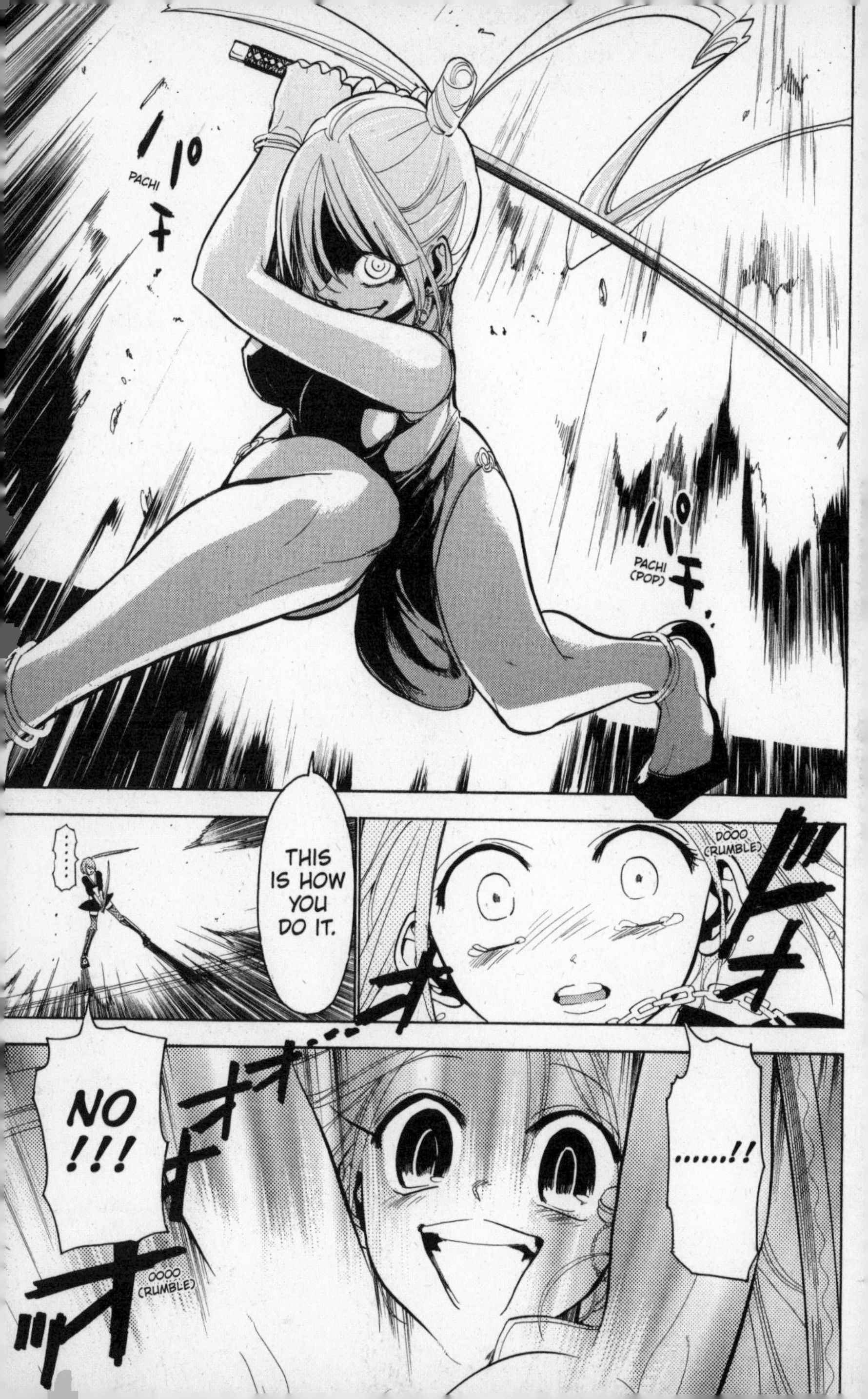
パチ
PACHI (POP)
パチ
PACHI
DOOO (RUMBLE)
THIS IS HOW YOU DO IT.
......
......!!
NO !!!
OOOO (RUMBLE)

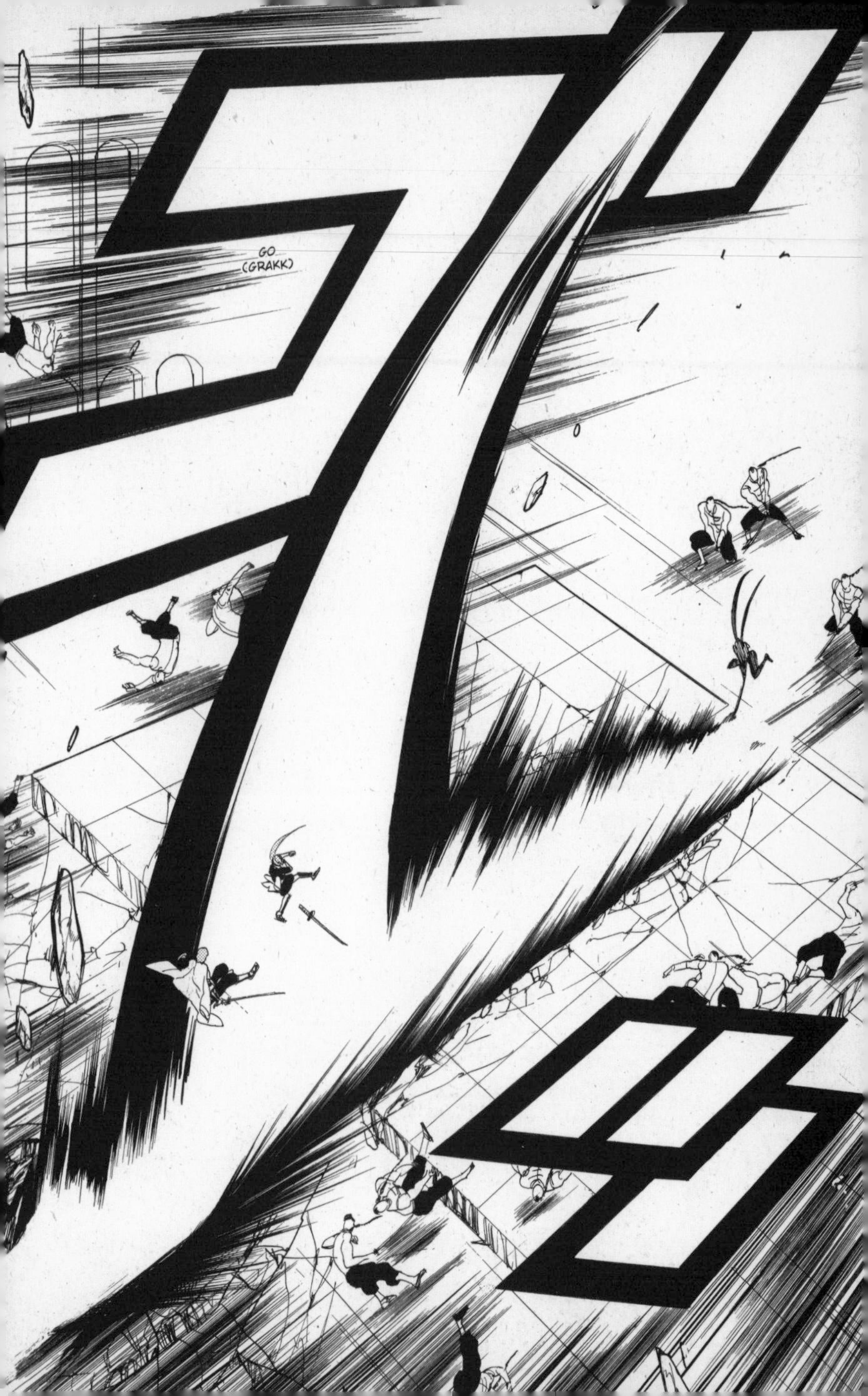
GO
(GRAKK)

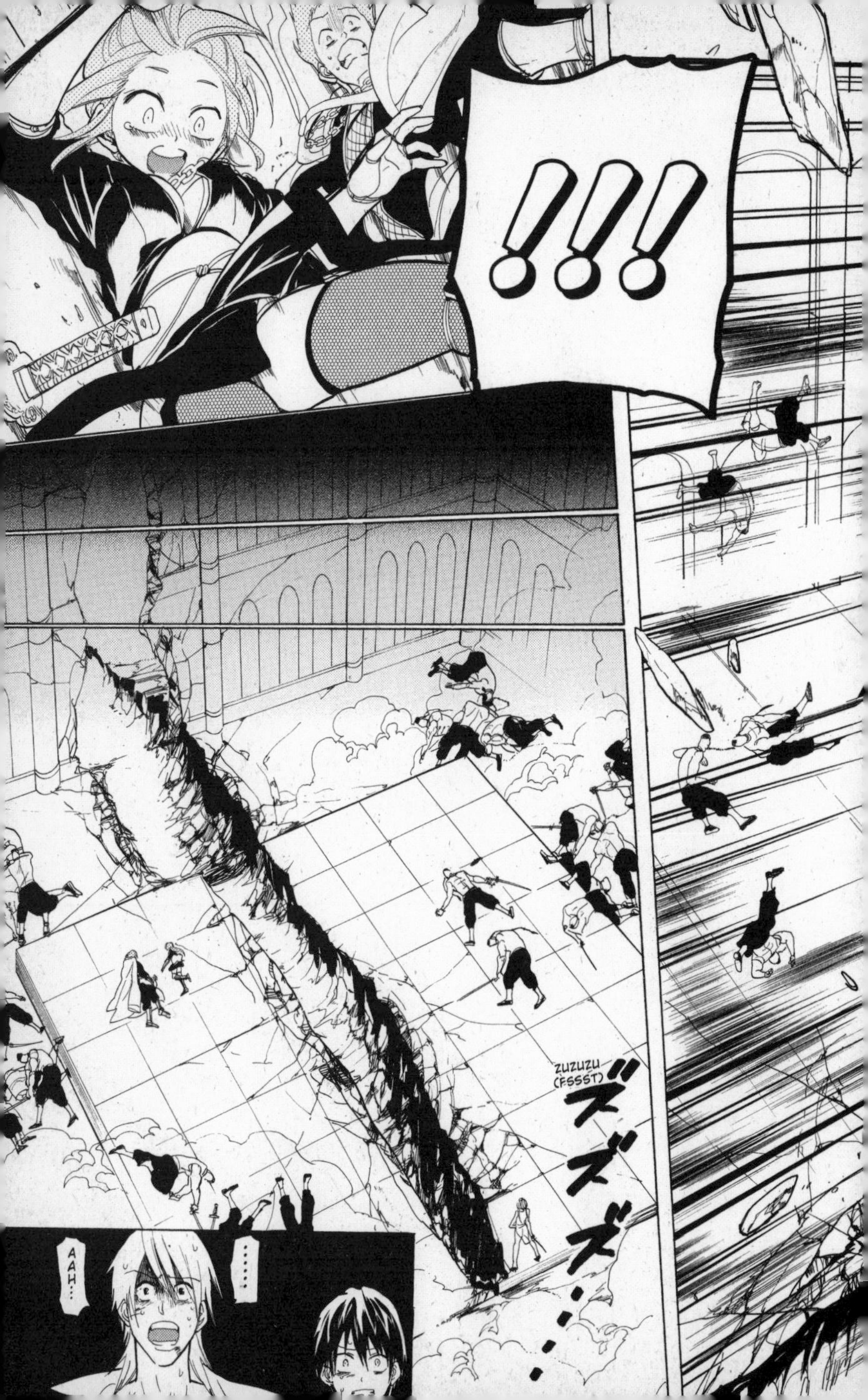
!!!
ZUZUZU (FSSST)
......
AAH...

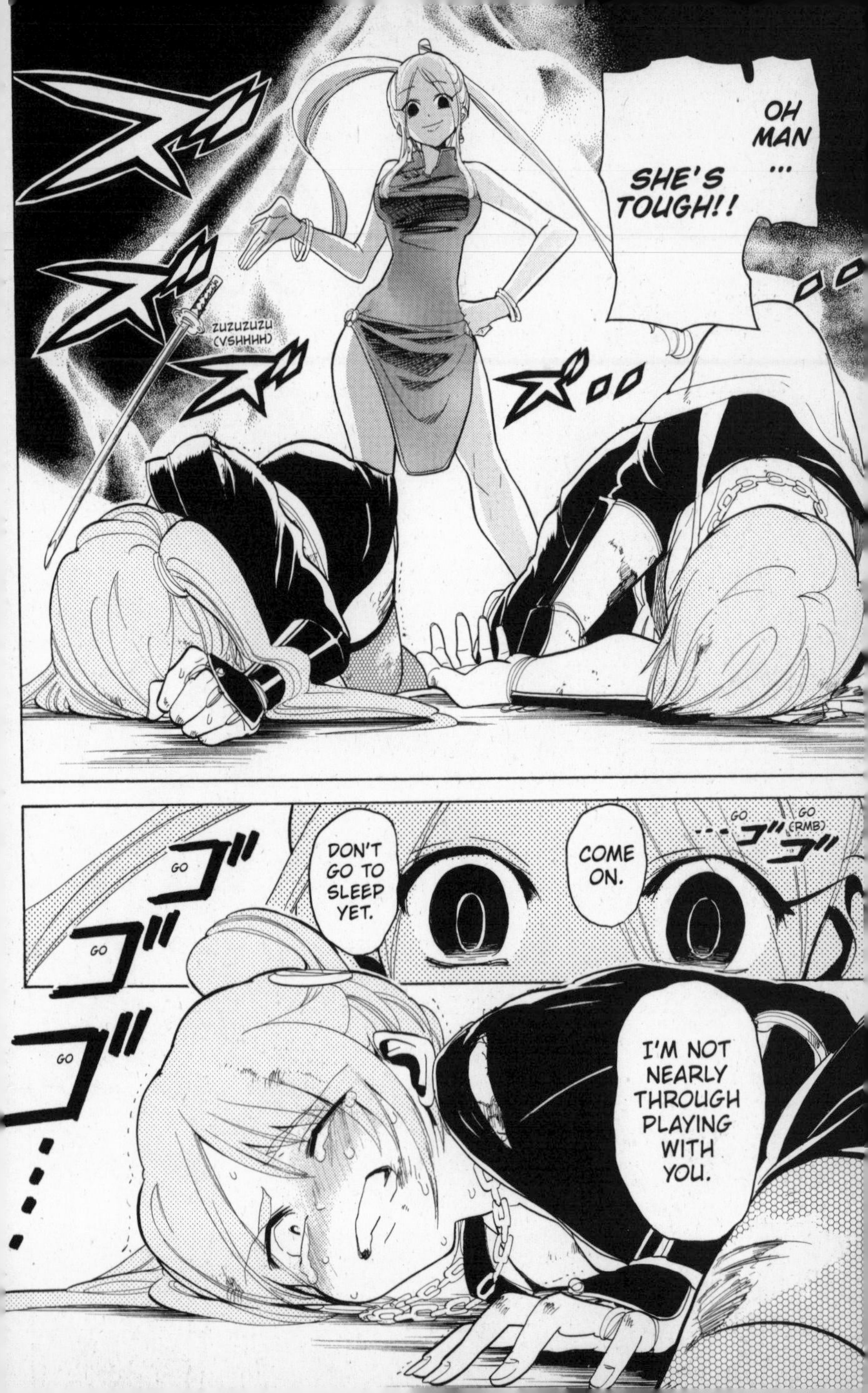
OH MAN ... SHE'S TOUGH!!
ZUZUZUZU (VSHHHH)
COME ON.
GO GO (RMB)
DON'T GO TO SLEEP YET.
GO
GO
GO
I'M NOT NEARLY THROUGH PLAYING WITH YOU.

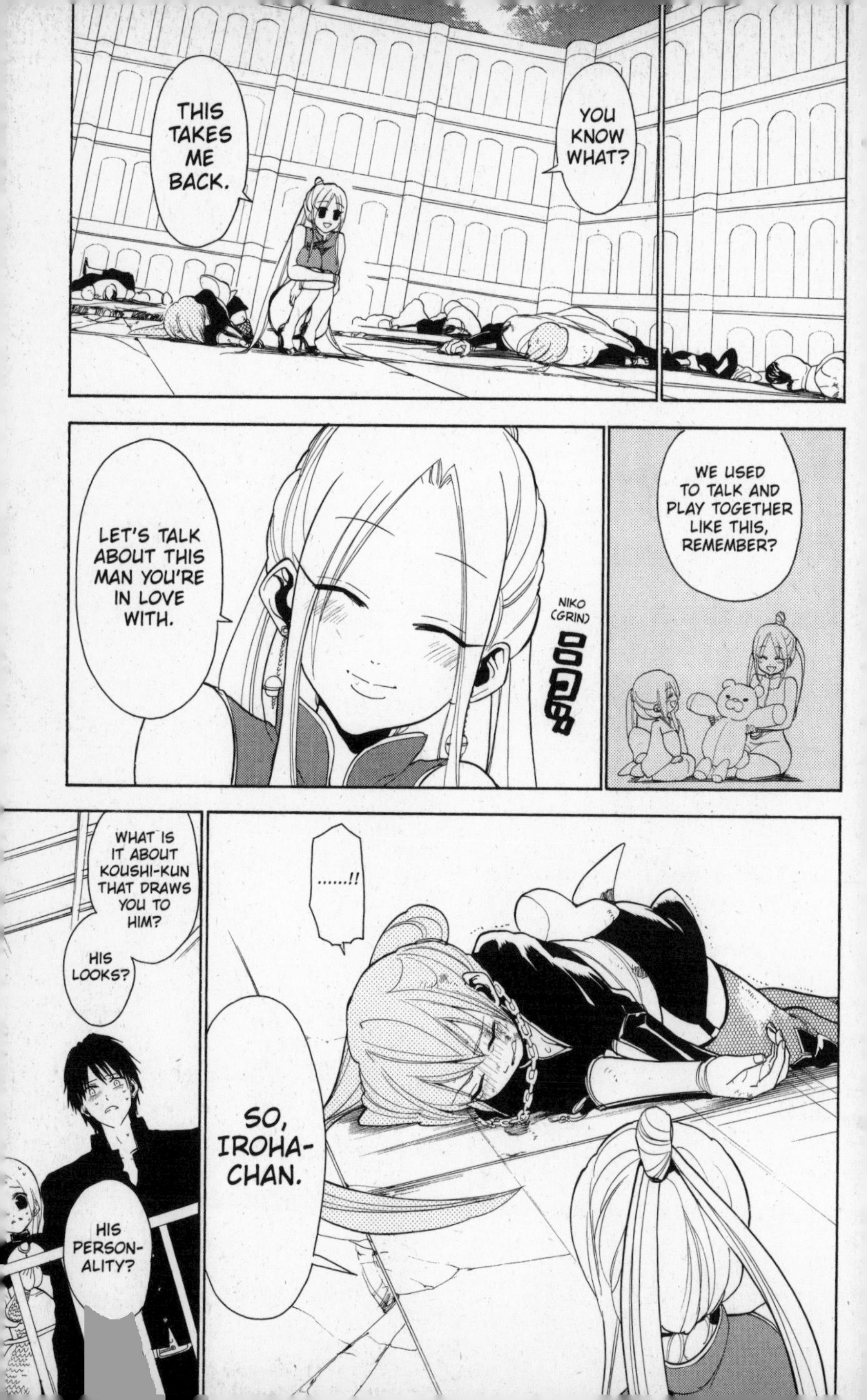
YOU KNOW WHAT?
THIS TAKES ME BACK.
WE USED TO TALK AND PLAY TOGETHER LIKE THIS, REMEMBER?
NIKO (GRIN)
LET'S TALK ABOUT THIS MAN YOU'RE IN LOVE WITH.
......!!
SO, IROHA-CHAN.
WHAT IS IT ABOUT KOUSHI-KUN THAT DRAWS YOU TO HIM?
HIS LOOKS?
HIS PERSON-ALITY?

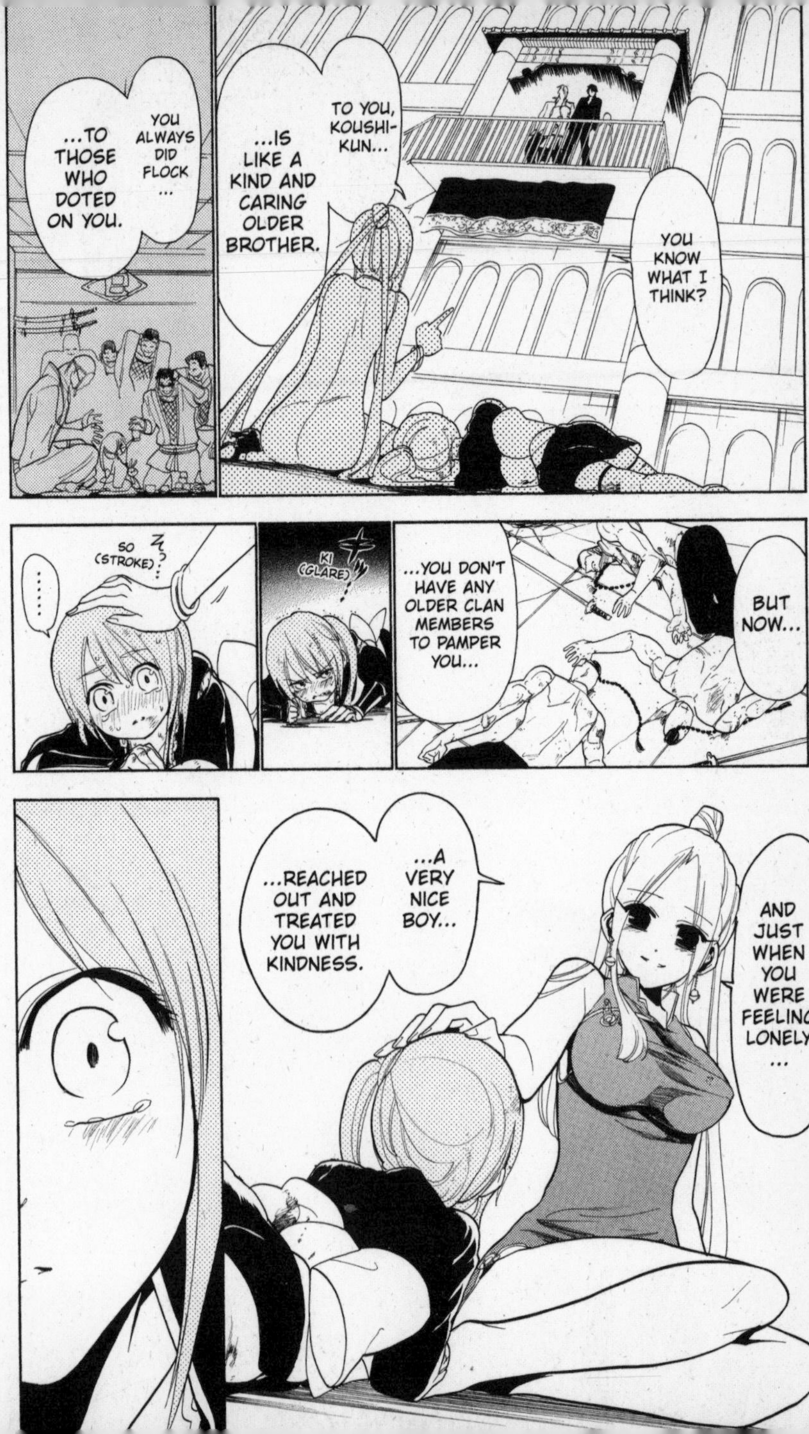
YOU KNOW WHAT I THINK?
TO YOU, KOUSHI-KUN...
...IS LIKE A KIND AND CARING OLDER BROTHER.
YOU ALWAYS DID FLOCK...
...TO THOSE WHO DOTED ON YOU.
BUT NOW...
...YOU DON'T HAVE ANY OLDER CLAN MEMBERS TO PAMPER YOU...
KI (GLARE)
SO (STROKE)
......
AND JUST WHEN YOU WERE FEELING LONELY...
...A VERY NICE BOY...
...REACHED OUT AND TREATED YOU WITH KINDNESS.

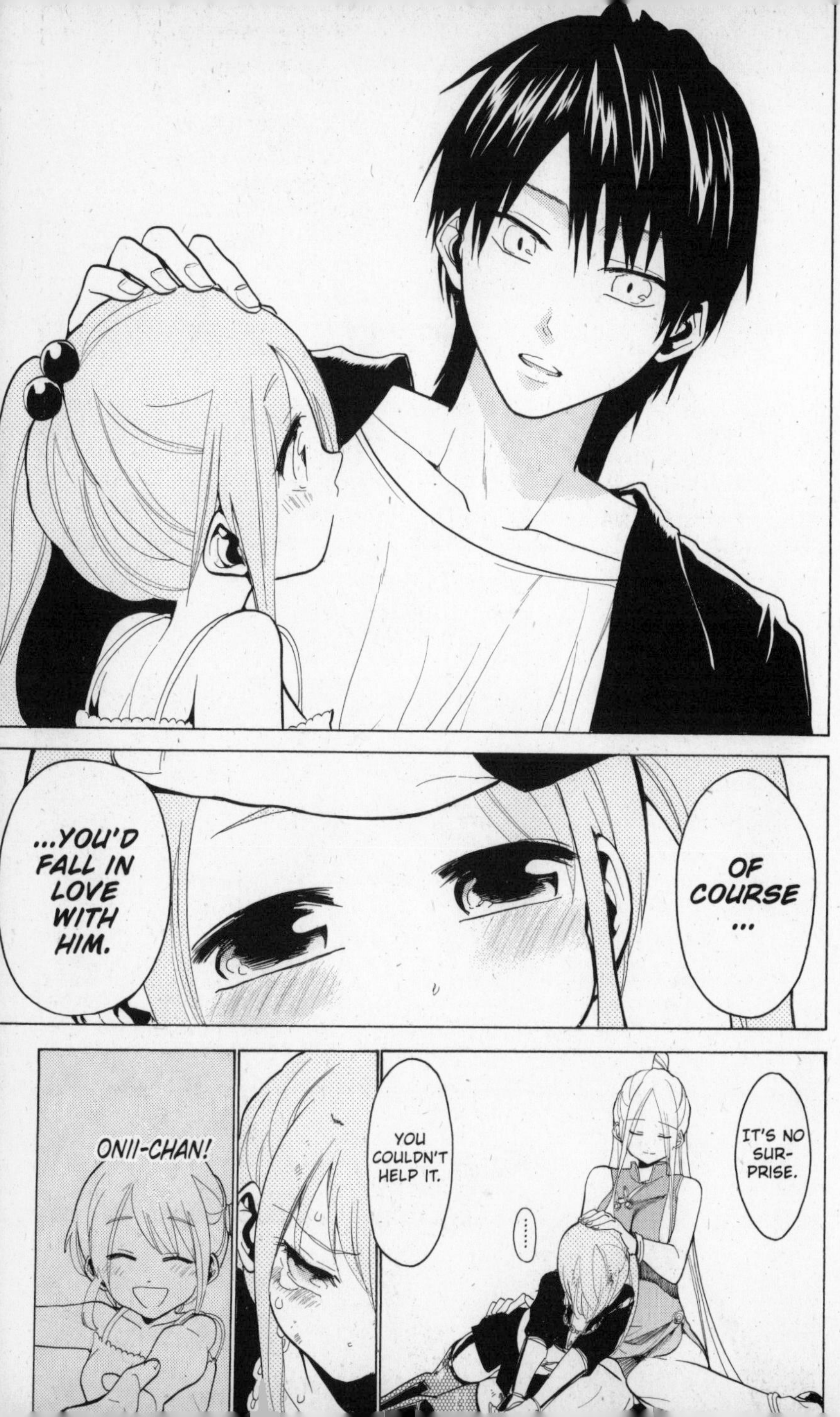
OF COURSE ...
...YOU'D FALL IN LOVE WITH HIM.
IT'S NO SUR-PRISE.
YOU COULDN'T HELP IT.
......
ONII-CHAN!

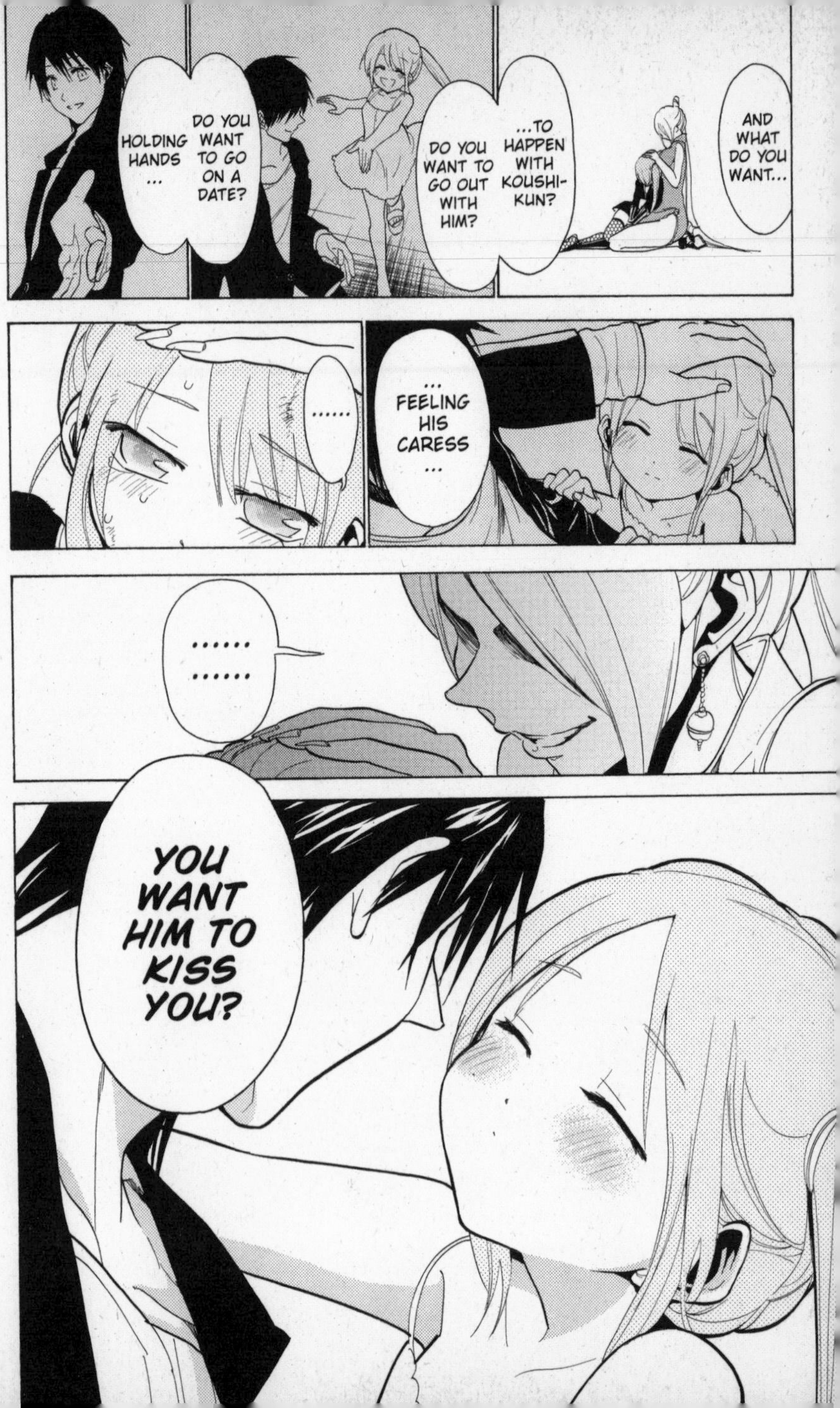
AND WHAT DO YOU WANT...
...TO HAPPEN WITH KOUSHI-KUN?
DO YOU WANT TO GO OUT WITH HIM?
DO YOU WANT TO GO ON A DATE?
HOLDING HANDS ...
... FEELING HIS CARESS ...
......
....
YOU WANT HIM TO KISS YOU?

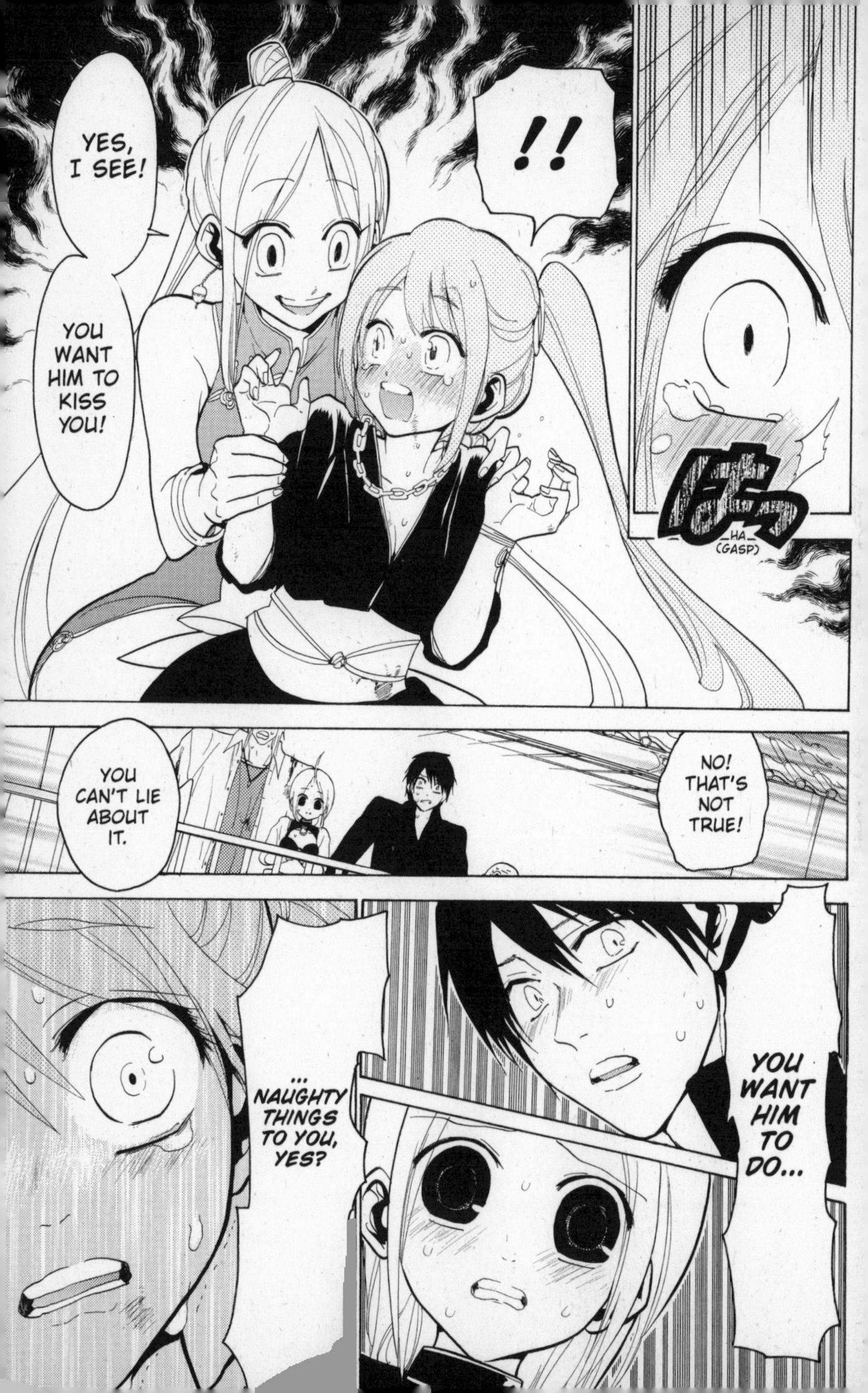
HA (GASP)
!!
YES, I SEE!
YOU WANT HIM TO KISS YOU!
NO! THAT'S NOT TRUE!
YOU CAN'T LIE ABOUT IT.
YOU WANT HIM TO DO...
...NAUGHTY THINGS TO YOU, YES?

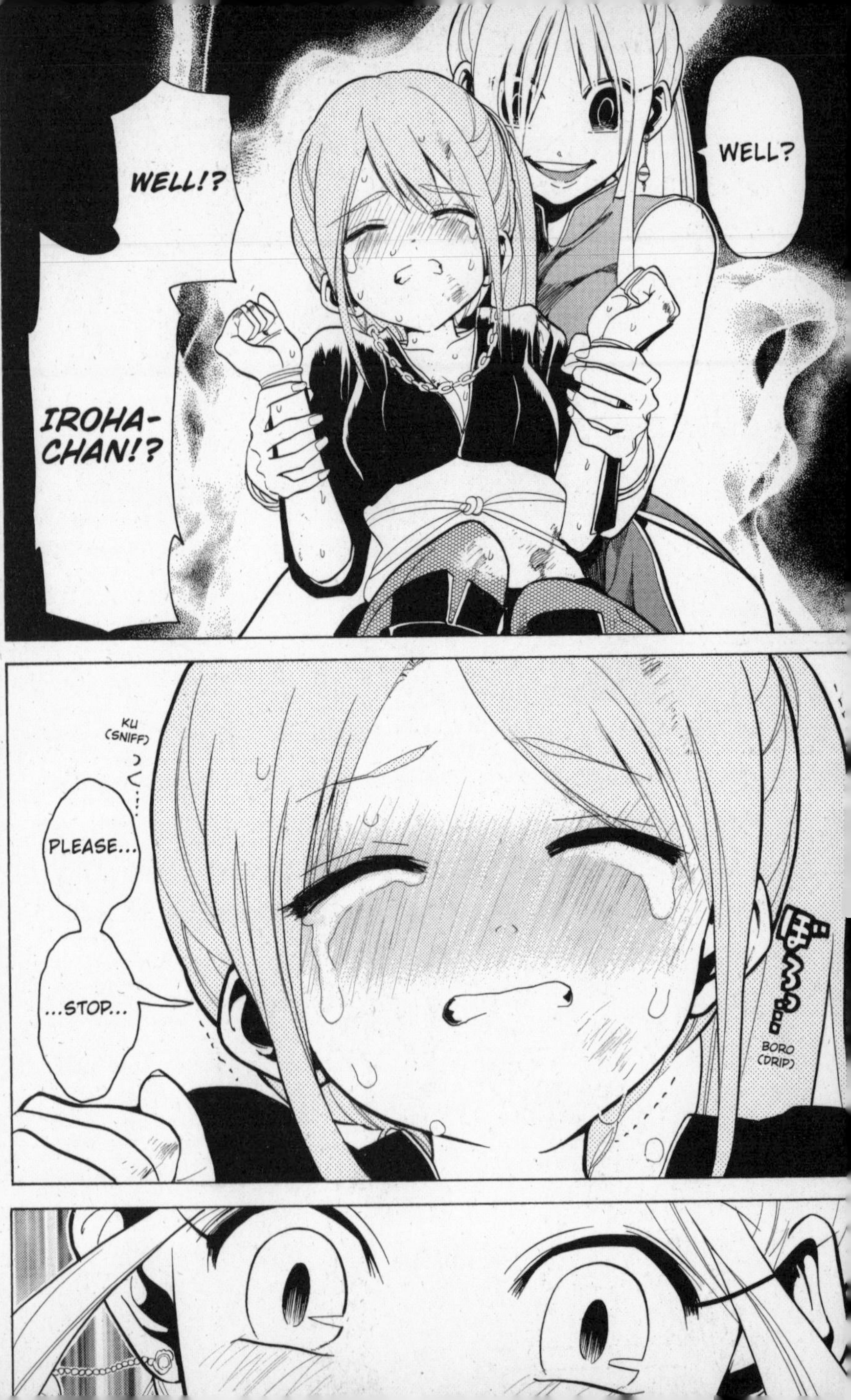
WELL?
WELL!?
IROHA-CHAN!?
KU (SNIFF)
PLEASE...
...STOP...
BORO (DRIP)

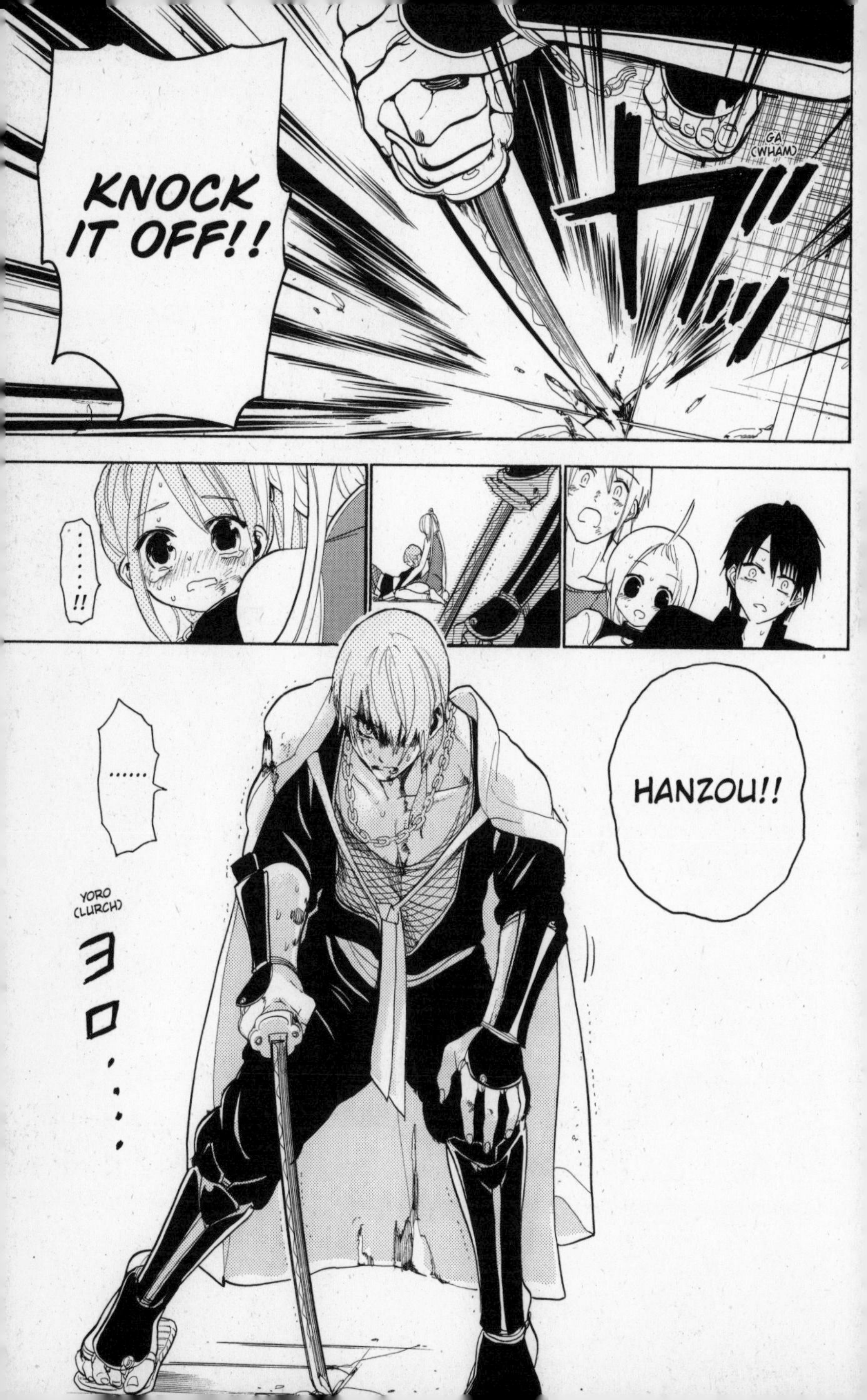
GA (WHAM)
KNOCK IT OFF!!
......!!
HANZOU!!
......
YORO (LURCH)

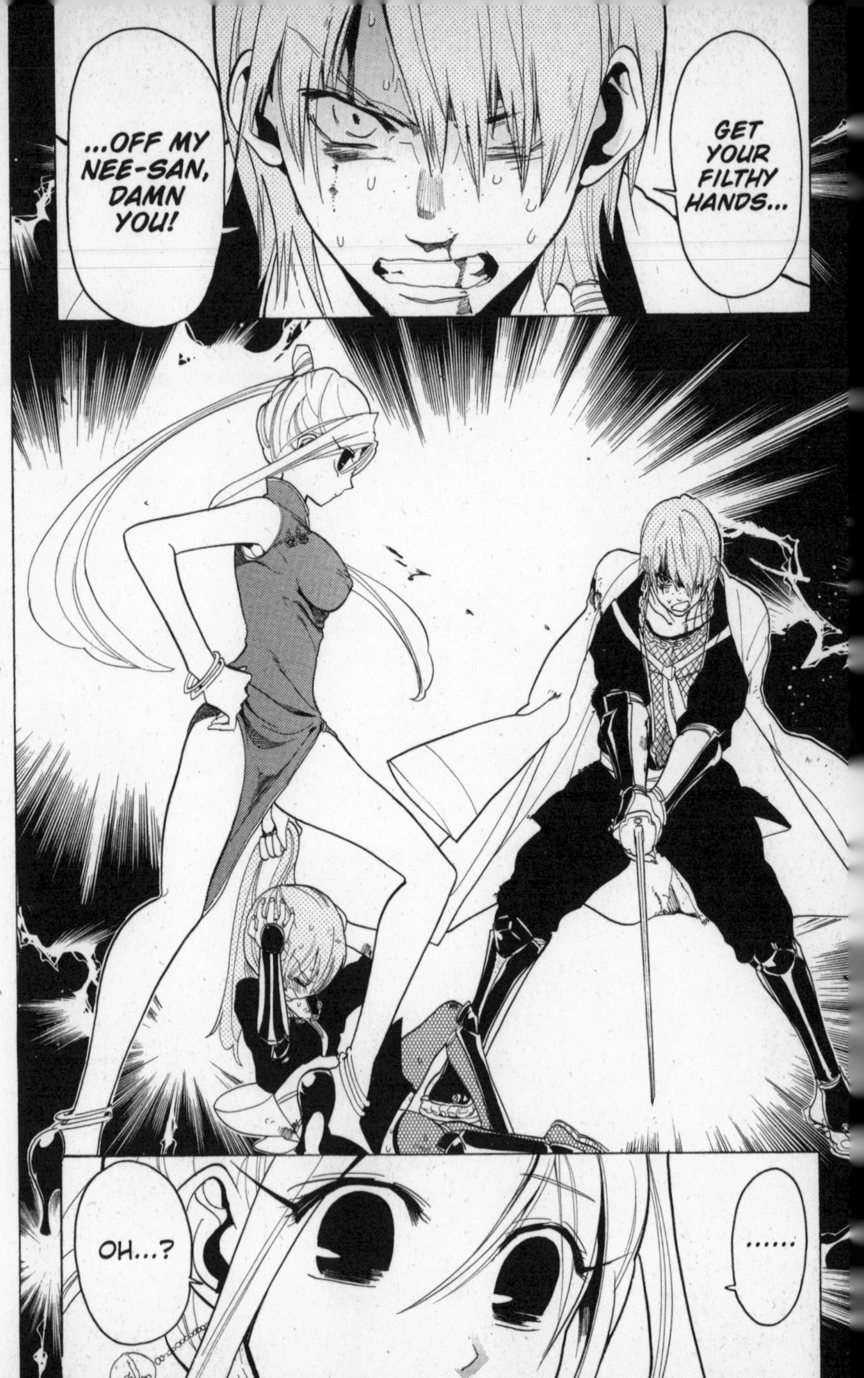
GET YOUR FILTHY HANDS...
...OFF MY NEE-SAN, DAMN YOU!
......
OH...?

CHAPTER 37. ONE-SIDED CRUSHER – END

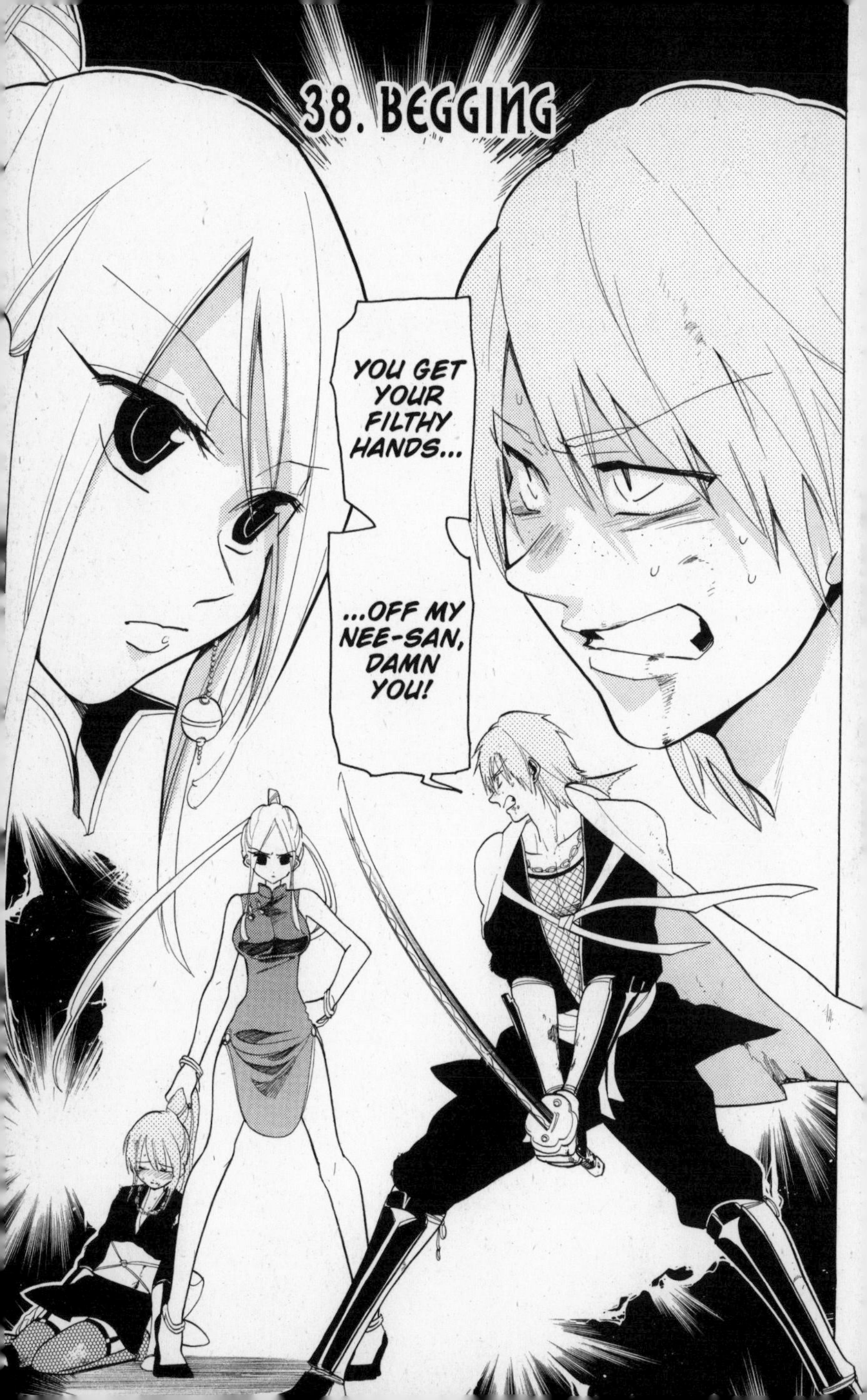
38. BEGGING
YOU GET YOUR FILTHY HANDS...
...OFF MY NEE-SAN, DAMN YOU!

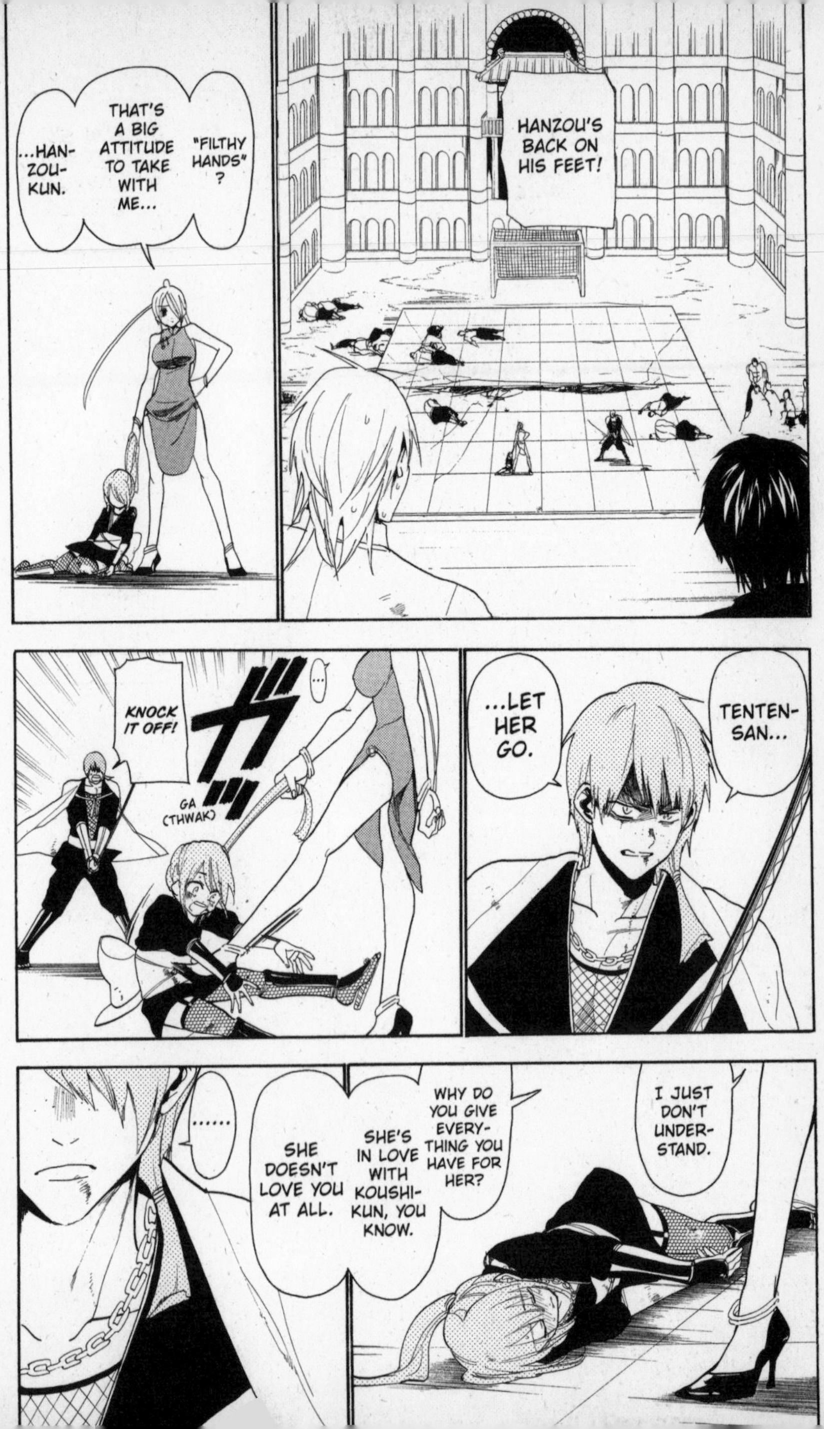
HANZOU'S BACK ON HIS FEET!
"FILTHY HANDS"?
THAT'S A BIG ATTITUDE TO TAKE WITH ME...
...HAN-ZOU-KUN.
TENTEN-SAN...
...LET HER GO.
...
KNOCK IT OFF!
GA (THWAK)
I JUST DON'T UNDER-STAND.
WHY DO YOU GIVE EVERY-THING YOU HAVE FOR HER?
SHE'S IN LOVE WITH KOUSHI-KUN, YOU KNOW.
SHE DOESN'T LOVE YOU AT ALL.
......

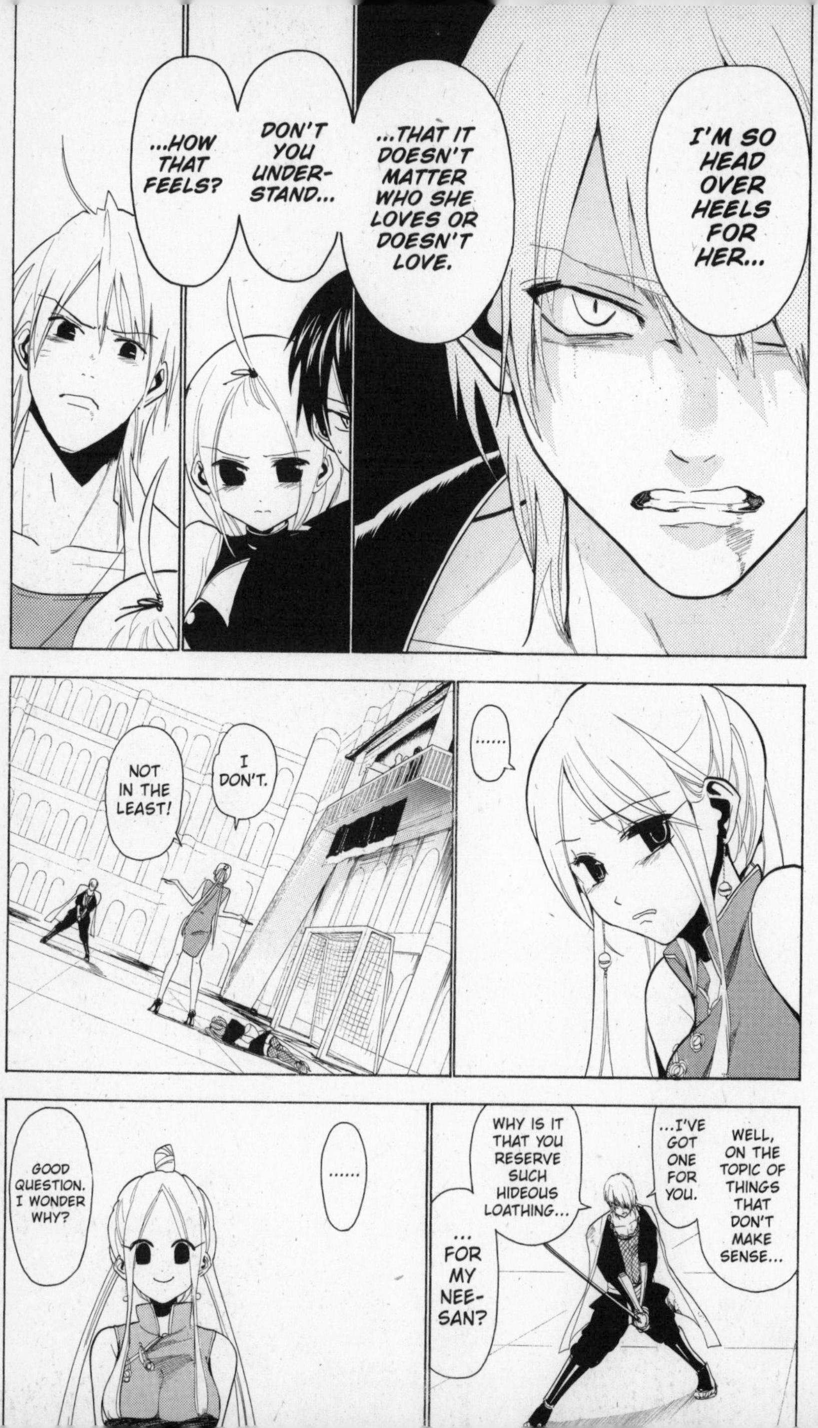
I'M SO HEAD OVER HEELS FOR HER...
...THAT IT DOESN'T MATTER WHO SHE LOVES OR DOESN'T LOVE.
DON'T YOU UNDER-STAND...
...HOW THAT FEELS?
......
I DON'T.
NOT IN THE LEAST!
WELL, ON THE TOPIC OF THINGS THAT DON'T MAKE SENSE...
...I'VE GOT ONE FOR YOU.
WHY IS IT THAT YOU RESERVE SUCH HIDEOUS LOATHING...
...FOR MY NEE-SAN?
......
GOOD QUESTION. I WONDER WHY?

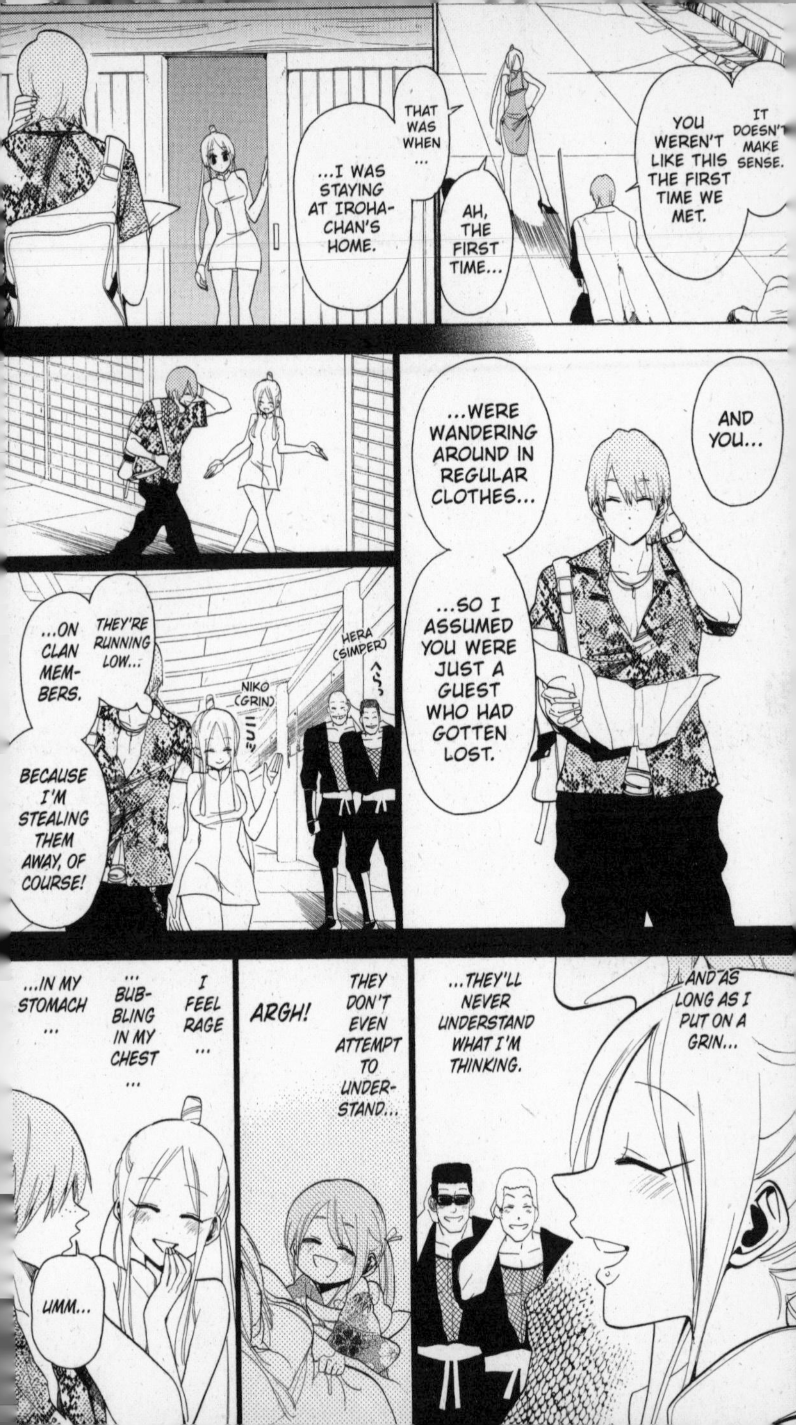
IT DOESN'T MAKE SENSE.
YOU WEREN'T LIKE THIS THE FIRST TIME WE MET.
AH, THE FIRST TIME...
THAT WAS WHEN...
...I WAS STAYING AT IROHA-CHAN'S HOME.
AND YOU...
...WERE WANDERING AROUND IN REGULAR CLOTHES...
...SO I ASSUMED YOU WERE JUST A GUEST WHO HAD GOTTEN LOST.
HERA (SIMPER)
NIKO (GRIN)
THEY'RE RUNNING LOW...
...ON CLAN MEM-BERS.
BECAUSE I'M STEALING THEM AWAY, OF COURSE!
AND AS LONG AS I PUT ON A GRIN...
...THEY'LL NEVER UNDERSTAND WHAT I'M THINKING.
THEY DON'T EVEN ATTEMPT TO UNDER-STAND...
ARGH!
I FEEL RAGE...
...BUB-BLING IN MY CHEST...
...IN MY STOMACH...
UMM...

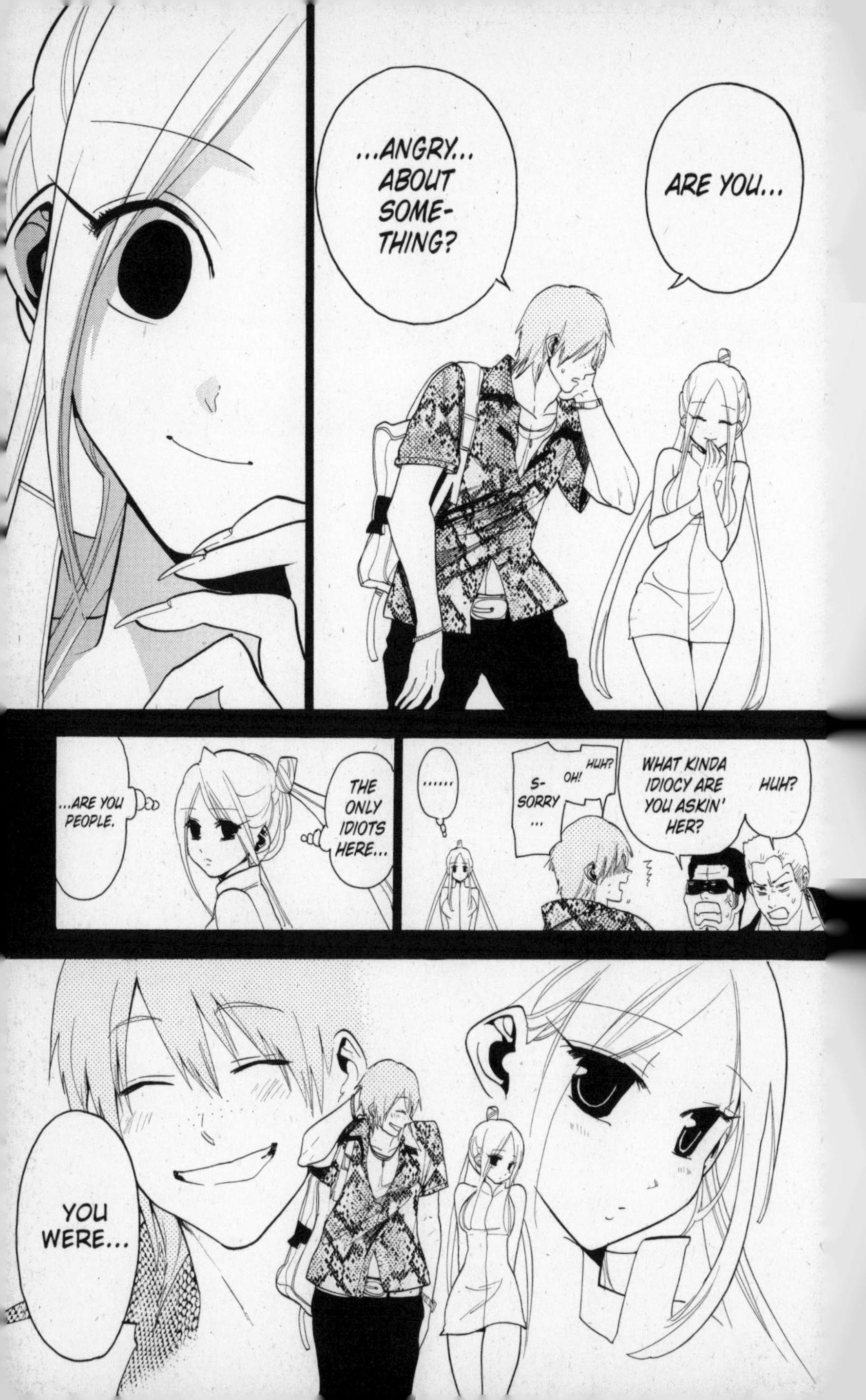
ARE YOU...
...ANGRY... ABOUT SOME-THING?
HUH?
WHAT KINDA IDIOCY ARE YOU ASKIN' HER?
HUH? OH!
S-SORRY ...
......
THE ONLY IDIOTS HERE...
...ARE YOU PEOPLE.
YOU WERE...

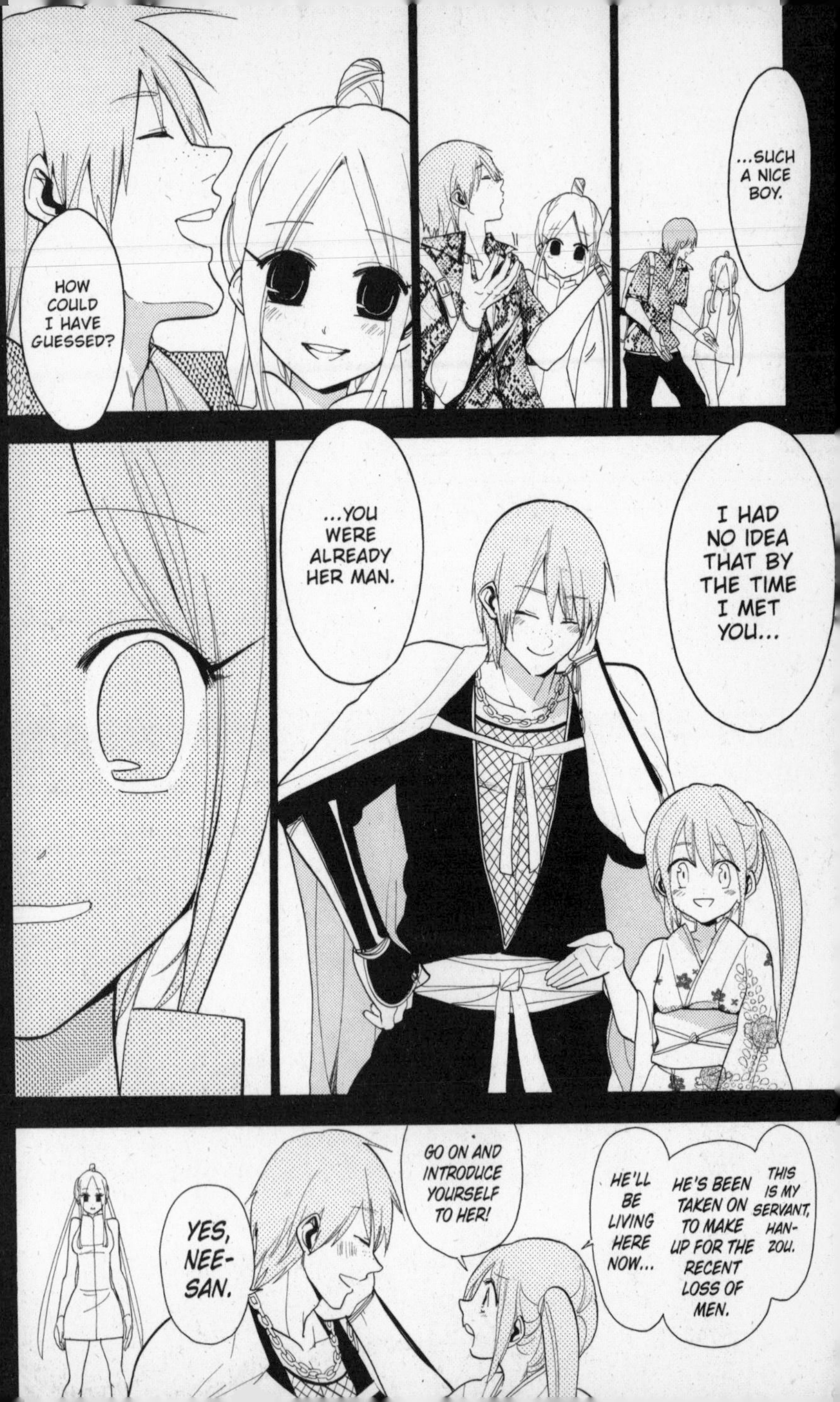
...SUCH A NICE BOY.
HOW COULD I HAVE GUESSED?
I HAD NO IDEA THAT BY THE TIME I MET YOU...
...YOU WERE ALREADY HER MAN.
THIS IS MY SERVANT, HAN-ZOU.
HE'S BEEN TAKEN ON TO MAKE UP FOR THE RECENT LOSS OF MEN.
HE'LL BE LIVING HERE NOW...
GO ON AND INTRODUCE YOURSELF TO HER!
YES, NEE-SAN.

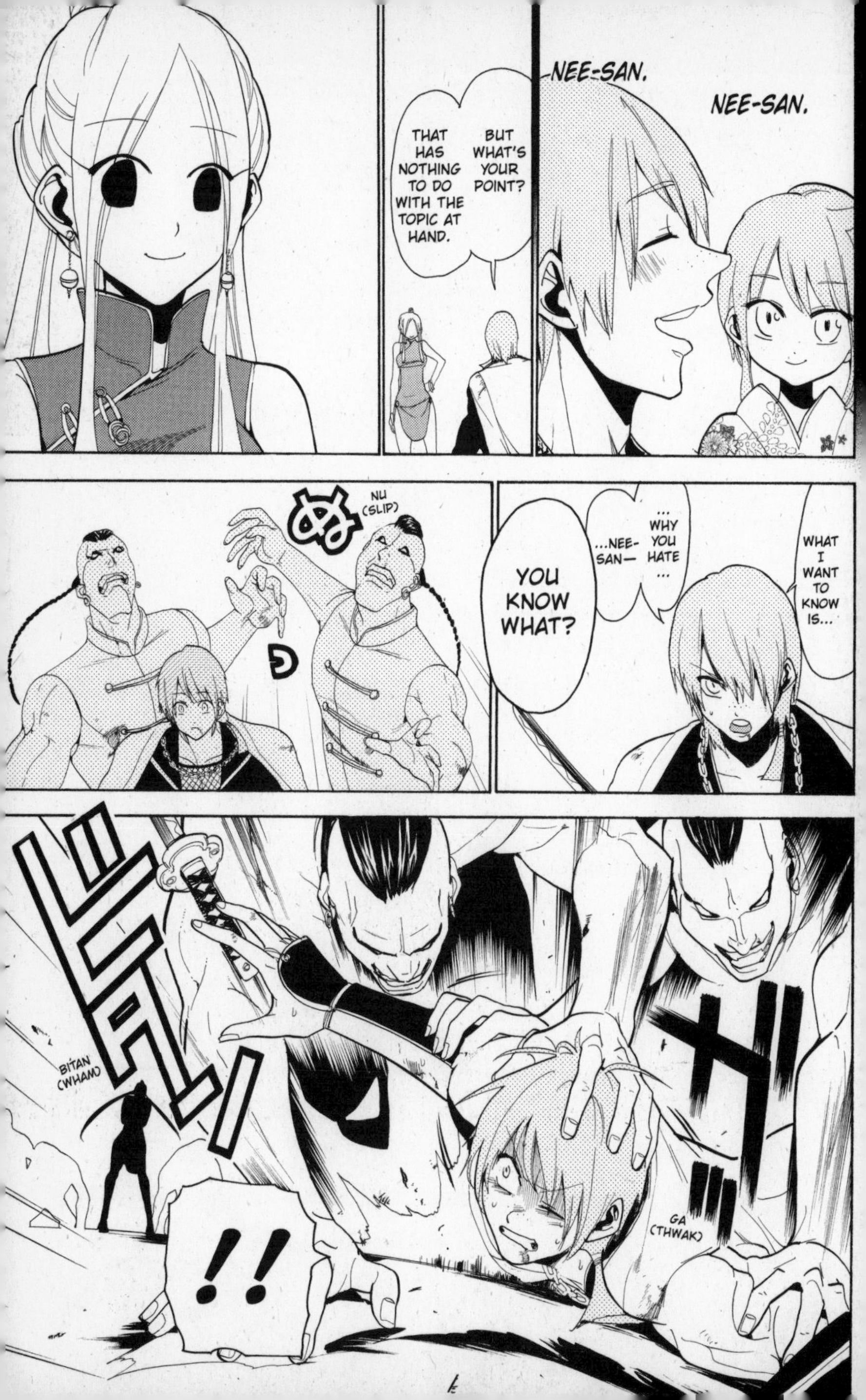
NEE-SAN.
NEE-SAN.
BUT WHAT'S YOUR POINT?
THAT HAS NOTHING TO DO WITH THE TOPIC AT HAND.
WHAT I WANT TO KNOW IS...
...WHY YOU HATE...
...NEE-SAN—
YOU KNOW WHAT?
NU (SLIP)
GA (THWAK)
BITAN (WHAM)
!!

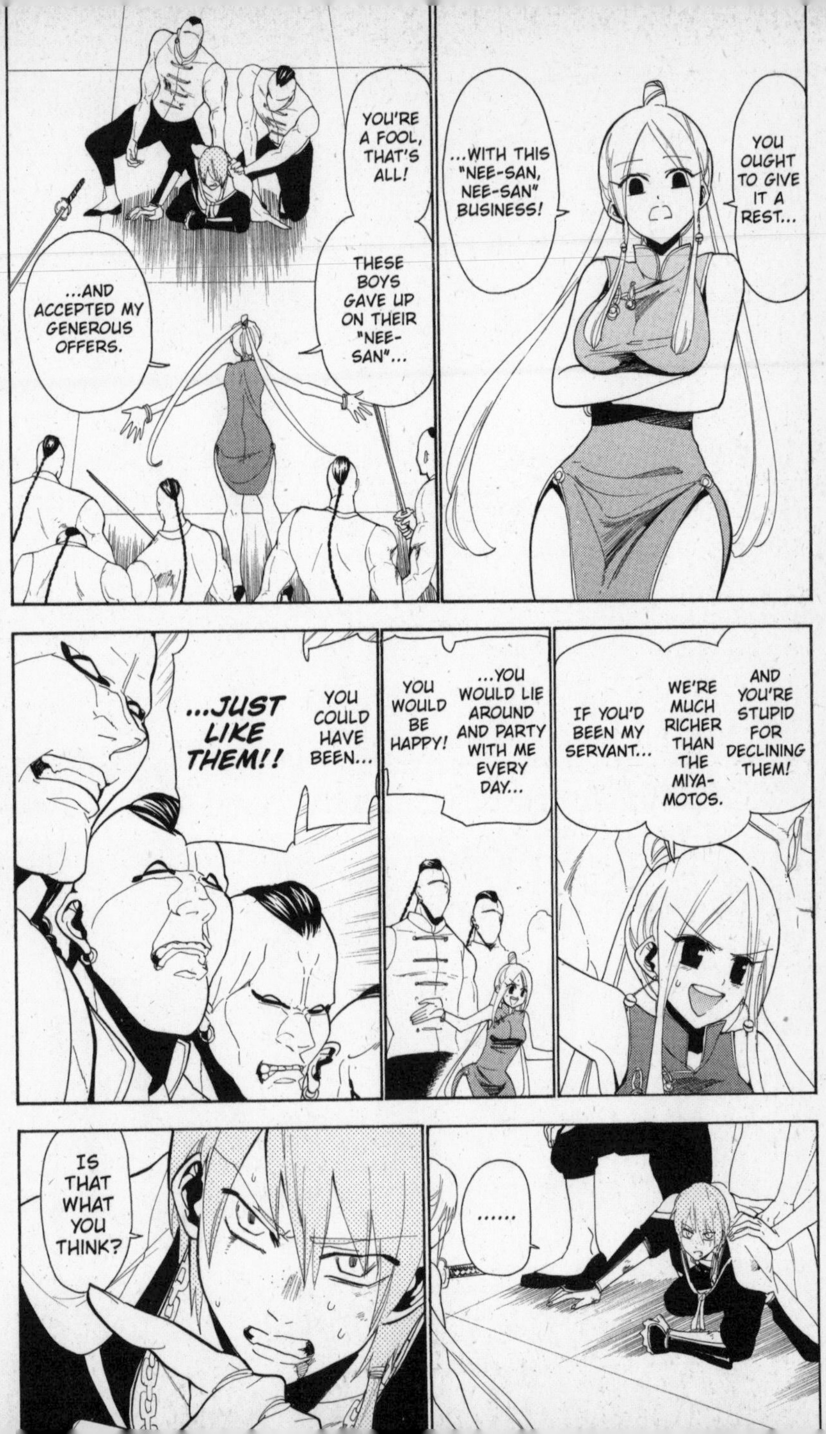
YOU OUGHT TO GIVE IT A REST...
...WITH THIS "NEE-SAN, NEE-SAN" BUSINESS!
YOU'RE A FOOL, THAT'S ALL!
THESE BOYS GAVE UP ON THEIR "NEE-SAN"...
...AND ACCEPTED MY GENEROUS OFFERS.
AND YOU'RE STUPID FOR DECLINING THEM!
WE'RE MUCH RICHER THAN THE MIYA-MOTOS.
IF YOU'D BEEN MY SERVANT...
...YOU WOULD LIE AROUND AND PARTY WITH ME EVERY DAY...
YOU WOULD BE HAPPY!
YOU COULD HAVE BEEN...
...JUST LIKE THEM!!
......
IS THAT WHAT YOU THINK?

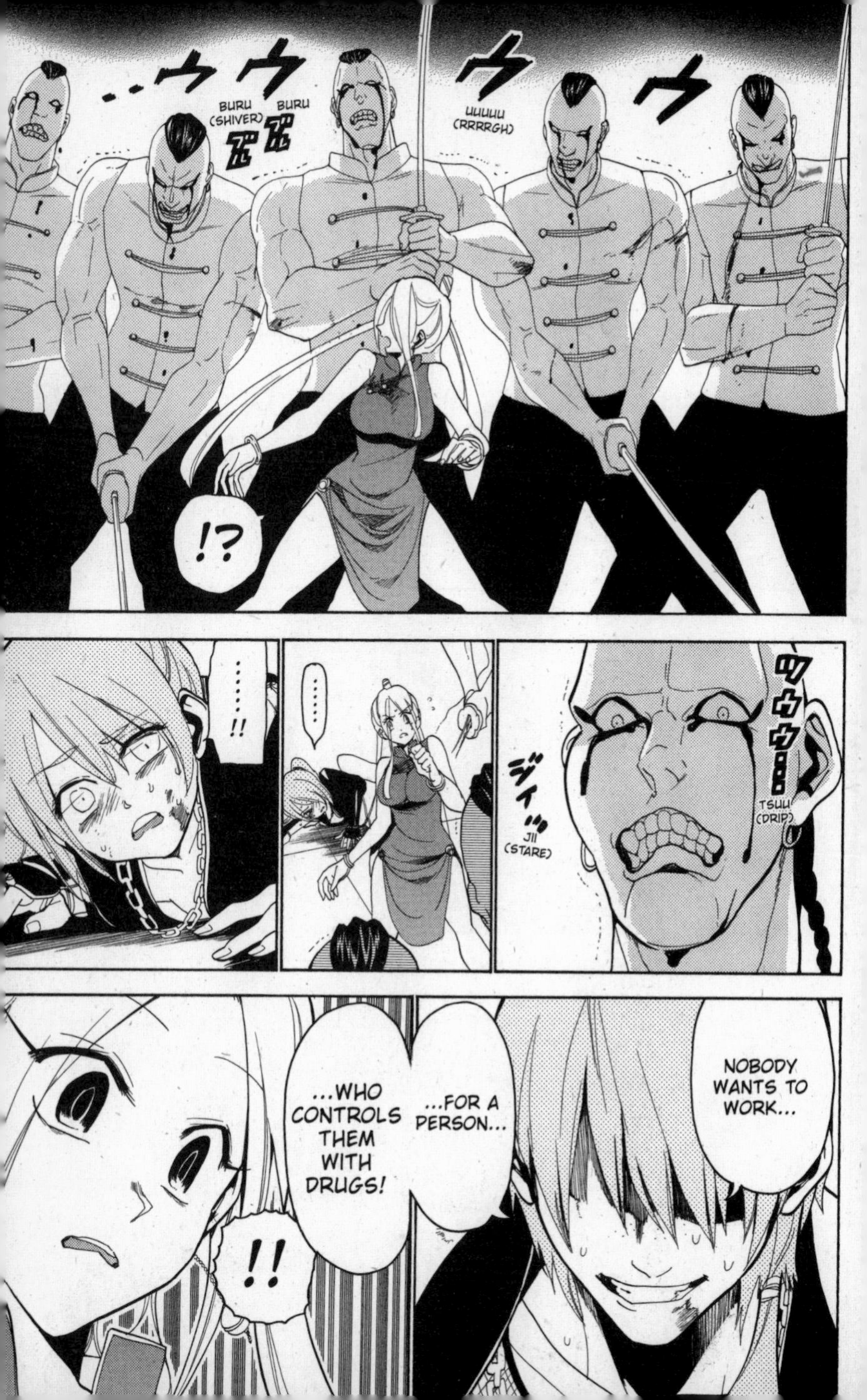

...ウウウウ
BURU (SHIVER)
BURU
UUUUU (RRRRGH)
!?
TSUU (DRIP)
JII (STARE)
......
......!!
NOBODY WANTS TO WORK...
...FOR A PERSON...
...WHO CONTROLS THEM WITH DRUGS!
!!

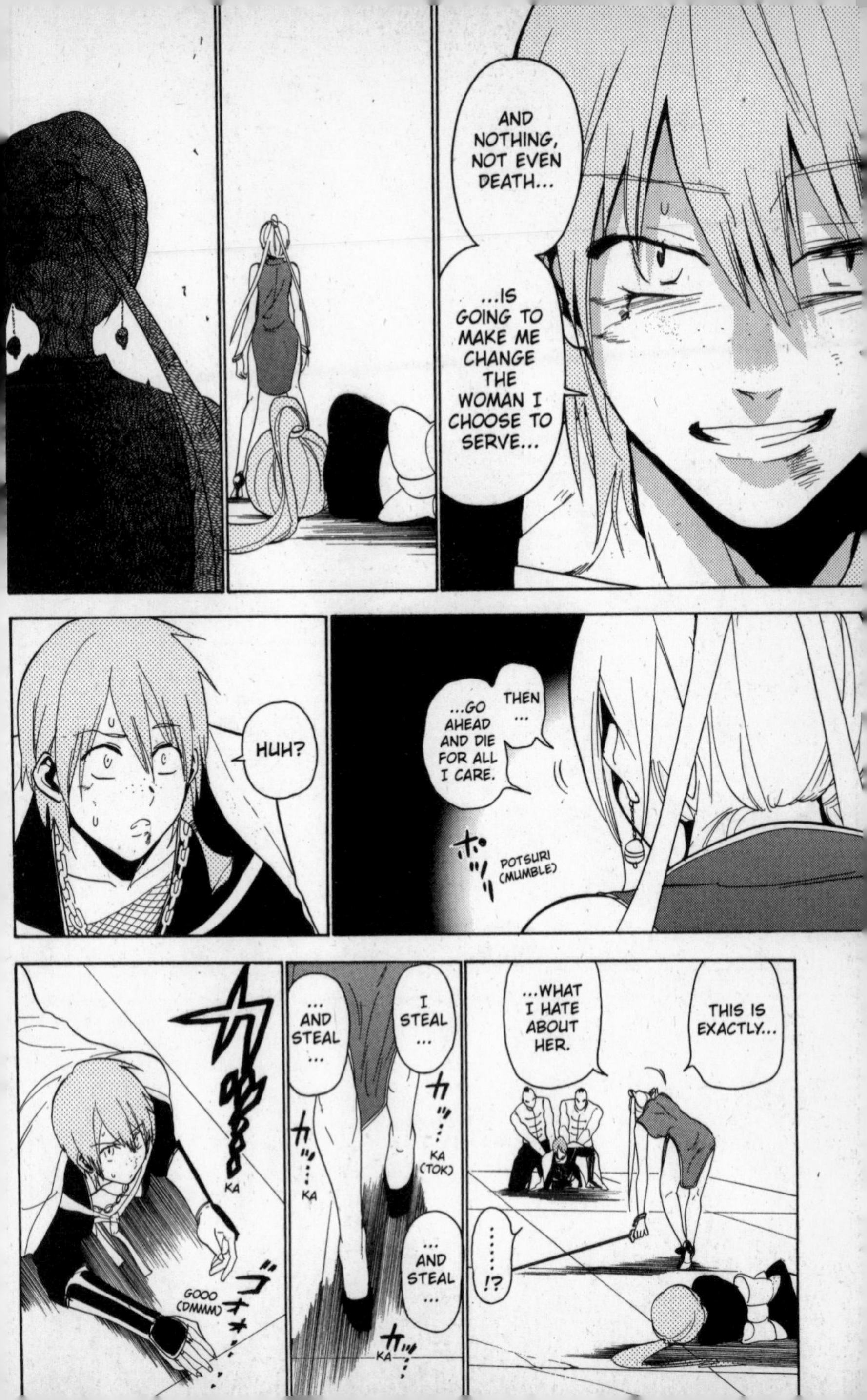
AND NOTHING, NOT EVEN DEATH...
...IS GOING TO MAKE ME CHANGE THE WOMAN I CHOOSE TO SERVE...
THEN ...
...GO AHEAD AND DIE FOR ALL I CARE.
POTSURI (MUMBLE)
HUH?
THIS IS EXACTLY...
...WHAT I HATE ABOUT HER.
......!?
I STEAL ...
... AND STEAL ...
KA (TOK)
KA
... AND STEAL ...
KA
KA
GOOO (DMMM)

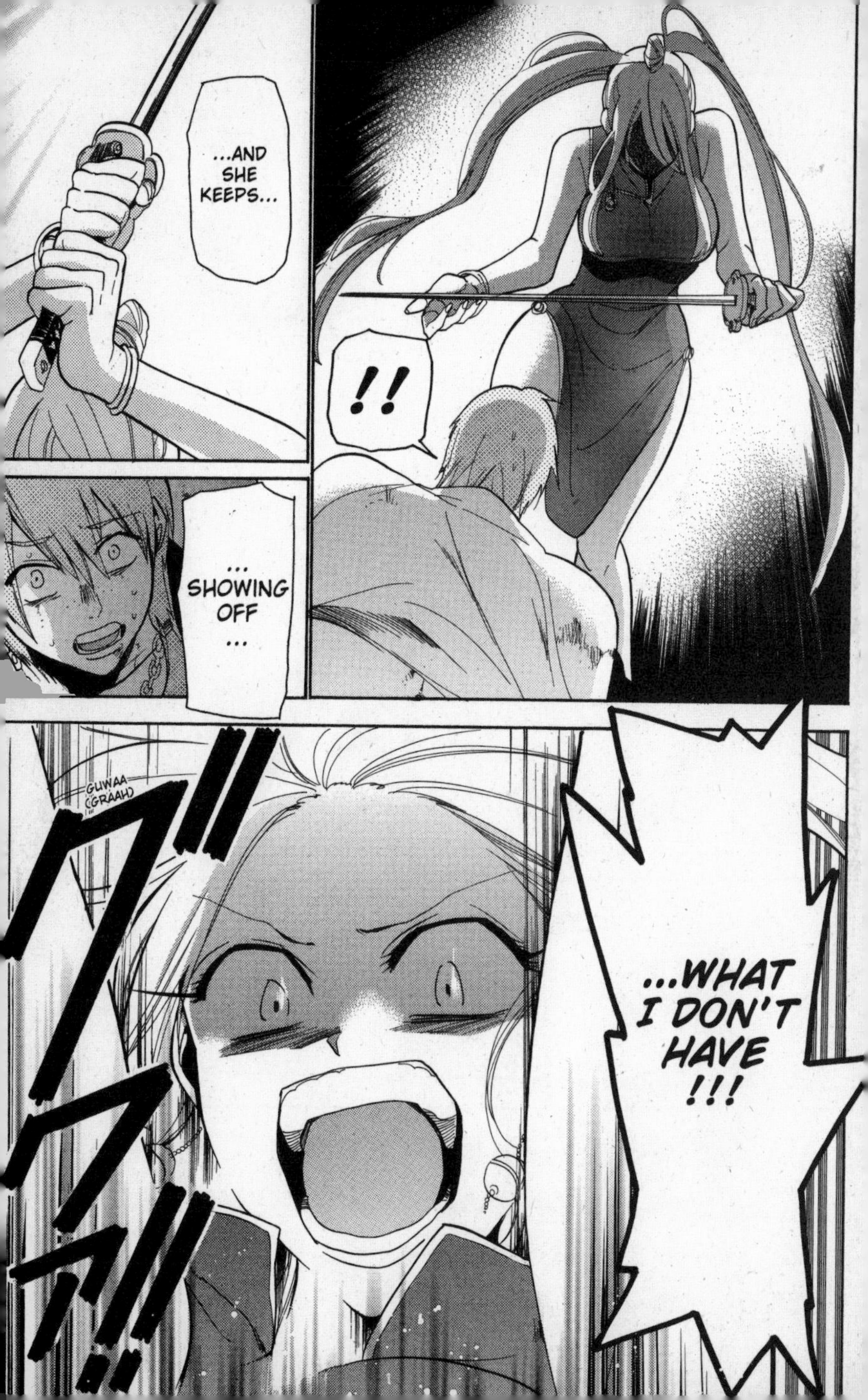
!!
...AND SHE KEEPS...
...SHOWING OFF...
...WHAT I DON'T HAVE!!!
GUWAA (GRAAH)

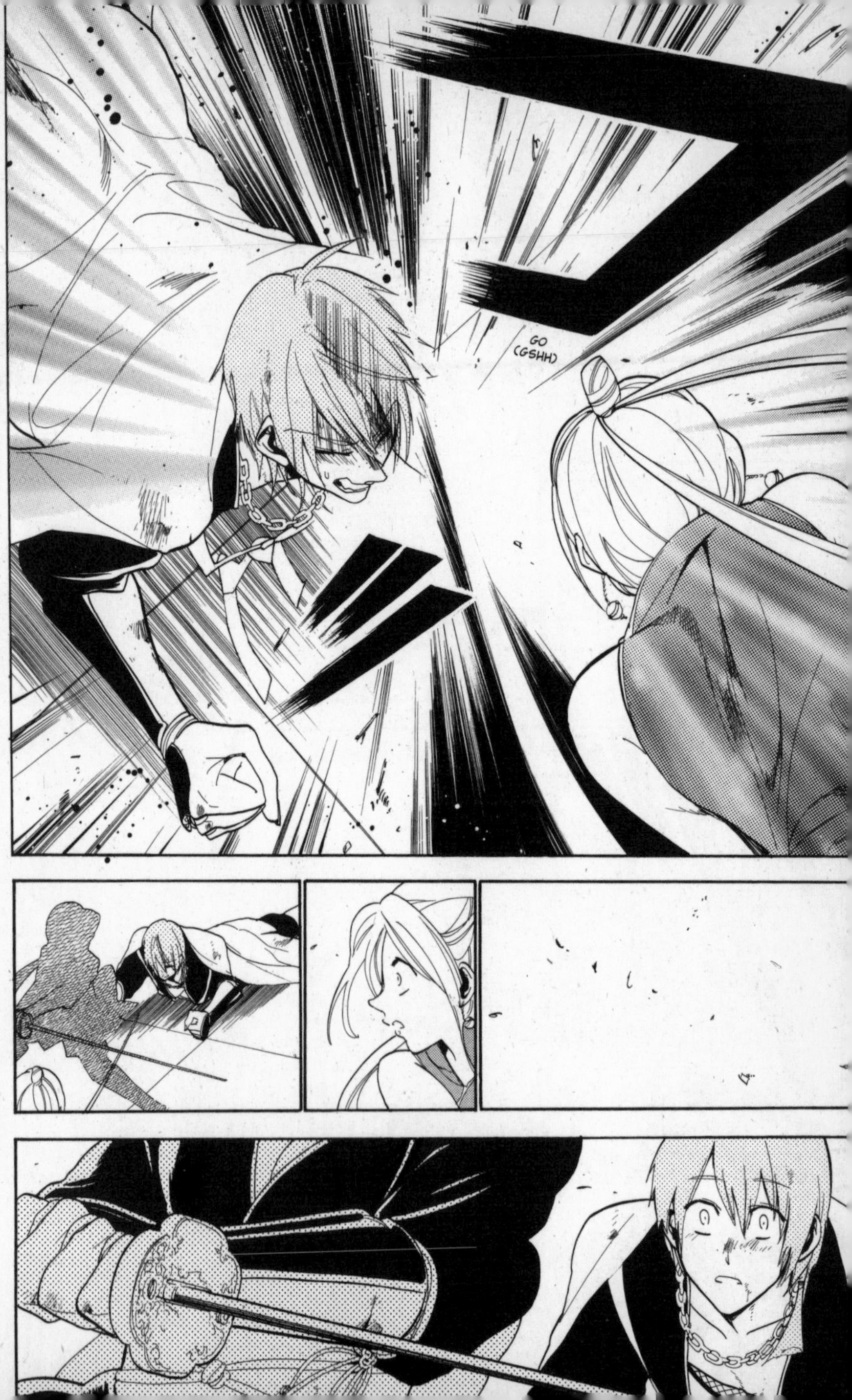
GO
(GSHH)

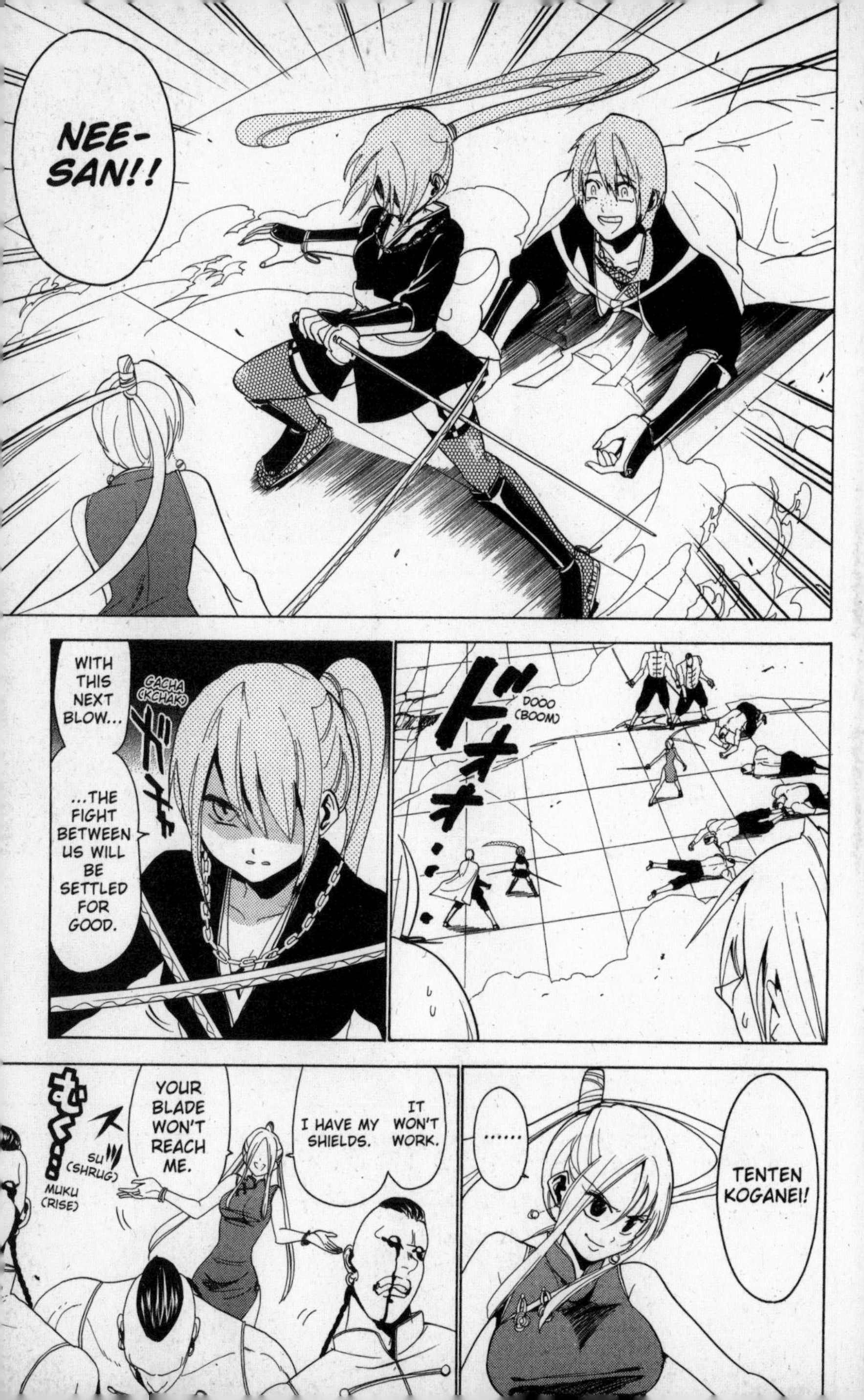
NEE-SAN!!
DOOO (BOOM)
WITH THIS NEXT BLOW...
GACHA (KCHAK)
...THE FIGHT BETWEEN US WILL BE SETTLED FOR GOOD.
......
TENTEN KOGANEI!
IT WON'T WORK.
I HAVE MY SHIELDS.
YOUR BLADE WON'T REACH ME.
SU (SHRUG)
MUKU (RISE)

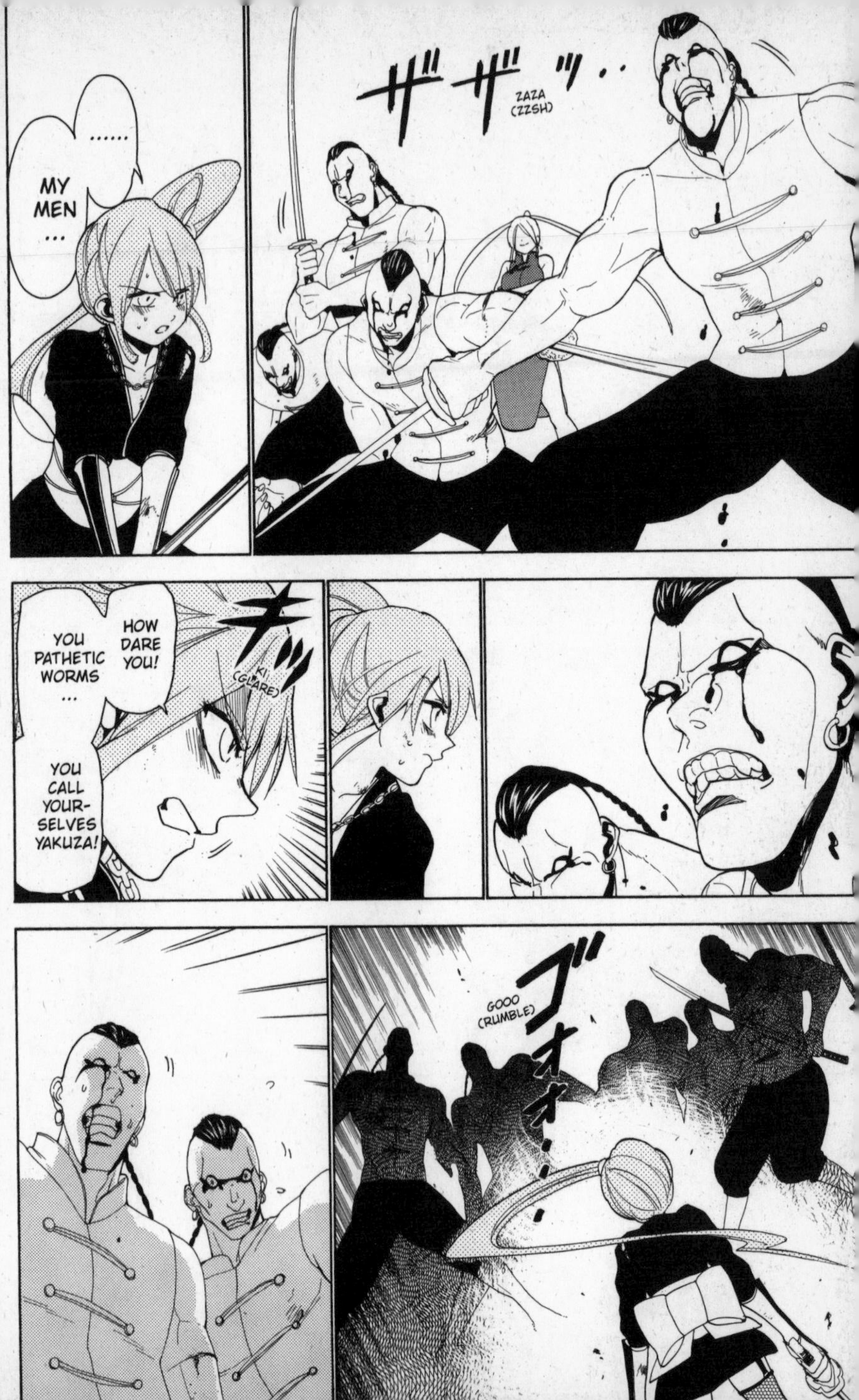
ザザッ..
ZAZA (ZZSH)
......
MY MEN ...
HOW DARE YOU!
YOU PATHETIC WORMS ...
チッ
KI (GLARE)
YOU CALL YOURSELVES YAKUZA!
ゴオオ...
GOOO (RUMBLE)

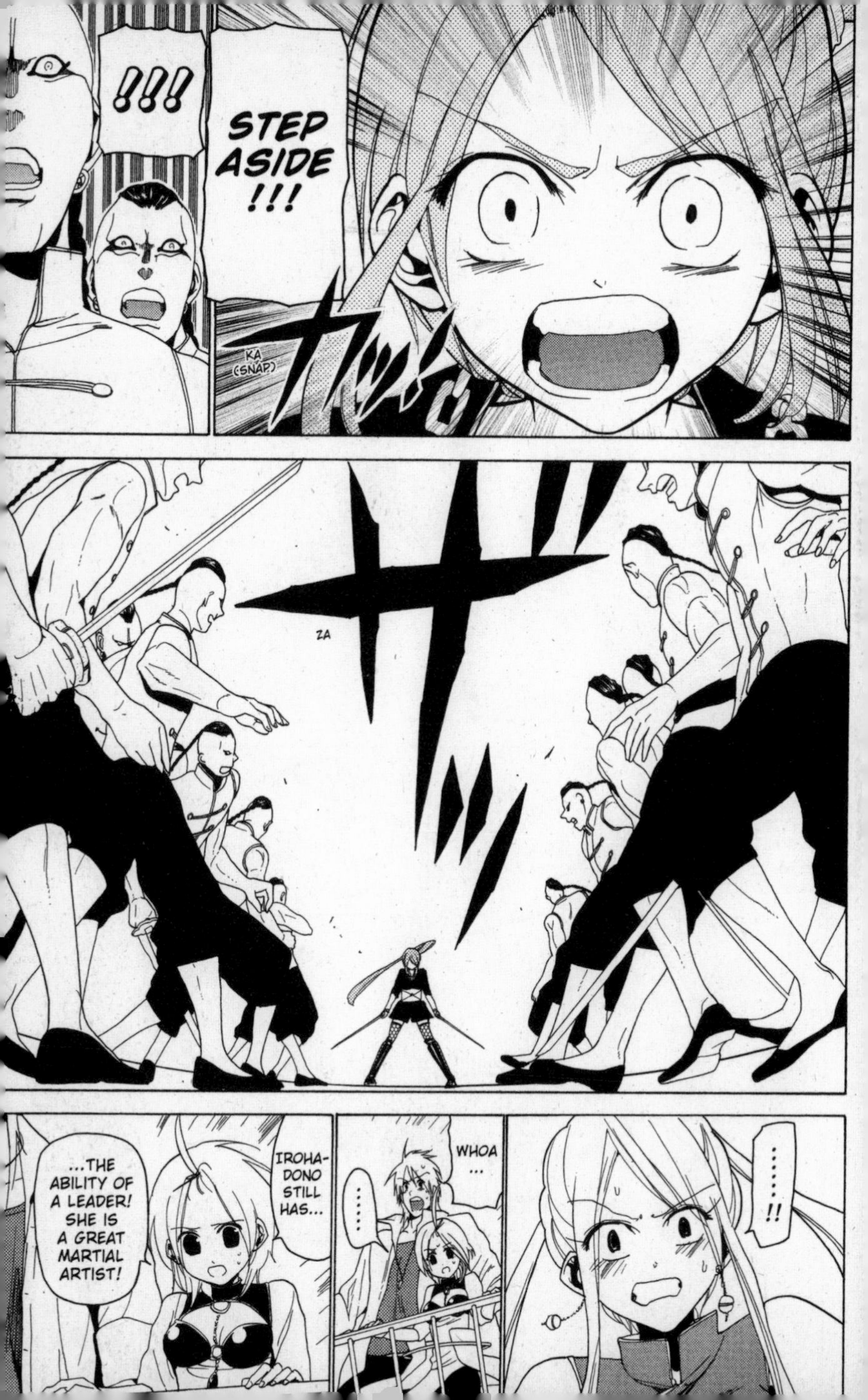
STEP ASIDE !!!
KA (SNAP)
!!!
ZA
......!!
WHOA ...
......
IROHA-DONO STILL HAS...
...THE ABILITY OF A LEADER! SHE IS A GREAT MARTIAL ARTIST!

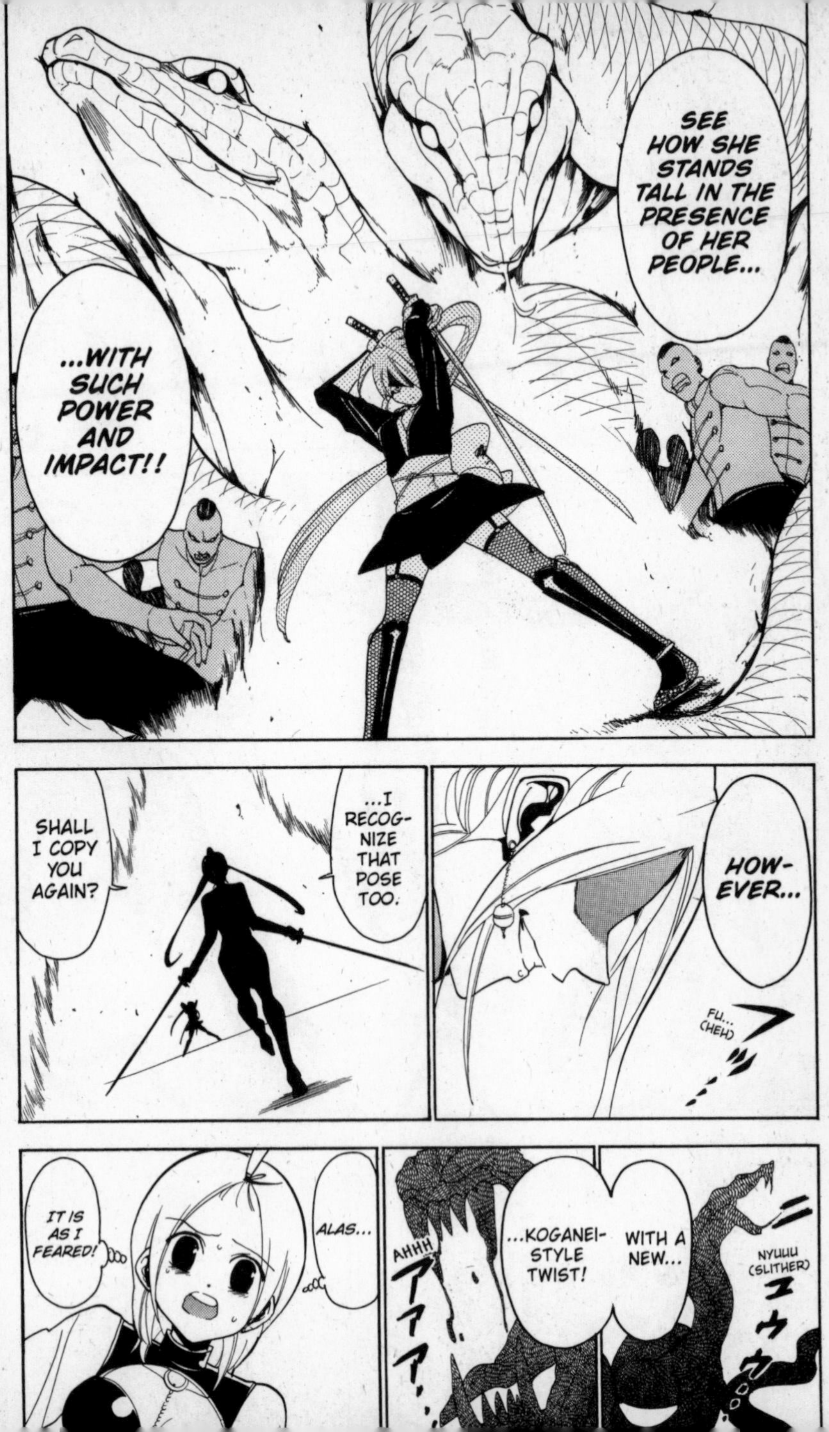
SEE HOW SHE STANDS TALL IN THE PRESENCE OF HER PEOPLE...
...WITH SUCH POWER AND IMPACT!!
HOW-EVER...
FU... (HEH)
...I RECOG-NIZE THAT POSE TOO.
SHALL I COPY YOU AGAIN?
NYUUU (SLITHER)
WITH A NEW...
...KOGANEI-STYLE TWIST!
AHHH
ALAS...
IT IS AS I FEARED!

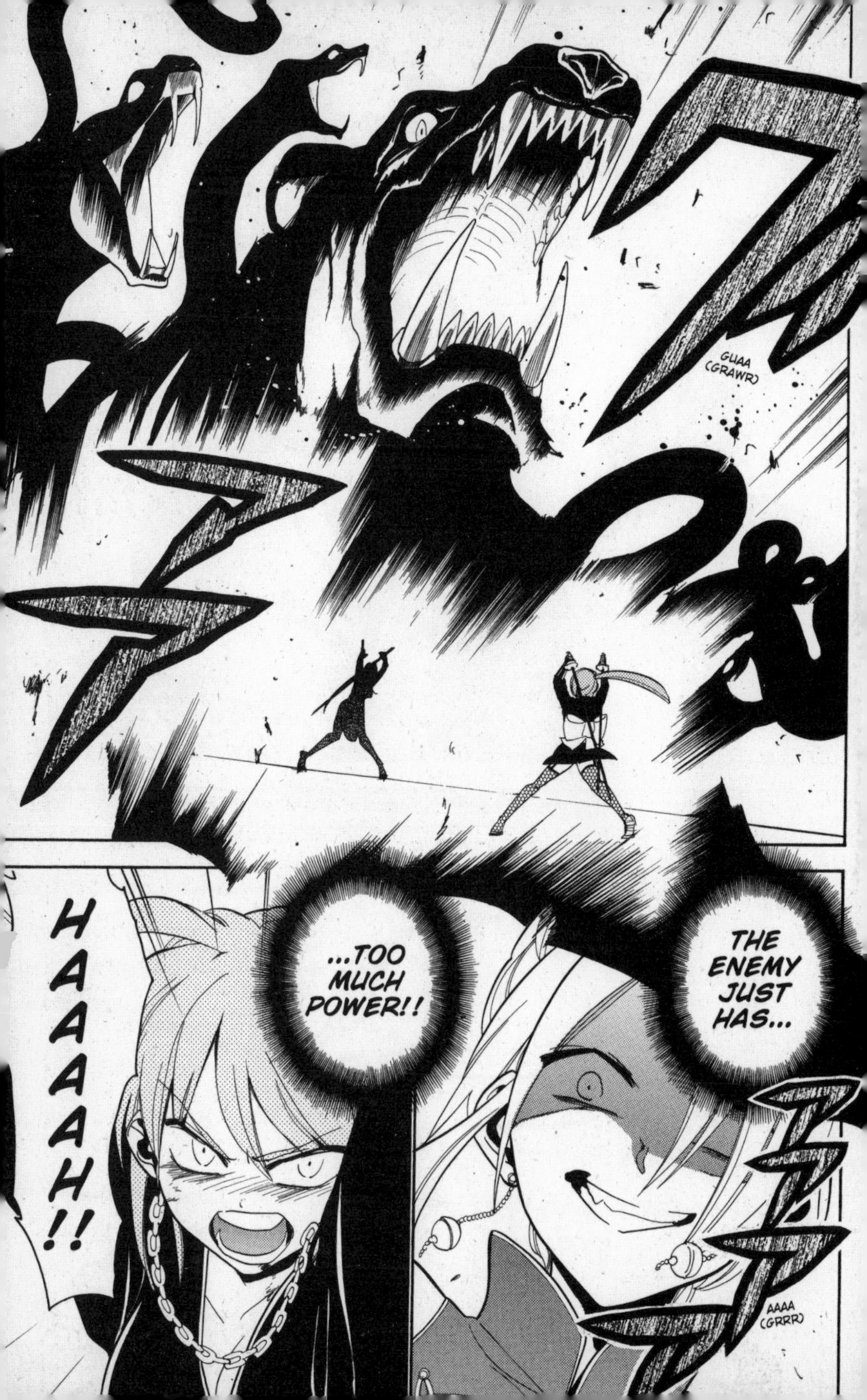
GUAA (GRAWR)
THE ENEMY JUST HAS...
...TOO MUCH POWER!!
AAAA (GRRR)
HAAAAAH!!

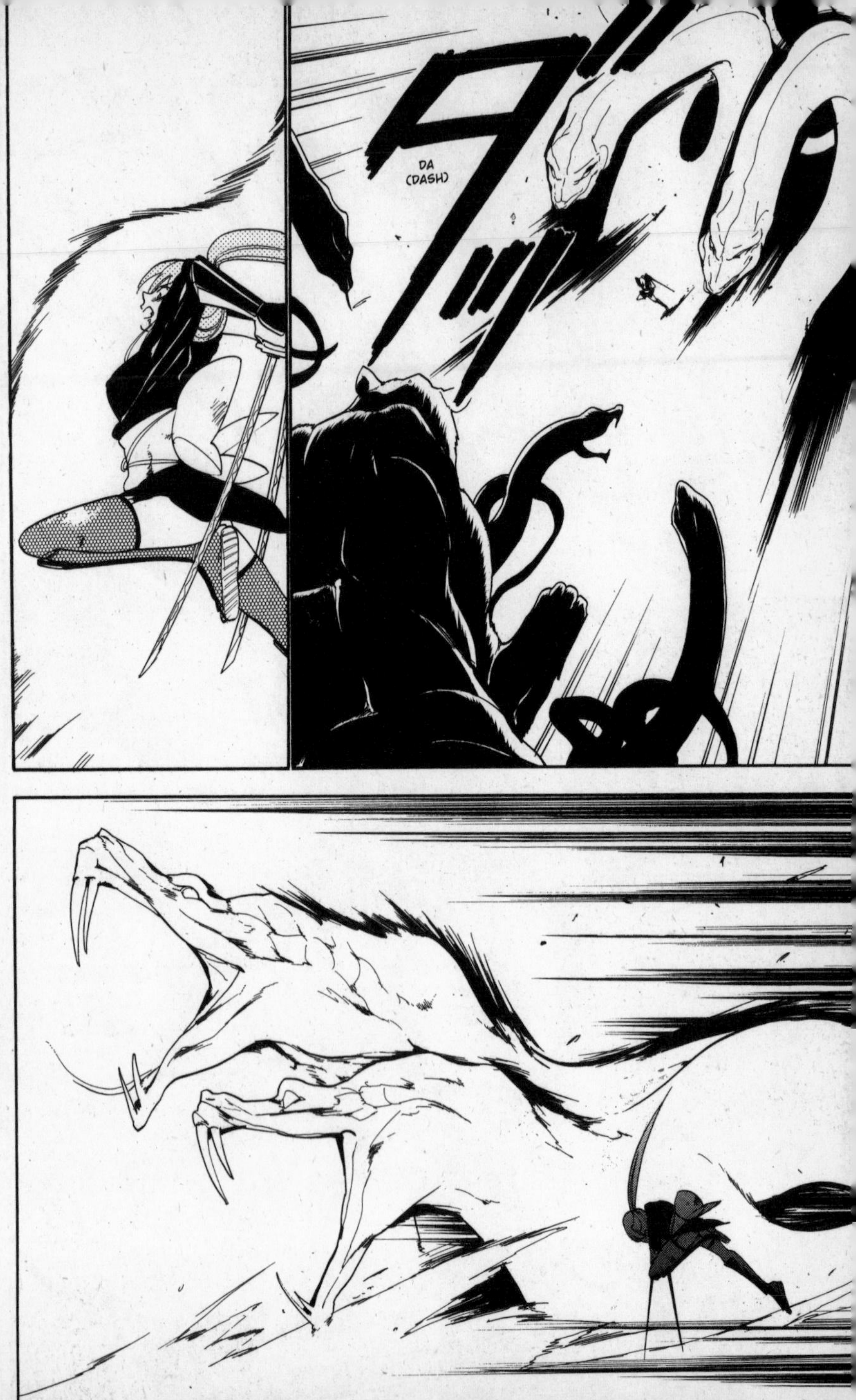
DA
(DASH)

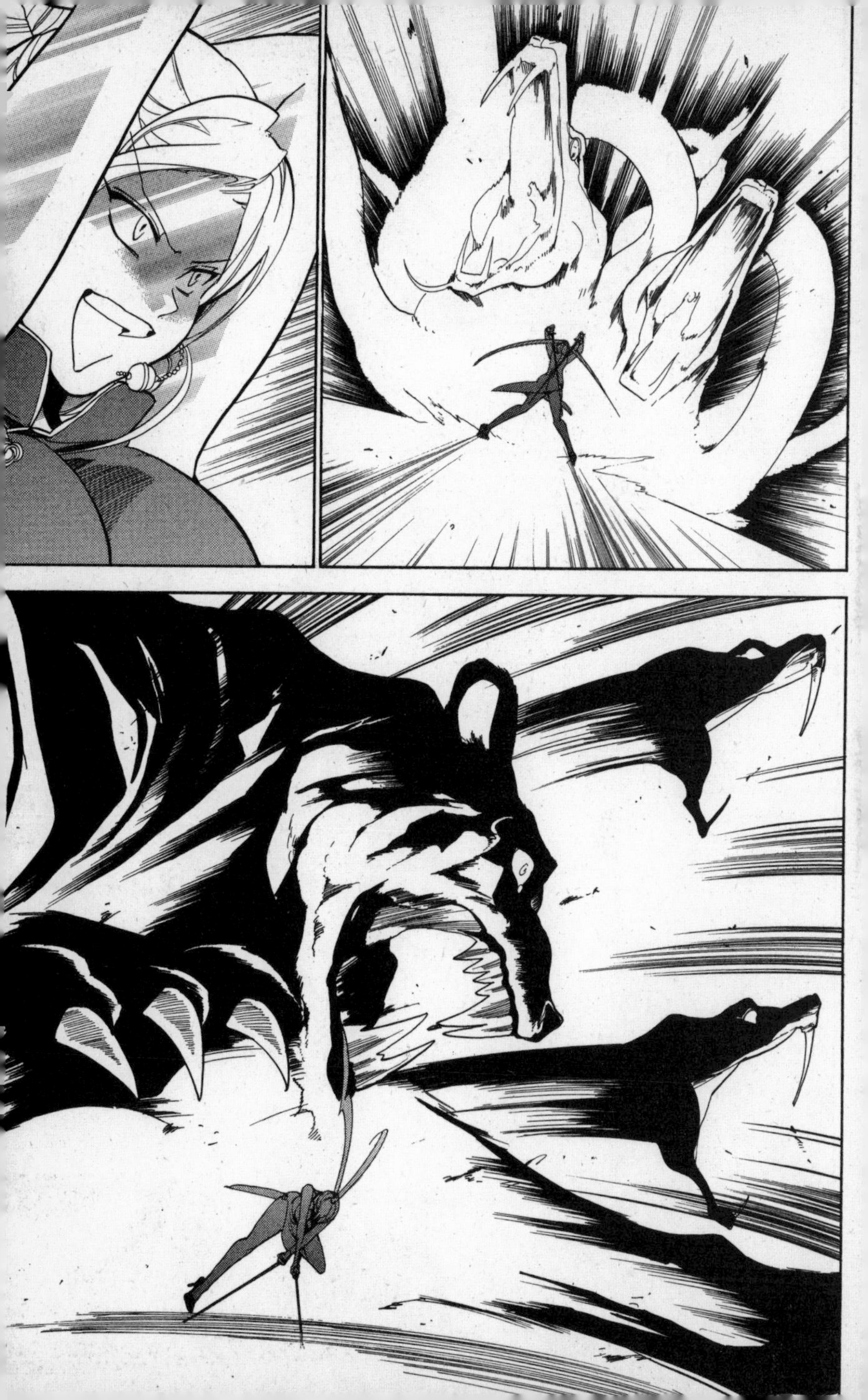

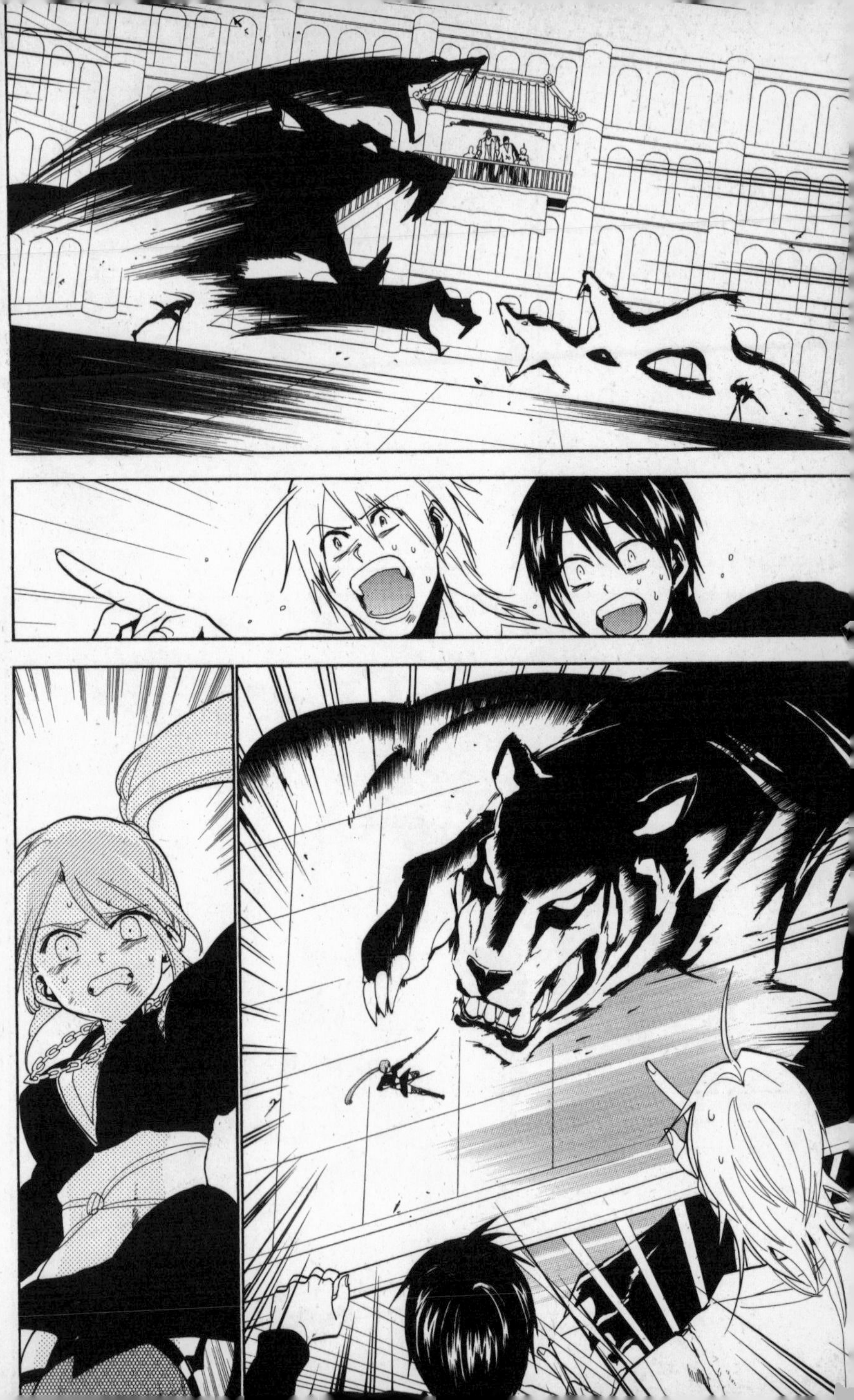

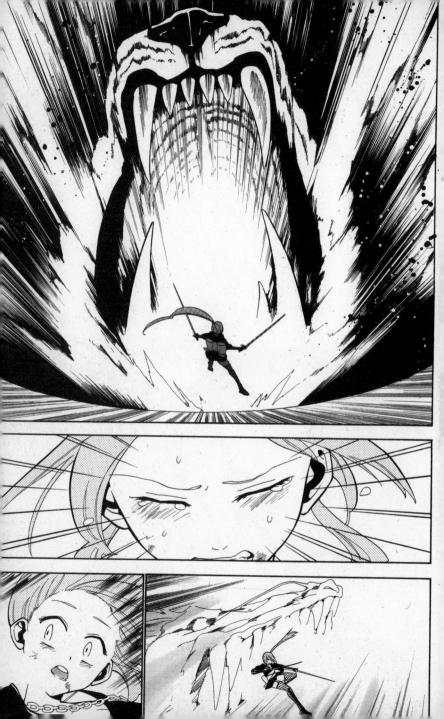

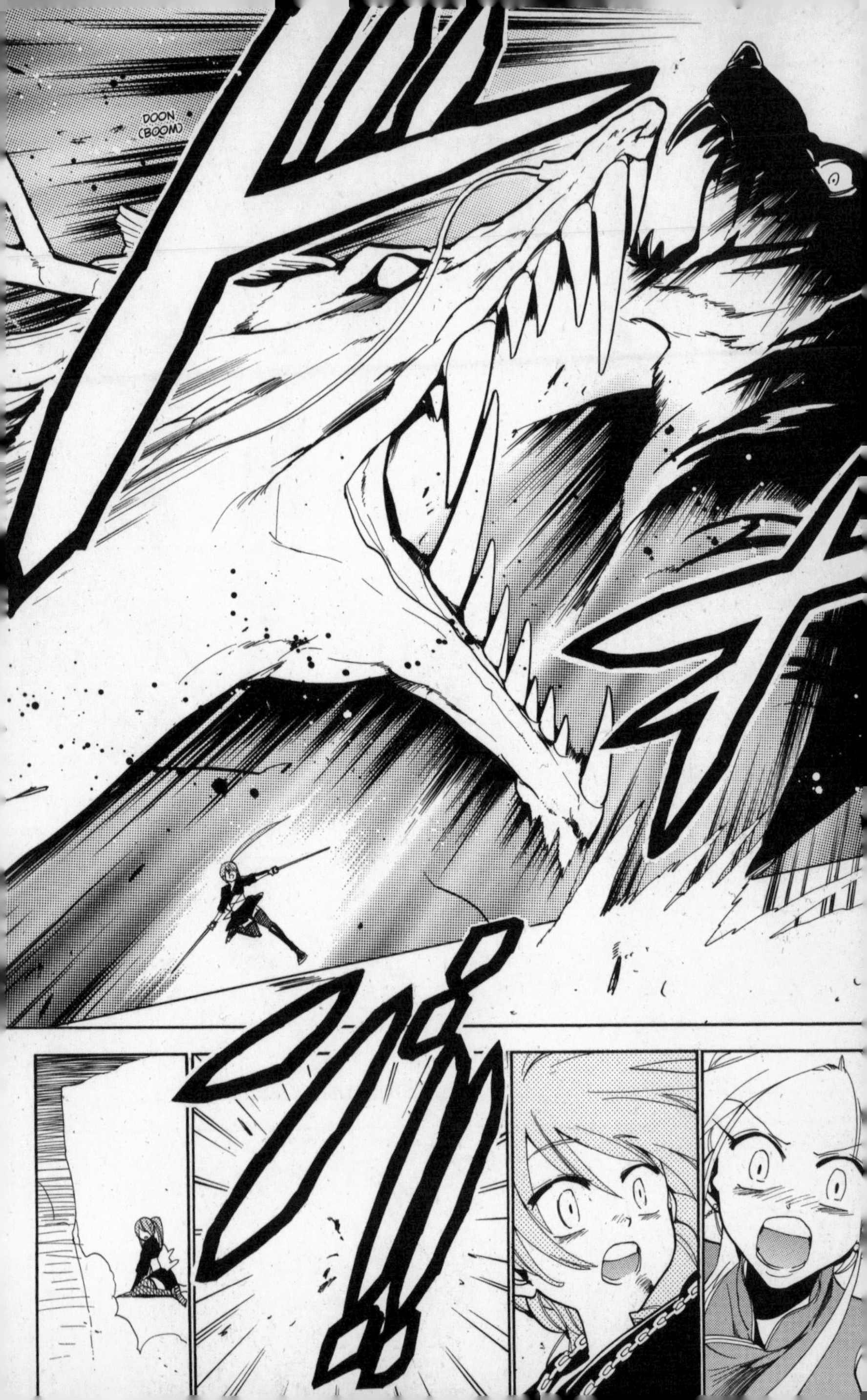
DOON
(BOOM)

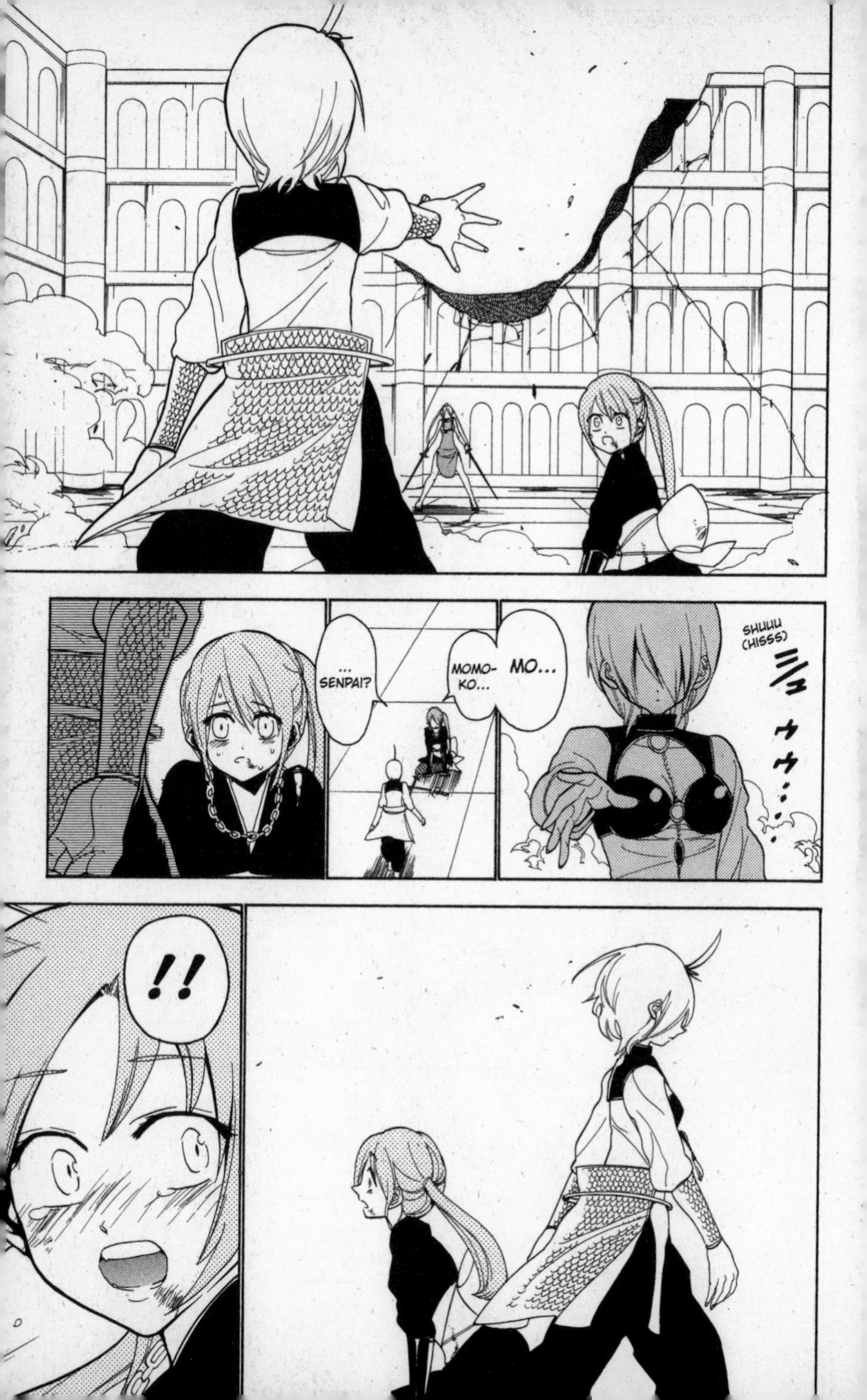
SHUUU (HISSS)
シュウウ…
MO...
MOMO-KO...
...SENPAI?
!!

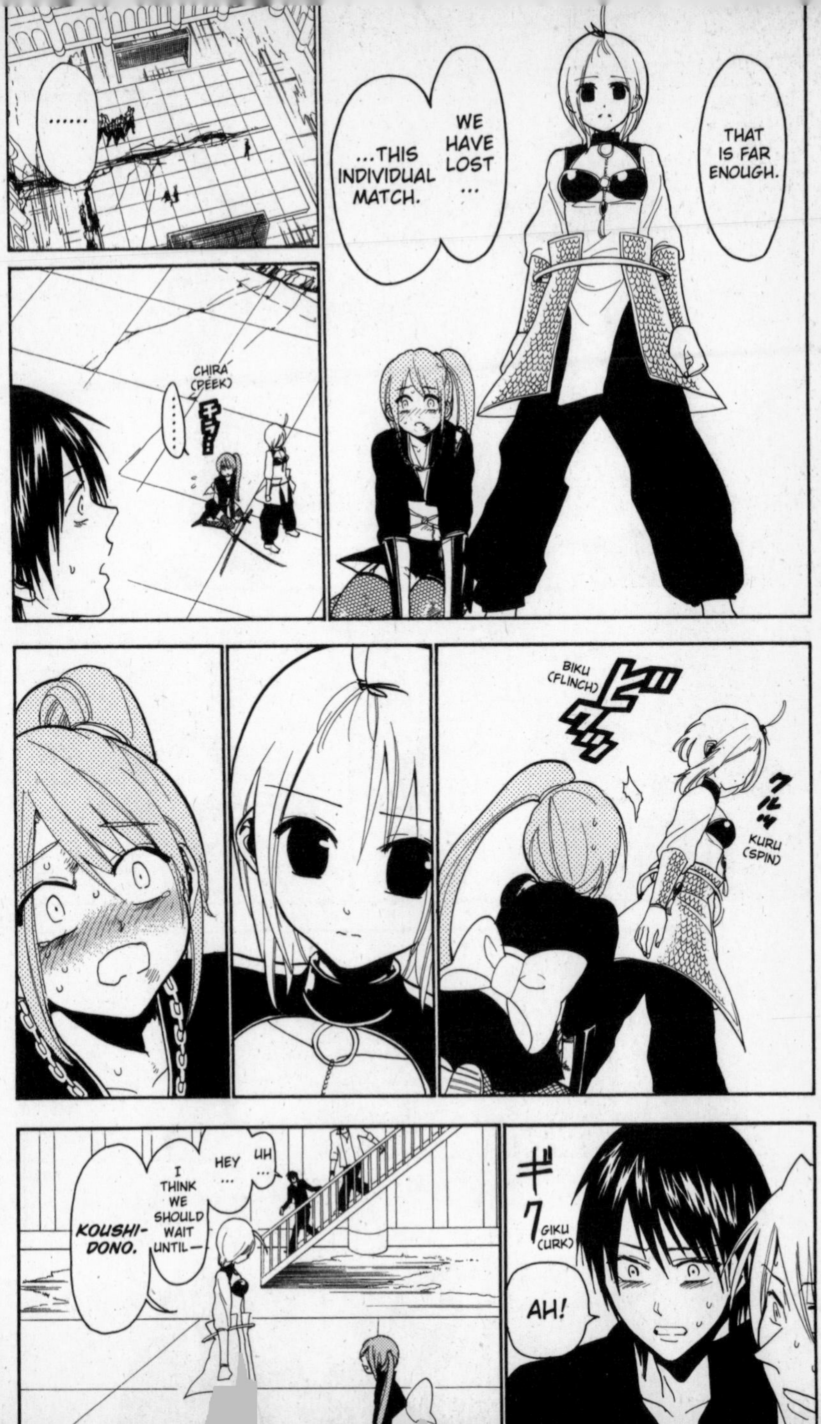
THAT IS FAR ENOUGH.
WE HAVE LOST ...
...THIS INDIVIDUAL MATCH.
......
チラ
CHIRA (PEEK)
......
ビクッ
BIKU (FLINCH)
クルッ
KURU (SPIN)
ギク
GIKU (URK)
AH!
UH ...
HEY ...
I THINK WE SHOULD WAIT UNTIL—
KOUSHI-DONO.

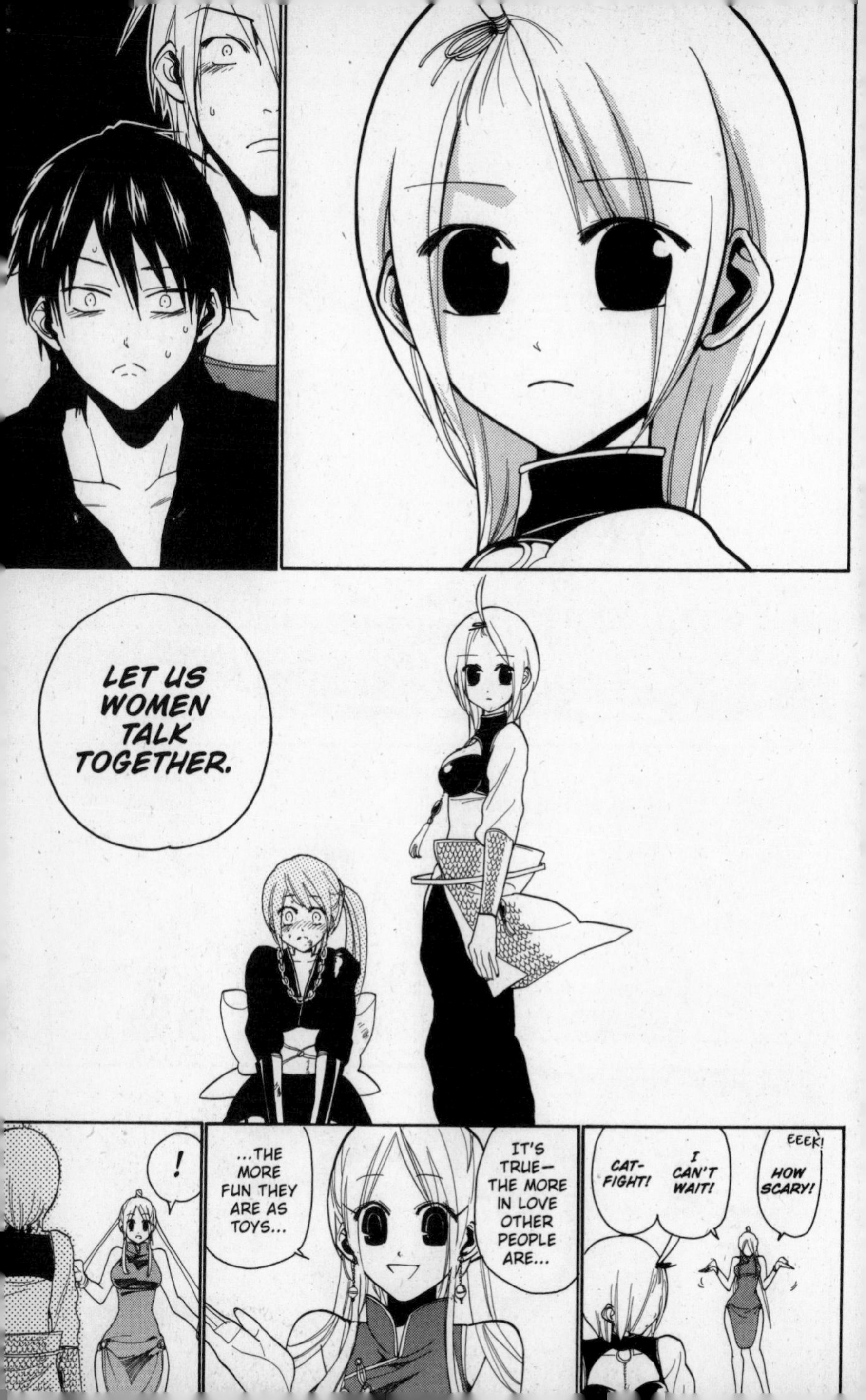
LET US WOMEN TALK TOGETHER.
EEEK!
HOW SCARY!
I CAN'T WAIT!
CAT-FIGHT!
IT'S TRUE— THE MORE IN LOVE OTHER PEOPLE ARE...
...THE MORE FUN THEY ARE AS TOYS...
!

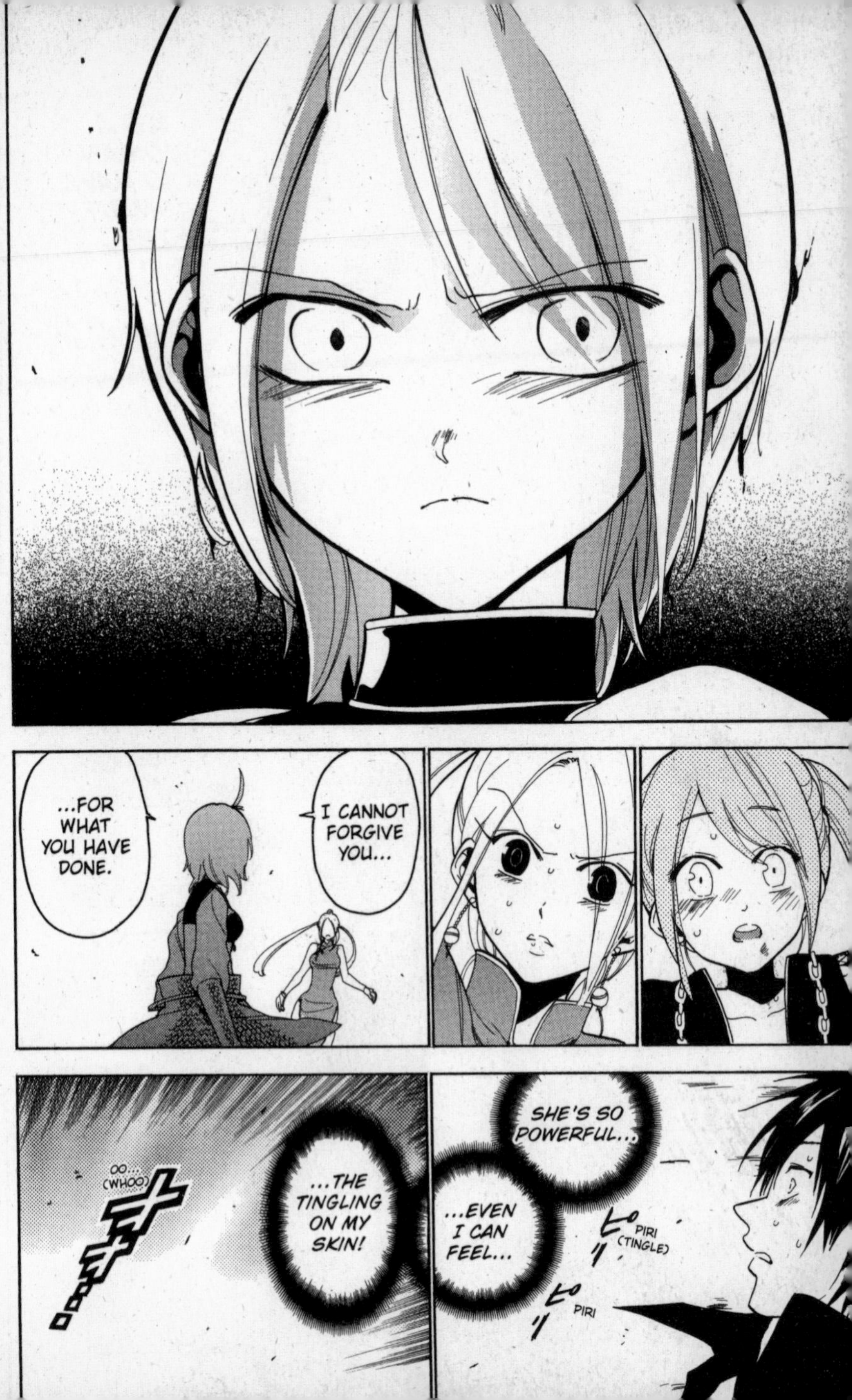
I CANNOT FORGIVE YOU...
...FOR WHAT YOU HAVE DONE.
SHE'S SO POWERFUL...
...EVEN I CAN FEEL...
PIRI (TINGLE)
PIRI
...THE TINGLING ON MY SKIN!
OO... (WHOO)

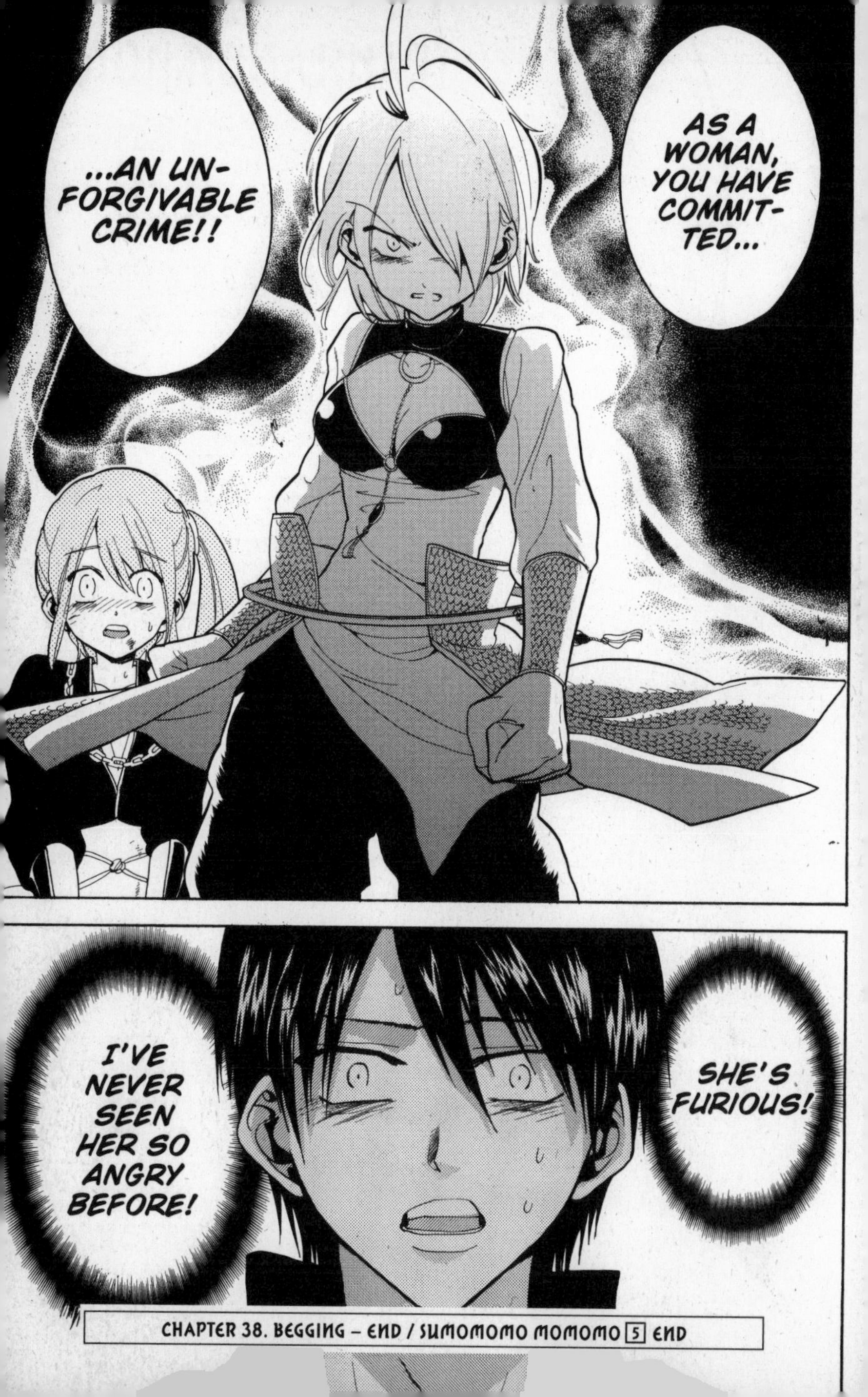
AS A WOMAN, YOU HAVE COMMIT-TED...
...AN UN-FORGIVABLE CRIME!!
SHE'S FURIOUS!
I'VE NEVER SEEN HER SO ANGRY BEFORE!
CHAPTER 38. BEGGING – END / SUMOMOMO MOMOMO 5 END

TRANSLATION NOTES

Sumomomo, Momomo is part of a well-known Japanese tongue twister which reads, "*Sumomo mo momo mo momo no uchi,*" and roughly means, "Plums and peaches are part of the peach family."

Common Honorifics
No honorific: Indicates familiarity or closeness. If used without permission or reason, addressing someone in this manner would be an insult.
-san: The Japanese equivalent of Mr./Mrs./Miss. If a situation calls for politeness, this is the fail-safe honorific.
-sama: Conveys great respect; may also indicate that the social status of the speaker is lower than that of the addressee.
-dono: A polite, formal honorific suffix.
-kun: Used most often when referring to boys, this indicates affection or familiarity. Occasionally used by older men among their peers, but it may also be used by anyone referring to a person of lower standing.
-chan: An affectionate honorific indicating familiarity used mostly in reference to girls; also used in reference to cute persons or animals of either gender.
-sensei: A respectful term for teachers, artists, or high-level professionals.
-nii, onii-san, nii-chan: Used to address one's older brother or brother figure.
-nee, onee-san, nee-chan: Used to address ones's older sister or sister figure.

Page 24
Cattail: In this case, the plant shown is actually known as a *nekojarashi,* meaning "cat-exciter." A tall grass with a large head very similar to that found on cattails, *nekojarashi* can easily be used as a cat toy, as shown here.

Page 38
Endou: The "*en*" part of this surname is written with the character for "monkey."

Antera Senpen-ryuu: In keeping with the pattern of the story, Antera is the heavenly general associated with the monkey in the Chinese Zodiac. Senpen-ryuu means "Infinite Changes Style."

Page 158
Sakazuki: The name of a special saucerlike cup that is used in the consumption of sake. It has a special place in rituals meant to bond people unrelated by blood — rituals that take their name from the cup itself. The sakazuki ritual is especially prized and utilized within the yakuza community, which traditionally forms itself into "families" within individual organizations.

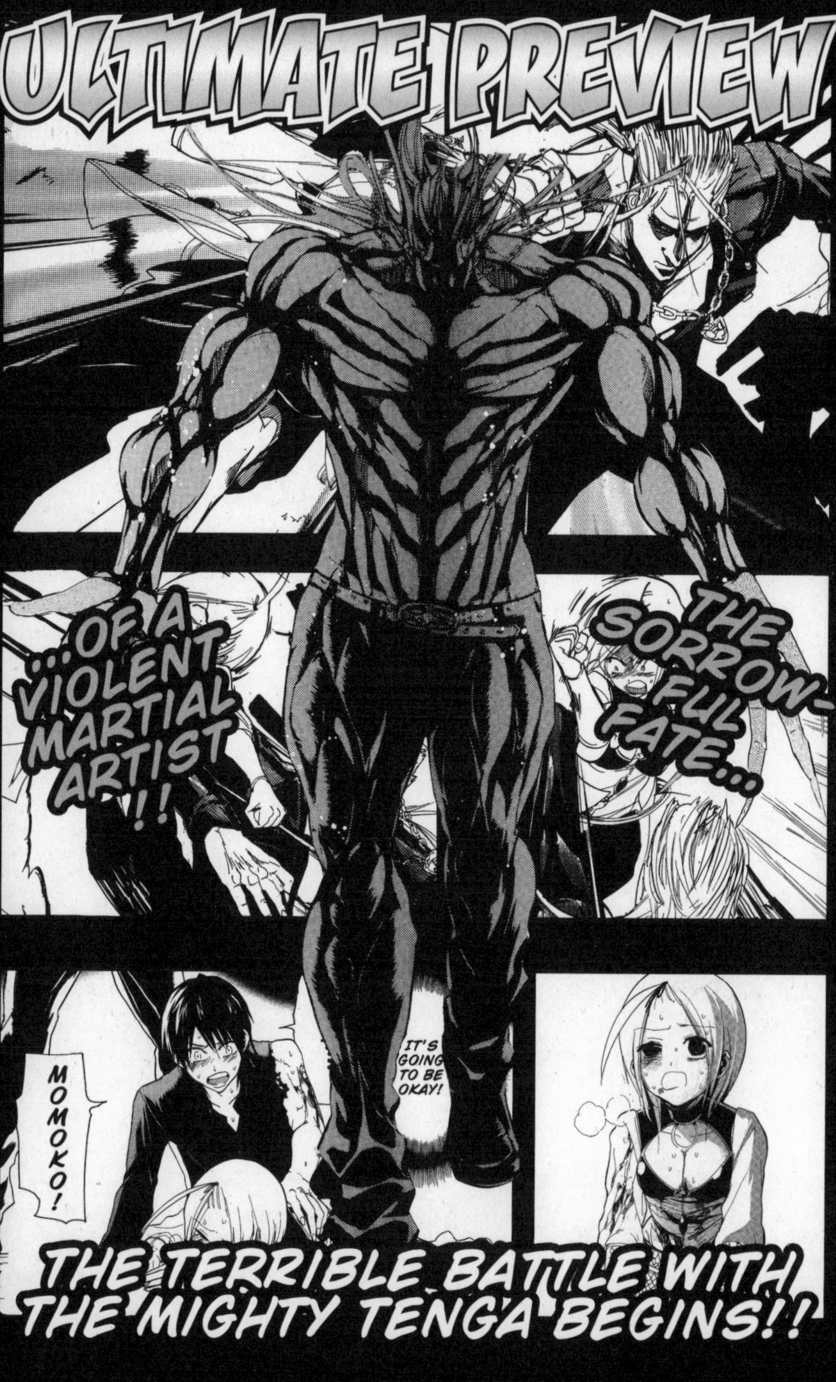
ULTIMATE PREVIEW
THE SORROW-FUL FATE...
...OF A VIOLENT MARTIAL ARTIST!!
IT'S GOING TO BE OKAY!
MOMOKO!
THE TERRIBLE BATTLE WITH THE MIGHTY TENGA BEGINS!!

FISTS CROSS AS TWO COLLIDE! EVEN IF THERE IS NO HOPE AGAINST A SUPERIOR ENEMY...
...WILL FINALLY AWAKEN!!
LOOK FOR VOLUME 6 IN NOVEMBER 2010!!

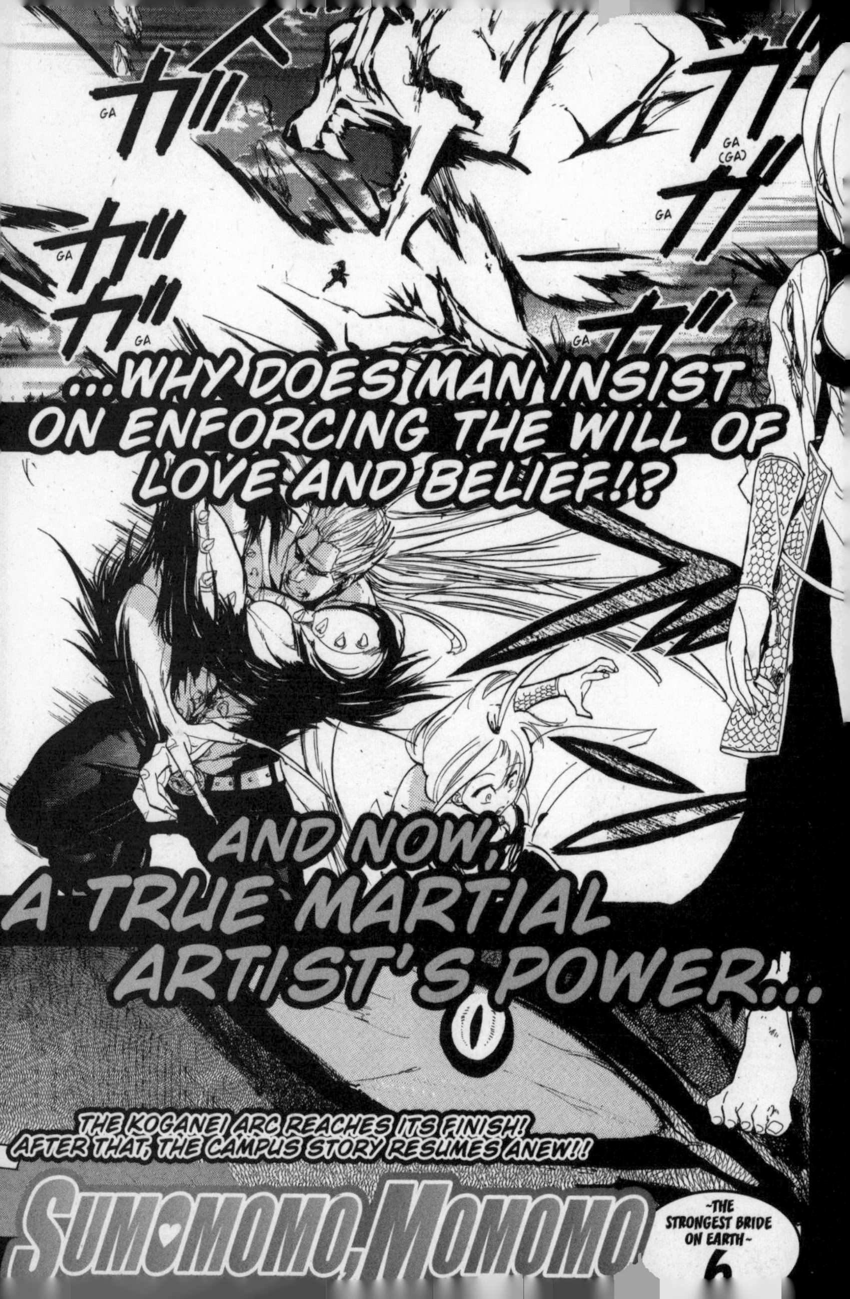

GA (GA)
GA
GA
GA
GA
GA
...WHY DOES MAN INSIST ON ENFORCING THE WILL OF LOVE AND BELIEF!?
AND NOW, A TRUE MARTIAL ARTIST'S POWER...
THE KOGANEI ARC REACHES ITS FINISH! AFTER THAT, THE CAMPUS STORY RESUMES ANEW!!
SUMOMOMO, MOMOMO
~THE STRONGEST BRIDE ON EARTH~
6

SUMOMOMO, MOMOMO ~THE STRONGEST (?) OMAKE ON EARTH~

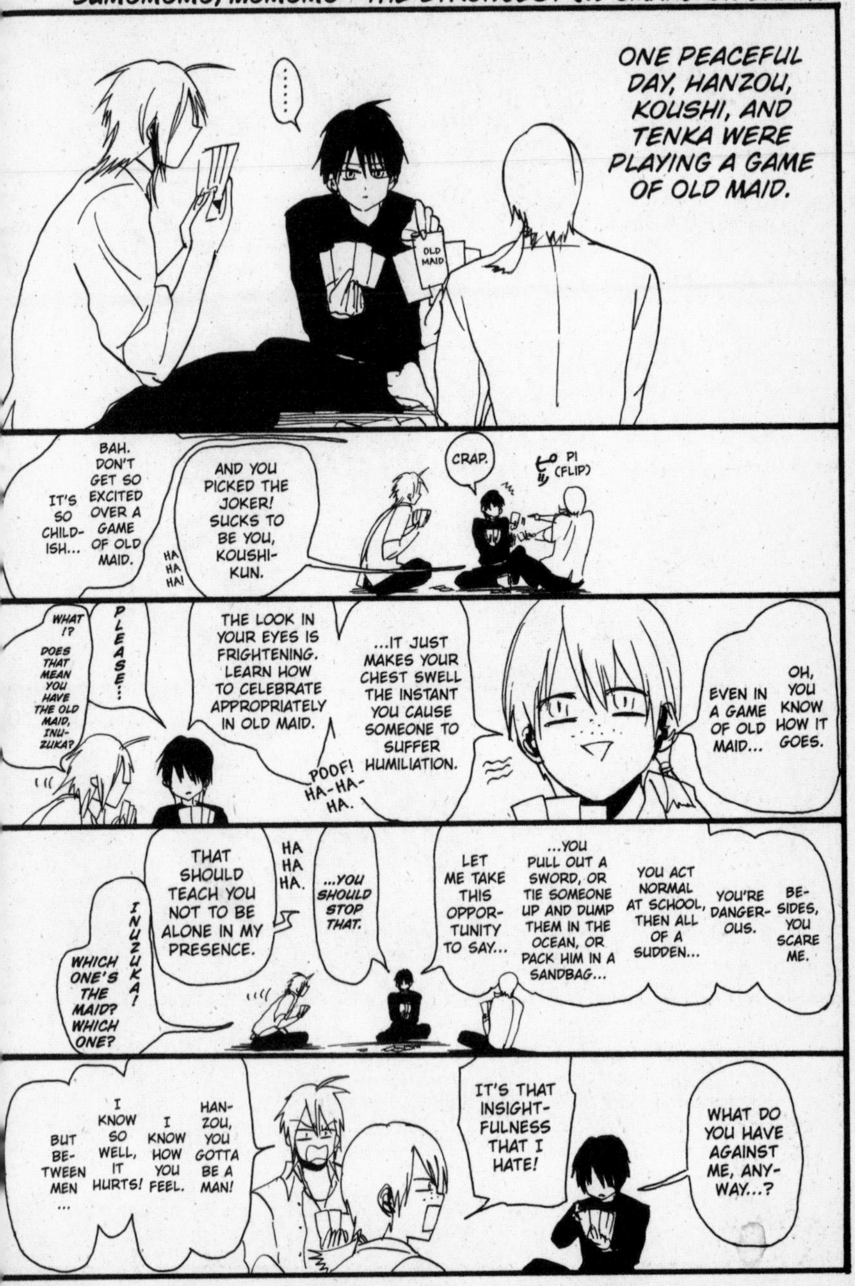

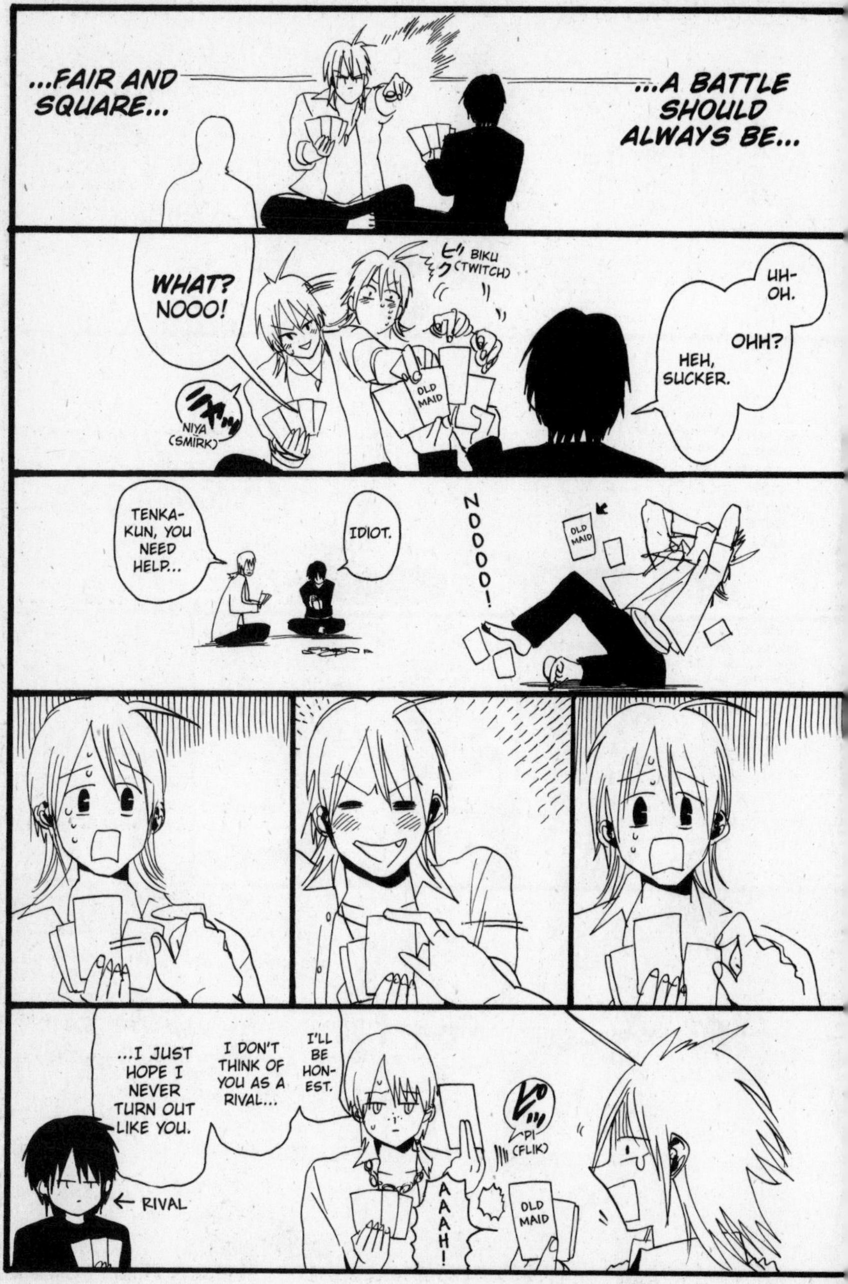
...A BATTLE SHOULD ALWAYS BE...
...FAIR AND SQUARE...
UH-OH.
OHH?
HEH, SUCKER.
BIKU (TWITCH)
OLD MAID
WHAT? NOOO!
NIYA (SMIRK)
OLD MAID
NOOOOO!
IDIOT.
TENKA-KUN, YOU NEED HELP...
OLD MAID
PI (FLIK)
AAAAH!
I'LL BE HON-EST.
I DON'T THINK OF YOU AS A RIVAL...
...I JUST HOPE I NEVER TURN OUT LIKE YOU.
← RIVAL

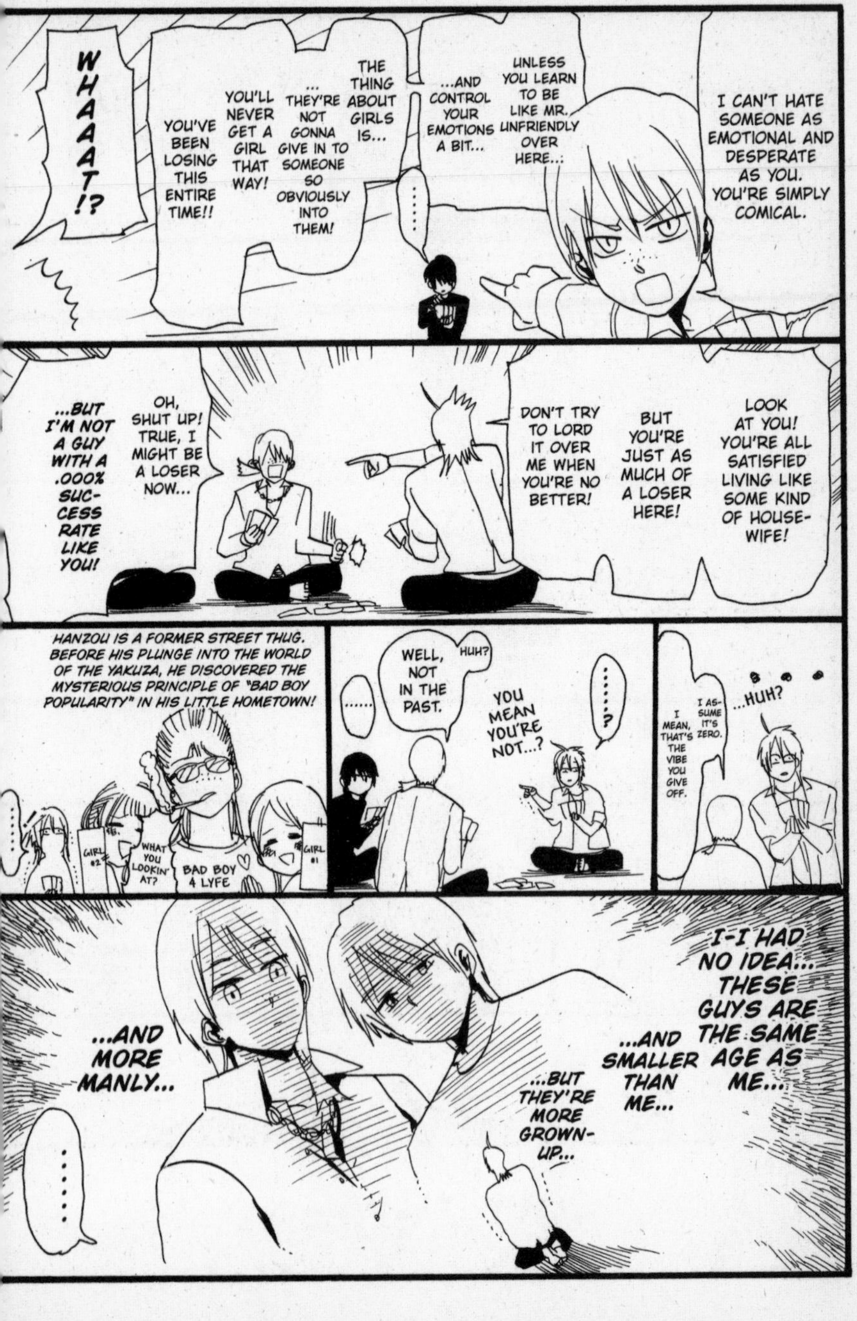
I CAN'T HATE SOMEONE AS EMOTIONAL AND DESPERATE AS YOU. YOU'RE SIMPLY COMICAL.
UNLESS YOU LEARN TO BE LIKE MR. UNFRIENDLY OVER HERE...
...AND CONTROL YOUR EMOTIONS A BIT...
......
THE THING ABOUT GIRLS IS...
...THEY'RE NOT GONNA GIVE IN TO SOMEONE SO OBVIOUSLY INTO THEM!
YOU'LL NEVER GET A GIRL THAT WAY!
YOU'VE BEEN LOSING THIS ENTIRE TIME!!
WHAAAAT!?
LOOK AT YOU! YOU'RE ALL SATISFIED LIVING LIKE SOME KIND OF HOUSE-WIFE!
BUT YOU'RE JUST AS MUCH OF A LOSER HERE!
DON'T TRY TO LORD IT OVER ME WHEN YOU'RE NO BETTER!
OH, SHUT UP! TRUE, I MIGHT BE A LOSER NOW...
...BUT I'M NOT A GUY WITH A .000% SUC-CESS RATE LIKE YOU!
...HUH?
I AS-SUME IT'S ZERO.
I MEAN, THAT'S THE VIBE YOU GIVE OFF.
......?
YOU MEAN YOU'RE NOT...?
WELL, NOT IN THE PAST.
HUH?
......
HANZOU IS A FORMER STREET THUG. BEFORE HIS PLUNGE INTO THE WORLD OF THE YAKUZA, HE DISCOVERED THE MYSTERIOUS PRINCIPLE OF "BAD BOY POPULARITY" IN HIS LITTLE HOMETOWN!
GIRL #1
BAD BOY 4 LYFE
WHAT YOU LOOKIN' AT?
GIRL #2
...!
I-I HAD NO IDEA... THESE GUYS ARE THE SAME AGE AS ME...
...AND SMALLER THAN ME...
...BUT THEY'RE MORE GROWN-UP...
...AND MORE MANLY...
......

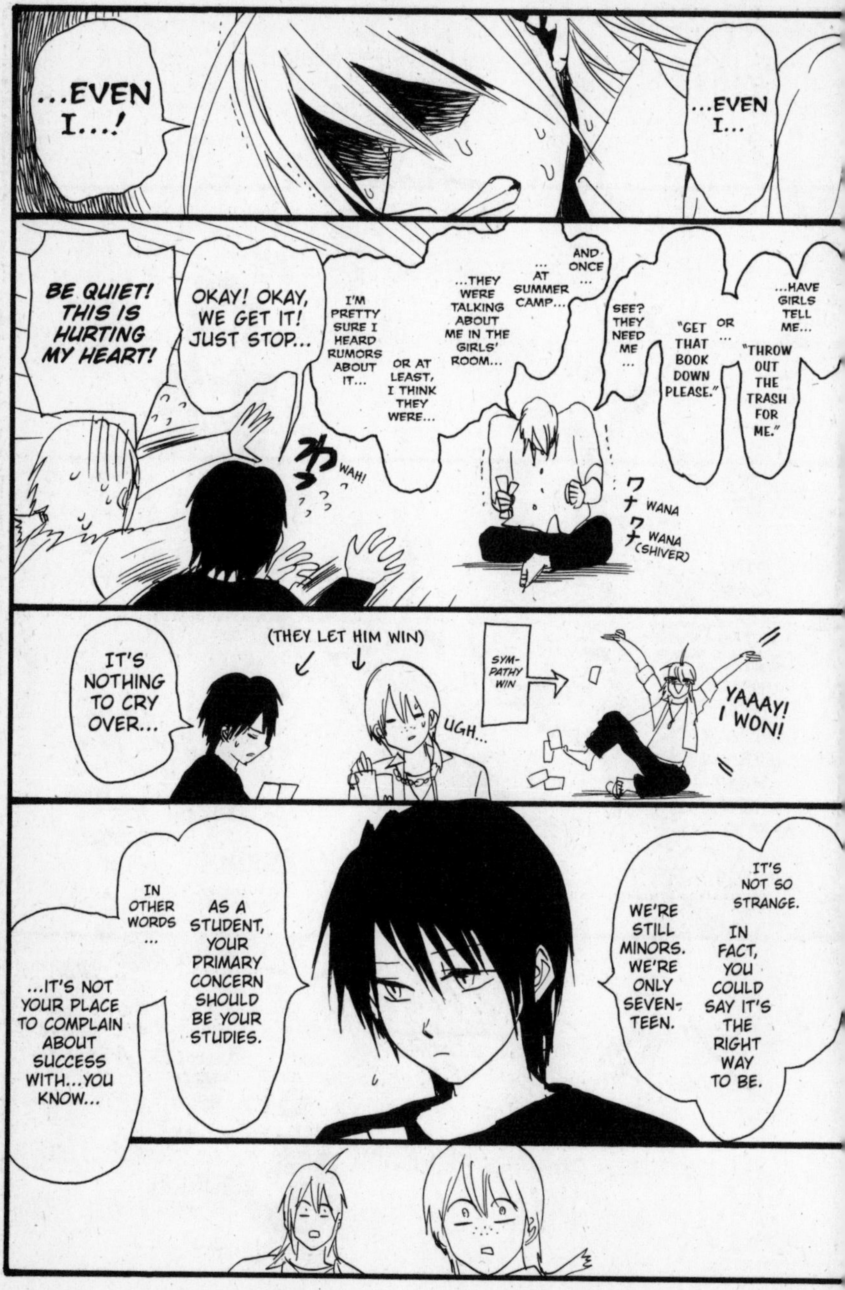
...EVEN I...
...EVEN I...!
...HAVE GIRLS TELL ME...
"THROW OUT THE TRASH FOR ME."
OR...
"GET THAT BOOK DOWN PLEASE."
SEE? THEY NEED ME...
AND ONCE...
...AT SUMMER CAMP...
...THEY WERE TALKING ABOUT ME IN THE GIRLS' ROOM...
OR AT LEAST, I THINK THEY WERE...
I'M PRETTY SURE I HEARD RUMORS ABOUT IT...
ワナ ワナ
WANA WANA (SHIVER)
WAH!
OKAY! OKAY, WE GET IT! JUST STOP...
BE QUIET! THIS IS HURTING MY HEART!
YAAAY! I WON!
SYMPATHY WIN
(THEY LET HIM WIN)
UGH...
IT'S NOTHING TO CRY OVER...
IT'S NOT SO STRANGE.
IN FACT, YOU COULD SAY IT'S THE RIGHT WAY TO BE.
WE'RE STILL MINORS. WE'RE ONLY SEVENTEEN.
AS A STUDENT, YOUR PRIMARY CONCERN SHOULD BE YOUR STUDIES.
IN OTHER WORDS...
...IT'S NOT YOUR PLACE TO COMPLAIN ABOUT SUCCESS WITH...YOU KNOW...

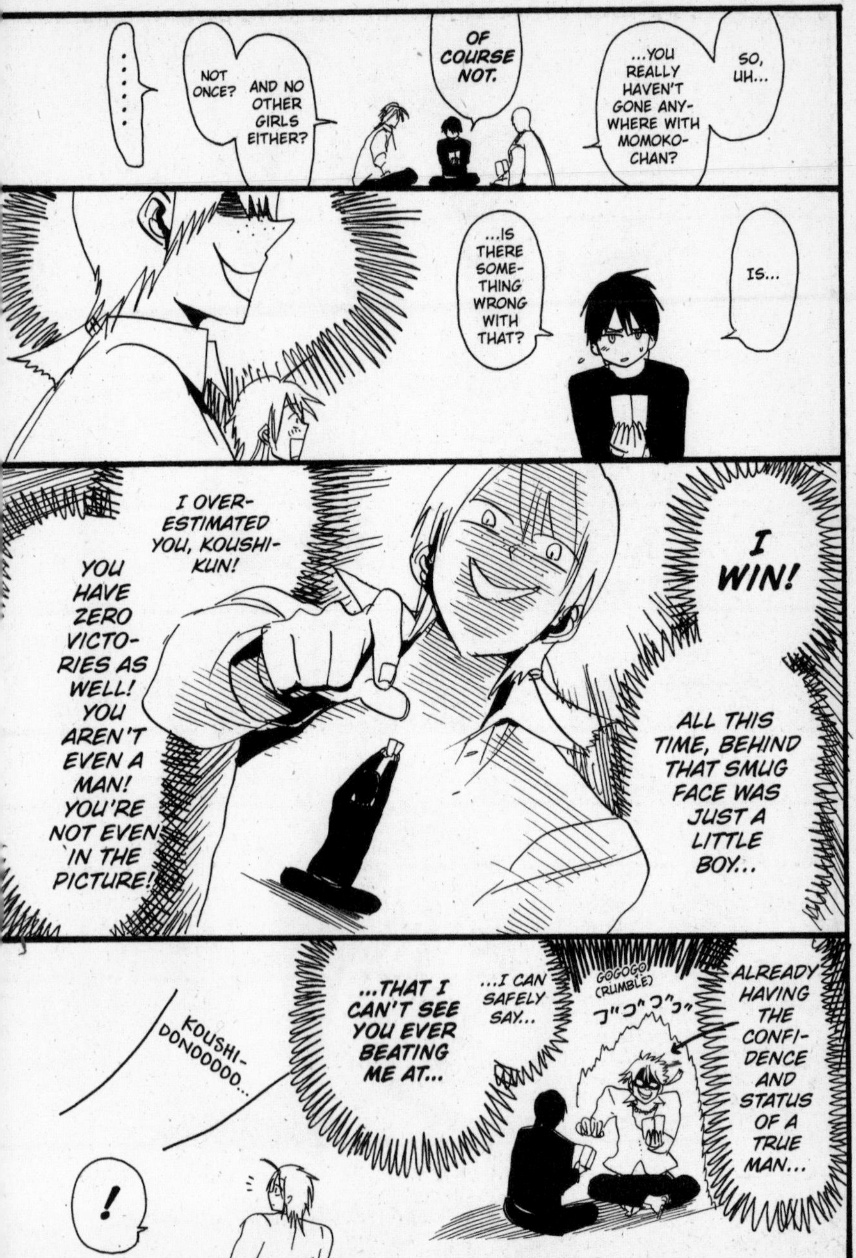
SO, UH...
...YOU REALLY HAVEN'T GONE ANYWHERE WITH MOMOKO-CHAN?
OF COURSE NOT.
NOT ONCE? AND NO OTHER GIRLS EITHER?
......
IS...
...IS THERE SOMETHING WRONG WITH THAT?
I WIN!
ALL THIS TIME, BEHIND THAT SMUG FACE WAS JUST A LITTLE BOY...
I OVERESTIMATED YOU, KOUSHI-KUN!
YOU HAVE ZERO VICTORIES AS WELL! YOU AREN'T EVEN A MAN! YOU'RE NOT EVEN IN THE PICTURE!
ALREADY HAVING THE CONFIDENCE AND STATUS OF A TRUE MAN...
GOGOGO (RUMBLE)
ゴゴゴゴ
...I CAN SAFELY SAY...
...THAT I CAN'T SEE YOU EVER BEATING ME AT...
KOUSHI-DONOOOOOO...
!

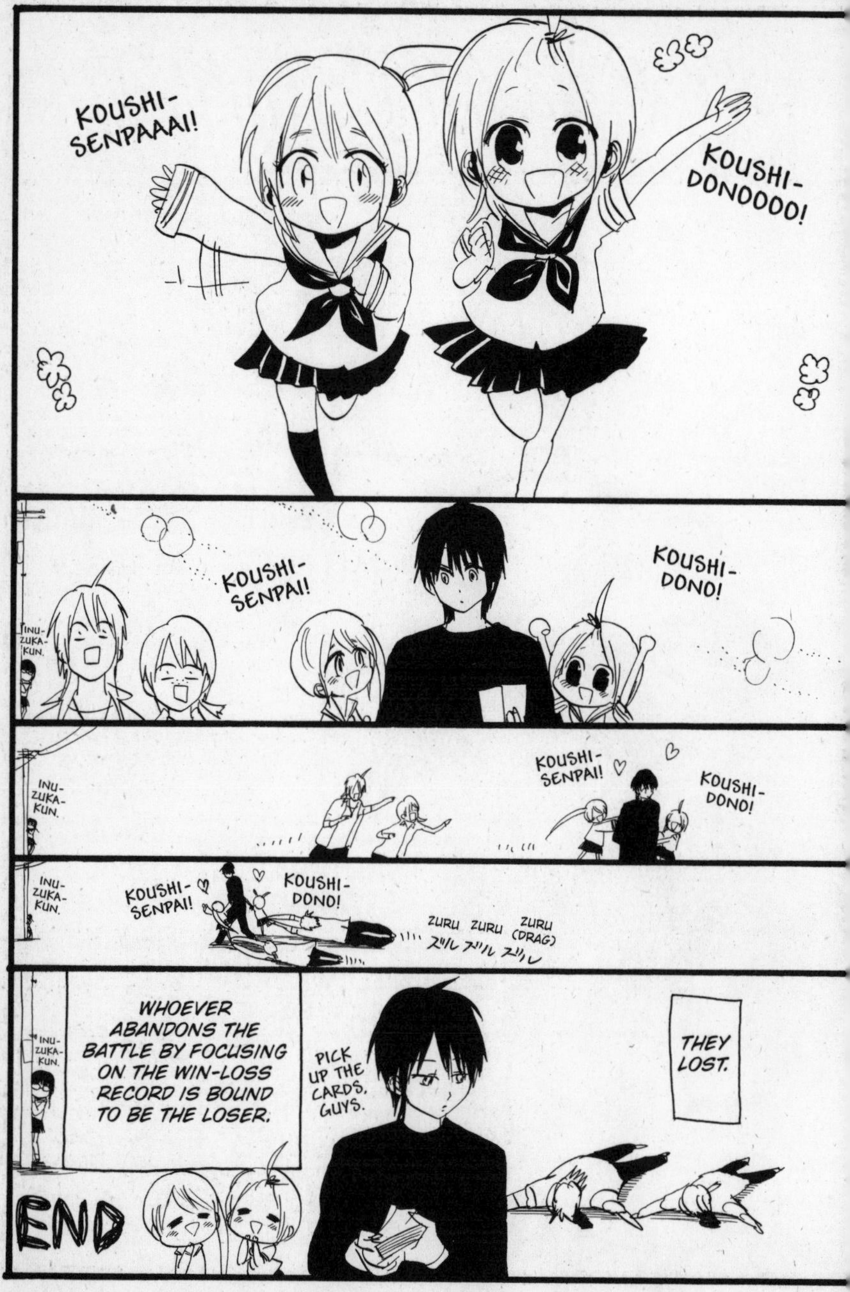
KOUSHI-DONOOOO!
KOUSHI-SENPAAAI!
KOUSHI-DONO!
KOUSHI-SENPAI!
INU-ZUKA-KUN.
KOUSHI-DONO!
KOUSHI-SENPAI!
INU-ZUKA-KUN.
ZURU ZURU ZURU (DRAG)
ズルズルズル
KOUSHI-DONO!
KOUSHI-SENPAI!
INU-ZUKA-KUN.
THEY LOST.
PICK UP THE CARDS, GUYS.
WHOEVER ABANDONS THE BATTLE BY FOCUSING ON THE WIN-LOSS RECORD IS BOUND TO BE THE LOSER.
INU-ZUKA-KUN.
END

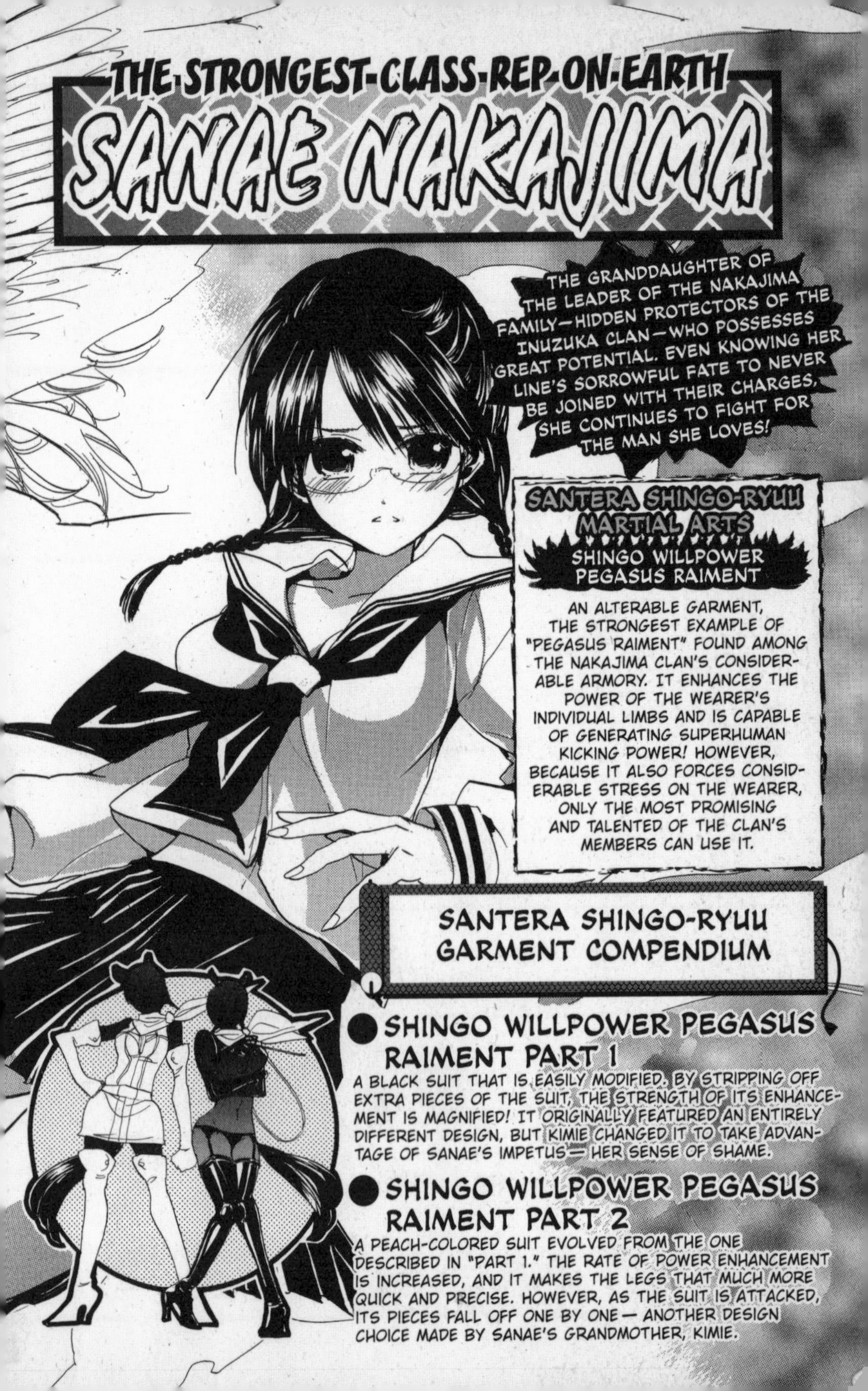
THE STRONGEST CLASS REP ON EARTH
SANAE NAKAJIMA
THE GRANDDAUGHTER OF THE LEADER OF THE NAKAJIMA FAMILY—HIDDEN PROTECTORS OF THE INUZUKA CLAN—WHO POSSESSES GREAT POTENTIAL. EVEN KNOWING HER LINE'S SORROWFUL FATE TO NEVER BE JOINED WITH THEIR CHARGES, SHE CONTINUES TO FIGHT FOR THE MAN SHE LOVES!
SANTERA SHINGO-RYUU MARTIAL ARTS
SHINGO WILLPOWER PEGASUS RAIMENT
AN ALTERABLE GARMENT, THE STRONGEST EXAMPLE OF "PEGASUS RAIMENT" FOUND AMONG THE NAKAJIMA CLAN'S CONSIDERABLE ARMORY. IT ENHANCES THE POWER OF THE WEARER'S INDIVIDUAL LIMBS AND IS CAPABLE OF GENERATING SUPERHUMAN KICKING POWER! HOWEVER, BECAUSE IT ALSO FORCES CONSIDERABLE STRESS ON THE WEARER, ONLY THE MOST PROMISING AND TALENTED OF THE CLAN'S MEMBERS CAN USE IT.
SANTERA SHINGO-RYUU GARMENT COMPENDIUM
● SHINGO WILLPOWER PEGASUS RAIMENT PART 1
A BLACK SUIT THAT IS EASILY MODIFIED. BY STRIPPING OFF EXTRA PIECES OF THE SUIT, THE STRENGTH OF ITS ENHANCEMENT IS MAGNIFIED! IT ORIGINALLY FEATURED AN ENTIRELY DIFFERENT DESIGN, BUT KIMIE CHANGED IT TO TAKE ADVANTAGE OF SANAE'S IMPETUS— HER SENSE OF SHAME.
● SHINGO WILLPOWER PEGASUS RAIMENT PART 2
A PEACH-COLORED SUIT EVOLVED FROM THE ONE DESCRIBED IN "PART 1." THE RATE OF POWER ENHANCEMENT IS INCREASED, AND IT MAKES THE LEGS THAT MUCH MORE QUICK AND PRECISE. HOWEVER, AS THE SUIT IS ATTACKED, ITS PIECES FALL OFF ONE BY ONE — ANOTHER DESIGN CHOICE MADE BY SANAE'S GRANDMOTHER, KIMIE.

STAFF:
MAKIKO HORI

SHUUGO
MURAKAMI

FUMIE ITOU

SEIKO KIZU

AUTHOR:
SHINOBU
OHTAKA

SANTERA SHINGO-RYUU SECRET ART COMPENDIUM

● WILLPOWER DRILLING LEG

A THRUSTING KICK WITH ALL THE ATTACK POWER CON-CENTRATED IN THE LEGS. WITH THE PEGASUS RAIMENT EQUIPPED, THE STRENGTH AND SPEED OF THIS KICK IS ASTONISHING. THE POWER AND STYLE OF THE KICK CAN BE ALTERED DEPENDING ON WHICH RAIMENT IS BEING WORN.

● WILLPOWER FLIGHT LEG

BY KICKING REPEATEDLY IN THE AIR AT ULTRA-SPEED, THE BEARER OF THIS MOVE CAN STEP INTO THE ATMOSPHERE AND CONTROL AIR AT WILL. AN EXTREMELY DIFFICULT ART THAT ONLY THE MOST TALENTED AND DISCIPLINED AMONG THE NAKAJIMA CLAN CAN ACCOMPLISH.

● WILLPOWER PEGASUS CONVICTION HOOF

BY KICKING REPEATEDLY INTO THE AIR WITH WILLPOWER FLIGHT LEG, THE USER FLOATS HIGH INTO THE SKY AND DELIVERS A RAINING BLOW AGAINST THE TARGET FAR BELOW. AN ENORMOUS BLAST OF DESTRUCTIVE AIR PRESSURE IN THE SHAPE OF A GIANT HOOF COMPLETELY FLATTENS THE ENEMY.

SUMOMOMO MOMOMO ⑤

SHINOBU OHTAKA

Translation: Stephen Paul

Lettering: Terri Delgado

SUMOMOMO MOMOMO Vol. 5 © 2006 Shinobu Ohtaka / SQUARE ENIX.
All rights reserved. First published in Japan in 2006 by SQUARE ENIX
CO., LTD. English translation rights arranged with SQUARE ENIX CO.,
LTD. and Hachette Book Group through Tuttle-Mori Agency, Inc.

Translation © 2010 by SQUARE ENIX CO., LTD.

Yen Press
Hachette Book Group
237 Park Avenue, New York, NY 10017

www.HachetteBookGroup.com
www.YenPress.com

Yen Press is an imprint of Hachette Book Group, Inc. The Yen Press
name and logo are trademarks of Hachette Book Group, Inc.

First Yen Press Edition: August 2010

ISBN: 978-0-316-07314-1

10 9 8 7 6 5 4 3 2 1

BVG

Printed in the United States of America